To Ride Hell's Chasm

Janny Wurts is the author of numerous successful fantasy novels, including the acclaimed *Cycle of Fire* trilogy and *The Wars of Light and Shadow* series. She is also co-author, with Raymond E. Feist, of the world-wide best-selling *Empire* series. Her skill as a horse-woman, offshore sailor and musician is reflected in her novels. She is also a talented artist and illustrates many of her own covers. Janny Wurts lives in Florida, USA

By Janny Wurts

Sorcerer's Legacy

The Cycle of Fire Trilogy

Stormwarden
Keeper of the Keys
Shadowfane

The Master of Whitestorm
That Way Lies Camelot

The Wars of Light and Shadow

Curse of the Mistwraith
Ships of Merior
Warhost of Vastmark
Fugitive Prince
Grand Conspiracy
Peril's Gate

With Raymond E. Feist

Daughter of the Empire
Servant of the Empire
Mistress of the Empire

Voyager

TO RIDE HELL'S CHASM

Janny Wurts

HarperCollins*Publishers*

Voyager
An Imprint of HarperCollins*Publishers*
77–85 Fulham Palace Road,
Hammersmith, London W6 8JB

www.voyager-books.com

This paperback edition 2003
1 3 5 7 9 8 6 4 2

First published in Great Britain by *Voyager* 2002

A catalogue record for this book
is available from the British Library

ISBN 0 00 710111 2

Typeset in Palatino by
Palimpsest Book Production Limited,
Polmont, Stirlingshire

Printed and bound in Great Britain by
Clays Limited, St Ives plc

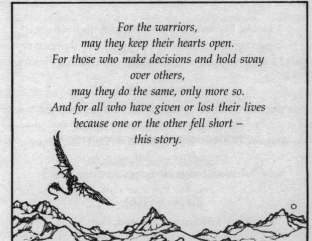

For the warriors,
may they keep their hearts open.
For those who make decisions and hold sway
over others,
may they do the same, only more so.
And for all who have given or lost their lives
because one or the other fell short –
this story.

ACKNOWLEDGEMENTS

I would like to thank the following individuals
whose interest, enthusiasm, support and dedication
walked in loving support alongside my creative footsteps.

My father John Wurts,
for the inspiration that led me to think outside the box.

Andrew Ginever, Justin Harrison, Dede McKenna,
Diane Turner, Jeff Watson,
Jane Johnson, Sarah Hodgson, Andrew Ashton
and the Voyager staff
Jonathan Matson,
and my unflagging husband, Don Maitz.

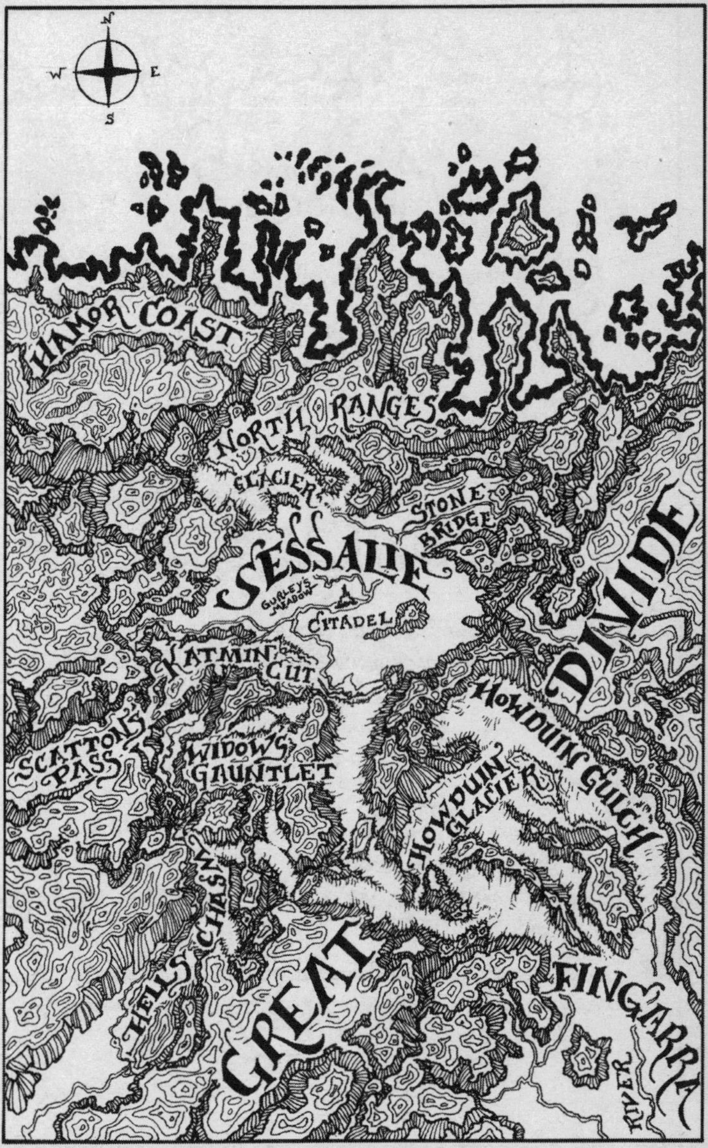
N
W
E
S
HAMOR COAST
NORTH RANGES
GLACIER
STONE BRIDGE
SESSALIE
GURLEY'S MEADOW
CITADEL
DIVIDE
KATMIN CUT
HOWDUIN GULCH
SCATTON'S PASS
WIDOW'S GAUNTLET
HOWDUIN GLACIER
HELL'S CHASM
GREAT
FINGARRA
RIVER

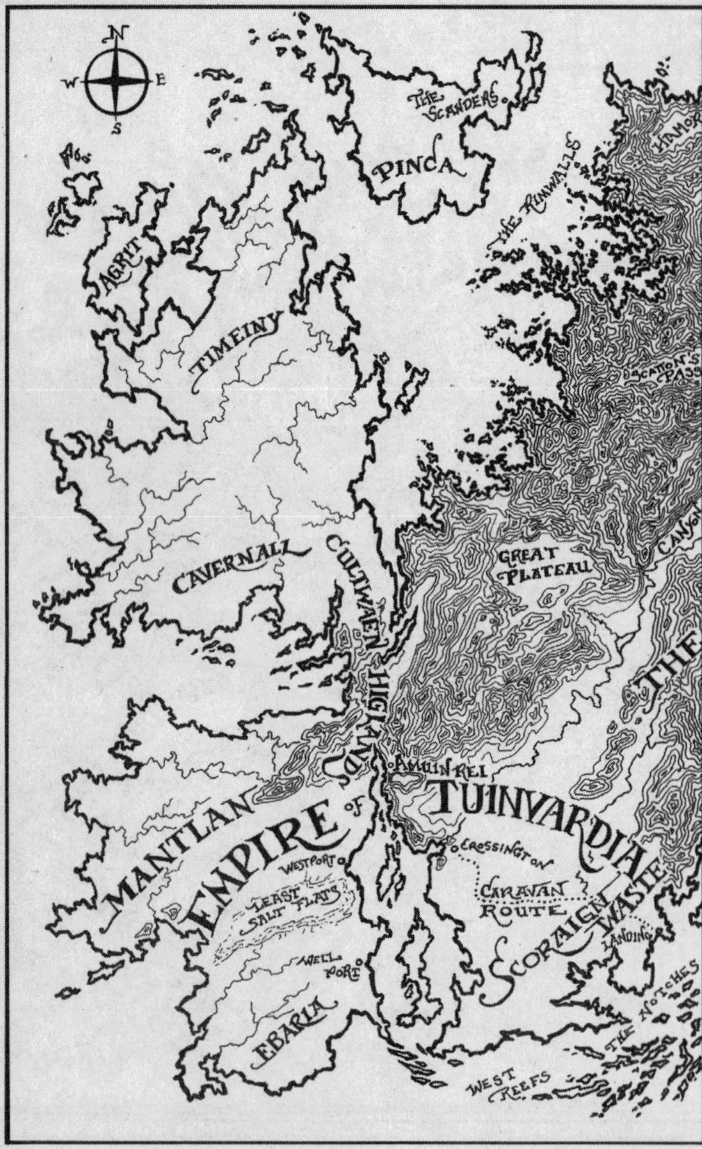

N
W
E
S
THE SCANDERS
PINCA
AGRIT
TIMEINY
THE RIMWALLS
HAMOR
CAVERNALL
CULTWAEN
HIGHLANDS
GREAT PLATEAU
THE CANYON
AMUIN REI
TUINVARDIA
MANTLAN EMPIRE OF
WESTPORT
LEAST SALT FLATS
CROSSINGTON
CARAVAN ROUTE
SCORAIGN WASTE
LANDING
MELL PORT
EBARIA
THE NOTCHES
WEST REEFS

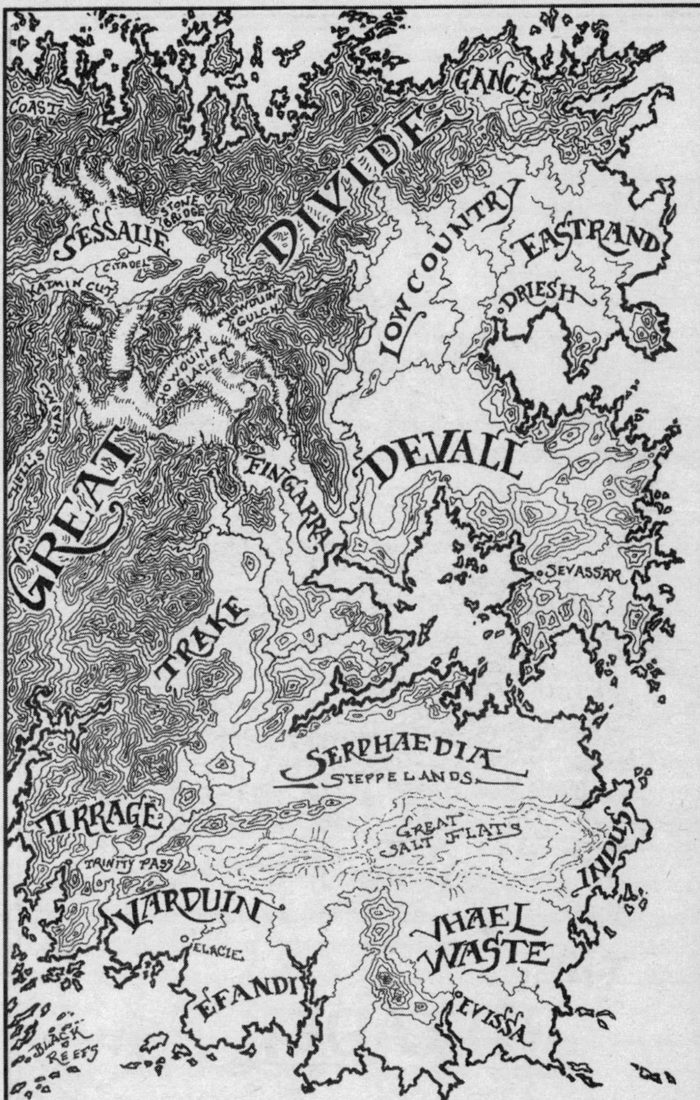
COAST
GANCE
GREAT
DIVIDE
STONE BRIDGE
SESSALIE
CITADEL
KATMIN CUT
HOWDUIN GULCH
HOWDUIN GLACIER
HELL'S CHASM
LOW COUNTRY
EASTRAND
DRIESH
DEVALL
FINGARRA
SEVASSAR
TRAKE
SERPHAEDIA
STEPPE LANDS
TIRRAGE
GREAT SALT FLATS
TRINITY PASS
INDUS
VARDUIN
ELACIE
VHAEL WASTE
EFANDI
EVISSA
BLACK REEFS

SANCTUARY PINNACLE
DEDORTH'S TOWER
BELL TOWER
COUNCIL HALL
COURTIER'S TOWN HOUSES
QUEEN'S GARDEN
ROYAL GUARD BARRACKS
KING'S PALACE
GUEST QUARTERS
HIGH GATE
SPRINGSTREET
MIDDLEGATE
MERCHANT'S MANSIONS
TRADE GATE
COCKATRICE
BULL TROUGH
FANE STREET
CRAFT QUARTER
FALL'S GATE
WELL
MARKET
GARRISON KEEP
LOWERGATE

THE CITADEL

The closet was dark, dusty, stifling, and the pound of her heart, ragged thunder in her ears. Her breaths went and came in strangling gasps. If death took her now, it would come filled with horrors, and strike without sound from behind . . .

I. Disappearance

IN THE LONG SHADOW OF THE MOUNTAIN SPRING TWILIGHT, UNDER THE GLOW OF A THOUSAND LANTERNS, ANJA, CROWN Princess of Sessalie, failed to appear at the banquet to celebrate her official betrothal. The upset and shock caused by her disappearance had not yet shaken the lower citadel, though more than an hour had passed since the midnight change in the watch.

The public festivities continued, oblivious. Farmwives and tradesmen still danced in the streets, while the unruly crowds spilling out of the wine shops teemed and shouted, a hotbed for fist fights and arguments. Mykkael, Captain of the Garrison, kept a trained ear on the tone of the roistering outside. He listened, intent, to the off-key singers who staggered arm in arm past the keep. The noise ebbed and flooded to the tidal surge of bodies, jamming the bye lanes and thoroughfares.

The racket funnelled into the cramped stone cell requisitioned as his private quarters. Captain Mykkael sighed, rasped his bracer across the itch of two days' stubble, then propped a weary hip against the trestle where his sword lay, unsheathed. The hard-used steel cried out for a whetstone and rag to scour a light etching of rust. Mykkael cursed the neglect, but knew better than to hope for the time to care for his weapon.

The taps in the taverns would scarcely run dry on this night. Landlords had stocked their cellars for weeks, while the folk from Sessalie's farthest-flung valleys crammed into the citadel to honour Princess Anja's brilliant match. Their exuberance was justified. A marriage alliance with the Kingdom of Devall promised them access to the coveted wealth of the sea trade. Yet if craft shops and merchants had cause to rejoice, no soldier who bore the crown's falcon blazon was likely to rest before cock's crow.

Twenty hours on duty, with no respite in sight, Mykkael grumbled, 'At least on a battlefield, a man got the chance to lay down his shield after sundown.'

He stretched his knotted back, steeled himself for discomfort, then clamped iron hands around his thigh above the knee. A grunt ripped through his teeth as he raised the game limb on to the plank trestle that served him as weapon rack and desk. There, forced to pause, he blinked through running sweat, while the twinge of pinched nerves rocked him dizzy.

Mother of all thundering storms, how he ached! Far more than a man should, who had no trace of grey. Still young, still vigorous, Mykkael kept his sable hair cropped from blind habit, as he had through his years as a mercenary.

Nonetheless, his career as a hired sword was finished. Cut short, with the spoils and pay shares laid aside not enough to sustain him in retirement. His fiercely kept dream, of an apple-bearing orchard and a pasture to breed horses, lay as far beyond grasp as the moon.

'Damn lady fortune for a cross-grained crone.' Mykkael glowered at his leg, stretched across the tabletop like so much worthless carrion. His infirmity disgusted him.

Three tavern brawls nipped in the bud, two street riots quelled, and a knife fight in the market started by a Highgate lordling who was fool enough to try to nab a cutpurse; scarcely enough exertion to wind him, yet the pain clamped down with debilitating force the longer he stayed on his feet.

'Borri'vach!' he swore under his breath. The uncouth, rolling gutturals of the southern desert dialect matched his savage mood as he unhooked the looped studs at his calf. No help for the embarrassment, that canvas breeches looked ridiculous under his blazoned captain's surcoat. Yet the more genteel appointments of trunk hose and high-top boots had proved to be too binding. Mykkael jerked up the cuff, laying bare his crippled knee with its snarl of livid scars.

Even in hindsight, he took little comfort from the troop surgeon's final prognosis. *'Powers be thanked, young man, you're still hale and breathing. With a joint break like yours, and a septic laceration, I'd have dosed you senseless, and roped you out straight and taken that leg with a bone saw.'*

Mykkael endured the lasting bitterness. Not to walk was to die. Even strapped in the mud of a drawing poultice, screaming half senseless with fever, he had kept that core of self-awareness. Others might cling to life, hobbling on crutches or a peg leg. For Mykkael, any handicap that rendered him defenceless would have wounded pride enough to kill him.

Alive enough to wrestle with his poisonous regrets, he groped through the clutter of bottles and remedy tins, while the cramps throbbed relentlessly through muscle and nerve, and the shattered bone that fastened damaged ligaments. Already the discomfort played the length of his leg. By experience he knew: the spasms would soon lock his hip and seize his back, unless the liniment just acquired from the nomad in the market could deliver him the gift of a miracle.

Hooves clattered in the outer bailey. Someone shouted.

A burst of agitated voices erupted in the lower guard-room, fast followed by the rushed pound of feet up the stairwell.

Mykkael found the dingy tin and flipped off the cap, overwhelmed by the smell of crude turpentine. 'Powers of deliverance,' he gasped. Eyes streaming, he scooped up a sticky dollop. The unnatural stuff blistered, even through his layers of callus.

Regardless, he slathered the paste over his knee. Its raw fire scoured, searing through entrenched pain. Mykkael kneaded in the residue, his breath jerked through his half-closed throat. He had no peace to lose. The fresh bout of trouble bearing down on his doorway was unlikely to grant him blessed ease in a chair, replete with grain whisky and hot compresses.

A staccato knock, cut off as the latch tripped. Vensic poked his snub nose inside, and grimaced in startled distaste. 'Captain, for the love of crown and country! This place reeks like a tannery.'

Mykkael pointedly hooked the tin closer. 'Should I give a damn who in the reaper's many hells finds my *off-duty* habits offensive?' He slopped another gob of liniment across his spasmed calf, and this time suppressed his urge to wince. 'Whatever complaint's come roosting this time, I'll remind you, Sergeant Jedrey has the watch.'

Apologetic, Vensic stepped inside. He shut the door, his easy-natured, upland features braced to withstand his captain's dicey temper. 'Jedrey's through the Middlegate, routing vandals from the merchants' quarter. You notice anything irregular on patrol?'

Mykkael shrugged, still massaging his wracked limb. 'The usual few brawlers and a bravo who got himself stabbed. A drunk was struck by a carriage. Dead on impact. The rest was all rumour, thankfully unfounded. Have you heard the crazy story that the princess ran away? Left her royal suitor abandoned at the feast, weeping on the skinny shoulder of the seneschal.'

Silence, of a depth to make the ears ring. Mykkael glanced up, astonished. The absurd notion of court curmudgeon and jilted foreign prince should have raised a howling snort of laughter. 'Better say what's happened, soldier!'

'You have a formal summons. Brought in by a royal herald in state livery, though he's masked his gold thread under a plain cloak.' Unwontedly deadpan, Vensic added, thoughtful, 'Shut-mouthed as a clam concerning the king's word, though we warned him you'd be sharp if we had to fetch you down to the wardroom.'

Mykkael's busy fingers stopped working in the liniment. 'A crown herald! Below the Highgate? Has the moat watch gone bashed on cloud wine?'

But the stunned rabbit shine to Vensic's blue eyes arrested his captain's disbelief.

'Of all the blinding powers of daylight!' Touched by an odd chill, Mykkael slapped down his turned cuff. He snatched up the rag meant for oiling his sword, wiped his smeared fingers, then hauled his lame leg from the trestle. A useless point, to argue that Princess Anja never acted the tart, or lowered herself to go slumming. Unlike her rakehell older brother, she visited the lower citadel only for processionals, surrounded by the gleam of her palace guard retinue, sweeping through to join the hunt, or to settle the petty grievances in the outlying hamlets that had languished as the king's health faltered.

'No one's mentioned an armed party of abductors in the wine shops,' Mykkael said with biting sarcasm. Tiny Sessalie was too hidebound to harbour a conspiracy without the busybody matrons making talk. So hidebound and small that every shopkeeper and servant knew his neighbour's close affairs, with half the blood in the kingdom related to itself by kin ties that confounded memory. 'Hard pressed, I'd be, to arrest a single miscreant who's sober enough to raise a weapon.'

Mykkael snatched up his naked blade, still loath to

credit rumour. Princess Anja was beloved for her light-hearted spirit. Already, her compassion had earned the same reverence the queen had known before her tragic death. To Mykkael, she was an icon who demanded sharp respect. He had needed his crack division and fully half of his reserves to restrain the cheering commons when the handsome Prince of Devall had arrived with his train to formalize his suit for her marriage. Everyone had noted the princess's flushed face. The trill of silver harness bells had shimmered on the air, as, radiant with joy, she had spurred her mount to welcome the match that young love and state auspices had favoured. The branding memory lingered, of the kiss exchanged upon the public thoroughfare. Her Grace's greeting had burst all restraint – an explosive storm of passion more likely to invite a lusty midnight foray to her bedchamber.

'Pretty foolish, if her Grace has stirred up the palace because she slipped off to the garden for a tryst.' Mykkael's amused chuckle masked the chilly ring of steel as he rammed his battered longsword into the sheath at his shoulder. 'Jedrey's better born, has the manners and diplomacy for that sort of social embarrassment.'

'Well, nicety doesn't man the walls, below the Highgate. If there's been foul play, the merchants are likely to work themselves into a lather, bemoaning the loss of Devall's ships. Suppose we faced a war?' Flippant though he was, to broach *that* jibing comment, Vensic jumped to clear the doorway. 'If the old king fancies he sees armies at the gates, he'll want your field experience ahead of any uptown bravo's breeding.'

Mykkael scotched the ribbing with his usual spiked glance, and prowled in hitched strides towards the stairwell.

'You won't have to go afoot,' Vensic added, dismayed as he noted the exhaustion betrayed by his captain's dragging limp. 'The herald's overbearing and snide with impatience, but his escort has a saddled mount waiting.'

'Well, the walk's the lesser evil,' Mykkael admitted, bald-faced. 'Bloody war's my proper venue. Crown orders aside, the drunks won't stay their knives. How in the reaper's hells can I keep the peace among the riff-raff if I'm called on to the proverbial royal carpet to act as a frisky maiden's chaperone?'

The wry conclusion stayed unvoiced. Taskin, Commander of the Palace Guard, was no more likely to appreciate a garrison man with desert-bred colouring treading on his turf above the Highgate.

Commander Taskin, at that moment, bent his ice-pale gaze upon the tearful maid who had last seen Princess Anja in her chambers.

'What more is left to say, my lord,' she despaired, her pink hands clasped and shaking. 'I've told you all I know.'

Tall, gaunt, erect as tempered steel, with a distinguished face and frosty hair, Taskin radiated competence. His silences could probe with unsubtle, scorching force. While the distraught maid stammered and wept, he stepped across the carpet and bent his dissecting regard over the clutter on Anja's dressing table.

The gold-rimmed hand mirror, the brushes and combs and tinted bottles of scent glinted under the flutter of the candles. No rice powder had been spilled. The waxed parquet floor showed no scuffs or other evidence of struggle.

In a cultured, velvet baritone that inspired chills of dread, Commander Taskin prompted, 'The princess was wearing bracelets adorned with golden bells. Her slippers, you say, had silver heels and toe caps. No rare jewels, none of the crown heirlooms, but she would have made noise at every movement. What else? Could she have masked a change of clothing under her court dress?'

The nervous maid curtseyed, though the commander's back was turned. 'Her Grace's gown had bare shoulders and laces down the front. Nothing underneath, but her thinnest silk camisole. Canna brought her smallclothes from the cedar closet. She stayed to empty the bath and gather towels while I helped her Grace with her wardrobe.'

Taskin added nothing, hands clasped behind his waist.

The maid swallowed and dabbed at streaming eyes. 'Her Grace sent me out to fetch the turquoise ribbons and a pin she said had been her lady mother's. By the time I came back, she had already left. Gone to the banquet, so it seemed, since nobody heard even a whisper of disturbance. If she's never been so thoughtless, well, new love would make her giddy. Her intended has the looks to scatter reason.'

The maid's distress was genuine. Anja loved a joke, but her style would not stoop to indiscretions that embarrassed her blameless servants.

Taskin prowled the chamber, his booted step silent as a wraith's. An uneasy pall of silence gripped the cream and copper opulence of the princess's private apartment. Such stillness by itself framed a stark contradiction to her tireless spirit and exuberance.

Anja's zest for life met the eye at every turn. The plush, tasselled chairs were left in compulsive disarray by her penchant for casual company. Gilt and marble tabletops held a riot of spring flowers, with long-stemmed hothouse lilies forced to share their porcelain vases with the weeds and wild brambles plucked from the alpine meadows. On the divan, a book of poetry had a torn string riding glove marking its vellum pages. Abandoned in the window nook, a seashell scavenged from the beaches of Devall overflowed with a jumble of pearl earrings and bangle bracelets. The playful force of Anja's generosity clashed with the constraints of royal station: the seneschal's latest scolding had been blatantly ignored. The massive chased tea service kept to honour state ambassadors had been shanghaied again, to cache the salvaged buttons for the rag man.

Even Taskin's impassive manner showed concern as he

subjected the princess's intimate belongings to a second, devouring scrutiny.

'My Lord Commander,' the maid appealed, 'if Princess Anja planned an escapade, I never heard a whisper. Her maid of honour, Shai, was the one who shared her confidence the few times she chose to flaunt propriety.'

'But the Lady Shai knows nothing. I've already asked,' a voice interjected from the hallway.

Taskin spun. His glance flicked past the startled maid, while the elite pair of guards flanking the entry bowed to acknowledge Crown Prince Kailen.

His Highness lounged in stylish elegance against the door jamb, still clad in satin sleeves and the glitter of his ruby velvet doublet. Fair as his sister, but with his sire's blue eyes, he regarded the ruffled icon of palace security with consternation. 'Don't dare say I didn't warn you, come the morning. Anja's surely playing pranks. She's probably laughing herself silly, this minute, enjoying all the fuss. Ignore her. Go to bed. She'll show up that much sooner, apology in hand. Did you really think she'd wed even Devall's heir apparent without any test of his affection?'

'That would be her Grace's touch, sure enough,' a guardsman ventured. 'Subtlety's not her measure.'

And the smiles came and went, for the uproar that had followed when her Grace had exposed the pompous delegate from Gance as a hypocrite. On the night he fled the realm, flushed and fuming in disgrace, she had asked the pastry cook to serve up a live crow inside the traditional loaf of amity.

'Furies, I remember!' But Taskin did not relax, or share his guardsmen's chuckles of appreciation. Instead, his tiger's stalk took him back to the window, where he tracked the distanced voices of the searchers beating the hedges in the garden. They met with no success, to judge by the curses arisen over snagging thorns and holly. 'No harm, if you're right, Highness. We'd survive being played for fools.' The commander inclined his head, meeting the crown prince's insouciance with deliberation. 'But if you're wrong? Anja taken as a hostage could bring us to our knees, drain the treasury at best. At worst, we could find ourselves used as the bolt hole for some warring sorcerer's minion.'

An uncomfortable truth, routinely obscured by Sessalie's bucolic peace: the icy girdle of the mountains was the only barrier that kept the evil creatures from invading the far north.

'May heaven's fire defend us!' the maid whispered, while the nearer guardsman made a sign to ward off evil.

If not for the peaks, with their ramparts of vertical rock, and the natural defences of killing storms and glaciers, tiny Sessalie would not have kept its stubborn independence. The hardy breed of crofters who upheld the royal treasury would never have enjoyed the lush alpine meadows, which fattened their tawny cattle every summer, or the neatly terraced fields, with their grape crops and barley brought to harvest through the toil of generations.

'Show me the sorcerer who could march his army across the Great Divide.' The crown prince dismissed their fears with his affable shrug. A drunk hazed on cloud wine might dream of such a prodigy; not a sober man standing on his intellect.

Even to Taskin's exacting mind, the worry was far-fetched. The flume that threaded that dreadful terrain was nothing if not a deathtrap. Foolish prospectors sometimes came, pursuing gold and minerals. They died to a man, slaughtered by hungry kerries, or else drowned in the rapids, their smashed bones spewed out amid the boil of dirty froth that thundered down the mouth of Hell's Chasm. Skilled alpinists occasionally traversed the high rim. Survivors of that route had been favoured by freakish luck and mild weather, since the arduous climb over Scatton's Pass required altitude conditioning for a crossing that took many weeks. Yet where storms and exposure sometimes spared the hardy few, the ravine killed without discrimination. The relentless toll of casualties had extended for time beyond memory.

'I thought you'd want to know,' Prince Kailen said at length. 'My father stayed lucid long enough to oppose the seneschal's complacency. His sealed order sent for the Captain of the Garrison.'

Commander Taskin left the window, his brows raised in speculation. 'Were you concerned I'd been pre-empted? Not the case. If you're wrong, and your sister's disappearance isn't an innocent joke, then we could have unknown enemies lurking in the lower citadel. Had his Majesty not dispatched the summons, I would have done the same. Has the garrison man arrived yet?'

'He should reach the palace at any moment.' Prince Kailen straightened up and jumped to clear the doorway for Taskin's abrupt departure. 'I expected you'd wish to attend the royal audience.'

The commander hastened towards the stair, in unspoken accord that the seneschal ought not to be left in sole charge. All too often, of late, the aged King of Sessalie lapsed into witless reverie. 'While I'm gone, Highness, have the grace to show my guardsmen every likely nook your royal sister could have used for a hideaway.'

The gate guard who emerged to meet the herald's band of outriders was the son of a noble, marked by his strapping build and northern fairness. His smart scarlet surcoat fell to his polished boots, which flashed with the gleam of gilt spurs.

'Captain My*sh*kael?' His aristocratic lisp softened the name's uncivil consonants. Cool, cerulean eyes surveyed the laggard still astride. 'The king's summons said, *"at once."*'

'Never seen a man limp?' Mykkael barked back, refusing to be hustled like a lackey. Bedamned if he would jump for any lordling's petty pleasure, aware as he was that his dark skin raised contempt far beyond the small delay for the care he took to spare his aching knee.

The guardsman disdained to answer. Once the captain had dismounted, he extended a gloved hand and brusquely offered a bundled-up cloak with no device.

Mykkael passed his winded horse to the hovering groom and received the hooded garment, his smile all brazen teeth. No one had to like his breeding. Last summer's tourney had proved his deadly prowess. Crippled or not, the challenge match that won his claim to rank had been decisive. If the upper-crust gossip still dismissed the upset as fickle, he could afford to laugh. His strong hand on the garrison manned the Lowergate defences. That irony alone sheltered Sessalie's wealthy bigots, and granted them their pampered grace to flourish.

Mykkael flipped the plain cloak across his muscled shoulders. The hem trailed on the ground. As though his slighter frame and desert colouring made no mockery of pretence, or the gimp of his knee could be masked, he gestured towards the lamplight avenue, its refined marble pavement gleaming past the shadow of the Highgate. 'After you, my lord herald.'

No streetwise eye was going to miss the precedent, that the Captain of the Garrison came on urgent, covert business to the palace.

'By every bright power of daylight, Captain! Try not to draw undue attention to yourself.' Through a tight, embarrassed pause, the herald gamely finished. 'The royal household doesn't need a sensation with Devall's heir apparent here to contract for his bride.'

'His Majesty commands my oath-bound duty to the crown,' Mykkael acknowledged. 'But isn't that golden egg already broken? To my understanding, we're one piece short for promising the man a royal wedding.'

Served a censuring glance from the ranking guardsman, the herald gasped, appalled. 'On my honour, I didn't breathe a word!' To Mykkael, he added, urgent,

'You'd better save what you know for the ears of the king and his seneschal.' He waved his charge along, taken aback a second time as he had to push his stride to stay abreast.

For Mykkael, the discomfort wore a different guise: beyond Highgate's granite arch, with its massive, grilled gates, he shouldered no citizen's rights, and no authority. Above the jurisdiction of the Lowergate garrison, he became a king's officer, pledged to bear arms in crown service. His claim to autonomy fell under the iron hand of Commander Taskin of the Royal Guard. That paragon was the son of an elite uplands family, handpicked to claim his title at his predecessor's death. His prowess with the sword was a barracks legend, and his temperament suffered no fool gladly.

A man groomed to stand at the king's right hand, on equal footing with the realm's seneschal, would have small cause to welcome an outsider and ex-mercenary, obliged to prove his fitness in a yearly public tourney until he scrounged the means to fund retirement.

'I hope your sword's kept campaign-sharp, and without a speck of rust,' the palace guardsman ventured in snide warning. 'If not, the commander will tear you to ribbons, in the royal presence, or out of it.'

Captain Mykkael raised his eyebrows, his sudden laughter ringing off the fluted columns that fronted the thoroughfare. 'Well, thank the world's bright powers, I'm a garrison soldier. If I wore a blade in his Majesty's presence, rust or not, I'd be tried and hung for treason.'

Stars wheeled above the snow-capped rims of the ranges, their shining undimmed as the face of disaster shrouded the palace in quiet. On the wide, flagstone terrace, still laid for the princess's feast, a chill breeze riffled the tablecloths. It whispered through the urns of potted flowers, persistent as the stifled conversations of the guests who, even now, refused to retire. Of the thousand gay lanterns, half had gone out, with no servants at hand to trim wicks. Silver cutlery and fine porcelain lay in forlorn disarray, where distraught lady courtiers had purloined linen napkins to stem their silenced onslaught of tears.

The staunch among them gathered to comfort Lady Shai, whose diamond hair combs and strings of pearls shimmered to her trembling. No one's calm assurance would assuage her distress, no matter how kindly presented.

Prince Kailen's suggestion of practical jokes had roused her gentle nature to fiercely outspoken contradiction. 'Not Anja. Not this time! Since the very first hour the Prince of Devall started courting her, she has spoken of nothing else! Merciful powers protect her, I know! Never mind her heart, the kingdom's weal is her lifeblood. She once told me she would have married a monster to acquire seaport access for the tradesmen. She said – oh, bright powers! How fortune had blessed her beyond measure, that the prince was so comely and considerate.'

A wrenching pause, while Shai sipped the glass of wine thrust upon her by the elderly Duchess of Phail. The ladies surrounding her collapse glanced up, hopeful, as Commander Taskin ghosted past on his purposeful course for the audience hall.

'Any news?' asked Lady Phail, her refined cheeks too pale, and her grip on her cane frail with worry.

Taskin shook his head. 'Not yet.'

Lady Shai tipped up her face, her violet eyes inflamed and swollen. 'Commander! I beg you, don't listen to the crown prince and dismiss my cousin's absence as a folly. Upon my heart and soul, something awful has befallen. Her Grace would have to be dead to have dealt the man she loves such an insult.'

The commander paused, his own handkerchief offered to replace the sodden table linen wrung between Shai's damp fingers. 'Rest assured, the matter has my undivided attention.'

He nodded to the others, found a chair for Lady Phail,

then proceeded on his way. Ahead, a determined crowd of men accosted the arched entry that led to the grand hall of state. The stout chamberlain sighted the commander's brisk approach and raised his gold baton. 'Make way!' His hoarse shout scarcely carried through the turmoil.

Commander Taskin lost patience. 'Stand down!'

The knot cleared for that voice, fast as any green batch of recruits. The chamberlain pawed at his waist for his keying. 'You've come at last. Thank blazes. The king is with the seneschal.' Still too rattled to turn the lock quickly, the fat official gabbled to forestall the commander's impatience. 'His Majesty sent a herald to the lower keep and summoned that sand-whelped upstart –'

Taskin interrupted, sharp. 'The Captain of the Garrison? I already know. He's a fighter, no matter what she-creature bore him. His record of field warfare deserves your respect.'

As the double doors parted, Taskin did not immediately walk through. He pivoted instead, catching the petitioners short of their eager surge forward. 'Go home! All of you. My guardsmen are capable. If your services are needed, I'd have you respond to the crown's better interests well rested.'

Through a stirring of brocades, past the craning of necks in pleated collars, a persistent voice arose. 'Is there crisis?'

Another chimed in, 'Have you news?'

'No news!' Taskin's bark cut off the rising hysteria. 'Once the princess is found, the palace guard will send criers. Until then, collect your wives and retire!'

'But Commander, you don't understand,' ventured the fox-haired merchant whose dissenting word rose the loudest. 'Some of us wish to offer our house guards, even lend coin from our personal coffers to further the search for her Grace.'

Taskin raised his eyebrows. His drilling survey swept the gathering, no man dismissed, even the foreign ambassador from the east, with his bullion brocade and his pleated silk hat, hung with a star sapphire and tassel. 'Very well. I'll send out the seneschal. He'll take down the list of names and offered services.'

Prepared for the ripple of dismayed consternation, Taskin's lean mouth turned, perhaps in amusement. The rest of his bearing stayed glass-hard with irony. Now, no man dared to leave, lest he be the first to expose his underlying insincerity. Once each pledge of interest was committed to ink, the commander could winnow the truly loyal from the hypocrites at leisure.

Beyond the broad doors, the throne and gallery loomed empty. The bronze chandeliers hung dark on their chains, the only light burning in the small sconce by the privy chamber. Outside its thin radiance, the room's rich appointments sank into gloom, the lion-foot chairs reduced to a whispered gleam of gold leaf, and the crystalline flares off the glass-beaded tassels a glimmer of ice on the curtain pulls.

Taskin's brisk footsteps raised scarcely a sound as he passed, a fast-moving shadow against lead-paned windows, faintly burnished by starlight. By contrast, the clash of voices beyond the closed door raised echoes like muffled thunder.

Taskin acknowledged the six guardsmen, standing motionless duty, then wrenched the panel open without knocking. He sized up the tableau of three men beyond as he would have viewed the pieces on a chessboard.

In the company of the King of Sessalie and the seneschal, the High Prince of Devall claimed the eye first. He was a young man of striking good looks. The hair firmly tied at his nape with silk ribbon hung dishevelled now, honey strands tugged loose at the temples. Though he sat with his chin propped on laced hands, his presence yet reflected the lively intelligence that exhaustion had thrown into eclipse. He still wore banquet finery: a doublet of azure velvet edged in bronze, and studded with diamonds at the collar. His white shirt with its pearl-buttoned cuffs set off his shapely hands. The signet of Devall, worn by the heir apparent, flashed ruby fire as he straightened to the movement at the doorway.

Taskin bowed, but as usual, never lowered his head. While the seneschal's ranting trailed into stiff silence, and the king's prating quaver sawed on, Devall's prince appraised the commander's rapid entry with amber eyes, dark-printed with strain. 'Lord Taskin, I trust you bring news?'

'None, Highness. Every man I have in the guard is assigned. They are diligent.'

The seneschal shot the commander a scathing glance for such bluntness. 'If you've heard about the herald dispatched to the lower keep, can I rely on your better sense to restore the realm's decorum? We scarcely need to raise the garrison to track down an errant girl!'

Taskin disregarded both the glare and the sarcasm. He would have honesty above empty words and false assurances. Nor would he speak out of turn before his king, whose maundering trailed off in confusion.

'Your Majesty,' Taskin cracked, striking just the right tone. 'I have no word as yet on your daughter.'

A blink from the King of Sessalie, whose gnarled hands tightened on his chair. His gaunt frame sagged beneath the massive state mantle with its marten fur edging, and the circlet of his rank that seemed too weighty for his eggshell head. Nonetheless, the trace of magnificence remained in the craggy architecture of his face; a reduced shadow of the vigorous man who had begotten two bright and comely children, and raised them to perpetuate a dynasty that had lasted for three thousand years.

An authoritative spark rekindled his glazed eyes. 'Taskin. I've sent for Captain My*sh*kael.' Brief words, short sentences; the king's speech of late had become wrenchingly laboured, a sorrow to those whose love was constant. 'You'll see soon enough. My seneschal objects.'

'I find the choice commendable, your Majesty.' Taskin

kept tight watch on the foreign prince from Devall, and recorded the masked start of surprise. 'Until we know what's happened, we are well advised to call out every resource we can muster.'

The high prince slapped his flattened hands upon the tabletop, but snatched short of shoving to his feet. 'Then you don't feel her Grace has played a prank for my embarrassment?'

'I don't know, Highness. Her women don't think so.' Taskin's shoulders lifted in the barest, sketched shrug. 'But Princess Anja being something of a law unto herself, her ladies have been wrong as much as right when the girl played truant as a child.'

The seneschal thrust out his bony, hawk nose, his stick frame bristling with outrage. 'Well, we don't need a scandal buzzing through the lower citadel! Find the herald, do. Pull rank at the Highgate, and turn the captain back to mind his garrison.'

'Too late.' Already alerted by the sound of inbound footsteps, Taskin's icy gaze fixed on the seneschal as he let fly his own sly dart. 'In fact, your service is the one that's needed elsewhere.' Two crisp sentences explained the gist behind the courtiers held under the chamberlain's watchful eye.

'Your Majesty, have I leave?' The seneschal bowed, shrewd enough to forgo his sour rivalry for opportunity. He thrust to his feet, his supple, scribe's hands all but twitching for the chance to wring advantage from the merchants' pledge of loyalty.

A short delay ensued, while King Isendon of Sessalie raised a palsied forearm and excused the gaunt official from his presence. As the seneschal stalked away, he peered in vague distress at the straight, stilled figure of his ranking guardsman, who now claimed the place left vacant at his right hand. 'Commander. Do you honestly think we might be facing war?'

'Your Majesty, that's unlikely.' Taskin's candour was

forthright. What did Sessalie possess, that could be worth a vicious siege, a campaign supplier's nightmare, destined to be broken by the early winter storms that howled, unforgiving, through the ranges? Only Anja posed the key to disarm such defences. Threat to her could unlock all three of the citadel's moated gates without a fight.

Within the royal palace, her loss might break King Isendon's fragile wits within a week, or a day, or an hour. Prince Kailen lacked the hardened maturity to rein in the fractious council nobles. The seneschal was clever with accounting, but too set in his ways to keep the young blood factions close at heel.

Sessalie needed the sea trade to sweeten the merchants and bolster a cash-poor council through the uncertainty of the coming succession.

Yet the petty slights and tangles spun by court dissension were not for Devall's ears. Anja's offered hand must not imply a bleeding weakness, or invite the licence to be annexed as a province.

Lest the pause give the opening to tread dangerous ground, the Commander of the Guard tossed a bone to divert the high prince's agile perception. 'The crown needs its eyes and ears in the sewers under Highgate. Captain My*sh*kael may be a misbegotten southern mongrel, but he keeps the city garrison trimmed into fighting shape. Knows his job; I checked his background. We want him keen and watchful, and not hackled like a man who's been insulted.'

The High Prince of Devall drummed irritable fingers, his ruby seal glaring like spilled blood. 'I don't give a rice grain if the man's low born, or the get of a pox-ridden harlot! Let him find Princess Anja, I'll give him a villa on the river, a lord's parcel of mature vineyards, and a tax-free stamp to run a winery.'

Commander Taskin had no words. His arid glance pricked to a wicked spark of irony, he had eyes only for the man in the plain cloak just ushered through the privy chamber door. The hood he tossed back unmasked his dark skin, the honesty a tactical embarrassment. Yet his brazen pride was not invulnerable. The soft, limping step – worse than Taskin remembered – was strategically eclipsed behind the taller bulk of Collain Herald.

That court worthy trundled to an awkward stop. Scarlet-faced, he delivered the requisite bows to honour vested sovereign and heir apparent. Blindingly resplendent in his formal tabard with its border of gold ribbons, and Sessalie's falcon blazon stitched in jewelled wire, Collain announced the person the king's word had summoned.

'Attend! In his Majesty's name, I present My*sh*kael, Captain of the Garrison.'

II. Audience

As the court herald straightened from his bow and stepped aside, Mykkael received his first clear view of the court figures seated on the dais. They, in turn, measured him, while his tactician's survey noted the Prince of Devall's suppressed flinch. Apparently the princess's suitor had not expected dark colouring, a commonplace reaction in the north. Mykkael gathered his own cursory impression: of smouldering good looks and tasteful, rich clothing, marred by a fine-drawn impatience. The proposed bridegroom seemed genuinely upset by her Grace's disappearance. His statesman's bearing showed signs of chafed poise as he paid deference to the reigning king of Sessalie.

As Mykkael must, also, though his war-trained awareness rankled for the fact Commander Taskin slipped away from his post and took position a half-step from his back. Mykkael had witnessed politics and intrigues aplenty, and court appointments far richer than Sessalie's. Yet where the close proximity of wealth and power seldom ruffled his nerves, the senior guardsman's presence raised his hackles. He felt newborn naked to be bladeless. Few kings, and fewer statesmen could size up his attributes with that trained killer's astute eye.

A pinned mouse beneath the commander's aggressive scrutiny, the garrison captain bowed. Foreigner though he was, his manners were accomplished enough to honour the crowned presence of royalty. Even when that worthy seemed a shrunken, dry armature, clothed over in marten and velvet. Sessalie's failing monarch might appear weak, might seem as though his jewelled circlet bound the skull of a man with one foot in the grave. Yet tonight, the palsied jut of his chin suggested an aware determination. The eyes Mykkael recalled from his oath-taking were dulled with age, but not blank.

The garrison captain met the king's wakened wits with the sharp respect he once granted to his war-bond employers. He assumed a patient, listening quiet, prepared to field the caprice of crown authority. Past experience left him wary. A ruler's bidding could cast his lot on the wrong side of fate, and get every man in his company killed.

The king drew a laboured breath, too infirm to waste time with state language. 'Captain. You are aware? My daughter, Princess Anja, is nowhere to be found.'

Mykkael inclined his head. 'Your Majesty,' he opened, his diction without accent, 'until now, I had heard only rumours.'

'You might wish to speak louder,' the High Prince of Devall suggested with hushed compassion. 'Of course, you would have tracked down the source of such talk.'

Mykkael paused. The king's alert posture suggested he had heard very well. Rather than break protocol, the captain settled for a polite nod as acknowledgement that Devall's heir apparent had addressed him.

Taskin smoothed the awkward moment. 'This is Sessalie, where the commons have been content for generations. If Captain My*sh*kael pursued every snippet of gossip, half the city matrons would be found guilty of treasonous words. His sleep might be broken five times a night, quelling false declarations that King Isendon was laid out on his death bier.'

The old monarch smiled and patted the prince's elegant wrist. 'My herald was forbidden from forthright speech.' A sly, white eyebrow cocked up, while the clouded gaze regarded the officer summoned in for audience. 'Even if Collain had broken faith, the crown's bidding left no opening to launch an investigation. Is this so, Captain? You may answer.'

Not deaf, or a fool, King Isendon, despite the clack of public opinion; Mykkael chose honesty. 'No need to investigate. I witnessed the source of the rumour myself in the course of a routine patrol.' At the king's insistence, he elaborated. 'One of the flower girls is in love with the driver of a slop cart. She went to have her fortune told, hoping for a forecast, or a simple to bind her affection. The mad seer who lives in the alley by the Falls Gate mutters nonsense when she's drunk. Her cant tonight said the princess was missing, but then, her talk is often inflammatory. Few people take her seriously.'

Taskin stirred sharply, and received the king's nod of leave. 'You think her words carry weight?'

'Sometimes her malice takes a purposeful bent.' Mykkael hesitated, misliking the prompt of his instinct. Yet Taskin's steely competence warned against trying to shade his explanation with avoidance. 'I've seen her prick holes in folks' overblown ambitions, or cause ill-suited lovers to quarrel. Occasionally, she'll expose the shady dealings of a craftsman. Mostly, her ranting is groundless rubbish. But one watches the flotsam cast up by the tide.'

'You will question this woman,' commanded the king.

Mykkael raised his eyebrows, moved to tacit chagrin. 'Majesty, I'll try. Until morning, the old dame will be senseless on gin. Cold sober, she can't remember the names of her family. I'll find the slop taker's sweetheart, if I can, and see whether she recalls something useful.'

The king regarded him, probing for insolence, perhaps. Mykkael thought as much, until some quality to the trembling, lifted chin made him revise that presumption. Those fogged eyes were measuring him with shrewd intellect. Mykkael keenly sensed the authority in that regard, and more keenly still, that of Devall's heir apparent, edged and growing jagged with concern.

Then Isendon mustered his meagre strength and spoke. 'Captain, you are the arm of crown law below the Highgate. My daughter has vanished. By my orders, you will do all in your power. Find her. Secure her safety.'

Mykkael bowed, arms crossed at his chest in the eastern style, that gesture of respect an intuitive statement more binding than any verbal promise. He straightened, bristled by a sudden movement at his shoulder.

The Commander of the Guard now flanked his stance at close quarters, no doubt mistaking such silence, perhaps even questioning his professional sincerity. Taskin's whisper was direct. 'You will answer to me, on your findings.'

The garrison captain inclined his head, not smiling. He waited until the King of Sessalie granted leave with the gesture of a skeletal hand. The dismissal closed the audience. Yet the gaze of the lowcountry prince did not shift, or soften from burning intensity.

Mykkael had time to notice that the man's hands were no longer clasped, but tucked out of sight beneath the tabletop. No chance was given to pursue deeper insight, or gauge the Prince of Devall's altered mood.

Taskin demanded his attention forthwith. 'We need to talk, Captain.'

Mykkael paid his respects to crowned royalty. As he turned from the dais, his words came fast and low, and without thought. 'Don't leave him alone.'

The commander stiffened. Only Mykkael stood near enough to catch that slight recoil. Taskin's hooded eyes glinted, hard as polished steel rivets. Clearly, he required no foreigner's advice. 'We have to talk,' he repeated, never asking which of the two royals had prompted the spontaneous warning.

That moment, the carved doors of the chamber burst

open. A flurry among the guards bespoke someone's imperious entry. Then a female voice cut like edged glass through the upset. 'Her Grace isn't hiding. Not in any bolt hole she used as a child, I already checked. Taskin! You can call your oafish officers to heel. They won't find anything useful tossing through everyone's closets.'

Belatedly, Collain Herald announced, 'Court worthies, your Majesty, the Lady Bertarra.'

'The late queen's niece,' Taskin murmured, for the garrison captain's benefit. 'A shrew, and intelligent. She's worth a spy's insights and ten berserk soldiers, and the guards I have posted at the king's doorway are loyal as mountain bedrock.'

Mykkael regarded the paragon in question, a plump, beringed matron who bore down upon the royal dais, her intrepid form hung with jewellery and a self-righteous billow of ribbon and saffron taffeta.

'Best we beat a tactical retreat,' Taskin suggested.

Mykkael almost smiled. 'Her flaying tongue's a menace?'

Taskin returned the barest shrug of straitlaced shoulders. 'I'd have the report on the closets from my duty sergeant without the shrill opinion and abuse.'

But withdrawal came too late. The matron surged abreast, and rocked to a glittering stop in a scented cloud of mint. Mykkael received the close-up impression of a round suet face, coils of pale hair pinned with jade combs, and blue eyes sharp and bright as the point on an awl.

No spirit to honey her opinions, Bertarra attacked the obvious target, first. 'You're a darkling southerner,' she accused. 'Some say you're good. I don't believe them. Or what would you be doing here, standing empty-handed?' Her glance shifted, undaunted, to rake over the immaculate commander of the palace guard. A plump hand arose, tinkling with bracelets, and deployed a jabbing finger. 'Our Anja's no hoyden, to be sneaking into wardrobes! Shame on you, for acting as though she's no more than a girl, and a simpleton!'

Taskin said, frigid, 'The closets were searched at her brother the crown prince's insistence. Do you think of his Highness as a boy, and a simpleton?'

Bertarra sniffed. 'Since when has a title been proof of intelligence? Prince Kailen will be drunken and whoring by morning. Simplistic, male adolescent behaviour, should that earn my applause?' Her ample chin hoisted a haughty notch higher. 'His Highness is a layabout who thinks with the brainless, stiff prod in his breeches. All men act the same. Here, our princess has been kidnapped by enemies, and not a sword-bearing soldier among you has the guts in his belly to muster!'

'Who's prodding, now?' Taskin grasped that perfumed, accusatory finger, turned it with charm, and kissed the palm with flawless diplomacy. 'Lady Bertarra, if you think you can stand between any grown man and his pleasures, you are quite free to curb the excesses of your kin with no help from my men-at-arms.' He bowed over her hand, his dry smile lined with teeth. 'As to enemies of the realm, give me names. I am his Majesty's sword. In her Grace's defence, I will kill them.'

Yet like the horned cow, the woman seized the last word. She slipped from Taskin's grasp and fixed again on Mykkael, silent and stilled to one side. 'That's why you brought this one? To sweep our sewers for two-legged rats? What did you promise for his compensation? A well-set marriage to raise his mean standing?'

Mykkael's slow, deep laughter began in his belly, then erupted. 'Now, that certainly would *not* be thinking with my man's parts.' His dismissive glance encompassed the jewellery, then the cascade of ruffled yellow skirt. 'A sick shame, don't you think, to dull a night's lust stripping off all that useless decoration? And, from some pale Highgate woman, who's likely to be nothing but fumbling inexperience underneath? That should require an endowment of land as incentive to shoulder the bother.'

Bertarra's mouth opened; snapped shut. She quickly

rebounded from stonewalled shock. 'Crude creature. Prove your mettle. Find our Anja and bring her home safely.'

A gusty flounce of marigold silk, and the matron moved on to upbraid someone else on the dais. Taskin resumed his interrupted course, his stride as sharp as any spoken order that the garrison captain was expected to follow. A pause at the door saw the guard rearranged. Two men-at-arms were asked to stand inside, in direct view of the royal person. The petty officer was dispatched elsewhere, bearing the commander's instructions.

That man angled his greater size and weight to jostle past Mykkael, standing withdrawn to one side. Taskin just caught the garrison captain's blurred move in reaction, an attack form begun, then *arrested*, too fast for the trained eye to follow. The ex-mercenary had already resettled his stance, when the commander's viper-quick reach caught the tall guardsman's wrist, and wrenched him back to a standstill.

'You give that one distance,' he cracked in rebuke. 'I won't forgive you a broken bone because you're careless on duty.'

The huge guardsman reddened.

Taskin cut off the flood of excuses. 'Not armed,' he agreed. 'Still lethal. Blowhard assumptions like that get you killed. Now carry on.'

Then, as though such a shaming display was routine, he finished his rapid instructions. 'I want to know who comes and who goes in my absence. If Bertarra leaves, or the seneschal returns, detail someone to fetch me.'

Moved off again, Mykkael's limp dragging after, the commander turned down a side corridor and whipped open the door to the closet chamber furnished for the king's private audiences. 'Sit,' he said, brisk, then rummaged through an ivory-inlaid escritoire for a striker to brighten the sconces. 'My man was a fool. Please accept my apology.'

Confronted by a marble-top table, and gold-leafed,

lion-foot chairs, Mykkael eyed the plush velvet seat he was offered. The scents he brought with him, of oiled steel, uncouth liniment, and greased leather, made strident war with the genteel perfumes of beeswax, citrus polish and patchouli. Since he saw no other option, he did as he was told; arranged his game leg, and perched.

Taskin chose a chair opposite, his squared shoulders and resplendent court appointments nothing short of imperial. His subordinate was dealt the same unflinching survey just given to his royal guards. 'I'd heard you had studied *barqui'ino*, but not the name of the master who trained you.'

Mykkael seemed less relaxed than tightly coiled, under the strap of his empty shoulder scabbard. 'There were only two living when I earned my accolade,' he admitted, his shadowed gaze regarding his rough hands, rested loose on the table before him. 'Both were my teachers, an awkwardness no one admits.'

'They both disowned you?' said Taskin, surprised.

Mykkael's sardonic smile split his face, there and gone like midsummer lightning. 'A northern man might say as much.'

'A vast oversimplification,' Taskin surmised. 'A stickler might ask you to explain. I will not.' With startling brevity, he cut to the chase. 'Our princess is in trouble. What do you need?'

As close as he came to being shocked off balance, Mykkael spread his fingers, lined by the shine of old scars. He delivered the gist. 'A boy runner, for a start, to ask my watch at the Middlegate to keep a list of who comes and goes. Next, I don't know what her Grace looks like, up close. A view of her face, if she sat for a portrait, could be sent on loan to the barracks.' He sucked a slow breath, then broached the unpopular subject dead last. 'An endowment for bribes, and extra pay shares for men whose extended duties keep them from spending due time with their families.'

'I expected you'd ask that.' Taskin was brusquely dismissive. 'The requisition to draw funds from the treasury is already set in motion. As to your runner, he's not needed. My sentries at the Highgate record all traffic to and from the palace precinct. They'll supply names until you can rearrange the Middlegate security to your satisfaction. As more thoughts arise, you'll send me the list.' Then, with a subject shift that rocked for its tactical perception, 'Now, how do you think your resource can help me?'

Thinking fast, Mykkael closed his fingers. 'If the Prince of Devall has foreigners in his retinue, I'd like permission to question them.'

Taskin sustained his stripping regard. Nothing moved, nothing showed. His aristocratic features stayed boot-leather still. 'You want to try cowing them by intimidation? Or do you presume we'd miss some nuance of testimony out of our northern-born snobbery?'

Mykkael was careful to keep his tone neutral. 'Actually, no. But I might address them in their own language.'

Taskin laughed, a rich chuckle of appreciation. 'My background check missed that.' He raised a callused thumb and stroked his cheek. 'I wonder why?'

'As a mercenary, sometimes, the pay's better if you let your employer believe you're brainless.' Mykkael watched the commander absorb this, pale eyes introspective with assessment.

'No doubt, such a pretence also helped your survival.' Unlike the speed of that formidable mind, the question that followed was measured. 'How many tongues do you speak, Captain?'

'Fluently? Five,' Mykkael lied; in fact, he had passed for native, with eight. The slight caveat distinguished that in the three Serphaidian tongues written in ideographs, he was not literate.

'I will see, about servants.' The commander never shifted, but a change swept his posture, like a pit viper poised for a strike. 'If you don't trust Devall, please say so, and why.'

Mykkael softened the cranked tension in his hands, reluctant and sweating under the cloak he had not snatched the chance to remove. 'I have no feeling, one way or the other, for her Grace's suitor, or anyone else. Just that cold start of instinct suggesting your king should not be left unguarded by hands that you know and trust.' A straight pause, then he added, 'It's battle-bred instinct. The sort of gut hunch that's kept me alive more times than a man wants to count.'

Yet if Taskin held any opinion on what his northern tradition considered a witch thought, no bias showed as he pressed the next point. 'My runners will keep you apprised of all pertinent facts from the palace. Whatever you find, I want to know yesterday. My duty officer will arrange for a courier's relay. The dispatches will be verbal. No written loose ends that might fall into wrong hands. If you stumble upon something too sensitive to repeat, you'll report back to me in person. Wherever I am, whatever the hour, the guard at the Highgate will arrange for an audience.'

Mykkael stirred in a vain effort to ease his scarred leg. His scuffed boots were too soiled to rest on a footstool, though the chamber was furnished with several, carved in flourishes, and sewn with tapestry cushions. *Barqui'ino*-trained to fight an armed enemy bare-handed, he still felt on edge, stripped of his blades and his sword. His absence from his post unsettled him as well. By now, the Lowergate populace must be seething. The princess's disappearance was too momentous to stifle, and the lives of Sessalie's servants too prosaic, to keep such an upset discreet.

Taskin's focus stayed relentless as he reached his conclusion, a summary drawn like barbed hooks from a spirit that placed little value on sentiment. 'I don't believe Princess Anja's playing pranks. I've known her like an uncle since the hour of her birth. Tonight, I fear she's in grave danger.'

'Her Grace is Sessalie's heart, I see that much plainly.' Where trust was concerned, Mykkael preferred truth. 'I may not know and love her as you do, but as I judge men, no garrison will keep fighting trim with the vital spirit torn out of it. That *does* concern me. I'll stay diligent.'

Commander Taskin slid back his chair and arose. A snap of hard fingers brought a page to the door, bearing Mykkael's worn weapons. 'If this kingdom relies on you, Captain, on my watch, you will not fall short. A horse is saddled for you in the courtyard, with an escort to see you through Highgate.' As the nicked harness and bundle of sheathed throwing knives were returned, Taskin delivered his stinging, last word. 'And clean the damned rust off that steel, soldier. Set against your war record, and your reputation, that negligence is a disgrace!'

The gelding in the courtyard was a raw-boned chestnut, fit and trained for war, but groomed with the high gloss of a tourney horse. Mykkael assessed its rolling eye with trepidation. Its flattened ears and strutting prowess might look impressive on parade. Yet in a drunken, celebratory crowd, its mettlesome temper was going to pose a nasty liability.

'Commander said not to give you a lady's mount,' said the leather-faced stableman, the reins offered up with a sneer. 'One that could stay in your charge at the keep, and not let you down under need. Your horsemanship's up to him? Lose your seat, this brute's apt to stomp you to jelly.'

Mykkael took charge of the bridle, annoyed. The challenge pressed on him by Taskin's guard escort rankled him to the edge of revolt. The smug urge, ubiquitous to men trained at weaponry, *to test his mettle*, was a trait he missed least from his years as a mercenary. Worse yet, when that puerile proving involved a tradition the more fiercely reviled: the handling of dumb beasts whose innate, trusting nature had been twisted to serve as a weapon.

The horse just straightforwardly hated. Conditioned for battle to use hooves and teeth, it swung muscled hindquarters under the torchlight. The chestnut neck rippled. A blunt, hammer head snaked around, lips peeled and teeth parted to bite.

Mykkael raised a bent elbow, let the creature's own impetus gouge the soft flesh just behind the flared nostril. 'Think well, you ugly dragon,' he murmured, his expert handling primed with a taut rein as the horse tried to jib and lash back. The striking forehoof missed smashing his hip, positioned as he was by the gelding's shoulder. For the benefit of the avid watchers, he snarled, 'In hard times, on campaign, I've been known to slaughter your four-legged brothers for the stewpot.'

One vault, off his good leg, set him astride before the brute beast could react. A jab of his heel, a braced rein, and he had the first buck contained, then redirected into a surging stride forward.

Behind him, the belated guards set hasty feet in their stirrups and swung into their saddles to catch up. Their dismayed northern faces raised Mykkael's soft laughter. 'Who's lost their beer coin to the rumour I can't ride?'

Both men looked sheepish.

The garrison captain was quick to commiserate. 'I'd buy you a brew to remedy your loss, if I had any loose coin myself.'

Yet the prospect of such camaraderie with a foreigner made the guardsmen more uncomfortable still.

Mykkael's grin widened, a flash of white teeth under the cloak hood just raised to mask the embarrassment of his origins. 'Think well on that,' he murmured in the same tone used a moment before on the gelding. He led off, reined the sullen horse through the archway. The clatter of shod hooves rang down the deserted avenue, bouncing echoes off the mortised façade of the wing that housed visiting ambassadors. The four-quartered banner of Devall hung limp by the entry, its gold-fringed trim tarnished with dew. Nor did the pair of ceremonial sentries stir a muscle to mark the passage of Mykkael's cloaked figure, attended by Taskin's outriders.

The ill-matched cavalcade passed out of the bailey, into the grey scrim of the fog that rolled off the peaks before dawn light. Stars poked through, a scatter of fuzzed haloes, punch-cut by the spires of the palace. At street level, the torches streamed, their smeared light gleaming over the dull iron sheen of wet cobbles.

That moment, a raggedy figure darted out of the shadows.

Mykkael's horse skittered, snorting. He slammed his fist into its neck, used the rein, and hauled its proud crest to the side to curb its lunging rear. His gasped oath slipped restraint, while the figure, *an old woman*, came on and made a suicidal grab for his stirrup.

Her hands groped and locked on his ankle, instead. 'Young captain,' she cried in a guttural, thick accent. 'A boon, I beg you! Please, out of pity, would you lift off a short curse!'

Mykkael kicked her away. As she fell, shrilling outrage, he slammed his heel into the raging horse. Before its raised forehooves came down, he drove it into a clattering sidle. Once clear, he sprang from the saddle, flung his reins to the guards, then forced his racked knee to bear urgent weight.

In two steps, he reached the woman and caught her skinned hands. 'I'm sorry, old mother.' Her tattered clothes smelled of dust and floor wax, and her hands wore the callus of a labourer. A cleaning drudge, bent and stiff with arthritis; his heart felt nothing but pity. 'My roughness aside, that horse would have killed you, leaving your family bereft. I regret also, for your disappointment. But I cannot lift any curses, short or long form.' Through her hiss of displeasure, he reached under the outraged tension of thin shoulders and braced her attempt to sit upright. 'Put simply, I lack the background.'

She rolled off a rude phrase in dialect; would have pulled away in her rage, had he let her. Instead, firmly gentle, he raised her to her feet, and steadied her through the shaken aftermath as she dusted her skirts back to rights.

The next question was his, spoken in the Scoraign tongue inferred by her lilting accent.

She raised filmed eyes, and stared at him, furious. The next insult she uttered was clipped.

While the guards watched, dumbfounded, Mykkael shut his eyes. He let her go. Masterfully calm, he repeated himself.

The drudge spat at his feet. She said five spaced words, then stalked away, the rustle of her threadbare garments lost in the muffling mist.

'Why did you lie to her?' The ruddy guard was forced to speak sharply to be heard through the gelding's rank stamping.

Mykkael snapped up his chin, aroused from blind thought, his brow knitted in puzzlement. *'Lie to her?'* Then his incomprehension broke. He swore under his breath. 'I can't raise curses! Powers of fury! I wouldn't know a desert shaman's singing if the spell weave it held slapped me breathless!'

When the guardsman stayed sceptical, and his husky colleague muttered a timeworn slur, Mykkael's temper frayed. He limped forward, snapped up the chestnut's rein, and glared in unvarnished disgust. 'I was raised by an uplands merchant who spoke the same milk tongue you did.'

Silence reflected the men's towering disbelief; Mykkael drew his irritation sharply in hand, made aware by the ragged intensity of his feelings that he was bone-tired. Two nights on duty without decent sleep would fray any man's judgement, never mind wreck the grace for diplomacy. He ignored the screaming twinge of his leg, fended off another snap from the horse, and, without mounting, marched it straight back towards the archway.

'Captain! Where do you think you are going?' Flustered again, no small bit annoyed, the pair of palace guardsmen spurred after him. 'The Highgate is *down slope*!'

'So it is. But I'm going back to the bailey.' While the ornery chestnut slopped foam on his wrists, and lashed its tail in thwarted temper, Mykkael turned his head. This time his smile held no easy humour; only purpose keen as a knife's edge. 'Or don't you believe Commander Taskin should be told that the storeroom closet where that drudge keeps her brooms has been scribed with a sorcerer's mark?'

III. Craftmark

THE RICH TRAPPINGS OF FINE MARBLE AND CITRUS-OILED PARQUET DID NOT EXTEND TO THE WARREN OF STORE cellars underneath the king's palace. Here, the close-set corridors had been chiselled into the mountain granite underlying the bedrock foundations. Cobwebs streamed from the soot-blackened ceiling, rippling sheet gold in the torch light. The floors lit by that flickering glow were rough stone, levelled with footprinted clay.

Mykkael lifted the flame of his borrowed spill and arose from his hurried survey. 'No tracks here but servants' clogs, and ones made by a heavyset fellow wearing hard-soled boots.'

'That would be the wine steward,' said the bearded soldier, standing with folded arms beside him. 'He's grown too fat for clogs. Can't see over his huge belly any more. Bercie – that's his wife – she bought him the boots. She feared he was likely to trip one day, and bash his old pan in a tumble.'

'Wise woman,' Mykkael murmured, cautious himself, as the yawning servant indicated the way towards a shaft with another frame stairway. The obstacle posed an unwelcome hazard for a man afflicted with lameness. 'We go down here?'

The disgruntled lackey bobbed his tow head, the pompom on his sleeping cap a dab of bright scarlet amid the oppressive gloom. 'For the store cellar, yes. Broom closet's just past the landing.'

Mykkael caught the sleeve of the fellow's striped nightshirt. 'Thank you. Keep the light. Go on back to bed.'

As the surlier of the two men-at-arms drew breath to disagree, the captain silenced him with a glance. His clipped nod dispatched the servant on his way. Then Mykkael waited, while the wavering glow of the rush light receded out of immediate earshot. 'You don't want more gossip.' His low voice emphatic, he added, 'Don't tell me, soldier, you aren't under discipline to keep tinder and spill in your scrip?'

The other guard stiffened, affronted. 'You don't give us orders, you sand-bred cur.'

Mykkael ignored the insult. 'Get busy with that flint! A sorcerer's mark can smoulder like wildfire. You don't leave one burning, once you know it's there. If you're frightened, just say so. I'll go on alone if need be.'

'But the light,' the bearded guard blustered, his ruddy face lost amid gathering shadow as the servant set foot on the upper stair and continued his shuffling ascent. 'We just carry birch bark. Burns out in seconds.'

'Stall a bit more, then you'll stand in the dark.' Mykkael shrugged, sardonic. 'Not a comfortable risk to be taking, where there might be a line of dark craft set at work.'

One balky man at last stirred to comply.

Patience gone, Mykkael reached out with blurring speed. He snaked a hand past the guard's fumbling fingers, and dug flint and spill from the unbuckled scrip. 'Don't you trust your commander? I doubt very much we'll expend what we have before Taskin arrives with pine torches. I hope he also brings men with strong nerves who will act without foolish argument.'

'We should wait till he gets here,' the surly guard snapped.

But Mykkael had already lit the rolled birch bark. He pressed the pace down the creaky board staircase, not caring if anyone followed. The recalcitrant guardsmen soon tramped at his heels, their grumbling stilled as they crowded the landing, and the broom-closet door emerged out of veiling darkness. The unvarnished planking had been inscribed: the scrawled figure demarked a crudely shaped lightning bolt, cut diagonally through an array of interlocked circles.

Mykkael loosed a hissed breath, rolled his shoulders, then forged ahead, resolute. He held up the spill. Bronze features expressionless, he traced the light over the wood, giving each chalky line his relentless inspection. No distraction moved him, even the fresh influx of voices and light, slicing down from the upper corridor. Taskin arrived. Five immaculate guardsmen marched at his heels, bearing oiled rag torches. Boots thundered on wood, the last stretch of stairway descended at a cracking sprint.

The commander rammed past the shrinking pair detailed as the captain's escort. He reached Mykkael's side in a glitter of braid and smartly polished accoutrements. There, he stopped, scarcely winded. His brushed grey head bent, stilled as filed steel, while the crawling progress of the hand-held spill inched over the outermost circle.

Then, 'No informative tracks, left pressed in the dirt,' Taskin observed in clipped opening.

Mykkael matched that brevity. 'I saw.' He pinched the flame out with his fingers, wiped the smutch of soot on his sleeve, then stated, 'The mark is a fake.'

'How are you certain?'

'It was done with dry chalk, not white river clay.' Mykkael raised his wrist, blotted the beaded sweat from his brow, then swiped his thumb through the pattern. He sniffed carefully. 'No spittle to bind it. No blood, or worse, urine. A sorcerer's lines can't hold any power without a minion's imprint to lift them to active resonance.'

'That's detailed knowledge for a man who just claimed

he lacked the touch to shift curses.'

Before the garrison captain could snatch pause to wonder how that fact had changed hands at short notice, Taskin's glance shifted. He took merciless note, when Mykkael braced a needful hand to the wall to forestall a sharp loss of balance.

'I can't lift curses,' the captain restated. He retreated an irritable, dragging step, not quite fast enough to shadow his fingers, which were splayed rigid and quivering. Taskin's stillness continued to jab at his reserve. Hazed like a fresh recruit, Mykkael found himself pressured to give far more than the simple answer. That loss of control ripped through his aplomb, raising temper just barely leashed. 'With luck, sometimes, I can ground them.'

Ice-cool, Taskin queried, 'At what cost to yourself, soldier?'

Mykkael flung up his head. The spark of trapped light in his eyes was chipped fire, under the crowding torches. 'I don't know!' Anger doused, he had less success with his exhausted, recalcitrant body. The seizing cramp from his overstressed knee rocked his frame through a running spasm. 'Trust me, if that mark had been a live cipher, you don't want the nightmare of guessing.'

A torch wavered, behind, as a man shifted grip to make a sign against evil.

The commander cracked, 'Hold that light steady! The man who just faltered, fetch this one a chair!'

Someone else muttered, 'That malformed get of a desert-whelped bitch?'

Taskin stiffened. 'No chair, then,' he agreed, his tone like taut silk run over a sharpened sword blade. 'My inept torchman will now fetch a camp cot from storage. The man who was insolent will *run* to the west wing and roust out Jussoud. In minutes, I want him down here with his oil jars, if he has to be hauled from bed, naked!'

The pair jumped as though whipped.

'You can open the door without penalty,' said Mykkael,

hoping the diversion might snatch him the interval to quiet his chattering teeth.

'I'll carry on,' Taskin stated, not moving.

The camp cot pulled from stores arrived seconds later. The men set up the frame by the corridor wall with no talk, only brisk and relentless efficiency.

'You'll strip, soldier,' the commander rapped out, his nailing regard still fixed on the garrison captain.

A sudden movement, *snatched still*, preceded the rage that rekindled in Mykkael's dark eyes.

Taskin stayed glacially immobile, throughout. 'You will remove your harness and peel your clothes to the skin. Then lie flat and stay there! My orders, soldier. On that cot, voluntarily. Or else my men will do that work for you, followed up by a lashing for insubordination.'

Mykkael forced a smile through hackled fury. 'You'd lose some. Not nicely. Let's duck the unpleasantness.' He reached up, slipped the fastening on the borrowed cloak, then the tang of the buckle that fastened his sword harness. 'After all, I did promise I would be diligent, and you have a princess to search for.' He undid the iron fitting, and removed his weapon with a crack of withering emphasis. 'The door is safe. Open it.'

The captain jostled a path through the closed ranks of the guards, and tried not to let sore embarrassment show as heads turned in riveted curiosity. Faced toward the wall, unflinchingly straight, he compelled wooden fingers to loosen the belt of his surcoat.

'You men!' snapped Taskin. 'Eyes forward! Whatever duty you have to this realm lies ahead of me in this closet.'

Exhibiting sangfroid enough to uphold his own order, the commander turned his back on the victim confined to the corridor. He positioned himself in front of the doorway and reached for the string latch, decisive.

'Don't trust that desert-bred,' blurted the red-haired sergeant who held the torch lighting his way. 'How do you know he's not lying?'

'You'll volunteer, then?' Taskin stepped sideways, inviting the man to approach the marked panel himself. The pattern's chalked lines glared a sinister white under the flare of the flames.

Bared to the waist, still unlacing his trousers, Mykkael observed the exchange. Unsmiling, he watched the burly sergeant shrink into the packed mass of his fellows. Just as uncertain, the others edged back, none among them prepared to shield him.

Taskin folded his arms, and regarded his finest with a glare to blister them pink.

Until Mykkael spun about. Half stripped and insolent, he shoved his way forward, and tripped the latch in their place.

'Thank you,' Taskin said, *almost* smoothly enough to mask his wound thread of unease.

Justifiable anxiety, which Mykkael forgave freely. The mountain terrain of the Great Divide kept Sessalie's subjects far removed from the horrors engendered by warring sorcerers. Folk here had likely lived their whole lives, and their parents and grandparents before them, never having experienced a live craftmark. They would not have witnessed the twisted devastation such workings brought down on the lives of the people they ruined. Hideous experience would make a man flinch. Given a backdrop of frightening tales and the gross distortions of rumour, such sheltered ignorance would be all too likely to invent conjecture much worse.

Brown eyes met blue, and locked through a moment of unexpected, spontaneous understanding.

Then Taskin said, crisp, 'That's one stripe coming for rank disobedience.'

Mykkael laughed, his other fist clutching at untied laces to stay the cloth that slipped down his hard flanks. 'No mercenary troop captain worth his pay would have slapped me with less than five.' He dodged back, beat a lively retreat towards the cot. But the move went awry as his bad leg gave way without warning under his weight. His clumsy next stride was reduced to a stagger that exposed him, full-length, to the torchlight. Since no man could miss the stripes on his back, laid down for some prior offence, he salvaged the gaffe with ripe sarcasm. 'Since I already know how the punishment feels, there's no thrill of anticipation. Let's spare the boring detail for later, why not? Quarter that broom closet, first.'

The shame-faced sergeant recovered his poise. He called a man forward to carry his torch, then drew his sword and shoved through the open plank door.

Brooms met him, their straw bristles struck upright in a barrel. The surrounding floor held canted stacks of hooped wooden buckets with rope handles. The torch light speared in, leaped across a second barrel stuffed to the rim with frayed rags.

'Search everything,' snapped Taskin. 'Slowly and carefully, one bucket and one rag at a time.'

To the rest, who continued to view Mykkael's disrobing with stifled whispers and outright suspicion, the commander stated flat facts. 'Our garrison captain is not your enemy. You will all stop regarding him as a tribal barbarian, or some sort of singing shaman. My*sh*kael's parentage is not known. His adoptive father was northern-born, a civilized merchant who picked him up by the wayside as an infant foundling. You can see the hard proof; he bears no tattoos. That's a rigid custom in the south desert.'

Left utterly stripped, made the merciless butt of eight strangers who pinned him with blue-eyed, superior scrutiny, Mykkael banished his last shred of pride. He sat, then lay back on the cot, and compelled himself to keep discipline. This hazing was not worth the grace of reaction. He had suffered far worse as a recruit. Iron-skinned under pressure, he did his practised best to support Taskin's tactical effort. Distrust, after all, could do nothing but impede the search to find Princess Anja. Better to disarm that fracturing influence before petty dissent could spoil troop unity, or someone got needlessly hurt.

'Your commander did his background check thoroughly.' Dry, sounding far more weary than he wished, Mykkael offered his wrists. The flesh on his arms and over his bared heart was clear brown, marred only by battle scars. 'As you see, my mother failed to mark me at birth with the blessing of her tribe. Tradition is strict. That sign proclaimed me unfit.'

Mykkael stopped speaking, shut his eyes, and braced in distaste to endure through the subsequent, scouring inspection.

Yet Taskin cut that embarrassment short. 'Unfit, likely due to an unsanctioned union. Not for a blemish or unsoundness.'

As the captain bore up, each over-strung muscle defined in the pitiless torchlight, no one could mistake that his crippling limp had been caused by a ruinous joint wound.

Easiest to tie off the final loose end, and force the review to its sorry closure. 'Fathers of infants who are not blessed and marked leave their get to die of exposure.' Mykkael finished, 'I survived because mine was inept, or a coward, or else soft-hearted enough to ditch me in the path of a caravan.'

He rolled over then, and masked his hot face behind the bulwark of his crossed forearms.

Left staring at the damp snags of his hair, and the welted scars crossing his shoulders and back, the crowding men quickly lost interest. They pushed ahead to explore the broached closet, drawn to pursue the more gripping evil that might lurk in the drudge's rag barrel.

They found Anja's beautiful, jewelled gown; her silver-capped shoes, her exquisite wire bracelets.

A shimmering chime of miniature bells trilled through the dust-laden air.

The sound touched Mykkael's ears with a sweet, haunting clarity, as he languished, face down on the pallet. He shivered, seized up as a cramp ripped his leg into mauling pain. Bared teeth hidden behind shielding forearm, he endured, exposed, but not bitter. At least he had Taskin's forethought to thank, that the paroxysm had overtaken him lying down. Had he been savaged while still on his feet, he would currently be sprawled under somebody's boots, curled into a whimpering knot.

Naked and cold, but held prone under orders, he could more gracefully withstand the public humiliation. While his hearing tracked the excited commotion unfolding inside the broom closet, more steps approached through the corridor above, then thumped down the dusty plank stair.

The arrival reached his side and stopped next to the pallet. Glass clinked, to the wafted fragrance of astringent herbs steeped in oil. Then a huge, warm hand closed over his shoulder, its touch trained and firmly knowing. 'I'm Jussoud,' said a voice of deep, velvet consonants, bearing the accents of the east. Cloth sighed with movement, as the speaker bent his massive frame and knelt on the rough stone floor. 'I serve as physician and masseur for the guard.'

No hesitation occurred over skin tone. Only the tacit, professional pause as the hand became joined by another, probing one wire-strung muscle after the next.

Mykkael turned his neck, opened one jaundiced eye. 'I'm sorry Taskin dragged you from your bed.'

'And so he should have,' that slow, cultured voice resumed. 'You're a mess, soldier. That liniment's for camels; did you know as much when you bought it? The gum's caustic, brings blisters. You'll have weeping sores, if you're stubborn and persist with its use.'

An inquiring poke near the hip socket raised a grunted oath from Mykkael. He continued to stare, anyway. He had the right, knowing just how it felt, to be foreign and billeted among northerners.

The giant looming over him was yellow-skinned, with

black hair braided down his back. He had the flat nose, broad lips, and silver eyes of the steppelands, which fleshed out the clues to his origins.

Another fingertip contact, this stroke moth-wing gentle at the back of Mykkael's thigh; except the result woke a nerve end, screaming. The garrison captain sucked an involuntary breath, half strangling the impulse to whimper.

'For pity.' But this time, the voice held compassion. 'You're a great deal worse than a mess. Without help, you're not going to walk out of here.'

The touch melted back. Mykkael pulled in a shuddering lungful of air, while glass jars chinked near his elbow. Then scented, hot oil splashed and flowed down his back, and the hands began work in earnest. Their gentleness almost wrung him to tears. He subsided, smoothed down by an expertise that made him wonder if he was back in a coma, and dreaming. His chest unseized. Shortly, he was able to speak. In the language Jussoud would likely know best, Mykkael murmured, 'How can I ever repay you?'

Jussoud gasped, his strong fingers shocked to a stop. 'How is this?' he exclaimed, overcome. Oblivious to the drama contained in the broom closet, he swept a searching regard over the desert-bred captain before him. 'How can you know the motherland's tongue?'

'Taught. As a child. My stepfather traded.' Mykkael raised himself on one elbow, straining to see what Taskin's soldiers had unearthed.

Jussoud's arm swiped him flat. 'Do not spoil my diligent efforts, you impertinent upstart.'

Working a bruised jaw, just banged on the cot strut, Mykkael grumbled a filthy phrase he had learned as a boy from a drover. Then he added, through bliss, as those hands worked their magic, 'Just don't ask me to write your distant relatives a letter. I speak, but I don't know the ideographs.'

'I do,' Jussoud stated, his dignity in place. 'They take

half a lifetime of patience to learn.' He caught Mykkael's elbow, planted a fist, then pressed down on one shoulder until something tight popped free in his client's upper back. 'Do you have patience, Captain?'

'Only as I choose. Thank you, for that. I'm much better.' Mykkael let his head loll in the crook of his elbow, warned as an icy shadow encroached that someone else came to stand over him. The near soundless step most likely meant that inimitable presence was Taskin.

The commander addressed Jussoud. 'Can you do aught with him?'

Sweet oil licked a channel down Mykkael's buttocks. 'Oh, I think so,' said the easterner, detached as a butcher who sized up the heft and weight of a carcass. 'If the muscles are eased, the pinched nerves will subside. The limp can be made much less noticeable.' His tone changed. 'Hold now.'

The hands grasped his leg, applied traction and torque. A reaming, white fire tore through his hip. Mykkael crushed his face to his forearm, and scarcely managed to muffle a scream.

Then something crunched and let go in his pelvis. Pain laced his bad leg, then subsided. On his face, slammed limp, Mykkael tasted blood on his teeth. For that, he said more words. Ones that had once made the incensed drover chase after a sprinting small boy, waving a lead-tipped ox goad.

'I can't make him civilized,' Jussoud admitted. Then he chuckled. 'No. Don't ask. I won't translate.' His hands moved, pressed a scar, testing with ruthless accuracy until a sharp flinch recorded the damage past reach of his skill. 'I can't ease the half of this knot of stressed tissue, certainly not overnight.'

'Who expected that miracle?' Taskin bent aside, clipped off an answer to somebody's question, then considered the prone body, stretched out at his mercy on the cot. 'If I send Jussoud down to the Lowergate barracks, will you make time for his services?'

Mykkael tipped up his face, disgruntled to be caught strapped with oil, and flat helpless. 'Yes. If Jussoud will agree to start teaching me ideographs.'

'That's Jussoud's choice.' Taskin tapped his chin with an immaculate thumb. 'Now, my choice. The whipping I owe you will wait. Can you stand yet?'

Mykkael flexed his leg with tentative care, then flashed Jussoud a glance of astonished gratitude. He shoved erect like a cat about to be served with a dousing, snatched up his dropped cloak, and covered his grease-shiny shoulders. 'I can stand,' he responded, running fresh sweat, but no longer wretchedly shivering. 'Exactly what did you wish me to see?'

'This.' Taskin moved.

Mykkael stalked after him, barefoot, and entered the crowded closet.

They showed him Anja's clothes, every one, down to the delicate, lace-sewn camisole, the fine, scented silk that had only hours ago kissed the girlish curve of her hips.

'What do you think, My*sh*kael?' Taskin demanded.

The garrison captain blotted his stinging, split lip. 'She took those off without help. Most likely willingly. Nothing's torn. The lace isn't hooked, or unravelled.'

'Is that all?'

As though the words goaded like searing hot wire, Mykkael knelt. He fingered a bangle bracelet, to a musical clash of gold bells. Then he picked up a silver-capped shoe, and arose with the dainty, scuffed sole cradled between his rough hands.

Princess Anja came alive to him in that moment.

Her presence combed over him, mind and spirit, and infused his rocked senses with the intimate essence of her exotic perfume. The aromatic blend of sandalwood and desert flowers framed a memory so vivid and distant, Mykkael knew of no tongue that had enough life in its spoken phrasing to capture it.

He sucked in a breath, overtaken by storm. The young woman, Anja, assumed tangible weight, a ghost presence spun from his living contact with the slipper cupped in his palms. Witch thoughts, Mykkael realized, then understood further: Taskin was deliberately testing him for wild talent.

Despite his fierce anger, he could not fight back. His fragmented awareness already dissolved, sucked down by a vortex of terror . . .

. . . clogging fear, filled with the sweat scent of horses, and fog, swirling dank off the river . . . Soaked clothes, dripping and clammy cold . . . A woman's heart pounding, her breaths jerked in gasps as she runs through the dark in hazed flight. She is desperate. Her taut hands grip damp strap leather, while behind her, the horses bump and jostle, their eager hooves clipping her lightly shod heels, and crushing the early spring grasses . . .

Drowning in horror, Mykkael wrenched his mind clear. Wrung dizzy, then falling, he spiralled back into the dusty cellar, and recovered his spinning wits. Enclosed by stone walls, and the scouring smoke thrown off the oiled rag torches, he crumpled. The shoe dropped from his grasp. It tumbled, clattering. Curled in a tight and shivering crouch, Mykkael fought back nausea, his nostrils clouded by the oiled sweat reek rising off his own skin.

His eyes were dry. Not blurred by a young girl's salt tears, shed in shattered panic as she fled headlong through the night.

Someone's fist clamped his elbow, jerked him back upright. The bruising grip savaged Mykkael's slipped senses with a wrench like the bite of cold iron.

'*What did you see?*' Taskin hissed in his ear.

Mykkael shut his eyes, still battling vertigo. 'Dark. She's outside. In flight for her life.'

'Witch thoughts!' someone gasped, close beside him. Light shifted as a torchbearer recoiled. Boots grated on gravel, as other men stirred and exchanged rounds of sullen whispers.

Then another torch, flaring, thrust into his face. '*What did you see?*' the commander repeated.

'Country clothes. Lightweight shoes. She's wet. Swam the river.' A shudder raked Mykkael. He thought about horses, then flinched as a sharp flood of warning coiled through him. Pierced by an icy stab of raw instinct, he closed his mind, hard, and shook off Taskin's probing. 'Witch thoughts,' Mykkael dismissed. 'Only fools trust them. I might be seeing a moment recaptured from the princess's early childhood. Or nothing more than a fanciful shadow, pulled in from one of her nightmares.'

'You claimed you weren't a slinking shaman,' the red-haired sergeant accused.

Mykkael shook his head. He swallowed back nausea. 'No shaman at all,' he insisted, his leaden tiredness pressing his scraped voice inflectionless. 'Not trained. Not brought up in tradition.'

Taskin's relentless gaze still bored into him. Mykkael sighed. He forced his scarred knee to bear weight, then reached out, *very gently*, and pried off the commander's insistent grasp. 'I never said, did I, that I had not inherited a pack of unruly, fresh instincts.'

Mykkael sensed sudden movement at the corner of his eye. He surged into a spin, hands raised, while the draped cloak gaped open at his waist. He caught a man's gesture to avert evil spellcraft, full on, then the sight of another signed curse, not completed. 'I am no sorcerer!' he cracked in fired rage. 'Don't you dare, in your ignorance, mistake that!'

Stares ringed him, unwavering. From men fully armed, and impeccably turned out, while he stood weaponless, half unclad, slicked in stale sweat and the itching residue of beast liniment and medicinal oil.

Mykkael uttered a word Jussoud would have appreciated, had the huge man still lingered in the corridor. Then, disgusted, he shrugged the slipped cloak back in place. To Taskin, he suggested, 'Find that drudge. Question her. She might have seen someone snooping here, earlier. If a witch thought bears weight, her Grace was not overpowered, nor was she smuggled out, naked. I'd guess your princess might have made her own way, masked in a servant's plain dress. See if someone else noticed the clothing.'

The ruddy sergeant bristled with outrage. 'Princess Anja would never indulge in foolish pranks! Nor would she be childishly stupid enough to leave Highgate without an armed escort.'

'Perhaps not,' Mykkael agreed. 'No harm, though, in checking.'

Taskin's searing regard on him lingered. 'The drudge has already been sent for,' he allowed. 'She could arrive in my wardroom at any moment. You ought to get dressed, or lie down before you fall over.'

Still fighting queasiness, Mykkael shot back a racked quip. 'No order, which?'

'Your call, soldier,' Taskin said, less generous than rigidly practical. 'If you drop, I won't waste a man, picking you up off the floor. Jussoud's gone home. He's sent back to bed. Can't lose the edge off him to exhaustion. Respect that, since I want you upright and alert, and for that, you'll need his attention tomorrow.'

'You do keep the rust polished off your swords,' Mykkael dug back without rancour. He rallied, gathered the trailing hem of the cloak, then ploughed ahead on unsteady feet until he won free of the closet. His scathing reply floated back from the corridor. 'You would have made a first-rate field captain, if you weren't cooped up guarding a citadel.'

Two men snapped fists to their swords, for the insolence; the arrogant sergeant bit back another slur.

Taskin, rod straight, took the ribbing in his stride. 'You serve under me, here above Highgate. Don't forget that.

Do you need a litter to reach your home turf? My groom can deliver the gelding.'

'No litter, no groom.' Caught with one leg thrust into his trousers, and his bad knee aching like vengeance, Mykkael unlocked the offended clench of his teeth. 'And forgetting your style of service is right tough, you high-handed, pale-faced bastard.'

But his heated, last insult was respectfully masked, its phrasing couched in the intricate tongue spoken in Jussoud's eastern steppes.

Two hours before dawn, the mist clung like wool, masking the snow-clad spires of the peaks that would restore her sense of direction. She huddled, shivering, in a pussywillow thicket, eyes shut to contain the fraught pitch of her fear, while patrols from the palace thundered past on the road, the smoke from their torches streaming . . .

IV. *Victims*

RETURNED TO THE PALACE ARMOURY, AND THE CANDLELIT ALCOVE THAT SERVED AS HIS TACTICAL HEADQUARTERS, Taskin resisted the urge to run agitated fingers through his hair. Before him, spread flat, lay the list of merchants' names and promises outlined in the seneschal's fussy script. A second sheet, sent from the Highgate watch officer, detailed the traffic moving to and from the palace. Beyond the balcony, Taskin also commanded a view of the wardroom, below. At this hour, the chequered floor was crowded by the relief watch, donning surcoats and arms for the upcoming change of the guard.

A hovering aide raised a question over the jingle of mail. 'Commander, you wanted the watch's list sent on to the Lowergate garrison?'

'To Captain My*sh*kael, yes. No need to waste time for a copy.' Taskin selected the rice-paper sheet, which dutifully recorded his own dispatched messengers bearing the locked chest from the treasury, along with a wrapped oil painting; Mykkael himself, and his two-man escort; then disparate groups of Middlegate merchants with their wives, their grooms and their carriage teams. Each of those entries had been matched against the seneschal's tally. The few names left over were accounted for: Crown Prince

Kailen, off to visit the taverns by Falls Gate. The other contingent included a robed dignitary and six servants clad in Devall's formal livery. They would be bound for the Lowergate keep, bearing the high prince's offer of funding and men to further the search for the princess.

The gesture was a breach of crown protocol, and a slight against Sessalie's aged king. Taskin assessed the move's brazen overture, then measured its impact against the desert-bred captain he had just given high-handed dismissal. The upright seneschal would have flinched to imagine the course of the coming encounter. Devall's smooth, lowland statesman might well fall prey to the brunt of Mykkael's outraged temper. The ex-mercenary was seasoned. He had demonstrated his astute grasp of royal hierarchy. Even disadvantaged and set under pressure, he had handled his share of political byplay down to a subtle fine point.

Devall's embassy was likely to suffer an unenviable reception down at the garrison. Not worried, his mouth almost turned by a smile, the commander slid the list across his marble-topped desk for dispatch through the messenger relay.

The aide left on that errand, and all but collided with an officer inbound through the alcove doorway. The arrival was early to be bearing word from the riders who quartered the riverbank. Taskin met the man's urgent salute, braced for bad news and already up on his feet.

'Report!' he demanded.

The breathless newcomer wasted no words. 'The palace drudge who discovered the sorcerer's mark? We've found her. She's dead.'

Taskin paused only to shout over the spooled rail of the gallery. 'Captain Bennent! Get me a task squad. Now!' To the winded officer, now forced to flank his commander's clipped stride towards the stairwell, he added, 'Take me there. I'll hear your details on the move.'

* * *

The hollow report of the destriers' hooves thundered over the planked drawbridge spanning the lower keep moat. To the rag men who netted for salvage on the bank, the noise posed a shattering break in routine. The Lowergate garrison were a division of foot. They used horses only for transport.

Not only the poor recognized the departure. As the breveted officer left in charge of the garrison, Vensic knew what his recent promotion was worth. By now made aware of the upset at the palace, he was at hand as the riders emerged through the dank swirl of fog at the gate.

The sultry glow from the bailey fire pans revealed them: two lancers leading in their immaculate palace surcoats, and a third man, cloaked and hooded, on a restive chestnut, whose slouched posture was not Mykkael's.

Vensic surged forward. He caught the bridle of the ornery horse before one of his horseboys got mangled. 'Where's the captain?' he demanded as the rider dismounted.

The palace guard escort startled, then stared at their charge, who flipped back the cloak's cowled hood to expose the light-skinned, wry face of the Middlegate's watch officer.

'When the captain stopped to take reports and give orders, we changed places,' the imposter confessed. His shrug as he slipped the cloak from his shoulders offered no grace of apology. 'Mykkael's habits force a man to stay keen. You'll learn, if you're here to serve under him.'

'We're Taskin's, assigned to the messenger relay,' one of the palace men rebutted. 'Where's your captain?'

'Had business, an errand,' said the officer, laconic. Then, to Vensic, 'Mind that rogue's ugly teeth. I'm told we're to keep him. Remember the drover that Jedrey caught trying to pilfer the stores? Mykkael says that one's appointed to tend him.'

Vensic laughed. 'That's just as likely to break his right hand as any formal sentencing.'

'Won't blight a man's conscience, that way, Mykkael said,' the gate officer explained in admiration. 'Captain wished that hooved snake all the wicked joy of war. Hopes it can scare better sense into yon light-fingered misfit.' Wary of the chestnut's lightning-quick strike, he surrendered the reins, relieved to let the keep's officer take charge, and muscle the brute through the bailey.

Vensic's brisk shout pulled a man from the muster gathered to relieve the street watch. 'Find a diligent boy who will keep the grooms clear,' he instructed, then secured the surly chestnut to the hitching post with the sturdiest rope and shackle. 'Someone from the armoury can have that pilferer brought up. Aye, the thieving little creep's to meet his punishment.'

To the Middlegate officer still beside him, Vensic said, 'Is the princess truly missing? Sorry prospect. What else did Mykkael give you?'

'A right mouthful of orders.' No smile, this time, as the Middlegate man assessed the yard's milling industry, orange-lit by the cinders whirled off the fire pans. 'First off, he wants you to double the street watch. No one's pulled from patrol on the walls. Mykkael's adamant, there. Draw a full reserve company, send them out straight away. I'll tell you the rest when we're settled inside.'

Vensic flagged the outbound sergeant, then belatedly noted the palace guards, who still trailed astride, looking miffed. 'Why not get down? Come into the wardroom and breakfast on cider and sausage. Captain Mykkael will be back on his own, before long. Slip in when nobody's looking, if he can, just to test if the men keep sharp watch.'

'Slinks like a desert cur,' agreed the guardsman on the grey, handing his mount off to a horseboy.

Vensic looked back at him, sober. 'He can, when it suits him. But be careful how you say so. Our garrison has a healthy measure of respect for the captain's outlandish habits.'

* * *

Mykkael, at that moment, was outside the town wall, standing knee-high in drenched grasses. The velvet shadow of spring nightfall masked him, heavy with mist, and the stench wafted up from the tannery. First overt sign of his presence, his sharp movement silenced the shrilling of peepers. The hurled flake of granite left his opened hand, sailed up in an evil and accurate trajectory, and cracked into a latched wooden shutter.

A painted slat splintered. The clatter of fragments wakened the dogs, kennelled in barrels behind him, and launched them into a frenzy. Chains dragged. The night quiet shattered to a chorus of barking.

Mykkael smiled, and waited. A moment later, the shutter slammed back and disgorged the irate face of a matron. If her hair was tied up in curling rags, her tongue was not bound. Keen as a troutman's flensing knife, her curses shrilled over the racketing hounds.

Mykkael winced. Since the misty darkness no doubt obscured the falcon device on his surcoat, he half-turned, resigned, and uttered the yip the steppes nomads used to round up their wandering stock. The barbaric cry transformed the dogs' snarling into yaps of riotous welcome.

'Fortune's pink, naked arse, it's yourself!' huffed the matron. The damaged shutter clapped shut.

Shortly, the downstairs door cracked, and a towheaded child admitted him. Mykkael ruffled her hair, then stepped into gloom redolent with wet hound, and the rancid aroma of ham and boiled onions. He said gently, 'I'm sorry. Tonight, I haven't brought butcher's scraps.'

The upstairs voice shouted down and upbraided him. 'You'll pay for that burst shutter in coin, if the silver comes out of your pay share.'

Then the house matron shuffled down the beam stairway, mantled in mismatched wool blankets. The feet under her night robe were callused and bare, with the lumps of the curling rags hastily stuffed under a drawstring cap.

Worse than mortified, she appeared outraged enough to snatch up a game knife and geld the importunate male who had rousted her.

Well warned as the spill of her pricket candle unveiled her purpled complexion, Mykkael spoke quickly. 'Crown business, madam. Your husband is needed.'

'Well, your murderer's bound to evade the law, this time. Benj is no use.' The woman plonked her broad rump on the settle, while the dutiful girl shoved the door closed. To Mykkael's raised eyebrows, the matron admitted, 'He's drunk. Flopped in a heap in the smokehouse, with my oldest son snoring off whisky beside him. They sipped their fill off the crown's largesse. Neither one's likely to budge before noontide, when they're finally driven to piss. They'll loll about with sore heads, after that. Take brawn and a handcart to shift them an inch, and not worth the thumping bother.'

'Where's the handcart?' Mykkael inquired, dead earnest.

The huntsman's raw-boned, vociferous wife stared back at him, gaping.

'Madam, tonight my quarry's no murdering felon. Her Grace Princess Anja is missing. I want the riverbanks quartered, but quietly. Taskin has three squads of outriders searching, crown guards, sent from the palace. They have city-bred eyes, and might see what's obvious, but for nuance, I need a trapper. Nobody other than Benj has the huntsman's knowledge to track her.' The pricket flame flared. Light brushed the cut angles of Mykkael's set face, then subsided, cloaking him back under shadow. 'I'll heave your man into the moat if I must, to shake him out of his stupor.'

'Benj'll waken, if it's for the princess.' The goodwife adjusted her blankets and stood, too canny to test Mykkael's barbaric temperament, or stall him with badgering questions. 'Or else, as I'm born, I'll help douse the layabout under myself.'

She shooed her girl off at a run to haul the handcart out

of the shed. 'We'll just strap my man into a dog harness, first. Benj, bless his heart, doesn't swim.'

The adrenaline prickle of raised hair at the nape was not a sensation Commander Taskin experienced often, although hazard had visited many a time through his diligent years of crown service. A poisoning attempt, or an assassin set on the run through the dark might unleash such a primal reaction. Taskin preferred the controlled clarity of sharp wits, applied with objective reason.

Yet the death that had followed Princess Anja's disappearance roughened his skin with untoward nerves as he pushed open the door to the drudge's cellar apartment.

The air inside smelled of hot grease and death, musty with closed-in dust. Straight as iron, Taskin peered into gloom scarcely cut by the flare of a tallow dip.

'Commander? She's here.' A striker snapped, setting flame to a second wick in an alcove off to one side.

Taskin crossed over the threshold. He almost tripped as his boot heel mired in a throw rug braided from rags. That ill grace nettled him worse than the exhaustion brought on by a night of extended duty. He pushed past a curtain of strung wooden beads, and at last encountered his duty sergeant.

The man knelt by a box bed tucked into the wall. Taskin stooped under the lintel and squeezed his tall frame into the stifling, close quarters.

The old woman lay straight as a board on stained sheets. Her eyes were wide open, as though the horror that had pinched out her life still lurked in the airless dark.

'Not a mark on her,' the sergeant said, his voice pitched taut with unease. 'Her extremities are cold and she's started to stiffen.' He pressed a palm over his nose and mouth to stifle the taint as he added, 'You know the men claim she was taken by sorcery? They've noted the desert-bred captain was the last to be seen in her living company.'

Taskin regarded those frozen eyes, gleaming like glass in the flame light. Again, gooseflesh puckered the skin on his arms. 'They think My*sh*kael did this?'

The sergeant shrugged. 'Well, our northern stock doesn't breed the rogue talent for witchery.'

'We have other foreigners inside our walls,' Taskin pointed out with acerbity.

'True enough.' The sergeant rubbed his bracers as though to shake off a chill. 'But we have only one of them born to bronze skin.'

Taskin rebuffed that statement with silence. He bent, sniffed at the dead woman's mouth, then resumed his unflinching inspection. Methodical, he pursued the unsavoury task, undeterred by the stink, or the whisper of draught that set the bead curtain clacking, and winnowed the glow of the unshielded candle.

The sergeant stared elsewhere, transparently anxious. 'What do you want done with the corpse? She has no close family; we already checked.'

Finished examining the dead woman's arms for a pox rash or signs of a puncture, Taskin gave his considered answer. 'Roust the palace steward. Tell him I want the use of a wash tub to pack the body in snow. Then fetch the king's physician. I'd have his opinion concerning this death, though the cause would seem to be poison.'

'Who would wish her harm?' The sergeant raised the candle, cast its wavering light over the poor woman's ramshackle furnishings. Her work-worn mantle draped, forlorn, on its peg, alongside two raggedy skirts. 'What did this drudge have that would merit an assassin who carried exotic potions?'

'If she knew anything about the princess's clothes, somebody wanted her silenced.' Taskin straightened, and wiped his long fingers on the corner of the fusty sheet. The glance he delivered along with his summary was stern as forge-hammered steel. 'If you overhear anyone else passing gossip, I want the talk stopped. No man mentions sorcery unless we have proof. The same rule applies to the matter of Captain My*sh*kael's integrity.'

Mykkael returned to the garrison wardroom in the black hour prior to dawn, but not with his usual style of cat-footed anonymity. His errand had left him soaked to the waist. No matter how silent, his presence brought in the miasma of green algae and raw effluent from the stock-yards.

Sergeant Cade met him, broad-shouldered and dependable, his gruff face drawn with concern. 'Bright powers, where were you?' His wry survey took in Mykkael's pungent state, and prompted a struck note of horror. 'Don't tell me you just dragged the Lowergate moat for somebody's unlucky corpse?'

'I was actually dousing a limp body under,' Mykkael admitted without humour. He pressed ahead by brute will, his exhausted leg dragging, and his voice raised over the screeling wail as the garrison's armourer refurbished a blade on the sharpening wheel. 'Is Jedrey down from the Middlegate, and where's Stennis? You did get my word, that I wanted the reserve roster called up for active duty?'

'Day watch is already dispatched, with reserves. Jedrey's back.' Cade gestured towards a pile of loose slates, jostled aside on a trestle. 'Assignments are listed for your review. You want them brought upstairs? Very well. I sent Stennis to head the patrol at the Falls Gate. The mad seeress you wanted to question wasn't asleep in her bed. Since her family couldn't say where she went, I presumed you'd want a search mounted, soonest.'

Mykkael gave the officer's choice his approval, then added, 'Not like the old besom, to wander at night.'

'Well, you have an immediate problem, right here,' Cade said, a nettled hand raised to shelter his nose from the stench brought in with his captain.

Mykkael stopped. He regarded his most stalwart

sergeant's dismay with a dawning spark of grim interest. 'You're suggesting I might change my clothing?'

Sergeant Cade gave way and threw up his hands, harried at last to despair. 'You won't get the chance. Devall's heir apparent sent an accredited delegate with five servants here to receive you. They've been cooling their heels with bad grace for an hour. Since the ward-room's too noisy to keep them in comfort, we put them upstairs in your quarters.'

The effort of dragging his game knee upstairs, weighed down by waterlogged boots, destroyed the lingering, last bit of relief bestowed by Jussoud's expert hands. Mykkael reached the landing, streaming fresh sweat. As his hip socket seized with a shot bolt of agony, he stopped and braced a saving hand against the stone wall by the door jamb. There, wrapped in shadow, reliant on stillness to ease his stressed leg, he all but gagged on the wafted scent of exotic floral perfume. The fragrance overpowered even his soiled clothes. Mykkael's first response, to indulge in ripe language, stayed locked behind his shut teeth. Cat-quiet, not smiling, he took pause instead, and measured the extent of his violated privacy.

Devall's servants had disdained to use the clay lamp from his field kit. Accustomed to refinements and lowland wealth, and no doubt put off by fish oil, they had lit the garrison's hoarded store of precious beeswax candles. The chest just ransacked to find them was shut, the lid occupied by a liveried adolescent, who buffed his fingernails with the snakeroot cloth Mykkael saved for polishing brass. More effete servants perched on his pallet. The largest pair had appropriated his pillows for backrests. Another one snored on the folded camp blanket, his pudgy hands clasped on his belly. The last rested boots fine enough for a lordling on Mykkael's straw-stuffed hassock, uncaring whether the bronze caps on his heels might scratch the painted leather.

The captain might ignore those self-absorbed oversights. But not the barebones necessity, that the high stool by the trestle he required to relieve his scarred knee was currently unavailable. The Prince of Devall's accredited envoy sat there, an older man with the arrogant ease ingrained by born privilege and crown office. His back was turned. The furred hem of a costly, embroidered robe lapped at his neatly tucked ankles, and his barbered head tilted with the air of a man absorbed by illicit reading.

The pain hounded Mykkael to a split-second choice, and efficiency overrode nicety. He drew his sword.

The grating slide of steel leaving scabbard whipped the dignitary to his feet. His raw leap of startlement whirled him around as the captain limped into the room, then sent him in stumbling retreat from a weapon point dulled by hard use.

Each dent, each scratch, each pit etched by weather lay exposed in the flare of the candles.

The servant on the stores chest gave a shrill squeak and dropped the polishing cloth in his lap.

'Not to worry.' Mykkael flashed his teeth, not a smile, snapped the cloth off the boy's trembling knee, then hooked his vacated stool just in time. Since his last, staggered stride towards collapse would be seen as a loutish breach of diplomacy, he turned the effect to advantage. 'This is a northern-forged longsword, as you see. Not a shaman's weapon, that must be appeased by the taste of living flesh when it's bared. I've only drawn it for cleaning, besides.'

While the High Prince's delegation eyed his bared blade with incensed apprehension, Mykkael met and searched six flinching glances one after the next, without quarter. 'Relax. Ordinary steel means nobody bleeds.'

As the dignitary smoothed down his ruffled clothes, and the servants nursed their shocked nerves, the garrison captain granted them space. He looked down, let them stare as they pleased while he scrounged after his oil jar.

The interval confirmed his suspicion that his papers had been disarranged. So had his quill pens, the keep's books, the ground pigments for inks, and his boxes of spare fletching and broadheads. Every belonging he kept on the trestle had been callously fingered and moved.

In deflected pique, Mykkael dipped the cloth and began to attack the rust on his weapon. The white snakeroot fibres quickly turned colour. To the untutored eye, the stains would appear indistinguishable from dried blood.

Soon enough, he was gratified by excitable whispers behind the servants' cupped hands. While the dignitary dared a mincing step forward and floundered to salvage diplomacy, Mykkael scarcely regretted the uproar aroused by his ornery leg. Dog-tired, in itching need of a bath, he allowed his ill humour to ride him. 'Since you didn't come down from the Highgate for tea, what can the garrison do for you?'

Gold chains flashed as the foreigner peered down his cosseted nose. Mykkael captured the moment, as the watery, pale eyes flickered over his person, and dismissed him. The man's shaved, lowland features showed his transparent thought: that Devall's greater majesty owed no grace of respect to desert-bred stock, bound by poor fortune to accept the paid service of an isolate mountain kingdom. Devall's suave overture would be dutifully delivered, though every word would ring hollow.

'His Highness, for whom I stand as crown advocate, wished to offer his assistance with the search to find Princess Anja. Armed men can be spared from his personal retinue, and gold, as need be, to loosen those tongues you might find reluctant to talk.'

Mykkael raised his eyebrows, his attention apparently fixed on his work with the sword. 'They'd crawl through the sewers at my command?'

The advocate stiffened.

The movement snapped Mykkael's head up. His brown eyes shone like hammered bronze in the excessive flood of the candlelight. 'Ah, there, don't take affront. Gold braid and velvet won't suit, I do realize. Why not offer Devall's guardsmen to Taskin?'

Unfazed by the servants' skewering regard, Mykkael watched, unblinking, while a man who was not thinking civilized words maintained his mask of state dignity. 'Commander Taskin has been offered assistance as well. In his Highness's name, I can say that gold braid and velvet are of trifling concern beside the royal bride's safety.'

'I agree.' Mykkael raised his sword, and swung towards the nearest candle to sight down the business edge. He set down the rag, then recovered the whetstone he also used as a paperweight. 'Tell your prince his generosity has my heartfelt thanks. If Sessalie's garrison requires his assistance, his men, or his bullion, I will inform him by way of Commander Taskin.'

Devall's envoy pursed sour lips. 'You don't care for her Grace's security, outsider?'

Mykkael took his time, primed the whetstone with oil, then ran it in a ringing hard stroke down the length of his blade. 'King Isendon, her father, cares very much. I work in his name.' Another stroke; the battered weapon's exceptional temper sang aloud with ungentle warning. 'Better that his Highness of Devall should be reminded not to forget that.'

'You were a mercenary, before this,' the delegate observed in contempt.

'Proud of it,' Mykkael agreed, reasonable. Proud enough to know, in Sessalie's case, that the keys to a kingdom were not in his purview to sell. 'Are you done here?'

'Apparently so.' The royal advocate snapped irritable fingers and rousted his bevy of servants. The industrious one elbowed his fellow awake. The others rose, yawning and scattering the pillows. As his indolent retinue assembled about him, the dignitary bestowed a crisp bow, then gathered his robes and swept out. The ruffle of air stirred up by his exit streamed the candles, and wafted the sickly sweet odour of hyacinth.

Mykkael swore under his breath with brisk feeling. Then he braced his left hand on the trestle and pushed himself back to his feet. He was still snuffing candles when Vensic arrived, bearing a flat item wrapped in a quilt.

'Come in, the door's open,' Mykkael snapped, resigned.

'Breached, more like.' The good-natured officer of the keep cat-footed inside, sniffed once, then grinned in farm-bred appreciation over the melange of bog reek and perfume. 'You asked for something from the palace?'

Mykkael turned his head, saw the package brought up from the wardroom, then nodded. 'A portrait. Her Grace's likeness, don't handle it carelessly.'

Vensic noted the scattered sheets on the trestle, frowned, then settled for propping his burden on top of the rumpled pallet. 'I see now why that dignitary left looking singed.'

'In the hands, or the tongue?' Mykkael finished his rounds, reached the stool, parked his leg. 'No shame in him, sadly. Only self-righteous contempt.' Since his fingers were trembling too severely to light the oil lamp, he was forced to waste, and leave the last candle burning.

'You should rest,' Vensic suggested in tentative quiet.

'Not just yet.' Mykkael clamped both hands on the trestle to stay upright as a cramp wracked his leg and shot fire through his lower back. The paroxysm subsided. He flipped through his papers, restoring their order, then paused. His fingertip traced down the list sent by Taskin, detailing the names of who had passed Highgate from the precinct of the palace. Prince Kailen's name appeared near the top. The entry beneath had been altered.

Mykkael's questing touch sensed the rough patch where someone had lifted the script. The name of a servant had been scribed in the blank, the ink on that line just barely fuzzed by the telltale hatch of torn fibre. The captain ran a testing thumb over the trestle, and encountered the trace grit of blotting sand.

That detail niggled. Here in the garrison, an erasure was more likely to be scraped with a knife, with the ink of an overstrike left to dry without any civilized niceties.

'Something wrong?' Vensic asked.

'Perhaps.' Mykkael resettled the whetstone on top of the list. Then he grasped his leg, hauled, and endured the flash of white pain as he propped the limb straight on the trestle. 'Send for Jedrey. If he's home, fetch him back.'

After a moment of expansive surprise, Vensic left on the errand.

Mykkael undid the bone buttons at his calf, jerked open his cuff, then ploughed his thumbs over the traumatized tissue knotted above his scarred joint. Given no better remedy, he reached for the tinned salve. Damn all to the fact he would hear from Jussoud, he had little choice but to keep himself upright and functional.

The night duty sergeant arrived at the threshold sooner than he expected. Born above Highgate, Jedrey was not wont to knock for the sake of a desert-bred's dignity. Still dressed, but not armed, the lordly man had not shed his grimed surcoat, a sure indication he had been in the wardroom, and not at home with his wife.

A stickler for propriety, he never addressed his ranking captain outright, but waited in surly silence.

Mykkael did not look up from his knee, which appeared to consume his attention. 'From the Middlegate sentry's report, by your memory, at what hour did Devall's party pass through? Say how many rode in that company?'

Jedrey scrubbed his chin with the back of one hand, to a grating scrape of blond stubble. He detested such tests. Yet he had learned along with the rest to handle the nuisance in his stride. 'The man serves as crown advocate for Devall's heir apparent. He passed the Middlegate with six servants in tow, just after his Highness, our Prince Kailen.'

Mykkael smothered his first impulse to look up. He said, through a grimace as the salve seared his skin, 'They went together? Be precise, Sergeant.'

'Perhaps.' Jedrey shuffled his feet, barely able to rein back impertinence. 'Devall's advocate could have stepped back to allow his Highness due precedence for royal rank. If so, your common-born sentry might not have recognized the finesse of a well-bred man showing good manners.'

The predictable note of admonition was there, for the late, callous handling of the lowlanders who were the captain's evident betters.

Mykkael stifled laughter, his face kept deadpan. Adept at keeping snob sergeants in line, he turned a drilling glance sideways. 'Tell me, how many of that party just left?'

Jedrey flushed, a patched red that made his blue eyes flash like gemstone. 'I did not count their individual backsides. They were angry.'

'Better worry quick on your own behalf, soldier,' Mykkael said with edged quiet. '*I* am angry. Inside this keep, off duty or not, I expect a man to keep his eyes open.'

A pointless exercise, to argue that Sessalie was not at war; that such vigilance was unnecessary for patrolling town streets; Jedrey choked back outrage, then found himself off-balanced again by Mykkael's next clipped question. 'Why are you still here, Sergeant?'

Jedrey succumbed to the prodding at last, rage couched in his upper-crust accent. 'You should be in bed. You're not. That's no man's business but yours, don't you think?'

Mykkael mopped the salve off his competent fingers, one mahogany knuckle at a time. 'I don't have a wife left fretting at home. That means you had business and purpose, for staying. Under *this* roof, soldier, you answer to me.'

No man in the keep contradicted that tone. Jedrey unburdened, his delivery professional. 'Your seeress was found. In the moat, stone-dead, no mark on her, no foul play.' He curled his lip, his insolent regard sweeping over his captain's stained surcoat. 'But you knew that fact already, did you not?'

Mykkael shifted his lamed leg to the floor. 'My swim happened outside the walls,' he said, quite suddenly dangerous.

That gleam, in his eyes, shot chills over Jedrey. His over-bred arrogance withered. 'The news just came in, this minute. You sent for me. And I've told you.'

'So you did.' Mykkael's tone was cut glass. 'Since, for self-importance, you delayed the delivery, you can stay on duty and execute my orders. I want the old woman's body brought here. Get Beyjall, the apothecary, also the physician who lives at the north corner of Fane Street. Let them see if the victim was poisoned or drowned.'

'She was piss drunk,' Jedrey stated, stiff under that peeling reprimand. 'Her heart probably stopped.'

Mykkael shook his head, saddened. 'The old besom hated and feared open water. Her family knows this. She never went near the moat, drunk or sober.'

'Foul play?' Jedrey said, his quick temper dissolved, as it must, to this captain's deft handling.

'I think so.' Mykkael's desert features were shadowed with pity, and an odd flash of recrimination. 'Powers deliver her sad, crazy spirit, I think she died very badly.'

'You act as though you killed the old fool,' Jedrey snapped.

He found himself summarily dismissed, and departed, brooding upon his captain's fiercely kept silence.

V. Daybreak

SPRING SUNRISE BROKE OVER THE KINGDOM OF SESSALIE, THE PEAKED ROOF OF THE PALACE A DIMMED GREY OUTLINE, masked over in fog. Inside the walled town, the streets lay choked also. The carved eaves of the houses plinked silvered droplets on to wet cobbles where the slop takers made rounds with their carts and their singsong chants for collection. If the seasonal mist shrouding the morning was normal, the spreading word of Princess Anja's disappearance cast unease like a spreading blight. The lamplighters had snuffed their wicks and gone home, bearing rumour to garrulous wives. The taverns that should have been shuttered and closed showed activity behind steamy casements.

Talk moved apace. Disbelief became shock, churned to wild speculation as the craftsmen unlocked their shops. Women veiled in the damp fringe of their shawls clustered in the Falls Gate market, while the vendors commiserated and shook puzzled heads. There were no eye witnesses. Even first-hand accounts from the feast yielded no shred of hard fact. No one could imagine a reason to upset the match between Devall's heir apparent and Princess Anja.

Least of all his Highness, Prince Kailen, who reeled in

drunken, vociferous bliss up the switched back streets towards the Highgate. Ribald echoes caromed off the mansions as he was led homewards astride a palace guardsman's borrowed mount.

The pair, immaculate man-at-arms and dishevelled prince, passed up the broad avenue, shattering the quiet and driving the ladies' lapdogs into frenzied yapping on the cushions of their bowfront windowseats. The procession clopped past the palace entry. It crossed the bordered gardens of the royal courtyard, where the seneschal awaited, a wasp-thin silhouette in sober grey, arms folded and slender foot tapping.

'Powers that be!' the prince slurred from his precarious perch on the horse. 'Why does it always have to be you?'

'Importunate offspring!' the seneschal huffed under his breath. He steadied the bridle, while Taskin's guardsman helped the prince down and supported his weaving stance.

The next moment became awkward, as, knocking elbows, court official and palace man-at-arms exchanged burdens; the one reclaimed his loaned horse, while the other assumed the jelly-legged burden of Sessalie's inebriated prince.

Too tall and thin to manage the load gracefully, the seneschal wrinkled his mournful nose. 'Sorrows upon us, your Highness. Each day, I thank every power above that your mother never lived to see this.'

'She's in a better position than you to make herself heard on that score.' Kailen laughed. His handsome, fair features tipped up towards the sky, which, to judge by his rollicking sway, appeared to be wildly spinning. 'At least dead, with her list of queenly virtues, she'd be more likely to claim the ear of omnipotent divinity.'

But the Seneschal of Sessalie was too old and lizard-skinned to shock; and Kailen, that moment, was a young man too dissolute to shame.

The guardsman stayed professionally deadpan throughout. Bound to deliver the messages he carried from Captain

Mykkael of the garrison, he remounted the moment he received his dismissal and rode off to make his report.

The seneschal turned Kailen around, then began the last leg of the journey to haul his charge to the royal apartments. He puffed, grunting manfully, taxed far beyond his frail build and aged strength. All his fastidious senses were revolted by the reek of the prince's clothes – below town smells of urine and stale pipe smoke; boiled onions, trout stew and dark beer.

'Why, oh why do you do this, your Highness? Now, more than ever, we need your subjects to see you as your father's trustworthy son.'

'Need me?' Prince Kailen snorted. '*Need me?* Nobody needs me! Only Anja.' He flung out an arm muscled fit from the tourney, too sodden to notice the woes of the courtier who sweated and struggled to brace him. 'Find my sister, get her wed.' He tripped, gasped a curse, then maundered into the seneschal's longsuffering ear. 'You'll have your coveted sea trade from Devall. My sister reigns as a wealthy queen over us, and I, her poor relative, steward no more than Sessalie's dirt-licking farmers.'

'You'll marry one day,' the seneschal chided, wrestling the prince's incompetent bulk up the first flight of marble steps. 'Who knows what alliance your betrothed might bring?'

Proceeding in comedic jerks and sharp stops, the mismatched pair passed the fountain at the arch, and missed falling in by a hairsbreadth.

'Oh, my intended will wed for a bride gift of turnips,' said Prince Kailen, morose. 'Who sends the princess of anything *here*, to marry a king who counts out his year's tithes in cattle?'

'Just let us get you into the hands of your valet.' Paused, gasping, the seneschal fumbled to grasp the bell rope, and summon a footman to open the door. He was tired himself, bone-weary of Sessalie's thankless, long service. Under damp morning mist, plagued by the ache of a near sleepless night, he had no ready answer to give to ease Kailen's maudlin grasp of the truth. 'Only pray your royal sister is found safe from harm, or she'll marry for turnips as well.'

At mid-morning, when sunshine struck through and shredded the mists into snags against the snow-clad peaks, Commander Taskin had rested and washed. Reclad in a spotless, fresh surcoat, he sat at his desk in the wardroom gallery, a light breakfast sent by his daughter reduced to stacked dishes and crumbs. The gold-leafed tray had been pushed aside. Folded forearms rested upon gleaming marble, Taskin listened to the guardsman who recited Captain Mykkael's report.

The official version was short and concise, covering the seeress found drowned in the moat, then the ongoing search for the flower girl whose petition for augury had coincided with the first unsettled rumour. Street watch had been increased. Informers were being interviewed. Mykkael expected results in by noon, along with opinions on the seeress's corpse from a reliable physician and a Cultwaen-trained apothecary.

The unofficial report ran much longer, and contained several unsatisfactory gaps.

This shortfall fell at the feet of the guard now sweating beneath Taskin's scrutiny. Unhappy with his assignment to Lowergate's keep long before Mykkael's shiftless absence, the weary man suffered the grilling review, his embarrassed features flushed the same hue as his blazoned palace surcoat.

Taskin's long, swordsman's fingers were not sympathetic, tapping in scarcely muffled irritation as he posed his string of questions. 'You say My*sh*kael's own men don't know where he went, though he came back soaked from the moat?'

'Well, the talk says the corpse might have something –'

Taskin interrupted. 'I don't want hearsay, or wild rumours from the lips of the disaffected! When I said I wanted that captain watched, I meant you to mind orders, soldier! I don't give a damn how My*sh*kael slipped your escort. Understand, and dead clearly: you failed in your given charge.'

'You don't trust that slinking desert-bred, either,' surmised the shamed guard.

The rebuke came, keen-edged. 'Trusting the man is not the same thing as knowing what he's about.'

A door opened, below. Taskin's relentless attention changed target to assess the arrival crossing his wardroom downstairs. The guardsman kept discipline, too chastened to risk a glance past the balcony railing. Faced forward, he made out the patter of slippered feet, approaching by way of the stairwell.

A gleam of sharp interest lit Taskin's eyes. 'At least now we're likely to fill in one bit of guesswork raised by your inept watch.' He grasped the papers stacked to his right, flipped them face down on his desktop, then weighted the sheaf with the warming brick filched from under the plate on his breakfast tray. 'Stand aside, soldier, but mind your deportment. You're not dismissed. My case with you will stay open until after I've settled the matter at hand.'

The man-at-arms moved, accoutrements jingling, and took position behind Taskin's shoulder.

Seconds later, the gallery door swung open. A man in gold braid and maroon livery stepped in with the peremptory announcement, 'His Highness, the heir apparent of Devall.'

Two more lackeys followed, then a rumpled-looking dignitary who appeared short on sleep. Next came a page-boy, groomed and jewelled, his costume topped by a tasselled hat that made him resemble a lapdog. At his heels, wearing costly black silk trimmed with rubies, the Prince of Devall stalked in like a panther.

The commander of King Isendon's guard did not rise, which caused his royal caller a flare of stifled pique. The fact that no servant had been sent in advance should have said, stark as words, that the business that brought him was sensitive.

'Your Highness?' said Taskin. 'I regret, without notice, steps could not be taken to seat you in proper comfort.'

There were no chairs. No fool, the Commander of the Guard did not volunteer to surrender his own. The High Prince of Devall swiftly realized he was required to stand, and his dignitary with him, like any other drill sergeant taken to task on the subordinate's side of the desk. He met the challenge of that opening play with an unruffled smile, though his gold eyes showed no amusement.

'I will not apologize for my inconvenience, your lordship.' The heir apparent snapped his ringed fingers, and a lackey jumped, removed his velvet mantle, and draped the lush cloth over the railing that fronted the gallery. There, still smiling, the lowcountry prince sat down. Throughout, he stayed untouched by the rancour that smoked off his dour court advocate.

That worthy held to his bristling stance, his caustic glare fixed upon Sessalie's titled defender. 'We have a complaint,' he announced, only to find himself cut off by the suave voice of his prince.

'Not a complaint, Lord Taskin. Rather, I bring you a heartfelt appeal.' Settled without a visible qualm for the twenty-foot drop at his back, the high prince handled himself with the aplomb of a sovereign enthroned in his own hall of audience. 'Princess Anja would not have us at odds over quibbling points of propriety. She is precious to me. This scandal has already shadowed our wedding. Should I not want her found, and restored to my side with all speed?'

'Precisely where do we stand at odds, your Highness?' Taskin steepled his fingers before him, eyes open in unflinching inquiry.

Rubies flashed to the High Prince of Devall's deprecating gesture. 'Your response to the crisis has been diligent, of course.' His handsome face shaded into uncertainty, a reminder that he was yet a young man, brilliantly accomplished, but with heart and mind still tender with inexperience. 'I refer to the fact that my help has been rejected at every turn.'

The dangerous insult, by indirect implication, *that perhaps King Isendon's daughter had been fickle by design*, had no chance to stay hanging between them. The smouldering advocate snatched at the opening to vent his affront.

'Not simply rejected, my lord commander!' Chalky, all but trembling, he served up his accusation. 'Your gutter-bred cur of a garrison captain had the gall to draw naked steel in my presence. I want him punished! Let him be publicly stripped of his rank for threatening an accredited royal diplomat.'

'He's owed a stripe, I'll grant you that much,' Taskin said, unmoved rock, against which hysteria dashed without impact. 'Not in public, however. In Sessalie, a soldier's chastisement is always determined by closed hearing. Nor will I ask my king to remove the captain from his post. My*sh*kael keeps his oath as a competent officer. Question that, though I warn, if you open that issue, you had better bring me hard proof.'

'I will not mince words.' The High Prince of Devall regarded his hands, clasped in jewelled elegance on his knee. 'Captain My*sh*kael came in from an unspecified errand, his clothing still wet from the moat. There, we are also given to understand, the seeress who started the rumour of Anja's disappearance had been drowned. Her corpse was recovered soon afterwards. Scarcely proof,' he admitted. His brass-coloured eyes flickered up to meet Taskin straight on. 'Perhaps those events suggest grounds for an inquest, at your discretion, of course.' His scalding censure suggested that in Devall, no ranking captaincy was ever made the prize of a public contest at arms.

Throughout, the commander maintained his taut patience. 'Sessalie's small, remote, and at peace for so long, our instinct for warring has atrophied. The Lowergate garrison in fact patrols the streets for thieves and disorderly conduct. An unsavoury pursuit, on our best days, and the crown's pay for the job is a pittance. Not having strife, without conquests or prospects for further expansion, we've maintained the summer tourney as hard training to mature the ambitious younger sons of our nobility. We have never, before this, attracted any foreigner, far less one approaching Captain My*sh*kael's martial prowess. Believe me, the upset has caused dog pack snarling aplenty, and no small measure of chagrin.'

'But now Sessalie has a missing princess, a tragedy also without precedent.' The High Prince of Devall held the commander's regard, no easy feat even for a man born royal. 'Dare you trust her life that this is a coincidence?'

Taskin cut to the chase. 'You're asking me to allow your men leave to lead inquiries below Highgate?'

His Highness eased at once with relief. 'Can that hurt? You would benefit. If your garrison man is innocent, my outside observation will clear him. I, in my turn, seek relief from helpless worry. I can't pace the carpet through another sleepless night! Not when we speak of the princess I would cherish as my wife, an intelligent partner befitted to rule Devall as a crowned queen at my side. Anja will raise the heir who carries my rule into the next generation. Her worth to me is beyond all price. Why should Sessalie stand on ancient pride, and refuse to acknowledge the fact that my future's at risk?'

'The authority you ask for must come from the crown,' Taskin said, unequivocal. 'Why did you come here, and not to King Isendon?'

'Have you seen the press in the audience hall today?' the prince's delegate broke in, scathing. 'His Majesty has been closeted with subjects all morning. Everyone from wealthy merchants' hired muscle to uncultured farmhand's sons – you have the whole countryside importuning the council for their chance to shoulder the adventure.'

'Princess Anja is beloved,' Taskin allowed. 'Is Devall's crown advocate surprised that Sessalie's people should respond in heartfelt concern?' He shifted his regard back to the distraught prince, then made his summary disposition. 'I'll give you one of my royal honour guards with a writ for Collain Herald. That should advance your Highness's petition to the head of the line.'

The commander stood, a clear signal the interview was ended.

Yet his Highness of Devall made no move to arise. His page exchanged a surreptitious glance with a lackey, and the advocate stared primly straight ahead.

'What else?' Taskin's frigid question met a pall of strained quiet.

Then, 'His Highness, Prince Kailen,' the heir apparent broached. Discomfited enough to have broken his poise, he twisted the rings on his hands. 'I'm sorry. Bad manners. But Anja is threatened. Her safety demands forthright speech.'

Taskin's mien softened, almost paternal with encouragement. 'Say what you've seen. Where lives are at stake, plain words will do nicely.'

The Prince of Devall quieted his fretful fingers, then unburdened himself in appeal. 'Kailen went down to a Falls Gate tavern to make inquiries after his sister. He was still there, and sober, when the servant I sent to buy wine for my retinue saw him. That meeting occurred some time after midnight.'

Taskin absorbed this, each item of testimony set against the report from the rigid-faced guard at his back. The commander was, if anything, too well informed on the outcome of that disgraceful affray: Prince Kailen had been plucked from the Cockatrice Tavern by Mykkael's duty sergeant, making his rounds. The royal person had been turned over to the palace guard, whence Sessalie's longsuffering seneschal had seen his Highness to bed.

Devall's heir apparent squared his neat shoulders, loath to dwell on the indelicacy. 'I realize Kailen likes to prowl like a tomcat. I also know him as a friend. To speak plainly, he has too much intelligence for the confines of his station. He acts frivolously because the peace and isolation here don't grant him any chance to test his wits. Appearances aside, I would credit his maturity this much. He loves his sister and this kingdom too well to have drunk himself into a stupor last night.'

'I would have thought so,' Taskin agreed, even that trifling confidence divulged with a reluctance that crossed his straight grain. 'On that score, my inquiry is now being delayed. Let me dispatch an honour guard to see you –'

But the High Prince of Devall raised a magnanimous palm. 'Spare your guardsmen, commander. I will seek Collain Herald myself.'

Taskin nodded. In person, the heir apparent would make himself heard, and receive the king's ear without help. Forced to acknowledge the young royal's earnestness, he unbent and ushered the contingent from Devall to the head of the balcony stair.

While the party made their way out through the wardroom, Taskin watched from the gallery railing. Once the lower door closed and restored his broached privacy, he addressed the guardsman his orders had held at attention throughout Devall's interview. 'What do you think, based on those facts you know?'

The man cleared his throat. 'Facts only? No one saw where Captain My*sh*kael went after he slipped our charge at the Middlegate. Prince Kailen was drunk when I set him on horseback. Sergeant Stennis had his Highness borne back to the garrison keep by two men culled from the street watch. No unusual report there – they'd scooped the prince from the arms of a whore, merry on too much whisky. The tavern was one of his usual haunts. Nobody mentioned him, sober.'

The commander held his stance, rod-straight and unspeaking as his survey combed over the vacated wardroom. Reassured that no bit of armour was out of place, and that each weapon rested keen on its rack, he attended the unfinished detail at his back with his usual cryptic handling. 'Very well, soldier. For your incompetence last night, ride down and find Mys*h*kael, soonest. On my orders, you'll tell the garrison captain he's to see me in person and address each point where his report failed to meet my satisfaction.'

Taskin spun and prowled back to his desk, the buffed braid on his surcoat a scorching gleam of gold, and his censure as painfully piercing. '*An unnecessary summons*, had you kept your watch, soldier. You'll suffer the fire of that desert-bred's temper as your due penalty for slacking. If the creature is contrary or difficult, and he should be, keep your professional bearing in hand. Your orders stand: make sure the man comes. Recall that I hold the outstanding matter of the captain's overdue punishment. When Mys*h*kael is finished with making you miserable, and only after you've brought him to heel through the Highgate, you can sting his pride with that fact, as you choose.'

'You want him sent into your presence well nettled?' the guard ventured, then caught Taskin's glare, and leaped in chastened strides towards the doorway.

The Commander of the Guard subsided behind his gleaming marble desk. He restored the papers sequestered beneath the brick, then finished his vexed thought in solitude. 'I'll pressure those war-sharpened instincts, damned right. The captain will answer me straight, if he's hazed. Easier to read through an unruly rage, and know whether he might be lying.'

Mykkael, at that moment, had not answered the thunderous knock that pounded the door to his quarters.

'He won't trust a lock,' admitted the fresh young officer

standing watch as Vensic's relief. 'No bar, either. The latch should open without forcing.'

'That's just as well,' Jussoud answered, 'since I dislike having to break things.'

The steppelands-bred foreigner seemed not to mind, that Highgate orders had assigned him to handle a demeaning round of service at the garrison. Nor had he asked for a lackey's assistance. His huge frame was still burdened with his basket of oils, a satchel of strong remedies, and the round, wooden tub the keep laundress used to wash surcoats. With unruffled dignity, he nodded to the stable-boys strung out behind, who carried yoked buckets dipped from the horse trough. 'Open up, lads. We're all going in.'

The ragged boys shrank back in wide-eyed hesitation, less afraid of the easterner's slant, silver eyes than of the dire prospect of disrupting the captain's peace.

'Damn you for a pack of cowards, boys!' snapped the officer to the column, that snaked halfway down the dim stairwell. 'Captain's not in, or quite likely asleep. And no wonder it is, if he's out like the deaf. Crazy desert-bred hasn't been off his feet for all of three days and two nights.'

'Easy for you to say,' the head stableboy sniped as his fellows jostled on to the landing behind him. 'You're not in front, and anyway, you were off duty the last time a man tried his luck barging in on the captain.'

Jussoud bared his blunt teeth in a grin. 'He got Mykkael's knife at his throat for presumption?'

The stableboy scowled. 'No knife. No sword, either. Just the heel of a hand, fast as lightning. Broke the man's nose all the same. Captain Mykkael didn't waste words, wasn't sorry. "Here's a rag for the bleeding," he said, "and what did the brainless grunt think he deserved, for crossing a doorway without taking soldier's precautions."'

'Here's proper precautions,' Jussoud said, agreeable, and offered the base of the wash tub as a shield.

Moved to awe, the skinny stableboy ducked inside the massive nomad's protection. At Jussoud's sly urging, he tripped the latch, and breached Mykkael's guarded privacy.

The captain was asleep, his lean form sprawled like a tiger's over the blanket that covered his pallet. His sword harness lay flat, at hand's reach on the mattress beside him. Surcoat, shirt and trousers were cast off on the floor, the heaped cloth exuding the ripe odour of bog slime through a lingering fragrance of hyacinth. Stripped down to his smallclothes, Mykkael had flouted the customs of his forebears and used fresh water to wash. Even there, field habits had trampled over nicety: the grime had been sluiced off with a rag and bucket, left standing in the bar of sunlight that shone through the arrow slit.

Propped at his bare feet, unwrapped, the princess's portrait regarded him.

Her exquisite likeness struck a note out of place in that rudely furnished chamber. The lush splendour of the oil paint glowed: the lucent sparkle in each rendered jewel, and the rich, velvet fall of her forest-green riding habit set into jarring contrast. Sessalie's court painter had done the young woman's grace more than justice; had captured the tilt of her refined chin, triangular as a waif's beneath her netted blonde hair. The jade eyes all but breathed with inquisitive mischief, the glint that peeked through her midnight-dark lashes seeming entranced by the subject of interest – just now, a fighting man's sculpted muscle, disfigured where mishap and the ravages of war had imprinted a uniformly brown skin.

The boys bearing the buckets stared agog. Then they elbowed and scrapped to claim the best view, amazed by a breathtaking display of scars no man born in Sessalie could imagine.

Unfazed, Jussoud set down the awkward wooden tub. He flipped back his long braid, shed the straps of his satchel and basket. As though he had ministered to lamed men all his life, he lowered the tools of his trade to the floor, not arousing a single plink from the glass. With the unhurried eyes of a healer, he read every sign of a man dropped prostrate from exhaustion. 'You say your captain has not slept in three days?'

'Near enough,' the duty officer allowed. 'The drunk and disorderly kept our hands full. We've been worked to the bone every watch, a night-and-day grind since the hour of Devall's arrival. Here, let me.' He pushed past, insistent. 'I should rightfully be the one to try waking him.'

Jussoud's huge hand shot out and caught the officer's shoulder. 'Not this way, you won't. The wrong move with that man could get us both killed.' Not pleased, as the stableboys burst into giggles, he took brisk charge and gave orders. 'Set down those buckets. Quietly, mind! Then I want every one of you down those stairs, quick! Tell the cook to brew me a cauldron of hot water. After that, get on back to your chores.'

As the boys shed their burdens and bolted, the nomad steered the duty officer back towards the doorway. 'When the water boils, you'll bring it, alone. I'll fill the tub and make ready, meanwhile. Best we let Mykkael sleep while he can. When the time comes, I'll waken him wisely, from a distance with a tossed pebble.'

VI. Morning

FALLEN ASLEEP UNDER THE BLACK-LASHED STARE OF THE PRINCESS OF SESSALIE'S PORTRAIT, MYKKAEL LAY immersed in thick darkness. HE forgot he still breathed. Hurled beyond mere exhaustion, his clogged senses felt sealed in a deadening field of black void. The featureless stillness did not last, but quickened to the unruly prompt of a witch thought. An uncanny movement twined through his mind and unreeled a ribbon of dream . . .

He knew her, felt the pounding race of her heart. His awareness flowed into the well of her most intimate self, until he felt the raw skin of her heels, chafed to burst blisters through the exertion of her headlong flight. Emotionally buffeted, he rode the crest of her terror, then shared her mind through a breathless interval as she snatched shelter in a hidden glen, touched gold under east-slanting sunlight.

The moving tableau of her thoughts spun and circled, flinching back from examining the grievous discovery that had shattered her life like a flung stone. Threat to Sessalie drove her beyond care for herself. Although sorrow knifed through her, vivid enough to sap her will to keep living, she battled its cry of futility. Through the salt sting of tears, and the ache in her chest caused by hours of running, she laid her head against the sweated neck of the mare who nuzzled her, begging for sweets.

Throughout, the horses surrounded her with their inquisitive warmth. Missing their accustomed ration of grain, they demanded, exploring her with the hay-scented puffs of their breath.

'You'll want for nothing,' she soothed, though her voice cracked.

The horses forgave the actual truth, that she had no such assurance to give. Their empathic herd sense stood as her mainstay against overwhelming despair. All three pairs, the horses' innate nobility gave her a gift beyond price: the generous trust of their confidence. She bespoke them by name to steady herself: Bryajne, the tall buckskin, who tucked his blunt, hammer head over the refined crest of Covette. She, a petite chestnut who flaunted the sculpted grace of her desert breeding; Vashni, the grey who carried on like the stud he was not; and Fouzette, whose stout forelegs still dribbled blood from a recent plunge through the briar; Kasminna, who delighted in nipping any creature caught unsuspecting, and Stormfront, whose dark coat gleamed with a silvery tarnish of dapples under the glare of the sunlight . . .

Then the flick of a pebble stung Mykkael's exposed side. Witch thought and dream shattered like glass, hammered through by the prompt of blind reflex. From his prone state of oblivious sleep, an explosion of ingrained physical instincts hurled him half dazed, not yet wakeful, through the practised response of a consciousness tuned by *barqui'ino.*

He grabbed and threw in one sinuous move, his raw senses reacting without the encumbrance of intellect. Sword and harness flew. Sheathed steel and strap leather scythed with deadly force back along the pebble's trajectory. The entangling missile slammed into the fast-closing wood of the door, followed hard by the throwing knife Mykkael always kept at close reach under his pillow. His schooled body hurtled after. Knuckles clenched and palms open, he poised the heel of his hand and the bone edge of his forearm to strike, while his bare skin sampled the flow of the air for the slightest warning of movement. He would kill by touch, his eyesight centred with absolute focus on the obstacles that could impede him.

He leaped the filled wash tub, one-footed, and landed without missing stride. Drill after drill, the brute course of his training had aligned his primal nerves to respond to what *was*, not what *should be*. Expectations were wrung still. The ferocity that propelled him was a high art: the unswerving clarity of an existence honed down to the pinpoint frame of the moment.

Mykkael reached the door, shoulder tucked to smash planks with a strength of will that ranged beyond flesh and muscle; and stopped. A hairsbreadth shy of destructive impact, hard breathing, he rocked on his heels and went still. The cold, feral force of his being became leashed. The change was distinct, as he released the taut stream of *barqui'ino* awareness and reclaimed the dropped thread of his reason.

The panel cracked open. Jussoud's silver eye dared a cautious glance through, followed by white teeth as he managed a smile of shaken appreciation. 'Two masters?' he said. 'I'd heard of one man who could claim that distinction.'

Mykkael pulled in a deep breath to arrest the jolting flash of adrenaline; his move *almost* casual as a sleeper just roused, but far too precise to seem ordinary, he braced a hand on the doorframe. The fingers, rock steady the instant before, now jittered with backlash withdrawal. 'To my shame,' he admitted.

'I could guess?' Jussoud dared. 'The one who first schooled you was better, in name. But he could not teach the technique you just used to cut short an entrained attack.'

'Certain steppelanders might suppose that.' Mykkael stepped back, bent, hissed a breath through shut teeth as he grasped at his spasmed muscle and tried to limber the seized joint of his knee. When that effort failed, he uttered a curse, gave in to necessity and hobbled. He raked up his thrown sword and harness from the floor, and released the jammed swing of the door panel.

Touched sober, Jussoud stepped inside. The trailing sleeve of his robe fluttered as he reached out and freed the stuck knife. He handed the blade back. Then he paused. Cool in the pale silk of his eastern dress, he provoked with no more than his patient stillness.

Mykkael's sultry glare met his silence like a slap. 'You want to know, truly? I wouldn't tell Taskin.'

'You don't have to tell me.' Jussoud's equable nature stayed limpid with calm. 'Your privacy is your own. No one else needs to know you. I don't give any man orders, whether or not he's hell-bent to destroy himself, body and mind.'

'I'm a practised survivor.' But the admission rang bitter. A disjointed backstep saw Mykkael to the wash tub. He caught the rim, now trembling like hazed game, and managed to brace his rocked balance before he fell over. Pinned down throughout an obstinate pause, he stared in fixed quiet through the arrow slit. Then he said, 'A beggar child wandered into the camp. One of the advanced aspirants was caught unawares. He reacted on reflex, and brained her.' Mykkael swallowed and stared down at his hands, as though they belonged to a stranger. 'I could not live with a memory like that. The shame of abandoning tradition was much easier. I broke oath and changed masters, left the first without asking permission for release, then spun lies to gain sworn acceptance with the second. I started again, on false pretext, as a novice. My first defection was found out, of course. Though I shared no secrets between the two *do'aa*, my name is still sealed with a death threat.'

He turned his head and regarded Jussoud, his pupils distended and black as sky on a starless night. 'Assassins come sometimes to strike balance for the dishonour of my broken oath. Either they die, or I do. There's no ground for compromise. Next time you waken a man with my history, call him by name before you toss stones. Much safer, that way. Unless you are addicted to thrill, and like taking an idiot's risk?'

'I was bred from wild stock,' Jussoud reassured him, smiling.

Mykkael burst into sudden laughter. 'Bright truth, like a spear point,' he agreed, the idiom taken from Jussoud's birth tongue. Indeed, every steppes nomad he had ever encountered seemed to court peril as an insolent pastime.

Embarrassed all at once by an unexpected intimacy, Mykkael glanced down at the steam that twined off the filled tub. 'You want me in there?'

Before Jussoud's reply, the captain peeled off his smallclothes. Naked, he made a desertman's sign against sacrilege before he stepped into the bath. 'That, for a man's urgent impulse to rut, that bequeaths us the ties to our ancestry.'

Jussoud untied his sash, and hung his silk robe. Stripped to the waist, he settled to work with his remedies. Immersed in warmed water, soothed under his skilled hands, Mykkael slept, slack and trusting as a baby. Later, gently roused and moved to the cot, he listened with half-lidded eyes as the nomad scolded over the scalds on his skin left by the beast drover's liniment. He slept again, under Anja's painted eyes, but this time his dreams brought no nightmares: only the soft burr of curses spoken in eastern dialect, and the mingled, sweet scent of medicinal oils.

Roused at length by an officer's tap at his door, the captain lay flat on his back and heard through the brisk list of the morning's reports. Jussoud tucked his knee into a support wrap of clean linen, then sewed the ends taut with silk thread. 'No more stupid doctoring with unguent for camels!' he snapped as he packed up his needle.

Mykkael flicked one finger, curt signal to excuse his diligent officer. Then he cocked himself up on one elbow, the damp ends of his hair slicked above the eased muscles of his shoulders. 'Thank you for your care of me,' he said, his gratitude left unadorned.

Jussoud towelled the excess oil off his forearms, washed his hands, then recovered his robe and adjusted the fall of his waist-length braid. 'I'll consider myself thanked if and when you respect yourself enough to spare that knee from further trauma.'

'What price, for the life of King Isendon's daughter?' Mykkael stated as he rolled on to his feet.

Jussoud paused, his hands burdened as he stoppered his oil jars and loaded them back in his basket. 'You know she's in danger.'

Mykkael nodded, unwilling to divulge the uncanny chill that witch thoughts had strung through his gut. 'When you see Taskin to account for my treatment – yes, he gave such orders! Don't insult that man's competence with denials. When you call on the tyrant to give him your gleanings, could you pass on the gist of my officer's report?'

Granted the willing assent he expected, Mykkael pawed into a clothes chest for a fresh pair of breeches and clean shirt. He dressed, still speaking, despite the discordant clamour of voices arisen in the downstairs wardroom. 'Relate the details you recall, as you wish. But the particulars I insist on are these: the Falls Gate seeress was murdered by drowning. The flower girl who sought her fortune knows nothing. My informers drew blanks. The streets show no sign of suspect activity.' He moved to the cot, retrieved mud-crusted boots. 'I have three lines of inquiry yet to pursue, and one more point I plan to tell Taskin in person. He can expect me. I'll be at the Highgate to meet him in three hours.'

The argument below subsided to grumbles, cut by the thump of someone's feet, climbing the inside stairwell.

Mykkael registered this as his fingers threaded the buckle that fastened his sword harness. Armed, now all business, he rebounded off his good leg, hooked the satchel of remedies from his path, and relinquished the obstruction into Jussoud's startled hands.

That forthright flow of urgency saw the captain through the doorway, a moving flicker of pale shirt doused into the shadow beyond.

What happened next, no man saw.

Jussoud's more orderly exit followed at Mykkael's heels. Bearing satchel and basket, the nomad began his descent of the spiral stair. He gained no more warning than a sigh of stirred air, then an indistinct sense of blurred movement. At the next step, he blundered into the falling, limp bulk of a sandy-haired palace guardsman. The wretch was unconscious. His unstrung frame crashlanded into Jussoud's dumbfounded embrace. The healer staggered. Half turned to save his precious oil jars from smashing against the stone wall, he narrowly managed to salvage his balance and sit with the dropped body sprawled in his arms.

'Jussoud, he's not harmed!' Mykkael assured him from below. Unrepentant, he spoke in low-voiced eastern dialect, as direct and brutal an admission of fact that his pre-emptive strike was deliberate.

'I'll have to tell Taskin,' the masseur warned, also using his native language.

'Your loyalty demands that,' Mykkael agreed. He stood his ground, all brazen, cold nerve, and sustained Jussoud's glare without flinching. 'Serve as my witness with the same honesty. You received my report, and heard out my intentions before this palace guardsman made his way over my threshold. Please see the fellow is properly cared for. My men downstairs will assist you. They'll dispatch a litter, as needed, to bear him in comfort through Highgate.'

Under his healer's questing touch, Jussoud felt the

vigorous signs of an angry victim starting to rouse. 'I will pray to my gods that you are a man who knows the full measure of trouble you stir. Little good comes of taunting the tiger.'

Mykkael spun without words. His step in departure made not a sound, a rare feat for a man who was crippled.

Jussoud sighed. As uneasy as though he had just sampled poison, he restrained the stunned guardsman's thrashing. He could not regret leaving the captain at large. No safe method existed to detain Mykkael. As a killer, the man was chilling, for his speed and his unrivalled competence. He might be the linchpin the crown required to save Sessalie's princess from danger. Yet if the contrary proved true: if the desert-bred was a traitor immersed in a covert conspiracy, the game piece haplessly caught in his path must survive to bear Taskin fair warning.

Prince Kailen suffered his punishing hangover immersed in his bath, the soaked hair at his nape crushed against the bronze rim, where he rested his pounding skull. Tendrils of scented steam rose about him, running sweat in rivulets down a complexion tinged greenish from nausea. When the crisp knock rattled the chamber door, Kailen whispered a curse. A crease stitched the corners of his shut eyes. Though he was in a sorry state to receive, the noise pained him worse than the prospect of unwanted company.

A dispirited flick of his Highness's finger dispatched his hovering valet.

The manservant deferred to the prince's condition. He moved on stockinged feet, and admitted the caller with hands that did their utmost to muffle the strident plink of the latch.

Cool air winnowed in. The draught puckered Kailen's flushed skin, bearing the fashionable hyacinth perfume used by Devall's court lackeys.

The Crown Prince of Sessalie decided his head ached

too much to endure any lowlander's penchant for ceremony. 'The heir apparent of Devall may enter, as he pleases.'

The draught became a breeze as several bodies filed in.

Kailen cracked open bloodshot eyes. Through parted lashes, he sorted the blurred but sparkling impression of Devall's maroon and gold livery. To the one pricked by the costly glimmer of rubies, he said, 'They haven't found any sign of her, yet. Not even that busy cur of a desert-bred, though he's got the whole lower garrison scouring the town. All the inquiries they've run down, every whisper they've culled from the streetside gossip has drawn nothing but blanks.'

The Prince of Devall looked haggard, as though he, too, had not slept through the night. Composed by the grace of iron will and state poise, he inclined his groomed head to request the dismissal of the valet. 'Might we speak of this privately?'

The fair royal in the bath tub shrugged streaming shoulders, then winced as his headache rebelled. He said testily, 'What's to hide? Every servant at court knows the details already. The kitchen maids bring back the lower town gossip on their return from the market.'

'Even so,' said the High Prince of Devall, his consonants considerately muted. 'My words, and yours, bear more weight than a commoner's.' He waited, smiling in gracious tolerance, until the red-faced valet accepted the hint, and bowed himself out of the chamber.

The Crown Prince of Sessalie surveyed his immaculate counterpart, his inflamed eyes a troubled china blue, and his clenched fists couched in soap suds. 'That's all I know, in my servant's hearing, or out of it. Nobody has a clue where my sister has gone, or what fate may have befallen her. We have no enemies, and no political significance to draw the interest of other nations. No one could have spirited her away without trace! Anja's much too resourceful to pack up her nerve and submit. It's not canny, to suppose she could have been kidnapped. Not in front of the nosy eyes of Sessalie's inbred society.'

'For myself, I prefer not to stand on presumption.' The High Prince of Devall gave way to his frustration and paced, fastidiously skirting the puddles splashed on the marble-tiled floor. 'Lady Shai is the princess's closest confidante. Some change in habit, or a detail of Anja's dress or mood may have caught her notice. An astute line of inquiry might prompt her recall. I wish, very much, to pay a call on her. Yet I need you along with me to observe propriety, do I not? Since the lady's a maiden, titled and wealthy, and not yet promised by handfast?'

Given Kailen's enervated sigh, the high prince's manner turned pejorative. 'You must come as I ask! I will not risk the least insult to Anja, or lend your court the mistaken impression that I would flatter another young woman with a visit in private company.'

'As if the sour opinion of Sessalie's matrons could tarnish Devall's reputation!' Kailen managed a lame grin. 'That's laughable.'

The heir apparent stopped, his regard sharpened by a turbulent mix of sympathy and censure. 'Her Grace is your sister, and the joy of her father's old age. She is also the paragon of wit and good character I have chosen as our future queen. For my sake, and for the pride of my realm, you will honour her by maintaining appropriate form.'

'Well then,' Kailen sighed, his puckered fingers clenched on the tub rim as he arose, streaming soap froth in a cascade down lean flanks, 'since I'm still too sotted to fasten my buttons, and you've excused my valet, your servants can kindly assist with my dress.'

Informally clad in his loose, white shirt, his sword harness and a labourer's knee-length trousers, Mykkael threaded a determined course through the late-morning crush in the streets. Though the thoroughfares under Middlegate were narrow, the traffic parted before him. Passersby always stared at his back, no matter what hour he passed. Even lacking his blazoned surcoat, he drew notice, surrounded by fair northern heads and pale skin.

He met that difference straight on, and nodded a civil greeting to the matrons out shopping with cloth-covered baskets. He asked the foot traffic to pause, allowing the straining mules of an ale dray smooth passage as they toiled uptown. By the public well, he caught the scruff of a sprinting urchin to spare an aged man with a cane.

The oldster's middle-aged daughter paused to thank him, then inquired after the princess. Mykkael gave his apology, said he had no news, then slipped like a moving shadow through the jostling press of women drawing water from the cistern. He kept a listening ear tuned to the snatches of talk that surrounded him: the idle speculation on bets for the summer game of horse wickets; complaints exchanged by servants concerning the habits of greatfolk; the chatter of young girls on the virtues of suitors; the irritation of a mother, scolding an unruly child. At random, Mykkael tracked the patterns of life embedded in Sessalie's populace.

Princess Anja's disappearance spun a mournful thread though the weave of workaday industry.

Mykkael let that tension thrum across his tuned instincts. Alert as a predator sounding for prey, he paused to sip a dipper of water in the shade, and overheard the Middlegate laundresses sharing news of a lost cat. His dark hand was seen as he hung the tin cup.

'Captain!' someone said, startled. Skirts swirled back as the women parted to give him space.

Mykkael nodded politely. Like most sheltered northerners, these folk met his glance with reluctance. If they had stopped challenging the authority he had never been seen to misuse, their hidebound tradition would not yet embrace the upset of a foreigner holding crown rank. Today, his appearance provoked a mixed reaction. While some folk still eyed him with outright distrust, or turned their shoulders to ward off ill luck, others met his presence with anguished appeal, as though the looming threat of a crisis forced them to a grudging trust. Now, his hardened experience offered them hope, that he might plumb their formless, uncivilized fears and retrieve their lost princess from jeopardy.

Mykkael surveyed faces, but found nothing suspicious. No furtive lurker dodged into the shadows. The crowd stayed innocuous. Nothing more than clean sun warmed the hilt of the longsword sheathed at his back. Only daylight nicked coloured fire through the women's drop-glass earrings. To the bold matrons who approached him with questions, he answered: no, he had no further news of the princess; very sorry.

The captain moved on through the racketing din of Coopers' Lane, where apprentices pounded iron hoops on to barrels. His step scattered a racing gaggle of children trying to catch a loose chicken. At due length, he reached the cool quiet of the gabled houses on Fane Street.

The physician lived on the corner, in a tidy two-storey dwelling with geraniums under the windows. Mykkael dodged an errand boy, hiked his strapped knee over the kerb, and chimed the brass bell by the entry.

A maidservant admitted him with punctilious courtesy and ushered him into a drawing room that smelled of waxed wood, and the musty antiquity breathed from the wool of a threadbare Mantlan carpet. Mykkael stood, rather than risk the pearl-inlaid chairs to the weapon slung from his harness. Hands linked at ease, he admired the animal figurines of carved ivory, then the ebony chests brought from the far south, with their corners weighted with tassels knotted from spun-brass wire.

The physician had been a well-travelled scholar, before he retired to Sessalie.

He entered as he always did, a plump, pink man with a myopic blink who moved as though shot from a bow. His clinical stare measured his visitor's stance, then softened to smiling welcome. 'Mykkael! Your leg's a bit better, today, is it not?'

The captain gave credit for that with his usual astringent humour. 'Jussoud's good work, not the bed rest your sawbones assistant prescribed me.'

'Cafferty meant well,' the physician apologized. 'That's his way of saying we don't have a curative treatment.' He glanced down, noticed his dripping hands, and sighed for the oversight that invariably made him neglect the use of a towel.

'Your seeress drowned,' he ran on, 'though you know that already. My report would have reached you at daybreak. More questions? Ask quickly.' He darted a glance sideways. 'I have a client waiting. A first pregnancy, bless her. She's perched on the stool half unclothed, anxious and not at all comfortable.'

Mykkael nodded. 'Quick, then. The apothecary agreed with your evaluation, but also concluded the old woman wasn't poisoned.'

The physician stopped, caught the nearest carved chair, then sat down at the glass-topped table and folded his hands. 'Oh dear. That's not what we expected to hear.' His brow furrowed under the combed fringe of his hair, gently faded to ginger and salt. 'You now have a vexing mystery to solve.'

Mykkael raised his eyebrows. 'Say on?'

The plight of his nervous client forgotten, the physician ticked off points on his fingers. 'She drowned. In the moat. Lungs were sodden with water tinged green with algae. But she did not fall in while she was still conscious. She had long nails. None was broken, or dirt-caked. I saw no evidence that she ever attempted to claw her way up the bank or cling to the slime-coated rock of the wall.'

'She could not swim?' Mykkael suggested. 'Sometimes panic sends that sort straight down.'

The physician blinked. 'They always struggle. This one's clothes were not torn or disarrayed. And she swallowed no water. Drownings do that, as they flounder.' He paused to rub at his temples, as though the fraught pressure of his fingers might ease the troublesome bent of his thoughts. 'Her stomach was empty, except for a pauper's dinner of beans and bread.' Silent a moment, he finally looked up, his mild face taut with sobriety. 'Captain, I'm loath to be first to suggest this, but –'

Mykkael voiced the horror without hesitation. 'Sorcerers can steal the mind, I have seen. Their victims are often reft of intelligence. A woman touched so might fall into the moat. She would not struggle, or swim, or cry out.'

The stout man at the table heaved an unhappy sigh. 'She would simply breathe in cold water on reflex, unaware of the fact as it killed her.'

'Thank you,' said Mykkael. 'I'm sorry to say you've confirmed my suspicions. At least the crown treasury will compensate you for the unpleasant service. The keep bursar will deliver your fee, at my order.'

Pale with distress, the physician stood up. 'Oh dear. You think that mad seeress knew something about the princess's disappearance?'

'I heard nothing about that, and neither have you!' Mykkael snapped. 'Where a sorcerer hunts, that is wisest.' On swift afterthought, he added, 'Does the apothecary suspect?'

'Master Beyjall?' The physician thought carefully. 'If he does, he stayed close-mouthed about it.'

'The man learned his trade in the Cultwaen Highlands,' Mykkael said, all at once pressed to urgency. Time fleeted past, while an unseen enemy moved apace. 'Beyjall should have seen a sorcerer's workings before this. He likely knows not to speak of such things and seed fear that might draw arcane notice. Listen to me. If you sense *any* creeping unease, or have the unsettled feeling you're being watched, go and ask the apothecary for a candle to burn after dark. If he doesn't understand what that means, or if he says he can't help, go to my personal quarters in the keep. Bring him along with you, and both of you stay there until I come back. Can you do that?'

No coward, the physician straightened stout shoulders. 'You have my promise. I'll see you out. Wherever you're going, I wish you bright guidance. I'll say this also. If King Isendon doesn't appreciate what you risk on behalf of his daughter, I do. We are fortunate to have you in charge of the garrison. Warded candle or not, I shall pray on my knees for your safety.'

'Pray on your knees for your own,' Mykkael snapped, then made his way out to the street.

The physician watched him go, professionally saddened by the halt in that fluid, athletic step. He stayed by the door until Mykkael's white shirt rounded the sunlit corner, leaving behind an uneasy stillness, astringent with the breeze riffling down off the glaciers.

VII. Noontide

MIDDAY SAW THE COURT LADIES RETIRED TO THE SANCTUARY TO HOLD VIGIL FOR PRINCESS ANJA. THE marble-faced building, with its queer, triangular portals and gold spires, crowned the highest point in the city. From the pinnacle at the stairhead, the view encompassed the three tiers of the walls, with the banners over the Highgate streaming like snippets of scarlet yarn in the breeze. Above, the sky hung like a bowl, the horizon notched by the serried ramparts of the peaks, dazzling under the sunlight.

'There, do you see them?' Sweating out the dregs of his binge, his face ashen from the rigorous ascent, Prince Kailen pointed from his perch on the paw of the stone lion flanking the Sanctuary's entry. 'Kerries will pluck mountain sheep off the high cliffs. You can tell where they nest by the middens of bones piled under the ledges.'

Far off, two pairs of black specks circled, the outstretched curve of their wings delicate as pen strokes in the clear air.

'They don't threaten cattle?' Devall's heir apparent leaned on the lion's tail, a touch breathless in his neat velvet. His retinue of servants, strung out below, still laboured to climb the steep stair.

'They can.' Eyes shut, since the stabbing brilliance played havoc with his pounding hangover, Kailen added, 'For centuries, the guard's archers fare out every spring to hunt down the fledgling young. Adults who lair in the close peaks are poisoned. Naught can be done with the mated pairs flocked in the rookeries over Hell's Chasm. The country's too rough to clean the nests out, so we'll never be rid of the scourge.'

'No boon to invaders,' the Prince of Devall observed. He peered into the shadowed interior of the Sanctuary where lighted candles flickered like stars. 'How long, before your court ladies retire?'

Kailen yawned. 'Not long.' He settled his broad shoulders against the lion's stone mane in a vain effort to ease his discomfort. 'The priest and priestess lead the prayers at midnight and noon. There, can you hear? They are ending the ritual.'

Inside, echoing under the cavernous vault, a male speaker cried praise to the powers above. Voices murmured in answer. Then the boys' choir chanted the final verses pleading for intercession. The singing rang out with a purity to scald human heartstrings, the liquid-glass harmony braided into the spruce-scented hush of high altitude.

The Prince of Devall inhaled the wafted perfume of the incense, ringed fingers tapping his knee. While the first of his puffing lackeys arrived, he bent his hawk's survey downwards. 'Merciful grace! In such close-knit quarters, how can one woman whose face is well known vanish without leaving a trace?'

'The king's men will find her. They must!' Kailen cradled his aching head, the heart of the realm he would one day inherit spread below like a model in miniature. The sun-washed tableau seemed peaceful as ever.

Only small details bespoke the grave trouble slipped in through the well-guarded gates. Taskin's patrols came and went, double-file rows of neat lancers threading through the carriage traffic in the broad avenues above Highgate.

In the queen's formal gardens, amid lawns like set emeralds, two dozen tiny surcoated figures enacted the midday change of the guard.

The sun, angle shifting, sparkled off the polished globe of a flag spire. The slate and lead roofs of the palace precinct dropped in gabled steps downwards, in cool contrast to the terracotta tile of the merchants' mansions, crowded in rows like boxed gingerbread above the arched turrets of Middlegate. There, the tree-lined streets ran like seams in patchwork, jammed by the colours of private house guards helping to search for the princess. Their industry seethed past the courtyard gardens, scattered like squares of dropped silk, and stitched with rosettes where the flowering shrubs adorned the pillared gazebos.

Farthest down, hemmed by the jagged embrasures of stone battlements, the lower town hugged the slope like a rickle of frayed burlap, the roofs there a welter of weathered thatch, and craftsmen's sheds shingled with pine shakes. Mykkael's garrison troops kept their watch on the outermost walls, the men reduced as toys, bearing pins and needles for weaponry.

Beyond spread the living panorama that was Sessalie, a terraced array of grain fields and pastureland carved into the sides of the vale, joined down the middle by the white tumble of the river. On the east bank, snagged by the planks of the footbridges, the trade road snaked towards the lowcountry.

The gong that signalled the close of the vigil sounded inside the Sanctuary. Devall's laggard retinue scrambled clear of the stair, while the priest and priestess filed out, bearing the staff with the triangle representing the trinity. After them, the veiled acolytes bore the symbolic fire in a golden pan lined with coals.

Prince Kailen clambered down from the lion's stone leg, astute enough to pay the recessional a semblance of decorous respect.

Presently the court ladies emerged, the deep shade of

the Sanctuary disgorging the sparkle of jewelled combs as they slipped off their white veils in the sunlight.

'There's Shai.' The crown prince moved in with athletic grace, despite his wasted condition. He breasted the flower-petal milling of skirts, bestowing kind words and sincere apologies, while the High Prince of Devall trailed in his wake, drawing a ripple of admiring glances.

The woman they sought was slender and retiring, clad in a shimmering bodice of roped pearls and a dress the shade of spring irises. She had paused by the entry, perhaps to commiserate, surrounded by a cluster of merchants' wives, who paraded their wealth in a peacock display of jewels and stylish importance.

For royalty, they gave ground with flattering speed. Swallowed into the pack, Crown Prince Kailen adroitly deflected their courteous murmurs of sympathy. 'Pray excuse us, we came to seek cousin Shai.'

Just as adept, Devall's heir apparent shed their female fawning with mannered good grace. As Shai turned her head, he captured her hand, his polished expression attentive and grave as he measured her burden of grief.

At close quarters, the famous violet eyes were inflamed, and the lily complexion expertly powdered to mask over traces of crying.

'Forgive me, Lady Shai,' the High Prince of Devall apologized. 'Our intrusion is scarcely a kindness, I realize. But is there a place nearby for us to retire to? Your cousin and I would appreciate the chance to address you privately.'

Shai touched her trembling fingertips to her lips. 'Not bad news?' Her eyes brimmed. 'You haven't brought tragic word of the princess?'

Hemmed in by the close press of women, and wary of Bertarra's peremptory inquiry from the sidelines, Prince Kailen interjected, 'Shai, no. We have no ill news. No word at all, in sad fact. Taskin's men haven't found any trace of my sister.'

'That's why we need you.' The High Prince of Devall

shifted his protective grip to Shai's arm and drew her into the shelter of his company.

Prince Kailen took station on her other side. 'The Sanctuary has a walled garden nearby, where the priesthood retire for contemplation.'

'The garden should do nicely. Shall we go?' The Prince of Devall inclined his head in salute to the hovering ladies. Then he smiled and moved Shai on through the press by the sovereign grace of his kindness.

In dappled shade, soothed by a natural spring that burbled from the flank of the mountain, the High Prince of Devall set Shai lightly down. He stood, Prince Kailen beside him, while she arranged the fall of her skirts over a marble bench. Her small hands flickered with filigree rings set with moonstone and amethyst. Neat as a doll, she could not have been more unlike the princess who was her friend and close confidante.

Where Anja was diminutively tough and outspoken, her frame slim as a boy's from her manic delight in racing King Isendon's blood horseflesh, Shai was like elegant fine china. She preferred her petticoats hemmed in thread lace, and her sleeves sewn with embroidered ribbons.

Once settled, she raised her beautiful eyes. 'I've already told Taskin everything I know, which is nothing.' She regarded the princes, her oval face drawn, and her intelligent, domed brow faintly lined with exasperation. 'Her Grace scarcely spoke to me since your Highness of Devall's arrival. Whatever thoughts she had on her mind, she had little opportunity to share them.'

The heir apparent knelt, his face level with hers. 'Did the princess not seek your opinion concerning the clothes she would wear for the banquet?'

'Powers, no!' Shai set the back of her hand to her mouth and stifled a small burst of laughter. 'That's a detail she would have left to her handmaid. Writing poetry interested her Grace far more than fussing over her wardrobe.

But even if that had not been the case, you must realize, she had no time!'

When Devall looked blank, Prince Kailen propped his back against a nearby beech tree and explained. 'Since our mother Queen Anjoulie died, my sister has held the keys to the palace.'

'She manages the staff,' Shai went on, the veil she had worn in the Sanctuary caught up and wrung between her tense fingers. 'For years, her Grace has made the decisions that run the royal household. The kitchen defers to her wishes. Visiting royalty meant stock must be slaughtered, with additional provisions bought in from the countryside, and perhaps a dozen village girls hired to help handle the chores and the linen.'

The High Prince of Devall absorbed this, then stated, 'Could such women have insinuated themselves in the palace, then acted in covert conspiracy?'

'Highness, no! They are no more than unskilled children.' Shai's tremulous smile came and went as she added, 'The oldest of them is barely fourteen years of age. The girls make up beds, and sweep cobwebs from corners the older drudges can't reach. The strongest ones haul the hot water for the laundresses, and probably stoke the fires under the cauldrons that scald your evening bath water.'

Prince Kailen agreed that the hirelings posed Anja no threat. 'The girls are the offspring of farmers known back to the seventh generation. They don't read or write. I doubt any one of them has travelled a step past the riverfront market, and Taskin himself runs the inquiry to make sure they are of good character.'

The heir apparent of Devall frowned and changed tack. 'What about Princess Anja? Lady Shai, you know her, none better. Did she show no sign of tension, no change in habits?'

'By glory, you men!' Shai regarded her paired escort in amazement. 'Princess Anja is madly in love! Every habit she had has been thrown topsy-turvy, which left every one of us guessing.'

'What about make-up?' the foreign prince pressed. 'Did her Grace use more powder or eye paint than usual, perhaps to mask signs of strain?'

'Of course she would, silly! For excitement, not strain!' Shai dealt the lowcountry prince's wrist a light slap with her veil, as though he were a dense-witted brother. 'Any maiden offered a match such as yours would take pains to maintain her best looks. Particularly her Grace, who never cared if she freckled from too much sun, or scratched her skin in the brambles.'

The Prince of Devall looked down, perhaps abashed, his ringed hands clasped in tight anguish. 'I want her back, safe! You must know, she is dear to me. Scrapes and freckles notwithstanding, I love her for her sharp wits, and her reckless humour, and for the sterling kindness that makes Sessalie's people adore her.' He glanced up, his features drawn to wounded entreaty. 'I could search my whole life and not take a finer woman to wife, or bring home a stronger queen for my realm. I need Anja because she has captured my heart, until I could look at no other.'

Shai touched her crushed veil to her lips; her violet eyes welled with tears. 'Oh, your Highness, I see how you cherish her. Don't you think I would give anything to restore her Grace to your side?' Shoulders bowed, she struggled to master her grief. 'Nothing I know could have caused the princess to leave us. Beyond any doubt, she must be in the hands of someone who seeks Sessalie's ruin.'

'You didn't notice anything amiss?' Prince Kailen pleaded, low-voiced and equally desperate. 'Anything, Shai, no matter how small. That one little detail might hold the clue to safeguard the princess's life.'

As the maiden shook her head in distress, the High Prince of Devall entreated, 'Think carefully, lady. You may not be aware, but last night, one of the palace drudges was found dead, with no mark on her of natural causes.'

Shai widened filled eyes. 'Mercy on that poor woman,

and upon all of us, for our failure. I've told Taskin I know nothing again and again!'

Torn raw, Shai appealed to Prince Kailen. 'Your Highness of Sessalie, I scarcely *saw* her Grace more than a moment, and only from a distance since the Prince of Devall rode with his train through our gates! On that hour, the princess was giddy, even breathless with excitement. I swear by every bright power above, she could not have suspected the least shadow of danger. She had but one thought, one dream, on her mind. That guiding star was the name of his Highness of Devall, who came to lay claim to her hand!'

'That's quite enough!' cracked an intrusive aged voice. 'Your Highnesses, yes! Both of you.' A stick-thin old matron invaded the grotto, fierce carriage as upright as any commander laying into brash recruits.

'The Duchess of Phail,' Prince Kailen murmured, a wry curve to his lips. 'Don't let her fool you. She's a treasure with steel principles, and an unbending penchant for kindness. Used to rescue the frogs I brought home in my pockets, and box the ears of the pages if she caught them at bullying spiders.'

The elderly woman bore in, her porcelain-fine frame stiff with outrage. 'Can't you rude brutes see a thing with young eyes? Lady Shai is already devastated. Your badgering questions just add to her heartbreak without helping the princess one bit.'

'Lady Phail, we are going,' Prince Kailen said, his hands raised in abject surrender. 'Trust me, we respect Lady Shai and have no desire to savage her feelings.'

Lady Phail gave a snort through her patrician nose. 'Well, that broth of tears has already been spilled!'

Her disgusted glance measured one prince, then the other, as though she debated which of the pair most deserved to be thrashed with her cane. In the end, Shai's distress put an end to debate, inept male minds not being wont to give ground for any wise woman's sensibilities.

Lady Phail ploughed straight on past, clasped her frail arms over the weeping woman's bowed shoulders, and delivered a glare like a lioness.

'Get along, boys! You're making things that much worse with your gawping.'

Hazed past the finesse of his lowcountry manners, the High Prince of Devall bowed and beat a retreat. Kailen, no fool, snatched his sleeve as he turned, and deflected his course down a bypath that wound through the shrubbery. The tactic was timely. Past the screening of leaves, a bouquet of coloured silk flashed in the midday sunshine. Bertarra's carping rose loudest over the chorus as the other court ladies descended to console Lady Shai.

The heir apparent of Devall glanced over his shoulder in bemused appreciation. 'Your sister rules that shark pack of harpies?'

'Oh, yes.' Kailen grinned. 'With all of our mother's cast-iron charm.' As though his sore head had begun to relent, his blue eyes brightened with fond memory. 'Bertarra's scared green of her.'

'Well, I see how your sister acquired her strong will.' Broken out of the fringing border of evergreen, the Prince of Devall approached the stone arch leading back to the sanctuary courtyard. 'We're no closer to finding where Anja might be.'

'Well, you've satisfied one point,' said Kailen, dispirited. 'Lady Shai doesn't know anything.'

'That,' said the high prince, 'or else she's a consummate actress.'

'Lady *Shai*?' Prince Kailen glanced sideways in unbridled surprise. 'She's intelligent, and no fool. But she's never dissembled, not once in her life.'

The gate's shadow fell over them. Gloom darkened the heir apparent's maroon velvet to black, and muted the shine of his rubies and gold studs. His profile, trained forward, showed no expression.

'The suspicion's unfounded,' insisted the crown prince.

'When my sister played pranks, it was always Shai's face that got her Grace into trouble.'

'Not this time, to our sorrow.' The heir apparent of Devall stalked towards the steep stair and began his descent, his fierce steps ringing on the carved granite. 'You do realize, I will find her Grace, *no matter the means or the cost*. If an enemy has marked her out for a target, I shall not rest until they are smoked out. Your realm's honour and mine are as one in this matter. As Devall's High Prince, I promise this much: when we catch the man who has dared to lay hands on my beloved, I will see him sentenced to the ugliest death allotted by law in my realm.'

By the change in the watch, Commander Taskin had questioned the wine steward's boys and ascertained that none had seen the sorcerer's mark on the broom closet. The bottled vintage brought upstairs for the feast had been fetched in the late afternoon the day prior. No one but the drudge who swept and mopped tables had occasion to visit the cellars during the evening. The old woman who was dead of an unknown cause, since the king's most learned physician had encountered no proof of a poisoning.

The patrols ridden out to search by the river had lamed a good horse, finding nothing. By now, any trail would be chopped to muck, since the seneschal's move to involve the crown council had posted an official note of reward. Brash adventurers from all walks of life scoured the brush, and talk of a scandal ran rampant. Princess Anja's plight was bandied by drunks in the taverns, while half of the Middlegate merchants tied black streamers to their doors, given over to premature mourning.

Taskin, short of sleep, weighed out his next options. He dreaded to face another interview with the king, with nothing conclusive in hand. The prospect of forcing a house-to-house search raised his temper to an edge that his officers knew not to cross. They shouldered the orders he saw fit to dispatch, and assigned men to the tasks without grumbling.

Jussoud sensed the subdued atmosphere in the palace wardroom upon his delayed return from his morning call at the garrison. The commander, he learned, had sent the day sergeant to grill the gate watch for the third time.

'Bright powers, they saw nothing,' the wizened old servant who polished the parade armour confided. Evidently the gallery above was not occupied, which loosened his garrulous tongue. He spat on his rag, dipped up more grit, and talked, while the helm in his hands acquired the high shine expected of guards in the palace precinct. 'Last night was a botch-up. All those carriages, coming and going, filled with greatfolk, and each one with their grooms and footmen and lackeys? Can't keep tight security on the occasion of a royal feast. Anybody forewarned and determined could have slipped in through Highgate unremarked.'

Jussoud set down his burden of remedies, hot and out of sorts from his uphill trek through unusually crowded streets. 'Where can I find the commander?'

'Himself?' The servant returned a glance, bird-bright with sympathy. 'He's up the east tower with Dedorth's seeing glass. You think you're going up there?' The oldster pursed his lips in a silent whistle. 'Brave man. Tread softly, you hear? Last I saw, our commander was in a fit state to spit nails.'

Dedorth's glass, at that moment, was trained on the fine figures cut by two princes, descending the steep avenue of stairs leading down from the Sanctuary. Taskin addressed the officer who stood in attendance without shifting his eye from his vantage. 'I want a watch set to guard Lady Shai. Also get two more reliable men and assign them to stay with the crown prince. Right now, soldier! As you go, tell the sergeant at large in the wardroom I plan to be down directly.'

'My lord.' The officer strode off down the steep, spiralled stair, armour scraping the stone wall as he gripped the worn handrail. His footsteps, descending, faded with distance, then subsided to a whisper of echoes.

Alone in the observatory's stifling heat, as the noon sun beat on the bronze cupola, Taskin swung the seeing glass on its tripod stand. Its cut circle of view swooped over the alpine meadows, then the scrub forests that clothed the rock pinnacles under the glare of the snow line. He scanned the folds of the glens, then the deep, tumbled dells with the leaping, white streamers of waterfalls. Deer moved at their browsing, tails switching flies; hunting peregrines traced their lazy spirals on outstretched slate wings. A mother bear drowsed near her gambolling cubs. Of human activity, he found none.

The trade road, repeatedly quartered, had yielded nothing out of the ordinary, and Dedorth, closely questioned, had been little use, immersed through the night in his vacuous habit of stargazing. The old scholar had not learned of the upset at court until his sleepy servant had fetched up his breakfast at sunrise.

By then, Princess Anja had been over ten hours gone.

Taskin laced frustrated fingers over the bronze tube of the glass. His circling thoughts yielded no fresh ideas; only rammed headlong against his enraging helplessness. Accustomed to direct action, and to successes accomplished through competence, the Commander of the Guard chafed himself raw. Scores of men at his fingertips, and an open note on the king's treasury, and *yet*, he could find no lead, no clear-cut outlet to pursue.

King Isendon's anguish tore at the heart. Taskin fumed, empty-handed, stung to empathy each time he encountered his own daughter, secure with his grandchild at home. Never before this had the quiet realm of Sessalie been rocked to the frightening rim of instability. The very foundation underpinning his life seemed transformed overnight to the tremulous fragility of cobwebs. Nor had the gossip of merchants and farmwives ever carried such a poisonous overtone of potentially treasonous threat.

The bitter sense gnawed him that he dispatched the king's horsemen over black ice, with no point of access to plumb the deep current that endangered the firm ground under their feet.

'Powers!' Taskin whispered, prisoned by the close air, with its bookish must of dried ink and unswept cobwebs, 'let me not fail in my duty to Isendon, to keep his two offspring from harm.'

Far below, the latch on the outer door clanged. A deliberate tread entered the stairwell. Taskin marked the step as Jussoud's, the muted slap of woven rush sandals distinct from the hobnailed soles of his guardsmen.

Loath to be caught in maudlin vulnerability, the commander spun the glass and reviewed the vigilance of the garrison watch on the crenels of the lower battlements. He found no man slack at his post, under Mykkael, which lent him no target upon which to vent his trapped anger when Jussoud reached the observatory.

Unmoving, his attention still trained through the glass, Taskin opened at once with a reprimand. 'You are late, by two hours.'

Jussoud leaned on the door jamb, his empty hands clasped. His reply held slight breathlessness from his climb, but no surprised note of rancour. 'If you've been at the glass since the midday gong, you'll have seen the press, above Middlegate.'

'I need not see, to imagine,' Taskin answered, now stubbornly combing the warren of streets by the Falls Gate. 'The seneschal's been very busy, all morning, setting stamps upon royal requisitions.'

'So I observed,' said Jussoud. 'Every man with a grandsire's rusty sword is abroad, seeking reward gold and adventure. They'll be clouding your evidence.'

'If we had any,' Taskin snapped, suddenly tired of watching the anthill seethe of the commons. 'Two leads, both of them slipped through our fingers. A dead drudge and a drowned seeress. The loose talk claims Myshkael killed them. Did you listen?'

'To what purpose?' Jussoud sighed. 'Could his talents enable a sorcerer's work? I don't know. Logic argues the desert-bred's not such a fool. Capable of setting a death bane, or not, why should a man with his training strike to kill in a way that would cause a sensation? As for the seeress, he had been in the moat. I saw his damp clothes cast off on the floor where he left them. For a murderer who supposedly drowned an old woman, he had taken no trouble to hide the incriminating evidence.'

Taskin lifted his head, his regard no less ruthlessly focused as he abandoned the seeing glass. 'Myshkael's true to his oath to the crown, you believe.'

'If I had to set trust in surface appearances,' Jussoud admitted, reluctant, 'the debate could be carried both ways.'

'I sent down a lancer to bring the man in. He is also delayed, by now well beyond the grace of a plausible excuse.' Taskin straightened, all business. 'Do you know what became of him?'

Jussoud stared back, his grey eyes unblinking. 'He waylaid Mykkael in a darkened stairwell.'

'Fool.' The commander's long fingers tightened on the seeing glass, sole sign of his inward distress. 'He's alive to regret?'

The healer nodded. 'Unharmed, and unmarked, in fact. Mykkael stopped him cold with a blow that stunned the nerves that govern involuntary reflex. Then he used direct pressure and cut off the blood flow through the arteries to the brain *only* long enough to drop your guardsman unconscious. I find that sort of efficiency chilling, a precision far beyond any nightmare I could imagine.'

'*Barqui'ino* drill alters the synapses of the mind.' Taskin stepped back, leaned against the stone wall, while the pigeons cooed in liquid murmurs from their roosts in the eaves overhead. 'Then you've seen this desertman use skills that can kill, and leave no telltale bruise on the corpse.'

Jussoud said nothing. His sallow skin shone with sweat in the spilled glare of sun off the sills of the casements.

'Where is my guardsman?' Taskin said, his probe delicate.

'On his feet, under orders, as far as I know still searching the town for the captain.' Reliant on trust earned through years of intelligent service, Jussoud dared a tacit rebuke. 'Shaken as your guard was, and exhausted after a night of rigorous duty, he was more afraid to return empty-handed. His search at this point will scarcely bear fruit. Mykkael left the garrison, masked under your officer's purloined cloak. The garment was found later, draped over the drawbridge railing. Even the keep gate watch could not say where the captain went, or what he pursued on his errands.'

Taskin grimaced. 'I'll have that guard recalled. How many more men should I send to accomplish the charge of fetching My*sh*kael uptown for review?'

'None.' Jussoud absorbed the commander's surprise, unsmiling. 'You won't have to collect Mykkael, even if his stiff-necked pride would allow it. The captain asked me to deliver his report from the garrison, and to add, he will meet you himself at the Highgate. You can expect him in person by mid-afternoon.'

The older campaigner's silvered brows rose. 'How arrogant of the upstart, to dictate to me. What facts has he chosen to deliver, meanwhile?'

Jussoud recited, choosing Mykkael's own words, and clipped sentences that did not elaborate. The close details he had overheard from the garrison's watch officer shed no more useful light on the knotted problems at hand.

'Nothing and nothing,' Taskin snapped, eyes shut through the pause as he gathered himself. His ascetic face looked suddenly drawn against its lean framework of bone. Then his eggshell lids opened. Direct as forged steel, he said. 'So much for bare facts. Now say what you think.'

Prepared for that command, Jussoud nonetheless chose his honest words with reluctance. 'I think Mykkael knows, or is hardset in pursuit of firm evidence that will reveal the fate that's befallen her Grace. He said she's endangered. Not why or how. I'd hazard two guesses. That he's loyal, but has a strong reason not to trust where he shares his information. Or else he's involved with an ugly conspiracy, and doing a magnificent job for the party that wants to obstruct us.'

Taskin nodded, relieved, his respect for the healer grown to the stature he would have accorded a peer. 'We aren't wont to warm to a man of his breeding. The court gossip condemns him. His background checks clean, but he was a hired sword and a mercenary. He might have been commissioned a long time in advance, and sent here to win his key position through the opening of our summer tourney.'

'He is a weapon, well sharpened to spearhead whatever cause buys his service,' Jussoud agreed in blunt summary. 'He could be the best chance we have to find Princess Anja, or he might be the cipher to cast Sessalie to the wolves that would tear her succession asunder.' A fraught moment later, he braved the soft inquiry, 'Will you leave the man free, or restrain him?'

'I don't know,' Taskin answered, his trim shoulders set to withstand an unprecedented burden of uncertainty. 'You're an astute judge of character, Jussoud. What do you feel this case merits?'

The commander watched, primed and sharp as a predator, and captured the nomad's split-second hesitation. 'Ah, Jussoud, you have doubts.'

The easterner sighed. 'Just one. Not substantial.' Mykkael had not *said* his own hand had killed a child; but the flicker of fear that had crossed his dark face well suggested the chance that he might have.

'No need to elaborate,' Taskin excused. 'As always, your thoughts and mine seem to move in lock step. I value that, even if, with this desert-bred, the waters are dangerously clouded.'

'Then what will you do?' Jussoud asked, well aware he might not receive a straight answer.

Yet Taskin chose to share his rare confidence. 'Let's first see if Captain My*sh*kael keeps his promised appointment at Highgate. If he comes in by free will, I plan to hear him. Should he have sound reasons for today's behaviour, I'll wait to see whether he chooses to disclose information I can use. The facts he delivers to my discretion had better hold value and substance. Once those hurdles are crossed, last of all, I must weigh the manner in which he answers to justly earned punishment.'

At Jussoud's wary glance, Taskin said, starkly grim, 'Oh yes, I will have to take that risk, won't I? The brazen creature has made sure he'll be tested. I have *no choice* but to handle him now that three counts lie against him, with only one of them mine, for an act of direct insubordination. He's incurred a diplomatic insult, formally registered, that for the realm's honour, I cannot ignore. You've just witnessed the third, a far more serious charge of striking a crown guard in obstruction of a royal duty.'

'Bright powers avert!' Jussoud warned. 'I respect your prowess, my lord, and your sound grasp of command, but I've also seen Mykkael in action. Do you actually know he can kill you, *that fast*, on the strength of an ingrained reflex?'

Taskin drew in a shuddering breath. 'I doubt my imagination falls short on that score. But Princess Anja's survival may come to rely on this southern barbarian's raw instincts. Either he's our best hope to recover her, alive, or he's a loose bolt of lightning, too deadly for any man's hand to restrain. If he's too volatile to bide under a crown soldier's discipline, loyal or not, we can't risk such a weapon among us.'

As the sun's rays slanted through the early afternoon, she huddled in the dank gloom of a rock cave. The tied horses rested with closed eyes and cocked hips. Chilled and exhausted, she snatched sleep in catnaps. Yet each time she drifted, fear stabbed her awake, sweating from the recurrent nightmare: of familiar faces tirelessly hunting her, their changed eyes ice-hard with cruelty . . .

VIII. Afternoon

THE GARRISON SENTRY ON WATCH BY THE FALLS GATE SCARCELY SENSED THE WHISPER-LIGHT STEP AT HIS BACK. Before he could turn, or set hand to his weapon, a small, furry bundle arrived on his shoulder, its sharp claws digging for balance.

The startled man-at-arms closed one hand on the scruff of what proved to be a young cat. Then he realized just who had crept up behind him. 'Captain!'

Mykkael flashed a smile from under the penitent's mantle that covered him from head to foot. He had been to the butcher's, to judge by the fly-swarming contents of the osier basket slung from one casual hand. 'Have that kitten sent up to the Middlegate watch officer, along with my updated orders, could you please?'

By now accustomed to the odd ways in which the captain saw fit to assert his command, the sentry secured the unsettled creature thrust into his grasp: a nondescript tabby with white paws and pink nose, sadly bedraggled, but bearing a braided cloth collar. 'Someone's lost darling?'

Mykkael nodded. 'Belongs to the little girl who lives on Spring Street, the house with blue shutters and stone walls smothered in grapevine.' He kept himself masked in the shadow of the keep, out of sight of the carters who jockeyed their drays past the foot traffic on the planked drawbridge. Through the cries of the vendors peddling grilled sausage, and the hoots of two sotted roisterers, he added, 'Tell the child not to let her pet wander again. I found him in the hands of the rat killer's boys.'

'Powers!' swore the guardsman, correctly faced straight ahead. 'I thought you'd ordered a stop to their cruelty?' Before Mykkael's tenure, such boys had trapped stray cats in the alleys, and lamed the poor wretches for rodent bait.

'As of today, those boys have received their last warning.' The captain's face hardened beneath the coarse hood. 'If they persist with their mishandling of animals, here's my updated word: the next offenders will be culled with a warrant. See that the change gets through to my sergeants.'

The guardsman on duty returned a clipped nod.

'Now,' Mykkael resumed, brought around to the business assigned to the watch by the Falls Gate. 'You have the information I wanted?'

The man's answer was prompt. 'The recent list of the seeress's clients, or at least the ones that her family recalls? The descriptions are scant. No one could agree on the numbers.'

'I don't care if the details were mixed up.' Mykkael measured the sun angle, his cloaked stance touched to scalding impatience. 'Report.'

The guard understood what his pay share was worth. He delivered the paltry summation. 'The old besom hosted a wide range of visitors, most of them commons who came to buy charms for luck in love, or talismans for prosperity and safeguard. Yesterday's list included five to eight merchant women from the Middlegate, all of whom came to her heavily veiled. Beyjall the apothecary visited once, perhaps to ask for a scrying. He often sought readings to locate rare herbs, but since the granddame kept her sessions private, the family can't swear the presumption in this case was accurate. They all remembered the page from the palace. He came, they said, in a craftsman's rough smock. But his shoes were a rich boy's castoffs.'

Mykkael's question slapped back, fast as ricochet. 'When?'

Taken aback by a stare of driving intensity, the guard breathed an inward sigh of relief that he was prepared with an answer. 'Two days ago. The night of the High Prince of Devall's arrival.'

'Well done. That will do.' Mykkael adjusted the hang of his sword blade beneath his voluminous mantle, a sure sign he had concluded the interview and now made ready to depart.

'Anything else, Captain?' Given a negative gesture from beneath the enveloping hood, the guardsman cast a distasteful glance over the clotted offal heaped in the basket. 'You're off on some errand outside the gates? Surely you aren't taking *that* as a gift to feed the blind storyteller who begs by the crossroad market?'

Mykkael tapped his chest, where he had a second wrapped packet stowed, beyond easy reach of the lower town's scourge of street thieves. 'The scraps are intended for somebody else. I'll be back in an hour, two at the latest. Tell your duty officer to have a saddled horse waiting, I expect to be in a hurry.'

Asleep in the sun after quartering the hills through most of the night with a hangover, old Benj the poacher stirred to the jab of a toe in his ribs. The sawing snore that rattled his throat transformed to a grunt of displeasure.

'Benj!' screeched a female voice that wrought havoc with his sore head. 'Benj, you damned layabout, wake up.'

The carping as usual belonged to the wife, shrill as a rusted gate hinge. The toe, which dug in with nailing persuasion and unleashed the fireburst of a pressed nerve, was no woman's. Benj shut his slack mouth on a curse. Aware enough to interpret the delirious yap of his dogs, he answered without opening his eyes. 'The only trail that matched your description runs into the western ranges. Six horses, led by a slight person who wore lightweight shoes, with soles stitched by a quality cobbler.'

'Benj, you rude wastrel, get up!' The wife caught his limp wrist with a grip like steel pincers and hauled. Her brute effort toppled him sideways off the kennel barrel currently used as his backrest. 'Benj, at the least, you can hold conversation within doors, like a civilized man of the house.'

'I'm not civilized,' the poacher protested. He opened bloodshot grey eyes, peered through his oat-straw frizzle of hair, then winced as the sunlight stabbed into the lingering throb of his hangover. To the cloaked desert-bred who crouched, feeding guts to his fawning hound pack, he appealed, 'I can talk just as well lying down. We don't need to go anywhere, do we?'

'In fact, we do.' Teeth flashed in the captain's face, though his grin showed no shred of apology. 'I'm a bit pressed, and would bless the favour if your woman could heat up a cauldron and boil a slab of raw beef.'

'You don't intend to feed a good cut to those dogs!' the woman yelped in shocked horror.

Mykkael laughed. 'Evidently not, since the thought seems to threaten you with a stroke! Here, let me.' He tossed the last gobbet from the basket, wiped his smeared hands on the grass, then replaced the wife's grip upon Benj's slack arm with a muscular pull that hoisted the lanky man upright. 'Come on, my fine fellow.' He braced the poacher's wobbling frame and steered a determined course through the dog piles dotting the yard. 'You'll be more comfortable inside, anyway, since those beef scraps will draw clouds of flies.'

The mismatched pair trooped into the house, the wife clucking behind, concerned for her rugs and her furnishings. Yet Benj arrived without mishap in his favourite seat by the hearth. Perched on the threadbare, patchworked cushion, he scowled at his feet, perplexed by the fact that the old nag had not forced Mykkael to pause and remove his caked boots at the threshold.

While the woman bustled to hook the cauldron over the hob, the poacher nestled his thin shoulders against the ladderback chair.

Mykkael sat on the settle. At home enough to push back his hood, he washed the suet and blood from his hands in the basin fetched by the poacher's tongue-tied little daughter. He did not press with questions. A rare man for respect, he stifled his need and waited for Benj to order his thoughts.

As always, that tactful handling caused the poacher to give without stint.

'Your quarry's holed up quite high in the hills. As you asked, we did not haze or close in. Just followed the trail from a distance. Good thing you forced me to start tracking last night. With every damn fool out there beating the riverbank, not even my dogs could unriddle the hash that's left of the scent.'

As though the report were as ordinary as the drone of the bees outside in the melon patch, Mykkael surrendered his packet of meat for the wife to stew over the fire. 'No one noticed you? No crown riders picked up on your back trail?'

Benj shook his head, cleared his throat, then demanded, 'Does a guest get no tea or hospitality in this house?' Before the wife could draw breath and sass back, he answered the captain's question. 'No one's wiser. I left my son in the hills, keeping watch. He will lay down fresh deer scent to turn any dogs, as you asked. If the searchers come near, he'll divert them.'

Mykkael released a deep sigh in relief. 'Benj, you're a hero.' While the wife scoffed at the untoward praise, the captain accepted the buttered bread set out by the towheaded daughter. He broke the hard crust between his scarred fingers, then raised eyes grown suddenly piercing. 'Listen to me, Benj. This business is dangerous, more than I ever imagined last night.'

The wife snorted again, bent to poke up the coals. 'Huh. What else is new? Benj has lived with the threat of the noose all his life, and damn all to sate his taste for the king's summer venison.'

But the captain shook his head, the bread chunk between his deft hands all at once a forgotten afterthought. 'No, Mirag, believe me. A hangman's rope would be merciful beside the perils that stalk Sessalie's princess.' His edged words cut the quiet like fine, killing steel swathed out of sight under satin. Without warning, his lean figure seemed set out of place, a jarring wrong note amid the fragrance of sweetfern brought in by her husband's jaunt through the brambles.

The small daughter retreated and clung to her mother's flax skirts. Mirag folded the child into a wordless embrace, and regarded the creature who ate bread on her settle, his poised calm transformed to a predator's stillness, a heartbeat removed from raw violence.

Mykkael made no effort to dismiss the fresh fear blown in like a chill wind between them. 'Already, two people have died for far less than your husband knows now. Keep your family at home. Talk to no one. Leave your son in the hills, under cover, and for your life's sake, hold to the very letter of my directions.'

'So long as I can sleep off the whisky that's pounding my brain to a pulp,' Benj said, wise enough to pretend to complacence before the wide eyes of his child. He tipped back his head, hands laced in his lap. 'That boy on the run, that's made off with the horses? He's somehow involved with the fate of the princess?'

'Her life may depend on what happens to him,' Mykkael admitted, unflinching.

Benj nodded, satisfied. 'Then I'll be here, for when you have need of me.'

By the time the water boiled, he was out cold and snoring. Mykkael snacked on bread and honeyed tea while his meat cooked, and Mirag badgered him to part with a chunk to enrich her stewpot for supper. The girlchild slipped out to play with the dogs, while Benj twitched in whisky-soaked dreams. Mykkael sat in thought, the odd finger tapping, while time fleeted past, and the sun slanted gold through the shutters.

'Meat's cooked almost through,' Mirag said at last. Since she had successfully cadged the best portion, she helpfully wrapped the remainder in yesterday's bread heels, then tied up the package with cheesecloth.

Mykkael arose. He extracted a filled purse from under his cloak and solemnly exchanged bundles. 'Here's compensation for the burst shutter, and the fee for Benj's tracking. There's more added on to cover additional service. Mirag, listen clearly. The coin stays in your hands until I send you word, do you hear? No drink for Benj. Keep him home and cold sober, with the dogs close at hand on their chains. I'll come back tonight with instructions.'

This once, the shrewd matron hesitated before she tucked the silver away under the lid of her milk crock. 'Captain, the danger to us has always walked with the power of your crown authority. I won't see my man hang for coursing royal game. Promise me this! Whatever happens, though you face your own downfall, you won't expose Benj's name, or say that he had any part in this.'

Mykkael pulled up his hood. 'I doubt that King Isendon would value a few deer above the murderers your Benj has helped the garrison bring back to justice.'

But the poacher's wife remained adamant. 'Captain, your promise! For my son's interference with Taskin's lancers alone, we could all lose our heads for crown treason.'

Sober now, sharply aware the woman before him was trembling, Mykkael reached out and gathered her clasped hands. 'You are brave as a tigress, and for that, on my honour: there is no act of treason in safeguarding the king's daughter's life.'

When Mirag's fear did not settle, Mykkael bowed his

head briefly. Then he laid the chapped skin of her knuckles against the sword belt slung over his heart. 'Madam, hear my oath. No man in Sessalie knows your husband has ever worked with me in liaison. Nor will they, I swear by the blood and the breath that keep the life in my body.'

The Seneschal of Sessalie received no warning beyond the desperate string of entreaties from Collain Herald, outside. Made aware he confronted an imminent invasion, but given no chance to order the scatter of state documents under his hand, he turned his head, lips pursed in harried forbearance. Then the latch tripped. The door to the chamber reserved for the king's private consultation wrenched open with a force that snuffed all the candles.

Bertarra charged in, turquoise skirts spread like sails, and her round face flushed with agitation. 'Guards, guards, guards, guards!' she burst out. 'Can't step an inch without tripping over the boots on their blundering feet.' Unabashed by the presence of four more men-at-arms posted by Taskin's select order, she marched hellbent towards the table where the seneschal marshalled the sheets of the afternoon's sensitive business.

'A waste of crown effort, guarding the barn door after the stock has been stolen,' the late queen's niece ranted on. 'I've counted a dozen or more brutes standing idle who ought to be outside the gates, scouring the countryside for kidnappers.'

The seneschal knew when not to waste his breath, arguing. He pushed up the spectacles slipped down his beaked nose, while the lady rocked into a belated curtsey before the chair that supported the king.

She addressed him at an ear-splitting shout: 'Your Majesty!'

Fortunate among men, King Isendon kept snoring, his eggshell-frail head tipped backwards against the throne's tasselled headrest. A bead of drool clung to his ruffled state collar. The thin hands on the chair stayed motionless, the sparkle of rings frozen still as jewellery set on a corpse.

The realm's seneschal fell back on longsuffering patience. 'Lady Bertarra, as you see, the day's trying events have left King Isendon overcome.'

The court matron narrowed her blue eyes and peered at the slackened face of her sovereign. 'His Majesty's fallen witless again?'

'Fast asleep, lady.' The seneschal sighed. 'He was wakeful, last night, fretting over the fate of his daughter. If you care to entrust me to deliver your message, I'll try to address his Majesty on your behalf when he wakens, if he is lucid.'

Bertarra sniffed, the jutted flash of her diamond combs lending emphasis to her disdain. 'No need to speak. Just give him this.' She uncurled the arm tucked over her bosom and slapped a rolled parchment on to the tabletop. Then, her errand accomplished, she spun and marched back towards the doorway.

At the threshold, she was jammed on her thundering course by the inbound arrival of Taskin. Fast on his feet, the commander nipped past her without snaring himself in her acres of ribboned petticoats. Before Bertarra regaled him with carping, he caught her plump elbow in a steering grasp, and murmured a gracious good afternoon as he backed her bulk clear of the chamber. Then his neat, swordsman's reflex closed the door in her blustering face.

Leaned back on the latch, one imperious boot heel wedged to jam the shut panel, he ignored the pounding commotion that ensued on the opposite side. His steely glance first raked over the king, then settled in nailing regard on the seneschal. 'You look like a pulped rag. Isn't Prince Kailen fit to relieve you?'

The seneschal poked up his spectacles again, and peered down the pinched flange of his nostrils. 'His Highness is closeted with the Prince of Devall, a wise enough choice, for the moment.'

Taskin folded his arms, a curt snap of his head indicating the rumpus that shuddered the wood at his back. 'What pearl of wisdom did Bertarra deliver?'

'Let's see.' The seneschal unfurled the parchment with fussy precision. 'A petition, signed by prominent court ladies and a select circle of merchants' wives. They send an appeal for a royal writ, demanding Captain My*sh*kael's arrest.' A blink of myopic, watery eyes was hard followed by the accusatory tap of a finger. 'You know the talk brands the man as a murderer.'

'Talk is not proof,' Taskin stated. The assault on the door at his back stopped abruptly, replaced by a furious screech. The commander laid a testing palm flat on the panel, too wise to shift his braced weight prematurely. 'She's broken a thumbnail, or bent one of her rings. Care to speculate which? We could wager.'

But the seneschal declined the diversion. 'We have a woman dead of a sorcerer's mark. Such a horror has never happened in Sessalie. The people are demanding to know what's been done in response.'

Tired himself, Taskin looked hackled. 'I don't arrest anyone for the clamour raised by hysterical servants. Nor will I act on the demand of an outcry that's fuelled by unfounded gossip.'

The seneschal squared off in earnest. 'Well, this particular document cannot be taken as hearsay.' He lifted a parchment from the welter of papers, one bearing an imposing wax seal and ribbons in Devall's crown colours.

'Diplomatic complaint, for Captain My*sh*kael's misbehaviour?' Taskin pushed erect. His clipped signal summoned one of his guards to stand by the doorway in case the Lady Bertarra renewed her attempt at forced entry. 'I know about that one. It's being addressed. Be assured that my own hand will administer the punishment. Its severity will *justifiably* match the offence. This concerns an offender under my right to remand into discipline. Not even for Devall will I subject a man to the lash without weighing his word on the matter beforehand.'

'What about this, then?' The seneschal passed across another state document, also set under Devall's royal seal. The writ underneath framed a formal request to King Isendon, asking grant for the High Prince's honour guard to exercise autonomous authority to conduct a private search for Princess Anja.

Taskin glanced at the king, still asleep, his circlet tipped askew over hanks of thinned hair, and his wristbones poked like bleached sticks from the glitter of his elaborately embroidered sleeve cuffs.

Sorrow and regret softened the response the commander returned to the seneschal. 'Lord Shaillon, don't set Sessalie's seal to Devall's request, not just yet. At least hold off until after I've had the chance to question the Captain of the Garrison. Although you hold the man in contempt, My*sh*kael may have had a sound reason for drawing his steel on the high prince's advocate.'

'No reason can excuse a rank breach of manners,' the seneschal fumed. 'Let me remind you, the official your desert-bred cur has insulted is an accredited royal ambassador! The wrist-slap penalty you're proposing is child's play! In Devall, by law, for the same offence, the wretch would lose his right hand.'

Taskin contained the quick flash of his temper. 'I'll remember, some time, to show you a man whose back bears healed scars from the whip. No pretty sight, I assure you, Lord Shaillon, with the sensible benefit that afterwards, the soldier can still bear arms in the kingdom's defence!'

'We speak of an outlander,' the seneschal bristled. 'Not one of our own, but a mongrel of low background, and questionable habits. Since *when* do we look to a desert-bred's brawling to conduct our affairs of state? How *dare* you suggest such a creature should taint a decision concerning a prince who stands to become our pledged ally, joined to our kingdom by the kin ties of wedlock!'

Yet even for royal protocol, Taskin refused to back down. 'Captain Myshkael is a red-blooded man, invested by oath, and in service as one of Sessalie's crown officers.'

'A mistake we should rectify. Should have done so, and long since. Shame on us all, that a penniless adventurer should be allowed to take rank advantage of the opportunity presented by our summer tourney. We cannot afford to risk a misjudgement. Not when the man might be the paid agent for some unknown enemy's plotting.' As Taskin took umbrage, the seneschal raised a stabbing finger and ranted straight on. 'We are faced with a crisis! At the least, such a foreigner ought to be set aside under lock and key. He must be removed from his post at the garrison, and a trusted man set in his place.'

'Fury and rhetoric will not grant Devall your endorsement, Lord Shaillon.' Taskin's gaze flicked past the seneschal's shoulder, towards the sovereign slumped in the state chair. 'The command to discharge Myshkael must arise from the hand of King Isendon himself.'

'A mumbling dodderer who drools in his sleep,' huffed the seneschal. 'When his Majesty wakens, confused, be sure I shall get the permission I need to set Sessalie's seal on these edicts. I'll have others drawn up in sensible language that will take steps to protect our security.'

Taskin gave back a wolfish smile, his posture held at smart attention.

'But I'm not asleep,' interjected King Isendon. 'Nor am I drifting, just at the moment.' He straightened his trembling shoulders, imperious, and snapped his fingers sharp as a whip crack. 'Give over those documents held in dispute. Yes. Set them in Taskin's hands. I leave the matter of Devall's complaints in his charge to address as he sees fit.' The damp, weary eyes tracked the seneschal's sullen capitulation until the requisite papers changed hands.

'That will do, Shaillon,' said the king, dismissing all argument.

'Commander,' he continued, 'you have mentioned a forthcoming inquiry over the conduct of Captain My*sh*kael? That is well. Treat with him fairly. If he brings any news of my daughter from the garrison, I expect an immediate audience.'

Taskin bowed. 'Your Majesty.' He tucked the state documents under his arm. By the time he turned in smart strides towards the doorway, the king's gaze had already lost focus.

The seneschal surged at the commander's heels in a bothered flutter of velvets. Ever determined to snatch the last word, he found his officious presence impeded by four immaculate crown guardsmen.

'Bertarra is right,' he snapped under his breath. 'All these sentries are a nuisance in the royal chamber.'

'Necessary, every man of them,' Taskin retorted as he breezed on his way down the corridor. 'King Isendon's safety is my bailiwick, Seneschal, and no subject for you or Sessalie's chancellors to lay open to mauling debate.'

The crossroads market outside the town wall was a noisy, sprawling event that bloomed on a patch of packed earth with each dawn, and melted away every sundown. The throng of itinerant pedlars, freebooting hucksters and farmwives who traded the odd head of livestock held no crown licence to sell. Too shiftless to maintain a stall in the town, they simply gathered and spread out their wares, or pounded in stakes for their picket lines. The result clogged the verge where the trade road met the cart track which snaked down from the alpine vales.

The regulars hunkered under rickety awnings, an ill-fashioned jumble of pegged burlap and canvas that fluttered and snapped in the breeze. Packs of raggedy children screamed and ran wild, through the singsong patter of the hawkers. On fair days, the blind beggar who told stories spread his blanket under the shade of the ancient oak that also, infrequently, served as the royal gallows. The dented tin bowl he set out for coppers always sat on the plank where the hangman's stair mounted the scaffold.

The hour, by then, approached mid-afternoon. Slanting sun fell like ruled brass through the branches. The odd scattered dollop licked the head and shoulders of the man in the hooded penitent's robe. He sat, one leg crossed and the other extended, in the dust at the storyteller's feet. The pair of them shared companionable talk, and a meal of bread crusts and boiled beef.

'Ah, then it's horses, now?' the beggar said, his rich voice slipped into the broad Trakish dialect learned from his mother in childhood. 'You're wanting to bet? That was the hot topic, rightly enough, until this sad tale of the princess overshadowed all else.' Paused for a sigh, he rubbed grease from his fingers, then recovered his dauntless, sly smile. 'Do you fancy the races, or maybe the outstanding team for the match of steed wickets next month?'

'Perhaps both, maybe neither,' said Mykkael in the same tongue. He folded the last slice of meat in a bread chunk, and laid the offering into the storyteller's outstretched palm. 'If I wanted to locate an animal of a certain description, perhaps to inquire if it was for sale, who would be likely to know where to look?'

'A rascal.' Moved to bursting laughter, the storyteller turned his face, sightless eyes bound with a scarlet rag to keep his affliction from upsetting the children. 'Vangyar, the horse thief, could answer your question. Knows every creature with hooves in this valley, and speaks like a breeder's textbook. Won't be so easy for you to approach him.' The beggar rapped the scaffold post at his back. 'Crown law sends his sort to dance with the rope.'

Mykkael shrugged. 'I don't know of any man or woman in Sessalie who is forced to steal out of hunger.' Hands clasped over his tucked-up knee, he waited until the beggar stopped chewing before he finished his thought. 'I'm seeking a horse with particular markings, not pursuing a writ for arrest.'

'Fair enough.' The storyteller dusted crumbs from his lap. 'Vangyar often drinks at the Bull Trough, by Falls Gate. One of the girls there's his favourite. If you can corner him, he'll know your horse. But I'll lay your king's silver against one of my tales, you don't catch him to pitch the first question.'

'Oh, you're on.' The garrison captain grinned under his hood. 'But I'll need a forthright description to have a fair shot at the take.'

'From a blind man? That's a joke.' But the storyteller delivered from the stock of detail he was wont to pick up from overhearing stray talk.

Mykkael listened, his sharpened gaze caught by the sudden moil of activity that swirled through the gaggle of potters, the stacks of grass basketry and the hunched cluster of women who laced oat straw into cheap pallets. When a shout punctuated that burst of disturbed movement, the captain uncoiled to his feet. 'My friend, we have a sealed wager between us. For now, I regret, I must leave you.'

The beggar returned a companionable nod, content to resume spinning tales from his dusty blanket.

Mykkael strode downhill. With brisk hands, he peeled off the penitent's robe and flagged down the man from the garrison, just reined in from a gallop, and towing a second mount on a lead rein.

'Captain! Thank the powers that be, the gate watch said you might be here.' Sergeant Cade spun his snorting, bald-faced gelding, and tossed Mykkael the bridle of the riderless grey.

'What's amiss?' Mykkael settled the reins and vaulted astride without touching the stirrup. Wheeled back towards the town, he heard out his sergeant's breathless report.

'Physician from Fane Street's showed up at the keep. They've got him in your private quarters, you asked that?'

'I sent him.' Mykkael pressed the horse from a walk to

a canter, then dug in his heels for more speed. 'Only one man? The apothecary's not with him?'

Sergeant Cade spurred his lathered mount to keep pace. 'The apothecary's dead, and your physician's not coherent. No one's been able to get him calmed down to explain how the tragedy happened.'

Mykkael swore. His face drained to a queer, greyish pallor, a precedent no man from the garrison had seen through any prior disaster. 'No help for the setback, I'm going to be late for my promised appointment with Taskin.' He hammered his dappled horse to a gallop, still shouting his fast-paced instructions. 'Go through the Falls Gate, pick up a task squad of eight men. I want the apothecary's house sealed off. No one goes in, do you hear me? No matter what seems to have happened inside, I want *nothing* disturbed by the ignorant.'

'Too late for that,' the sergeant yelled back, his words breathlessly pitched over the rolling thunder of hooves. 'There's been a small fire. Burned like merry hell. No brigade dumping water could douse it. Went out by itself, finally, and left an unnatural, smoking crater that destroyed the back wall of the house.'

'Get the bucket brigade out.' Mykkael leaned over his mount's wind-whipped mane, still urgently snapping directions. 'Take a list of their names. Round up each one. Force them to step through the smoke of a cedar bonfire, then bathe head to foot in salt water.'

Sergeant Cade stared. 'Have you gone mad?' The cost of pure salt, this far inland, was extortionate.

'No, soldier. Forget about questions. Just follow my plainspoken order!' Mykkael balanced his horse, then changed its lead to sweep right at the moat and take the main road through the Lowergate. 'I'm off to the keep to settle the physician and secure his immediate safety. If you can, dispatch a rider to Highgate. Tell Taskin I'll be delayed.'

'Done, Captain.' Cade veered his mount and set off.

Mykkael urged the grey underneath him still faster,

railing at fate in snatched curses. Beyjall's sudden death carried damnable timing. The chance was slim to non-existent that a message passed through the watch at the Falls Gate could be relayed uptown in time to defer Taskin's rendezvous. Mykkael resigned himself. The reprimand he would earn for the lapse seemed hellbound to become an ordeal of savage unpleasantness.

IX. Late Day

HOT, SOAKED IN SWEAT, MYKKAEL FORCED HIS GAME KNEE AT A RUN UP THE KEEP STAIR, THEN BURST THROUGH the door to his quarters. He swept the chamber with one raking glance and fixed on the forlorn figure perched on the edge of his pallet.

Sadly rumpled, the physician slumped in his shirt-sleeves. He looked like a fluffed robin blown in by a storm, elbows set on his knees, and hands pressed to his brow.

The scuff of the captain's lame step aroused him. He bounded upright with a cry, palms raised in startlement. Behind the skewed glass of his spectacles, his china-blue eyes were dilated to black from the adrenaline jolt of his terror.

Mykkael stepped back. Checked to thoughtful calm, he tipped his head past the lintel and directed a shout down the stairwell. 'Vensic! Send one of the armourer's boys up here at once with a torch!'

Relief suffused the physician's blanched face. 'Light of deliverance!' he gasped, all but sobbing. 'On my soul, now I know you're not one of them.' His wobbling knees gave way all at once. Dropped back to his seat on the captain's coarse blankets, he rushed on in breathless hysteria. 'At least, the word goes that most sorcerers' minions will avoid the sight of a natural fire.'

'Some will flinch from an unshielded flame,' Mykkael agreed. He watched with the fixated stare of a lynx, his wary hands poised at his sides. 'Except for the oldest, and most powerful. But even ones bound to the dark arts for centuries can't abide the smoke from green cedar.' Cued by the tap of the boy's running footstep crossing the landing downstairs, the captain spun and moved back past the threshold. He returned in an eye blink, a lit torch in hand, which he touched to the frond of cut evergreen, stashed out of sight on his hurried way in.

Smoke billowed as twigs and needles ignited. 'Forgive me,' Mykkael snapped, as the resinous fumes caught the draught. The scented blue smoke billowed up in a cloud and wafted over the rattled physician. 'I had to make certain you carried no taint.'

'No bother at all,' croaked the neat little man, lightly coughing. 'Precautions are nothing but rock-hard good sense. Dear me. Until now, I thought Sessalie lay too far north to be threatened by demonic plotting and craftwork. That's why I chose to retire here. Very peaceful.' But horror had shattered his idyllic complacency. He trembled to realize that his days of tranquil practice might be for ever undone.

While the cedar smoke thinned in the breeze through the arrow slit, the physician removed his fogged spectacles. He buffed the glass with a limp handkerchief pulled from his waistcoat pocket. Shaky fingers restored the wire frames. Behind thick lenses, his bright, blinking gaze tracked the desert-bred captain, each move. Mykkael doused the torch. Then he crouched by his pallet to drag out a strongbox tucked underneath. The lock had no key, but worked through a puzzle array of brass levers fashioned by artisans from the far east.

'You seem to possess an impressive experience,' the physician observed at due length. 'That's most reassuring.

I suppose, in your past, you were probably hired to fight in a sorcerers' war?'

Mykkael nodded, terse, head bent and hands busy sorting the contents of his opened coffer. 'Against the Sushagos, yes, and after them, Quidjen and Rathtet.'

'You fought *against* Rathtet?' The physician dropped his crushed linen, startled. 'I didn't know any defenders had survived that unspeakable bloodbath.'

'Very few,' Mykkael said, his voice cranked and tight. 'A miserable, unfortunate few.'

'Oh dear. Not a subject you like to dwell on, I see.' The tactful pause lingered, while the physician recovered his dropped handkerchief. He was a worldly man, informed well enough to know that mercenaries steered clear of countries invaded by sorcerers. Lavish pay lured only the brashest young fools. The ones who signed on were quick to regret. Spellcraft could inflict worse than ruinous losses. Scarred veterans, returning, were wont to avoid a repeat of their wretched mistake.

Mostly, such conflicts levied trained troops from the far south, where skilled viziers could grant them defences. Aware his repeat record of paid service was unusual enough to seem suspect, Mykkael gave a short explanation. 'My contracts were arranged by a *barqui'ino* master, who considered high risk and extreme danger to be part of an aspirant's training. The eastern despots always hired. Paid swords were preferred, even prized for their use in covert reconnaissance. The ones who fell into enemy hands couldn't be tortured to spill secrets they didn't know to begin with.'

'Yes, I see that.' The physician huddled into his sweat-dampened shirt. 'You would have been valued for that sort of work, dark-skinned as you are, and facile with your gift of languages.'

Mykkael straightened up, bearing a worn leather sack with a drawstring. He fished inside, and withdrew a grimy copper disc strung on a scraped length of rawhide. The thong had been cut more than once, and rejoined. Three mismatched knots interrupted its contiguous length. 'Here,' said the captain. 'Wear this for protection.'

The physician gave the token his dubious inspection. Under verdigris tarnish, the wafer of metal had been finely scored with overlaid circles, interlocked through a series of triangles. The leather looped through it was darkened with stains, faintly rancid with a dried rime of sweat. 'What is it? These are bloodstains?'

'Talisman,' Mykkael answered, 'a potent charm, fashioned to guard against the assault of cold-struck sorcery.' He had his fingers thrust deep in the sack, apparently counting the contents. 'These were made for the foot troops who fought Rathtet.' Confronted by the physician's masked shudder, he said in offhand reassurance, 'Yes, they're still potent, dried blood notwithstanding. The men who wore these died of arrows.'

His inventory complete, Mykkael closed the drawstrings, then tied the sack on to his belt. 'Don't change the knots. They were ritually done to protect against theft and mishap.'

As the physician's unease progressed to reluctance, the captain stepped close, lifted the artefact from the man's shaken grasp and slipped the thong over his head. 'There. Relax, now. You're safe. Wear that talisman next to your skin, and don't take it off when you wash.'

Mykkael stepped back. The physician watched with mollified eyes as the captain eased his game leg on the stool beside the plank trestle. The keep officer had left a pitcher of cold water on a tray. Mykkael poured, not troubled by the lesser scars on his arms as he offered the terracotta mug. 'Drink?'

The physician refused, still afflicted by over-strung nerves.

Mykkael sucked down a deep draught for himself. 'Now,' he said calmly. 'Tell me what happened to Beyjall.'

The little physician's poise crumbled utterly. 'I didn't see much,' he confessed. Shaking hands clasped, he cleared his throat, and manfully started explaining. 'When I finished the last of my morning appointments, I went round to ask for a candle. Not that I needed one. I hadn't sensed trouble. But better, I thought, to apply for the remedy before the onset of first symptoms.' He trailed off, his dough face flushed to crimson.

'Go on,' Mykkael urged. 'What's done is over.'

The physician braced up, his eyes glassy with recall. 'When I arrived at the apothecary's shop, the door was ajar. That was not usual. He liked to have customers let themselves in. But when I mounted the steps, the front room was empty. The iron-strapped door to the stillroom was closed, a surprise, since the place appeared open for business. That's when I first realized something was wrong. I called Beyjall's name. When he failed to appear, I looked closer. Scribed on the plaster beside the door's lintel, I encountered what looked like a sorcerer's mark.'

The narrative ground to a painful halt. Mykkael waited, stone-patient.

'Glory preserve us,' the physician gasped. 'You know how it feels to encounter pure evil?'

'I know,' Mykkael answered. Just that; nothing more.

The physician shook his head, shivering. 'Powers forgive me, I ran in blind panic.'

'Well you should have,' Mykkael said with bracing force. 'Such craftmarks are volatile and unspeakably dangerous!'

The physician huddled, forlorn on the pallet, unable to shake off his misery. 'Dear me, to my sorrow, so I have seen. Those voracious, *unnatural* flames, and the smell – one doesn't forget.' He swallowed, then mustered frayed nerves and faced the garrison captain straight on. 'The apothecary was alive, and most likely locked in. He must have realized someone had entered. I heard his cries, and his pounding as he begged for help to escape.'

Mykkael showed the wretched survivor nothing but sympathy. 'You came straight here?'

'Directly.' The physician dabbed moisture from behind his fogged lenses. 'Captain, I hoped you might know what to do.'

Mykkael paused through a dreadful, brief silence, run through by awareness that his men from the garrison *had* responded; the squad that had rushed to the apothecary's rescue had shouldered that lost cause in disastrous ignorance. By the narrowest margin, they had missed being swept to their deaths in the explosive first conflagration.

Only the choking press in the streets and the gift of blind luck had preserved them.

At uneasy length, the captain said gently, 'Beyjall died, very horribly. You couldn't have helped him. Nor could I, had I been present. That mark you saw was pre-set to ignite within a matter of seconds. You are more lucky than you know to be here at the keep, safe and breathing. Caught out of his depth, let me tell you, Doctor, the wisest man first saves himself.'

The physician braced up. Sound sense notwithstanding, his torn heart would take more convincing. 'Poor Beyjall. You believe he was murdered because of the drowned seeress we examined?'

Mykkael shook his head. 'Not entirely, no. I think he was killed for his knowledge. Just as she was. They were the two people in this placid realm who were first to notice the works of a sorcerer afoot.'

'Dear me.' The physician blinked, his prim, worried glance on the captain. 'The unnatural creature might strike at you next.'

'I expect that he will.' Mykkael drank the last of his water and stood. 'You'll be all right? One of my men will escort you home, and stay to keep watch at your doorway.'

The physician rose also, and hooked up his crushed jacket. His bobbing stride trailed the captain's lamed move to depart. 'Will he carry a talisman like the one you gave me?'

Mykkael stopped. He turned his head, the tigerish glint in his almond-dark eyes crushed out by the force of his pity. 'I don't have enough of them to go around.'

The physician sucked a breath, raised to chilled understanding. 'Thank you for that honesty. I can manage well enough on my own. Heaven preserve us! What a sorrowful thing, that such evil should invade these quiet mountains and stake out a foothold in Sessalie.'

'My task,' snapped Mykkael, 'is to see such power thwarted. You'll go home with my man-at-arms as your escort, and sleep with him guarding your doorstep. On your way, would you stop on an errand for me? You knew the apothecary better than most. Someone must pay a call and inform Beyjall's widow the crown will pay for his funeral.'

Eight centuries past, one of Sessalie's queens had desired a rooftop garden. She had grown sunflowers to feed gleaning birds, and shared their winged company through hours of contemplation. The king who was her great-grandson added topiary, and an array of formal flowerbeds, which, years later, the kitchen staff claimed to grow herbs under glass for winter seasoning. No one recalled which subsequent sovereign had added the turrets, and planted the first of the trees.

By Isendon's reign, the oaks had grown ancient, their gnarled trunks halfway fused with the stonework that vaulted the entry. A confection of wicker tables and chairs scattered under the shaded branches now became the afternoon refuge for Sessalie's ranking courtiers. Just now the primary occupants were royal, Crown Prince Kailen and the heir apparent of Devall, attended as usual by the deferent circle of his liveried retinue. Only the saturnine advocate was absent, dispatched on an unspecified errand.

On the table, banked in a bowl of shaved ice, a serving of strawberries sweetened their conversation. The Prince of Devall had asked for red wine. The gold tray held a bottle of the famed cloud grape, just emptied. Another one had been opened to breathe, when the seneschal arrived, puffing from his three-storey ascent from the council hall.

'My Lord Shaillon, you look as tried by the day's frustrations as any man on two feet,' greeted Devall's heir apparent, his dauntless good cheer a brave effort to lift the elderly statesman's flagged spirits.

Prince Kailen sighed and pushed back the blond hair tumbled over his forehead. 'Still no word on my sister.'

The seneschal nodded, exhausted beyond platitudes.

Too polished to show disappointment, Devall's heir apparent lifted the bottle, selected a clean goblet from the tray, then poured in a dollop, and swirled it. 'Sit, my good man. You're just in time. We needed someone with a fresh palate to taste this superlative vintage.'

The seneschal drew out a chair and perched like a mournful sparrow. Polite to the bone, he accepted the wine, then cast a frowning glance on the emptied glass next to Prince Kailen. 'His Highness ought not to be drinking after last night's indulgence.'

Devall's heir apparent smiled with sheepish charm. 'The lapse is my fault. I can't be truly sorry. Your kingdom produces exceptional wines. Bereft of my bride, who can blame me for seeking such exquisitely seductive consolation?'

Sessalie's seneschal tasted the sample, then nodded his reserved approval. While the Prince of Devall filled his goblet in earnest, he asserted, 'A wine haze won't help Princess Anja's recovery.'

'No,' Kailen murmured. 'But it does dull the ache.' He bunched up his napkin, wiped the dregs from his glass, then slid it forward, inviting a refill.

The foreign prince complied, then set down the bottle. His tapered fingers still nursing the goblet that stood all but untouched before him, he broached softly, 'What news of my current petitions to King Isendon?'

'They have not been refused outright.' But the seneschal's braced posture suggested an edge of stonewalled exasperation. 'I could wish the issue had been handled differently.'

'Why don't you address my documents of appeal and their outcomes one at a time?' suggested the Prince of Devall.

'The diplomatic complaint cannot be ignored. There will be a punishment extracted. However,' the seneschal qualified stiffly, 'the garrison captain who enacted the offence will be dealt with by military discipline.'

'That means Commander Taskin's been appointed to call the damned desert-bred on to the carpet.' Kailen dashed down a swallow of wine, and grimaced. 'That upright old stick doesn't cut an offender much slack. He'll execute the verdict along with the sentence, and won't relinquish his right to keep privacy inside the ranks of his guardsmen.'

The heir apparent of Devall said baldly, 'The commander won't consent to an extradition.'

'Never.' Prince Kailen gave a tight laugh, drained his goblet, then fixed haunted eyes on his counterpart. 'Powers above, this is Sessalie! Here, we hang only murderers and livestock thieves. Our dissenters certainly don't include traitors. What brangles we settle between foreign diplomats are mostly disputes over how much of our best wine should be sold for export. We don't have the *occasion* for criminal extradition, far less any precedent concerning the inequities of law that exist between outside kingdoms.'

'Your Highness, you can't have the desert-bred captain turned over to Devall's bailiffs,' the seneschal summed up with acidic dignity.

'Are you trying to tell me he won't be locked up?' Brows raised by incredulity, the heir apparent sipped wine to douse the fire withheld from his language.

The seneschal sighed. 'Taskin maintains his crown

soldiers to fight. He keeps malcontents in line with the lash, and remands them for state prosecution only if they have incurred a direct threat of injury to a person of the royal family.'

'But this captain is the mongrel get of a darkling southerner!' Kailen burst out in protest. 'Surely a citizen's entitlements won't apply?'

'They shouldn't.' The seneschal sustained both princes' regard, his expression bitter as ice. 'But Taskin stepped in at a sensitive moment. He stood on his prerogative to handle the trial, and King Isendon charged him to redress the misconduct with fairness.'

'Well, no blood was drawn,' the High Prince of Devall admitted. 'Short of a dead advocate, I cannot submit an appeal to the primary complaint. No, the case must rest. If the outcome is lenient, I will placate my ambassador. He'll receive my reminder that he shouldn't expect formal protocol when dealing with low caste on errands.'

Gracious in capitulation, the heir apparent offered the last of the strawberries to brighten the seneschal's mood. 'Now, what of my appeal to help search for the princess? Surely that met with a warmer reception?'

'Sadly not.' The seneschal declined the blandishment, the deep, sour lines that bracketed his mouth hardened to dole out more bad news. 'The king has made disposition and given the request over to Commander Taskin's discretion.'

'Then the writ will die there.' Sessalie's crown prince jammed aggravated fingers through his corn-silk blond hair. 'Taskin's nothing if not a cast-iron despot. Never has fancied anyone's boots trampling over his turf. Devall's honour guard will not be permitted to deploy, no matter how sensibly competent.'

Devall's heir apparent absorbed this, pressed at last to withdrawn silence.

The seneschal fell back on aristocratic poise, grasped his goblet, then used the wine to ease his dry mouth. 'On a good day, the commander would pose an obstructive impediment.'

'A good day!' The High Prince of Devall shoved the berry bowl aside. Bolt-upright and incensed, he pulled in a deep breath, but could not quite rein back his lit temper. *'There's more?'*

'Oh, yes.' When balked, the seneschal could deliver a setback with vicious brevity. 'Taskin made plain he'd withhold all opinion until after his appointment with the Captain of the Garrison.'

Crown Prince Kailen rocked out of his chair, swaying and flushed. *'Myshkael! What does Myshkael have to do with this? My sister is missing, and past doubt in grave danger, and* Lord Taskin *takes pause to consult with an outlander concerning* Devall's *right to assist?'*

The high prince grasped Kailen's strained wrist, bristling with autocratic authority. 'Sit down!'

'Bright powers above!' The younger royal dropped rigidly into his chair. He accepted the filled wine glass pressed into his hand, and knocked back a vengeful swallow. 'Taskin ought to be down on his knees, singing praises for Devall's generosity.'

The high prince set down the bottle, not shaking. His rage stayed ice-cold, and his bearing immaculate. 'I'm worried. Very much so, for Anja's sake.' He locked eyes with the seneschal in earnest regret. 'I don't like to suggest what may be spurious nonsense, but has anyone raised the question of whether your southland captain may have connections to a sorcerer? If your staunch commander appears to be acting outside of the ordinary, if in fact he's shielding a criminal, that could be the first sign of warning. A man who wields craft might start off by casting spells of influence over another to further his nefarious ends.'

'My*sh*kael could well be the catspaw of such an enemy,' Kailen broke in, morose. 'Defend us from evil! Lord Shaillon, I'm not the only one to suggest that Anja's abductors might be aligned with a demon.'

The seneschal inclined his groomed head. 'It is true, near enough, that two women have died of questionable circumstances since yesterday. There is evidence pointing to Myshkael, but no actual proof. The danger, as you correctly infer, is that the case might lawfully fall to Commander Taskin to prosecute.'

The Prince of Devall interjected the first breath of fresh air. 'Well then, in good sense, something must be done to instil a proper avenue for oversight.' His attention encompassed the seneschal, the need in him suddenly piercing. 'For the princess's safety, could I trust you to appeal as my emissary to King Isendon? I could offer my crown advocate to stand in on proceedings to guard against biased judgement.'

'His Majesty has retired to bed,' said the seneschal. 'He's unlikely to entertain anyone's audience before morning. Taskin would be the exception, bearing word of the princess. Only the duchess, Lady Phail, attends the royal person throughout his informal light supper.'

Prince Kailen banged down a fist, upsetting the dregs in his goblet. 'Balefire and damnation!' While the wine spilled and ran, bleeding drips through the wicker, he added, 'If that desertman's a killer, Anja could already be dead! Powers preserve, we can't wait till tomorrow.'

'No,' the heir apparent agreed in leashed quiet. 'But we dare not tip our hand, or arouse a dangerous traitor's suspicions by running roughshod over Sessalie's court protocol. If Anja's alive, such thoughtless action might actually kill her.' He righted Kailen's glass, spread his napkin over the spill, then tucked the crown prince's unsteady hand over the stem of his own goblet. 'Drink, settle down. We shall handle things quietly. If My*sh*kael's not honest, he will have a past. Unearth one incident that casts doubt on his word, or demonstrate that his record lacks integrity, and we can build a case to strike him from his post upon grounds of his questionable character.' Devall's heir apparent caught the seneschal's nod of approval, and responded with an affable smile. 'We're agreed, then. My servants are trained to be expert at listening. My honour guard, as well, is on forced, idle time. The generous man would allow them a night's liberty to sample the joys of the town. Let them visit the taverns in plain clothes, and see what seamy facts they might garner.'

The seneschal arose, his censure directed at Kailen as he collected the half-finished wine bottle. 'You'd do well to get started, though if fortune favours, you may not need to look far afield.'

Devall's high prince stood also. While a servant restored his pert velvet cap, with its ruby brooch fastening and pheasant's barred tail feathers draped stylishly over his shoulder, he asked, 'Is something afoot?'

'We'll see,' said Lord Shaillon, Crown Seneschal of Sessalie, leaving the garden with purposeful strides. 'Taskin was scheduled to meet with the desert-bred captain two hours ago. So far as I've heard, the slinking cur hasn't shown up.'

On station at the Highgate, now nettled down to his blue-blooded bones to be forced to wait upon Captain Mykkael's delinquent appointment, Commander Taskin had not passed the stalled time in idleness. As late day shadowed the mansions fronting the avenue that led uptown from the Middlegate, he had seen his contingencies covered both ways. Behind the walls, a task force was positioned to ride down a fugitive and make an arrest; at his side, a dependable sergeant attended, equipped with shackles and a whip in a canvas bag.

Since the breathless message sent from the garrison brought word of the captain's delay, nothing changed, except that Taskin ceased his wolfish pacing.

Subsided into a glacial stillness at the arrow slit fronting the belltower, he held on to see whether the errant offender would bend desert-bred pride and ride in.

At streetside, no telltale sign showed to reveal any

change in the gatehouse watch roster. The sergeant was bored, and displeased by the prospect he might have to manhandle a commoner. Hot in his surcoat, he stood at attention until his boots pinched, and his patience frayed into rags.

'The wretch isn't coming,' he insisted at last. 'Why should we waste the whole day? You can't honestly expect proper conduct from a dog who was bred on a nameless chit in a sand ditch.'

Taskin said nothing. His narrowed eyes measured the activity in the avenue as the late afternoon press of foot traffic and carriages began thinning out before sundown.

'There,' he whispered under his breath. 'Sadly late, but not lacking honour.'

The distempered sergeant belatedly sighted the horse, driving uphill at a prudent trot that would cover ground, but not threaten unwary pedestrians. Its rider was not wearing Sessalie's hawk surcoat, nor did he use his crown rank to commandeer a more timely passage. Mykkael was clad in a sweat-damp, plain shirt, his preferred longsword slung from his shoulder. The casual dress at first seemed a statement of raffish effrontery, which regarded lightly the stature of a crown commission. Yet as the foreign captain breasted the rise, that impression was undone by his air of rapacious concentration.

Watching him, Taskin felt the hair on his arms rise up in primal warning.

Then the horse bearing Mykkael flung up its head, jerked short by his hand on the bit. It curveted sideways, while its rider raked an irritable, sharp glance over the sun-washed gatehouse.

'Bright powers curse him!' the sergeant remarked. 'He's noticed our archers. I'll have the fool whipped whose careless move has served him an idiot's warning.'

'That's my crack division posted up there,' Taskin murmured in instant correction. 'Not one of those bowmen twitched a finger. Probably nobody had to, given My*sh*kael's experience. Any veteran who ever mounted a siege would measure those gatehouse embrasures. Were they empty or full, he would take pause to assess his exposure.'

Down the thoroughfare, Mykkael cranked the horse's head sideways. Rein and heel used in concert, he dragged its weight into a wheeling rear.

'That's not a man acting on possibilities!' the gate sergeant snapped in dismay. 'If our nerve-jumpy quarry saw no sign of threat, then he's sure as daylight running flat scared out of guilt.'

'Do nothing!' said Taskin, his tone scraped to ice. 'If we react, we'll never see how this man handles himself under the check rein of lawful authority!' Beyond that cryptic statement, the commander chose tact. Now was scarcely the moment to mention the desert-bred captain's predisposition for witch thoughts.

Downslope, the horse skittered on clattering hooves, its rider a blurred form masked behind a tossed flag of black mane. The pair sidled into an oncoming dray, whose six-in-hand team shied aside and milled over a fruit seller's handcart. Its upset freight of melons tumbled and rolled, to a chorus of curses as chaos unravelled the peace. The dray team bucked in blinkered panic, while spilled fruit bounced and smashed, slicking the cobbles with crushed pith. The two carts behind entangled themselves to avoid trampling down hapless bystanders. While the watch in the gatehouse was diverted by the course of unfolding disaster, the lone horse re-emerged. It trotted a zigzagging, riderless course, with trailing reins looped under its forehooves, and vacated stirrups thudding its ribs.

'He's gone!' yelled the sergeant. 'Fled belly-down for the gutter.' He drew in a breath to signal the archers, only to have Taskin's hand clamp with bruising restraint on his wrist.

'Do *nothing*, I said!' the commander cracked, urgent. 'A show of armed force will only unleash that man's lethal instincts. Stay here. Hold *hard*! I won't risk a bloodbath.

Nobody moves on that captain before I'm dead certain he's running.'

The sergeant stared aghast at the Commander of the Guard, whose granite face displayed tension, but not yet any fire of alarm. 'You're possessed!' he exclaimed.

But Taskin spared no breath for debate. 'Soldier! Mind orders! Pull all the archers out of the battlement. Yes, every one! Assemble them in the bailey beyond Highgate. Keep them quiet and prepared. Wait for my express signal to disband, or deploy through the streets as a search party!'

X. Sunset

As the armoury sergeant stamped off to mind orders in self-righteous disapproval, Commander Taskin instructed the gate watch to handle the fracas outside by routine procedure. The brute effort became theirs, to unsnarl the bunched wagons that obstructed the royal roadway. Crown men-at-arms lent their muscle to unlock jammed wheels, redirect the stalled traffic, and to round up the runaway horse.

The residual chaos was sorted with dispatch. While the recaptured mount was tied to a hitching rail, the most vocal dissenter passed under Taskin's critical review. 'Tell that benighted vendor to stop howling! At my word of surety, the crown treasury will bear the cost to repair his smashed handcart. If he's going to miss supper, the gate-house strongbox can settle the loss of his fruit.'

The Highgate petty officer knew that tone too well, and jumped forthwith to comply.

The upset was contained, and the ale dray's riled team coaxed to work its way clear of the thoroughfare. Guardsmen remained to steady their bits, while the driver jumped down to make stopgap repairs to torn harness. The inevitable bystanders paused to assist. Laughter lightened the atmosphere of chagrined frustration. Like the shine of a jewel, casually dropped, Taskin saw the qualities that made Sessalie flourish set into brilliant display. Simple gifts, born of an abiding deep peace, where life was not required to pass in a rush; where taxed tempers could be vented through teasing and jibes, and lost time was unlikely to harm anyone's long-term prosperity.

Set under the shadow of unknown threat, Taskin bore the burdensome charge of his office as never before. If he failed to uphold crown security, these trusting folk would be shattered. An open-handed generosity instilled over thousands of years would be undone by fear and the horrors of bloodletting strife.

While the lowering sun burnished the gate spire's brick belfry, the carriages with locked wheels were untangled, and set rolling back on their way. Foot traffic resumed. The strutting pigeons that fed on squashed melons wheeled aloft as the carters behind whipped up their idle draught teams.

Taskin held firm, lightly sweating, in the masking shade of the sentry's box. His tense inspection measured the servants, returning uptown from market, and the bakers' women with their wicker baskets, who sold scones in the palace precinct. He scrutinized each of the lampblacks' boys, and made sure of their pale skin and fair hair. He eavesdropped upon conversations, as well, until the first team and vehicle rolled past. The grinding barrage of iron-rimmed wheels raised deafening echoes in the stone passage that pierced through the gatehouse battlement.

Throughout, the errant Captain of the Garrison failed to make an appearance.

The palace commander wrestled his unsettled disappointment. The staked risk was unthinkable, if he should allow his intuitive judgement to lead him too far. A realist to the bone, Taskin faced his self-made disaster. He had no bird in hand. Nothing remained but to bow to defeat, and shoulder the round of rough consequence. Once the dray passed, he must take direct action: order his archers to hunt down a fugitive whose motives were now highly suspect.

'Merciful bright powers!' he swore, pitched to anguish. He would have to weigh the ugly choice quickly, whether to spend lives and attempt to bring in the desertman living; or if he should cut losses and have the guard shoot to kill on first sight.

The dray rattled clear of the uptown archway, admitting the blued haze of the late day. Braced by the clarity of mountain air that seemed strangely unsullied by peril, Taskin gave in and retreated through the Highgate. He entered the icy shade of the passage, hardened to bitter resolve.

'Commander Taskin,' said a quiet voice by his ear. A ghost-light hand tapped his shoulder.

Taskin whirled, sun-blind, and peered into the gloom.

There, Mykkael stood, close as shadow itself, his features veiled under darkness.

Surprise snapped all poise. Taskin clamped a fast hand to his sword hilt. Shocked reflex had the blade halfway cleared from the scabbard before he recovered control.

'Peace,' said Mykkael. 'I had requested a scheduled appointment?' Palms turned outwards, he added, 'If I'd wanted you down, you'd be dead. My knife would have just cut your throat.'

Bristled like a hazed hornet, Taskin relinquished his grip on his weapon. The well-oiled blade slid home in its sheath, ringing counterpoint to his dry speech. 'You're past two hours late, soldier! That's slipshod timing. Better bless your freak luck that I am still here to receive you.'

'Evidently not without a few righteous doubts,' Mykkael stung back. The spring-wound alertness instilled by the placed archers did not fade through the first flare of contact. In bald-faced disregard of his senior officer's antagonism, he dared to lower his hands. His nonchalance remained too dreadfully crisp as he rubbed a film of greased grit off his knuckles, then assessed the pith stains splashed on his shirt.

Taskin watched, not amused. 'You clung all this time to the jackknifed dray's undercarriage?'

'Not without penalty. Yes.' Mykkael scrubbed a scraped knuckle on his breeches, then fixed his raptor's regard on the immaculate crown officer before him. 'We need to talk. Somewhere in strict privacy. Where? Choose quickly. I haven't much time.'

Taskin's strained equanimity recoiled. 'Soldier, your nerve is past tolerance! Just what gives you the right to dictate your meaningless preference to me?'

Mykkael stared back, unsmiling also. If he had the urge to slash back with argument, no such heated blood moved him. 'You've trusted me this far. I thank you for that.' Then he waited, hands empty, in silence.

'Damned well, you know I need information,' Commander Taskin relented. 'I will grant what you ask, with conditions.' He signalled for the captain to march ahead through a sallyport. Beyond lay an arch with a strapped wooden door, and the steep spiralled stairway that mounted the Highgate belltower. 'Go up to the top. I'll join you there, shortly.'

Mykkael's piercing quiet showed he was not fooled to complacence. Nonetheless he went willingly. As his gimping stride assayed the steep stair, Taskin redressed his near failure, and tightened his iron-clad sureties.

He set a sentry on guard by the sallyport, then halted the traffic that flowed through the gate. After, he crossed back through to the bailey, where he collared his waiting sergeant.

The huge man was dispatched to stand watch with the sentry, alongside a quartet of the troop's most accomplished bowmen. Though night had not fallen, Taskin had torches set alight in the wall brackets. He asked to take charge of the shackles and whip. Then he laid final emphasis on his precautions. 'I'm going up alone to speak with the captain and to mete out his sentence in punishment. If I call you *by name*, you will join me directly. No one breaks that instruction. The stair won't be climbed without my express order. I expect to return with Myshkael in my company. If he comes down alone, have these men loose to kill. No mistakes! Drop him fast, with a heart shot. You'll have no second chance. If he's alive, and inside arm's reach, believe this, you're going to be dead men.'

'What if the sly lizard scales the stone of the belltower?' the sergeant objected, taken aback.

But Taskin had already matched that contingency with a shocking array of brute force. 'I have the remainder of your company of archers posted outside to prevent him. If Myshkael bids for escape down the wall, he'll hit the ground as a riddled corpse.'

'What does that leave you?' the squad sergeant pressed.

'Your duty comes first,' the king's commander declared. Then he set off through the belltower's entry without second thoughts, or a pause to look back.

Taskin mounted the winding stair, careful to measure his pace and arrive without being winded. He had cut off the bell ropes, two storeys up, the foresight an act of solid good sense, or a move made in rampant paranoia. The debate was moot: the desert-bred he proposed to meet on equal footing posed too dangerous a cipher. Even a minor misjudgement might trigger a deadly reaction in consequence. If the crown's first commander chose to risk his own person, he would not hazard the wellbeing of the realm. He backed his position. No man set to flight could jam the rope and climb down. If he tried, he would find himself stranded.

Yet even the most stringent set of precautions failed to ease Taskin's nerves. Like a cat caught mincing across a hot roof, he wrung small assurance from logic: that if the war-hardened creature Sessalie's need must put to the test had not asked in good faith for this conference, he would scarcely have consented to be trapped like a rat inside a cordoned keep.

The closed granite gloom of the stairwell gave way at due length to the airy, gold slant of the westering sunbeams that pierced through the tower's cupola. Taskin emerged on the landing beneath the last risers that accessed the trapdoor to the belfry. Ruled by ruthless caution, he stashed the shackles and whip. Then he squinted upwards, letting his eyesight adjust to the flood of the outdoor light. No sound came from above, where Mykkael awaited. Taskin surveyed the gaps in the planked platform tied into the brick walls by hewn beams. The lit cracks showed no telltale shadow to reveal where the desertman might stand to meet him.

Warning gooseflesh prickled across Taskin's skin. The hitched breath caused by smoke touched his senses that half instant too late. Before he could react, a blazing frond of evergreen plummeted downwards and landed, shedding sparks at his feet.

He yelled, leaped forward, and stamped out the blaze before the dry boards ignited.

Coughing through clouded fumes, he scrambled up the last steps and snapped hoarsely, 'What damn *fool* act of idiocy was that?'

Mykkael was seated above, on the brick sill of one of the arches. His back to the sheer drop outside, and an insolent foot dangling over the beams that hung the brute weight of the bells, he answered, 'I don't trifle with foolery. Forgive me. There's a sorcerer's minion at large, and no space left for mistakes. That sprig of lit cedar was *my* act of surety, to test beyond doubt you're not one of them.'

'And are you quite done?' Taskin grated, irritably slapping out the live cinders that seared holes through the hem of his surcoat.

'You still have your archers,' said the desert-bred, reasonable. 'Call out the order to shoot, as you wish. But I had to be certain the commander who can order me killed is one I can trust, and not tainted.'

Taskin rubbed at his neck, found the muscles strained

rock-hard with tension. 'You realize you're treading on dangerous ground, soldier.' Irate enough to attack out of hand, he planted his stance on the platform and regarded the deadly creature above him. 'Nor have I posted my bowmen at whim. Jussoud warned straight out you could drop me.'

Mykkael faced him, not arguing. His defenceless back stayed presented towards the open arch of the belfry. An archer's prime target, in his sunlit white shirt: the only assurance in his power to offer, to back the credential of Taskin's security. One that, even still, fell woefully short. Keen hearing would warn if a shaft launched to take him. The steep arc as it flew would grant time for evasion, long before its flanged point could strike home.

His dark face turned downwards, unreadable, Mykkael stated, 'We all tread upon dangerous ground.'

'Then are you the snake set into our midst?' Taskin ripped back in blunt challenge. 'Have you failed to notice that's what the court factions are claiming? No one holds any scrap of hard evidence against you. But you realize, at this point, that's not a clear-cut reason for me to stand down the outcry for your arrest.'

Mykkael snapped an oath in some guttural dialect that ground on the ear like scraped gravel. 'Let me say what I know. Your princess is in dire peril *this moment*. For her sake, hear me through. As we go, you can ask me whatever you wish. I will answer as your subordinate.'

'You can spare me my reasonable doubts on that score!' Yet Taskin stepped back. He braced his squared shoulders against the brick wall, still flushed with fury. Only his gesture suggested the chance he might balance his options by listening.

'All right.' Mykkael expelled a stiff breath. 'Protections, first.' He shut his eyes, turned his face away to disarm any inference of threat. With placating, slow movement, he untied a wash-leather bag from his belt, then removed something strung on a stained rawhide tie. He dropped the object with a metallic clink on the platform at Taskin's feet.

The commander dragged the thong close with his boot toe. Still without touching, he examined the queer pattern of geometry etched into the green copper disc. 'What's this?'

'A talisman,' Mykkael answered. 'You'll wear it next to your skin night and day, do you hear? Ignore what I've said at your peril.'

Taskin looked up, his eyes like forged steel. 'Where did you get such a thing? Whose hand made it?'

'That's the vizier Perincar's working.' Mykkael swallowed. As though the words burned him to undying bitterness, he answered as he had promised. 'The artefact came from the wars with Rathtet.'

Taskin raised startled eyebrows. 'But I thought no survivors –' His breathing hitched through a disastrous pause, as the most likely bent of plausibility ran a grue of dread straight through him.

'No!' Mykkael shook his head, looking anguished. 'I never fought for Rathtet! No mercenaries did.' Again, he closed his eyes; not to blunt hair-trigger reflexes, this time, but visibly wrestling an unutterable weariness. As though the forced explanation seared him to inward pain, he met Taskin's bidding and qualified. 'Eighteen of us lived. I fought at the side of Prince Al-Syn-Efandi. He died with his head in my lap.'

Merciless, the commander snatched the opening to interrogate. 'If that's the truth, then what were his last words?'

Mykkael stared back, outraged and unblinking. 'A royal command, to flee the country bearing his daughter to safety. That's why what remained of my company survived. We ran, while the rest of the defenders manned the walls until the capitol was overcome.'

Such simple phrases, to map an abyss of sheer horror; the nightmare weeks of privation and flies; the days that came riddled with traps that ripped men into screaming fireballs and husked them to twitching, seared meat. The harsh facts of geography, which a man born in Sessalie might not know, that such a flight had to forge a path *through* Rathtet's battle lines, and cross the city of tents that encompassed the sorcerers' encampment. The very ground underfoot had been shackled in conquest, rock and soil laced through by a morass of vile craft that opened the earth as the conduit for demonic powers. Even years later, bathed in clean, alpine sunlight, Mykkael's shadowed eyes masked the terror endured through that flaying line of retreat.

And still, Taskin tested him. 'What became of the daughter, the Efandi princess?'

'She still lives,' Mykkael whispered. 'Don't ask me to name her, or say which country has sheltered her. The Rathtet sorcerers would kill to extinguish her bloodline, and they have a powerful, long reach.'

Frost-sharp from the dimness beneath the stilled bells, the commander's inquiry pursued him. 'Perhaps long enough to have trailed you to Sessalie?'

'I don't think so.' Mykkael shook off the grip of untenable memories to outline his reasonable certainty. 'They won't know my name. I didn't experience the mark which killed Beyjall. Without seeing, I couldn't hazard the first guess as to which demon's sorcery made it.'

'Ah, yes,' Taskin pounced. 'The Cultwaen apothecary, that your message bearer explained was struck down. We'll get to him, later. I have accusations already in hand. They insinuate you killed the palace drudge with that mark in the cellar, a working made with intent to conceal the princess's clothes.'

Mykkael frowned. 'I already told you the mark was a fake!'

Taskin nodded. 'You did. But how do we know you're not lying?' He pinned the copper talisman under his boot, not yet convinced he should wear it. 'The woman lies dead. Not from poison, although she had no sign of violence upon her.'

'A craftmark won't kill that way,' Mykkael said, distressed. 'They burn. Never consume tinder like a natural flame, but destroy all that lies in their circle of reach. You can see for yourself, if you care to inspect the damage done to the house where Beyjall met his end this afternoon.'

'But we saw no smoke from our watch towers here,' Taskin persisted, relentless. 'My guard heard no cries of fire and no alarm bells in the Lowergate precinct.'

'You wouldn't,' Mykkael agreed. 'There's no smoke to be seen. A mark raises a conflagration no dousing by water can quench. Once unleashed, their spelled forces burn unchecked, igniting all things in their path, even metal and stone. They rage until they have consumed everything within the range of their pre-set intent. Such death is ghastly, beyond all imagining. Must I plead? Commander, for love of your king, accept the grace of that talisman!'

Taskin left the disc where it lay and relentlessly stabbed his point home. 'I don't see you wearing one.'

'Fair enough.' Mykkael forcibly curbed his raw nerves. He bent his neck, and regarded his hands, while the breeze fanned across the mouths of the bells, and brushed their resonance to an atonal whisper. 'Do you trust Jussoud?' Shown his adversary's startlement, the southland captain might have laughed, had the straits not been volatile between them. 'If you don't, you should. He was born to an ancient and honourable line of eastern princes.'

'What nonsense are you talking about?' Taskin huffed, thrown off balance. 'The man's a masseur, a paid healer, if one with exceptional skill. I agree he's well educated. But *royal*?'

'Oh, yes.' Mykkael smiled. 'Jussoud is the son of a noble, old house. The nomads of his homeland don't teach commoners literacy. Among their close society, the use of the ancestral ideographs is a time-honoured secret.'

Odd knowledge, for this upstart desert-bred to cast at large without thought. Yet its edge set a sting that jabbed through to the commander's well-guarded heart. As long and as well as Taskin had employed Jussoud, as often as he had divulged the rare gift of his personal confidence, the healer had not shared any such fact from his nomad parentage.

'He didn't tell me, either,' Mykkael ventured, unasked. 'Except to admit, when I pried, that he knew how to write his birth language.'

Shadow flickered, from behind.

Mykkael whipped taut, head turned sharply, then subsided as a pigeon flew through the arch. It settled to roost in the rafters, cooing to a dusty flutter of wings. Lit by the last, dying rays of the sun, Mykkael probed, still more gently, 'My question remains, do you trust him?'

'More deeply than most,' Taskin admitted, nettled to reveal even casual intimacy.

Perhaps eased by the grit of that honest reluctance, Mykkael shifted position, his back angled against the stepped brick of the arch. 'Then ask Jussoud what he might know of the marking tattooed under the hairline above my nape.'

'A talisman?' Taskin asked, well aware that an arc shot tried now would not ensure a fatality.

'Better. A warding. Done by Eishwin, first, then augmented later by Perincar for my defence of the Efandi prince.' Mykkael averted his face and shoved up his cropped hair to expose an uncanny pattern of geometry, thin lines overlaid by a sequence of indigo curves that twisted into a spiral. 'I have another mark laid into my sword. Yet I could not bear the weapon in King Isendon's presence. A mistake. Last night, no one realized the dread powers possessed by the princess's enemies. I had no sense of forethought to guess how significant the oversight would become.'

More pigeons roosted. This time, the desert-bred

captain did not flinch. Arms folded, set against the lucent backdrop of sky, he held himself still as struck bronze, and as silent. Taskin stared back at him, forced to measure that razor-cut face through the golden blaze of the afterglow. He quelled a brisk shiver; vainly prayed the effect was no more than the chill of the breeze blowing down off the glaciers.

'Oversight?' he pressured at careful length. 'I'd have you define that.'

Mykkael spoke, his turned profile expressionless. 'The warding tattoo will protect me, even make me invisible to a scryer. But without the mark on that sword hilt beside me, I'm exposed. A sorcerer, or his minion planted in Sessalie's court, will have seen everything that I am.'

'We don't *know* what you are,' Taskin snapped. 'That's the stinging thorn at the heart of the problem!'

'But that thorn is your dearest advantage, perhaps.' Mykkael's quiet laughter held startling warmth across the gathering darkness. 'Blinding powers of daylight! How you hate to sully your immaculate resource with the wild-card tactic of chaos!'

Taskin smiled also, surprising himself. 'Yes, you rankle. If I don't give the court your axed head on a plate, you're going to have to convince me. Very well. I am listening. Speak your mind, Captain. Start to finish, with no wretched detail left out.'

'Trust first,' Mykkael insisted. 'Or else call on your archers, or better, step back and release me. My first obligation is to the king's daughter. I can't risk what I know falling under the sway of a sorcerer.'

'Demon!' Every inch as exposed as the creature he held under ruthless threat of his bowmen, Taskin bent down and snapped the artefact up from the planking. He slipped the knotted thong over his head with brusque warning. 'If you're playing me false, you're a dead man.'

'We could all wind up dead men, or something much worse.' Yet Mykkael accepted the capitulation as genuine.

He vacated his reckless perch in the archway, and swung down from the dusty crossbeam, his balanced landing on to the platform slightly marred by his damaged knee. He adjusted the jostled weight of his sword. Then he sat down, one leg folded beneath him, and the other extended to ease the strain of his injury. Shoulders hunched, both hands busy kneading cramped muscle, he launched into clipped recitation.

'First of all, I don't think your princess was abducted. Something she saw, perhaps something she heard, made her realize there were enemies at court, poised with intent to cause harm. I believe she grasped the severity of her danger, and arranged her own flight in secret.'

'The obstacles ranged against such a feat would have been close to impossible,' Taskin said. True sorrow chafed through as he agonized, 'Why would she bolt and tell no one? Merciful glory! I've guarded that girl, and protected her family for more years than she's been alive!'

'I realize that much.' Mykkael loosed a hissed breath and resettled his game knee, unable to make the limb comfortable. 'Why, I don't know yet. How, I hope to ascertain tonight.'

'She's alive?' Taskin slipped the talisman under his surcoat, disliking the uncanny warmth of the thing as it nestled against his bare skin.

Mykkael replied through the gathering gloom, while the sky past the cupola deepened from aqua to indigo. 'With reasonable certainty, I expect so.'

Taskin dogged him, relentless. 'Witch thoughts or hard facts?'

'No hard facts,' said Mykkael. 'As yet, nothing more than a string of probabilities that point in a similar direction.' Whiplash-curt, he cut off the commander's immediate demand. 'But I will pursue none of them! Not now! Until we expose *just what* drove her Grace to flight, she's far better protected if no one knows where she's gone to ground.' He shifted again, needled by the incessant pangs of his leg. 'The double-edged question, whose answer *will* kill without hesitation or mercy: find out why she ran, and roust up a snake's nest of danger.'

'Go on,' Taskin said, as the stillness spun out. 'You still have three deaths to account for, and an alibi to explain your foray in the moat.'

'The apothecary was eliminated because he owned the skilled knowledge to track sorcerers. The seeress and drudge both died of drained minds. A sorcerer or his bound minion can do that. They don't always kill by it. When the damage left by their prying is minor, their victims will sometimes seem drunk. If a sorcerer wants her Grace flushed out of hiding, I believe he'll suck anyone dry, seeking leads. The seeress was a clairvoyant who haplessly picked up the wrong scrap of vision. The drudge would have been the most likely to encounter the princess's clothing. Presupposing her Grace stashed a change of plain garments well in advance of the feast, the rag barrel had to be guarded. The princess may have scratched the fake sorcerer's mark herself, both as warning to us, and as a decoy to scare passing servants away from the closet. The drudge didn't know anything. If she had, she would surely have told me when we exchanged words in the street. I think the enemy drained the poor woman simply because he was desperate.'

The desert-bred captain abandoned the effort to ease the complaint of his leg. He regarded the crown commander who loomed over him, arms crossed at his chest as though his clamour of doubt might be stifled by physical pressure.

'I don't like the deaths, either,' Mykkael stated outright. 'But they have served your king. Those murdered are the one best assurance you have that your princess is alive and still running. No conspirator slaughters with such wanton callousness! Not unless he is caught in extreme disarray. Your princess has quite likely upset his plots and thrown him into scrambling disadvantage.'

Taskin seized on the detail left dangling. 'Then what of your swim?'

'No, Commander.' The words, velvet-soft, held an adamance no posed threat of violence could gainsay. 'I've said all I can without compromise to her Grace's safety.'

The explosion which followed was silent. Taskin slipped a fluid step back, passed through the open belfry door, then returned with the canvas bag and steel shackles. Smoothly as he engaged his next tactic, Mykkael moved faster, uncoiled to his feet in a lightning surge of reaction.

Hands up, backed against the platform railing with the bells cloaked in dark at his back, he measured the commander who advanced to restrain him. 'No. I ask you, don't do this.'

Pinned like prey under that lion-fierce stare, Taskin felt the hair rise at his nape. 'Give way. At once. You do realize, you cannot run.'

Mykkael tested his footing on the gapped planks, taut as a coiled adder. 'I will kill any man who lays hands on me.'

'Stalemate. In the event my orders fail to constrain you, my archers will shoot you on sight.' No fool, Taskin realized he could be dead in an instant. He sustained the dread crux, as the desert-bred captain faced the sure prospect of capture. As well, he recorded the slight, warning flicker that whipped through taut muscle in rebellion: *Mykkael was not going to back down.*

Taskin risked all and pressed for full forfeit. 'Submit, soldier. By crown law, I command you.'

Well braced for the blow, hand poised at the sword he would likely have no chance to draw, Taskin saw Mykkael's features twist with horror and despair. 'Forgive, oh, *Mehigrannia*, forgive!' And that cracked cry of entreaty to a foreign goddess woke the king's commander to fear beyond measure.

Taskin dropped the shackles. '*Mykkael!* Submit.'

That stopped the spring of the tiger, just barely. Mykkael's dilated eyes still searched his adversary's pale face; stayed fixed there, unblinking, while his mind wrestled to gauge the significance implied by that impulsive shift to correct accent. He fell back on hair-trigger caution, and rechannelled his response into speech. 'This is not an arrest?'

'Right now, a just detainment for punishment.' Taskin loosed an explosive, pent breath and unleashed the full force of his strained exasperation. 'I owe you a lashing for last night's insubordination, and another for a formal complaint made to the king under Devall's royal seal. Powers above, man! You've made *damned* sure by your fractious behaviour that I'd have no choice but to handle you!'

Mykkael's taut expression changed from shock, through astonishment, to a look of flat set distaste. 'All right. But no cuffs. I will stand for it.'

Taskin stayed unmoved. 'You object to restraint?'

That elicited fury. 'I'm a foreigner, not an animal!'

'A good soldier,' Taskin allowed. 'But I've checked the more striking details of your background. My fears are well founded. The reflexes ingrained by your *barqui'ino* training do not answer to your humanity.'

'They can,' Mykkael argued. 'Otherwise, I would be nothing more than a dangerous beast.'

'Then you do see my problem.' The commander continued to haze him, ungently. 'Men with your skills have turned on their masters, before this. Should I entrust my life to your cocky self-confidence? Should I risk King Isendon's daughter's?'

Mykkael laughed. He lowered his hands, a blurred whisper of movement in darkness. 'Commander, you already have.'

A stinging, fierce truth; the archers set in the embrasure earlier had *not* been ordered to fire. Neither had the desert-bred struck down the man who provoked him with such savage adherence to principle.

Taskin kicked the dropped shackles off the edge of the platform. 'Very well, soldier. Let's have this over with. Remove your sword harness and shirt.'

Awakened from the torment of her nightmares, she arose and tended the horses. The strangling anxiety did not leave her. She must risk her precarious freedom, and flee again through the coming night. The evening star shone overhead, as it had throughout happier hours in childhood when she had tagged after Dedorth to his tower. Now, the same memory wracked her with chills. For her enemies would assuredly use the old scholar's seeing glass to scan the slopes of the mountains and seek her . . .

XI. Twilight

While Mykkael stood, half stripped, with hands braced on the rail, Commander Taskin took his leisurely time. He shouted downstairs for his sergeant to fetch up a lit torch. Through the interval while the huge man climbed the stairs, he unbagged the whip, a braided lash on a wooden stock, the tip end bearing no saving silk tassel to soften the bite of its punishment.

When the breathless sergeant arrived with the firebrand, the commander cut short the man's staring interest. 'Socket that torch and return to your post. No loose talk, and no changes. My first orders stand as I gave them.'

No movement, from Mykkael, as the seconds spun out, though his skin wore a sheen of light sweat. He stared rigidly forward, the mute bells looming over him. Taskin went on to pry one of the flat, bronze studs from his scabbard. He then drew his dagger, and shaved the soft metal to a razor-keen edge. His eyes stayed on Mykkael, all the while knowing how trapped nerves would rasp at a man, forced to wait. He crimped the sheared fragment of metal to the whip end; watched like a snake as the desert-bred noticed the unpleasant fact that the stilled bells above caught and amplified sound. Faithfully cast, they magnified clarity, returning the clamped tension required to force each breath into even rhythm.

Put to the test of such cruel anticipation, most men would succumb to their crawling anxiety: the coward worn down to a plea for reprieve, and the courageous, snapped to a temperamental demand to get on and finish the unpleasantness.

Mykkael said nothing. Only the sweat that dripped down his flanks belied the appearance, that he had been born without nerves.

Taskin unreeled the whip without warning, brought the first stroke whistling down. The end of the lash cracked into the railing, and slapped tight, wrapped by whistling impetus. The dangling end with its ugly, sharp tip scribed shining arcs in the torchlight.

Mykkael did not break. His hands gripped the rail, pressed taut, but now faintly trembling. Still, the scrape of forced breathing adhered to the discipline of his imposed calm.

Taskin stepped close. He unwound the bound lash from the wood. Still inside reach, deliberately taunting for the volatile flaw that might crack the captain's temperament, he said, 'That one was mine, the stroke I promised for last night's act of insubordination. The next must draw blood, for raising your hand against the crown guardsman you dropped on the garrison keep stair. The rest must redress Devall's slighted honour. I won't know how many of twenty you've earned, unless you would care to speak?'

'For the drawn sword?' Mykkael asked, teeth locked as the lash fell again, this time striping him clean. The sliver of metal sliced a stinging line from left shoulder down to right hip.

Taskin gave cool assent as he coiled the whip. 'The high prince's stiff-necked advocate filed protest like a circling shark. If you knew the man was a hidebound, proud fool, *why* did you leave me no option? What did you think, when you drew your brash steel on his Highness of Devall's accredited spokesman?'

Mykkael answered, fists clamped to the railing. 'To force him to stop reading my private papers, and prying into the garrison's business.' When the lash did not fall, he sucked in a sped breath and held braced.

'No pride?' Taskin pressed. 'Only tactics?'

'Yes, there was pride, but not for the reason you think.' Mykkael shut his eyes, flinched but a hairsbreadth as the whip struck, another weal laid crosswise over the first. 'Remember, I don't have to stand for this.'

'I am not a fool, prideful, or otherwise.' Taskin readied the whip, the frost in his question confrontational. 'Were you justified?'

'Perhaps.' Mykkael fought his tone neutral. His bad knee was shaking, locked rigid by stress. 'Afterwards, I found that an entry was altered. I don't know by whose hand. The changed notation was yours, concerning the number of Devall's servants who passed through the Highgate last night. By my watch's count, a name was deleted.'

'Three stripes will do, then.' The last, expert stroke fell alongside the first, a considered decision which left the uncut, smooth shoulder a right-handed swordsman required to fight unimpaired.

'Hold fast, soldier! Your sentence is finished, but I have not given you leave, yet.' Taskin crossed the platform, bent, and hooked up Mykkael's discarded shirt. 'Don't move, now.' The commander shook out the garment, and with brisk, steady pressure, blotted the running blood into the cloth. Then he waited. The fresh welts still welled and dripped scarlet. Though the captain had finally started to shiver, Taskin repeated the process thrice more.

Then he draped the marked shirt over the railing. 'Put that back on.'

Mykkael took up the stained cloth in scalding distaste; pulled it over his head, not missing the artful subtlety. The commander's deft ploy lent the credible appearance that he had received a full dozen lashes in punishment.

'Make sure the blood shows when you leave here,' Taskin insisted, relentless, as he stripped the metal from the end of the lash, and restored the whip to its bag. 'Nor are you to remove that shirt, soldier, or touch the fresh wounds underneath. You'll keep the badge of your shame in plain sight. Sessalie's crown honour depends on it.'

'You feel Devall's retinue has unwarranted, sharp eyes?' Mykkael grimaced, and gave up his attempt to ease the chafe of the cloth on raw flesh. 'I urge you to treat that lot with extreme caution. They have certainly earned my suspicion.'

Taskin sighed. 'No proof, soldier?'

Mykkael shook his head. 'Not yet.' Still constrained by the thread-slender technicality, that he had not received dispensation to bear weapons, he held, against the grain of his nature.

Taskin said, 'Well, at least we can rely on the fact you'll be watched. The evidence must assure his Highness of Devall beyond doubt my professional word carries weight.' The commander regarded Mykkael's sweat-damp face. Unafraid to look into the eyes of the man he had just served a humiliating penalty, he closed with professional respect. 'I'll send Jussoud down to your quarters in three hours. He will dress your back properly. Afterwards, you are under my orders to wear your king's falcon surcoat. That should stop the complaints I've received that you meet your duties by skulking.'

Released to recover his weapons at last, Mykkael strapped on his sword, his jaw set as the burden pressed into the sting of his shoulder. He eased the sheath flat. Then, without rancour, he asked the commander's indulgence, and slipped off the bag containing the rest of the copper disc talismans.

'Take these,' he instructed. 'Give one to the king. Distribute the others at your discretion, with my stringent suggestion that none goes to the Prince of Devall or his retinue. Test every candidate with cedar smoke first, and be prepared to kill failures by ambush. They will be the made tools of a sorcerer, and unmasked, they'll become *deadly* dangerous. Tell your chosen who pass, keep the discs out of sight! Also, don't trust anyone who's drunk, or acting the slightest bit changed from the ordinary.'

Taskin hefted the sack, realized there could not be more than six pieces left inside. 'How many of these have you given to your garrison men?'

Mykkael looked at him. 'None. I can't secure the gate against sorcery, nor shield a walled town with only six men! Yet six, chosen well, might stand guard for the king.'

'But not Crown Prince Kailen?'

The two men locked eyes, with only Mykkael's bitter black with the doubts inflicted by harsh experience.

'I can't make that call,' admitted the desert-bred. 'His Highness's habit of drink could be harmless. Safest of all, to hold back and not pose the first question.'

Taskin received that assessment, thoughtfully deadpan. Then he said, 'You're not excused, soldier. Not before you have shared the ongoing evidence that suggests where her Grace may have fled.'

'No.' Mykkael stepped back, pushed at last to snapped patience. 'I've said all I intend to. Impasse? How trying. At least, earlier, I could have been thrown to your archers without bleeding for the stuffed head of Devall's spying lackey.'

Taskin lost grip on his fury, as well. 'You madman! Are you *trying* to press me until I've no choice but to kill you?'

'Security,' Mykkael argued. His fleeting glance sideways assayed the distance from railing to dangling bell rope. 'Don't waste precious time! Once I find out why your princess has bolted, then, *only then* will I know if I have the skills to protect her!'

'Jump, soldier, go on,' goaded Taskin. 'You'll find the rope's cut. Not to mention the toll of that bell will roust all of Sessalie against you.' Aware the deterrent was not going to stay the captain's decision to leap, he spoke quickly. 'You would hold your ground against me, and for the sake of your towering arrogance, defy Sessalie's king?'

Mykkael never hesitated. 'I would stand against anyone. Commander, you gamble with risks you cannot possibly imagine!'

And *again*, came that sawn note of grief, as though a man turned at bay faced the bittermost end of wrecked hope.

Stymied by that obstructive precedent, Taskin wrestled to recover his ranking authority. 'You do realize,' he warned, 'that you might force my hand. On crown directive I could be commanded to make your arrest.'

'Powers forefend, and deliver the ignorant from all manner of hideous destruction!' Mykkael broke at last, desperation driving a commitment as firm as a death sentence. 'Commander, hear this clearly! You hold my trust. But with one reservation: if you order my person set under restraint now, or at any time before this crisis is over, I *will* have no choice but to kill any man who lays hands on me. This includes yourself. I'll not be set in irons while your princess is threatened. I take my oath to King Isendon seriously, and that means my freedom to act for Sessalie's safety must come before *everything else*.'

'Bright powers show mercy!' Taskin cried in anguish. 'You're asking me to trust you to guard Anja's life when *nothing* you say can be verified!'

Mykkael shook his head, helpless. 'I can't ease that choice from your shoulders, except to urge you to question Jussoud. If anyone can, he might speak for me.'

A whiplash of mockery, the righteous demand of Sessalie's loyal crown officer: 'How?'

Again Mykkael looked down, the gesture now recognized as a tormented need to guard privacy. 'I did not ask your nomad the name of his tribe. But if he is Sanouk, he will have a relative who served under me against Rathtet.'

'Dead?' Taskin snapped.

Mykkael swallowed, and again shook his head. 'No. Alive, at least the last time I saw her.'

Torch-lit against the thick darkness, the desertman seemed almost harmlessly diminished, a limping figure in a soiled white shirt, with eyes scored by lines of exhaustion. Yet the unvanquished quality to his silence somehow still demanded respect.

'Stalemate,' stated Taskin. The admission rang bitter. No man, before this one, had shaken his seasoned experience, or undermined the ferocious pride of his competence. 'You are granted a stay, upon Jussoud's word, and my honour now rides on your freedom.' The commander stepped sideways, opening the way towards the door. 'To appease my archers, we'll descend together.' He shouldered the bag with the whip, then raked Mykkael head to foot with a last, savage glance of assessment. 'Just have the damned *grace* to look chastened, will you?'

By the preference of his deceased queen, Anjoulie, the king's private chambers had wide casement windows overlooking the snowcapped peaks of the Great Divide. On clear nights, under starlight, the flares where the kerries breathed fire streaked like comet tails over the summits. When the gusts off the glaciers rattled the glass, a log fire always burned in the grate.

In late spring twilight, with the casements cracked open, and the mild air wafting the fragrance of jasmine from the stone terrace outside, a pageboy still tended the coals for the warming pan that comforted Isendon's chilled feet. Installed at the royal bedside, the Duchess of Phail shared a tray of light supper for the purpose of pleasant company, and the pursuit of refined conversation.

When his Majesty suffered maundering wits, she coaxed him to eat. If he sat, blankly staring, she spoonfed him like a child. She adjusted his blankets and managed the warming pan to ease his poor circulation. Her eagle-eyed vigilance and tireless, kind manners had earned the undying respect of the servants. Most evenings, except for the guard at the door, she attended the aged king in private.

Tonight, the upset caused by Anja's disappearance had broken that gentle routine. The page had been reassigned to the armoury, to forestall the excessive gossip. Two muscular guardsmen flanked the inside entry, with four more stationed in fully armed vigilance along the corridor outside.

King Isendon sat wakeful, propped up in his favourite oak chair. No tactful diversion had enticed him to eat. The folder of poetry in Lady Phail's lap had failed to lull him to sleep. Conversation did nothing to quiet the palsied fingers that traced fretful patterns on the coverlet. The clouded eyes held a febrile spark, struck off the tinder of fiercely kept hope and the flint of numbing despair.

'She is the light of Queen Anjoulie's virtue, still shining,' the king said, repeating the same words of five minutes ago. 'Powers stand guard for her. She often hares off on impulse. But even her boldest pranks are well planned . . .' The quavering voice trailed, then resurged with a fire many years younger. 'I *must* believe that my daughter's alive! Without her, the heart of this kingdom will be cast into darkness.'

In his prime, spurred by anguish, King Isendon would have paced. Now shrunken with grief, he tugged uselessly at his blankets.

'The guard will find her.' Lady Phail laid aside the loose sheaves of verse. Her firm fingers captured the king's paper-dry hand. 'No man has sired a more beautiful daughter, or one as intelligent and resourceful. Whatever has happened will come right, in time. Lord Taskin won't rest without answers.'

The king jerked up his nodding chin. 'Who comes?'

Lady Phail cast a pert glance towards the guards, to see whether they had heard footsteps. None had. The taller redhead returned a negative jerk of his helm.

'Nobody's there, sire. Do rest easy,' Lady Phail soothed him.

'Someone comes!' King Isendon shoved bolt upright, scattering his blankets and tumbling his silk-covered pillows on to the carpet.

'All right, sire, we'll see.' Lady Phail gestured for one of the guardsmen to oblige by checking the corridor. Then she bent with her usual sweet patience, and gathered the dropped bedding from the floor.

The click of the latch as the guardsman returned rang too loud in the mournful quiet. 'No one,' he stated softly. 'The guards outside say the same.'

King Isendon permitted the duchess to cosset him, though his frown remained welded in place. 'Taskin's expected shortly with news. I can't be asleep when he gets here.'

'We'll waken you, sire, never fear.' With genteel grace, the old lady fluffed the last pillow, but refused the indignity of smoothing her sovereign's hair. As though his Majesty still retained all his faculties, she honoured his rank with a curtsey, then swept back to reclaim her stuffed chair. 'Do you favour a team for the horse wickets yet? Kailen has picked Farrety's to wear his badge. That's raised some heat between Muenice and Lord Tavertin. Each of them hopes you'll bestow royal favour.'

For a moment, the king brightened. 'Anja thought Tavertin's team would wash out. His master of horse trains the animals too hard. Wears the high fettle right out of them.' Isendon turned his drawn face towards the window, where stars, but no kerrie fires, burned. 'Would that Anja were here. Her young eyes would judge which team's fittest.'

'Well, you managed to better the team she liked last year.' Lady Phail's smile turned wistful. 'Such a close match.'

But King Isendon's mind had wandered again. His staring eyes scanned the richly appointed chamber. Whether fogged vision showed him shadows or shapes, no one knew. His seeking inspection quartered the carved scrolls that crowned the pilasters, then the lavender silk adorning the chair seats, and the marquetry table with its tracing of mussel-shell inlay. He squinted at the clothes chests with their tapestry coverings, examining each tassel with razor-sharp inquiry. His gaze stalled at last in the nook by the armoire. 'Someone *comes*, I tell you!'

'Very well, sire. We shall see.' Lady Phail arose, caught up her cane, then moved with a whispered rustle of skirts to check the outside doorway herself. Sometimes the king would subside at her word. Other times, his unpredictable perception captured subtleties missed by the guardsmen. The wits that had scattered with his infirmity were wont to present them with vexing puzzles. If the seneschal found his Majesty's idiosyncrasies a constant irritation, the men Taskin posted to watch the royal chamber were faultlessly staunch and supportive.

The tall redhead lent the duchess his courteous assistance and unlatched the door once again. Yet this time, as the bronze-studded panel swung open, the tap of rapid footsteps approached, rolling echoes down the vaulted corridor.

'That will be Taskin.' King Isendon pushed at his blankets, tumbling pillows helter-skelter once more.

'His Majesty's right,' said the blond guard, relieved.

The crown commander and two immaculate officers shortly breasted the stair that led from the anteroom. They reached the king's door at a cracking fast clip, with Taskin more than usually brisk, and an edge like a sword on his temper.

'Lady Phail.' Formally crisp, he touched the old woman's palm to his lips, then tucked her wrist over his elbow and bowed his white head to the king. 'Your Majesty, have I leave?'

King Isendon's demeanour perked up to recapture the semblance of regal presence. 'As your duty commands you.'

Taskin signalled to the blond guard, then one of the officers beside him. Both men stepped out at his low-voiced instruction to post a sharp watch at the stairhead. 'If anyone comes here, delay them. Make plenty of noise. I want no one approaching his Majesty's chamber without warning.' Next, the commander called one of the guards in the corridor by name. 'Step inside, please.'

The appointed man replaced the one just dispatched with the seamless poise of the elite. A nod from their commander placed the remaining officer in armed readiness at their backs, a stark oddity. But the men entrusted with the king's person knew better than to serve such a change with remarks. Taskin himself ushered Lady Phail to her seat.

Glittering in his surcoat and gold braid, the Commander of the Guard bowed again to his king, this time with rigid correctness. 'Your Majesty, I ask your indulgence with a precaution.'

'Trouble, Taskin?' the aged sovereign asked, his fingers settled with laced dignity into his blanketed lap.

'Perhaps, sire. Kindly bear with me.' Given the regal nod to proceed, the commander knelt by the hearth. He used the fire iron to shut the flue damper, then reached under his surcoat and withdrew a sprig of evergreen, which he tossed on to the flames.

Fragrant smoke billowed, clouding the room. Back on his feet, Taskin stood his ground before his two guards, his chiselled regard trained upon Lady Phail, and the invalid form of his sovereign. No one moved. No face showed a flicker of trapped fury; only puzzlement and restrained anxiety, as the cedar smoke wafted a spreading pall on the draught let in through the casement.

The commander released a slow breath, while the officer by the doorway eased his tense shoulders, and relaxed the taut grip on his sword hilt.

'Lock the door,' Taskin said. 'I would have our discussion kept private between those of us here in the room.'

The king raised a weak forearm and fanned at the fumes. His fragile cough spurred Taskin to attend the necessity of releasing the closed-off flue. Smoke swirled at his movement. Tendrils combed into the gloom by the armoire, and *there*, something embedded unseen in clear air met and tangled.

Like the hissed shriek of flame doused in ice, a whirlwind of sparks shot upwards. The eruption scored across startled eyesight, *there and gone in an eyeblink.*

'What was *that*!' Shocked, Lady Phail dropped her cane.

The thud as it landed upon the thick carpet jarred the guardsmen's cranked nerves. The officer by the door yanked his blade from his scabbard, while the others surged on to their toes. Yet their readiness encountered no visible target. The king sat with his knuckles clenched on his knees, with Taskin like cast ice before him.

The smoke billowed up and licked the groined ceiling, then dispersed to a pall that misted the shine of the candles, and dimmed the surrounding furnishings.

'Glory preserve us!' King Isendon grated, distraught. The sharp scare appeared to have focused his wits. 'That I should have lived to see Sessalie befouled by a sorcerer.' His faded glance encompassed his commander. 'We are in grave danger, indeed. I trust we are reasonably safe at this moment? That the smoke has effected a banishing?'

Shaken to pallor, Taskin knelt. 'Your Majesty, what little I know may not be enough to stave off a threat to your life.'

Isendon's gesture suggested impatience. 'Rise. You are trusted to handle what must be done. Carry on. Have you news, or fresh hope for my daughter?'

'Very little, sire.' Taskin stood erect, his lifetime habit of unflinching nerve maintained by relentless courage. 'I have no direct facts concerning the princess, or any clue to her whereabouts. Only the report from your garrison captain, who maintains the emphatic belief she's alive.

My*sh*kael's battle experience against warring sorcerers suggests he has knowledge to support this.'

Isendon nodded, his sunken chest wracked again by a feeble cough. 'You knew he fought against Rathtet?' At the commander's stark surprise, the aged sovereign showed the ironic humour that had once been famous for scalding unwary courtiers. 'Oh, yes. He saved the Efandi princess, it's said, though her survival is a close-guarded secret.'

'You *knew* this?' Satisfied that the smoke had penetrated every last remaining cranny in the room, Taskin directed his officer to release the damper blocking the flue.

'A king has his own ways to acquire information,' Isendon said. 'Ambassadors trade in state secrets to buy favours.' Forced by shortened breath to speak in clipped sentences, the king battled his weakness and qualified, 'The man won the summer tourney with formidable skills. Now he guards my keep gates. I had better know whether to trust him.'

Still rocked by discovery that the old fox had outflanked him, Taskin blurted, 'And do you, sire?'

'Within careful limits.' King Isendon's smile was given to Lady Phail, who quietly straightened his blankets. She tucked a pillow to prop his frail shoulders in response to the reed-thin exhaustion that frayed through his phrases. 'One can never trust any foreigner, fully. His nation of birth is not Sessalie. Yet Mykkael has sworn my oath of crown loyalty. I pay him for fair service. Which, so far as I've managed to trace, he has delivered to all his employers.'

Taskin released an explosive sigh. 'I found no evidence on him of oath-breaking, either. That doesn't mean he wasn't hired beforehand to assay an outsider's plot against Sessalie.'

Isendon tapped his fingers on the arm of his chair, the tremors now sorrowfully pronounced. 'Do you think so, Taskin?'

The commander stood, struck to stillness, the platinum shine of his hair hazed under the tarnish of fug in the air. 'No,' he said at strained length. 'Blinding glory, I've pushed him! Yet by the pernicious fact that he won't crack, I cannot be wholly certain.'

This time, the play of irony over Isendon's features came shaded by relentless grief. 'Then, my old friend, you understand very well how to shore up the burden of Sessalie's crown. I can't, for much longer. The fates of my heir and my daughter must reside in your hands, meanwhile.'

Remanded to address that harsh duty, Taskin inclined his head. 'Very well.' He slipped the coarse leather bag from his belt, which contained Mykkael's gifted talismans. 'These artefacts were brought by the garrison captain from his service against Rathtet. He claims they will offer protection from sorcery. Sire, will you consent to wear one?'

Lady Phail's gentle voice broke the widening pause. 'His Majesty's awareness has slipped again, Taskin. I'm sorry.' She patted the king's knee, but aroused no stir in response. 'If my opinion matters, I believe our liege would have done as you asked.'

Taskin nodded, struck grim as he shouldered a decision he found abhorrent. He passed two of the copper discs into Lady Phail's keeping. 'One for the king, Duchess, and, if you're willing to share the same risk, the other for you. I trust you to stay by his Majesty's side and stand guard for his wandering wits.'

'A sharp ear on the court gossip can't hurt,' Lady Phail agreed with stout courage.

Taskin's smile of gratitude was heartfelt. 'I would never have asked that much, Duchess, but yes.' He added instructions to keep the talisman hidden, and to wear it always next to the skin. While the elderly granddame donned the vizier's talisman, then gently attended the king, the crown commander distributed the last two discs to the best of his men, appointed to stand guard at the door.

'You will wear these, soldiers, and not disclose them to anyone! Here forward, you don't leave your king's bedside, ever! You'll eat in his chamber, and sleep *in his presence* by turns. You'll flank his litter as he goes to hear audience. Only those in this room are protected. That means, you keep impeccable secrecy! Speak to no one outside of the five of us, am I clear? I will have the servants bring wood, and you will see that a log fire burns in this chamber at all times!'

'Sorcerers can't stand such?' the red-haired guard asked.

'Some of them. Their minions are said to avoid chance exposure to wood smoke.' Taskin nodded to the taciturn captain who stood as his second in command. 'Bennent, you can unbar the door.'

'What of our crown prince?' inquired the fair guard. 'For the security of Sessalie's succession, should his Highness not wear a talisman before one of us?'

Worn to hag-ridden tension, the commander met that inquiry squarely. 'I'm sorry to say that Prince Kailen can't be trusted to keep his shirt on for the whores.' He matched eyes with the guardsman, whose gaze flicked aside, unable to refute that sad truth.

'I know our prince. Beneath inexperience, there is no man better. Under happier circumstances, his Highness could be forgiven the feckless adventures of youth.' Taskin stifled his deep grief, and delivered his iron-clad conclusion. 'But this sorcerer who stalks Sessalie is utterly ruthless. If King Isendon falls to his spellcraft, such an enemy could prey upon every subject in this realm through his sovereign rights to the throne. I grieve for the necessity. But the protection of Sessalie's people *must* come first. I will guard Prince Kailen as I can, but against this danger, the weak game piece wearing the crown must be the most stoutly defended.'

Under the wax-bright flare of the candles, Taskin regarded each guardsman in turn, and measured their commitment and courage. 'Stand your post with due vigilance, soldiers. The king's safety relies on your hands.'

He signalled his officer, prepared to depart, when an outburst of arguing voices arose in the corridor outside. Taskin surged forward and jerked open the panel, all but bowled aside by the breathless arrival of Sessalie's seneschal.

The irate official ploughed straight in, determined to demand royal audience.

'Lord Shaillon!' Lady Phail sprang up with cane in hand to enforce the king's violated privacy. 'How thoughtless of you to barge in with no consideration for the hour! Your liege is asleep, and needs his rest sorely! I will not see you task him with burdens, my lord. If you should press his Majesty's health, he may not be lucid to sign the documents the council requires in the morning!'

Stalled on his course, the seneschal spun and bristled at Taskin. 'You let that slinking desert-bred go free! How *dare* you flout this kingdom's incurred debt. You've let Devall's slighted honour be slapped aside for a pittance!'

'I'd scarcely call any lashing a pittance,' Taskin stated in acid correction. 'Have you had occasion to see a man whipped? Your accusation does nothing but expose your cosseted mind and rank ignorance.'

'Only twelve strokes!' The seneschal sniffed. 'The last guard with the effrontery to brawl with a foreign royal's servant received twenty. Or don't you recall how to count?'

'You will not bring your childish bluster in here,' Lady Phail snapped with stout righteousness. 'Out! Now!' She gave Taskin a jab in the small of the back, then hooked the seneschal's arm in steel fingers and urged him back towards the doorway.

'Duchess, would you obstruct the king's greater interests?' The seneschal planted his feet. 'I implore you to use better sense. The heir apparent of Devall is not pleased by the commander's cavalier treatment.' After a rancorous glower towards Taskin, Lord Shaillon plunged on in appeal.

'His Highness of Devall could stand on his rights and take offence. Should he annul his suit, Anja's heart would be broken. Would you risk seeing her Grace jilted?' Harried backwards another step by the indomitable granddame, the seneschal snarled, 'Is this scruffy dog of a desert-bred captain worth casting our rights to the sea trade into jeopardy?'

Lady Phail tapped her foot. When her staunch manner threatened to enlist the royal guardsmen for help to clear the king's chamber, the seneschal accosted Lord Taskin, who stood obstructively next to the moulded door jamb.

'That foreign captain is a liability to this kingdom's prosperity!' the seneschal ranted. 'I insist, he should be clapped into irons.'

An astute tactician, Taskin saw the withering, cold fire that sparked Lady's Phail's narrowed eyes. Wise man, he bowed and stepped clear, the image of the genteel courtier in his impeccable falcon surcoat.

Yet the seneschal was sunk too far into his tirade to keep pace with his rival's acuity. His impudence was caught short: the old lady rapped her ivory cane on his wrist, the same treatment she allotted to importunate boys caught stealing jam in the scullery.

'For shame, Lord Shaillon!' said Lady Phail. 'Your behaviour lies beneath well-born dignity, to raise such a row against a *common* man who is innocent. King Isendon has already given the matter the swift disposition it deserved.'

'*What?* His Majesty was lucid?' Lord Shaillon's beaky face jerked sideways, once more brought to bear on the commander's upright serenity. 'What has the king said? You were present?'

Cool as the sheathed sword, Taskin answered. 'You won't lack for witnesses. We were all here. His Majesty pointed out that the garrison captain has never mishandled his oath. Since My*sh*kael's past record bears no charge of treachery, he is held by the crown to be trustworthy.'

Defeated, the seneschal stalked to the door. 'This will not end here, I promise!' Faced straight ahead, unwilling to spare a disdainful glance for the other armed captain, who paced like a predator at his heels, Lord Shaillon pronounced, 'That desert-bred cur is a liability to the realm and I will not stop until I hold proof to expose his deceitful nature.'

XII. Evening

STARS SALTED THE SKY OVER THE PALACE PRECINCT, YET NO NIGHTFALL HAD EVER SEEMED BLACK AS THE ONE THAT followed Princess Anja's disappearance. Without news, the rampant explosion of rumours spread a climate of blanketing fear. No carriages rolled in the avenues, or pulled up before the marble fronts of the mansions. Shadow and gloom hung over the door yards, where the welcome lanterns set out for guests should have cast jonquil circles of light. No candles illumined the glass panes of the salons, and no laughter trilled on the air.

The peacock splendour of Sessalie's court stayed withdrawn behind locked doors on the hour the seneschal hastened to pay his next call.

He arrived on foot at the east wing of the palace. There, the High Prince was installed in the lavish apartment allotted to visiting royalty. Out of sorts, the seneschal knocked at the door beneath Devall's quartered banner.

A butler in a velvet tabard cracked the panel. He peered down his pampered nose before letting the seneschal in, his practised eye busy as he sized up his visitor's vexed bearing. By smooth rote, he chose the appropriate words to acknowledge the jammed wheels of state. 'Your plea went unheard? Then I have to warn your lordship in advance, the high prince's mood is not sanguine.'

'He has every right to express his distress,' Sessalie's seneschal soothed him. 'I will see him, regardless, provided he is willing to receive an official from Isendon's court.'

'Would you offer condolence?' Prepared to stay planted with superior obstinacy, the butler considered the matter. 'How should I present you?'

'I don't bear good news,' the seneschal admitted, too well seasoned at handling prickly foreign diplomats not to manage an uppity servant in his stride. 'Say the ruling that balks his Highness was made by the king, but explain that a resourceful young man might hear the details, if he wished to probe for a loophole.'

The butler bowed. 'My Lord Shaillon, wait here, if you please.'

Smoothly as butter left on a plate, the seneschal found himself cooling his heels on the carpet in the front hall. If that pre-emptive treatment stuck in his craw, he made himself swallow the sting. It was *Sessalie's* shamed grace that begged Devall's indulgence, sadly not the other way around.

Yet his cause was not lost. The butler trundled back before long, bringing word that the high prince would admit him. The seneschal was ushered into the elegant small dining room, where busy staff were clearing the dishes that remained from his Highness's supper. The heir apparent of Devall sat, informally clothed, while another servant poured tea. He looked hag-ridden. Stripped of rings, his hands seemed too slender and still. His plain tie-string shirt with its facings of satin clothed the posture of a despondent young gallant.

He glanced up, the sovereign gold of his eyes shadowed beneath tawny hair. 'I was not expecting state visitors,' he apologized, not asking forgiveness for his maudlin mood. 'Be comfortable. Sit. Would you care for some tea?'

While the butler vanished, the Seneschal of Sessalie

accepted the chair presented by another ubiquitous manservant. Not a seat at the prince's table: crown officers in Devall were not treated with any such familiarity. But the placement set him an intimate distance to one side, where two men could speak eye to eye. 'Tea would be nice.'

A porcelain cup was set into his hand, then sweetened with a dipper of spring honey. His royal host constrained his impatience, while the table servant awaited the seneschal's nod that his personal taste had been satisfied.

'My butler informed me you bring no fresh news,' the High Prince of Devall said in opening. Hope in him blazed anyway, a simmering tension that shifted him anxiously forward. 'Did you perchance have something more you thought should be delivered in private?'

'I'm sorry, your Highness.' The seneschal's lanky knuckles engulfed the gilt cup, lending the appearance of threatened fragility. 'The king's grace endorsed the decision of his crown commander.'

'They place their trust in that dark foreign captain, then. *Why?*' Too well bred to pace before another realm's titled delegate, Devall's heir shifted his burning gaze, consumed by frustration and worry. 'The man has shown nothing but suspect behaviour. What does he know that we don't?'

The seneschal shook his head. He would not offer platitudes, though concern for the princess was quite plainly chafing her young suitor ragged.

The exhaustion shading his handsome face was laid bare without the appointments of his state trappings. 'Powers of mercy! Why must my hands stay tied? *The princess who will share my future's at risk!* Each passing minute weighs on me like torture. Even your commoners are free to ride out, encouraged by the crown's bounty. Prince Kailen has the relief of questioning the adventurers who come in claiming to have information.'

'Well that's no boon, really,' the seneschal allowed, his mood raised to arid amusement. 'Listening to every pig farmer and his cousin, insisting he's found tracks in his barnyard, or the signs someone's slept in his loft.'

The high prince glanced down, his silence turned searing, and his tea cup jammed between rigid hands.

'I'm sorry,' the seneschal said lamely.

'If this were Devall, I would have every man in my father's guard under orders, rousting those crofters' barns with a warrant! In Sessalie, my marshal-at-arms is forced to sit idle, while, it appears, the best I can do is rely on a misfit ex-mercenary who comes and goes at his secretive whim, and who answers to no man's authority.' Crushed under pressure, the porcelain gave way. The prince hurled the fragments on to the tray, his face turned away to mask bursting anguish as a servant stepped in to stanch his gashed palm on a napkin.

The lackey inquired, 'Your Highness, should I fetch your physician?'

'Thank you, not now.' The heir apparent of Devall knotted the stained linen tight, then regarded his visitor with flaming embarrassment. 'My Anja is in danger, or worse! And I can do nothing at all but sip tea, wrapped up in the silk ties of protocol!'

The seneschal sighed. Kind-hearted beneath his thick crust of propriety, he cleared his throat and expressed sympathy. 'Your straits are understandably difficult, your Highness. Yet Isendon's officers are scarcely incompetent. Taskin has never failed Sessalie's crown. His intelligence cannot be faulted. We may not know Captain My*sh*kael as one of us, but his triumph at last summer's tourney was a feat of spectacular skill. The commons have granted him sharp respect. They will answer his questions, where, truth to tell, your polished lowlanders might awe them to self-conscious silence.'

'Well, what good is a war-trained swordsman against a nefarious covert plot?' Lost to poise, deaf to statecraft, the High Prince of Devall jammed tense fingers through his hair. 'Anja is everything to me. I cannot love and do nothing but wait for some desert-bred dog to paw through the sewers sniffing for clues!'

Again, the seneschal strove to console him. 'The man impressed the king enough to win his royal trust. Until quite recently, his Majesty's rule has been sound. Even failing, his wits are not always scattered.'

The high prince stayed sunk into cankerous despondency.

Spurred by his plight, the seneschal burst out, 'Well, it is a fact that My*sh*kael fought in the wars with Rathtet.'

'*What!*' The High Prince of Devall jerked up his head. 'Did I hear you say *Rathtet*? But that's not possible!'

'Apparently so,' said the seneschal.

'Not possible!' The heir apparent surged to his feet in agitation. '*Where did you learn this?*'

The seneschal blushed. 'I overheard my king say so, months back, through a closed door in a private conference with his ambassador.'

'By the nine names of *hell*!' the prince swore, his face turned sheet-white, and his beautiful hands trembling beneath the lace hem of his cuffs. 'If what you say holds the least grain of truth, then your realm of Sessalie lies under the shadow of an unspeakable threat!'

The seneschal blotted slopped tea from his robes, dismayed, but still striving to placate. 'Your Highness, what are you saying?'

'About Rathtet?' The High Prince of Devall stalked up and back down the carpet. 'Prince Al-Syn-Efandi was killed, along with all of his family. His people *died* when the capitol was savaged by Rathtet's lines of raised sorcery!'

Shot to his feet, also, while the saucer and cup rattled in trembling hands, the seneschal stated, 'Then you think Captain My*sh*kael *fought for the sorcerers?*'

'He had to!' cried the prince, driven to shrill despair. 'That war of invasion left not a single survivor among the Efandi defenders!'

The seneschal stared back, aghast. 'Powers above! Then our Anja is in terrible danger, indeed. She could be dead, or far worse, a live puppet in the hands of a sorcerer.'

'She won't stay there!' Ripped to steel determination, the High Prince of Devall rammed a path towards the door, scattering anxious servants. 'By glory, for Sessalie's imperilled safety, now I must act! You need that desert-bred captain *contained*! I tell you, he's unspeakably dangerous.'

The seneschal thrust his burden of porcelain aside. 'My*sh*kael can be arrested, and by the king's writ. We only need proof of his perfidy.'

The high prince turned down the hall towards his officers' quarters, his brisk strides streaming the sconces. 'Any proof?'

Trailing him, breathless, the Seneschal of Sessalie affirmed with sped haste, 'The king's case for trust is based on the foreigner's record of honest service. Show he broke faith, or acted for evil, Lord Taskin will turn out the guard and not rest until the fell creature's arraigned.'

The High Prince of Devall glanced sideways, his gold eyes angry as balefire. 'I will have your proof! Whatever it takes. Can I ask your support?' Contempt crossed his chisel-cut features, then sly irony, there and gone in a heartbeat. 'At least you can't mind if we listen at doorways to gather the facts to seal the arrest.'

Then and there, a gaunt form clothed in the night's looming shadow, the Seneschal of Sessalie granted the High Prince of Devall his trembling assent. 'Bright powers, for the sake of our princess, I'd do anything to see that sand-bred cur delivered to justice in irons.'

'*Justice*?' The high prince slammed open the door to his guards' quarters, ripped to a snarl of laughter. 'Oh, not justice. For Anja's *life's sake*, give the wretch over to me.' The princess's suitor clapped his hands to summon his marshal, his explosive, cold fury a force to prickle the hairs at the nape. 'Do that, and I'll have an accounting under

Devall's crown law! With knives and hot irons, I'll tear out what your false captain knows from the cords of his screaming throat!'

Across the palace precinct, behind the west wing, the warren of servants' tenements overlooked the block of the guards' barracks. Commander Taskin mounted an outside stair that led to the one-room apartment where Jussoud had chosen to settle since leaving the steppe country far to the east. The windows were lit. Clay oil lamps brought from the tents of his homeland cast a carmine glow on the sills, hung with their boxes of medicinal plants, and the vines cultivated for tinctures. More pots of greenery crowded the landing, their sweet, mingled scents a mélange on the crisp spring air.

Taskin knocked at the entry, painted red in the eastern tradition, with the Serphaidian ideographs for prosperity and peace set into a gold-leafed cartouche.

A barefoot step answered. Jussoud opened the door, his silk robe tied by a broad sash, woven with an insignia of dragons. His hair was unbound, tumbled in braid-crimped black waves to his waist.

'Commander,' he said, his greeting surprised, and his silver-grey eyes turned inquiring. 'You need me again? There is trouble?' When Taskin did not immediately answer, he widened the door without hesitation.

The commander accepted the welcome, his dress and bearing no less than parade-ground precise. Yet the tension that rode the trim set of his shoulders suggested the distress of a man unaccustomed to losing his bearings.

Jussoud crossed his patterned carpet, the bracelets worn on his ankles a thread of gold light against his saffron skin. Not owning chairs, he offered the commander a grass-stuffed cushion. 'Sit. You look like you need to. I can't recall ever seeing you appear this confused.'

Taskin showed no offence. Only a note of clipped exasperation inflected his upper-crust speech. 'By every word for the havoc of hell, I can't recall feeling this way, either.'

An iron pot steamed on a coal-fed brazier next to the flame of the oil lamp. 'I have *sennia*, brewed from Sogion beans. Will you have some?'

The commander shook his silver head. 'Thank you, no. I can't fathom how you drink that damned tar, far less acquire the taste for it.'

Jussoud laughed. 'Inborn habit, no doubt.' He retrieved his goblet from the windowsill, a delicate vessel fashioned of shell and artfully twisted wire. Then he settled on to the opposite cushion, his innate grace a startling trait for a man of his massive stature. 'Our mothers mix a black paste from the flowers to ease pain when their children cut teeth.'

Across the saffron glow of the lamp, Taskin sat still and said nothing.

'Troubled, indeed,' Jussoud observed. 'What has Captain Mykkael done, now?' At the commander's snapped startlement, the healer's round face showed a smile just barely suppressed. 'No other man's capable of testing your nerves. Did you come here for insight or facts?'

'Truth,' Taskin blurted, amazed by the stumble the moment he opened his mouth. As often as he had watched the masseur pry open a man's heart to facilitate healing, he had never experienced the skilled technique applied to his guarded reserve. No use but to fling wide the floodgates, now, since emotion had sprung the first breach. 'Mykkael said you were born to a royal house.'

'Why have I never confided?' Jussoud's threatened smile became a soft laugh that wove through the hiss of the oil lamps. 'Because the blood of my origins is a manyfold blessing, common as grass on the steppe. Kings there are measured by the wealth of their harems. The old despot who fathered me has no fewer than one hundred and eighteen wives. That was the count of four years ago. The old terror will assuredly have more women, now, and eight times their number in grandchildren.' The healer sipped at his goblet, his measured gaze thoughtful as his northern-born friend strove to assimilate his explanation. 'Nomad children from the great houses are encouraged to leave home and travel the world, and return one day, bearing knowledge. That is my heritage. Choice brought me to Sessalie. Preference keeps me. Your crown serves my pay. However, you have become a great deal more than my employer.'

As Taskin's relief swelled the following pause, Jussoud added, 'No, don't speak! What's the use? You haven't the words in you, anyway.'

Taskin shook his head, astonished as the depth of compassionate friendship soothed him back into contentment. He relaxed, made at home amid the shelves of stacked scrolls, and the cedar boxes crammed with glass jars of rare oils and remedies. 'Well,' he confessed, 'I came for an inquiry, after all.'

'I thought as much,' Jussoud said. 'You had Mykkael cornered, did you not? Or why else would he strike out with that chosen fact to upset your self-assurance?'

'Why? You tell me.' Restored to business, Taskin rested his chin on the steepled tips of his fingers. 'The man's too *damned* secretive. He refuses to give sureties. The demands that he makes tear holes through my security wide enough to let in an invasion!'

'Why don't you start at the front of the problem,' Jussoud suggested with equanimity.

'Very well.' Taskin shrugged. 'You'll have to bear with the tangents.' He dug into the scrip at his belt, and removed a sprig of fresh cedar. 'Could you burn this for me?'

Jussoud accepted the snippet of greenery without question. He touched the frond to the oil lamp, then let the haze of fresh smoke flare up and winnow around him. 'I routinely burn certain herbs for protection in this space,' he admitted. 'An added round of cleansing won't be taken amiss.'

The commander shifted his weight, discomfited by much more than his barbaric perch on a cushion. 'Such uncanny precautions are necessary, where you lived on the steppe?'

'Sometimes.' Jussoud scooped a clay bowl from the shelf. The flat bottom was lined with sand and used ash. The nomad stuck the burning evergreen upright and allowed the small fire to consume itself undisturbed. 'We don't suffer attacks by cold sorcery, if that's the assurance you seek.'

Satisfied the room held no uncanny sign of demonic visitation, Taskin emptied the leather bag from Mykkael and handed over the last copper talisman. 'What do you make of this?'

Jussoud noted the disturbing pattern of the knots straight away. Turned cautious, he examined the disc in his palm. One glance at the engraving cut into its face, and he closed his large hand, eyes shut as he sucked a deep breath.

'You've seen this sort of talisman before,' Taskin stated.

The masseur's fingers stayed clamped, though his silver eyes had reopened. 'Yes, I have. It's an artefact from the wars with Rathtet.'

Taskin scowled, eyebrows bristled above the blade of his aristocratic nose. 'You were there *also*?'

'No.' Jussoud sighed. The mane of dark hair spilled over his shoulders shadowed his sobered expression. 'My sister owns one.'

'Sister!' Taskin stiffened, shocked, prepared to apologize. But the nomad lifted his unburdened left hand, and banished the need with a gesture.

'No words. It's all right.' The knotted thong swung as Jussoud extended his shut fist into the lamplight. 'By this, I presume that Mykkael has asked me to speak for him?'

'He didn't ask,' Taskin qualified quickly. 'He hoped, if I made the approach, that you might.' Every inch the commander of the king's guard, he marshalled his unruly resources. 'As you say, let's begin at the front of the problem. First of all, that disc may be needed for your protection. I have one also. So does the king. Three have gone to my finest guardsmen, including Captain Bennent. Another is held by the Duchess of Phail. Will you wear the last, and become my silent observer, unknown to all others but me?'

'Mykkael gave these to you?' Jussoud asked. 'If he has, you are honoured. They indicate you might hold something more than his personal trust.'

'Better say what you mean,' Taskin said, oddly ruffled to discover he might have been granted an unsought burden of commitment. 'I have given the captain his provisional freedom, bearing on what you care to tell me.'

'Nothing's changed, since we spoke in Dedorth's observatory.' The talisman still snugged inside his bunched fist, Jussoud spread his hands. 'I don't *know* whether Mykkael came to Sessalie under the pay of another employer. If he has, or has not, his mere presence is deadly.'

'Then why not tell me what you know of the man?' Taskin's insistence was gentle, warned as he was that the ground he assayed must be guarded by emotional pitfalls. 'I'll bear the tactical burden of decision myself, whether the captain should be entrusted to uphold his crown duty to Sessalie. The desert-bred told me, if your tribe was Sanouk, you might have a relative who served under him. Am I right to believe that person may be your dead sister?'

'Not dead,' Jussoud corrected, his delivery made rough by reluctance. 'She was one of the unlucky survivors.'

Taskin held, unblinking and still, by the wavering fire of the oil lamps. 'Unlucky?'

'Yes.' The healer unsealed his tight fist. While the breeze through the casement breathed chill off the glaciers, the clean shear of ice interwoven with the incongruous summer sweetness of flowers, he regarded the engraved copper disc. Then he looped the stained thong over his head as though the uncanny metal might burn him. He pulled his midnight hair clear of the leather. The copper talisman dropped over his heart, framed between the embroidered dragons stitched on his wide sash and the open lapel of his robe. He spoke then, his proud face trained ahead, and his unfocused eyes staring into a grim past. 'Orannia was one of the eighteen who walked out of the Efandi capitol alive. Like most of the rest, she suffered from madness beyond any power to remedy.'

'My*sh*kael was her acting captain?' Taskin probed carefully.

'More.' Jussoud arose. Barefoot, he strode to the window. For a racking, drawn interval, he regarded the black rim of the mountains reared above the faint, starlit shine that defined the slate roofs of the barracks. 'Mykkael was in love with her,' he said at last. 'They had expected to marry. My father, the old despot, forbade the match, and banished Mykkael from the Sanouk.'

Taskin would not soften his driving impatience. 'Dishonoured?'

'No. Nothing like that.' Jussoud changed his stance, faced back into the room, his features brushed gold against the night casement. 'He had brought her home through great difficulty. Like the desert tribes, my people have trained shamans. But their chanting could not cure her, or restore her to her right mind. Our law says the mad may not marry, and Mykkael would not abide.'

Taskin looked at him, testy. 'Bright powers! Then you've known that desert-bred's background and name all along?'

Unmoved to rancour, Jussoud shook his head. 'I never met him, you understand. Only heard of his history by way of correspondence with my distant relatives.' The nomad healer left the window, paced past his boxes of remedies, and pinched out the flame on one of the lamps, which was failing. While he scrounged for the phial to refill the reservoir, he resumed his measured explanation. 'We are an insular folk, not apt to welcome a stranger. The written record inscribed in the tribe's chronicle used the

Serphaidian ideograph for "dark foreigner" to reference Mykkael's petition to wed into the royal clan. Orannia and I share a father, a name. She chose the road to her heritage as a fighting sword among mercenaries. I had not seen her since girlhood, and I did not revisit the family until after the year she returned.'

Taskin glowered through the flare as the lamp was relit. 'Well, certainly you must have suspected Sessalie's captain might be the same man!'

'Not really. Even last night, when I saw the vizier's mark under his hair, I could not be sure. The captain who loved Orannia was a southern-born swordsman. The troops who fight sorcerers often bear Scoraign blood, since the culture lends an advantage. Many veterans wear similar tattoos, laid down for shielding protection. Our tourney champion might have been a survivor from any one of a dozen campaigns. Though he bore two styles of geometry, overlaid, Eishwin's lines are more subtle in nature, and the light in the cellar was dim.'

Taskin tracked Jussoud's deliberate tread as he returned to his cushion and sat down. While the healer recovered his goblet of *sennia*, the commander inquired with acid tenacity, 'Just when did you know your bold fellow for certain?'

Jussoud set down his drink with a nettled clink. 'Fires of mercy, *would you have asked him*?' Before Taskin's straight silence, which said beyond doubt, that no measure was too stiff for Sessalie's security, the nomad healer tucked his robe under his folded knees as though to ward off a chill. 'I knew when I went to the barracks this morning, and found the shaman's ward on his sword hilt.'

Taskin leaned forward. 'Not desert work?'

'No.' Jussoud returned a stunned shake of his head, as always bemused by the commander's exhaustive, sharp faculties. 'Mykkael is not tribal, his birth people never owned him. The lines he bears on his sword are Sanouk. A protection like that could only have been sung by our shamans, in gratitude, on the hour Mykkael left our camp.' Finding his goblet depleted, Jussoud used the oil lamp to refire the coals underneath his squat iron pot. Then, easy nature restored, he provoked, 'Had I known you were holding an interrogation, I'd have offered a pitcher of water.'

'No water,' said Taskin. 'We're trying to forestall tears. I promise I'll pay you a social call once Princess Anja is safe, and this threat posed by sorcerers is over.' He wrinkled his nose at the pungency of warmed *sennia*. 'If you don't burn your vocal cords drinking that stuff, I'm not done with today's round of questions. What of My*sh*kael's history with Prince Al-Syn-Efandi? Do you know aught of his flight from Rathtet?'

Jussoud stared. '*From* Rathtet? Bright stars of my ancestry, did he say that? If he did, that should show you his bitter reluctance to speak.'

Taskin handed over the padded cloth to allow the heated pot to be handled. 'Go on.'

Jussoud refilled his shell goblet, swirled the melted liquid inside until it assumed the consistency of hot glue. 'To win free, *your captain had to cross* through *the battle lines*. Our record, taken from Orannia's ravings, says this: he took twenty-five. They were his best fighters, the core of his troop, and closer than brothers, or family. One by one, he watched them die. Or go mad. He had Eishwin's mark in his favour. Most didn't. The few who stayed sane arranged the diversion, and Mykkael pressed through, alive. He kept those struck to madness upright on their feet, made them bear weapons and keep fighting. He endured horrors our shamans would not suffer our scribes to record to keep his oath and bring the Efandi princess to safety. He cosseted his band of survivors through, drove them beyond near starvation and disease to get back into friendly territory. Perhaps he held on out of hope their ruined minds could be recovered. Perhaps he did so because he had no one left, and the Efandi princess still to guard.'

'They couldn't be cured, then?' Taskin asked quietly.

Jussoud shook his head. 'Most killed themselves, after. What use to grieve? They had no future, no hope to win free. But my sister had family with Sanouk beliefs. Our customs will not embrace suicide. Mykkael tended her needs, saw her through the long journey home. Yet even our shamans could not recall her to reason. The Rathtet lines of sorcery burn in her mind without surcease. She still wakes up screaming from nightmares and deranged memory. Night and day, she is guarded from sharp objects.'

The last question fell light as a whisper against the backdrop of quiet. 'My*sh*kael would not leave her before he was banished?'

Jussoud sighed, ran a troubled hand through his hair. 'The last entry in the record was sealed by the ideograph for everlasting endurance. Mykkael had no place to go, after all. No troop, no cadre of specialized, trained officers. All his savings and supply trains were lost when the Efandi capitol was sacked. The princess he saved holds his debt, but no revenue. He became a lone sword, with no standing, then finally no hope, I should think. The subsequent wound that ruined his knee would have forced his retirement from mercenary service.'

'Why can't you swear to his honesty, then?' Taskin pressured.

Jussoud's eastern face showed the bitterest grain of his sadness. 'Because I know him through my sister's letters, the sane ones she wrote through the years when she served with his troop. Her heart saw the truth with all of love's dangerous clarity. Mykkael is a man who holds to integrity before honour. Ethics mean more than his promise. He will act on his human principles, first, and see himself damned if an oath, and right choice, should come to be set into conflict.'

Taskin heard through the last testimony, the braid trim at his shoulders straight as ruled brass in the flame light.

His gratitude stayed silent. He held no regret. Nor would he demean the scouring exchange pressed to closure with the syrup of pretentious apology. 'I am satisfied,' he said. 'As long as no man comes forward with evidence that My*sh*kael has broken his sworn bond, the king's word of trust can be used to stay the prejudice of the crown council.' He arose, then, regretful for the last order he must issue before leaving the healer in peace.

'Jussoud, would you take one further duty amiss? I need you to call down to the gate keep tonight to dress that insolent desertman's back.'

The nomad pushed his filled goblet aside, his black brows set into a frown of thunderstruck tolerance. 'I'll braid up my hair, then. How many stripes did he make you lay on him?'

Taskin answered, his proud head faced forward, that not even Jussoud should observe the irritation and grief that made shreds of his iron-clad bearing. 'On the streets, you'll hear twelve. I'm not known to deceive. For the sake of the kingdom, and my peace of mind, please make *damned* sure you strip him in private.'

XIII. Night

THE LATECOMERS WHO TURNED OUT TO HELP SEARCH FOR THE PRINCESS PILED UP AT THE MIDDLEGATE guardhouse. Drawn by the reward, or else moved by concerned generosity, their press in the street almost rivalled last night's crowd of celebrants. On foot, since Taskin's industrious watch officer had dispatched his horse back to stabling, Mykkael paused in the shadow outside the flood of the gatehouse torches. Still stinging from the commander's cavalier handling, he sized up the adventurers who had gathered for audience with Crown Prince Kailen. They were a mixed lot.

Grizzled farmers who smelled of hayfields and sweat came to loan their leashed hounds for tracking. Dairy maids and goatboys who had been searching the hedgerows rubbed shoulders with velvet-clad merchants and liveried servants. Jammed chock-a-block against the Middlegate's brick wall, weather-beaten caravan guards in dusty leathers swapped tales of road hazards and bandits with itinerant tinkers and wagoners. Two red-cheeked laundresses gossiped with a frocked housemaid, while a young girl with emerald ribbons flirted with a bravo bearing a sword that looked like an ancestral relic.

Mykkael mapped their collective mood: caught the

notes of disaffected anxiety, deferred hunger, and strained temper that would jealously guard the established position in line. No slinking tactic acquired in the field would let him slip past unobserved.

The garrison captain snapped off a coarse phrase in dialect, damning Taskin under his breath. Then he shifted raw shoulders beneath his sheathed sword. Chin raised, face bare, he prepared to brazen his way through.

At first, darkness covered him. The harsh shadows thrown by the torches masked the vivid stains on his shirt. As he worked into the press, recognition drew surprised murmurs of 'Captain!' followed by the inevitable flurry of movement as petitioners shifted aside. Brisk, but not hurrying, Mykkael reached the gate keep; and like the stir of cold breeze from behind, the first voices exclaimed. Fingers pointed in salacious discovery.

Unflinching, the captain arrived at the checkpoint. He met and passed by his posted sentry's shocked gasp; disregarded the sharp looks of inquiry. The watch officer's stunned questions were handled the same way: Mykkael ignored them. As if the bleeding marks of fresh punishment were nothing outside of the ordinary, he demanded a summary report of the traffic since sundown, point blank.

The officer gaped, caught Mykkael's bark of reprimand, then snapped to and started reciting. When his list was complete, with the abnormally high numbers of Devall's off-duty honour guard duly noted, the captain revised standing orders. He dispatched his gawping gate sentries to sort out the adventurers and free the clogged street. Then he strode on his way, without rising to comment, as speculation sparked like wildfire between the men-at-arms left at their posts.

'D'you think they'd have shackled him?'

'No man would dare!'

'If he did, he'd be dead, no doubt about it.'

'. . . without chain, who could hold him?'

'. . . suppose it was Taskin. Old icicle dick. Sprang from the womb with a sword in one hand, and a pair o' steel bollocks in the other.'

'Could've handled our captain, maybe, but powers of glory! What disgrace on the record could have remanded a commissioned crown officer for a lashing?'

A burst of rough laughter from the gatehouse wardroom echoed down the dark street. 'Oh, get real, man! A sand-bred cur holding a crown captaincy on his merits, and *that's* not a rank provocation?'

Mykkael chose the straightest route down the thoroughfare, past the lit fronts of the wine shops. Hard-tempered nerves from his years as a mercenary let him ignore the jeers of the dandies; the derision elicited from tradesmen and shopgirls; the vindictive hoots from the derelicts his men-at-arms had often collared for feisty conduct. Of far more concern to his wary ear, the sword in the sheath at his back: he listened, intent, to its silence. Yet no hum of warning arose from the shaman's lines sung into its warded hilt.

That quiet provided him small reassurance. Mykkael's senses crawled. Each passing second touched a pulse of tingling dread through his skin. Danger moved on the wind, a coil of moving intent that lurked, *waiting*, just under the range of his instincts. Attuned to the triphammer beat of his heart, he grazed against the black reflection of Anja's terror, *as somewhere in a bramble-choked meadow, she stumbled uphill in the dark.*

The rumble of iron wheels dispelled the odd current of witch thought. Mykkael dodged clear of the outbound slop wagon, sharpened by the awareness that the oldster on the driver's box was not whistling. The captain moved on, pushing the halt in his leg, and testing the texture of Sessalie's calm with an ear tuned and listening for change.

The mild night around him might have seemed ordinary, but for the wound pitch of a tension that sang underneath the ingrained habit of normalcy. Trade folk spoke in lowered voices on the street corners, their faces frowning and serious. Babies wailed from the lower town tenements, their cries muffled behind snugly barred shutters. Lovers stole kisses in the nooks between streetlamps, yet their embraces tonight seemed more frantic. If the tavern boys hung jaunty baskets of flowers above the doors of the taprooms, the talk at their backs held no ribald jokes, and no treble female laughter. Tin lanterns cast their circles of light, gilding the first shine of dew on the cobbles. Ahead of the mist, the air was dipped crystal, alive with the calls of a nightjar floating down from a rich merchant's garden, and the knifing chill breathed off the ice fields above Howduin Gulch.

While time fleeted.

Arrived at the keep gate, Mykkael heard bullfrogs in the moat, sure sign the night's crew of rag men were not out on their rounds netting salvage. Across town, the gist of the overheard gossip had wound to the same grim thread: Sessalie wore a deep-seated unease underneath her long-standing peace. People still tried to cling to complacency. They might shrug off fear with a smile of self-derision. False security blinded them. Amid the snug sanctuary of their mountains, the notion of deadly peril had been dismissed as unfounded fancy for too long.

Such innocence had no language to measure the magnitude of its helplessness. If Commander Taskin had ever once glimpsed the terrors these folk might suffer under usage by cold-struck sorcery, the iron courage of his commitment must surely falter, outfaced.

His face like cast stone, Mykkael greeted his alert sentries. Since, by his order, no torches burned by the watch post to spoil their night sight, he was spared their remark on the state of his back. Ahead, the plank bridge wore snags of mist risen off the black water below. Mykkael crossed the span, a scrape introduced to his stride by the knee overtaxed by the belltower steps. Yet tonight, far deeper concerns eclipsed the trials of his physical discomfort. The qualm in his gut as he stepped back on to stone paving served him the clear-cut warning: that he walked over ground wracked by the uncanny currents that moved where a sorcerer worked.

Mykkael approached the lighted bustle of the keep, pursued by haunted thoughts. He held no illusions, not now. His paper-thin tissue of peace had been torn since the moment he broached the locked coffer holding the Rathtet war's artefacts. From Highgate, he carried the bone-deep awareness that his baiting ploy with Taskin's crack archers had gone beyond brazen tactics. Each breath, he wrestled the stripped cry of his nerves. For King Isendon's oath, and for a princess who pleaded with painted green eyes from a portrait, he wondered if he had the resilience left in him to withstand the challenge a second time.

Behind the balefire burn of Anja's live fear, he still heard Orannia's screaming. The fierce pain he had no power to remedy still bled him, a scalpel cut through the heart.

Two paces beyond the portcullis archway, the glow off the fire pans set him on display. Men trained to a hair-trigger edge of response took note of their captain's entry. The white shirt hid nothing. Mykkael stepped across a lightning-struck silence, fast followed by thunderclap as the first, amazed whistle creased the stilled air at his back. The irritation all but unleashed his temper, that the guard had changed roster at sundown. Reliable, taciturn Cade was off watch. Which stroke of fouled timing launched Sergeant Jedrey to crowing satisfaction.

'Insubordination, striking a crown lancer in the line of duty, insulting royal ambassadors, and oh, yes! While we're at it, how many stripes decorate your dark hide for upstart insolence? How delightful to see Commander Taskin's delivered the lashing you've richly deserved of your betters!'

'Uncreative as all the rest of them,' Mykkael agreed, his derision astonishingly amiable. He added, 'Get me a task force of thirty men, soldier, armed and at the ready. I'm inside to the wardroom for a fast bite to eat. They'll march on the moment I come out.'

Stalled in mid-diatribe by the brisk shift in subject, Jedrey lost words for rejoinder.

'Duty!' cracked Mykkael. 'I'm calling a raid on a Falls Gate tavern, and you, dandy man, get to flash that spotless new surcoat at the forefront.'

'Which tavern?' asked Vensic, arrived for the bloodbath, and richly enjoying the flush that steamed Jedrey's ears.

Mykkael smiled, all teeth. 'The Bull Trough's overdue for a mucking, I think. There's still some stew left in the kettle inside? That's good. To ream out that dive, a man doesn't march without sustenance.'

Unlike the paved avenues in the upper-tier neighbourhoods, the warren of byways adjacent to Falls Gate were packed dirt, entangled and narrow as dropped string. Shopfronts battled for space to hang signs beneath the roof beams of the tenements, strung with their raggedy lines of hung laundry. No lamplighters visited these twisted, dimmed alleys, where starving rats scavenged the midden heaps. Citizens who braved the district at night brought candle lamps of wrought tin, or better, pine torches less apt to extinguish if dropped in the heat of a fracas.

The garrison's task squad marched with oiled lint cressets, unlighted. Sessalie's unbroken peace notwithstanding, Mykkael would have no man in the king's falcon surcoat pose a target for covert assassins. The lesson had gone hardest, to teach men to walk quietly, with weapons and mail shirts damped silent.

For that reason, even the most furtive of whispers carried through, as the plan for the raid was mapped out.

'Did you *see*, man, he leaned back in his chair, marked like that, and ate sausage as though nothing pained him.'

Mykkael snapped a finger against the strap of his sword

harness, which forced Jedrey to jump *fast* to still the loose chatter. Whether or not the sergeant regretted his impulse to select the most dissident names from the watch list, the garrison had been tuned for obedience. A war-hardened captain never slackened his discipline to insist a man under his charge had to like him.

'Who wants to cover the bolt holes?' Mykkael asked. His question cut through the barrage of coarse laughter that rolled from the packed taproom beyond the alley. 'The Bull Trough has three.'

'Three!' exclaimed Jedrey, attentive at last to his duty. 'Powers of daylight! Is that why you've never raided here?'

'No.' Mykkael's answer showed tolerance. Under the faint shine of starlight, he glanced overhead and surveyed the row of gallery windows, curtained in lamplit, rose chintz. 'The proprietor lies, cheats, waters his brew, even spices his cider with aphrodisiacs. But the madam who runs his upstairs brothel doesn't prostitute children.'

Given the fifteen volunteers he required, the captain described the buildings whose cellars housed the escape routes. Jedrey reorganized the remaining men, some to seal off the doors and windows, with the coolest heads held in reserve for the frontal assault on the tavern.

'We raiding for unpaid crown revenues, then?' asked the bold man just forcefully silenced.

'If you can pry out the proof there's a deficit,' Mykkael replied. A woman's throaty chuckle drifted downwards, while the outline of a lissom body crossed the candlelit glow of a curtain. Beneath, the alley was poured pitch. If the captain's form melted into the darkness, the stillness about him suggested the tension of a stalking lynx. 'That's your job, soldier.' To Jedrey, he added, 'Position your men quickly. Move them in the moment you hear the noise come back up in the taproom.'

'You won't be with us?' the sergeant asked, startled.

Mykkael turned his head. Not smiling, with teeth or otherwise, he said, 'There's a man inside I wish to interview.

You'll raid the bar and keep a lid on the bolt holes, while I bag my game in the brothel.'

'You're climbing in by way of the *wall*?' someone broke out, incredulous.

'What in the reaper's thousand hells for?' Eyebrows raised, Mykkael laughed outright. 'Easier, surely, to use the front door and go in as a paying customer.' Before Jedrey's look of poleaxed astonishment, he said plainly, 'Why else keep the splendour of my spoiled shirt, if not to wring a martyr's applause from the riff-raff? On my chosen signal, Sergeant. Have the men ready.'

Mykkael strode off, the hitch of his worsening limp masked under the alley's clogged darkness. The men left in place by the windows, and the strike force poised under Jedrey, watched their captain take pause only once, his sharp, desert profile outlined in the light that spilled from the Bull Trough's taproom. That split second gave him the bearings he needed. A man on a mission far removed from the lusty pleasure of dalliance, Mykkael tugged his snagged shirt from the grip of a scab, resettled his sheathed sword, and strode in.

The smell and the noise assaulted the senses in an overpowering blast: the fat reek of tallow like warm glue, binding the miasma of heated bodies, spilled beer, yelling voices and shrieked laughter, underlaid by the pitch tang of sawdust. The wolf pack seethe of roistering patrons wore drab motley and homespun, or the worn leather aprons of craftsmen. Seated on benches, or leaned in fierce argument across the rough trestles, they spoke the tough dialect of woodcutters and drovers, and wore the sweat-shiny muscles of smiths. Dice throwers rubbed elbows with shirtless men, arm wrestling, while wagers were counted, and cheeky barmaids swayed through the press with trays laden with foaming beer steins.

Until Mykkael's entry provoked a sharp recoil. Sight of his features cast a hush as dense as a thrown blanket. The heave of boisterous movement stalled. Pale faces turned, flushed red with stunned recognition. Here, his dark skin framed a shout that spoke louder than the crown's falcon surcoat, or his vested authority as captain of Lowergate's garrison.

One too many of tonight's rabid gamblers had lost a year's coin to the upset at last summer's tourney. Nor had the insult subsided without strain. The changes flushed through the stews by the Falls Gate by Mykkael's worldly experience had curbed the freebooting licence left ingrained by decades of slipshod enforcement. His steel-clad patrols redressed those inequities, which kept the smouldering sparks of old rancour well fanned.

'Well, well! Look what an ill wind just blew in off the streets,' ventured a heckler towards the rear. A man at one of the front trestles spat, while, staring challenge at Mykkael, a blowsy seamstress pushed the stained hands of a dyer's boy into her gaping blouse. His surrounding friends hooted, applauding with drunken encouragement. Once past the shock of Mykkael's entry, the Bull's patrons realized they were a multitude, pitched against one.

Sparks ripe for dry tinder, they were primed to react.

Mykkael's strategic review had assured that the horse thief he sought was not in the crush on the benches. Met on all sides by aggressive hostility, he broke into full-throated laughter. 'Are you pigeons starving for cheap entertainment? Never saw any lot stare like green boys at a man who walks in to scratch the ripe itch.' He reached out, snake-fast. While near bystanders flinched, his tossed coin rang on to a serving girl's tray. His follow-through snagged a filled tankard. Mykkael sampled the brew. Eyes shut in a grimace of striking contempt, he returned the vessel in nearly unbroken motion. 'The whores better have nicer kick than the brew, here. Which skirt's got steaming magma beneath? Only one, I hear tell, is worth asking for.'

'And which one's that, mongrel?' a roisterer shouted. 'For you, she may not be in heat.'

But Mykkael had well hooked their male curiosity. He swaggered towards the railed gallery, where the establishment's ringleted madam set her nubile collection on display.

Taskin's left signature could not escape notice. 'Looks like you been whipped out of one bed already,' a doxy remarked from the sidelines.

'Just frisky, first round,' Mykkael disagreed. His tigerish smile went and resurged as his dark eyes roved over the mountainous form of the madam. Admiring her roped pearls and pillowed, pink bosom, he leaned over the railing, kissed her rouged cheek, then chided before she could speak. 'Ah, mother, relax. The hard edge is sawn off. I'm nice for the women, tonight.'

The burst of coarse laughter shook dust from the ceiling beams. Limp notwithstanding, Mykkael disdained the stair and staged a fluid vault on to the platform. The onlookers were presented with his insolent back as he inspected the live goods, half naked and simpering as they flashed sheer lace petticoats, and preened in their ruffles and glass beads.

A few baited their prowess with cutting enthusiasm, the boldest ones fingering his soiled shirt, or jostling his stance with swayed hips.

'I'll cure that limp, soldier.'

'You walking three-legged, boy? C'mon. Let me ride you.'

'Let's see how long I take to melt your hard muscles to jelly.'

A coy redhead tucked a spray of daisies through the strap of his harness. Mykkael plucked out the flowers with a gallant's bow, then shied them into the crowd. He moved on, measuring the line-up with jaded provocation, neatly sidestepping the vixen in scarlet who tried to rake her nails down his shoulder. Her glare of contempt fixed full on his face, she spat; and again, her stabbing spite missed its mark, turned aside by his stunning, fast reflex.

'Try again?' Mykkael goaded, then frowned towards the madam, his eyes shadow-dark and unreadable. 'I prefer my fights with some steel in them, yes? So, how much for Vangyar's hot favourite?'

The huge woman smiled. 'Too late, randy dog. She's already with him.'

'Is she, then?' Mykkael raised his eyebrows, tossed one, two, three crown sovereigns with the sweet *ching!* of gold, into the silk-covered trough of her lap. 'In that case, second best will have to stand in.' He shot out a hand, clamped the wrist of the hussy who had spurned him, and laid her fingers against the rough stubble of his jaw. 'This one will do.'

The madam nodded her triple chins, granting obscene acquiescence.

His outraged selection screeched and spun like a cat. She tried to savage him, and lost her other hand to his iron grip. 'Spit again?' the desert-bred captain invited. His expertise peerless, harangued at each step by a shrieked tempest of curses and the glitter of snagged beads, he manoeuvred his catch up the stairway.

He flung her off at the top of the landing, then foiled her lunge for his throat by showering coins on the floorboards. 'Which room is Vangyar's?'

'What? *Are you crazy?*' Dropped to her knees, her fingers scrabbling under his boots to recover his scatter of silver, the doxy glared upwards through tumbled hair.

'Dogs usually are.' Mykkael flicked one last coin through the gloom, this one a gleaming crown sovereign. 'You looked like you needed the night off the most. I trust you're well paid? Then enjoy a good sleep.' Downstairs, the noise in the Bull's taproom resurged. The captain spoke through its boisterous roar, each word punched with urgent clarity. 'Which door, right or left?'

'The one straight ahead,' snapped the whore, left kneeling and breathless at the speed by which her lush charms were abandoned.

Mykkael quartered the corridor with soundless strides, the wasp hum of steel as he drew his sword at one with the move that tripped the latch and eased open the panel. Slick as a wraith, he slipped inside. The door he had barged clicked closed at his heels, a triumph of timing, as Jedrey's launched raid broached the taproom downstairs, to a thunderous burst of pandemonium.

For Vangyar the horse thief, the night's pleasure turned sour between heartbeats. A callused hand grasped his naked shoulder, and flipped him like a fish off the yielding, ripe flesh of his woman. Thrown on to his back amid twisted bedding, his roaring shove to arise was stopped cold by the edge of a longsword, touched against the shocked thrust of his manhood.

'Stay put,' demanded the demon-dark swordsman; then, 'Be still,' to the woman, whose painted eyes flew open as a draught chilled the throb of desire left unpartnered between her gaped thighs.

Before her last moan shattered into a scream, Mykkael snapped, 'Cover yourself. Leave. Do as I ask. If he does as well, I won't harm him.'

A rushed flurry of cloth, as the whore snatched a wrap, and fled on rouged feet through the doorway; then a *bang* on the floorboards, as something downstairs rammed into the ceiling in the course of the ongoing fracas.

Mykkael regarded the long face of the horse thief, dripping sweat off the trailing tips of his moustache. 'My soldiers are raiding. They won't come upstairs unless I change their orders. Nor do I bear a crown warrant with your name under seal as a criminal. *Not yet,*' Mykkael emphasized, the relentless sword pressed to cringing, drooped flesh as Vangyar rebounded from shock into venomous fury. 'You will answer some questions, first pass, with the truth. If you don't, if you lie, on my word, I'll draw blood you'll regret for the rest of your useless life! Now, you don't want to ruin your manly joy? All you need do is stay reasonable.'

Propped akimbo on braced elbows, Vangyar glared past his belly, and into those pitiless desert-bred eyes. 'Ask, bitch-bred cur. Then bend your stiff neck looking over your shoulder for the rest of your days, which are numbered.'

Mykkael blinked, flashed white teeth through curved lips without smiling. 'Fair enough. If I wanted to buy a particular black horse with silver leopard dapples, four white stockings, and a chevron-shaped star on its forehead, could you get him?'

Vangyar flopped backwards, the bristle of beard on his chin thrust against the damp pit of his throat. 'I could,' he said, sullen, 'except the brute beauty's been stolen.'

Mykkael tweaked the placed sword. 'Elaborate. Quickly.'

Through the shrieks of a woman, slashed through the chorus of male bellows from below, the horse thief reassembled his scattered wits and applied his professional knowledge. 'Horse you want's part of a steed wicket team, three blooded pairs who used to be pastured upriver, in the meadows behind Gurley's cow farm.'

'Owner?' prompted Mykkael. The blade in his hand stayed, a needle of fire by the fluttering dip by the bedside.

Vangyar shook his head, swallowed. 'Don't know. The wicket team was assembled several months back, and set into training in secret.' To ascertain the unpleasant foreigner understood, the horse thief took pains to qualify. 'Rich folk like to do that, enter what they call "dark pairs" to tip the odds and enliven the betting. Sometimes they upset a favourite to humble a rival. Blood's sometimes let, to keep such surprise challenges under wraps. The batch with your black was close handled, that way. Someone's rich boy from the Highgate brought coin for their upkeep to Gurley. His sons did the riding to fit them, under lists of detailed instructions.'

Mykkael absorbed the gist. 'This black horse I'm wanting was stolen, you say?'

'Not only him. The whole team of six was just lifted.'

Vangyar jerked his chin, snarling his resentment. 'Let me free, you mad dog. I can try to find out who did the take. Wanted to anyway. Six culled off one pasture is ravening greed. Don't need this territory stirred by the heat as crown law sets the countryside boiling.'

Mykkael narrowed his eyes. 'When was this wicket team stolen?'

'Last night.' Vangyar glanced with exasperated rage at the sword blade, then assayed a broken-toothed grin. 'I could get this horse, surely. With the princess gone missing, I much doubt the king's magistrate has troubled to register the theft on the rolls. Likely fat Farmer Gurley never got through the hubbub to file his complaint.'

'Then consider the incident registered, now.' Mykkael lifted his sword blade. One fluid motion saw the steel run back into the sheath at his shoulder. Throughout, his hard gaze stayed pinned upon Vangyar, as though the man's narrow nose and slab cheekbones could be engraved into permanent memory.

Downstairs, the noise rose in a crescendo, then fell back like spent surf towards order. Mykkael spoke at length. 'I know your face, Vangyar. That says you're a marked man. If you can't make your way in an honest profession, I suggest you leave Sessalie tomorrow. Stay, lay your hand on another man's livestock, and take my promise as your fair warning. Your nice lady will weep at your hanging and sleep with another the day of your burial.'

'Bitch-bred mongrel!' Vangyar kicked free of the sheets, shoved bandy legs to the floor, and snatched in blind rage for his clothes.

'Might do well to bide.' One moment more, Mykkael grinned over his victim's stung pride. Then he strode to depart, all flaunting grace in his disreputable, blood-stained shirt. 'Unless you want to be snagged in my raid? Somebody downstairs tags you for a horse thief, Sergeant Jedrey might haul you in.'

Hand on the latch, he sensed the sharp movement. He

had already engaged on trained instinct, as the thrown knife parted the air. Dropped down, spinning back, even before the blade impaled itself in the door plank, he embraced the crystalline state that framed the reflex of *barqui'ino* awareness. Two blows of his hands: one placed to stun nerves, and the next to drop his attacker with a broken neck.

Vangyar reeled backwards, scarcely aware he was dying until his head thumped into the bed frame. Out straight on the floorboards, he realized he *couldn't* be staring straight down at his own naked buttocks.

'Damned *fool,*' snapped Mykkael, voice like iron above him. Then metal spoke, whining clear of its sheath. The swift cut of the sword let in the night ahead of the throes of last suffering.

XIV. Strike

THE DOWNSTAIRS RAID HAD REDUCED THE BULL TROUGH'S TAPROOM TO THE TUMBLED WRACK OF A BATTLEGROUND. Tallow dips still burned in the bar's chandelier. Beneath their sultry glare, the upset trestles, spilled food, and smashed crockery lay scattered over the sawdust, poked through by the splinters of benches destroyed in the throes of combat. If not peace, then the semblance of order prevailed. The last protesting bystanders were being turned out by the fist of crown authority. Others, less innocent, were being detained. Their railing objections raised mayhem enough to keep Jedrey's task force preoccupied. The man-at-arms posted on guard by the stair became the first to notice the captain's reappearance on the landing above.

Paused at the newel post to rest his game knee, Mykkael surveyed the activity with professional acuity: the barmaids who knelt with damp rags to minister to the bludgeoned fallen; the alert cordon surrounding the bar, where, on the only upright stool, the garrison's quartermaster scowled beside a salvaged candlestick, crosschecking the establishment's books. The whores had all fled. Their provocative splendours had been replaced by a sorry collection of scofflaws, roped by the wrists to the platform rail, until an escort could be assembled to march them back to the keep.

The loose end still remained. Mykkael gritted his jaw, gave up his leaned stance, and pressed his limping step down the stairway. His order collared the attentive young guardsman. 'Upstairs, soldier. An exceedingly stupid man threw a knife.'

The man-at-arms signalled to a companion, resigned. 'Fetch a plank, Paunley. We've got a corpse to haul down for a pauper's grave.'

'Sadly,' Mykkael affirmed. The female shriek to his left spun him round, prepared for a fit of hysterical grief, or the mindless assault the bereaved sometimes launched to vent their outraged denial.

Yet no lissom sweetheart leaped to savage his face. Only the Bull's indomitable madam stood her ground, unmoved as the mountain rooted to earth in her acres of flounces and skirts.

Eyes on her streaked face, the captain inquired, 'Did Vangyar have any family?'

The madam shook her ringleted head. 'None that I knew.' Her dimpled hands blotted the stream of her tears with the wad of a sequined shawl. 'Haul him out as you please. His girl won't be claiming the body.'

'She was a professional, I saw that much.' Mykkael gathered his balance to pass on his way, then stopped stiff as the madam's sensuous fingers clasped the wrist underneath his loose sleeve.

'You didn't lay.' She sniffed, her sorrow replaced by a glare of ferocious offence. 'Did my dearie in scarlet not please you?'

Mykkael laughed, not missing the wise, queenly dignity underneath her run paint and histrionics. 'You have your pride; I see that also.' Though in evident haste, he permitted her grasp long enough to address her question. 'Your vixen has charm, but unfortunately, she also has grit and integrity. I suggest you retire her. Some are born with too much spirit for whoring. They're the ones who always get hurt, no matter how forcefully you warn your johns you won't allow their rough handling.'

The madam sighed. 'I know that.' She released her touch. Her searching pause reassessed him, blue eyes sharpened by an intelligence at odds with her surface display of distress. 'But Maylie has nowhere else she can go. Her brother's a halfwit who needs cosseting.'

'Send the fellow across to the garrison keep,' Mykkael said. 'If he can sweep floors and not make useless trouble, he'll earn his day's bread. He can sleep by the fire with the cook's brats.'

He moved on, then, without a glance back, and demanded a summary report from the man set in charge of the prisoners. The captain listened, as he had to the madam, with one hip braced to the railing to ease his bad knee. If his stance seemed too easy, his attention maintained its unswerving intensity. One wretch, he set free. If clemency ruled him, the sheeted burden brought downstairs on the plank refuted the presumption he might keep any slipshod habit of leniency.

All at once, his head turned. 'Who is that?'

The officer just interviewed followed his glance: saw the broad-shouldered man in plain clothing who had just raised the sheet from the corpse. The jostle as the bearers paused for his review caused the victim's head to roll off the board. Unsupported, it dangled, wrong way around, like a melon hung from a string.

'Powers!' The officer minding the prisoners swallowed fast. Through the scald of churned bile, he grated, 'That man, standing there? He's the marshal of the high prince's honour guard. Came here on leave time, until Sergeant Jedrey accepted his help.'

Before the last word, the captain was moving. Mykkael crossed the wrecked floor, his limp grown pronounced as he hoisted his leg across an overturned trestle. No such hitch marred his reach, as he clamped a fast hand on Jedrey's immaculate shoulder. The grip must have ground on a nerve, for the large man went boneless. Spun around and bowed backwards against the bar, he lay gasping, the sweat springing down his blanched face.

Behind, the keep's quartermaster shot straight, his finger still pinned to the disputed sum in the ledger. He drew breath, stopped, thought the better of speaking, then wisely moved back out of range.

The captain's dark eyes kept their merciless focus. Instinct deferred, shown a cold-cast ferocity that *would* act before mercy or reason.

'Devall's marshal leaves. Now!' The order held a warning past compromise. 'No questions, and damn protocol. I'll have no stranger's meddling given the sleeve to stir into garrison business!'

Released, Jedrey straightened. His face was wrung pale. The stoop to his shoulders seemed flaccid and aged, and the arm he required to brace his slack knees shook in spasms as he clung to the bar top. 'The high prince is our *ally*, you slinking, dumb mongrel. Offend his Highness, and you'll turn our merchants to paupers. No lowland port will ship goods out of Sessalie if your post-pissing ignorance turns Devall's monarch against us.'

Mykkael said no word. Just moved, a blur sprung from stillness no wary reflex might track. A snap cracked the air. The sergeant toppled. Jedrey's frame hit the floor like an axed tree, his left forearm snapped clean through both the long bones between elbow and wrist.

'Carry on,' Mykkael said to the dumbstruck quartermaster. 'You heard my orders. Henceforward, you have the watch.'

At his feet, Sergeant Jedrey's stunned effort to rise tangled with his horrifically mangled appendage. His shriek of fainting shock sliced through the ignominy, as the garrison captain stepped over him. 'You're relieved. Where I trained, we don't waste the time pissing posts with citations and whippings.'

The raid on the Bull Trough Tavern took over an hour to wrap up. Mykkael chose not to be present throughout, but came and went, one man-at-arms or two at his heels, to prowl the back streets above Falls Gate. The taverns he sampled seemed chosen at random. He quartered their packed taprooms as though testing their mood, taking note of which patrons did what, with no inclination to make more arrests. The Cockatrice, favoured haunt of Prince Kailen, seemed more than usually raucous and jammed. There, Mykkael lingered, absorbed by something he encountered in a dimmed corner, though the guardsman beside him saw nothing.

Before the toll of the watch bell at midnight, the garrison captain was at hand to enforce the quartermaster's order to march, as the Bull Trough's catch of malcontents were moved under guard to the gaol in the Lowergate keep. The straggling prisoners could not be moved smartly, roped as they were, the tied wrists of each man attached to the left ankle of the one in procession before him. Any wretch who tried bolting would trip half the line, with the fallen as living anchor. By the time the coffle reached the plank drawbridge, the night mists descended like layers of dropped gauze. Mykkael's stride was visibly dragging, no longer quite noiseless as he traversed the span over the moat.

For that reason, he led the way into the gate arch, with guardsmen flanking the prisoners on each side, and the quartermaster and a squad of six stalwarts holding position as rearguard. Beneath the dank stone, thick with the rust taint of iron and the gritted smoke of spent torches, the darkness was a jet shroud, punch cut by the ruddy glare from the fire pans in the bailey beyond. What warned Mykkael, whether the brush of stirred cloth, or the note of chance-struck metal, or some whispered change in the air, no man knew.

His reverse was too sudden. The front pair of captives jammed into each other, shouting, as his evasion crashed backwards into them.

Whatever sprang without sound from the shadow lunged after him, thrusting with murderous steel.

Moving with the assault, his shoulder already twisting to narrow the available vital target, Mykkael took the stabbing strike for his heart as a graze across chest and shoulder. The tip of the blade jabbed a prisoner's arm, raising an ear-splitting yell.

Mykkael dropped, palms flat on wet stone, then rebounded upwards, away from the trampling scuffle of roped legs. He drew, sword screaming from sheath, met and parried attack, to a pealing shriek of clashed steel. The blows exchanged came one after the other like licked fire, scribed out in chance-caught reflection. The clamour belled in a crescendo, then ceased. Something dropped, rolling, to a gurgle of drowned breath, jetting stone walls and panic-stricken men with a spray of let blood.

By the time the roused watch sprinted into the sallyport with lit torches, the dropped body drummed its heels through the spasms of death. Mykkael bent above with his sword slicked bright scarlet. With no pause to survey the carnage before him, he hoisted his fallen assailant by the ankle, and began hauling him shoulder down towards the bailey. The lead captives, milling behind in stunned shock, saw a stranger's face, still spasmed by its final rictus. The dragged fingers, limp and weaponless, trailed over the stone, splashed with the blood and urine that flooded, still steaming, from the opened viscera.

'Dark powers of hell!' gasped a man, while two of the tied captives dropped retching. The inbound guard with the torch recoiled clear as his captain shoved past with his burden.

'Assassin!' snapped Mykkael, his temper shaved thin. 'A boring damned nuisance, now that he's dead. First, there's a captive with a stabbed arm that wants binding. Next, I want to know what the moat watch was doing, that this crafty visitor slipped by them. Last, I want a plank set up in the wardroom under good light. I will know what sort of creature dared an ambush on my turf with the thought he could strike without penalty.'

The gate watch scurried, somewhat green at the gills, as Mykkael proceeded with his fresh kill across the width of the bailey. Soon engrossed in his promised review of the corpse, he snapped off more orders. Stablehands were dispatched with buckets and brooms to sluice away the spilled effluent. A boy caught staring was sent to recover the dropped sword, and a knife, if he could find it. The moat watch was called in for reprimand; then the rattled quartermaster was reminded to assert his authority. Men who had never seen battle-raw violence mustered their shocked nerves, and resumed their dropped purpose under their captain's brisk bidding. Chaos receded. The jangled knot of prisoners began to be sorted, the wounded one doctored by Vensic's firm hand, while Mykkael retired upstairs. Settled industry ruled for scarcely a minute before upset erupted all over again.

The keep sergeant was left on his own as the next sheet-wrapped body borne on a plank trailed in on the tail of the crisis.

'He killed *twice* tonight?' Vensic sucked in a vexed breath, and swore as he knotted the linen over the captive's unlucky puncture. 'Holy powers of mercy.' He tried not to look at the hacked mess that lay, dribbling gore on the wardroom trestle. Then, 'Don't go up there,' he snapped to the quartermaster, who ventured an unwise step towards the stair. 'You need watch orders? I'll handle the dispatch. Captain'll be a rank bundle of nerves. Let him unwind first. Trust me, he'll come back down when he's ready.'

'You hear yet, he broke Jedrey's arm?' said a man, somewhat shrill, as the neck-broken corpse was manoeuvred inside and laid out alongside the first. More guards milled about, shaken and exclaiming.

'Poke a dog with a stick, it'll snap. Sergeant Jed was a fool to provoke him.'

'Blighted bad call, for those wretches on moat watch!' a bystander griped in commiseration. 'You hear what

Captain Mykkael *said* when he dressed down their sad hides for negligence?'

In no mood for gossip, Vensic cracked orders. 'Canvas and needles, boys, keep it smart! We've got two stiffs to sew up for the gravediggers. And this place to scrub down in the meantime. No man sits on his arse till, floor to ceiling, we're mopped clean as the late queen's pantry!'

As the room cleared, and the fascinated pack broke away from Mykkael's morbid handiwork, the keep sergeant collared the quartermaster to hear the official report.

Jussoud padded into the lull of the aftermath, still wearing his fine robe and silk sash with the dragons. He quartered the room once, reviewing the two corpses with unmoved professional quiet. Even under the fluttering candles, the loose tunic and drawstring trousers on the gutted one could not be mistaken for northern dress. As though foreign assassins were commonplace visitors, the tall nomad met Vensic's leashed-back distress with a calm like unruffled water. 'Since these two lie past need of my services, where's your captain?'

'Taskin sent you?' Vensic shut his eyes, released a pent breath, then set down the duty slate in his hand. 'I thank glory for that.' Exhausted and troubled, he placed the chalk alongside as though it was explosively fragile. 'Mykkael's upstairs. Mind how you handle him. He isn't inclined to want company.'

'By nature, is he a man who craves a woman to let down from the tension of violence?' Jussoud shrugged, the chink of glass in his satchel too strident amid the strained quiet. 'Then bide easy. I'll manage well enough on my own.'

Vensic rubbed his stubbled face with taut hands, nodded, then moved with intent to roust stableboys. 'You'll be wanting the wash tub?'

Half turned away to proceed up the stair, Jussoud glanced back in surprise.

And steady, sensible Vensic gave way, his voice cracked

rough by an onslaught of shaking. 'Last I saw, Mykkael looked as if he'd walked through an abattoir. *What's happening?* Who sent the foreigner that just tried to kill him?' Then, as the braced set to those eastern-bred features reached through, his distress snapped to shattering fear. 'Bright powers, what's troubled you? Jussoud?'

But the nomad had no assurance to salve his deep worry, that fresh bleeding could be masked by the gore of a kill. 'Send up filled buckets. Hot water. Leave them outside the door. If I need aught else, I'll send down to you.' All business, he spun and mounted the stair, leaving Vensic, struck desolate, behind him.

The door at the top of the landing was ajar. The feeble glow of the clay oil lamp beyond spilled carmine light over the stairhead, where Jussoud took pause to consider the difficult prospect of entry. He shifted his satchel, to a faint clink of glass.

That distinctive sound, or perhaps the earlier tread of his grass sandals, reached Mykkael's overstrung senses and woke recognition. His flint voice came muffled, from behind that gapped panel, the phrasing in high-caste Serphaidian. 'Jussoud? Come ahead. Only you.'

The nomad contained his stark apprehension, pushed open the door, and stepped through. The sweet-burning fragrance of incense filled his nostrils, underlaid at next breath by the coppery tang of let blood. Jussoud all but flinched as his tentative first footfall mired in Mykkael's dropped shirt. The fabric was sodden, more scarlet than white. Rinsed in hellish tones by the lamp on the trestle, Mykkael knelt before what looked like a clothes chest. His posture was upright, buttocks propped on the heel of his good leg, with the bad knee extended at a sideways angle that suggested the scream of pinched nerves. His naked, marked back showed Taskin's three stripes, the scabs rubbed raw where his harness had chafed. His head stayed bowed, and his hands, tucked before him, were not visible.

He might have been settled in meditative contemplation, except for the tremors that chased in sharp waves through the musculature alongside his spine. 'There is always reaction,' he said, almost steady. 'It will pass. Take care to move slowly until then.'

Jussoud took a deep breath, sampling the incense for narcotic drugs. He smelled none, only the mild blend of herbals used in southern physics for calming. Left to wait, allowed no direct outlet to allay his concern, he softly set down his bundle of remedies. The stained shirt, untangled, showed him two rents: one across the left-hand side of the chest, and beside that, another razor-clean slice through the upper sleeve. Anxious about bleeding, but granted no invitation, the healer crushed down his urgent impatience.

The incense unreeled serpentine smoke, tinted rouge in the flutter of the oil lamp. Mykkael drew in the scent with shuddering long breaths, as though all five senses could be condensed down to one, with the meadow-flower fragrance the ephemeral nail upon which he hung his strained consciousness. Cued by the intuitive awareness that tonight, the ritual was not going to ease him, Jussoud dared a cautious step forward. 'I'm coming across.'

The captain did not forbid him; only the tremors grew worse as the healer's slowed step approached. Jussoud reached, ever so carefully gentle. He touched the unmarked right shoulder, felt the animal flinch of recoil, then the lightning-fast surge of roused sinew as the man underneath his poised fingers strangled down the reflexive *barqui'ino* response.

'All right,' Jussoud said. 'Settle back. You can trust me.'

'Orannia's brother,' Mykkael whispered, the next wracking shudder all too close to the wrench of a sob stifled silent.

Jussoud knelt, gathered the tortured knot of bronze flesh into his steady embrace. 'In a kinder world, we should have been family.' There he held for long minutes, while Mykkael trembled against him, head turned aside in choked grief. Over his shoulder, on the lid of the clothes chest next to the incense, Jussoud saw the object that had held the captain absorbed: an intricate wooden seal inlaid with gold patterns, until what looked like an axe blow had hewn its symmetry into quarters. 'Brace up, now, Captain. I'm going to raise you.'

Mykkael cursed his knee, which had forced his collapse, then swore with more venom as he saw the silk sleeves of the robe Jussoud had just spoiled with bloodstains. The inventive, rich phrasing startled the nomad to laughter. 'I can see we won't waste any candles testing your eye reflexes for a concussion.'

'My head wasn't dunted,' Mykkael agreed. Leg under him, his wrecked balance back under command, he managed to perch on the stool with his bloodied hands braced on the trestle. 'Did you know Anja?' he asked, point-blank.

'Yes. Forget memory. She is not like Orannia. Let her quandary bide for the moment.' Jussoud withdrew his steadying touch, caught blindsided as an explosion of tuned instinct whipped Mykkael back to his feet. The move erupted too fast to resist. The nomad stopped cold, awareness shocked through him that, had he owned the speed of reaction to try, the attempt might well have destroyed him. Since the aggression seemed caused by someone's step on the stair, he chose words in rapid Serphaidian. 'It's a boy bearing buckets. Hold fast, do you hear?'

Mykkael disarmed reflex, spun, and propped his stressed frame on the trestle. His hurt tucked into a protective posture, chin averted, he said, 'I should send you out.'

'You're not going to. Stay still.' The nomad moved, intercepted the boy on the landing. He returned with the steaming buckets, shut the door, then recovered his satchel of remedies. He rummaged inside, trimmed the wicks of four candles, and set them alight one by one. Now able to see clearly, he approached Mykkael and started his treatment in earnest. 'Do the *do'aa* ever poison their blades?'

Mykkael turned his head, jerked stiff with surprise. 'You knew that assassin was oath-sworn?'

'To mark you? He had to be.' Jussoud completed his cursory assessment, then selected a soft rag, several herbals and two oils. He tested the first bucket, and made an infusion with the hot water. 'Answer.'

'They don't.' Mykkael subsided, eyes shut, while those quick, knowing fingers probed at the gash on his chest, then the shallower graze on his bicep. 'The swords they carry are quite sharp enough.'

'So I see. Nothing you have here should cause undue worry.' The nomad dipped his clean rag and pronounced, 'This will sting. I am sorry. But stitching would badly impair your mobility, and naught else will reliably stanch such a razor-clean cut.' Fast and sure, he wrung the hot linen and began the unpleasant chore of cleaning the open flesh wounds. No need to waste words to note how a hairsbreadth change in angle would have let the sword's point pierce the chest wall. Mykkael surely knew how close he had come to the death that had danced with him in the dark.

As often happened, Jussoud's steady silence invited the overstrung mind to unburden.

'Had they sent a southerner, I would have died,' the captain admitted straight out. 'The fact he had northern skin let me place him.' He sucked a sharp breath, as Jussoud's ministrations moved on to the angry slice on his arm. 'A man sent from that *do'aa* may have known of the knee. Even odds, and surprise, he should have been able to take me.'

'Yet he did not.' Jussoud rinsed his rag, packed the wounds with clean lint, then added a salve that eased the virulent sting like a tonic. 'Life's too short to waste looking back.'

'The two masters I flouted don't think so,' Mykkael said, his sadness turned savagely wrenching.

Jussoud rummaged for dry linen, then uncapped a tin with turpentine gum, and softened the contents over the candle. 'Well, they must get tired of losing trained men.'

'You saw the seal?' Mykkael retorted. 'Smashed crosswise, that means they will quarter the known world. It is sent as an oath-breaker's promise of vengeance. I had hoped, of the two, Kaien's *do'aa* might release me.'

Jussoud dipped the linen into the tin, let the melted gum soak through the fabric. 'Do you care very much if you itch as you heal?'

Mykkael curled his lip at the strong reek of pine gum. 'That concoction you've got's going to spare me from having my torso done up in strapping? Great glory. I'll scratch like a dog, and be grateful.' Then he flinched, gasping swearwords, as the healer plastered the heated strips over his traumatized flesh.

To divert him from the pain, Jussoud posed a sensitive question. 'What made you think Kaien might grant you release?'

Eyes shut, head thrown back, with the sweat rolling off his temples in drops and soaking his sable hair, Mykkael jerked out his answer. 'Such a seal is given, master to student, on the swearing of oath. It is kept on display, then awarded with ceremony upon completion of training. I did not finish my schooling. Not then, not ever, with Kaien's *do'aa*. When I deserted without given leave, the master smashed my seal, for dishonour. The first assassin he sent delivered that token. Though that aspirant died by my hand, I sent his disc back, unbroken, along with his ashes. For the second man, I did the same. By my respect for their dead, they would understand I had never shared secrets between *do'aa*. Tonight, as you see, they dispatched their reply. Third is final. My appeal is not going to be heard.'

'Outcast,' Jussoud said. 'Did you murder that beggar girl?'

That snapped Mykkael out of pain-shocked stupor.

Riled beyond hurt, his eyes open and angry, he slammed his taut fists on the trestle. 'With these hands? No! The spilled blood stained another's. But, by allowing such knowledge to exist in the world – yes. Which weapon strikes down the victim, the living man or the sword? All of us in that *do'aa* killed that child. Saddest of all, maybe, that I was the only one there who was shamed enough to walk out.'

'I spoke for you, today, when I wasn't sure,' Jussoud said, in one measured sentence drawing the sting from his test of the captain's integrity. 'Brother I lost to Orannia's madness, I say here, you were good enough to have wed as a prince of the clan.'

That undid Mykkael. He stared, thrown off his balance in surrender, while the nomad's deft touch steered his unsteady steps towards the pallet. Settled, face down, the tears *almost* came that the past had never wrung from him. 'Demon, begotten of demons,' he murmured, exhausted down to the bone. 'I had better be good enough now, to recover Isendon's daughter.'

Jussoud moved in staid calm and fetched the clean bucket. Endlessly patient, he sat on the edge of the cot, sorted among his oils and remedies, and made up a second infusion. This one did not sting, as the warm cloth tenderly swabbed the three livid welts on the desert-bred captain's back. Jussoud cleaned the spatter of bloodstains, also, everywhere else he could reach. 'You cannot help her Grace by any means if you don't keep your head and stay free.'

Mykkael sighed, eyes half lidded and weary, now that he was stretched prone. 'By that, you know I have a garrison man turned informer?'

'Do you?' That steady, soft touch scarcely faltered.

'The assassin's dropped sword wasn't found in the archway when I sent a boy to recover it,' Mykkael stated, and this time the bitterness blistered. 'You learned the fact I had two masters from your tribe? Not Taskin.' Satisfied once that point had been clarified, the captain closed his eyes fully. 'How much is my oath-breaking likely to cost? If Taskin kept silence, I have to expect the unpleasant truth that somebody knows how severely I'm forsworn with one, if not both of the *do'aa*.'

With practised mercy, Jussoud ripped off a stuck scab to cleanse the festering flesh underneath. 'The bald truth you've asked for is ugly enough. The king's trust in fact rests upon your past record of loyalty, and you are foreign-born, which draws enemies. That could see you bound in chains on an implied charge of treason at the slightest hint of provocation. Will you go if you're summoned?'

'I don't know.' Mykkael shifted his knee, fretful, the fine tremors now more due to pinched nerves than the backlash of excess adrenaline. 'As your people have said, it's the ancient problem facing the starving snake who foolishly swallowed its own tail. Go or not, I would find myself damned. Break my oath of crown service by jilting Taskin's authority, or submit to the chain of command by free choice – Sessalie's chancellors would clamour for my arraignment either way.'

Jussoud blotted his handiwork dry, then set to with more lint and salve. 'Short-term decision,' he pronounced at due length, breaking through the strained quiet. 'Cover these, you'll feel more comfortable, later. After the last, can you bear it?'

Mykkael swore. 'Do your worst, healer. By such grace, the doomed man counts his blessing of life. If I pass out, asleep, just be sure that my sword is left underneath my right hand.'

Arisen to warm his tin of congealed resin, Jussoud recovered the harness and blade from the floor. He could not avoid the tragic glance sideways, or fail to acknowledge the sad altar made over the battered wood of the clothes chest. The stick of lit incense had long since burned out. Under the lucent flames of wax candles, the smashed token disc blazed like a brand. Moved by sharp impulse,

Jussoud bent and veiled it. He snatched up the stained linen just used to swab down Mykkael's back, and saw, amazed, that his hand was unsteady with anger.

For long minutes, he walked the floor, after that. He paced until he was certain his hackled emotions had dispersed back to centring calm.

Mykkael watched, eyes slitted with irony. He slept the moment the cold mark on the sword hilt was slid underneath his slack hand. Lightly breathing, he scarcely stirred as Jussoud sealed his back under strips of resin-soaked bandage. Battered unconscious by blinding exhaustion, he thrashed once in a dream, and called Anja's name. Or perhaps his appeal was Orannia's. His whisper ran on in an unknown tongue, a wracked cry of desperate, hoarse agony.

Jussoud wept, then blotted his run tears in relief for the gift of blank silence, restored. His hands faltered, then moved on, careful, so careful, not to brush against the bronze skin with the knife blade he required to cut away the stained wrap that supported the lamed knee. Mykkael rested, oblivious. His hands on the coverlet stayed slack and trusting, as perhaps they had during childhood. As the candles burned low, and the mist spun white tendrils past the arrow slits, the masseur finished his labour in unstinting quiet. He eased what he could. At the end, when the oils and the strength of his hands had achieved all the healing he knew, he sewed a fresh binding over the damaged joint with its crippling scars.

This time, with no pang of regret, he used the fine eastern silk embroidered with the Sanouk royal dragons, cut away from the sash at his waist.

The horses gave her their hearts under cover of darkness. Their shod hooves struck sparks, clambering over sharp rock, and sliding on perilous footing. The game trust that risked slender legs to a lameness brought tears to her anxious eyes. Should a misstep cause injury, the distressed animal would draw marauding kerries, an event sure to betray her desperate flight, and cast her, helpless, back into the reach of her enemies . . .

XV. Charges

RETURNED THROUGH THE HIGHGATE IN THE STILL HOURS BETWEEN MIDNIGHT AND DAWN, JUSSOUD MADE HIS WAY through the stately streets that wound behind the east wing of the palace. The houses here belonged to old blood nobility. Even so late, the candle lamps cast fuzzed light over dooryards and carriageways, glinting on the glazed panes of sash windows. The beautiful town home surrounded by cherry trees had been in Taskin's family for centuries. Though the seat of the earldom bestowed on the patriarch was a hall on a country estate, the house in the citadel was never unoccupied. Younger sons often served in the royal guard, or held a chancellorship in the crown council. For this generation, the tradition of palace residence fell to Commander Taskin.

Jussoud passed the carved lions flanking the entry, tired down to the bone. He knocked quietly, knowing a servant would answer, despite the uncivil hour. Admitted by a punctilious bald man in an immaculate jacket, the nomad healer shed his grass sandals. He accepted the house stockings he was offered, relieved that the servant had the grace not to comment on the spoiled state of his clothes. Then he padded where he was led, over floors spread with antique carpets, past ancestral portraits and darkened doorways that smelled of walnut oil and lavender. The servant admitted Jussoud to the drawing room, where Taskin's widowed daughter sat beside a lit candelabra, the quilted wrap in her arms filled with a squalling infant.

'Teething,' she explained. Her shy glance towards the nomad held genteel apology, while the scarlet-faced child in her slender arms hiccoughed and kept on howling. 'The little warrior wouldn't quiet for his wetnurse.'

Jussoud smiled. 'If I offered the remedy we use in the steppelands, your father might never forgive me.'

'A Sogion bean mash?' The young woman smiled, rocking the babe, as she probably had been, for hours. 'The old soldier came home muttering the substance must be addictive, or why else would any sane human being suffer the hideous taste.'

'The plants themselves aren't narcotic,' Jussoud said, searching the scatter of rich furnishings for a chair that was not ancient, and delicate with carving. 'Infused, the roots and the leaves act as a tonic. Only the seeds react on the nerves. They cause numbness along with a mild euphoria, which is why they work best to ease pain.'

Porcelain fair, the young mother watched with amusement as her nomad guest awkwardly perched his large frame on a tasselled tuffet. 'Well, that explains Father's rigid disdain. He has always distrusted ebullience, wringing his happiness out of hard work.'

'He's awake, still?' Jussoud inquired, hopeful.

The daughter shook her head, hands adorned with sapphire rings smoothing the child's corn-silk hair. 'Your commander's asleep. He needs the rest. This uproar over the princess's disappearance has worn him until he is driven.' She regarded the healer's stained sleeves, her social verve clouded to apprehension. 'I expect you've come to report from the garrison? Is there aught that can't wait until daybreak?'

Jussoud measured the pleading love in her eyes,

sparked by a concern that was also fuelled by an unsettled, formless fear. 'I can imagine Taskin would be exhausted. He was strained when I saw him, earlier.' Too worn himself to shoulder another round of dissecting interview, the nomad firmed his decision. 'Let the man rest.'

'Father will be duty-bound to rise before dawn,' the daughter said, gracious. 'If you wish, I can have a spare place laid at breakfast. Be here, and I promise you'll see him before anyone.'

Jussoud stood, a towering figure robed in spoiled silk, and the remnants of a sash that had once borne a magnificent work of embroidery. The uneasy trouble his presence implied sat ill in that chamber, amid the inherited comfort of genteel years of tradition. 'I'd be grateful. Expect me. Only one message I carry is urgent. Tell Taskin by my word, sealed upon the blood of my ancestry, to trust Captain Mykkael above everything.'

'Your commander will hear what you ask upon waking,' the young woman avowed, while the attentive servant arrived at the door to attend the tall nomad's departure.

Jussoud crossed the palace precinct and retired to his quarters, where, ground down by weariness, he warmed a goblet of *sennia* to soothe his lingering tension. Then he slept through the night, unaware of the price his kindly solicitude might exact from two men whose sworn vigilance defended the realm.

Two hours before dawn, when the teething grandchild at last quieted in the arms of the exhausted young mother, a thunderous pounding at Taskin's front door upset the household's routine. The same well-groomed servant answered the knock. This time, the candle lamp scattered reflections on jewels and gold, the maroon velvet of Devall's royal livery, and a tight pack of official faces still puffy with sleep. No chance was given to make civil inquiry, or to observe the custom of house stockings. All but bowled aside, the servant could only bow and make way before birth-given rank and urgent authority.

Heading the pack, the High Prince of Devall eschewed court manners and demanded the Commander of the Guard. Just behind his shoulder came the seneschal, Lord Shaillon, looking harried in yesterday's creased finery. At his heels trouped Devall's perfumed retainers, half a dozen mail-clad lowland honour guard, and two of Sessalie's chancellors, brought up from the rear by Captain Bennent in his falcon surcoat.

The invasion aroused Commander Taskin. He arrived in the hallway, no less competent for the fact the disruption had caught him in bed. His silver hair was combed. Without slippers, he had thrown a dressing robe of dark wool hastily over squared shoulders. 'Lord Shaillon, what is amiss?'

The seneschal spun, brandished a rolled parchment, then bobbed in deference to the High Prince. 'Tell him, your Highness.'

'Perhaps we should retire where your lordship can sit down?' Devall's heir apparent suggested. His veneer of state courtesy masked smouldering rage.

'By all means.' Commander Taskin inclined his head.

The flustered servant led the way into the formal dining room, then scrambled to light sconces and arrange chairs. Royal rank assumed precedence; Devall's prince led his glittering retainers. Taskin granted a host's deference and permitted the disgruntled chancellors to follow, the stout one shaking his head in apology, and the gaunt one stone-faced and silent. As the seneschal stalked past, the commander ventured an ice-clad whisper: 'You had better hold a writ from King Isendon's own hand to excuse this uncivilized intrusion.'

Lord Shaillon fielded the pressure in silence, his face showing smug satisfaction. Taskin trailed the ranks of his uninvited company, his last word to his captain to stand at the doorway. 'Do you know what's happened?'

Bennent's demeanour stayed grim. 'Let their own words inform you. It's not good.'

Fine cloth rustled, and jewels flashed through the moving tableau, as the household servants scrambled to accommodate the party of distressed dignitaries, and foreign-born courtiers sorted their disparate stations. They settled at last, the high prince installed in the high-backed head chair, with his marshal and his advocate at right and left flank. Taskin selected the foot of the table, and by preference remained standing.

Lit from behind by the flare of fresh candles, he measured his guests with a glance coldly hard as any bestowed on his guardsmen. Then he addressed the High Prince of Devall. 'Your Highness, I would hear what has passed, stripped of the dance steps of protocol.'

Through a disruption at the door, as Captain Bennent forestalled the distressed inquiries of the household, the High Prince of Devall inclined his fair head. His sculptured features seemed haggard, his circlet of rubies blood red in their burnished gold settings. 'Your Captain of the Garrison has been charged with treason. The Seneschal of Sessalie holds the royal writ commanding his immediate arrest.'

Taskin advanced and received the parchment from Lord Shaillon's lizard-thin hand. He snapped off the ribbon, unrolled the document, and read, quick to ascertain the fact the seal at the bottom was genuine. 'I don't see the king's signature,' he admonished.

While the partridge-round chancellor squirmed in his chair, the thin one cleared his throat. 'My Lord Taskin, five of the high council have stood as signatories. Of eight, that presents a majority.'

Taskin slapped the parchment down on to the table, where it rolled itself up with a hiss. 'Where are the other three worthies who did not set their mark? Still in bed?' His blue eyes flickered back to Lord Shaillon. 'As the king surely is, also, at this hour.' Arms folded, he stalked back to his place, his sangfroid unmoved by the hot-blooded haste crowding the chairs in his dining hall. 'I will breakfast, and dress, and consult with his Majesty once he arises.'

Which unhurried authority at last broke the high prince's patience. 'Shining powers above!' His fists slammed the tabletop. The cut-glass salt cellar jumped, sheeting costly white crystals over the lace doily beneath. 'Your princess is in deadly danger! While this desert-bred officer stands at the heart of conspiracy, free to seed ruin at will, how can you *think* of delay? Action is required, not breakfast, not dalliance with consulting a witless old man!'

'Who is my sworn king!' Taskin cracked. 'Take care how you speak of the sovereign whose realm graces you with guest welcome.'

'You will act to guard Anja!' the high prince erupted, 'or by the nine names of the demons of hell, I will see you cut down for obstruction.'

The mismatched pair of chancellors pitched into the clamour, one stammering to placate, and the other adding the threat of high council authority. While Devall's retinue coalesced, seething, the seneschal's distressed appeal to see reason razed through the noise.

'Commander, you hold a lawful writ, set under seal of the realm!'

Taskin glared. 'I have seen a sealed parchment scribed with empty words. No proof! No grounds whatsoever to depose a crown officer.' As his rebuttal imposed a strained silence, he added with forceful finality, 'Nor will I stir one man of the guard to call down another for treason with no shred of evidence in hand.'

'But we do have evidence,' said the seneschal with shattering dignity. His expectant glance swung towards the head of the table, where the heir apparent of Devall nodded his affirmation.

Taskin returned no trace of thawed warmth. 'Show me.'

Rubies glittered as the high prince gestured to his marshal-at-arms. 'Bring the sword.'

That muscular worthy arose at his prince's bidding. His hands were a fighting man's, ringless and direct, as he laid a cloth-wrapped bundle on the tabletop.

'Lord Taskin,' invited the high prince. At his gesture, the marshal slid the object across the waxed wood. 'See what you make of this weapon.'

Heads craned, while Sessalie's crown commander flipped back the cloth. The folds fell away to unveil gleaming steel, raised to an exquisite temper. The sword's handle was strapped in black leather, the guard ring at the hilt a foreign style engraved with symbolic patterns.

'Assassin's blade,' Taskin identified. 'Though I don't know what sect.' He glanced up, his eyes as relentlessly ruthless as the sheen on the weapon before him. 'Does this belong to Captain My*sh*kael? If so, I would ask how he came by it before I jumped to suspicious conclusions.'

'That blade is not My*sh*kael's,' the high prince corrected. 'It belonged to the man just dispatched to kill him.'

Unmoved by drama, Taskin shrugged. 'Dead?'

'Violently so,' burst in the seneschal. 'Your desert cur all but slashed him in half before the eyes of the Lowergate garrison!'

'This should concern me?' Taskin provoked. 'If the captain's still standing since the attack, he's certainly competent to mind his affairs without intervention on my part.'

The seneschal bristled, all but launched from his chair. 'If his affairs run counter to Sessalie's wellbeing, your concern becomes paramount.'

'Then get to the point!' Aggressive, impatient, Taskin poised to stalk out. 'Show me there's a threat to the realm beyond circling, cat-and-mouse rhetoric.'

The High Prince of Devall raised a placating, ringed hand. 'I'll speak. My marshal assembled the evidence, after all. If the princess is restored to us, living and well, her recovery may ride on the fact he recognized the pattern on that hilt for the mark of a *barqui'ino do'aa.'*

While the seneschal subsided, and the chancellors watched with uneasiness, Taskin's blistering glance encompassed the marshal's bull-necked complacency. 'How do you know? You have no such training.'

The prince quelled his man's nettled surge to arise. 'No training, that's true. Yet Devall has wealth, exposure and enemies. My lineage has lost kings when men bearing such weapons crossed inside of our borders. When the powers that hired them found us, or our allies, too troublesome, necessity compelled us to know things your backwater realm need never address in detail.'

Taskin hooked a chair, and conceded enough to sit down. 'I am listening, your Highness. Tell me facts, not conjecture, since I am informed enough to realize that no *barqui'ino* master ever sells his oath-sworn as assassins.' As though he wore royal surcoat and sword, and not a plain woollen dressing robe, he directed his drilling regard down the length of the table.

The High Prince of Devall inclined his head, bright as a gilt icon against the dark panes of the casement. 'Let my marshal explain to your lordship directly.'

'The *do'aa* don't hire out assassins, this is true,' Devall's ranking guardsman conceded. 'But they do send them to carry out deaths on their own account. An oath-sworn who breaks their tradition of integrity is cut down so, without quarter. Since an outcast initiate *will* sell his sword, and since his trained background makes him all the more deadly, we in Devall have studied *barqui'ino* traditions. Your My*sh*kael is such a creature, forsworn.' The high prince's officer concluded his case with patronizing assurance. 'The man your desert-bred gutted tonight was sent from Kaien's *do'aa* to dispatch him. Your proof is the pattern engraved on this sword. That your captain broke loyalty is beyond any question. Three men at the Lowergate garrison saw him search the corpse. He found and removed a seal fashioned of wood and gold wire that had been quartered in fragments. Such a token would have been ritually broken by the master whose tradition he dishonoured. Sergeant Jedrey has the names of your witnesses, if you wish to crosscheck for veracity.'

The seneschal rushed to drive home the inequity. 'The king's trust was based upon My*sh*kael's past record. You heard his Majesty state that condition, with the Duchess of Phail in attendance.'

'Sessalie's council must support the arraignment,' ventured the slender chancellor down the table. His pearl studs and lace emphasized his distress, as he swept a hand towards the unwrapped weapon. 'Here we have proof the foreign captain is forsworn, and unfit to invest in crown service.'

'That's a long leap, from the inference of one broken promise, to cry a man down for treason,' Taskin remarked. His glance raked over the assembly. 'Should King Isendon choose to dismiss him, and we don't know that his Majesty will – the case has not been heard – My*sh*kael would be still entitled to freedom. The council's writ for arrest is not legal. I cannot call out my guardsmen against a man who has committed no crime against Sessalie.'

'Then it is my realm's honour your planted feet will offend!' the high prince interrupted with heat. 'I want that desert-bred captain detained! Let the wretch answer to my charge of treason against my future wife's standing as queen of Devall.'

'Your suit for marriage has not yet been signed,' Taskin responded, unmoved. 'Your slighted honour at this point rides upon nothing more than conjecture.'

Accosted by a spitting explosion from the chancellors, and condemnation from the seneschal concerning disastrous losses to trade, the crown commander held firm. His enamel eyes bored into Devall's high prince. As his survey detected the masked signs of unease, reflected again by the slight, fretted movement that stirred through the royal retinue, Taskin resumed his sharp challenge. 'What aren't you telling us, your Highness? What hidden motives lie outside Princess Anja's feminine charm? For whatever harm has breached our borders, I presume to suggest that Devall's might and wealth would be the more likely attraction to set her Grace under threat in the first place.'

'You place our high prince's dignity below an outcast foreigner whelped like a stray dog in a ditch?' the crown advocate pealed in struck shock.

Before Taskin's withering contempt, the heir apparent flushed, pride reversed into startling contrition. 'No, this is not what you think! I don't speak out of spiteful prejudice.' He adjusted his chair, then glanced down at his hands, torn and suddenly reticent. 'Devall has enemies,' he confessed in discomfort. 'Very deadly ones, at this jointure.'

Taskin sharpened his nailing regard. 'Better talk plainly, your Highness, and fast, since you think they've endangered our princess.'

'Who else could have possibly struck at her Grace?' the high prince cried with breaking anguish. 'I value her spirit, would never have risked her to harm! But the burdens of crown responsibility sometimes cause a man to make unpleasant choices. Yes, I love Princess Anja! Yes, I courted her for her exceptional wit and her exquisite beauty. But I must tell you now, she is also desirable to Devall because Sessalie could offer my heirs a safe haven should our lowcountry lands be invaded.'

Taskin cut across the shocked clamour that ripped through the gathering. 'You say Devall has attracted the enmity of a sorcerer?'

The high prince swallowed, his stiff bearing in shreds. 'I fear so.' Pinned down under Taskin's relentless scrutiny, he divulged the shaming truth. 'Mercy on us, we have. The threats are direct, but not public. For that reason, your garrison captain could easily be the hand of that evil, among us. Mys*h*kael is an oath-breaker, condemned by

Kaien's *do'aa*. And our enemy has been well known to contract such outcasts and send them as weapons against us. For the wellbeing of your princess, I beg you, constrain him! If he has been hired as catspaw to strike down my alliance with Sessalie, your royal family will see blood and tragedy, I promise.'

The heavyset chancellor appealed directly to Taskin. 'Can you swear, or show proof that this desert-bred's not acting under the pay of a foreigner?'

'No.' Taskin addressed that shortfall without flinching. 'Such things can be checked.'

'But an investigation in depth will take time,' his lean colleague argued. 'Dare we allow the creature his liberty, with Anja's safety in question?'

'The council can appoint Sergeant Jedrey to take charge of the garrison,' the seneschal pressed, the parchment bearing the writ for arrest tucked back under protective fingers.

'Cade's better suited,' Taskin snapped, while the High Prince of Devall stood back from the argument, and Captain Bennent, from the doorway, gave professional opinion that even young Stennis handled the men more effectively.

'But Jedrey's their senior, and born above Highgate,' the seneschal took pains to point out. 'On the heels of a traitor, the nobles would raise less complaint over one of their own.'

'I will agree to detain Captain My*sh*kael!' Taskin cracked across the raised climate of vindication. 'He'll be held for questioning until his word to the crown can be tested. Yet until my investigation establishes guilt, or unless King Isendon's personal ruling sets the crown seal to his arraignment, he is a commissioned officer of the realm, and not to be named as a traitor.'

'We are satisfied.' The High Prince of Devall flicked a nod at his marshal, and as one, his liveried retinue arose. Although he was entitled to royal prerogative, he graciously allowed the seneschal and chancellors to leave the chamber ahead of him. As they filed towards the doorway, conferring in subdued tones, Taskin signalled for Captain Bennent to let the room clear without hindrance. Unmoved, except to rise to his feet, Sessalie's Commander of the Guard waited, dispassionate, as the heir apparent of Devall detached from his retinue, and strode to confront him face on.

'We have been at odds, your lordship. I am regretful for that.' Chin raised, his neat hair caught back in a ribbon beneath the diadem of worked gold, the high prince displayed his wealth and refined breeding with unabashed grace in adversity. 'Can we lay our differences aside? Sessalie and Devall are now joined as allies. We share the same wish for her Grace's secure future. The hope of her swift recovery assuredly aligns us on the same side.'

Taskin returned his most freezing regard. 'We may hold the same wish for the princess's safety, your Highness. Yet after the truths you have disclosed today, never again presume to suppose that we might join hands in alliance.'

The handsome prince stiffened, gold eyes flashing fire. 'I will marry Anja. She will be honoured as queen in my realm. If she dies, or sees hurt because you stayed your hand, or if you fall short of your word to kennel your desert-bred captain, then I promise: I will see redress. In Devall, such insolence as yours would be broken, one bone at a time, on the wheel.'

Taskin smiled with a punctilious precision that mocked. 'But this is not Devall, your Highness. Since my service to Sessalie does not involve making arrests in a dressing robe, you alone are responsible for preventing me from direct execution of my duty.'

'Then I commend you to action, your lordship. I insist, we should not be at odds.' As a last, gallant gesture, the prince extended his hand.

The crown commander no more than looked on, his stance stilled to frosty amazement.

Stonewalled, as the young royal jerked his offered touch

short, a recoil as abrupt as a scalding. 'Forgive me, your lordship! I should have expected your insular pride might refuse a foreigner's familiarity.'

Taskin returned a bow of dispassionate correctness. 'As a foreign royal, given guest right under my sovereign's protection, I must ask your Highness to remain under guard in your quarters. I will assign men to address your security. For if Devall's enemies have moved against Sessalie through your proposed suit to our princess, logic follows that the acts of such heinous conspirators might also place you at risk.'

The prince stiffened. 'You overstep your authority, Commander!'

'Do I, your Highness?' Taskin matched the younger man's fury, his features unmoved as cut marble. 'Then present your complaint to the king when he wakens. I'd ask you in for the audience, anyway. Whether or not you'd choose to be present when Captain My*sh*kael answers your charges, be certain I will have Isendon's ear when I interview you at exhaustive length. Once I return, you will explain the peril you have drawn to our heart through the ties to your kingdom's enemies.'

Unasked, both marshal and retinue moved in. They surrounded their prince, then escorted him out in their circle of liveried protection.

To Bennent, still on station by the door, Taskin gave disposition. 'Hear my orders, Captain. See to the high prince's security. Assign eight men with sharp eyes and keen ears. I will dress, and attend what needs to be done to fetch My*sh*kael in from the garrison.'

Captain Bennent absorbed this, the implication of posting surveillance turning his frown deeply troubled. 'You don't completely trust Devall's motives?'

Stepped back to the table, Taskin regarded the sword, then snatched the veiling cloth overtop as though the sight of the steel gave offence. 'His Highness of Devall is a coward,' he said.

'That's harsh,' Bennent murmured. 'The princess adores him.'

'Oh, yes.' Taskin tugged the lapels of his robe close, as though he suffered a sudden chill. 'A statesman will always use his best attributes. This one has shamelessly snared her Grace's affection and wrangled our merchants' ambitions to buy the toehold for an alliance. The prize glittered, and blinded us. Our failing king blunted sound judgement. We saw our princess as a jewel of incalculable worth, and quite failed to weigh our kingdom's stability as our most precious asset. Powers above! Who thought rich and powerful *Devall* might broker a bid for survival? Shame on us all, if our Anja should pay with her life as the pawn of lowcountry entanglements. How dare the crowned King of Devall think so low, to play Sessalie's peace on a game board encroached on by sorcerers!'

A jagged pause followed, while the candle flames shimmered, and the stilled air hung like liquid glass.

'Do I trust his Highness?' Taskin straightened trim shoulders as though to dislodge a stinging fly. 'Captain My*sh*kael does not. By his ornery nature, he's told me straight out. Now, that could be because he's employed by Devall's enemies. Or he could be loyal, and Isendon's sworn man, in which case, I want the high prince kept under tight watch until we know whether these accusations hold any substance.'

Framed against the dimmed corridor, Bennent showed surprise. 'You think Devall's charges are spurious?'

Taskin scarcely hesitated. 'Let's just say that, given what I know, I don't see that desert-bred accepting the employ of any faction that associates itself with a sorcerer.'

Now Bennent looked troubled. 'Without the king's direct intervention, you have no legal choice but to bend to the will of the council. The arrest their hasty vote has demanded will have to be carried out.'

'That's the meat of the problem, exactly.' Taskin brushed past towards the stair, the hem of his dressing robe slapping his bare calves to his tempest of testy irritation. 'If you say prayers for any one thing, beg the powers that be for a miracle. Let Captain My*sh*kael be convinced to abide by convention, and come into custody quietly.'

XVI. Pre-dawn

WORD OF TASKIN'S ARRIVAL AT THE LOWERGATE DRAWBRIDGE REACHED VENSIC AT THE GARRISON WARDROOM. Caught with chalk slate in hand, upbraiding a laggard, the breveted officer stared at the man sent in with the news from the watch.

'The king's first commander? *Here!*' he exclaimed, disbelieving.

'Himself,' the messenger affirmed, winded yet from the sprint that had brought him ahead of the cavalcade. 'He's got ten outriders with lances behind. To judge by their mounts, they mean business.'

The demands of meeting Captain Mykkael's stringent discipline taught a man to respond to the unexpected. Vensic cast down the slate where he stood, and sprinted flat out for the bailey.

He burst out of the keep just as the task squad from the palace drew rein inside the archway. Mist hung, blanket-thick. The hour preceded the change in the watch, when the yard stood all but deserted. Men out on patrol had not yet returned, with their relief, soon to arm, not quite due to call in for duty. The stone enclosure as yet held no bustle of industry, no drills or sparring recruits, no cook's boys or washing women, and no busy clamour of armourers. Against early silence, the crack of shod hooves on the cobbles raised deafening thunder.

All Highgate guard veterans, the riders pulled up in formation, then held there in ominous quiet. Vensic peered through the fog, attentive to the man at the head of the column who dismounted and tossed the reins of his grey charger to the first groom who rushed from the stable.

Taskin strode over directly, the gleam of his helm marked by hellish reflections thrown off the coals in the fire pans. His blue eyes raked over Vensic just once: a scouring assessment that mapped the young sergeant's neat surcoat and immaculate weapons, and no doubt discerned the farm mud on the boots of his origins.

Still, the crisp challenge would have done Mykkael proud. 'I'm acting officer of the keep, Lord Commander.'

Taskin returned a clipped nod, his glance showing tacit approval. He would have already noted the keen stance of the sentries minding the walls. Now, his scrutiny swept over the bailey, noting the rigorous tidiness, the cord of piled wood, the ready response of the grooms and the vigilance instilled in the gate watch. 'I've come for your captain. Is Mykkael asleep?'

Struck to unease by the precise choice of accent, Vensic breathed easier, that this summons at least would catch no one in bed. 'Captain's up and gone out, lordship. Sergeant Stennis has the Falls Gate patrol. Sergeant Cade reports with the relief in an hour. Meantime, what can I do for you?'

The guard's first commander gave no inch of slack. 'Tell me where Captain Mykkael has gone.'

Vensic's crown oath foreclosed the evasion that even Mykkael's imposed standard of conduct would have expressly forbidden. 'He dreamed badly, he said. Something he wished to investigate took him out to the tourney field beyond the walls.'

Taskin fielded this news in his stride. 'Stay here. Mind the garrison. When Cade comes on duty, as there's news, I will send.'

Footsteps approached; someone's hasty arrival tossed a restive disturbance through the closed ranks of the horsemen.

Vensic noted the upset without time to react. As foreboding broke into a clear jab of warning, he had eyes for nothing except the commander before him. 'Bright powers, what's happened, to bring such as you down from Highgate?'

'I'll tell you what!' Sergeant Jedrey burst in, just returned with his arm bound in splints, and his temper combative with malice. 'Mykkael's now under the king's writ for arrest. He's being charged with treason.'

'You've been relieved,' Vensic said without heat, his attentive inquiry still fixed on the crown's first commander. 'Go home, Jedrey.'

'Oh, I'll stay,' the outraged sergeant said, self-righteously indignant. 'The council will shortly hand me the garrison. Trust me, farm boy, when that happens, I'll burn the letter that gave your promotion, and you'll be the one cut from rank.'

Taskin never deigned to glance sideways. 'You're breveted?'

Vensic took heart from the commander's steel nerve. 'Yes. Last week. Under Mykkael's signature, on grounds of merit. The note was to go before his Majesty along with the bursar's monthly lists for requisition.'

'I see,' Taskin said. His chilly regard swept the keep officer again, measuring with a depth that raised dread, though the bailey, the gates, and the garrison grounds were all well in hand, each detail kept in sharp order. Decision followed, as surgically swift. 'Then under my auspices, you'll swear your officer's oath to your king. Today. Have your letter on hand at the change of the watch. You'll go with my riders through Highgate.'

Courage spoke, then, despite that hard gaze. 'I stand behind Mykkael.' Vensic lifted his chin. 'My captain has not betrayed Sessalie.'

For one brief instant, amid rag-thick mist, Taskin's features seemed something less than frost over chiselled granite. 'The accusation of treason is specious, I do realize. King Isendon's faith in the captain is not compromised. Yet to dismantle the council's distrust fully, Mykkael has facts he must verify in front of a Highgate magistrate.'

'Let them wait,' Vensic pleaded. 'His mood's worse than brittle. There's something uncanny abroad in this kingdom. Mykkael's in pursuit with an unswerving focus that's frankly been frightening.'

'A mad dog that wants chaining,' Jedrey interjected. 'Broke my damned arm in a crazed fit of temper. If your lancers are here to drag that one in, I suggest you arm them with boar spears.'

Yet again, Lord Taskin refused the distraction. To Vensic, in closing, he said, 'Have your letter in hand at the gatehouse when my riders return. We act on parchment law, without shackles. Once Mykkael agrees to submit to my custody, I'll see you through to stand for your captain as witness.'

Vensic nodded, not relieved, but at least reassured that Taskin's handling of crown justice would be fair. 'Expect me. The discipline problem in this garrison, meanwhile, I claim as wholly mine.'

Taskin's sudden, spontaneous laughter cracked through the oppressive darkness. 'By all means, soldier. For myself, I'd have tested the suggestion of boar spears on the whiner, were your insubordinate something more than a weakling, and not tasked with a broken arm.'

The crown's first commander snapped his fingers to signal the waiting groom. He remounted his gelding forthwith. In stark disregard for the outflanked dismay of the garrison's disgraced sergeant, he wheeled his outriders through the main gate, and vanished into the mist.

The fading grip of night still cloaked the valley outside the citadel. The misted tree limbs shed their burden of dew in a whispering patter of droplets. Sound carried. The snorts of the horses and the jingle of harness would have warned any war-wary man of the company now clustered at the verge of the tourney field. The smells of skinned grass and oiled steel struck through the tang of hot horseflesh.

'I am not stalking quarry!' Commander Taskin snapped, irritable as his hovering officer attempted one last round of protest. 'I go forward alone. If I fail, if the man under writ has sworn a false oath to the kingdom, or if he refuses to bend for lawful –'

'You'll be down, likely injured,' the lance captain argued in sharp misery. 'All for the sake of a ditch-bred mongrel outcast from his tribal background. Why in the nine names of hell should you shoulder such risk in your king's gravest hour of need?'

Taskin forced a deep breath. 'Stand fast, by my order! If I'm wrong, if that desert-bred kills me, you may all hunt him down at will. Yet until the unlucky hour I fall, remember that I'm in command here!'

'Your lordship, don't go!' The lance captain swallowed, glanced aside, and with wretched reluctance, backed down.

Taskin passed the soaked reins of his horse to the rider who normally bore the king's banner. 'If I need you, if backing is wanted, I'll shout. Damned *well* hold your line unless you receive my clear summons.'

Straight back turned, the commander strode off through the dew-sodden grass of the tourney field. He knew what he risked in the darkness ahead. At the crux, he understood well enough that he might face worse than a wounding. Resolve firmed his step. He would not yield for politics. The killer he had disarmed in the belltower had been anything else but a madman.

Overhead, the mist showed the first murk of grey dawn. Still mantled in gloom, the ground stretched ahead, the greensward gouged here and there by the hooves of the horse wicket teams brought out for gallops and practice. The tang of manure was not out of place, except for the fact it was fresh. Taskin heard the creak of saddle leather first, then the whisper of equine breathing. His cautious sally soon encountered the horse, no less than the war-trained chestnut sent on loan from the palace stables.

The rank creature had been hobbled, steppeland fashion, in ties of leather and felt. Its bit rings and stirrups were muffled in rag, with the knotted reins run under the leathers, and the empty saddle left girthed. The rider was nowhere in evidence. Taskin avoided the beast's surly kick, well warned in advance. Whatever activity Mykkael pursued, he had taken pains to ensure his mount would not wander.

Taskin pressed onwards, constrained to caution. Because he moved slowly, he did not entangle himself when he encountered the first line of staked string.

The twine was strung on thin wooden palings driven into the ground just under waist height. An exploratory touch established another, set at an angle to the first. The intersection where the two lines crossed had been tied with a white twist of rag. Utterly mystified, Taskin took pause; and so heard the nearly soundless footfalls approach his position from the left.

'I am mapping the contours of pattern and flow,' Mykkael explained, conversational. 'You can help.'

'How?' Taskin raised his eyebrows, amazed by the note of restrained calm from a man who *would not* be unaware of the nervous lancers grouped at the edge of the field.

'Hold this.' Mykkael approached, a wraith disgorged from the gauze layer of mist. If dark hair and features kept his expression invisible, his spare form was clad in the spotless, crisp cloth of Sessalie's falcon surcoat.

Taskin suffered a pang of regret, to see an order delivered as punishment observed to the letter of obedience.

'The sword is sharp, too,' Mykkael assured him, his humour shaved thin by dry irony. 'I give you my word I cleaned off the rust. Shall we not set the proof to the test?' He knew of the lancers; yet his touch was quite firm as he passed over the rough ball of twine. 'Draw the slack taut, will you?'

Taskin grasped the string, equable enough to let matters unfold in due course. The string, he noticed, held the pungence of fish; had in fact been soaked in cheap lamp oil. Curiosity piqued, he followed Mykkael's lead, watched as the clever fingers tied off a fresh streamer to mark the site of another junction. He forbore to question. The desertman forged onwards, his carriage suggesting the listening intensity of senses trained into stripped focus.

Mykkael hailed him, next stride. 'Come ahead. Can you feel this?'

Still bearing the twine ball, Taskin approached. A dark hand grasped his wrist, gently guided until he felt a ranging chill pour down his skin. 'That's no breeze,' the commander admitted, uneasy enough to pull back as the captain released him.

The answer came quiet, out of the murk. 'No wind, truly. Such energies flow through the ground and the air when a sorcerer works. The closer the spacing, the more powerful the lines of his casting. Yet after sunrise, through the day when the wind moves, the disturbance we feel now will become almost too subtle to measure.' A rustle of cloth, as Mykkael set another stake into the turf. Then he reached out, accepted the twine, and deftly tied off a half hitch. 'This way, most likely.' He bent his lame step leftwards, and added, 'Though, truth be told, I'd prefer if my hunches proved wrong.'

Guided past a drain swale by a hand on his arm, Taskin shivered as another chill ruffled his skin.

'Bright blazing *hell*!' Mykkael stopped, crouched down. He ran questing fingers over the earth, then rammed in another wooden marker. 'That's close, too damned close. Tie the string,' he instructed. 'Then, if you pray, appeal to your trinity the pattern we're mapping ends here.'

In fact, it did not. More stakes were set. Soon a webwork of string fluttered with cloth knots at the multiplicity of revealed junctions. While the clinging mist slowly dampened his surcoat, Taskin realized he sensed the nexus points most clearly when the desert-bred happened to touch him.

'Shared resonance,' Mykkael explained. 'Probably the effect of Perincar's mark, though I can't say for sure, not knowing what untamed gifts ride my fate by way of my bloodline.' His sudden grim bitterness could not be mistaken as he fixed the last stake, then tied and cut off the oiled string. 'We don't have much time. Since you didn't come down here just to talk, we'd better hold serious conversation.'

Overhead, the sky showed the first gleam of pearl, too ephemeral to read the stance or expression of the dark-skinned man close beside him. Taskin fought back his pervasive dread, and forced his speech to stay mild. 'You have a report to make, soldier?'

Mykkael chafed his hands, as though easing an ache touched through the live flesh of his fingers. 'This much. You have a powerful sorcerer at work, definitely. His spellcraft grows bolder. I found a watch vortex set at the Cockatrice Tavern, where Prince Kailen drinks. Didn't dispel it. The taproom was too crowded not to cause widespread panic. Just realize: whoever speaks in that place, your sorcerer's going to be party to every whisper.'

Then, too acutely aware that the silence had acquired a cut-glass intensity, Mykkael pressed the question. 'What's wrong? Commander?'

'Such watch marks,' Taskin said, gruff. 'Can they be seen?'

'In low lighting. Sometimes. Better say why you're asking.' Mykkael listened with an unsettling, stilled patience, while Taskin explained King Isendon's queerly insistent behaviour, then the fountainhead of pent energy released when the cedar had been burned and the fumes swept through the royal chamber.

'Watcher's mark,' Mykkael affirmed, 'which you unstrung with a banishing. That means your sorcerer's now warned your king's guarded. He'll move openly, very soon.' Then the bitterness resurged, starkly caustic. 'Perhaps already has. You're here, after all, with your troop of armed lancers. Which faction at court wants me captive?'

'Political formality,' Taskin reassured him quickly. 'You'll be granted a royal hearing the moment the king's lucid, with my earnest expectation you'll be discharged.'

Mykkael's interruption sheared across his next line. 'No. Don't speak. Hold the wretched details for later. You've said things that raise questions which have to be answered.' Without waiting, he plunged on. 'Does your king seem to see things that others do not?'

Discomfited, Taskin braced his trim shoulders, scattering droplets off his sodden surcoat. 'His Majesty used to make light of what he called his "cold starts". Now, since the onset of his affliction, the courtiers attribute his maundering to spells of blank wits.'

'He sees things,' Mykkael stated in stripped apprehension. 'Powers, of course! It makes sense that his daughter has likely inherited that attribute. *That's why she ran!* Her Grace would have sensed the invasion of Sessalie's court. She certainly realized her life was in danger.'

'But you can't show me proof,' Taskin snapped, immovably cornered by the frustration served up by the high council's writ.

'I can try.' Aware of the challenge pending against him, Mykkael fought to contain ebbing calm. He assessed the brightening sky overhead, the last shadow fading moment by moment as sunrise broached the east rim of the peaks. 'Within a few minutes, we'll have enough light.'

'To discern the pattern?' The crown's first commander folded his arms against the encroaching chill. 'Yet I'll scarcely know what I'm seeing, will I?'

Mykkael dug into his scrip, used his flint to strike

sparks and ignite the cut length of oiled string he planned to use as a touch match. 'I may not know, either, except that by complexity and close spacing alone, I already sense something shaping that runs outside the concept of frightening.' Here, he paused, string cupped in dark palms as he blew to make the spark catch. Then he held, his stance coiled, as though measuring the air for the slightest suggestion of movement. 'The greater flow of a sorcerer's energies is reflected in mirror image, at nexus points. Without wind as influence, when we set the string alight from its easternmost point of alignment, we'll see which direction the flow of the energy draws the flame. You'll know which junctions are crossings, and which are divisions. A sorcerer's lines always stream towards his origins, and run to ground through the site of his primary bonding with power. As the string burns, you will clearly discern where Sessalie's enemy has come from.'

The sky overhead turned from pewter to silver. The tips of the near stakes were now visible in hazed outline against the grey scrim of the ground. The white cloths tied at the junctions hung limp, already burdened with moisture.

'Now,' Mykkael murmured. He bent, set the flame to the string, then stepped back as the oiled fibres caught.

The fire raced down the twine, consuming fuel at a pace that outstripped any natural combustion. Spitting into the first junction, the damp rag burst into an explosion of sparks. Split runners of the flame rushed down the string on both sides, and *also* carried on down the centreline. Dew-dampened cloth posed the conflagration no impediment. Taskin, as onlooker, felt an ugly prickle of dread raise the hair at his nape. No word need convince him that he stood witness to the play of demonic powers.

The next junction passed, a division, and the third proved the very same. When the fourth and the fifth split the energy further, with no doubled-back loop for renewal, Mykkael began swearing in tongues; as the sixth, then the seventh rag raged into fountained sparks, and the energy paths only widened, he lapsed into a more ominous silence.

'Have you seen a pattern like this one before?' Taskin asked, all but desperate to crack the unbearable tension.

The captain returned a stressed whisper. 'Never. Merciful powers, *nothing* determined as this. *There are no crossings, only branches*. We are looking at conquest on a scale unimagined.'

'Beyond Sessalie?' Taskin demanded.

Mykkael regarded the remnants of his laid strings, the rushed lines of fire a reflection imprinted in his eyes as the last junctions flared, the revealed branches fast flying towards immolation. 'Mehigrannia show us the will to preserve, your Sessalie's no more than the stepping stone to launch an invasion across the barrier of the Great Divide!' His stunned horror lingered, pervasive as the stink of plumed smoke, while the last span of twine fizzled into wisped ash, with one stake left burning like a torch.

'There,' Mykkael pointed. 'Sight a line from where we stand through that post and extrapolate, and there lies your sorcerer's origin.'

'Lowcountry,' Taskin affirmed. 'Devall, most likely. The high prince came clean, damn his pride and his reticence. He finally admitted his kingdom has earned a savage array of strong enemies. Still, how do you know the sorcerer's origin is not on the same line, but behind us?'

'Because the east stake's gone cold.' Mykkael stowed his twine, then plucked a twist of grass and wiped the residual oil from his fingers. His features remained in cut silhouette as he took fate in hand and tested the current of Highgate's prevailing politics. 'Was his Highness of Devall behind the outcry that's called you out with your lancers?'

Taskin sighed. 'From the start, each of you has entreated me not to trust the other party to act in Sessalie's best interests.'

Mykkael stepped back. He replaced his flint, then refastened his scrip with controlled deliberation. 'Then you'll have to decide on our merits, Commander.'

'Captain, I already have.' Against brightening day, the commander confronted him, his unwavering stance that of an icon wrought out of antique silver. 'My lancers are here bearing arms, but they don't carry prisoner's shackles.'

The dark captain weighed this. 'You're asking me to come in, voluntarily?'

'Not asking.' The steel in that tone was not malleable. 'The seneschal, Lord Shaillon, is an inflexible man. His sway leads the voice of detraction. The lure of Devall's sea trade has won the high council's backing, and cited proof off the assassin you just foiled has framed a writ demanding your arrest. King Isendon can overturn the document through a hearing.' Pressured by Mykkael's undivided attention, Taskin finished his case with crisp delicacy. 'I know first-hand that his Majesty trusts you. On my assurance, you must stand down. Come back through Highgate under the protection of my lancers, and bide under guard until the king's lucid word sets you free. You have my fair backing. Stand firm on your sworn oath to Sessalie, and Devall's case fails. You can be restored to your post in the garrison with no loss beyond a few hours.'

Mykkael turned his head, regarded the forlorn array of his stakes, and the last, sullen glow of the burned one, as the flames subsided to embers against the lead backdrop of mist. 'Tell me, Commander, has the High Prince of Devall ever once tried to touch you since you accepted my talisman? And if he has, did his Highness draw back from the contact as though he was burned?' Aware of the answer before Taskin spoke, the desert-bred hurled down his conclusion. 'Your enemy is flushed, Taskin. Whether the creature has cast his influence through Devall's heir apparent as a catspaw, or whether his Highness has become a bound minion pulled on puppet strings, the attack upon Isendon's crown is going to move into the open. Go back to the Highgate! Protect your king. As you love Sessalie, leave me at large to safeguard the life of your princess.'

'Your case cannot be made to stand *in absentia*,' Taskin was swift to point out.

Mykkael stepped back another pace, the poised change in his carriage unmistakable. 'Find a way. Understand me! This charge to entrap me is part of a sorcerer's plot to extend the range of his power. Hold me in restraint, you will doom your princess. *Your enemy knows me, surely has since the moment I entered the royal presence without the protection of the shaman's mark on my sword!* Force me above Highgate, and I very much doubt that I'll be set free with my life.'

'You realize you're asking a traitorous act of me.' Taskin raised his opened palms. 'Until the king speaks, I'm bound by realm law to enact the will of the council.'

Mykkael shook his head. His fist closed, with distress, on his sword hilt. 'Choose. I can't plead.'

Shown the bared force of character behind Jussoud's assessment, Taskin drew a breath just as shaken. *Here was a man, a trained killer, who would hold his integrity above spoken promises.* The question demanded an accurate answer: which faction claimed the weapon of this desert-bred's resolute initiative?

Taskin collected the strained cloth of his faith. Only one course of possibility remained to dismantle the council's ruling, based in law, by the king's witnessed word. 'For Anja's life, then, answer me truthfully. Can you swear to me, Mykkael, that you *never* broke oath to Kaien's *do'aa*? That the assassin you felled was not their man, sent out to call your life forfeit?'

The reply, forced through anguish, seared for its straight honesty. 'Oh bright powers and Mehigrannia's mercy! I breached honour with Kaien, but not for the cause you might think.'

'Then the only shred of hope you have to establish your innocence is to hold your crown oath to Sessalie inviolate.' Aware of the tenuous, last rags of trust shredding like tissue between them, Taskin extended himself beyond pride in appeal. 'Captain, you won't plead. I will, for your honour! Show me the loyalty you gave the Sanouk for Orannia. Come in with my lancers and testify!'

'Save your king as you can,' said Mykkael with regret. He turned his back, walked, but not in submission. Ahead of his dreadfully purposeful, limped stride, the smudged form of his hobbled gelding loomed through the mist.

He would mount up and ride, Taskin realized, overwhelmed by his shattering failure. Sessalie's fate no doubt rested still on the unknown, unproven alignment of this desert-bred's fixed allegiance. A split second of time, to enact the decision: whether to reject the case in the untested belief set in foreign talismans, and arcane patterns of fire and string, or to hold out for the bedrock surety of evidence that this killer was not the tool of Devall's shadowy enemy.

This, boiled down to the one damning fact: that Mykkael had not chosen to lie. '*Save your king as you can.*' The last sentence became too ambiguously damning. Taskin understood, in cold fury, that he was outfaced without quarter. He would have to bid for hard proof.

'Stand fast, soldier!'

No response; Captain Mykkael advanced. Deaf and blind to persuasion, he rejected just hearing under King Isendon's ear, and the ties of his oath to crown law.

Taskin closed his hand on his sword hilt and cleared the blade with a warning ring from the scabbard. The next word he uttered must summon his lancers in command to ride down a fugitive.

Except Mykkael stopped. Faced about, he held his bared sword in hand, though no sound had attended its drawing. He did not speak. In the waxing light, through the dense mist, his features were expressionless stone. Eyes locked to the form of the crown's first commander, he took a deliberate step back, then another.

Three more, and Mykkael would reach his saddled gelding. A single, swift stroke would sever the hobbles. His vault astride would happen before any mounted troop could cross the tourney field, far less react in armed strength to prevent him.

Pressed beyond options, Taskin shouted, and sprang.

His steel met the captain's experienced parry with a virulent clangour. The sound would spur the lancers to charge. Crack men, each one devoted to Taskin, they would converge at a gallop to attack and cut down a traitor.

XVII. Sunrise

SOUND CARRIED WITH BRUTALLY MAGNIFIED CLARITY, UNDER THE STRANGLING MIST. THE SHRILL CLANG OF STEEL meeting steel in close combat rang over the oncoming hooves of the destriers. Fist closed on his lance, the wet sting of his horse's mane lashing his wrists, the guard captain urged his troop on at a gallop. Though Taskin's skill as a swordsman was legend, the fast-paced exchange veiled under the fog bespoke a ferocity that outmatched every gift of trained reflex, and defied every skilled trick of intellect.

The select troop of guardsmen racing to intervene heard crossed blades scream, again and again, without let-up. Blow met tortured counterblow at breathtaking speed. The clamour of stressed steel left no opening for mercy. The desert-bred creature who attacked their commander was *barqui'ino*-trained, a war-hardened butcher without conscience. Ten men-at-arms spurred their mounts with one thought: to cut the cur down without quarter.

'The mongrel foreigner's got a lamed knee,' gasped the rider alongside the lance captain. 'Taskin will take him, he's bound to!'

Yet the belling fury of each passage described nothing else but a ruthlessly desperate contest.

'Hyaa!' screamed the captain, and drove his mount harder. But the horse underneath him jibbed and broke stride, forced to swerve to avoid a diabolical array of placed stakes. The air smelled of char. Through veiling grey, a sullen flicker of orange shone where a grass tussock had been set burning. Chilled by the thought he might ride over ground worked by a sorcerer's lines, the lance captain bellowed a terrified warning.

As he grappled the agonized question of whether or not to rein up, he heard, close at hand, the dissonant scrape of a blade yanked clear of a bind. There came no following chime in riposte. The mist cloaked a field draped in terrible silence, ripped across by advancing hoof beats.

One man would be down. Not knowing which of the two fighters had fallen posed his lancers a lethal danger.

The troop captain shouted the order to halt. He dragged his mount, sliding, on to its haunches, only to feel the reins give way in his hands. He yelled for back-up, already too late. Emerged from the fog, a shadow wearing the king's falcon surcoat had sliced the strap leather clean through. While the captain rocked, off balance, and clawed to grasp mane, an iron grip closed over his wrist and jerked him headlong from the saddle.

Spun, reeling, then thrust with brute force to the ground, he fell sprawling across a limp body.

'Stanch his wound!' snapped a voice from the air just above him.

Stunned breathless, the lance captain realized the sodden, warm bundle beneath him was none else but the crown's first commander.

'Taskin!' He groped, felt the hot gush of blood drench his hands. 'Merciful powers, he's killed you!'

Yet the commander's tortured breathing rasped on. The blue eyes stayed open, demanding. Alive, he still fought. The strong flood of bleeding affirmed a vitality fast ebbing with every rushed heartbeat. 'Taskin, hang on! We'll fetch Jussoud.'

Yet the toll of inflicted damage wrecked hope. The lance captain snatched the long hem of his surcoat in desperate fingers, and crushed wadded cloth to the gash that had all but severed the commander's right arm at the shoulder. Then he shouted to order his company. 'Grigori, Mistan, to me! I have Taskin. He's down and in need of a field dressing! You others, *ride*! The traitor's on foot, running east!'

Through the mazing impediment of mist-cloaked stakes, amid confusion and yells of disbelief, the lance company wheeled and gave chase. The two men singled out spun their horses and came. They stripped off their surcoats with hurried hands, and took over the grim task of bandaging. Taskin shivered, not lucid, then lay slack and chilled. While day brightened the fog to a tissue of silver, the surge of his pulse turned erratic and shallow.

'Powers that be damn that murdering desert-bred!' Mistan cursed in frustration. 'We can't lose the commander, not now!'

'We won't,' murmured Grigori, determined. Against daunting odds, he wiped scarlet hands and bent to the grim work of necessity.

Beneath his frantic efforts, the laboured draw of Taskin's breathing sawed on, the rushed blood flow contained by hard pressure. While the pound of galloping hoof beats receded, and men's shouts diminished with distance, the ugly, deep wound was strapped in tight bindings.

'Stay with him. Don't quit! Mistan, go. Get Jussoud down here fast as possible.' The lance captain left the fate of his fallen commander in Grigori's capable hands, and plunged into the white pall of mist. He caught his loose horse, unbuckled both stirrups, then fixed the stripped leathers to the bit rings to replace the slashed ends of his reins. Remounted, he charged in pursuit of his company, heartset to ride down the criminal foreigner who had spurned his crown oath.

He found bodies, first off: three fallen riders cut all but

in two, and past help, where they sprawled in pooled blood and the stink of rent bowels. The steaming, spilled viscera flung over drenched grasses became graphic evidence of the violent stroke that had dropped them. Lashed to wild rage, the lance captain raked his mount with spurred heels. He pelted ahead through the cotton-thick mist. Across the verge of the tourney field, he crashed into a stand of woods, a brush-choked windbreak that bordered a village steading of hamlets and farmland. The next lancer he encountered was limping on foot. He reined in and called him by name. 'Ebron! Where's that fugitive desert-bred?'

'Gone for the low road, flat out like a fox. The pace he's set's likely to run the horse underneath him to blazes.' The lancer managed the rest in harsh gasps, his forearm pressed against four cracked ribs from the drubbing blow that had felled him. 'Kills like a fiend. Nobody gets near him. He ducked under *Kevir's* lance, the damned spider. And he's riding that ugly hammerhead chestnut. Our horses know that brute's heels much too well. Spurs or not, the creatures refused to close in, or stand their staunch ground when we cornered him.'

'Your mount?' snapped the captain.

'Dead,' Ebron said, heartsick and furious. 'Slaughtered from under me like worthless meat. I was lucky not to be crushed as she crumpled.'

'How many of ours are left standing?' the lance captain snapped.

'At best count?' Ebron's voice broke. 'Maybe none. Under mist, we're blind targets. The murdering creature still wears the king's surcoat. He can't be marked out unless he's on top of us, and nobody realized until much too late: he carries a desertman's blowpipe and darts, and shoots tips that are certainly poisoned.'

'Go back!' cried the lance captain. 'Take Grigori's horse and ride for the garrison. I want reinforcements. Trackers and dogs. Get a runner to Highgate. Have Bennent send archers. Mistan's already gone for Jussoud to do what he can to save Taskin.'

'You're pressing ahead?' Ebron asked, his concern over-riding the misery of grief and the seizing pain as his chest cramped.

'No choice for it.' The lance captain wheeled his mount onwards, his last words hurled over his shoulder. 'The desert-bred wretch has now shown his true coat. I'll enlist help from Devall's guard, if need be, and see him chased down like hazed vermin.'

A prodigy blessed with keen judgement, Vensic had Jedrey confined under house arrest, with four unflappable garrison men dispatched to stand by his door as enforcement. Then he sent a messenger sprinting to Cade, bearing the summary report of the night watch's worrisome developments.

That insightful forethought brought the day sergeant in early. He strode through the keep gate, his sheathed sword in hand, along with the belt that had not yet fastened his billowing surcoat. Though his mood seemed disgruntled, only the foolish presumed that the same disarray ever clouded his mind in a crisis.

The guard lancer, Ebron, encountered this fact at first hand, arrived aching and hot from his savage ride in from the tourney field. Used to Taskin's brisk handling, he delivered a terse account of Mykkael's defection. Then, lulled by Cade's laconic quiet, he tried imposing his lance captain's demands for trackers and dogs, and armed search parties.

'Soldier,' Cade stated, unmoved as fixed stone, 'this is Lowergate's garrison. By rank and crown standing, I am the watch officer. If Mykkael is disgraced, I don't see lawful discharge. If Taskin fell to his sword, who stood witness?'

The Highgate man stiffened in outraged disbelief. 'Powers preserve!' He suppressed a pained cough, his discomfort made worse by the fumes from the garrison cook's insane practice of burning evergreen under his stewpot. 'Are you *daring* to shield a proved felon? Most of my mounted company are struck down! Three were just gutted by your murdering desertman's sword. Three others lie paralysed, dart-shot. I've got broken ribs, at your captain's hand. His was the blow that unhorsed me. If that's not firm evidence, you all risk your necks as a sorcerer's willing collaborators.'

Sergeant Cade sheathed the knife he had just inspected for sharpness; went on to fasten the baldric that hung his well-used, classic broadsword. 'But Mykkael's no sorcerer. Quite the opposite, in fact.'

Ebron sat, shocked, by that quiet delivery. The ward-room bench was too hard to ease him, and the noise of the dawn watch arriving, too disruptive to let him field setback with equanimity. 'You've been duped by witch-ery,' he accused, his voice rising.

'You're an expert with spell lines? How amazing. Where in Sessalie did you find the experience?' Bald, stolid Cade stared Ebron down. He seemed not to care that any man in the garrison might overhear such a sensitive confronta-tion. 'Before you spout off your pig-ignorant hysterics, you might wait to see how Captain Bennent weighs up the facts.'

'Mykkael has fought sorcerers three times before this,' Vensic filled in from the sidelines. He stepped back, making way as the cook's boy shoved past, arms laden with more fronds of cedar. 'He's taught us the means to lay down tight banishings, and left instructions to safe-guard this keep. Has the guard above Highgate taken simi-lar precautions? No? Then who's to say, but an expert, that your high council, and even your lance captain, weren't suborned?'

Ebron shoved to his feet, drawing stares from the men who snatched breakfast before they marched out for duty. 'I have comrades cut *dead*! Some were wretchedly poisoned. And Taskin's down, gravely hurt with a wound that might kill him, or worse, cripple his sword arm past mending.'

Cade took that ugly news in stiff stride. 'Vensic will appoint a task squad to bear litters. They'll take up your fallen and assist with the living. Oh, yes,' he resumed, before Ebron's hackled startlement. 'We've been well versed, and by Mykkael himself. Your dart-shot companions could pull through and survive. Not every nerve poison is fatal, and of those that are, all but the worst ones have antidotes.'

The lancer's enraged protests were strangled mid-word, as Sergeant Cade gave the matter his adamant dismissal. 'You'll have a fresh horse to ride up to Highgate. Make your report in due order. Until Captain Bennent responds with a direct command, my obligation to the crown of Sessalie is quite clear. Every man in this garrison will secure the city gates. If, as you say, Captain Mykkael's a turncoat, he's already outside and running. Inside keep walls, the safety of the king and his lawful subjects must claim my highest priority.'

Cade called for a groom to saddle a remount. Next, Ebron was hustled off to the stables, still viciously fuming, his arms clamped to brace his cracked ribs.

For one stricken moment, amid the purposeful racket brought on by the change in the guard, Vensic and Sergeant Cade shared a deep glance of frustration.

The older man, as senior officer, was the first one to speak. 'Your take and mine would appear to agree.'

Vensic's frown remained grim. His reply rang with venomous irony. 'That Taskin's not dead outright must mean that Mykkael thought the guard was misguided, and not suborned by the enemy. He would have counted the princess's safety over everything else. How much time can you give him? And how long do we have, before we might face a sorcerer attacking our flank?'

Cade rubbed his pink head, uneasy as he measured the desperate pitfalls that mired the course of the future. 'I can send out green trackers. Mykkael won't be found right away, at least by any of ours. If Devall's men ride, they won't know the country, and they'll be several hours behind him. No more can be done, beyond minding the walls. Here's acting orders, on behalf of this garrison. You'll accompany the litter-borne lancers past Highgate. Find Bennent. Be sure, if you can, that Taskin stays under warded protection. The commander alone holds the power to muzzle the guard, and unconscious, he's desperately vulnerable.'

'I'm away,' Vensic answered, cued at last by the nod from his staffer that his picked squad of bearers were assembled and ready to march. 'Stay firm. We'll survive this.'

The careful, strong sergeant who handled the day watch arose, all his gear set to rights, and his manner as stern as forged iron. 'Powers keep you close, man, and save your damned prayers. It's your captain's survival that's cast into jeopardy. The only way he can clear his name, now, is to deliver King Isendon's daughter alive, and keep faith that the crown doesn't fall in his absence.'

Flat on his belly in dew-drenched brush, Mykkael crumpled up the tail of his surcoat and muffled the frantic rasp of his breathing. He had two darts left. Around him, the mist swirled in heavy white billows, that soon would disperse under sunlight. His bad knee shot fire down the nerves of his leg. Without the chestnut just turned loose as decoy, he had no chance at all of outrunning the lance captain's rabid pursuit.

Worse still, Taskin's sword had left him well blooded. An ugly stab wound punctured his thigh. His right knuckles were opened, a surface gash that promised to stiffen like vengeance as swelling impaired the tendons. Altogether too many hurts marred the focus of his attention.

Eyes shut, shaking through the whiplash reaction from

use of his *barqui'ino* reflexes, Mykkael strangled back the distraction of grief. He could not change fate, must not torment himself with the useless wish, that the commander's skilled swordplay might have left him *one* opening for a less drastic response. Remorse did not ease the demands of necessity. Ahead, Mykkael measured the daunting odds set against Princess Anja's survival.

Behind, first of the unpardonable string of casualties, the crown's most loyal defender was down with a crippling wound, and in peril of losing his life.

Stretched out in damp leaves, the desert-bred captain marshalled the cold force of his discipline. He breathed until his raced panting and pulse rate subsided. Subservient to his mind, his stilled body melded into the natural landscape. Overhead, a foraging sparrow flitted through interlaced branches. Patient as a stalker, Mykkael eased the cloth away from his face. He grasped the blow tube, then drew out his last darts. These had been simply fashioned, no more than a tinker's needle fixed into a dowel plug, with a wisp of fletching attached. Since the sparrow showed no sign of alarm, he snatched the moment to his advantage. With the needle of one dart used as a stylus, he scratched a row of small characters into the wood stock of the other. Chance stayed in his favour. His tremors had steadied enough to allow his rushed hand to stay legible.

Then he dipped the point of the marked dart into the phial of poison tucked into the flap of his scrip. No instant too soon; after he loaded the blow tube, the sparrow spread slate wings and flew. Mykkael waited, listening. This thicket masked him like countless others, snatched as havens in enemy territory. As he had through defence of the Efandi princess, he sensed the live thrum of a sorcerer's lines course through the earth and the air. That uncanny, sawing awareness flicked and snapped at his sensitized nerve ends. Mykkael held, touched by witch thoughts, and racked into sweat by the brushed sense of Anja's raw fear.

Too late for regret that high council politics had sparked the fire to precipitate crisis: his choice to escape for her Grace's survival was a cruel, two-edged bind that must raise the stakes and cause Sessalie's enemies to unmask.

The garrison, the royal guard and the failing old king would all too likely become torn apart by that consequence.

Mykkael strangled the ghosts of old sorrows, along with new ones that cut him as fiercely. As he once had, bound by Prince Al-Syn's death wish, he took charge under ruthless priority. He shifted his breathing, as he had trained, and suspended his mind, a heartbeat removed from the primal state of trance that would unleash his volatile reflexes.

The crackle of disturbed brush that had startled the bird approached the thicket, moving uphill. An equine snort tagged the determined last guardsman, pursuing his quarry, alone. Mykkael poised the blow tube against his lips. His motionless body went nerveless. Fixated, he watched the drift of the mist.

The lancer came on as a stalking shadow, blurring the gapped trunks of the aspens. Mykkael hung back. Shoot too soon, and his dart might bounce off the man's armour, or snarl amid the bunched folds of surcoat or cloak. The desert-bred waited, unmoving, until the horse was all but on top of him, and the man's florid face plainly showed through the film of the fogbank.

The mind, stripped of reason, recorded details: fair moustache, blue eyes, a lance captain's insignia above the crown's falcon blazon on the breast. Highgate ignorant, or else sheltered by parade ground arrogance, the officer had couched his pennoned lance forward, ready to charge. The hunter lying in ambush weighed out the pitiless odds, knowing the unwieldy length of the weapon would hamper the horse's instinctive evasion. Attuned into passionless, *barqui'ino* reflex, Mykkael spat the dart at the optimal moment.

The lancer flinched, slapped his neck where the sting bit. That unthinking response drove the needle point home. Not entirely foolish, as he reeled in his saddle, he reined left, *towards* the source of attack.

Moving already, Mykkael launched from cover, the snatched length of a stick deployed like a short staff between his spread fists. He hammered the braced wood into the rider's upper arm, backed by the hurled weight of his body.

Shocked nerves threw the lancer's muscles into spasm. He toppled, while the horse kited sideways and bolted, emptying him from his saddle. Mykkael pressed his fallen prey flat in the bed of soaked leaves. Throughout the bucking throes of locked struggle, he jammed his palm over the dart embedded in the lance captain's neck. The moment the rider's downed bulk ceased from thrashing, he eased up. He jerked out the needle, and left the point nipped like a pin through the collar of the man's surcoat.

'Mehigrannia forgive,' Mykkael whispered, then arose, skinned moss and dead leaves stuck to his gore-splashed surcoat. 'Let Jussoud find you in time.'

Campaign warfare had tempered all of his skills. Sessalie's guard scarcely tested his ruthless experience. Eight men down had bought him the narrowest interval to outpace the roused wrath of a sorcerer. Mykkael recovered the fallen lance, used the stout shaft to brace his bad knee. Later, if he lived, he could attend to the puncture Taskin's sword had jabbed through the meat of his leg. For now, stark necessity forced him to take flight. If he could, he would have to catch the loose horse, and use it to lay a false trail.

The morning mist lifted. While the valleys lay cloaked, the shimmering snow of the peaks etched a flawless blue sky, and cleared sunlight streamed into lace-curtained windows. Rainbow refractions shimmered through a crystal vase of cut flowers, except as the shadow of Taskin's daughter swept past. Her fretful pacing had not eased since Jussoud had arrived to discover his promised conference at breakfast would be deferred. Though her teething infant at last slept in peace, the young mother could not bear to settle.

Not after seeing the healer's anguish on the moment he learned Commander Taskin had ridden out before dawn with a sealed writ for Captain Mykkael's arrest.

The household had been upended by the nomad's agitated demand for a horse.

'Bridle only!' he had shouted after the servant who raced for the stables to comply. 'Don't waste one second for a cloth or a saddle!'

When, minutes later, the clatter of hooves by the entry informed of the horse's arrival, Jussoud had given the daughter's alarmed questions no satisfactory answer. 'Just pray to your trinity that I'm not too late.' He squeezed her hand, an inadequate comfort, then thanked the plump steward, and breathlessly sprinted outside. The sleepy groom who led in the gelding was shown an astonishing display of steppeland horsemanship as Jussoud vaulted astride in a whirl of silk and pitched the horse to a scorching gallop.

Early morning wore past. Under the dappled shade of the cherry trees, the great house lay in wait, secluded from the palace precinct and the wildfire eruption of rumour.

The knock, when it came, was loud and direct, not the tap of a genteel visitor. Too anxious for restraint, Taskin's daughter entered the carpeted hall as the steward opened the door. Outside stood a distressed man-at-arms, wearing the plain linen surcoat of the garrison. He did not shove inside, or display uncouth manners, but bent his blond head and broke his news with straightforward gravity. 'Your king's first commander has been grievously wounded, a sword cut in the right shoulder. He's alive, though not conscious. Jussoud is bringing him up in a litter. I'm here to ask, can a room be made ready? With him, as well, are four fallen lancers, including their ranking officer. For expediency, is it possible to ask whether the healer can treat them together under this roof?'

The door steward deferred as Taskin's daughter stepped forward. Her blue eyes reflected her terrified anxiety. Only the steel of her family heritage sustained her steady reply. 'You require four additional beds? The servants will provide for the wounded as necessary.' Her graceful gesture excused the steward, who departed on hurried feet.

The lady was left with the Lowergate messenger, to master the hurdles of courtesy. 'Taskin would make you welcome inside. In his place, what can I offer to ease you?'

The young officer surveyed her imploring expression, then answered the cry of her heart. 'I have seen your father. He is in the best hands. I'm sorry I can't offer more hope.'

Tears trembled, unshed, on her lower lashes, though her remarkable voice scarcely wavered. 'You are called –?'

'Vensic, my lady.' He came in, braced her arm, and eased her into a nearby chair. 'I am here on garrison Sergeant Cade's direct order to stand guard by Lord Taskin's bedside. Will you allow me?'

She stared at him with her father's eyes, the granite behind unmistakable. 'You are Myshkael's man, Vensic? *And Myshkael's sword struck my sire down?'* She had not missed the demeaning detail, that the tall man before her was weaponless. Assumption followed, that the Highgate guards must have disarmed him as a precaution. 'Why should my father require protection from such as you, in the security of his own house?'

The officer gave his pained effort at truth. 'The one man who might have answered that question is now set on the run as a fugitive.'

She said, 'Who are Sessalie's enemies, then? Has her Grace fallen foul of a sorcerer?'

'I fear so, my lady.' Where her father had been haggardly reticent to speak, Vensic faced worse without flinching.

'Men have died out of ignorance, with the king's council backing the wrong side to fulfil their self-righteous need for a scapegoat.'

'Bold words, with no proof,' said the lady, her lace collar trembling to the raced beat of her heart. 'Bold man, to expect I should trust you.'

Vensic bowed his head. 'You are Lord Taskin's daughter. I am Mykkael's loyal officer, sworn, as he is, to uphold an oath to the king. The same as your sire, you'll have to choose.'

Her grief all but broke her. 'If your father lay dying, how could you?'

The young garrison man looked away, anguished, all of a sudden flushed with the unease of a hamlet-born farmer thrust into a setting of titled wealth. His hobnailed boots held their stance in the hallway, heedless of the priceless carpet. 'My lady, I could not speak for my father. His spirit already rests with the trinity. For yours, since he still clings to life, I will beg in the name of my captain. Don't repeat the mistake that might kill him.'

Silk slid with a sudden, whispered scream as the lady covered her mouth with taut fingers. Then she gathered her courage, gripped the shreds of her dignity, and questioned with crisp asperity. 'Jussoud was the one who sent you as messenger?'

Vensic affirmed, straitly still.

'Then you'll answer to Captain Bennent on the matter,' the lady said in conclusion. 'In the event of My*sh*kael's defection, or in his blameless absence, the Highgate's second in command becomes your acting officer.' She arose, forewarned by the uproar outside that the litter-borne wounded were arriving. 'For now, I expect you'll stay busy as the rest of us, nursing your desertman's rough handiwork.'

The front door cannoned open. Bearers streamed in, directed at once by the cohort of house servants sent by the steward to accommodate them. Jussoud's towering frame ploughed through their midst, the sleek tail of his braid striking as midnight amid the sunny preponderance of towheads. He saw Vensic first, then the strained presence of Taskin's daughter.

His compassion answered her desperate composure without a second's delay. 'My lady, your father still lives. The litter that carries him follows, more gently. Join the bearers, as you wish, even walk at his side. He's not conscious. Please don't try to rouse him. He's at worst risk from blood loss, and must be protected from jostling.'

As Taskin's daughter broke and ran in a flutter of marigold skirts, Jussoud's next order was addressed to Vensic. 'Sergeant! I want this household set under the same protections your captain detailed for the garrison.'

'Done!' Vensic surged forward, collared a servant, and listed his urgent requirements.

Milling chaos resolved into industrious order. The stricken were installed in the parquet ballroom that Taskin kept unfurnished to practise his sword forms. The steward had already brought cots from the servants' wing. Staff from the kitchen trooped in with braziers and pots. These were trailed by three red-cheeked laundresses, bearing the linens the housekeeper's thrifty eye had culled from the closets for bandaging.

Candles were lit. Piled blankets were unfolded. Hands shifted the prostrate men from the litters, while Taskin's taciturn valet gathered cloaks and unbuckled spurs, and pried off four pairs of boots.

Jussoud himself knelt at the lance captain's side, dictating symptoms to the house's elderly secretary, who set fast-paced notes down in ink. When Vensic returned, wafting a torch of lit cedar, the huge nomad looked up, his hand still clasped to the guardsman's slack wrist, and his grey eyes sharply beseeching. 'Which nerve poison did your captain use on his darts?'

Chilled despite the close heat of the flames, Vensic recognized the flaccid pallor of a man unmistakably dying.

'Mykkael knew them all.' Undermined by a surge of terrible doubt, he forced the discouraging answer. 'How can I guess? The fast-acting ones were most fatal.'

Jussoud swore, turned back to his work, and addressed two hovering houseboys. 'Get this man stripped. The last hope I have is to force him to sweat. The effort won't save him. But heated towels may ease the rictus that's starting. He surely can't die any faster.'

The healer's rapt face showed compassionate sorrow, seared through by self-poisoned regret. Even still, his care did not falter. Working to loosen the victim's tight collar, the nomad encountered the minuscule dart, deliberately pinned through the fabric. 'That torch! Vensic, hurry! Bring the light closer.'

Under the flood of illumination, the line of tiny characters showed clearly, scratched into the stained wood of the shaft.

'What do you make of this?' Jussoud's urgent gesture invited the secretary to lend his considered opinion.

The wispy man traced the letters, lips moving. 'Fane Street.' He blinked and looked up, his pouched face apologetic. 'But I don't know the foreign symbol that follows.'

Vensic expelled his stopped breath, hope revived. 'A physician from Fane Street sometimes serves the garrison. He could read that, I'm sure! Powers preserve! You're probably holding Mykkael's coded key to the antidote.'

'I know that fellow. He's a worldly, learned man.' Jussoud surged to his feet, his voice raised like a storm over the bustle of activity. 'I need a groom with your fastest horse for an errand down to the Falls Gate!'

The cry of the horns rebounded off the peaks, each clarion call a torn strand from the life left unravelled behind her. For of course, the notes framed the heartbreaking reminder of the carefree days when she had ridden out hunting. Now, as she thrashed through the thickets, the same music lashed her to terror: the ox horn of Sessalie's master huntsman blended into the descant bugle of the crown prince's trumpet, sounding to muster the hounds. When she also picked out the deep, belling tone of Devall's distinctive conch shell, she bolted in sweating panic . . .

XVIII. Fatal Stakes

THE PORTLY LITTLE PHYSICIAN FROM FANE STREET TUGGED TO STRAIGHTEN HIS DISHEVELLED JACKET, THEN BENT under the light of Vensic's held candle. His soft hands stayed gentle as he prodded and murmured. He presently asked Jussoud to cradle the sick man's head. Then he knelt with his elbows braced on the pillow and peeled back the lid of the unconscious lance captain's eye.

'No, keep on with your work, child,' he encouraged the aproned cook's girl, who had hesitated to give him space. She reddened, then resumed squeezing a vile-smelling remedy from a rag into the flaccid man's mouth.

'Don't worry, the poor fellow's not going to feel this.' The physician pressed the red flesh on the inside of the eyelid, and measured the interval as the capillaries refilled. He peered, his brow furrowed, as the pupils he examined for reflex stayed sluggish beneath the flared spill of the flame. 'You saw this?' He pointed out the tinge of dull yellow that sullied the whites of the lance captain's eyes.

'Distressed liver,' Jussoud murmured from his hovering stance, as he unclasped his hands and resettled the victim's lolled head. He addressed the next question without flinching. 'How long? The symptom only just started to show the hour before your arrival.'

'Oh dear. That's not good.' The physician tucked the blankets back up, and by habit ran a soothing hand down the stricken man's arm. 'Your fellow might suffer impairment of balance, or perhaps, a lingering numbness of the skin. Time and rest will eventually heal all the damage.'

At Jussoud's expression of naked relief, the pink-cheeked physician hastened to give reassurance. 'Oh, my, yes, he'll survive. All four victims will. This one just might take a bit longer to pull out. The venom from black-legged spiders kills gradually, after paralysis sets in. Knows his poisons, does Mykkael. He's dosed this just right. What criminal charges lie over these men, to have called for such drastic measures?'

The silence that followed rang on the ears.

'You don't *know*?' Vensic grated, stunned speechless by the iron-clad discretion shown by Taskin's household servants.

The physician blinked in mild offence. 'I was treating an elderly man with a boil when your message boy hammered my door in! I left the poor fellow soaking in salts, while my housekeeper rushed to drag my assistant away from his breakfast. Cafferty's steady, but sour as crab apples on mornings when he doesn't eat. Will somebody tell me what's happening?'

Vensic swallowed. 'I apologize.' Since no one else volunteered, he stood as his captain's spokesman. Even given the gentlest phrasing, the debacle that had occurred on the tourney field seemed an act of unparalleled ferocity.

'You've driven out *Mykkael*?' The portly physician thrust to his feet. 'Powers save us, that's madness! That desert-bred knows more about marauding sorcerers than any man I've ever known who's survived the vile touch of experience. Hates spell lines so deeply, he's scarred from within. He would lay down his life before serving such evil!'

Jussoud stared at his empty fists. 'We already know. It's Sessalie's high council, and northern-born prejudice, that's forced Captain Mykkael to take flight.'

The physician stared, poleaxed, his dimpled hand pressed to his shirtfront. 'Such stupidity could kill us,' he whispered point blank. 'I would offer to testify, though I see you don't think words of character will be any use to mend a good man's maligned standing.'

The nomad healer extended a massive, warm palm, and steadied the physician's rocked balance. 'Come upstairs,' he urged. 'Help me treat the wound in Commander Taskin's right shoulder. I'd appreciate your trained touch. After that, if you think Mykkael's plight is not hopeless, we will all weigh his problem, and hear through your list of suggestions.'

In the upstairs seclusion of Taskin's bedchamber, the mullion windows stood open to let in the light. Morning breezes flowed off the ranges, sharp with the ice scent of snow. The air carried sound with high-altitude clarity: the echoes of horn calls drifted up from the vales, cut by the baying of hounds.

Vensic tried not to let the distant progress of the hunt drag his thoughts to fretful distraction. He trailed Jussoud into the brightened room, where Taskin's daughter kept anxious vigil from a quilted chair by the bedside.

'You may not wish to stay,' the nomad opened. 'Your father's wound is severe. The treatment he needs will be difficult.'

The young woman straightened, determined. 'I will stay, if you will permit, and hold his hand throughout the duration.'

The physician from Fane Street resettled his spectacles. 'Brave heart, your presence can do nothing but help.' He sized up the room, with its lofty ceiling, its dyed carpet, then the four-poster bed spread across with fresh linen and bleached wool, which couched the stricken commander.

His uncertain glance flicked back to Jussoud. 'Are you sure the setting's appropriate?'

Jussoud tempered his answer as much for the distraught lady. 'I can't promise that the procedure will be neat. However, the commander will do best not to be moved. This east-facing chamber provides the best light. If you wish, ask the servants to spread canvas.'

Taskin's daughter arose, fingers laced through her father's limp hand. 'I thought you just said it was dangerous to move him.'

'I can't do the fine work of stitching on a mattress,' Jussoud explained, unwilling to hide his deep apprehension of the trial that must lie ahead. 'Your father will need to be strapped to a plank to hold him perfectly still.' The nomad swallowed, grey eyes locked to the woman's pinched face. 'We don't dare dose him numb with a soporific. His vitality is already too low.'

The daughter gamely lifted her chin. 'I won't leave him.'

'Very well.' Jussoud signalled to Vensic, who admitted the servants to make preparations. Swift hands rolled aside the rich carpet. Under the house steward's tireless efficiency, plank and trestle were readied, and trays and tables arranged within a matter of minutes.

When Jussoud and the rotund physician moved at last to shift the stilled man on the bed, Vensic trailed them. 'I might help support him, if you wish.'

The physician nodded encouragement, then noticed the daughter's small start of alarm. 'Don't worry. The garrison men have been rigorously trained. The young sergeant knows how to handle the injured.'

She released Taskin's hand, stepped aside with reluctance. 'The desert-bred's work?'

'No one else's.' Vensic took charge of the rag strips, hung them over his sturdy shoulder, and moved close as Jussoud peeled back the sheets.

Two stout servants steadied the plank, while three pairs of hands moved in smooth co-ordination and eased Taskin's prone form on to the rigid support. The commander showed no sign of awareness throughout. The sculptured, lean limbs they arranged at his sides stayed cool to the hand as grain marble.

'Nice job, with the field dressing,' the physician admired. 'The shoulder wound has cut terribly deep?' He absorbed the details of Jussoud's murmured answer, while Vensic dispensed strips of flannel rag and helped bind the commander's slack frame across chest, wrist, thigh and ankle.

'Support his head, please,' Jussoud requested, then asked Vensic to bear up one end of the plank.

Slowly, with no jostling bump, the delicate burden was transferred to the waiting trestle. The cook's boy brought wooden stools from the pantry, then filed out with the other servants. Only the grizzled head stableman stayed. He had handled enough ugly wounds with the horses to manage the requisite steadiness. Bashfully silent, he stood by the brazier, ready to heat irons for cautery, or shed more light with a mirrored candle.

Jussoud shed his silk robe. The fitted garment he wore underneath was fine linen, tied with a sash at the waist. From his satchel, he added thick cotton wraps to catch sweat that might stream down his wrists, then a brow band tucked around his head. Last, he washed his hands in a bucket of salt water, then dipped them in a soak of strong iodine. 'Do the same, if you please,' he asked of the physician. 'I expect you've seen use of clamps, before this? That's good.' Next, the nomad tipped a nod towards Vensic. 'You wash as well. Do you think you can mind the tray with the instruments? Just pass over those items I ask for.'

'Should I falter, I'll tell you.' The garrison man tried not to look at the face of the proud man Mykkael's sword had left senseless. Taskin seemed far removed from the vigour of life. His chest scarcely stirred with the effort of breathing.

The daughter was already poised at his side, her fingers clasped to her father's hand, and her head held high as a spirited hawk's in the grip of unflagging hope.

'Make sure he stays warm,' Jussoud instructed her. 'Over there, on the stool, do you see? I've got bladders of hot water folded into the blankets to heat them.'

'All right then, we're ready.' The nomad reached out, slipped the tight knots binding the bandages, while the physician, unasked, unwrapped the bundle containing the healer's instruments.

The bleeding gushed no matter how deftly the sodden wrapping could be eased away. Jussoud's swift touch moved and pressed down on a point at the shoulder, and another between the layered muscle above Taskin's elbow. The physician proved to be deft with the clamps, in spite of his stubby, plump fingers. In terse bursts of movement, the deep, severed veins were pinched off in the grip of locked tweezers.

'I'll need that lamp,' Jussoud said to the stableman.

Despite clammy palms, Vensic threaded a strand of gut filament on to the smallest, curved needle. Time trickled by in strung tension. No one spoke, as Jussoud's patient hands tied off the severed veins, and one by one, stopped their bleeding. The delicate task was accomplished at last, without falling back on the scarring expedience of cautery.

'Amazing, how the swordsman managed to avoid cutting the exposed artery,' the physician murmured, rock-calm. 'You have damage, assuredly, but most can be sewn.'

Vensic stole one fleeting glance at the wound, and wished in sick fury that he had refrained. The tendons were sliced just over the joint, with the gaping, raw meat of the muscle sheared from the bone to lay bare the cartilage cuff of the shoulder.

A moment longer, the two healers conferred, cross-checking their store of skilled knowledge. Techniques might differ, and yet they agreed in their cautious prognosis.

'We can save the use of his arm, perhaps, lady,' Jussoud informed Taskin's daughter. 'If blood loss, or infection, don't bring him down first, he could heal strong enough to bear weapons. But I warn you, if he lives through the shock, the convalescence will be severe and prolonged. No remedy can make such a shoulder wound comfortable. If he wakens, and I can't promise he will, he'll face a fortnight of intractable pain. Many weeks after that, he can't be permitted to lift anything, or raise his right arm, even to put his wrist through the sleeve of a dressing robe. If he tries, he will tear these slashed tissues past mending. If we do the hard work, can you handle him?'

'If she can't, I will,' Vensic vowed in dead earnest. Across the stilled chamber, the door latch clicked open, but failed to draw anyone's notice. 'I can't believe Captain Mykkael intended to leave the king's first commander a cripple.'

'Bright powers!' cracked an incredulous voice from the threshold. 'How can you and Cade still maintain the belief that your disgraced captain is innocent?'

Vensic turned his head, the tray bearing the instruments jostled by his startled movement. 'I don't know what Cade thinks,' he said, icily truthful. 'Though he may well feel as I do, having served under the man for eight months.'

Guard Captain Bennent strode into the room, imposing and angry, and wrestling unrestrained grief. 'And how *do* you feel, soldier?'

'Not here!' Taskin's daughter implored. She thrust to her feet, ready to spring like a wildcat to keep peace in her father's sickroom. 'No discord, I beg you. Please hold your argument elsewhere.'

Yet Bennent was too riled to placate. 'Lindya, go out. This is become a matter of crown security.'

Raised with the unmalleable tempers of fighting men, Taskin's daughter had the wisdom to realize when she had no choice but give ground. She bestowed a razor-edged glower of warning before she slipped from the room. Bennent's jerked nod excused the staunch stableman, who set down his candle lamp and left as well, without daring a murmur of protest.

Bennent's attacking tread advanced across the stripped floor. 'Catspaw? Or worse, a traitor's accomplice? Answer my question at once!'

Vensic stood his silent, rankled ground, and passed Jussoud a freshly strung needle. The extreme tension built, while the physician looked on with shrinking apprehension. Only Jussoud stayed unmoved. Raised outside dissent by intense concentration, the eastern nomad applied steady hands to his work. The example of his determined calm restored the footing for patience and reason.

Vensic drew breath, and *somehow* held on to his temper. 'How do I feel?' he repeated, accusations put aside before the looming threat facing his endangered homeland. 'That I have never in my life known a fighting man of such unparalleled competence. Mykkael is direct. He's hurtfully honest with everything he undertakes. If he were the ally of Sessalie's enemies, by now, we would lie under conquest.'

Bennent's heavy footsteps snapped to a stop. What he saw, raw and brutal, under Jussoud's skilled fingers disallowed any grounds for appeasement. 'Then why should your vaunted outsider draw killing steel against Taskin?'

'Ask Taskin!' snapped Vensic. 'If Mykkael cut him down, the mere fact he's not dead begs the question.'

'There's truth, if you'll hear it,' the physician interjected. 'In my time, I have served on my share of battlefields. Your commander stands a reasonable chance to survive. The foe who wished harm would have severed his arm, and with far less effort than the friend with the presence to pull the hard stroke that inflicted this desperate damage.'

Yet it was Jussoud's soft testament that defanged the aggression bristling between the two officers. 'I would have been proud to count Mykkael my brother.'

Forced to take pause, aware as he was that Taskin himself had respected the desert-bred's competence, the guard captain loosed his clenched fists. 'I have to pursue him as fugitive, regardless. The council is adamant, and the High Prince of Devall won't be satisfied. His Highness's honour guard has already mustered. They ride out under Prince Kailen's backing, and no power short of King Isendon's word can raise the authority to stay them.'

Vensic cut off a fresh length of gut. On flat courage and nerve, he bent to the task of threading another fine needle. 'You can at least keep the garrison from Jedrey's brash hands?'

Again Bennent demurred, this time with sincere irritation. 'I can press my influence, but not guarantee. Until the king's lucid, the council's writ rules.'

He refused to elaborate the grim prospects. Princess Anja's disappearance had fanned Highgate prejudice the hotter, and cast fresh suspicion on the foreigner's upset of the past summer's tourney. Worn raw from an obstructive encounter with the seneschal, Bennent knew best of any: the storm winds of politics were unlikely to reverse in Cade's favour any time soon. His pause turned thoughtful as he marshalled what resource he could in retreat. 'I can reassign you, as Taskin's ranked second.' To the garrison man, who showed evident character, he offered by way of apology, 'Where would you serve, given choice?'

Vensic's frank startlement changed to resolve. 'Appoint me to guard Taskin's door, if you please. His lordship must have a sharp sword to stand by him, and someone without court ambitions will need to make sure his sickroom stays warded with cedar.'

Even Bennent was forced to acknowledge such fierce heart. 'You do realize, if Taskin dies, you'll be blamed as a traitor's accomplice.'

Vensic's jaw tightened. 'That's why Commander Taskin can't die,' he agreed. 'On Highgate turf, Mykkael has enemies who may not act for Sessalie's best interests. Cade dispatched me here with sound forethought.'

The unpopular fact that the commander's staunch

loyalty had the audacity to shed doubt upon Devall's motives now left him a helpless target. Captain Bennent was anything but a fool. 'All right. Under my auspices, Cade's assignment will stand. You stay to guard Taskin's safety.' His blue eyes were flint, as he finished. 'To uphold that honour, one of mine would not hesitate to lay down his life, if need challenged him.'

Vensic nodded. 'I've already helped carry such devoted men here, three of them laid out for burial.' He passed the readied needle to the physician, who had seamlessly offered to spell Jussoud's efforts. Freed, for the moment, to match Bennent's regard, the young officer returned a calm that was almost provocative. 'How dare you expect I would do any less, for your man, or the captain who trained me?'

Bennent gave back his rapacious approval. 'Powers! You'll serve. I'll have the Highgate watch release your held weapons.' He paused, shook his head, then mused somewhat rueful, 'You'll stand out in this house, looking coarse as a farmer. I realize you're not shamed by your Lowergate origins, but unfortunately, right now, appearances carry a bloodletting weight of significance. You'll unbend your loyal neck for necessity? Good. Then go downstairs at once. Tell the first servant you find to fetch you a palace guard surcoat.'

While Vensic relinquished the instrument tray and let himself out of the sickroom, Jussoud murmured, 'No, that talisman stays. We'll tuck the disc and the cord out of sight underneath the cloth strapping we use to bind up the shoulder.'

'I was already aware,' the physician answered, leaving the copper disc undisturbed against Taskin's wax skin. 'Mykkael left me one also, I'm grateful to say, after the sorcerer's mark claimed poor Beyjall.'

Jussoud glanced up, startled. 'You're protected as well? Bright powers, and give thanks for the blessing! I feared I might have no learned help.'

Across the gaping wound that engaged their shared efforts, spoken words fell disastrously short. Allied by their store of worldly experience, the healers who tended the king's stricken commander both sensed the pressure unbearably building: unless Mykkael was brought down, either killed or discredited, the sorcerer that had targeted Sessalie's crown for destruction would strike openly, turning unimaginable power upon innocents with horrific and violent force.

The sound of horns and the baying of hounds always made Benj the poacher querulously restless. If game was being coursed, or a man hunt was in progress, he liked to observe from the hilltops, or follow along from the covert thickets. If the affray was no commoner's business, he always insisted his livelihood required such prying vigilance.

A man who trapped out of season ought to know where the crown's wardens were treading. Benj preferred his lazy time in the taverns, rather than waste himself tramping over disturbed ground unlikely to harbour worthwhile quarry for days. Never mind that a fool might get caught red-handed, if he returned to collect from a snare the crown's huntsman might have discovered.

That Mykkael's silver confined him at home left Benj in a pacing bad mood. He was particularly vexed, since the clever man himself had broken last night's promised rendezvous.

'Well, he's paid you enough for the privilege of sitting,' Mirag scolded, cheeks flushed as she drubbed dirty shirts in the wash tub. 'You should kiss the soles of your boots and be grateful. While the rest of us work, and the girl weeds the melon patch, you get to rest on your arse doing nothing.'

'I could do that part better at the Bull Trough, or the Cockatrice,' Benj carped. He stalked away from the window, shot a liverish glance at his wife, and then added,

'As for well paid, I've not seen a copper! How should I know? This stash of coin on your bragging tongue may not even exist!'

Mirag unloaded a sopped wad of cloth and brandished her soapy fist. 'Just because you lie like a fish? Doesn't mean all the rest of the world acts dishonest and mulishly brainless!'

'Woman, you're a trial on all of my nerves, not to mention everyone else's.' Benj lashed a kick at a footstool. Deprived of his gin, and ornery as a bagged viper, he relished a bloodletting argument. 'A cow with a bee-stung udder's more reasonable. If this bribe Mykkael left us is more than a figment, show me the hard silver, woman. Else I'm going out, and bedamned to your louse-ridden promise that I shouldn't drink!'

'No boozing.' Mirag wrung out the suds, then heaved the sodden clothes into the rinse bucket. 'Nor have I wool plugs stuck in my ears. Married to you all these desperate years, I can hear if a hound pack's coming or going. That lot's not coursing the forest at all, but hellbent down the road towards the lowcountry.'

'Not all of them,' Benj contradicted her. Awake or asleep, his ear stayed attuned to a pack's belling music. He stomped an undaunted course to the doorway and snatched up his mud-crusted boots.

The wife dropped her laundry and bolted to stop him. 'Just where do you think you'll shove off to, old man?'

Benj flashed her a glare. 'Outside,' he answered. 'Have to cut loose the hounds. You want my pack requisitioned on crown business? Those are Highgate horns. Hear them?' In Benj's opinion, the king's uppity officers were pinch-fists. They took what they pleased upon grounds of privilege, with no thought of hard use on the dogs.

'My pack's better off out scaring up rabbits,' Benj insisted. 'Won't risk leaving them tied for the taking. They're wont to pick up bad habits like ticks, mishandled by Highgate's slack huntsmen.'

Mirag frowned and clawed back a stuck wisp of hair. Her crafty awareness had noted the horns, as well as the call of the conch shell sounded by Devall's overdressed retinue. That a foreigner's men rode out in armed force boded trouble, by all common sense. 'I promised Mykkael.'

'Bedamned to the wind in your nagging mouth, woman!' Benj shoved through the doorway, still talking apace. 'I don't loose the pack quick, we'll have none to offer if and when yon dark foreigner gets here.'

Sharply afraid for no tangible reason, Mirag hiked up her splashed skirts and plunged out of the cottage, hard on the heels of her husband. 'Here, Benj. I'll help.'

As the oddly matched couple dashed into the yard, the dogs burst into yapping pandemonium. Leaping and yammering against their chains, they surged towards a man whose shadowy form emerged from the breaking mist. He carried a sword, worn shoulder-slung over the crown's falcon surcoat.

'Damn all to the nethermost pit of red hell!' Benj cursed. 'We're too late off our arses to make any difference.'

Mirag snatched his wrist. 'No. Maybe not.'

For when the figure knelt down and offered a hand, the mastiff bitch stopped her snarling and quivered with exuberant welcome.

'Well expose me for kerrie bait!' Benj slapped his gawping jaw with relief. 'About damned time that scoundrel of a captain showed up to claim his due service.'

The rangy poacher hastened his stride, Mirag puffing beside him. They reached the kennelled pack just in time to see Mykkael himself bending down to free the hounds' shackles.

'They'll be requisitioned,' the desertman warned, untying rope collars at speed. He was out of breath, and hampered by a gash that had recently laid open his knuckles. More bloodstains marred his surcoat and breeches. 'Hurry on. We don't have much time.'

Where Benj had no eyes, beyond liberating dogs, Mirag's sharp wits never rested. 'They're after you, Mykkael?'

'Yes.' His sharp face stayed absorbed, and his flying hands did not falter. 'The result of misguided politics and an enemy who's by far too clever and dangerous. I've been framed.' Passing the stripped collars into Mirag's stunned grasp, the desert-bred added, contrite, 'You don't have to shelter me, or shoulder the risks of an innocent promise made yesterday. Here and now, you're released from my claim over Benj's skilled service.'

Through the instant that Mirag stood fish-eyed and speechless, Mykkael unsnapped the last brace of chains, peeled off the final two collars, then pushed erect with a forced hiss of breath. He looked like a man who was hurting as he gave Benj his strait-laced apology. 'I can settle for information alone, and be gone. Keep the coin. You'll have earned it if you still know where your boy has holed up near those horses I'm chasing. But we're going to have to speak quickly.'

Mirag stiffened, offended. 'That's unworthy nonsense!' Never before had she turned off the needy, or delivered a friend to crown justice.

Her husband agreed. 'You can hide in the straw at the back of the mastiff's barrel. No fool searches there. Lose a hand if he tries. Old bitch likes nothing better than mauling a meddling stranger.'

Mykkael glanced from husband to wife, his eyes obsidian-hard, and his tension as ruthlessly measuring. 'I can't do this. Far too dangerous. The High Prince of Devall's lured a sorcerer to Sessalie. You could both be condemned to die, or much worse, if you're caught harbouring me as a fugitive.'

Benj surveyed the desert-bred with professional acuity, then delivered his withering assessment. 'You try to run, cut and bloodied as you are, even those fat, stupid hounds down from Highgate can't help but nose you out.' He scraped his jaw, spat, shared a glance with his wife. 'Never took you for foolish, Captain.'

Mykkael said a word in blistering dialect, then winced as he tested his bad knee. 'You're right, of course. I've no choice but accept.' He looked up again, his bronze features desolate. 'No coin I have can repay you for this selfless kindness.'

'No matter,' said Benj, already moved on to eye the stained surcoat, then the holed breeches and splashed boots. 'Strip,' he said, terse. 'Every damned stitch. Have to bury your clothing under the midden. No way else to keep the damned tracker's pack off you. Wife!' he bellowed, though she still stood beside him. 'Shout up to the melon patch. Tell the girl to fetch out the phial of fox piss I use to mask scent for my trapping.'

The woman glared at her spouse, both her ham fists jammed with dog collars. 'Oh, you wouldn't!' Her eyes widened, horrified. 'The idea's a straight cruelty.'

Benj shrugged. 'Unpleasant, I warrant.' His pale eyes shone, adamant, through his lank forelock. 'Nonetheless, I'd rather be safe than rock-stupid.'

The raw-boned woman sighed in apology. 'I'll wash the clothes, Captain. Don't fret for your dignity.' Still, she shied from Mykkael's too direct gaze as she faced the errand just asked of her. 'For your poor, abused person, I'll promise to have the lye soap and hot water waiting.'

'Mirag, I'm grateful.' The desert-bred caught her hand one brief moment, and touched her chilled palm to his cheek. As he let her go, his smile burst through, swift as lightning flashed through a stormfront. 'No doubt I've smelled worse in my time on campaign.'

Old Benj slapped his knees in uproarious delight. 'Oh, no, my fine fighting cock, you surely haven't. The recipe in that phial's a trade secret, besides. I'm going to enjoy every moment, watching your eyes stream with tears as you sluice yourself down. The gagging aroma's my rightful revenge, I tell you. Fair penance for the wretched dunking you served me the past night in the moat!'

XIX. Cipher

BY MIDDAY, WORD OF THE DESERT-BRED'S BUTCHERY HAD SPREAD FROM THE FALLS GATE TO THE SALONS ABOVE Highgate. Mykkael had always aroused stirring controversy. Sown in the wake of his discredited character, new rumours sprouted apace. Opinions were bandied about in the market, or across idle glasses shared in the wine shops. Conjecture turned vicious, until Sergeant Cade was forced to rein back heated talk in the garrison. For the handful who maintained that Mykkael might be innocent, others insisted his hand lay behind the abduction of Princess Anja. Men-at-arms voiced their outrage by chafing to join the Prince of Devall's rabid man hunt.

The belief Mykkael practised dark sorcery was widespread, since the uncanny construct made of stakes and singed string had been found on the blood-soaked tourney field. Such lines had too likely been some fell snare, drawing men like live prey to their doom.

Above Lowergate, servants returned from their shopping agreed: the uncanny foreigner had surely been a paid conspirator all along. The misfortunate princess's fate, at his hands, ranged the gamut, from a captive held for extortionate ransom, to a victim earmarked for torture to feed the dire evils of spellcraft.

The litters seen bearing up wounded and dead had quashed the last whisper of uncertainty. Through bloodshed and poison, one ditch-bred savage had just butchered a company of lancers. The Middlegate merchants who shipped goods to the southern coast aired their entrenched distrust of the Scoraign Wastes' scattered tribesmen. Such creatures lived rootless as wandering beasts, with their singing shamans and queer fetishes and their clannish, uncivilized ways. As wealthy matrons gathered for their morning teas, the old tales resurged: yet no desert warrior in their husbands' experience ever slaughtered as wantonly as this one.

Above Highgate, where discussion of lurid detail was considered unseemly manners, the privileged court ladies were compelled to react with constraint and circumspection. Taskin's house staff was notoriously close-mouthed. With his stately wife departed for the season to the duchy's lavish estate, social callers were firmly discouraged. Lady Lindya's retirement to attend her father forestalled direct questions after the noon vigil held at the Sanctuary. Inquiries were pursued with gloved velvet discretion, until a court lady with a relative in the guard at last confirmed the sad news.

'Yes, the vile rumours are true. The low-caste Captain of the Garrison has struck down a brave company of the king's men-at-arms.'

Closest to the palace, Lady Shai affirmed, 'Lord Taskin lies gravely wounded, and there were deaths among the guard. Since Lady Phail deemed the trouble too distressing for the king's ear, the seneschal was forced to press charges for treason through the council, then call for the precedent of having Prince Kailen sign the death warrant on behalf of the crown.'

'Four more companies of lancers have been commandeered from Captain Bennent,' the guardsman's relation ran on. 'They are scouring the countryside for the fugitive, with assistance from Devall's elite honour guard.'

Since the sorry affray was now public knowledge, the wife of a prominent high chancellor added in lisping sorrow. 'Oh, yes, we have harboured the minion of a sorcerer, or his accomplice, all along. A dreadful tragedy, that Princess Anja should be taken by such evil on the eve of her formal betrothal.'

Her veiled face turned sideways to acknowledge Bertarra's insistent question. 'Indeed, Lord Taskin is far gone. Sadly, he may not survive.' Commiseration followed for young Lindya, who had already lost her gallant husband to last year's fever.

Moral duty demanded the charitable response. Of one mind, the court ladies gathered, bearing baskets of food. They assembled clean linen, helping hands, and cut flowers to ease the burden set on the afflicted.

Taskin's house staff intercepted their offerings at the door, then dispatched volunteers to assist in the sickroom. The refined manners of Highgate did not condone uselessness. With cheerful good grace, the court ladies shouldered the unpleasant chore of cleansing and feeding the bedridden convalescents.

The Fane Street physician patted their ringed hands, and gave calm reassurance that the infirmity they witnessed would pass. One man had already started to stir, and required diligent oversight to keep him from mindless thrashing.

Lady Shai knelt at the tormented man's bedside. 'Here, let me,' she murmured. Her violet eyes unflinching in kindness, she took over the physician's place on the stool.

'Bless your care,' he said, grateful, and moved on his way to mix remedies.

Shai graciously nodded. She soothed the sick man's flushed forehead with lavender water and made no complaint for the stains on her embroidered sleeves. Sessalie's security had ever allowed such selfless charity to flourish. Wakened to threat by the loss of their princess, and now shown the first ugly casualties, the ladies of

Highgate fought for their graceful lifestyle the only way that they could. They made themselves useful tending the helpless, and eased cruel infirmity and suffering.

Except for Bertarra, whose kin ties to royalty would bow to no living impediment. She brushed aside the importunate servants. Arms clasped to a gargantuan vase of fresh flowers, she barged up the stairs like a siege ram. There, she all but cannoned into the young guardsman posted outside Taskin's bedchamber.

Her attempt to plough him aside met blunt force, and a farmhand's uncivilized accent. 'Woman, I don't care blazing powers if you're cousin to ten royal donkeys. You could be born marked with the trinity's blessing, and not pass this doorway without Jussoud's word, and Lady Lindya's approval.'

'Take your hand off my wrist!' Bertarra bristled. She tipped her powdered face past the flame blooms of the lilies, and bestowed a withering glare. 'Wrap a pig in a crown guard's surcoat, he still stinks of the sty.'

Vensic returned his best imitation of Mykkael's razor-toothed smile. 'Dress a milch cow in jewellery, she's still a cow. What's your name, Bessie? Who shall I say's come ploughing the gate?'

Bertarra blinked, stonewalled. 'You insolent sprig! Move aside! Apologize at once, or I'll see you publicly gelded.'

'In a crown guard's surcoat? Now wouldn't that show set a farmyard precedent on the elegant lawns above Highgate!' Vensic tucked her plump wrist back over the flower vase to forestall its alarming tilt. 'Since I won't apologize, and you can't shove past, you need not threaten my bollocks, madam cow. Looking at you would dismast any bull who ever had the healthy urge to rut.'

Flustered to outrage, Bertarra flounced. The vase disgorged a dollop of chilled water, which slopped down her bulging cleavage. Her furious shriek all but cracked the ceiling's antique plaster.

Brisk footsteps approached from behind the shut door. Then the panel snatched open, and Jussoud appeared, black eyebrows snarled into a frown like a stormfront. 'You'll be quiet, or I'll come out with a gag. Choose which, lady. Quickly! My patience is spent.'

'Jussoud, leave be,' interjected a female voice from the top of the stairway. 'Everyone at court knows it's useless to thwart Lady Bertarra's curiosity.'

The Duchess of Phail had slipped up from behind, discreetly dressed in robin's-egg blue, with peacock feathers tucked through her netted white hair, and her leaning hands crossed on her cane. 'Bertarra, please! Your noise is a trial to Lindya, whose child has awakened. One wailing infant cutting new teeth is quite enough to upset the peace.'

Bertarra flushed pink. While she shed her vase on a side table and routed the spill from her bosom with a handkerchief, Lady Phail tipped up her diminutive chin and cast her inquisitive glance over Vensic. 'Stand aside, soldier. I promise to keep Lord Taskin undisturbed, and to answer to Jussoud's instructions.' Then, in polite expectation the young guardsman would yield, she called past the nomad's obstructive form into the curtained chamber. 'Lindya, let me spell you. Take your time, dear. Go on and wash up, and visit your son in the nursery.'

Jussoud stepped aside, and Vensic backed down, clearing the doorway as Taskin's daughter emerged, looking wan and transparently grateful. 'My Lady Phail, you're sent by divinity itself. I've left a bowl and a rag on the tray. Could you try and drip broth into Father's mouth? He's lost blood, and needs to take fluids.'

'Out, Lindya, I'll see to him.' Without looking aside as Taskin's daughter departed, Lady Phail added, acerbic, 'Bertarra, the lilies look lovely right there where they are. Downstairs, the ladies are serving cake to the neighbours who have come asking for news. Your help would be greatly appreciated.' With no further ado, the Duchess of

Phail hefted her cane and pattered into the commander's sickroom.

Bertarra craned her neck this way and that, to peer past Jussoud's thwarting bulk.

'Do you wish to follow?' the nomad said, deadpan. 'I could use assistance emptying the slop jar.'

Yet the late queen's niece gleaned little from the dimmed room, beyond an uncouth reek of cedar smoke, and a pale and motionless form masked in tucked sheets to the chin. No bloodied bandages showed; no bustle of life-and-death drama. In fact, Bertarra found the astringent quiet of Jussoud's management dull.

'I've mopped up enough water already, thank you.' After one scathing, last glower at Vensic, Bertarra beat a mollified course back downstairs.

Jussoud granted his Lowergate sentry a broad grin for diligence, then gently closed the chamber door to restore Taskin's dignified privacy.

Lady Phail, in her inimitable way, could put Bertarra's brash nature to shame. Her first, shocked assessment of the commander's low state caused no hitched breath, and no outcry of feminine sympathy. She simply stood by the bed with closed eyes, perhaps recalling the exuberance of today's stricken man, when she had doctored his skinned knees during boyhood. Then, in upright resignation, the duchess marshalled her poise. She checked the comfort of Taskin's blankets and pillow, and assumed the lapsed duty with broth bowl and rag that Lindya had left in her charge.

Before the nomad could regroup and sit down, she demanded, 'What can you tell me that might grant an opening to settle the seneschal's hysterics?'

Jussoud blinked, clasped the palms he had scoured shiny from strong liniments, and tempered his chafing distress. 'Nothing Lord Shaillon would regard as substantial. He's not much inclined towards a foreigner's opinion concerning Mykkael's sterling character.'

'The bright stars of your ancestry aren't going to

impress him,' Lady Phail agreed with acute honesty. 'Not that you would waste such an oath on the cause of this morning's debacle.'

'In fact, I do swear, and my oath is not wasted,' Jussoud said, his scarce buried rage the surprise of a whipcrack unleashed across silence.

Rings sparkled to the bounding start of old hands as the duchess dropped the linen in the broth bowl. 'Blinding glory, Jussoud! How can you demean the honour of your family name for the sake of a renegade savage?'

The nomad laced his strong fingers in taut effort to stay his explosive frustration. 'Mykkael,' he said, firmly, 'is the most civilized man I have the privilege to know. He was to have married my sister, who is royalty. Before a misfortune ended the match, my clan viewed his suit favourably. By my word, as a legitimate blood son of Sanouk, your Taskin lies here through the fault of the council, and the impetuosity of the High Prince of Devall. They led the factions that forced your commander to undertake Mykkael's arrest.'

Yet the duchess showed that strong endorsement short shrift. 'Someone had to drag in that misbegotten desertman.' The disturbed bowl resettled, and rag back in hand, she gently began to administer broth to the comatose man on the bed. 'If Lord Taskin realized the degree of his peril, he was a rash fool not to delegate. The risks should have fallen to others who bear Sessalie less critical responsibilities.'

'You don't understand.' Jussoud's grey eyes shone fierce in the dimness as he, also, reclaimed the solace of work, and took up mortar and pestle to grind herbs for a poultice paste. 'Captain Mykkael is the one grievously wronged. The sealed accusation for treason set a bind on the desertman's honour. He had to choose between a lawful detainment that would assuredly see him condemned, and the freedom to act he dared not set at risk, to defend the life of Princess Anja.'

'And her Grace perchance is still alive?' cracked the duchess, no room in her grief for vain hope.

Jussoud spared her astute mind no grace of ambiguity. 'Mykkael struck down Taskin upon that belief.'

The granddame who had succeeded Queen Anjoulie as mistress in the king's bed weighed that startling viewpoint in silence, while the scent of crushed tansy wafted through the pungent smell of cedar burning in the brazier. Her voice was steel, when finally she spoke. 'You're suggesting I made a mistake to shield Isendon from the unpleasantness?'

'Lady Phail,' said Jussoud, his threadbare anguish revealed, 'how could I presume? My word does not offer one shred of proof to appease the High Prince of Devall, or to sway the unsettled fears of the council.'

The duchess sopped more broth from the bowl. Her profile still recalled the sweetness of youth, as with tender patience, she nursed her unconscious charge through another lifesaving swallow. 'The seneschal would not bend now for hard proof. Nor will the council risk the advantage to trade by leaving the high prince dishonoured and slighted.' Her head turned. Blue eyes held the sorrow of hard wisdom as she said, 'Time passes. The day must arrive when Sessalie's welfare is no longer our burden, but our legacy. Would you leave Crown Prince Kailen the role of a child? Force him to back down from his first test of sovereign authority, and I tell you, the strength of his spirit will stay stunted.'

Yet Jussoud remained adamant. 'His Highness can't blood his sword on this peril. Do you know what we face? *Have you words for the concept?* Mykkael is the only weapon we have to stave off a cold-cast invasion by sorcery.'

Lady Phail sighed. Her aquamarine earrings flashed like iced fire as she raised her chin in staunch resignation. 'If the tiresome strivings of politics matter, the king never came lucid this morning. I pretended otherwise. The implied threat, that his Majesty might intervene, was the only tactic I had to restrain the irate tenor of the council. If the High Prince of Devall and the seneschal had prevailed as they wished, Crown Prince Kailen might have received council endorsement to stand as legal regent of Sessalie.'

The duchess let that bald-faced effort to placate work through the widening pause. Ever tactful in aggression, she reached for a napkin and blotted an undignified dribble from Taskin's slack lips.

Yet the nomad's scorching rage failed to abate, a departure of shattering precedence.

Though mystified by his doomed loyalty to a murderer, the Duchess of Phail could not abandon her backbone of moral compassion. 'If the king wakens tonight, I can ask his Majesty whether he's willing to hear your appeal for the cause of Mykkael's good character. Oh dear, Jussoud, no! This affray is too cruel to allow for such hope. I've known his Majesty since we were children together. He is not going to rule on this matter quietly. With eight guardsmen down, and one of them Taskin, I can already say that your desertman stands little chance of receiving a royal reprieve.'

'Someone must try,' Jussoud insisted. He broke off as a heavy tread approached from the corridor outside.

Captain Bennent's bass tones carried through the closed door as he broke the morning's ill news to young Vensic. 'I'm sorry, soldier. I did all I could, but Jedrey's been reinstated. Command of the garrison now lies in his hands, unless King Isendon reviews the case and countermands council edict. You haven't eaten? By all means, go on down to the kitchen. My sword will guard Taskin throughout your absence.'

When the expected sharp rap demanded an entry, the nomad arose, wraith-silent, and lifted the latch.

Captain Bennent strode in armed in chainmail and sword, the immaculate gleam of his spired helm catching the slice of light through the curtain. His surcoat brushed the waxed shine of his boots, a sure sign he had come straight from the council hall.

The fresh pungence of horse wafted from him, regardless, ingrained in the stained saddle blanket draped in the crook of his forearm. 'I need you to look at this,' he announced point blank, and offered the item for Jussoud's inspection. 'The physician downstairs could translate the lettering. But the language as written was strange to him.'

Never one to be hurried, the nomad set aside his mortar and pestle. He flattened the horsecloth against his crossed knee, his eyes running down the fuzzed strings of characters under the glow from his brazier. 'Where did you get this?'

'The trapping came off the lance captain's mount, recaptured at large in the countryside. The groom found the marks when he stripped off the saddle. As you see, the message was scrawled on the underside, where no casual observer would find it.'

'Mykkael's?' Jussoud's inquiry was sharp as he moved to the window, and widened the curtain to let in more light.

'The physician thinks so.' Armour flashed, blinding silver, as Bennent nodded to acknowledge the duchess. Then he settled with laced hands on the brocade chair, away from the rippling blaze on the hearth. 'It doesn't carry worked sorcery, so he said, since the talisman we wear doesn't warm to it.'

'This is no sorcerer's line,' Jussoud affirmed.

Bennent turned his harried glance towards the figure swathed in the bed. The face, with its imperious hawk nose and wide brow, remained still as a carved marble effigy. 'How's Taskin? No change?'

'His pulse has strengthened, an encouraging sign.' Jussoud stated without looking up. 'The progress is slow, but we've managed to lessen some of the shock caused by blood loss.'

Bennent shifted his boots, distinctly ashamed for the

haste that deferred the propriety of house stockings. 'No wound fever?'

'Too soon to tell.' The daylight limned the nomad's absorbed profile, and nicked leaden highlights through his jet braid. He shifted the horsecloth, and spoke at last, his heartsore regret leashed behind an unshakable dignity. 'The message is Mykkael's, and yes, I can translate.'

The desert-bred warrior he had embraced as a brother might lack birthright knowledge of the Sanouk royal ideographs, yet he spoke all three castes of Serphaidian dialect with native nuance and fluency. The words written here had been framed in that tongue, but marked in the phonetic characters used by merchants for trade correspondence.

Lady Phail broke through the conflicted pause. 'Did My*sh*kael send an appeal for a stay of clemency?'

'He did not.' Jussoud's gaze stayed fixed on the cloth, as though the sight burned. Or else he still agonized over the script, stained into fabric with an ink mixed at need from blood and crushed charcoal. The eastern-bred nomad roused himself finally, shook his head, then resumed his lagged explanation. 'By Mykkael's strict code, he has not broken faith with King Isendon.'

'Three slain lancers, and five others wounded would give that specious statement an argument.' Captain Bennent jerked off his helm, worn ragged from battling unsubtle intrigue and the outcries of shaken chancellors.

The Duchess of Phail pressed the anxious question. 'Presuming we aren't being duped by a liar, what did the desert-bred send?'

'Instructions. In depth.' Jussoud gentled his wounding delivery as hope died on the old woman's face: that the renegade captain had not, after all, delivered first news of the princess.

'Just share what he says,' Bennent barked, out of patience.

Silk shimmered in the draught through the casement

as Jussoud closed his eyes and recited. 'Mykkael warns that the balk of his capture will cause the sorcerers against us to unmask. We must prepare ourselves for attack. Devall's enemies will most likely seek to unseat Sessalie's crown at one strike. The common folk should remain unmolested, at first. Chosen targets will be King Isendon and his trusted circle of warded supporters, for the plot as it stands is spearheaded to unseat the crown quietly. According to Mykkael, the realm's best chance, and ours, to bid for survival, is to withdraw to the tallest, most fortified stone tower, and to lay down drastic measures in warding. The particulars brought to our attention are precise, and clearly listed.'

The nomad smoothed the horsecloth beneath disturbed hands. When he steeled himself to confront Captain Bennent, his affable features showed fear. 'Guardsman,' he ventured in sober entreaty, 'I beg you to take this advice seriously.'

For the closing, scrawled line, now decently masked beneath the damp clasp of his hand, had used desperate words, couched in the most sacred privacy of the Serphaidian idiom. *'Jussoud, as you read this, my breath as word, sworn under the sure vengeance invoked by the fires of Sanouk royal dragons: had Prince Al-Syn-Efandi done these few things, as advised by his vizier Perincar, he may have held out with his life. Willing servant, under the stars of your ancestry, consider my sword your right arm. After Isendon's charge to safeguard Princess Anja, expect I will try to send help.'*

'Isn't that nesting the good eggs in one basket?' said the Duchess of Phail, smashing through tensioned silence. 'Quite a risk, to place the king's life at the bidding of a foreigner we have no firm proof we can trust.'

Jussoud strangled his rushed protest. Denied Taskin's cool intellect, he must rest his appeal on the palace guard's ranking captain. Yet hope crashed headlong. Through the experienced eyes of a healer, Jussoud watched Bennent weigh Mykkael's warning, not as information dispatched at great risk by the hand of a hard-pressed ally, but coloured by the prevailing suspicion of outside blood cast as adversary.

'Bad tactics,' said Taskin's second in command with the flint of a fixed decision. 'We dare not hole up with the king in a tower. We'd just become sitting targets. What better way for a sorcerer to destroy Sessalie's crown, than to mew up the royal defenders? If we didn't die in the pre-emptive first strike, we'd be pinned down to starve in confinement.'

'We'd stay alive,' Jussoud stated in clashing reproof.

'I will not see King Isendon held hostage on my watch!' Bennent arose, resolved, and offered his arm to the Duchess of Phail. 'Lady, you'll have my escort back to the palace. Please stay with his Majesty, as Taskin directed. I'll be rearranging the guard and bolstering the noon watch.' As he eased the old woman's frail step towards the door, the guard captain issued his last order. 'Jussoud? You are to burn that horsecloth, forthwith. Best not to take foolish chances.'

Left alone to guard Taskin behind the shut door, and bearing the distress of a loyal man's earnest message, the nomad wrestled his shocked disbelief. The saving grace of this hard-won knowledge, wrested out of the ruin of a shattering past failure, had been repudiated at one stroke. The rejection begged a repeat of the tragedy that had once destroyed Mykkael's life. Jussoud could have wept for the terrible irony. The desert-bred's effort to settle in obscurity as a garrison captain in Sessalie had not brought him the respite of peace.

Lamed and alone, he would shoulder bad odds and strive under his oath of protection to another doomed king. And if he survived, and again he won through, his sacrifice would be wasted. He would live to see another royal family slaughtered, and a second proud princess reduced to a lifetime of purposeless foreign exile.

Jussoud stared straight forward, stunned beyond

thought. First-hand, he had witnessed the horrific damage a sorcerer could inflict on the living. *With the sight of a healer, he had looked into Orannia's eyes. There he had sounded a madness of such scope, the dark depths would have shredded and drowned him.* He masked his bleak fury, that he had renounced the way of the Sanouk warrior. Taskin's helpless trust stung his heart like reproach, set alongside the lesser betrayals that galled like stuck thorns in the flesh: that Vensic had not been allotted due time to finish his meal in the kitchen, nor Lindya, to return from her promised leave to visit her child in the nursery.

Jussoud flung the horsecloth aside as though scorched, his anguished entreaty a whisper bent towards the commander laid out on the bed. 'Taskin, my friend, you must waken and fight. More than ever, your king's people need you.'

For the sorcerer who stalked Sessalie had been freed to step through the breach of a sheltered courtier's rank ignorance.

The palace guard captain appointed for his staunch reliability under pressure now danced with a peril outside the scope of imagined precedence. Faced by the unknown, Bennent lacked the courage to grapple the shadows, where precepts of honour became entangled with the mercy of human integrity. So often, the still, quiet doubts of the heart became strangled as the rigid assumptions of law struck them mute.

In all of Sessalie, only Taskin had the tenacious perception to question appearances with unbiased strategy. His anxiety became a springboard for deeper thought. He mined fears for their hidden advantage. In daring to see past tried ground and experience, he accepted the pitfalls only as they became proven as facts. The flexibility left at play between mistrust and honesty had let him discern Mykkael's unassailable character.

Jussoud took up the condemned square of horsecloth, and hissed a scalding oath through his teeth. Moved by the hammering force of his grief, he shoved to his feet, ripped open his satchel, and dug out his notebook of remedies. Then he took up stylus and ink. Before he enacted Bennent's rash order, he committed the words of Mykkael's scribed warning into Serphaidian ideographs. Empty-handed at last, while the flames in the hearth performed their voracious office, he busied himself with Taskin's welfare, and took up the broth bowl and rag.

'It's tragic how the lack of imagination so often shapes our defeat,' he confided, though the friend who languished near death on the bed was in no state to respond with his usual insightful rebuttal.

XX. Quarry

AFTERNOON SUN BLAZED DOWN ON THE KENNEL BARREL, BAKING THE INTERIOR TO STIFLING HEAT. BENJ'S MASTIFF lay belly down in the dirt, hackled growls interspersed with her panting. Between snarls, she rested her muzzle between her splayed paws in the sliver of shade cast by her water trough.

Mykkael could secure no such marginal respite, with the yard outside crammed with lancers.

Sweating under thick straw, knees tucked to his chin, with his nostrils inflamed by the gagging stench of the poacher's concoction of trap scent, he endured parching thirst with equanimity. His limbs stayed relaxed. The company of guardsmen milling outside scarcely excited his pulse. This mounted party was the third pack of man hunters arrived to raise a crown inquiry. The renegade captain remained unconcerned, as long as the sword hilt under his hand showed no warning hum of raised resonance. Since Mirag's house had been searched twice over by armed predecessors, and the mastiff had already dispatched one zealot home with a savaged wrist, the Highgate voices declaiming outside sought fresh dogs for the trackers, not fugitives.

Mykkael closed his eyes and let himself drowse.

Paradox almost raised his smile of sympathy for the lancers' confounding predicament. He had once experienced their frustration at first hand: old Benj could spin his laconic lies one after the next like a champion. His hounds were long since gone into the hills. Any huntsman must realize they would answer to no man until hunger wore down their exuberance.

Soon enough, the king's riders untied their mounts and departed. The mastiff bitch lapped a drink from her trough and subsided back to her panting. The desertman wedged at the back of her barrel lapsed into exhausted sleep.

Time's flow suspended, and he slipped unremarked into the half-world of dream . . .

Dogs hounded her trail. She had fled their baying for hours, as they worked her scent through the foothills. Hunkered down, breathless, behind the screen of a stunted tangle of balsam, she understood she would be run to earth like any other doomed prey chased down by a fervent pack. Harried into the stripped rock of the ranges, she wrestled to stem the panicked awareness that her position was fast growing hopeless.

Only the horses were safe, left grazing in a hidden glen.

'May the threefold light of the trinity keep them,' she gasped between stabbing breaths.

She had thoughtfully kept them well guarded from dogs, tucked away between the clefts of two tumbling streamlets. Huddled into herself, and fighting despair, she cursed the weakness that had prompted her downfall. Hunger had driven her out to try foraging. Had she stayed in the glen, the quartering search party would not have crossed over her trail. Now their pack had wind of her, they were not going to let up . . .

Mykkael aroused, gasping, the cry on his lips instinctively muffled behind the clamped force of his hands. Anja's terror still gripped him. His heart raced too fast, and his breathing ran ragged, attuned to the rush of her panic. Cast back into himself with a plummeting wrench, he fought for the presence of mind to regain his own sense of identity.

The fust of straw mould still clogged his turned senses, laced through by the ammonia reek of Benj's prized trap scent. Mykkael blinked stinging sweat from his eyes, then shuddered through a spasm of nausea. His knee pained him. Jussoud's pine-gum dressings itched his wounds like hell's vengeance, and everywhere else the cloth strips did not cover, his stinking, bare skin had been nipped by the mastiff's shed fleas. He shifted, unable to make himself comfortable. Inside the cramped barrel, the pain of pinched nerves wrung him dizzy, while the puncture from Taskin's sword-thrust throbbed, tight and hot with fresh swelling.

Outside, he still heard the belling of hounds. Mykkael cursed their ill-starred persistence. He tipped back his head, rubbed sweat from his brow, and pitched his crawling nerves to endure. He had suffered far worse in his past. No risk undertaken to ease his distress would excuse the mistake if the citadel's searchers should trap him.

Time fleeted. He measured the cost of each second passing, and wrestled to bind his fraying awareness to the immediate present. Weariness defeated him. Or else the attrition of stress let in chaos, and witch thought sucked him under again.

The cries of the pack hunting near at hand melded into the yelps of another, far distant . . .

Her efforts to circle behind her pursuit had led to disastrous failure. Again and again, the steep gash of the ravine forestalled any chance of escape. Though she tried, she could not flee down the back of the ridge. Her shins were scraped and bruised, from the tumbling fall she had suffered the desperate time she had tried. Old rock slides had scoured the unstable slope. The scarred rubble left behind was a precarious trap of loose scree, dead trees and smashed boulders.

Her hag-ridden flight had pressed her too far up the mountain.

The scant cover provided by storm-ravaged evergreens could not hide her from mounted riders. The huntsman in charge of the pack at her heels knew his grim trade too well. He worked his hounds with unshakable patience, undeterred as the sun and wind leached away the moisture binding her scent. Each time the dogs circled in baffled checks, he whistled encouragement to his lead couple, and cast his seeking pack wider. Patiently thorough, he covered each hollow and patched scrap of shade until her path was unravelled again.

On bare rock, where the trail had gone cold, her pageboy's shoes had crumbled the dry lichens. The tracker's diligence found those faint signs, and the hunt dogged her heels without let-up.

She sweated, wrung by exhaustion and crushed hope. While the hounds relentlessly zigzagged up the ridge, hied on by shouts from the riders, she faced the futility of trying to run. The scoured rocks of the peaks held no haven. While she panted, pressed to tears of trapped rage, she glimpsed furtive movement on the slope down below her.

A boy in brown homespun slipped out of a thicket, dragging what looked like a bundle of stained hide over the ground with a pull rope. Too young for a beard, he moved like a wild thing, blending into the minimal shelter of tree and stone and dry gulley. His towhead stayed attentively turned, as though he gauged the cry of the hounds and measured their closing distance.

At the crest of the ridge, where the scars of the slides had savaged the flank of the mountain, he paused and rolled his bundle over the brink. Then he bolted, dodging towards the ravine, perhaps agile enough to clamber down, or else aware of a hidden cleft with the saving grace of a footpath. She watched him go, and considered the risks of attempting to follow his footsteps.

Yet before she could act, the hounds burst upslope. Scattered and questing to trace a cold trail, they struck the fresh line the boy had just dragged across their path of pursuit.

The lead couple nosed the hot scent. Their wild tongue rallied the pack like a torrent. Seized by primal instinct, they swerved and ran riot.

The huntsman frantically sounded his horn. His shrilled call was ignored. The dogs plunged away in hysterical frenzy, straight for the rim of the scree slope. Running flat out, they charged over the brink, nose to ground in yapping, full chorus.

'Powers of hell, they've picked up a deer!' the huntsman yelled in frustration. He spurred through the scrub, too late to head off the disaster.

Before his eyes, the hounds plunged ahead. Intoxicated by the scent laid to trap them, they streamed through a rattling fall of loose stone. Rocks and boulders shifted, turned over, and rolled. The pack scarcely faltered. Their belling changed pitch to shrill yelps as they tumbled, milled head over heels as the unstable footing let go with a ground-shaking roar.

More riders pelted out of the woods. These wore guard surcoats, polished helms and mail byrnies, and with them were Taskin's crack archers.

'There!' cried the huntsman. He pointed towards a disturbance that shivered the brush. 'That could be the two-legged quarry we're tracking!'

'Bring him down!' snapped the officer leading the company. 'Whether or not he's the man on crown warrant, he's run interference on behalf of a criminal and destroyed the king's favourite hunting pack.'

At his order, four men reined up short and nocked arrows. They bent their bows, aimed, and released a tight volley after the fleeing boy . . .

The flight of the shot arrow snagged the thread of his dream, and consciousness plunged into darkness. The tug of blind instinct let Mykkael sense the choked-off cry that Sessalie's princess stifled to silence.

'Your Grace, stay still!' he gasped in warning, as though the fierce will behind whispered words might pierce through to her distant awareness.

Anja's peril was desperate. If she gave in to fear, if she moved or called out, the armed party of hunters who chased down the boy would resume their diverted pursuit.

Deprived of their dogs, they still had a skilled tracker, and hours of remaining daylight.

Mykkael thrashed in his sleep, his oath-sworn charge to defend her safety granted no outlet for release.

'Anja!' he whispered.

Frustration tore through and broke the connection. The princess's lingering anguish remained, seared through his being, heart-deep. Remembrance of another woman's suffering woke his past, and unleashed the dire force of his nightmares.

Crammed in the dank straw at the back of the kennel barrel, Mykkael rode that slipstream of horror. Again, he experienced the rolling grass of the steppe, where a camp-circle of painted elkhide tents slapped in the tug of the breezes. The harmonic chanting of Sanouk shamans lapped him under layer upon layer of raised power. Their quickened conjury crackled over his skin, and that of the woman he cradled. Song swelled and subsided, all to no avail. No shimmering ward of unbinding could lend him the foothold to speak her name and be heard. Try though he might, all the love he possessed could not lift the fires that raged through her violated mind. Again he beheld the mad, silver eyes of Orannia, whose days and nights framed a prison of agony, lost to the torment of Rathtet spell lines that no power he knew could release.

Crushed by helpless despair, Mykkael caught her hands. He subdued their blind fight. As he had, countless times, he fell back on endurance and constrained her reasonless thrashing. When she finally wore herself down to a state of limpid exhaustion, the shamans broke their circle again. They laid quiet hands on his shoulders, dusty and bronze and streaming with sweat from the throes of his adamant striving.

He remembered, unwilling. The sun had poured down like liquid gold, as the silenced Sanouk singers filed out one by one, and left him with their defeat.

The dream ended, as always: Mykkael buried his face

in the warmth of his beloved's tangled black hair. Wrung mute in every language he knew, he yielded to grief, and begged that blank darkness to drown him . . .

An unknown interval later, Mykkael wakened, jerked back through the focus of *barqui'ino* trance by the vibrating thrum of his sword hilt. He tossed off choking straw. The darkness framed a punched circle of twilight, and the kennel barrel rocked, slammed by the mastiff's snarling lunge as she hit the fixed end of her chain.

Spurred by a flooding jolt of adrenaline, Mykkael erupted on lethal reflex and launched out of the barrel behind her.

The cottage windows glowed orange, unshuttered and spilling soft light through the shadow of dusk. Five horses stood tied by the melon patch, dismissed in the stream of stripped-down perception, rote-trained to seek only targets. Two guards in Devall's livery lounged by the door, engrossed in idle talk with a leather-clad fellow, bearing a huntsman's bone-handled skinning knives.

Naked, and shedding a flurry of straw, Mykkael charged. If the knee slowed his pace, his bare feet scarcely rustled the dew-drenched grasses.

His sword rammed the huntsman point blank through the kidney. The low thrust angled upwards to pierce through the diaphragm, and emerged just under the heart. The killed man slammed into the right-hand guard, and knocked him half-senseless into the door jamb. The sword's out-thrust tip pierced him, also. His cry was ignored. Mykkael used the first victim's dead weight as fulcrum, jerked upwards, and widened the damage. He followed through with a twist of his wrist, and a wrenching yank sideways. The bound blade struck bone, ripped the nerves of the spine, and the paralysed huntsman dropped, gagging. Mykkael stomped the air from the expiring corpse, foothold for a leap that hurled him into close quarters. A blow to the standing guard's wristbone slapped his drawn sword wide, and laid him open for a hammering punch to the larynx. The blow crushed the cartilage. He reeled away, choking blood.

Mykkael spun, cleared his blade from the downed huntsman's body, and finished his whirling pivot. The spinning force of his cut slashed the punctured guard at the waist. The body collapsed, spilling entrails, while the desertman bore through on his unspent impetus and smashed shoulder down through the doorway.

The mastiff's ongoing, hysterical racket obscured the groans of the dying. Warned by the crashed door, allowed a blurred second in which to react, the lowcountry guard posted inside the threshold died first, of a chopping stroke to the neck.

Mykkael hurtled over the falling remains. Sluiced in the rained jet from a severed artery, he felt the warding tattoo at his nape come alive with a razor-edged tingle. Light flared through his aura. Made aware he had blundered across the proximity of a sorcerer's active spell lines, he let the burst run to ground through the ward's sphere of shielding. The fact the effect momentarily blinded him was not going to make any difference. The glimpse as he entered had already mapped out the lay of the room. *Barqui'ino* reaction drove him ahead on the flow of subconscious awareness.

While the whine of shed sorceries hazed his nerves like live fire, he relinquished his mind, let go of identity, and gave his schooled instinct free rein.

His hands encountered live flesh, and killed, before thought could track the result.

Stopped, hard-breathing, Mykkael blinked through the glaring blaze as the disrupted spell line shredded away. Then the shivering force of *barqui'ino* backlash broke over him. He held still, hurled into the wrenching shift as the sluggish process of reason re-engaged, then laboured to sort the meaningful aftermath written into his spattered surroundings.

The man who had carried the sorcerer's power lay, neck broken, under his feet. Catspaw, not minion: the cold link had severed with death. The wasp hum from his sword had faded to silence, leaving the mastiff's outraged barks, and a woman's hysterical weeping.

Mykkael looked up from his scarlet hands. Five horses, five kills; all threat seemed dispatched. He dismissed the odd fact he was naked. Then he noticed the victim stretched prone on the settle. The man's stubbled face seemed familiar. He lay stretched out and strapped at wrist and ankle with the twine a trapper might use to bind otter snares. Mykkael sucked in a shuddering breath. Another layer of deep training let go. Recognition seeped back, followed by the clumsy recovery of speech. 'Benj? Are you lucid?'

The gaunt poacher shut his eyes, which spilled over with helpless tears. He answered, voice quaking, 'Hell's fury, you'd best ask yourself that.' He swallowed, and turned his head with strained anguish. 'Help Mirag. See to the boy.'

Mykkael followed his glance. He saw the arrow-shot child sprawled on the floor, then the matron, knelt over him, keening with grief.

Full cognizance slammed back. Sorrow and regret flooded into the emptied expanse of his mind, leaving Mykkael winded and speechless. Next moment, thought came, and his battle-trained senses recorded the fact the boy's stillness was not unbreathing. He lay gravely wounded, not dead. The frenetic, bright tint of foamed blood at his lips suggested that he had been lung-shot.

'What happened?' Mykkael raised his clogged sword. While he pressed his gimping step over the splashed floorboards, Benj flinched, jerked short by the cruel restraints.

Mykkael read the fear inspired by his movement. He stopped still; waited. While his friend recoiled in stark fear from his presence, he recovered the requisite gentleness.

'Benj, what happened?' he repeated.

The distraught poacher continued to stare as though he confronted a stranger. At length, he managed to frame words. 'Timal turned the king's pack as you asked, and they caught him.'

Mykkael surmised the rest out of heartsick conjecture. 'Since he couldn't be questioned, they brought him back here? Then tried to pry answers from you?' Shown a terse nod, the desert-bred forced a taut grip from his blood-slippery fingers. He acted fast, to shorten distress: two neat cuts slashed the ties holding the captive. 'Benj, I'm your friend. Why didn't you wake me?'

'No chance,' gasped the poacher, still trying to conceal the embarrassing fact he was shivering. 'And anyway, the damage was done. Timal was already grievously hurt. Mirag saw the risk. If they captured you here, the crown might see us hang as collaborators.' He shuddered, the lingering shock of his panic still darkening his distended pupils. 'We didn't guess we'd be tried by a sorcerer.'

'A catspaw, borrowed as puppet, no more. Rest easy, he's now destroyed.' Mykkael braced the goodman's quivering shoulder, and allowed the firm contact to restore reassurance. 'Let's think about Timal. I'll need the remedies you keep for the dogs. Also any herbals you have that I might use to make compresses.'

His firm tone let Mirag recover a semblance of her shattered poise. 'Devall's huntsman already dug out the arrow.' She raised reddened eyes, wiping her wet cheeks with the back of a palsied hand. 'The point had wedged between ribs, so he said. He assured us the puncture was shallow.'

'The boy's still bleeding,' Mykkael stated, his urgency carefully tempered. 'Keep him warm, Mirag. Above anything, don't try to move him.'

The desert-bred helped to prop her husband erect, and wisely withheld the unpleasant prognosis that too often attended a lung wound. Instead, he called on his field experience and urged the stunned household to regroup and take needful action. 'Benj? Build up the hearth. Then shove the fire tong under the coals. We're going to need it for cautery. I have to attend a brief errand outside. Fast as I can, I'll be back to assist you.'

The poacher rubbed the chafed skin at his wrists, and gamely struggled to rally. 'Unshackle the mastiff as you go by, before she breaks her damned neck.'

Mykkael nodded, already going. As he bent to clear the hacked dead from the doorway, he noted the face of the sorcerer's catspaw, a hapless victim claimed and used by an evil compulsion, who had *almost* succeeded in channelling a spell line to break old Benj in submission. A split second only, the desert-bred paused, regarding his kill in fierce irony. Naked and dirt-smeared, still reeking of the poacher's rank potion of fox piss, and with the blood of five men unwashed from his hands, he vented his barbaric thought.

Three stripes marred his back for drawing his steel in the presence of Devall's crown advocate. 'But what laughable penalty will I have earned for snapping the man's neck with bare hands?'

'A scolding,' carped Benj, thrust back to his feet, and desperate to restore balance to a world turned hideous with crawling shadows. 'Yon advocate, there, he's passed beyond suffering. But you've tracked a right mess of dog dirt and blood all over Mirag's clean floorboards.'

Mykkael's labour outside took a handful of minutes. He sluiced off at the well, stripped the horses of trappings, and fashioned makeshift hackamores of rope to tie them out of sight in a fir copse. When a foray to the midden failed to unearth his clothes, he thrashed through the brush, swearing and slapping at midge bites, and shortly turned up at the cottage, his arms loaded down with cut cedar.

He re-entered the burst door, too spent to duck as a bundle of hyacinth-scented cloth struck him foursquare in the face.

'Put that on, you rank savage!' shrilled Mirag from the hob. One hand on her hip, she stood pouring water from the kettle into her battered wash tub. 'The girl is upstairs, still, but when she comes down, I won't have her exposed to your scars and your outlandish nakedness.'

Mykkael tipped his head past the greenery. He surveyed the maroon cloth of the advocate's cloak puddled on freshly mopped floorboards, and stated, 'I won't wear that.'

'You will,' Mirag argued. Her puffed eyes saw red.

'She's convinced the child will take fright at the sight of you,' Benj apologized, coarse-grained with tiredness. He sat on the floor at the side of his son, who now whimpered in fretful pain. 'Bend foreign pride and cover yourself, will you?'

Mykkael limped around the offensive garment, crouched down an arm's length from Mirag, and tossed his cut greenery into the fire. He spoke with his back turned, dark skin marked across by the well-soiled strips of Jussoud's resin dressings. 'No. I will not. Fetch back my surcoat and trousers. I don't care a damn if they're reeking of garbage.'

Mirag's glower suggested her ire on the subject was not going to be placated for any man.

'That cloak has a hood,' Benj pleaded, reasonable. 'The disguise could help your survival.'

Limned by the haze of plumed smoke as the evergreen sparked into flame, Mykkael shot to his feet. His eyes glittered, wide open and wild, and the set to his shoulders stayed adamant. 'I won't wear that, I tell you, though I died this second! The cloth bears the taint of a sorcerer's touch, a fine point that's lethal to compromise.' He moved, snapped up the fire tong, and used the glowing hot tip to jam the offending garment into the cedar-laced flames.

Then he stood on his rankled dignity and added, 'You can hand me a second-rate blanket.'

Mirag glared back at him. 'A blanket's too good, you uncivilized madman.' Shaken to the brink of hysteria, she shouted down his astonished, hurt protest. 'Whatever you touch won't be left fit for rags, with you reeking of fox piss and bear scat. Climb into this tub and scrub yourself down. When you're clean, we can talk about clothing.'

Mykkael drove his limping step to the wash tub, wet his finger, and flicked a sizzling droplet to test the heat in the fire iron. 'I'll bathe for you later,' he suggested, calmed at one breath as he grasped the denial that caused Mirag to fixate on trivia. No comfort held the power to ease what her instincts already told her.

Her boy on the floorboards was dying.

'Benj,' Mykkael urged with the utmost soft clarity, 'please lend me your help. If we don't stop the bleeding, there's no chance at all. Let Timal not go without trying to save him.'

The poacher clung to his son's chalk-pale hand. 'You know what you're doing? You've done this before?'

Mykkael shut his eyes, swallowed. 'In war. On the battlefield, more times than I wish to recount.'

He chose not to broach the imperative precaution, that when he was done, the cottage and all of its unsalvaged contents must be burned to the ground. He had not survived three conflicts with sorcerers without learning the bitter necessities. Lacking the permanent presence of wards, or the protections afforded by talismans, he could not shield Benj or his family from the enemy's arcane scryers. That left no choice but to eradicate every last shred of evidence that the patrol sent by Devall had come here. Fire laced with green cedar must cleanse the trace imprint of the recent dead, and all that remained of the corpse of a catspaw, infused flesh and bone by the deadly, left sign of a sorcerer's lines of compulsion.

Day wore away, and sundown had faded to twilight, with Jussoud still unable to share Mykkael's warning message with the learned physician from Fane Street. The strain of that urgency wore at his patience. He opened the curtains, while the early stars burned above the high peaks of the ranges. The gold flare of kerrie fires plumed against the indigo sky as the creatures soared through their aerial hunt on outstretched, scimitar wings. While darkness gathered, and lights from the palace spilled through the boughs of the cherry trees, Jussoud listened to the draw of Taskin's breath. He noted small signs of improvement. The rhythm had strengthened, with the depth of each inhalation approaching the reflex of natural sleep.

Encouraged, the healer made rounds to brighten the candle lamps. He weighed the risks, undecided whether he should snatch the brief chance to slip out. Taskin's delicate state still demanded attendance. The dosage of remedies and herbals required constant adjustment to keep pace with each shift in his life signs.

Vensic's watch at the door could not address setbacks, and Lindya's adamant vigil forestalled every chance to summon the physician in privacy.

Time passed. The windows darkened. Jussoud nursed his silent, agonized fears, until the opportune servant sent up from the nursery asked Lindya to help settle her son.

'Go, lady,' the nomad was quick to assure her. 'Right now, your father's condition is improving. Your child needs you far more. You could help most by retiring to the nursery, and showing a composed face to the household.'

Lindya stirred in the looming shadow by the bedside. Deep-set weariness and heart-torn appeal conflicted her delicate features. 'You won't leave the room?'

'Rely on that.' Jussoud arranged his lamps on the marquetry table used for a makeshift pharmacy. He sorted through his herb packets and tinctures, and began the demanding, meticulous process of mixing an elixir by the eastern method of imprinting subtle substance as catalyst into the essence of water. 'If you're worried, you could do me the favour of calling for the physician. He mentioned earlier he had obscure knowledge that might speed your father's recovery.'

Released from her quandary of pained indecision, Taskin's daughter left with the servant. Jussoud waited, using the fixed steps of his recipe to constrain his scalding impatience.

The physician arrived shortly, pink-cheeked and alert, but lacking his usual ebullience. His greeting to Vensic was perfunctory, and his cautious manner as he latched the door bespoke his masked agitation.

'I don't like the complacency shown by this court,' he opened point-blank. 'The crown council and the palace guard have no concept to fit the gravity of their situation.' He pushed up his spectacles and rubbed tired eyes, then added in embarrassed afterthought, 'Your lancers downstairs are recovering nicely. I think by tomorrow two can be released into the care of their families.'

'Actually, my primary concern was the lack of sound wardings,' Jussoud reassured him. 'That's why we need to consult.' Finished counting the requisite droplets of essence into a phial of purified water, he lifted silver eyes from his work and shared a glance of suggestive gravity.

The physician fielded that wordless appeal. He closed the short distance from doorway to table, all the while maintaining the thread of casual conversation. 'You know eastern remedies?' His interest stayed genuine as he surveyed the array of fine essences, sealed in their blown-glass jars. 'Which school? Indussian?'

'The same.' Jussoud's shut eyes expressed his relief, as he corked the fresh tincture and began to agitate the contents, shaking the solution end for end for a count of one hundred strokes. 'I also have notebooks compiled by the seers of the Pinca.'

The physician pulled up a rush-seat chair. 'Now there's a rare body of scholarship. My own notes are sketchy. I'd appreciate the chance to share knowledge.'

Jussoud managed the briefest of smiles. 'You'd be welcome. Do you read Pinca?'

'Not as fluently as I'd like.' The physician heaved a

soulful sigh, his thinning hair like floss in the dimness. 'I used to have Mykkael help translate.'

Granted his circumspect opening, the eastern-bred nomad lowered his voice and explained the gist of the message the discredited desertman had sent by means of the saddlecloth.

The physician listened through to the finish, unblinking. 'Blinding glory!' he whispered. 'Why under the light of the risen sun hasn't anyone acted?'

'Ignorance.' Jussoud uncapped the phial in hand, selected a clean dropper, and proceeded to measure the next sequence of dilution into a fresh measure of water. 'The rote habit that clouds human nature,' he concluded in saddened disgust, 'sealed into fixed orders by Captain Bennent's distrust.'

The physician crossed his arms as though chilled. 'You do realize there was purpose behind every one of Mykkael's instructions? The western viziers have written that Perincar's markings hold mathematical properties. Their geometry will guard the bearer independently, but also, they're said to cast a ring of protection that grows in exponential proportion when assembled in multiples of three.'

Jussoud all but faltered the count of his next agitation. Lips tight with worry, he withheld from comment until the last hundred strokes of his remedy were complete. 'Mykkael left us eight, under warded protection.' Then he set down his phial with dawning dismay. 'The captain himself was the ninth, don't you see? Or has he not shown you the pattern that Perincar tattooed at the nape of his neck?'

The physician stood up. 'Well, he's set on the run as a fugitive, now, sealed under a legal death warrant. Truth be told, his prospects look poor.' His quick wit observed that the nomad perceived every daunting political obstacle: that the crown prince was too green to handle the council, and the seneschal too hidebound to see past the blandishment dangled before Sessalie's landlocked trade. 'It's not canny. That young peacock from Devall still has his retainers out scouring the countryside. Everyone seems convinced that Mykkael's hand harmed the princess. His Highness's anger's inflamed to the point where I fear the crown's archers will shoot on first sight.'

'Only Taskin might stop them.' Grim as cold iron, Jussoud set his new remedy on a tray. He added a clean glass dropper, and moved to attend the unconscious charge in his care. 'As things stand, we are helpless targets. I think King Isendon will be lost, and each of us will be dead, if we can't find some way to enact the precautions Mykkael sent us in warning.'

'You wrote them down, Jussoud?'

Both nomad and healer stopped short between thoughts. For the words, faint but clear, had issued from amid the pillows of Taskin's sickbed.

XXI. Setbacks

The nomad dropped to his knees with a startled cry, and all but scattered his neat tray of medicine. '*Taskin*?'

Better poised without the heart's burden of friendship, the Fane Street physician bore the candle lamp towards the invalid on the bed. Under the golden spill of the light, the commander's grey eyes were open.

'You still trust that desert-bred, *after this*?' Though weak, the whispered demand was imperious. '*Tell me why*.'

'Gently,' Jussoud chided him. Quick to recover his sensible equilibrium, he set his remedies aside on a footstool. 'I could ask what made you try the stupidity of attempting Mykkael's arrest without backing.' He touched the pale forehead, found no fever, then added, 'If you rest, and maintain a slow convalescence, your sword arm could heal without damage.'

Yet if he expected the hopeful prognosis to disarm the commander's suspicion, Taskin rejected all inclination to settle in peaceful relief.

Jussoud cut off his strained effort to speak. He brandished the dropper of remedy, then smiled as the familiar, irascible spark enlivened the commander's wide eyes. 'This won't make you sleep, I assure you.'

The physician adjusted the lamp, also carefully gauging the response of the wounded man's pupils. He added, helpful, 'The essence has no sour taste, and will only help build your strength.'

Taskin gave way, too depleted to argue. His glower of forbearance stayed fixed on the ceiling, while he suffered the nomad to slip the remedy under his tongue. Once the dosing was finished, his husked voice seemed fractionally stronger. 'Kaien's *do'aa*. The garrison captain was proved forsworn. Devall's interfering marshal brought evidence.'

'You never asked why? By the stars of my ancestry, I thought so!' Jussoud settled back on his heels. He gathered Taskin's left hand, and laid finger to wrist to measure the pulse. 'Now listen to me. No excitement, understand? Your condition is fragile. We are blessed to have you wakened and lucid, but you cannot withstand undue stress.'

Taskin's wax forehead pinched into a frown. 'You want my backing to salvage that desert-bred?' The pale eyes flicked sideways, still furious. 'Then speak for him.'

Jussoud bowed his head. 'Mykkael forswore Kaien's *do'aa* for the death of a child.' In measured phrases, he explained the particulars, while the silence grew thick enough to suffocate.

Taskin stared straight ahead. His chest rose and fell. The raced pulse under Jussoud's tacit touch fluttered light as a moth's wing. When speech came at last, the scraped words were reduced as the rustle of breeze through a feather. 'Mykkael would have entered the second master's *do'aa* under a false claim of autonomy.'

'He had to.' The nomad swallowed and closed his vibrant clasp over the commander's fingers. No glance could he spare for the stilled presence of the physician from Fane Street. His eastern voice remained firm as he resumed a discussion that must turn revealingly private. 'The master who finally finished Mykkael's training was the only man living who knew the technique to curb the conditioning of *barqui'ino* reflex. His *do'aa* alone taught the sequence to allow a roused warrior to stop short of a killing blow.'

'"*An awkwardness no one admits,*" Mykkael told me.' Taskin's confession emerged with demanding effort. 'That was his fair wording, when he affirmed his past course of study under two masters.' The commander attempted to turn his head, prevented by Jussoud's quick restraint before the move pulled at his bandages. The ascetic face on the pillow grimaced, ripped by sorrow too late to redress. 'I was wrong,' Taskin finished. 'The Captain of the Garrison never once lied to me as his senior officer.'

'They have not made his capture,' Jussoud assured him, an inadequate effort at solace. 'He will have gone on to save Sessalie's princess with all the resource he has left.'

Taskin's expression showed wounding remorse. For in fact, the direct order given to Mykkael in his audience with King Isendon *had been to do all in his power to safeguard the life of the princess.*

Taskin sucked a taxed breath, the spirit that infused his faltering flesh fanned to incandescent resolve. 'Get me to the king. I don't care how.'

The distressed physician dimmed back the lamp, and broke silence to offer a warning. 'If we try to move you, please understand, you're likely to slip into a coma.' The anxious glance he shared with Jussoud underscored the life-threatening risk, that if the wound tore and started fresh bleeding, additional dehydration and shock would foreclose any chance of recovery.

Yet Taskin rejected the prudence of cosseting. He would but argue, and waste precious strength. The sorcerer's plot would not rest through the pause for a stricken man's health to be guarded.

Jussoud matched his friend's courage, his demeanour grim as hammered gold in the flame light. 'If we do this, you realize, your daughter Lindya is going to claw us to shreds.'

Taskin shut his eyes, adamant. 'Strap me to a plank with

a sheet overtop. Damn well claim I'm dead if you have to! Keep me here, and the fact I am wearing a talisman will draw in a pre-emptive attack. This house and its occupants would suffer the brunt!' A bald truth, followed hard by another, as bitter. 'Nobody else can force Captain Bennent to reverse his misguided decision.' Taskin opened his eyes again, pleading. 'Jussoud, you must! For Sessalie's security, *we have no choice*! You have to help me carry through Mykkael's instructions to safeguard the life of the king.'

An hour's tense labour saw the poacher's young son strapped in bandages, and wrapped under layers of warmed blankets. If his colour looked grey, and his breathing stayed clogged, the emergency cautery had accomplished its desperate office. No more flushed blood bubbled from the boy's mouth. He would rally from shock; or he wouldn't.

While Benj scrounged up canvas and poles for a litter, Mirag flitted about like a gadfly, gathering untidy piles of provisions, and fretfully hovering beside Timal. Throughout, the male target of her railing tongue maintained his unruffled composure: Mykkael perched on the settle and attended the neglected wound in his thigh. A patter of curses hissed through his teeth as, head bent, he cast aside the cut reed just used to flush out the puncture. He tipped back his head, waited with fixed patience for the wave of fresh pain to subside.

'You think we're daft, or just dumb as squabs to swallow such outright foolishness?' Mirag upended a basket of leeks to fish out the one turned with rot. 'Do as you say, and Timal will perish for certain.'

The desert-bred she accosted stayed tolerant. 'Timal should not be moved,' he admitted, point blank. 'But if he stays here, if you choose not to abandon the cottage, every one of you will lose much worse than your lives. This I promise.'

His conviction left no room for ambiguity. 'This site has

been fouled by a sorcerer's long spell. When I go, the wardings I carry move with me. Would you leave your family at risk, stripped of every protection? Unless you allow me to banish the last trace imprints with fire, you will be tracked down. Such a creature will have a bound scryer.'

'Mirag, please, we can't argue.' Benj looked up from lacing a patched length of canvas to a litter pole, his eyes overshadowed by lingering fear. He had lost more than his son's carefree health to the unclean works of the enemy. The trauma of his narrow escape from the horrific force of a spell line might not, now, ever leave him.

'The sorcerer will dispatch a minion, or worse, when his catspaw fails to return.' Mykkael could not mourn what had already passed. As a warrior, he turned the sum of his skills to salvage the course of the future. 'Unless drastic steps of prevention are taken, an etheric trail of disturbance will remain. A sorcerer will use that cold trail to bind you, the same way he snared Devall's advocate.'

Clad in one of Benj's castoff nightshirts, the desertman stretched out his hurt leg and tested the mash of warmed herbs just prepared for a drawing compress. Each move methodical, he slathered the paste over the swollen puncture. Then he rinsed his hands in a bucket, and bound up the wound in clean cloth.

'If I survive to clear my reputation, and if Sessalie remains free of conquest, I promise to see that you receive the crown's fair restitution for damages. You have your dogs, and the pay I left, meanwhile. That should be enough to sustain you.' Mykkael knotted the ends of the bandage, looked up with his insolent smile, and finished, 'You buried the coin, Mirag? It's safely concealed somewhere outside the cottage?'

She ignored him, offended, and folded her arms, well braced for the irate glare from her husband. 'There's no more secure place, Benj! I dug out a hidey hole under the mastiff's barrel.'

Yet the fact the poacher looked mollified did nothing to appease her attacking rancour towards Mykkael. 'What about Timal?'

'See him settled with the nearest trustworthy neighbour. Then send to the physician on Fane Street. His assistant, Cafferty, is competent with wounds. Ask him to visit the boy's bedside.' Mykkael stood up, tested his scarred knee, then sat down again. He borrowed upon Jussoud's example and used more binding to wind a support wrap. As he worked, he continued his effort to wear down the goodwife's hostility. 'Tell the physician's man that Sergeant Vensic at the garrison will see his fee paid from my personal funds.'

'Go to the *garrison*? Are you mad?' Benj paused in the act of tying off the sewn canvas. 'My boy was cut down for a criminal act!'

Mykkael looked up, uncompromising. 'No, Benj. This day, Timal fell as a hero, serving my loyal oath to the king. If Isendon's reign withstands this assault, and Sessalie endures to find triumph, make no mistake. Your family's strength and hard sacrifice will have played a vital part.'

Mirag dropped the onions she had been sorting. They rolled helter skelter over the tabletop as she reached out on shocked impulse, and touched Mykkael on the forearm. 'Wait, please, one moment.' Then she bolted upstairs, wiping the moisture that welled up in her eyes.

While Mykkael stared after her, mystified, Benj slapped his knee with relieved satisfaction.

'Oh, I knew she'd come round, the old besom. Sure enough, the wife's had your clothes washed for you all along. They'll be strung out to dry in the attic.'

Yet when Mirag returned with her burden, the cloth had been tidied beyond cleaning. Plain shirt and breeches were ironed and folded. The falcon-crest surcoat lay piled on top, painstakingly mended and crisp. She heaped her offering onto the settle, then smoothed down the swatch cut from Jussoud's silk sash, its intricate embroidery pressed flat.

'I've told Benj,' she forestalled before Mykkael could thank her, 'if he's going to keep bringing me shirts marked with bloodstains, I'd ease the brute work, and dye his light linen with walnut.'

The boots and sword harness she thrust into the captain's hands were freshly oiled and gleaming, with the desert-bred now the one forced to mask his fierce upsurge of gratitude.

'I've been expertly humbled,' he said as he dressed, donned and buckled his harness, then sheathed his sword at rest over his shoulder.

'You men never stay that way more than a minute.' Mirag kept her back turned, although he was clad. Yet this time she did not shrink from his presence as he assisted with packing the rations.

Preparations were finished with whirlwind expediency, with foodstuffs, hunting bows and selected necessities cleansed with sprinkled salt, then run through a hazing of cedar smoke. Mykkael ran testing fingers over each separate item until he was satisfied that no taint of the sorcerer's working remained. Then he strapped the provisions on to two of the horses and helped load the wrapped boy in the litter. The girl was fetched down from her bed in the attic. Crying with confusion, she was bundled outside to join the forlorn family gathered with Mykkael in the yard.

'Go,' he said, urgent. 'Don't stop to look back, for your lives' sake. I'll shoulder the needful work with the fire, then ride escort and see that you reach your friends safely.'

The seneschal paced up and down the plush carpet, a crow in dark robes against the gilt and white furnishings that appointed the salon maintained for state guests. His emphatic fingers stabbed at the air as he railed, while the high prince sat with his lace sleeves turned back, elbows braced on a marble tabletop.

The heir apparent of Devall still wore his briar-scratched

boots, though servants had taken his soiled shirt at the door and reclothed him in damascened silk. They had added an earring with a teardrop ruby. The jewel dangled like snap-frozen flame, with no jaunty suggestion of swinging. Such leashed stillness, beside the seneschal's ranting, showed a preternatural patience.

Crown Prince Kailen, who also observed, was not fooled. From the comfort of the room's cushioned windowseat, he recognized the dangerous, self-contained fury of a hunting cat balked of its prey.

'What you say points towards a deep-seated conspiracy,' the Prince of Devall interjected.

The seneschal stopped short. He stared at the foreign prince, horrified. 'Commander *Taskin*? Betray King Isendon or Sessalie? That's not possible!'

The high prince tapped his fingertips one after another to a rippling sparkle of rings. 'That's the impression a clever conspirator would surely hope to convey. Or the opposite. Taskin might have been loyal, until something changed him. Don't forget, he was alone in the mist with that slinking desertman. Nobody actually saw what occurred, though I've heard enough ugly rumours. Were there not wooden stakes strung over the ground from the practice of some unclean rite?'

The seneschal digested that statement, flummoxed as though he had just burned his tongue on a sherbet. 'The Commander of the Guard was half killed by a sword cut, not sorcery.' He tugged his robe about his bowed shoulders, as though brushed by a sudden chill. 'Captain Bennent himself saw the wound.'

Devall's heir apparent glanced towards Prince Kailen, then sighed with quiet forbearance. 'I keep forgetting I need to explain what should be painfully obvious. Your people here have too little awareness of how a sorcerer works. Taskin possessed an upright, strong character. To bind his will and make him a subservient catspaw could be easily done if he was in a weakened state, or unconsciousness.

Your desert-bred shaman would have had his trap well laid and waiting. Once he had Taskin alone and at his mercy, what better way to mask a conversion than to give his victim what looked like a life-threatening sword wound?'

'I do find this odd,' Prince Kailen ventured. 'Two carriages bearing the commander's daughter and servants passed through the Highgate an hour ago.' Since the afternoon's hue and cry after Mykkael, he had bathed and changed, then spent a watchful interlude easing his parched throat at a wine shop. 'To judge by the baggage I saw strapped to the roof, the household seemed bound for retreat to the family duchy.'

'Why send them on such a hard journey at night?' The seneschal made way with bad grace for the servant just arrived to refresh the candles. 'I've seen no sign at all that violence might arise inside the walls of the citadel.'

'But you won't see the crude gesture of blood in the streets!' the High Prince of Devall said with high feeling. 'Since your crown prince was denied legal power as regent, one strike at King Isendon would give our enemy his foothold to break the succession. While your chancellors scrabble to sort out the confusion, an invading sorcerer would simply step into the breach.' Rings sparked gold fire to a snap of fine fingers. 'Like that, he would topple the kingdom.'

'A bizarre flight of fancy,' the seneschal scoffed. 'Particularly since Taskin has been at death's door ever since this morning's attack. The court ladies who helped tend the wounded insist that he's never stirred from his bed.'

'This afternoon, maybe,' Prince Kailen broke in. 'But what, pray, do you make of that?'

His gesture encompassed the view through the window, which overlooked the main thoroughfare, where the paved avenue branched off to meet the arch of the palace entrance. There, a small, guarded portal led into the royal grounds from the streetside. Beyond lay the sequestered preserve of the late queen's hothouse and gardens. From there, if a man knew the warren of buildings and byways, and could speak the right words to the guard, a roundabout route could give access to King Isendon's private chambers.

'You should take a look,' Devall's High Prince challenged. 'What harm, if my fears are proved wrong?'

The seneschal unbent and stalked over the carpet. Making no effort to hide condescension, he peered past the crown prince's shoulder and saw the tightly knit threesome bearing the litter as they passed under the gate lamp. The jet fall of Jussoud's tribal braid caught his eye, as words were exchanged with the posted sentry. Then the sheet which covered the litter was turned back. The pressured guardsman gave way at first sight. When he slipped the bar, granting the party admittance, even the seneschal's stuffy façade cracked into consternation.

'What's happening?' demanded the heir apparent from his imperious seat at the table.

Prince Kailen turned his head, no longer amused. 'A setback, your Highness. Two foreign healers, and a Lowergate man masked in a palace guard surcoat appear to be taking Lord Taskin by the back way to King Isendon's apartment.'

'My*sh*kael's creatures, all of them.' The high prince fixed his scalding regard on the seneschal. 'Do you need further proof? Or will you and your chancellors continue to dither, while a wolf pack of low-born, outland conspirators attempt an assault on your king?'

Mykkael dragged the dead bodies indoors, then followed with their assortment of horsecloths and trappings. He made his work thorough: affixed bundles of cedar to each door, each shuttered window, and at the four corners of the condemned cottage. He had just kindled the torch to fire the thatch when the first of the loose hounds straggled in. The dogs knew him. They harkened to his voice, bounding in through the darkness to fawn in a muddle at his feet. He paused long enough to fasten their chains, then resumed his grim rounds with the torch.

War had well taught him the business of reiving. The greedy pattern of fires he seeded rippled over the cottage, then consumed roof and plank with a roar. By the time the conflagration slacked off, naught would be left of the home of a friend, but a scorched patch of carbon, with not one stump of timber left standing, and only the chimney stones left as a shell.

Mykkael spared no second thought for regret, that Benj and Mirag might never forgive him. The couple had left with their daughter unharmed, and a wounded son still gamely breathing. Were they lucky, they might live for the rest of their days, weeping tears for those sorrows that decently ended with death. If they cursed his name, Mykkael had no balm for the blame their torn hearts might lay on him. He watched the crackle of cleansing fires, and prayed for Mehigrannia's mercy, that the poacher's family should never experience the evil that could enslave a human spirit beyond mortal life.

At the finish, assured by the quiescent chill of his sword hilt that no such untoward power ranged at large, Mykkael led the remaining three horses out of the covert thicket. He unshackled the hounds, then called them to heel, and mounted bareback and rode on his way.

The lanes by that hour were nearly deserted. He was able to cover ground swiftly. If lategoing wayfarers were wont to stare, nightfall mantled his features. Under wan stars and the setting new moon, a hound pack accompanied by a garrison surcoat made him seem just another diligent searcher, empty-handed and homeward-bound. He overtook Benj's family beyond the first crossroad, to the garrulous joy of the pack, and more tears from Mirag as she noticed the smell of smoke that clung to his hair and clothing.

'Come, now,' urged Mykkael. He dismounted, passed

the ends of the hackamores to the girl, who was leading the two laden horses. Then, while the mastiff bitch nosed at his boots, he commandeered Mirag's end of the litter, and insistently pressed for more speed. 'You've got to move on, Benj. Believe me, you can't risk a moment's delay.'

When the girl tired of walking, Mykkael boosted her on to a horse, and cajoled Mirag to take charge of the lead ropes. He saw the bedraggled family of four safe to the house of the charcoalman's wife before moonset.

Mirag and the children were hastened inside, folded into warm blankets and sympathy. Benj lingered in the dank chill of the yard, his black-and-tan hounds piled in heaps at his feet, and his flaying tongue suddenly tied. He had always been clumsy at leave-taking.

Mykkael was obliged to speak for them both. 'Keep a lit fire with cedar greens, always! Do you hear, Benj? Except for your errand to Fane Street, for the boy's sake, promise me you'll keep close.'

The grizzled poacher sucked in a shivering breath, for the first time in his criminal life uneasy in shadows and darkness. 'You need not convince me,' he said in cracked fear. 'It's Mirag who won't bear things quietly.'

'Then handle her.' Mykkael grinned. 'She's no worse, really, than your ornery mastiff. Feed her with kindness, she'll be placated.' His dark face turned serious. 'I have one last favour to ask in the name of Sessalie's princess. Benj, can you loan me the use of your lead hound?'

Benj looked at him, dumbstruck. 'You want Dalshie? For what? To track that forsaken boy and his horses, that almost cost Timal his life?' When the desert-bred failed to soften, he cursed. 'Perish your ancestry, foreigner, not Dalshie! She's the breath and the life in my veins!'

'I need her,' Mykkael said, his voice flint-struck iron. 'Crown requisition, or as a brave favour done by the hand of a friend. Or is the life of her Grace not worth your best dog? If Princess Anja is claimed by the sorcerer whose catspaw just glancingly touched you, I can't begin to describe the horrors that might befall her by morning. This I can promise, at bitter, first hand. Your fair land of Sessalie will be crushed by conquest. The good people you know will suffer an evil beyond your most terrible nightmares.'

'Go! Mykkael, go now! I can't bear to watch.' Shoulders bowed, old Benj turned his back. His eyes stayed averted, bitter and streaming. Nor did he give way to heartbreak and plead. He stood like a rock as the captain called Dalshie, and the dog, ever true to her gallant, long lineage, left her pack to answer his perilous summons.

'She's already exhausted,' Benj insisted, unmoving, his arms folded over his chest. Savaged beyond comfort, he received the softly spoken answer.

'I know, Benj. I'll not spend her carelessly.'

Mykkael chose the fittest pair of dark geldings, and the laden one bearing his choice of provisions. He knotted their lead lines, then mounted and whistled for Dalshie. As she leaped at his leg, he caught her by the scruff and hauled her up into his lap. Then he dug in his heels with no shred of mercy, and drove headlong from the yard.

The princess's flight had turned straight upcountry from Farmer Gurley's unkempt back meadow. Mykkael made his way avoiding the road. Where his knowledge of the landmarks fell short, he was guided by the poacher's description of the game trails that led to the alpine meadows where cattle were grazed in the summer. Few patrols searched the deep woods, after dark. Of those he encountered, none expected a fugitive to be outbound from town at this hour. Guardsmen from the Highgate disdained to question a rider wearing garrison colours, particularly one ploughing through brush and briar apt to tear the fine cloth of their surcoats. The one who called a query across a field accepted his shout concerning remounts for some officer whose horse had gone lame. The hound was excused as an animal sick with exhaustion.

The patrols from the keep had been dispatched by

Jedrey, whose sheltered mind held poor grasp of strategy in rough country. The easier ground had been assigned to his favourites. Those given the harder sweeps in the hills rode in predictable patterns, which let Mykkael slip through with an ease he should have found shameful. He had night to lend cover, and mounts with dark coats. Forest shadow and moonset helped mask him.

He pressed upwards at a relentless fast clip. When his first mount flagged under him, he dismounted, slipped the headstall and vaulted on to the spare one. Then he set off again, the hound trotting on foot. The packhorse laboured, winded, behind him.

The rising ground showed the first spurs of grey rock, mantled with copses of fir trees. Mykkael clung to the verges, where the blanket of shed needles would keep the horses' shod hooves from striking chance sparks. He felt as though eyes watched his back at each step; as they might, if an enemy lurked in Dedorth's observatory and commandeered use of the seeing glass.

As Mykkael gained altitude, the game trails narrowed, until the faint tracks that snaked through the thickets would not allow passage for horses. The captain picked his way up the gulches carved by spring snowmelt. His mount clattered over the deposits of loose rock. The scratches its iron shoes chalked on the stone left a beacon for a sharp tracker. Yet no time could be spared for stealth. One catspaw destroyed would just prompt an adept sorcerer to create another to stand in his place. The crown's archers would know where their shot struck down Timal. Inside a matter of hours, or less, more searchers were bound to ascend.

Mykkael had no weapon beyond flight and speed in his race to find Princess Anja before them.

He reined his horse down another steep bank, spurred into the froth of a freshet, and there, the riptide of witch thought overwhelmed him . . .

* * *

He was Jussoud, bearing the poles of a litter down a path in the palace garden. Awareness chilled him, that his grass sandals were making more noise than he wished. Behind him, the Fane Street physician glanced side to side, rabbit-scared, the nervous shine off his spectacles glancing against the black shapes of the topiary. Vensic's tiger-soft tread moved at his left flank, each step taken with stalking wariness.

'We should hurry,' the young sergeant whispered. 'Something's not canny. The crickets are too quiet.'

Which fact was not new, to Jussoud's steppe-trained ear. He kept his tread steady. Although every instinct urged him to run, he held out, unwilling to risk unwise haste that might jostle Taskin's hurt shoulder.

The next moment, brisk footsteps approached down the path. The way ahead came alive with the jingle of spurs, and the chance shine of weapons by starlight. Four palace guardsmen accompanied the robed form of a council chancellor.

'Set Taskin down!' Jussoud cried, words scored by the metallic scrape as Vensic cleared his sword from his scabbard.

Then the talisman worn at his chest came alive, tingling with active warning . . .

'No!' Mykkael cried, 'Vensic, no! Don't attack!'

For the garrison man had no shred of protection. If he stayed with the companions minding the litter, he had a chance to be saved. The copper discs worn by the others would cast a limited field of protection. Drawn as passive talismans, their pattern would shield, but could not counterward an assaulting spell engaged in an active attack.

'Vensic, hold!' Mykkael whispered, anguished by his helplessness. He had seen too much horror: *the boldest and best of his field troop most hideously destroyed, one after the next, by the binding lines spun by Rathtet.*

If this latest officer engaged his brave sword, if in armed defence he made contact, he would perish, the consumed prey of a sorcerer's long spell.

Yet shouted words could not bridge the separation; a

witch thought lent no saving power to warn.

Mykkael broke out of unruly, tranced vision, reeling back into himself with a wrench that left him gasping and sick. For a moment he could do nothing but cling to the sweat-dampened crest of his mount. While grief and distress ran him through like live fire, he recontained his shocked nerves, thrust back upright, and pressed the horse onwards.

Distraction could not matter; death and sorrow could not claim even tears of acknowledgement. Jussoud, who was brother, and Vensic, who was protégé, and Taskin, who held his respect, and not least, the meek physician who displayed such terrified courage – all must suffer their fates without salvage. One man and a dog bore Isendon's charge to safeguard a royal daughter. Now, nothing less than the peace of a kingdom rode on the unwritten outcome.

Mykkael forged ahead, though he ached for the price of necessity. Since the disastrous defeat of Prince Al-Syn-Efandi, he had fought to bury his wounded heart in sealed solitude. Sessalie's peace had leached through that resolve. His circle of newly forged friendships had made inroads, and were now, yet again, all he had resembling a family.

'Benj, Benj,' he whispered, torn ragged, while the gelding splashed and scrambled up the ravine. 'I always understood how you felt about Dalshie.'

How much harder to bear, when the next sacrifice claimed was likely to be a perceptive and talented young sergeant.

XXII. Assault

THE ODD SENSE OF URGENCY REACHED OUT OF NOWHERE AND SEIZED JUSSOUD BY THE HEART. HE HAD BEEN BORN to a tribal tradition that honoured the unseen world known to shamans. On trust and impulse, he moved at speed, grabbed Vensic's surcoat and yanked backwards with all of his strength.

The garrison man's attacking lunge was jerked short. The brisk parry effected by his crown guard opponent whistled short of connection.

Vensic crashed off balance into Jussoud's braced shoulder, shouting his outraged surprise. There, the huge nomad pinned him, just as the rising spell line fully unfurled. The three men guarding Taskin's downed litter came under attack by a crackling explosion of fire. The shielding geometry written into three talismans turned its brute force, deflecting the thrust from the party surrounding the litter. No natural conflagration, the licking whirlwind that engulfed them seemed to feed upon nothing but air.

Enveloped by the shrieking noise and scalding heat of a shredding assault, besieged by a relentless power that surged to consume, Jussoud screamed into Vensic's ear, 'Cross that flame with a blade, you're a dead man!' He kept his arms locked until the young man's furious struggle subsided to understanding. Then the healer added, 'Take up the litter and give me your sword.'

Trained touch countermanded the stiff surge of resistance. 'Now!' Jussoud cried. 'No argument, Vensic! I carry protection. You don't hand me your weapon, we die here.'

The spelled fire closed in. Its uncanny, mindless surge to destroy ripped and seared with a savagery beyond parallel. The thin ring sustained by Perincar's defences withstood the onslaught, just barely. Its limited range hemmed them in like trapped rats. Such tight shielding could not ground the roused force of the element, or break the cast line of demonic power summoned in from the shadow realms of the unseen. Fire howled and raged, balked but not quenched. Its heat would scorch cloth and peel skin, if not scald the lungs with each drawn breath. By now the Fane Street physician was shouting with ragged hysteria.

Vensic released the sword, just as Jussoud's fierce yank wrenched the weapon's grip from his hand. 'Bear up the litter,' the nomad gasped, frantic. 'Then stay at my heels. Rely on the vizier's pattern we carry, no matter what mayhem should happen!'

Jussoud shouldered ahead. The blade in his grasp was an ill-suited match, too small and too lightly balanced. The swords he had used to train on the steppe had been curved, forged with more weight at the tip to make slashing strokes more effective. Sanouk warriors always wielded such weapons in pairs. One blade left him hamstrung and guardless.

Worse, the nomad dared not pause to mourn his broken integrity. He must cast off the grace of his healer's oath, that forbore to cause harm through violence. A failure to act would destroy three more lives, with the innocent populace of a whole kingdom left to the plot of a sorcerer.

Either the geometry worked into the talisman could withstand the line of spell-cast destruction, or within seconds, Taskin's protectors would succumb to a fate beyond horror to imagine. Standing firm was no option. Delay would see them all roasted. Jussoud closed his eyes, stepped forward, and *trusted*: first the defences Mykkael had left, that had once held strong through all but the worst lines of hot conjury spun by Rathtet's bound sorcerers. The nomad relied on his tribal ancestry, that understood the deep realms of the spirit world. Last, he fell back upon childhood training, that had taught him the warrior's way of the sword.

The effort to walk was like ploughing into a padded wall. Resistance arose at the interface, where the talisman's guarding influence ran against the hurled balefires summoned by cold-struck spell lines. Jussoud firmed his will and leaned into the pressure.

'Stay with me. Follow!' he gasped, then blessed the response as the others rallied behind him. Sterling result of Mykkael's tempered discipline, Vensic had managed to calm the physician. The pair of them resumed the delicate task of bearing up Taskin's litter.

Jussoud pressed forward, and the fire line shifted. The combined advance of three matched vizier's talismans pressed into the gyre of spelled forces and yielded a grudging span of clear ground. Another thrust forward, another hard step. Each footfall felt set in glue. Jussoud steeled his courage, and leaned on the strength of his nomad heritage. He was the son of a Sanouk royal house, born to an ancient and honourable ancestry. Through closed eyes, using mind, he groped for the shape of the otherworld, the unseen context of subtle energies that underlay the solid existence known to the animate senses.

He expanded his awareness outside human flesh. Across the first veil, he encountered the desperation and fear mirrored by his committed companions, then their more subdued counterpart: the one man, gravely wounded, lying helplessly unconscious. Jussoud traced out the ephemeral threads, where his thoughts and theirs ran in sympathy. He used mental imagery to refigure the weave, where jeopardy spun common lines of need and survival. Then he embraced those strands shared by his companions, mentally wound them into his own, and projected the flow of them forward. He angled their matrix to strengthen the forces that actively stood off the fires; and Perincar's pattern captured that willed influx, and flowered, and resurged to a blaze of cold blue.

The fires roared and fell back. Streaming sparks, and flaring in unnatural colours, the aimed brunt of the long spell yielded. The barrier gave way in grudging retreat as Jussoud pressed his advance. He gained one step, two, over stinking, charred earth. Heat blistered his soles. He stamped out the flare of caught embers as his grass-soled sandals ignited.

The next moment, Jussoud sensed a sharp shift in the hostile conjury. Deflected by the reverse spin of Perincar's geometry, the line of demonic attack streamed into live contact with the thrusting steel of two sword blades as the lead pair of palace guardsmen bore in on the misguided chancellor's order.

Their blades flared up, instantaneously consumed. The flash of ignition raised tearing screams, as the nexus of otherworldly destruction flowed across the bridged steel, and claimed the hapless men holding the weapons.

Their suffering described unimaginable agony. The Fire, elemental, unbound living matter. It left not a wisp of charred ash. No smoke billowed. No crackle of flame masked the victims' shrill cries. As the flux of wild energy immolated their bodies, Jussoud beheld the abomination in its wrenching entirety. He had known the spell lines of a sorcerer drew on demonic intelligence. Never, before this, had he grasped the foul truth: that such power was bartered in exchange for men's souls, devoured in shredding torment.

To die of the body brought healing peace. To be killed by the unclean forces of hell was to suffer a fate that transcended time.

While the screams of the guardsmen shocked through the scorched air, Jussoud sensed their wailing echoes resound past the boundary of the unseen. Demons served sorcerers, so men said in their ignorance. Made witness to the act of forced crossing at first hand, a healer's perception beheld the reverse: that the hunger of such beings had no limit. Their 'masters' *in harsh fact* existed as slaves, perpetually constrained to feed them. If a sorcerer exhausted the lands under his conquest; if *ever* his supply of fresh victims fell short, he would, in his turn, be consumed. Each innocent death let the sorcerer live, one half step removed from the powers that sealed his irreversible pact with damnation.

The cruel irony that Mykkael must have borne from the Efandi defeat crashed hard against humane preference, as tribal knowledge let Jussoud comprehend the poisoned victory bought by his survival. A successful defence against sorcery permitted no saving grace of empowerment. Like the desert-bred captain before him, Jussoud could protect helpless lives, yet do *nothing* to spare suffering as the doomed guardsmen were inducted by the spun fury of a sorcerer's cold-struck spell line.

No horror prepared the initiate observer. Jussoud recoiled, retching, while unspeakable, fell forces chained the matrix of two human spirits, and denied them the transition of death. Shrieking in agony that had no voice, their shades were sucked down, shackled into undying captivity to fuel the insatiable will of the demon.

'Jussoud!' screamed Vensic. 'Go forward. You have to! Like it or not, we're all Sessalie has on the front lines guarding the breach!'

Taskin alone held the power to stop this; wrest command of the guard away from the council, and out of the sorcerer's influence. Yet the cool course of logic justified by necessity could scarcely assuage raw emotion. Jussoud pressed ahead, but not out of courage. He jammed his heart closed, shut his eyes and stepped over the razed ground out of shrinking cowardice. At the crux, he could not bear to face the abyss that yawned under his sister, Orannia.

In that dreadful moment, her brother understood the full scope of the terror that pursued her. For the first time, he realized why Mykkael had been adamant to stay by her side to prevent her from suicide. Half trapped, still alive, her madness suspended her over a death that *was not going to buy her deliverance.*

Worst of all, as Jussoud lived the choice that consigned two human spirits to perpetual suffering, he knew *that Mykkael his brother would forgive him.* Of all men, the captain well understood this moment's poisonous self-loathing.

How many times had the desert-bred been forced to enact such hideous destruction? How many strangers and loved ones alike had been delivered to perpetual bondage by his sworn charge to save the Efandi princess?

The tainted thought followed with punishing clarity: that his decision to distribute Perincar's talismans had invited fate to replay his most terrible nightmare. Alone, Mykkael had weighed the unbearable choice. How long had he wrestled the face of his nemesis? Where, amid screams as wrenching as these, had he found the fibre to repeat the untenable past, and attempt to guard Isendon's daughter from the perils of a sorcerer's conquest?

How many others must be consumed, or go mad? How many must shoulder the price meted out, suffering past the reach of a lifetime, beyond hope of reprieve, like Orannia?

For two more palace guards blocked the garden path in the company of the chancellor. One of them would be the puppet claimed and used by the sorcerer's minion, to sustain the potentized spell line.

'Jussoud!' Vensic shouted. 'Keep moving! You must! Lose ground now, and the sorcerer kills wantonly. What fate will befall the people of Sessalie if their king goes down in defeat?'

A thought fragment answered, arisen from the unseen fabric of the otherworld. Its source was no ghostly reflection prompted by ancestral wisdom. The vibrant echo received by Jussoud held the searing, explosive remorse of Mykkael's living experience . . . *'my brother, by the stars of your ancestry, may you never hear such screams as these from the throat of an infant, or a child . . .'*

Jussoud shuddered. Horror forced him to assay the next step.

The third stride saw the wall of fire collapse with a whistling rush of stressed air. The forces driving the demonic assault ripped away like a curtain of tissue.

Two more armed guards faced them, a half step behind the stoop-shouldered old man who served as Sessalie's most venerable chancellor.

'Be wary, Jussoud!' the physician cried.

Yet the son of an ancient nomad bloodline would sense peril birthed from the unseen. Instinct raised the hair at Jussoud's nape the instant he locked eyes with the spell-bound creature before him. The frail gentleman in his fussy silk doublet had once been a timid, retiring philanthropist. He would not have stood firm through such fire and storm, except as the used glove for a minion. The immediate presence of danger roused Perincar's talisman to spontaneous heat. Jussoud felt every scored mark in its pattern as though graven into his skin. He acted before thought, before fear, before primal reflex prompted panic-stricken flight. He balanced his mind inwards, and cried out for the guidance of ancestral instinct to steer his raw will to survive.

The timid old noble *who was a live catspaw* cracked out his imperious demand. 'Guardsmen! You will set this party of traitors under arrest!'

'We go nowhere for the hell-spawned puppet of a sorcerer,' Jussoud said, teeth clenched with desperate defiance. Then he levelled the sword, and touched the rounded steel pommel to the talisman disc at his breast. Contact inducted its searing vibration through the forged length of the weapon. Jussoud sensed the timed moment. As the stressed metal sang aloud in his hand, he moved in the way of the warrior, and ran the elderly chancellor through his thin breast and defenceless heart.

Shock followed. The pierced body wrenched backwards and toppled. No catspaw remained, and no danger. Only an old man, dying. He sprawled on to the white gravel, convulsed by traumatic agony. Warm blood and vomit gushed at Jussoud's feet. He recoiled, gagging, while the sword locked fast in his grip jerked free with a sucking wrench. He staggered back, overcome by the raw stink of slaughter, and crashed, numbed with shock, into Vensic.

Nor did the untried garrison man fall short as the demands of necessity fell on him.

'Take the litter!' The breveted sergeant's shout struck a note of command to shore up faltering nerves. 'Do it now! Jussoud!' He jammed a pole into the nomad's left hand. When the easterner's shocked fingers failed to respond, Vensic let his grip slide. He used crisis and *forced* stunned confusion to resolve, engaging the healer's instinctive reflex to guard the gravely wounded from jostling harm.

Then Vensic reached over the salvaged litter and wrenched the blooded sword out of the nomad's stunned fingers. 'My job, now, fellow!'

The garrison man twisted. His stopgap parry just blocked the first guardsman's attacking lunge. The fouled steel turned the murderous thrust, barely. The bind of stressed metal slid screaming, past Jussoud's silk-clad shoulder.

'You handle Taskin!' Vensic gasped, rushed. 'I'll clear the pathway.' As the remaining pole of the litter changed grip, he surged to the fore, sword raised to guard point to engage the assault of both palace guardsmen at once. They came on, crying treason. Their shouts rang on the night air, charged with chilling conviction. Belief fuelled their aggression. They were convinced they had just witnessed clear proof: the uncanny slaughter of two fellow guards, and the murder of an unarmed high chancellor.

'Sure enough,' Vensic gasped through the chiming clash, as his angled steel hammered into the first lunging blade. The turned sword shrieked aside. He ducked under the second, and lashed out with a kick. The blow caught the opposing swordsman's wristbone. As the weapon sailed free of the victim's bashed hand, he finished, 'we have no choice but get out of here.'

Taskin's guardsmen were superbly taught. Yet Mykkael's matchless training had instilled the savagery required to survive on a battlefield. Eight months of the captain's ruthless surprise drills had found Vensic a gifted pupil. Even disadvantaged by green nerves and stacked odds, even thrown the uncertainty of darkness, he closed in with deft speed. Once inside a man's reach, a longsword became either a cudgel, or a disastrous hindrance. Brute infighting let Vensic turn fists and battering knees against opponents best schooled for elegant blade work. He struck to disable. Smashed joints could stop a skilled swordsman faster than landing a stroke with an edged weapon.

The two guardsmen were down, moaning, and the fouled steel wiped clean on the dead chancellor's robe before anyone noticed: the sword that had been a garrison-forged blank now bore the faint tracery of Perincar's geometry on the pommel.

'Resonance,' the little physician explained, as the litter supporting Taskin's slack form was rushed onwards through the dark garden. 'Jussoud picked up the aroused vibration of the talisman through sympathetic touch. Then he thrust the blade into the suborned flesh of a sorcerer's acting catspaw. Passive protection encountered a potentized line of spellcraft, and reconfigured that energy, forcing an imprint.'

'Do you think the new mark might grant shielding properties?' asked Vensic, all at once overtaken by shivering dread, and the shock of his desperate action. His face looked haunted as he cut his own question short. 'Never mind. After this, I'd be a stark madman to invite the fool's chance to find out.'

Paused to water his mount at a freshet, Mykkael rested his brow against the forearm braced against the pack-horse's lathered shoulder. The black-and-tan hound he had borrowed at need sprawled panting next to his feet. The poor beast was likely as hard-used as he was. He had covered the last league to the ridge crest on foot to spare his exhausted gelding. The stony ground had savaged his knee, and done the stabbed thigh with the compress no favours. Plagued now by the running fire of pinched nerves, Mykkael cursed the brute legacy left by his scars. If he pushed too much harder, the leg would collapse. Here, he would have no saving help from Jussoud if his overstressed resources failed him.

Thought of the nomad closed a sharp spark of contact, raising a flicker of witch thought: *of searing grief, and the captured impression of the aftermath of a deadly fight: two men had burned, consumed by a sorcerer's spell line; and a sweet-natured old chancellor taken as catspaw now lay dead. The corpse sprawled alongside two staunch palace guards, brought down by Vensic's expedient infighting. Jussoud shouldered the weight of Taskin's litter, his steadfast nature cruelly torn: that necessity had granted no time for a field splint to ease the injured men's agony . . .*

'Ah, my brother,' Mykkael gasped, his astonished relief over Vensic's survival made bittersweet by the penalty of Jussoud's remorse. 'I weep for your sorrows. If we survive to share *sennia* together, I'll tell you the sore truth: two men down, but alive, is a blessing beyond measure. And the spell-ridden chancellor was much worse than dead on the sorry moment you struck him.' Perincar's mark, and the clean steel of the sword, had actually delivered the old man to the mercy of a natural crossing.

By now high upcountry, Mykkael breathed deep to

resettle his unruly awareness. The cold air ran thin as a knife-blade into his overtaxed lungs, chilled by the ice on the rims of the peaks. If the sky showed no moon, the snowfields reflected a measure of ambient light. Stars pierced the black zenith between the whispering needles of evergreen.

The scrub was too thick to permit a view downwards. Yet when Mykkael glanced back, he felt a grue of unease chase his spine, as though arcane pursuit searched the ground near his backtrail.

When the saddled horse lifted its dripping muzzle, he urged the pack animal to the streamside, and scratched its soaked neck while it drank. Then he cajoled the tired hound on to her feet and pressed relentlessly onwards, up the boulder-snagged spine of the ridge. To judge by Benj's description of landmarks, the most likely glen to conceal six horses lay another two leagues further on. Mykkael must decipher the poacher's instructions and discover that hidden cleft ahead of the questing sorcerer. Four more hours of hard going, provided his knee held, and two winded horses could withstand the rigorous ascent.

Mykkael wound his grip through the gelding's damp mane, clamped his jaw, and forced his aching leg to bear weight. As he limped through the dark, over flint rocks and gnarled roots, he sensed the distanced, jumbled impression: *of stone stairs, walled in by the rippled glass panes of the late queen's conservatory. Stars shone through, distorted as run silver, as three men, breathing hard, groped upwards by touch. They climbed with urgent, desperate care, bearing a wounded man on a litter. The air wore the humid must of mulched earth and the ethereal fragrance of roses, woven through by the rank tang of danger . . .*

A jarring, slipped step regrounded strayed thoughts. Mykkael hissed a ragged curse through his teeth. No oath could do aught to relieve the pain that lanced through the small of his back. Since the shuddering tremors were not going to release, he chose prudence before pity, and remounted the tired gelding. Higher he wound, through the stands of stunted evergreen, while the lit windows of Sessalie's scattered farmsteads glimmered through the mist silting the vale far below.

When the ridge back sheared into a near vertical ravine, Mykkael shifted the load off the stumbling pack horse. He slipped the hackamores and let both exhausted animals go free. Hereafter, the clanging scrape of shod hooves and the falls of loose stone dislodged by their passage would cause too much noise. He dared not risk hazing the fugitive princess into a needless, blind panic.

Light flooded out of the council hall windows, a setback Jussoud noted with stark apprehension. By the muffled clamour of voices inside, and the coming and going of servants in Devall's livery, Collain Herald was losing the thankless task of maintaining lawful order. Like undertow during a shifting tide, the cascade of events had disrupted the secure process of Sessalie's succession.

'That's the guard for the crown prince's formal retinue, parked over there by the entrance,' the Fane Street physician pointed out. His gloomy whisper cast echoes off the glass roof, as he mopped his round face with his coat tail. 'Inevitable, I suppose, that young Kailen should press his right to his father's authority.' Worried, since Jussoud still bent over the stilled form of Commander Taskin, he added, 'His lordship is slipping deeper into shock?'

'Yes. The foreseeable difficulty.' Jussoud sighed. 'His blood pressure's low from severe loss of blood. The elevated pulse rate won't come down, I'm afraid, until we have him settled and still.'

'Well, the bandage is still dry, he's not started bleeding,' the physician assured him, his stubborn optimism seeking for good amid an increasingly grim situation.

Paused to rest, with the litter shafts braced on the overhead balcony above the shadowed beds of the queen's roses, the healers attending the wounded commander faced the raw brunt of their predicament. For the unexpected session held in the council hall made the direct route to the king's chambers impossible to attempt.

Moments later, Vensic's light tread returned, grating over the gritted planks under the roof where the royal gardeners forced seedlings in flat boxes. 'No going by way of the back corridor, either. There are now posted guards flanking each of the doorways. I can't fight them all.' His strained distress reflected his dread, that he might face a cold-blooded repeat of the tactics just used in the garden. 'Bad business to try, since they're probably sentries following reasonable orders, and not suborned by the enemy.'

'We won't risk more killing,' Jussoud agreed, a decision that brought small relief.

For they now confronted the fallback position that Taskin had outlined with bald-faced reluctance: to unseal the ancient brick passage in the walls, then access the concealed vault underlying the late queen's apartments. *'Go that route,'* the experienced commander had husked, *'you'll be vulnerable. If the king has fallen to the sorcerer's faction, you could find yourselves trapped without recourse.'*

'Soonest started, then,' murmured the Fane Street physician. He finished buffing his clouded spectacles. Then he bent and shouldered his end of the litter, even his dauntless nature subdued by the perils lying ahead.

The balcony ended where the glass conservatory met the buttressing wall of the wing that housed the grand ballroom. In daytime, the row of high lancet windows let the light stream downwards in striated patterns across polished hardwood floors. By night, the windows were jet wells, poked with mud-speckled straw where the jackdaws had nested. Vensic was forced to his knees, to grope for the wrought-iron grating.

'We don't dare use a candle,' Jussoud replied to the physician's disturbed query.

The dusty panes of the upper conservatory could be seen from the guardpost at Highgate. From here, even the briefest struck light would shine far and wide like a beacon.

The grate Vensic encountered was crusted with rust. He scraped his knuckles against rough brick, prying to free the obstruction. Worse, a light bobbed at the far end of the conservatory, trailed by a flurry of voices.

'If they're in here, we'll flush them,' a searcher assured an unseen commanding officer.

Vensic worked at the jammed grate with desperate focus. The marginal gain when it gave and pulled free was followed by crushing defeat, as the aperture in the wall opened into cobwebs and bottomless darkness. The musty spokes of a ladder descended, too steep to accommodate an unconscious man on a litter.

'We can't do this,' Jussoud gasped, tortured. 'We can't carry Taskin down in his state! The shoulder is going to tear.'

'Surrendered alive, his fate will be worse if he falls to a sorcerer's minion.' The physician shook his head, brisk. 'No choice,' he whispered. 'We'll have to set him into a sling.' To the eastern nomad, who had not served in war, he added his brusque reassurance. 'I've solved this before. It's the way wounded men are brought down from high battlements when no one can access the stairs.'

'I've practised the technique,' Vensic added. Sword drawn, he worked fast, slicing through the soft ties binding Taskin into the litter. 'Mykkael's drills were more thorough than anyone imagined we'd ever need.'

The physician added his agile assistance. In short order, Taskin's body was shifted, and the canvas drawn from the poles. Quick cuts fashioned two crude leg holes. Another, higher up, was positioned to support the upper body, slung by the unwounded arm. Then the canvas was folded in half, the commander's slack frame supported within like a child in an oversized nappy. The torn shoulder was left tightly strapped to his chest. The canvas could now be raised by the corners, overlapped at each side. A pair of strong men, from above, and another to guide Taskin's legs from below, could now ease his unconscious weight down the ladder.

'Jussoud and I will handle the work from above,' Vensic instructed the physician. A glance over the balcony showed more lights, streaming steadily closer. 'You go first, and if you pray, beg the powers of *grace* we won't stand on a dry-rotted ladder.'

No time for second thoughts, and no breath for regrets or recriminations, as the three harried men hoisted Taskin and descended into the ink-dark shaft leading down to the hypocaust. From there, they must make their way under the floor, and find the vent that accessed the warren of passageways carved beneath the old wing of the palace.

Nor did they dare, even then, strike a light. A chance gleam cast through a chink or crevice would give their position away. Progress was reduced to a groping trial of cramped quarters and unrelieved darkness, broken by the clomp of the searchers' boots, or the dusty fall of strayed torchlight through the gaps in the sagging floorboards. The hypocaust was a warren for rats, festooned with dense cobwebs, and shining with foetid puddles leaked by the terracotta pipes. The space was too tight to sit upright. A task force of guardsmen creaked over their heads, showering down grit and stirred spiders. The fugitives made their way at a tortuous crawl, with Taskin inched forward in tender, slow stages, either laid over two men who slid on their backs, or else pulled along on the canvas sling, with one man or another on hands and knees at his side to guard his strapped shoulder from mishap.

They escaped the conservatory through a hatch at the back of the caldarium, then ploughed through the pits where the ashes were piled for fertilizer. Vensic and Jussoud bore up the litter, with the pink-faced physician masked in his handkerchief, in desperate straits not to sneeze. Persistence saw them across the conduit of the old sewer by way of a plank that threatened to crack at each step. From there, they traversed the drain from the laundry, creeping in single file down a narrow ledge of slicked stone, while noisome waters lapped at their ankles.

Beyond, the dank shaft of a stairwell ascended to the wardrobe of the late queen's apartment.

'How's Taskin?' whispered the physician through the pause at the landing to recoup taxed breath and wrung nerves.

Jussoud sat with the commander's bare feet in his lap, pressing reflex points with skilled fingers. 'He can't handle much more of this.'

'Two storeys,' Vensic murmured. Soaked leather squelched as he shifted his weight in the darkness, perhaps to make sure of his weapon. 'We should go. Delay's just as likely to kill him.'

For the muffled sound of raised voices carried down through the stairwell, dire warning the binding dispute in the council had ascended to storm the king's chamber.

'Taskin's stable as he's going to get in these straits.' Jussoud peeled off the marred silk of his overrobe, and fashioned a sling to support the wounded commander's dangling legs. 'Let's get him up where there's light, and a bed. I can't do any more for him here, but watch him lose ground he couldn't afford in the first place.'

The game little physician shoved erect, faintly wheezing, and muscled his share of the burden. The climb up the narrow, turnpike stair passed with relative ease, while the rising argument in progress above unfolded with alarming clarity.

'... in league with the sorcerer!' cried the seneschal's excitable tenor. 'The two guardsmen maimed in the garden just swore they saw that steppeland nomad raise balefire and burn two hapless souls to oblivion!'

Bennent's gravel bass tendered a reply, a rumble too low to decipher.

The seneschal's ranting broke in again, cranked to the shrill edge of hysteria. '... commander *told* you to burn all this cedar? You know that such smoke could call in fell spirits, even attract the most dangerous of conjury! If you don't quench that fire and post additional guards to stand watch at the royal bedside, I'll have to advise Prince Kailen that your better judgement may have been compromised. You could be suborned by the selfsame sorcery that overthrew Taskin this morning!'

'Hurry!' gasped Vensic, his steady nerve shaken. 'If I have to bear steel within the king's presence, you realize they'll drop us with crossbows.'

Above the last risers, a chink of light leaked past the concealed panel in the wardrobe. Jussoud squeezed aside to give Vensic space to search for the recessed latch.

Yet the panel gave way without touch or fumbling. The hinges creaked wide, and a candle lamp glared in dazzling brilliance upon them.

The three squinting fugitives made out the gleam of two guardsmen's helms, then the form of an elegant old woman bearing a cane. 'I wondered if you'd try to sneak up the back way,' stated the indomitable Duchess of Phail.

Jussoud bowed his head. He gathered himself, spoke, even through the despair of dashed hope. 'My lady, Commander Taskin is sinking. Would you deny him the right to his final bequest? He has risked his life for the chance to speak to the king, words he counted above his survival.'

'To condemn that slinking desert-bred?' snapped the duchess, past patience. 'A cause scarcely worthy of his lordship's last breath!' Her clipped gesture signalled the guardsmen.

'Perhaps to clear a staunch man's defamed character.' Jussoud matched the aged duchess's scorn, the grave dignity of his ancestry backed by his courageous regret. 'Choose wisely, grandmother. For want of the truth, the cost could extend to uncounted innocent lives.'

'We've lost three such already, so I understand.' The duchess thumped her cane and pronounced with snappish asperity, 'How fortunate for you Lady Lindya was born with a woman's good sense! She sent word ahead. We've all been anxiously expecting your arrival for the better part of two hours.'

The granddame tipped her white head to the pair of standing guardsmen. 'Come along, help them through. Glory preserve us, if I'd realized the ruffians planned to traipse through the sewers, I'd have asked the servants to make up Taskin's sickbed using the second-best linen.'

In Sessalie's palace, three men escorted their unconscious companion into the royal apartments; and the eight living, who bore talismans fashioned by Perincar's hand, and a ninth man, who carried another imprinted by resonant transfer into a sword blade, crossed into regional proximity. A circle of power interlaced with itself, and a warding arose, pealing a note whose clear intonation sounded across the unseen world known to shamans . . .

XXIII. Fugitive

MYKKAEL SENSED THAT BEACON WHERE HE KNELT, SOAKING HIS INFLAMED KNEE IN THE GUSH OF A STREAMLET tumbling off the high glaciers. The chill that combed over his skin and ran *through* him had nothing to do with cold water. His unschooled, blood instinct understood that a change had just knitted through the fabric of the world's energy. On his feet before thought, he snatched up the trousers and boots left heaped on the bank, and jammed them on over his wet skin.

The hound whined, uneasy, touched by her animal awareness that somewhere, a primary balance had shifted. She circled, anxious to pursue the cold trail picked up amid the grazed grass of the glen.

His soft word restrained her, until he had hoisted the bow and provisions on to his back. If the shaman's mark on his sword remained silent, he could not shake his vague sense of dread. Stalking powers stirred through the unseen interface between the air and the earth. The drawing pull of that subtle disturbance rippled through the patterns of natural current, sure sign of the demonic powers entrained through the drawn lines of an active sorcerer.

Mykkael hastened onwards. The prod of his urgency increased at each stride. Even without knowledge to read into the flux, his inborn sensitivity was teased by the sense that a point of balance had shifted in Sessalie. Somewhere, the stream had altered against the sorcerer's favour. Balked on one front, the thrust of the conflict must now narrow its target. Again, the enemy's attention ranged outwards, the spearpoint of its focus turned in single-minded pursuit of the princess.

Before the insatiable drive of the predator, she would be the hare helplessly running.

By now, she was hungry, tired and worn. Crushed hope left her vulnerably defenceless. The challenge she faced had exhausted her resource, until she had nowhere to turn. Mykkael shared the lit flame of her desperation. Witch thought delivered the cold sweat of her nightmares, sown by the despair that had followed her exhausted collapse. *Anja knew she was doomed*. Flight into the rugged wilds would break her, a bodily failing that could not keep pace with the unflagging strength of her will. In whimpering sleep, she still bid for escape, stubbornly ploughing ahead through dreamed landscapes of storm-barren rock and scrub balsam. Yet even such adamant courage could no longer stave off the certainty of defeat.

Mykkael pressed upwards, embraced by the high mountain silence. Across weathered stone, and dense mats of fir needles, or ankle-deep cushions of mosses, he followed the trail worked by Benj's best hound, step by unbalanced, lame step. Survival in war had taught him endurance to match the demands of necessity. Miles of scouting through enemy territory had schooled him to make his way quietly.

In time, Dalshie quickened. The white scythe of her tail threshed the brush as the scent she unravelled grew stronger. Mykkael kept her close. The advantage of using a poacher's prized hound, she would track without giving tongue. Her exceptional nose at last brought reward: the pawing stamp of a horse broke the stillness ahead, from a hollow screened in by evergreens.

A hand signal brought Dalshie back to heel. Mykkael eased the supplies and the bow off his back, left them propped against a shagged boulder. The hound, he tied with a pack strap. Then he made his unencumbered way forward, one hand lightly clasped to the mark the Sanouk shamans had sung into his sword hilt. Its ward stayed quiescent. The vizier's tattoo at his nape did not rouse.

A stalking, wolfish shadow, Mykkael entered the dense grove of pines. Their resinous fragrance washed over his senses, closed in by the blanketing darkness. A horse snorted warning. Shod hooves scraped on rock. Mykkael froze, waiting out the herd's alarmed challenge in poised stillness.

Starlight shone down, and he saw them: equine forms cast into ephemeral outline, erratically slashed by the glimmer of white blaze, and star, and leg stocking. Emerged from their restive movement like smoke, the lone grey shook out his flax mane, his coat a gleam of tarnished pewter among them. The black with the chevron-marked forehead tossed his head to a glitter of bossed silver buckles. He was haltered, or bridled, his picket line tied to a tree that shivered with each nervous tug. Mykkael peered through the gloom, past the jostling horses. He surveyed the ground with quartering patience, and finally found Princess Anja.

She was crumpled in an exhausted heap against the loom of a boulder. Wrapped in a dark cloak, she was all but invisible, except for the rat-tailed stripe of blonde braid, spilled over her huddled shoulder. A slackened hand was tucked over bent knees, fingers tangled in the cuff of a sleeve too long for her delicate wrist.

Asleep, Mykkael realized, her wary spirit overwhelmed by an exhaustion that served him the gift of surprise. He moved on her quickly, before the uneasy horses could startle her fully awake.

She roused anyway. Shoved to her feet with the surge of flushed game, her oval face turned in confusion.

Widened eyes sighted his falcon surcoat. At once, her pale features went rigid. Every trace of wit and intelligence drowned under a flood of blank terror.

Bristled by witch thought, wrung breathless by the strangling, shared impact of a fear that overwhelmed the base instinct to scream, Mykkael reacted on *barqui'ino* reflex and launched as she whirled to run. He caught her wrist, hauled her short, called her name without title. 'Anja!'

She slammed against his hold, twisted and thrashed, a creature gone mad with panic. When his grasp remained firm, she gouged his skin with her nails, then hammered his boots, lashing out with desperate kicks.

'Anja, Anja, *Anja*!' Mykkael reeled her in before she unbalanced him. As he had, *countless terrible times for Orannia*, he bundled her flailing body against his chest. Wincing for the hurt to last night's strapped sword wounds, and the knuckles laid open that morning, he clamped her bucking struggles under his interlaced forearms. 'Anja! Princess! *Anja look at me!*'

She had no choice. Her anguished green eyes met his own, with scarcely a handspan between them.

He held on. Granting her wild fight neither quarter nor space, he made her behold him fully: a dark man of desert descent who smelled of pine gum and balsam. Whatever she expected, he was warm-blooded and human, possessed of a calm deep enough to stand firm, even through mindless hysteria.

She broke all at once, like a puppet unstrung, and sagged sobbing against his shoulder. He held her, rock-steady, not moving a hair. His embrace caged her wracked frame, while the emotion stormed through, bursting the dam of choked-back desperation. When finally the tempest had played itself through, he braced her gently back on to her feet.

'Your Grace of Sessalie, at your sire's command, I am Mykkael, Captain of the Garrison.' He granted the honorific due her royal station, hands crossed at the heart, as he had for the king who held his sworn service.

'You're not one of them,' whispered the princess, her tone scraped and hoarse, and her proud carriage utterly shaken. A hand bare of rings arose, trembling. She swiped back the wisps of gold hair caught in the elfin curve of her eyebrows. Her features had sharpened under privation. She looked like a starveling waif, except for the poise that straightened the shoulders under her ripped shirt and skewed cloak. 'Blinding glory, Captain, I'm sorry. I tore at you just like a harridan.'

'No harridan born had the reason that you did,' Mykkael said with simplicity. He never once glanced at his bleeding wrists, still respectfully crossed at his breast.

That shook her to tears. This time, she blotted the silenced outburst away with a soiled sleeve, and forced a deep breath. Her steadied, next phrase showed incredulity. 'You know why I ran. *My sire sent you?*'

Mykkael answered the last question first. 'His Majesty charged me to stand guard for your life. I've guessed why you ran. But the details still matter. We're both better off if you can explain using your own words, your Grace.'

The princess hugged her clasped arms to herself as though raked by a savage chill. She subjected Mykkael to a scouring survey that lasted uncomfortably long. Then she shivered again, a violent spasm that shook her from head to toe. 'The High Prince of Devall met me at the gate . . .' She fought through reluctance, then swallowed. 'His Highness was not the prince. Oh, he looked like the man in all ways that matter. Except, when he came close and kissed me, I *knew*. He is not my beloved. No longer human. Not any more.'

Those open, jade eyes regarded Mykkael, awaiting the word of disbelief that never came. The desert-bred did not speak, or prompt, or fill her strung silence with platitudes. He made no courtier's effort to distance her jagged grief. He just watched her. Anchored by rooted quiet, he offered her all that he owned: the inadequate solace of his acceptance.

Anja stirred finally, her scorching gaze lowered to the trampled moss underfoot. She resumed in the soul-wrenching tone he remembered too well, from refugees who had beheld the impossible, and found their lives upended by fears that were going to mark them for ever. 'I went to confide in my brother, the first chance I could get him alone.' Again those expressive green eyes overflowed. *'Kailen was changed also.'*

'You see as your sire does,' Mykkael stated gently. 'Things that others don't know are there.'

Her speechless nod answered him. A resilient spirit let her rally inside of a moment. 'Oh yes, I see things.' Anja raised her chin, fired to blazing rage as she fought to shake off an unnatural horror that no flight and no distance could wring back the hope to excise. 'The brother I know is not there any more. Something else looks out of his eyes. That's when I realized I had to run. An uncanny power is at large within Sessalie, and it threatens to destroy more than our lives.'

Mykkael absorbed this, aware of sudden discomfort as the skin on his scalp tightened into contraction. Each line of Perincar's warding tattoo felt written over in fire. Though the sword at his shoulder showed no response, his ruffled nerves would not settle. 'Shape-changers,' he murmured, the taste of the word hammered iron and blood. 'Mehigrannia's mercy, your Grace, you have given me very bad news.'

The young woman, who had once laughed and worn silver bells, rubbed dispirited hands on the tunic she must have purloined from a page. 'We have to get out. Into the lowcountry. I don't know how I can do this alone. But I'll have to seek audience in a foreign court, and try to bind an alliance.'

She had little to barter, as a younger sibling. Her tiny kingdom could not pay a sumptuous dowry, or attach her with marriageable estate. The shame burned her red. As a foreigner and a man, he must realize she held an empty hand, beyond her own female attributes.

Lest he laugh, or disparage, Anja showed him steel challenge. 'What other way do I have to buy my people a vizier's protection from sorcery?'

Mykkael did not argue the flaws in her premise. Starvation and day upon day of blind fright had left her too painfully brittle. 'Princess, bide easy. You'll eat something first. Then, yes, we'll have to keep moving.' Her dumbfounded stare raised the sharkish, clipped smile that had won over another scared royal heiress before her. 'Did you believe I would run you to ground in these hills, and not trouble to think of provisions? Your Grace?'

'I didn't think half so wisely, if at all,' Anja confessed, sadly chastened.

'I beg your pardon, Princess, but you did.' Mykkael's humour vanished. 'A sorcerer does not allow for mistakes. The timely escape you accomplished alone has so far spared Sessalie's freedom. A victory you may not credit, perhaps. My knowledge says otherwise. The strength to take flight without pause to share confidence has been all that kept you and your sire alive.'

Anja stared at him, differently this time, as though, all at once, his unaccented speech and crisp manners smashed through her presumptions concerning an officer with a Lowergate commission. 'Sire once mentioned that you were experienced.' Her straightforward regard became piercing. 'Are you telling me you have fought sorcery before?'

'More than once, Princess.' Mykkael saw no reason to embellish the statement. The truth he delivered omitted the bald fact: that no conjury he had ever opposed had commanded the skills of a shape-changer, far less an assault brought to bear by a pair of such murderous minions. He masked his anxiety. Guardedly still, he watched Sessalie's princess try to measure the man behind his exotic southern breeding. In forthright self-honesty, she encountered the pitfall: that her sheltered background left her unprepared to assess the least compass of his experience.

'Forgive me, Captain, but I've been remiss.' Anja tucked her bright braid back under her cloak as though embarrassed by her northern ignorance. 'I should be the one asking pardon in turn. You won our summer tourney with the arts of a champion, yet we in Sessalie have never troubled to appreciate your formidable assets.'

'Good tactics,' Mykkael excused her with velvet-clad equanimity. 'Can't be the thorn in the side of an enemy if you leave the choice weaponry set out on public display.' To keep her diverted, he addressed the essential point first. 'I carry a warding attached to my person, and a shaman's line in my sword hilt. Their properties will offer defence, and mask us from scryers, but with limited range. Listen carefully. You must not stray from my presence, Princess. The warding starts to thin at ten paces. Its active power dissolves altogether another five paces beyond that.'

Since the pack with the provisions lay outside the pine grove, he could no longer conceal his appalling limp. His turn, now, to shrug off embarrassment for the flawed gift of his fighter's protection. A king's daughter would be too proud to comment, he thought, or too well bred to disparage a man she perceived as a low-caste foreigner.

Anja matched just three of his dragging steps before proving him wrong. 'If the injury is an old one, I am saddened.' Her glance at the captain's face stayed unflinching. 'If you're hurt, let me know how I might help.'

Discomfited by her forthright compassion, where Orannia would have thrown him off balance with scorching words, then followed with a gamine's smile, Mykkael skirted a leaning rock rather than highlight the shortfall posed by his battered leg. 'Rest will improve things,' he admitted, then caught himself frowning. He made himself rise to match Anja's rare grace. 'The loan of a horse would be timely. I'm perfectly well able to ride.'

Whether or not she accepted the evasion behind his request, they had reached the tree where he had tied Benj's hound, and stashed the bow and provisions. Anja paused only to ruffle the dog's ears. Then she turned and closed her fists on the bulging pack alongside his one-handed grasp.

'To keep your grip free for your weapons,' she said.

Since that showed the bare-bones good sense she was going to need to survive, Mykkael stood back and approved. He took charge of the arrows and bow. Then he untied the hound, mindful of the way Anja muscled her burden through the dark, upon uneven ground. Tired, half starved, she still carried herself well.

Unlike the pampered Efandi princess, King Isendon's daughter would not require his assistance each time the footing turned rough. Mykkael's sharp relief raised the burn of old bitterness, and whipped his mouth to a hardened line. Anja's resourcefulness would do very well, since his game knee could scarcely support even her diminutive frame. Stinging where exertion pulled at his scabs, he trailed the sylph who mastered the wretched terrain with no complaint, and who shoved the cumbersome pack overtop of the boulders she was too slight to scale.

Such relentless, tough spirit demanded respect, and affirmed Mykkael's short-term decision. Though foreboding prodded his instincts to urgency, he understood he must chance the time to shore up Princess Anja's equilibrium. Small use to attempt the harsh perils ahead, if the shattering truth of her straits fell upon her when she was half starved and dispirited.

The food he delivered was hurried and cold, a link of Mirag's hard sausage, some cheese, and a crumbling crust of coarse bread. Mykkael ate his share in impersonal silence, aware of the princess's inquisitive regard through the moments when she thought him too busied to notice. He allowed her to stare. Since the short reach of his wardings was destined to undermine privacy anyway, he endured the revealing discomfort as he rolled up his trouser cuff and retied the binding that braced his bad knee. Darkness, at least, masked her sight of the scars, if not the extent of infirmity.

Manners triumphed. The princess let her unanswered question abide. Mykkael chose not to mention his spiking unease as he sensed the first signs of a foray made by the enemy.

The sorcerer worked, seeking through the unseen, an uncanny awareness that combed across the dark landscape and measured all things in its path.

To the trained eye of a shaman, the subtle energies underlying the tangible world would have burned with unfurling lines. Mykkael could not perceive their clear pattern. Yet even uninitiated, he felt the whisper of change ripple across the unseen. A sensation like vertigo tugged at his mind, as the questing trace of uncanny forces deflected the flow of earth's natural alignment. The disturbance spun closer. High-pitched tension sang through him. He well knew the instant his wardings engaged, and the short spells written into the vizier's tattoo stirred into active defence.

Sweat flushed him. He had to force his jaw to unclench. The desperate, long weeks he had been stalked by Rathtet had imprinted too many hideous memories. The flare of his wardings did not flicker quiescent, but increased. As though this new sorcerer *expected* a barrier, the probe of hostile forces tested and pried, yearning, searching, *demanding* to grasp the slightest opening for entry.

Mykkael resisted his impulse to shout. His head felt clapped under the maw of a bell whose dissonant tone vibrated just above hearing. Perincar's workings touched him that way, when he sat in their raised field of resonance. As the vivid memories of the past's gristly horrors resurged through his jangled mind, he held his ground. *This was Sessalie, not the rocky vista of the Efandi plains.* The power that tested for entry was *cold-struck*, a line sustained over distance; not a hot contact sourced out of warped ground, suborned to serve in demonic alignment with the nether realms of the unseen.

The raw edge of immediate fear was too real, that these were *shape-changers* he faced, full-fledged minions of a sorcerer of unknown name and origin. Not Rathtet, who still wielded a living matrix of influence; not the working of the defeated Sushagos; nor Quidjen, consigned to languish in oblivion after bloodshed and terrible loss had dispatched his bound sorcerer to final demise. Mykkael fought down sweating dread with grim logic: that Eishwin and Perincar had both held formidable experience with multiple styles of long spell. The geometries jointly twined through his flesh would be fashioned to counter the forms each vizier had mastered throughout the wise course of a lifetime. The powers wielded by Sessalie's attacker *might* derive from a demon their lore could encompass.

Or might not.

Mykkael shut his eyes. He made himself sift for what nuance he could, sounding the depths of unpleasant sensation. He derived the vague sense that a scryer had cast testing lines, then noted the pulse as the warding geometries spun their threads into tangles that thwarted. Not cleanly, not fast; but the bulwark sustained him.

Where the princess breaking coarse bread with her fingers knew only an ordinary night, and cool winds sighing through the scrub forest, Mykkael caught the sudden, subliminal sting as a breach tore through the primary ring of protection. Instantaneous, sharp vibrations woke and ran through his sword hilt. The warding notes sung by the Sanouk shamans rang through air and cleared the intrusion, then stood fast, holding the breach. Their persistent ache buzzed through his marrow, low as the whine of a wasp trapped in glass. Mykkael loosed his pent breath. Saved though he was, he could not seize respite. The subtle resonance raised by the nomad singers never failed to exacerbate his blood instincts. The powers of the unseen pressed on his mind until he *felt* the probe of Anja's curiosity, intrusive as an itch playing over his flinching skin.

Jumpy as a cat, Mykkael nursed his patience. He checked the hang of the bow; made sure that quiver and arrows were securely clipped to his belt. Then he sorted through the supplies in the pack, and fetched out the sacks of barley, corn and oats he had filched from Mirag's pantry.

'You brought *grain*?' Anja said. 'Powers bless you, for that. The horses are worse off than I am.'

He nodded, not letting her see his unease. Since the combined strength of his wardings seemed to be holding firm, he blotted the seeping scab on his knuckle, and fished out other items requisitioned from Benj's condemned cottage: a pair of Timal's sturdy boots, leather breeches, a clean shirt, and a heavy felt jerkin. On top of the pile, he laid a sharp skinning knife, borrowed out of the smoke-house.

'Here, Princess,' he said, gruff. 'These ought to make you more comfortable.' Not to mention the blessing, that changing her raiment would also divert her incessant staring.

Then, a narrow brush with disaster: Mykkael almost let himself laugh as the princess's gratitude changed to dismay for the close proximity forced by the warding. Fume though she might, she could not leave his presence, even to guard her maidenly virtue. Since his smothered amusement was bound to enrage her, Mykkael snatched the saving excuse to acquaint himself with her horses.

He befriended them shamelessly, using the drive of their empty stomachs. Small rations, fed slowly; too much would cause colic. He let them snuffle the grain from his hands, and lip at his hair. All the while, the curse of his witch thought barraged him, and heated his cheeks with the echo of Anja's flaming embarrassment. Though he kept his back most scrupulously turned, he *felt* her uneasy distress, *knew* the slide of each garment and the kiss of chill air against every last private patch of bared flesh.

His silenced humiliation seared worst, for the intimate violation he could not prevent. To suppress the shared flush of the young woman's outraged emotion, Mykkael immersed himself in the crowding warmth of her magnificent animals. They were tethered into the traditional pairs that made up a steed wicket team. No mare alive had foaled finer than these. Mykkael surveyed quality breeding drawn from the four quarters of the world, from the cloud-dappled black with his steppelands stature, to the racing blood of the west, to the delicate, fine beauty raised in the deserts, that deceived for the strength of its hardihood. He ran appreciative hands over the iron gloss of six proud necks. Felt the cool elasticity of firm tendons as his cursory check encountered a loosened shoe. He used the flat tang of his knife hilt, and his boot sole, to tighten the clenches, then set down the clean leg, admiring.

Whoever had conditioned these animals had brought them to an exceptional peak.

His comment raised Princess Anja's reply, as she tugged at lacings to adjust the boy's clothing. 'Gurley's lads followed my training instructions, when I could not ride them myself.'

Mykkael straightened, surprised, one hand fending off the impudent grey, who butted to relieve the itch of the tack her preparedness had wisely left on him. 'These horses are yours?'

Anja approached, rubbed the nose of the sturdy northern mare some daft romantic had named Fouzette. 'They were to have been my surprise gift to the high prince, following our formal betrothal.' She blinked fast, turned away, then shrugged like a stoic. 'I wanted him to share the glorious thrill of watching an upset team win the wickets.'

The aggrieved note of passion behind her flat voice said she might have been running them now; would have left these proud beasts to claim their due victory, had they not been the only mounts she could take without drawing notice. She laid her face against the satin hide of the buckskin, Bryajne, who turned his blazed head, comically flummoxed to realize she carried no stashed gift of carrots. 'They'll serve to carry me over the border. I can ride post once I get to the lowcountry, where people won't know my face.'

Desperation rode behind those stark words, and witch thought derived the gist of the unspoken necessity: that a fast, timely sale must raise enough gold to regale her Grace in state clothing. She would stretch those scant funds, hire the minimal retinue a princess must have to present herself at a foreign court.

Mykkael seized the bitter opening. 'You won't need to sell them.' The hurt lashed him, as hope transformed her thin face, and lifted her flagging spirit.

He braced himself to deliver a cruel string of facts that foreclosed any tactful kindness. 'Princess, I'm sorry. But your plan to circle back down to the lowlands will bring nothing but death and destruction.'

Her wrenching shock stung him. 'Oh bright powers! You aren't telling me the palace has already fallen! Or that Sire –'

'Not dead!' Mykkael gasped, defenceless and fighting to breathe through the anguish of her grief at close quarters. The reactive connection aroused by Sanouk song lines was now haplessly bound to his person, lidded under the ranging fields of the active viziers' wardings. 'King Isendon lives, Princess! Your capital is imperilled, but not yet brought under conquest.'

Uncertainty ripped him, *hers*, as she whispered, *'How do you know?'*

Anja's need seized his vitals, demanding response: the primal attachments to blood family and survival framed a drive too overpowering to deny. Mykkael shuddered, hurled off centre. His inborn talent unfurled into witch thought, searing a line of vibrant awareness across the unseen, towards the source of her deepest affection . . .

King Isendon aroused in the royal chamber, dizzied by the resin pungence of cedar smoke. As always his eyes would not focus, at first. There were people around him. He could hear loud voices, clashing in argument.

'. . . pure folly trusting that murdering desert-bred!' The reedy tone belonged to the seneschal, immersed in habitual complaint. 'Such "instructions" could get us all killed.'

Someone the king did not know murmured answer, cut short by the Duchess of Phail, whose shrewd instincts seemed to have faltered. Danger would follow if anyone listened to her bitter condemnation.

King Isendon filled his weak lungs, and forced speech. 'But Myshkael has found Anja. He guards my daughter under my charge of protection.'

'Your Majesty?' said a deep, gentle voice, close at hand. A warm grasp supported his shoulder.

King Isendon blinked. His hazy sight cleared to unveil the anxious face of a steppeland nomad he recognized. 'You can't feel him, Jussoud? Tell my courtiers the truth. Captain Mykkael is no murderer. His skill on the field against sorcerers is legend. A fact quite well guarded, among eastern monarchs. Few wish the particulars of that history made public. The man's been privy to far too many state secrets. Often guarded the chambers of royalty.'

'He's maundering,' an authoritative officer in palace armour broke in.

'Not a bit! Damn your insolence, soldier!' King Isendon thrashed erect, assisted by the timely arm of a pink-faced man wearing spectacles. Short of breath, too short, *to be asking strange names, Sessalie's sovereign resumed cogent speech. 'Captain Myshkael's worth any ten of you, officer! His sword alone spared Prince Al-Syn-Efandi's daughter from falling to Rathtet. Who better, to guard my own Anja?'*

Spent, sorely trembling, King Isendon sank back. While the darkness pressed him, narrowing down his fuzzed vision, he clung to his ebbing awareness. 'By royal decree, Myshkael's instructions must stand.'

Then blackness descended, let in by a roaring red maelstrom. Isendon's consciousness sank and drowned. He let the dark swallow him, grateful, while the world beyond his blanketed senses crackled with tendrils of fire . . .

King Isendon's distant awareness cut off, snapped like a strand of chopped string by the shrieking descent of spelled fires. The kin tie that had drawn Anja's consciousness to her sire frayed away, dividing Mykkael's perception: as witch thought showed him the royal apartments, set under siege by a spell line, he also felt the princess beside him, bereft, and ripped into shock.

He reacted before thought, caught her shoulder and spun her, then clapped a hand to her mouth to stifle her keening outcry. 'Your Grace, be still! Your sire's not harmed!'

Mykkael had no time to ponder the warding he had sensed, springing cold blue over Isendon's chamber; no chance to describe the dread perils of spellcraft, or warn against the dangers let in by voiced panic. Witch thought still showed him the thrust of cold sorcery, guided in by the perilous, ephemeral connection forged out of his volatile talent, and Anja's overpowering desire. A raging attack *that could not touch Isendon* now ran wild, reaching, stretching, seeking: yet the destructive assault of the enemy found no weak point of access to claim Sessalie's king. The reflective, joined force of nine gathered talismans, and a chamber fumed with green cedar, turned the strike of the spell line aside. Too focused, too strong, too murderously fashioned to dissipate, the stream of attack spilled down the path of least resistance: the thinning, last trace of the contact that had linked a father's anxiety to his daughter's distanced distress.

Mykkael foresaw disaster. A split second shy of full

impact, he suspended thought and let go into *barqui'ino* reflex. One move hurled Anja astride the grey horse. The next drew his sword and slashed through the picket line. He grabbed mane, vaulted on to the sturdy Fouzette. Yelling like a crazed nomad herder, he drove horses and princess to headlong stampede, while Benj's best hound showed her innate good sense, and bolted flat out alongside them.

Fire struck at their heels. Flames crashed roaring over the trees, igniting hemlock and fir like dry tinder.

'Go! Move!' Mykkael shouted, drummed heels into the mare and whipped the horses from under the edge of the conflagration. He yanked rope, slapped rumps with the flat of his wailing sword. While the combined effects of three sets of wardings ringed his presence in shielding force, he charged the shying animals through springing wildfire and a hellish rain of splashed cinders. His protections unwound the raw balefire of sorcery. Their proximity was sufficient to guard Anja's person, himself and all seven terrified animals. But the *place* in the cleft where the princess had stood through the vulnerable mischance of contact now became a naked target, packed with acres of volatile timber.

The dense stand of evergreens roared up like a torch, as balked spellcraft seeded a forest fire. If the lethal impact of cold-struck power was sent to ground, or quenched out by the captain's wardings, no beast could escape getting ravaged by burns, if the wall of natural flame overtook them.

'Ride!' Mykkael hauled hard on the picket rope, kept the horses together, and steered Anja's wild-eyed grey to close quarters. With its nose jammed in matched stride at his knee, he shouted, 'Ride, don't look back. If you can't stay astride, or if your mount falters, we're not going to escape this.'

The Princess of Sessalie proved herself then as a woman of mettle and courage. She grabbed up loose reins, found the dangling stirrups. Then she ran the game grey over rocky terrain with the nerve of a woman possessed.

XXIV. False Refuge

THE ASSAULT WROUGHT OF SPELL-BONDED FIRE PROVED SHORT-LIVED. ITS MAELSTROM OF ENERGIES ACCOSTED the frail circle of Perincar's configured ward ring, then departed, there and gone like a wind-blown match. Its wake left the duchess's steel nerves in shreds. Her ragged breathing and the seneschal's distraught whimpers tore through the stunned silence cast over the king's private chamber. All the candles had blown out. The ruby glow of fanned coals in the grate shed the only light in the room. Of the ten shocked and shaken survivors, the only two not wrung white with terror were the invalids who remained unconscious.

The physician was first to clear his dry throat. 'That was not defeat, but withdrawal,' he ventured in tremulous distress. The skewed glass of his spectacles flashed in the gloom as he appealed to the armed authority of Captain Bennent. 'Pray don't drop your guard. Our peril is not one whit lessened.'

'We aren't vanquished, either. The king is unharmed,' Jussoud said from the royal bedside. Outside, a tumult of shouting erupted. Doors crashed down the corridor. More disturbed voices arose from the stairwell that accessed the grand hall of state. Despite the uproar, the nomad healer stayed calm. 'While his Majesty lives, Mykkael warned we were likely to be kept under constant siege.'

Too rattled for argument, the seneschal helped guide Lady Phail to a chair.

Only Taskin's distraught first captain stood stunned, at a loss for intelligent reaction. 'Merciful powers, that saddlecloth . . .'

Jussoud answered, crisp, 'You ordered it burned. But the contents weren't lost.' He arose and took charge, addressing the steadfast guards flanking the doorway. 'You men! Keep these chambers secured. No one enters! Vensic? Please build up the fire. The warming pan can be used to make cedar ash. Lord Shaillon, if you would please light the candles? Your commander needs my attention.'

Lady Phail snugged her shawl over quaking shoulders. Her contrition was practical, and her courage a force far beyond her frail strength. 'What can I do?'

Jussoud crossed the floor and presumed, as a healer, to gather her clammy hands. 'Duchess, you'll be needed to comfort the king. Your sharp wits are our indispensable asset, but please, for your sake, let me brew you a tonic. You've suffered a terrible shock.'

'No, thank you!' the granddame snapped in offence. 'Bitter tea never fails to upset my digestion.'

She snatched back her hands, which the raised pitch of her anger now flooded with lifesaving warmth; a mule's kick of a blessing, Jussoud saw in dismay. He had no remedies to offer. Apparently he had lost his hip satchel during the crawl through the hypocaust.

Though the seneschal still fumbled to ignite the first candle, the Fane Street physician noted the nomad's crestfallen despair. 'We're not entirely bereft, Jussoud. My jacket pockets hold a few simples I keep at hand for emergencies.'

'You shall not lack for medicines.' The duchess smoothed her skirts and arose. 'His Majesty's physician keeps a stocked chest in the linen closet. Bennent! Make yourself useful. I'll need a man's strength to help move it.'

'Tactics, first, Duchess.' The royal guard's acting captain discarded bruised pride and faced Jussoud, rigidly braced to salvage his mistaken judgement.

Yet the nomad now crouched beside Taskin's prone form insistently endorsed Lady Phail's first request. 'Fetch the remedies now, Captain. Before I speak further, you must understand. If Taskin slips from us, the warding that just spared your king will collapse.'

Spurs clinked as Captain Bennent stood aside to let the seneschal brighten the wall sconce. 'I don't understand. If one of us fails, could Lord Shaillon not assume –'

As the seneschal turned, recovered enough to respond to his name, the Fane Street physician cut off Bennent's words with a headshake, then offered, 'Jussoud, attend Taskin. I can explain this.' He caught the royal guard captain's wrist and towed him aside with brusque firmness.

'What's this?' Striker in hand, Lord Shaillon turned his suspicious regard towards one, then the other foreign healer. As the tumult outside became more intrusive, he pursued his querulous inquiry. 'More conspirators' secrets?'

'By command of your king!' That weak, rust-grained whisper still carried the peal of a lifetime's authority. Under Jussoud's skilled hands, Taskin had achieved a tenuous return to consciousness. 'Captain Mykkael's instructions will be carried out!' Eyes shut, his gaunt face like wax on the pillows, the commander whispered, 'Dedorth's tower.' He coughed weakly. 'Move. Safer refuge.' Then he added, 'Bear the king promptly.'

'Impossible,' said Jussoud, too hard-pressed for dismay. 'My lord, your condition is fragile and should not be stressed. Another move would be dangerous, and our party of nine *must not separate.*'

If Taskin did not yet realize the virtues of Perincar's talismans relied upon close proximity, Jussoud could but hope the commander could interpret his strained tone as imperative. He dared not speak more openly, or broach the fact that the guarding properties of the pattern required nine *living* bearers to achieve its full strength. One death would cause the structure's collapse. Even the momentary delay as a disc was transferred to a successor would grant a fatal opening for the enemy sorcerer to exploit, a detail the Fane Street physician now took pains to conceal from the seneschal's distrustful interest.

Taskin's face tightened. 'We cannot stay here.' His imperious eyes were glazed over with pain and a febrile exasperation. 'Did you notice, Jussoud? The palace is in flames.'

The breath the nomad drew to cry protest in fact carried the tang of fresh smoke, an acrid influx no longer masked by the resinous fumes of the cedar that Vensic was burning to ash in the warming pan. Outside, shrill voices raised the alarm, fast joined by the pound of running footsteps. The two guardsmen braced the king's door with stout furniture, while Bennent and the Fane Street physician returned with the remedy trunk slung between them. Lady Phail trailed in their wake, looking frayed.

More shouting arose from the corridor, as the council broke session in panic. A chancellor screamed for a task force with buckets, while another, backed up by Prince Kailen's honour guard, sowed the disastrous belief that King Isendon was under attack. Devall's marshal could be heard mustering more men from the grounds to mount an immediate rescue. The palace sentries were bound to rally to the High Prince's claim that a sorcerous assault, spearheaded by traitors, had taken Sessalie's aged king as a hostage.

'They can't get in,' Captain Bennent assured them crisply. 'I've seen through the window. We're surrounded by fire.' Beyond the king's chamber, where the perimeter of the geometry had shed the volatile thrust of the sorcerer's attack, the beams and the tapestries had been seared to flame. Heat and smoke would stand off the misguided intervention of the men-at-arms for a short while.

'That's why Mykkael insisted we seek refuge within a stone tower.' Jussoud clasped Taskin's wrist in tacit assurance that he could be trusted to deliver the requisite facts. 'Once inside, we'd be removed from ground contact, which weakens a sorcerer's spell line. Even if everything under us burns, stone walls will hold firm. If we place ourselves wisely, Perincar's pattern will spare the boards of the floor where we shelter. The royal quarters offer no such protection. We're far too exposed to be safe, here.'

'That's raving nonsense!' the seneschal cracked. 'What have we to fear from *Prince Kailen's honour guard*? Or from the lowlanders under Devall's marshal-at-arms, for that matter?' Imposingly robed to preside in state council, Lord Shaillon jabbed an accusatory hand at the nomad, half clad in stained breeches and the smutched linen of his underrobe. 'This *sorcerer* is the High Prince's enemy, after all. Our interests are one and the same!'

'Be quiet!' rasped Taskin.

But the seneschal nattered on. 'I cannot agree that My*sh*kael is no traitor. The king, spare his wits, was behind on current events when he spoke for the desert-bred's character.'

'*Be quiet!*' barked Bennent. He left the remedy chest in the care of the frowning physician, and knelt next to Taskin's bedside. 'Orders, Commander. I'll carry them through.'

The wounded retainer drew a laboured breath. 'Foremost. Trust Mykkael. Follow Jussoud's directions.'

'He has asked a retreat to Dedorth's tower,' the nomad supplied in saving intervention.

'All of us go. Now.' Taskin's pale forehead glittered with sweat as he reached the end of his strength. 'Don't trust Devall. Keep Kailen away. Bind Shaillon's mouth, if you have to.'

'Not necessary!' snapped the Duchess of Phail. As the

seneschal surged forward to vent his stunned outrage, she banged her cane in his path at an angle that threatened to rap shins. 'I shall see that Lord Shaillon keeps himself in hand.'

The Fane Street physician froze in the act of buffing his spectacles. 'This talk of moving is utter madness! If the effort doesn't kill your man with the wound, the sorcerer who's marked this kingdom for conquest has planted his minion among you. That creature could seize every one of those confused men-at-arms, twist their minds, and use them to attack us. If we stir outside bearing an unconscious king, we risk being ripped up like crow bait!'

Captain Bennent stood erect, his competence restored by the gift of subordinate command. 'Stay here, we'll go down like trapped rats in a barrel. The stairs are in flames. So are the floor beams that shore up the corridor. That leaves us a stand-down that we can't escape. We're going to be vulnerable the moment the watch sergeant recalls his recruit drill with the scaling ladders.'

'That leaves us the sewers,' said Vensic, his manic face underlit by the glow of the cedar he was methodically reducing to ashes. 'That stairwell is stone. If we can mount a side foray to the laundry, a few wash tubs might serve us as boats.'

'Better,' gritted Taskin, his eyelids clamped shut. 'The king's private wine cellar. Below us. Get casks. Use bed slats or tear up the floor planks.'

'Make a raft?' Jussoud's snarled frown unravelled at last. 'He's right. We can float our two invalids.' An easy, soft ride for the one gravely wounded, with six able-bodied left free to wield weapons, or assist the aged duchess and the seneschal. 'We can slip out through the cut where the spill meets the moat.'

Bennent's face cleared. 'That might save us.' Two ancient sallygates pierced the wall, there. He could pull rank, appropriate the sentry, and send him with orders to the acting watch officer posted at the Highgate. 'We'll commandeer an armed task squad to help us reach Dedorth's tower, and stock it with food and supplies.'

Jussoud sucked a deep breath, glanced towards Vensic, then plunged straight away into planning. 'Defences, first. We're going to need ashes, lots of them. Water. Salt. Torches can be made from the bed linens. Just make sure they're well laced with cedar.'

'On it,' said Vensic, grim as stamped bronze as he tipped another load of glowing embers into the king's porcelain chamber pot. Skirts rustled, beside him. He glanced up to discover the Duchess of Phail standing over him, arms laden with bundles of cedar, and her slender back straight as a post.

'Show me what's needed, young fellow,' she said.

Vensic's smudged features brightened with provocative delight. 'Can you bear it? Someone's got to tear up the linens for rags, and soak them in the melted wax of your mightily expensive white candles. Do you think your seneschal could unbend and help? Birch kindling is nice, but will burn much too fast. I'm afraid it's no use. We might have to unroll a shelf load of book scrolls for torch grips.'

Lady Phail choked, then rebounded with a snort of laughter. 'Captain My*sh*kael should be proud. If the crown of Sessalie survives this crisis intact, remind me to commend his barbaric ingenuity. He's served us with a first-rate field officer.'

'Ah, Duchess,' Vensic murmured, 'you have sorely misapprised him. If my captain had to choose to spoil a book to save a king, the necessity would as likely make him weep.'

That struck tone of grief, couched in country-bred accents, caught the elegant duchess off guard. She regarded the farmboy turned swordsman who sat with head bent to his work, surprised to impulsive, mad hope. 'You truly believe that your desert-bred is hardy enough to prevail?'

Vensic's hands paused. His grave gaze encompassed

the activity as Sessalie's frail king was bundled up and transferred to a litter. 'Mykkael must, don't you think? Without Princess Anja, alive and free, what resource will you have left in hand to steer the kingdom through Isendon's succession?'

A sparkle of gems scored the dark as the duchess laced her prim fingers over the bundles of cedar. 'You don't set much store by Prince Kailen, do you?'

'I was born on a pig farm.' Vensic set his jaw, well braced to resist. 'Ask me anything you want about a hog farrow.'

Yet the old lady's imperious patience could have stung the silence out of a corpse.

Vensic hissed a vexed sigh through his teeth. 'Duchess, I don't know his Highness's character as you do.' The garrison sergeant accepted her disconsolate offering of greens, his good-natured face sorely troubled. 'But Mykkael was blunt, the one time he mentioned the crown prince. Since the royal sister fled, he said the tactical question still rankled. *Why did Prince Kailen stay?*'

The wind swept with cruel force over the barren heights above the timberline. Stopped in a stony cleft to ease the winded horses, Mykkael took grim stock of his salvaged assets. The bow slung alongside his sword was still with him, likewise the quiver attached to his belt. The tightly packed arrows had not jostled out. He still had the grain bag strung over his arm, and Benj's game dog, who lay chewing the bruised pad of a forepaw. The horses had kept all their shoes, which turn of luck bespoke divine blessing, considering how recklessly he had run them.

Sessalie's princess had come through, unharmed. She presently crouched, capturing a trickle run down off the ice packs, and sipping from her cupped hands. The melt water would set an ache to the bone. Despite this, her Grace raised no murmur of complaint. Said nothing at all, though she surely believed the loss of the pack with the food posed a disastrous setback.

Mykkael weighed the greater threat, while the wind hissed down, and the black sky glittered with starlight. Though at present both of his wardings had calmed, the sorcerer had tested their measure. The demon that bound the fell creature would know where to aim his next search. This moment of snatched respite could never last. Pursuit would resume, a relentless joined contest that would kill a fugitive far faster than any depletion caused by starvation. Mykkael still carried flint and steel with the kit in his scrip. If a safe refuge could be secured in these heights, he could forage and trap to gain sustenance.

The horses' needs were less easily satisfied. No meadows grew amid the high peaks. The mixed grain he had left was a pittance, once the ration was divided six ways. To let these magnificent animals starve was too dismal a sacrifice to contemplate. Nor could Mykkael slaughter them for their meat. The brave heart they had shown in their dash up the slope had displayed their breathtaking generosity. These animals freely gave of themselves with a trust that overruled natural instinct. Because their human riders had asked, they had galloped, unstinting, at breakneck speed, over rocks where a misplaced step could have shattered their slender legs.

Anja rinsed her flushed face. Still without speaking, she sat on a rock, and blotted her dripping fingers. Tucked in her dark cloak, her pale hair wisped like floss in the wind, she measured Mykkael's tensioned stance.

When the quiet extended, and he volunteered nothing, she broke her reserve and asked outright, 'How long do you think we have?'

Mykkael weighed her resilience, and told her the truth. 'I can't say for certain, not knowing which sorcerer covets Sessalie, or what style of conjury he spins to align his attacks. Expect this much. He will strike fast, now his plot is unmasked. You have become a detail he must eliminate, your Grace. No sorcerer I've seen ever leaves a blood claim that could rally an outside invasion. Your enemy must make certain no foothold remains to upset his chosen conquest.'

That condensed explanation withheld the bare worst: that Kailen was already bound as a full-fledged minion. *If Sessalie fell, and his sister remained living, her blood ties of kinship would see her hunted down by the minions of other demons who stood as her first enemy's rivals. Outside Sessalie, she became the contested weak link, a tool through which the invading sorcerer could be counter-attacked and made vulnerable.*

Unaware of the hideous gravity of her peril, Anja clawed fallen hair from her eyes, jerked her chin in annoyance, then tugged the frayed tie from her braid. 'We'll have to escape. Do you have a plan?' Head tipped aslant, she shook out her long hair, finger-combed the strayed wisps, then began to rebind its luxurious length. That she handled the task without help from a maid showed the quality of her self-reliance.

Encouraged to encounter such cool practicality, Mykkael scrambled down from his vantage. 'Your first assessment was sound thinking, Princess. Sessalie requires the protection of an accomplished vizier, or a shaman. We'll have to seek elsewhere to petition for help.' He knelt by the cleft, his game leg extended, and assumed her place at the small stream. 'The unpleasant difficulties have to be faced. The valley's no option. Even if we slipped past the armed company that's bound to ride in pursuit, we cannot try the road, or win through the bottleneck pass to reach the eastern lowlands. If we try, we'll run into armed cordons, at strength. I can't fight such numbers. No foray by stealth can see us across the cataracts at Stone Bridge.'

'But that's nonsense!' Anja whipped off the end of her plait, and securely knotted the tassel. 'Sessalie's guardsmen should answer to me.'

'Should,' Mykkael said, 'does not mean they will.' He plunged his slashed knuckles under the chill water, and sucked a fast breath at the sting. While the cold slowly numbed his outraged flesh, he outlined the pernicious difficulties. 'This sorcerer's intrigues have swayed your high council. The lure of the sea trade is driving the politics. Suppose, at Stone Bridge, you met Devall's marshal? Or troops that are Sessalie's, but under the command of your brother, invested as lawful regent?'

'Save us!' gasped Anja. Her terror resurged. 'If Sire's incoherent, the council's sealed writ could overrule even Taskin.'

Mykkael was blunt. 'That's already happened.' How to tell her? *The crown's first commander fell to my sword, in defence of my charge to protect you?* He strangled that thought, along with the resurgent ache of his grief. What use, to lament his false arraignment and defamed character, if Princess Anja did not survive? He could die beside her. His failure would make him Taskin's murderer in more than an empty name. The straits that entangled him framed the harsh quandary: how could any lamed, disowned swordsman protect a northern-born princess if she was shown cause to doubt his integrity?

His rough curse in dialect did nothing to ease the ragged edge from his nerves. Nor did Anja's awareness of Sessalie's geography offer the kindness of ambiguity. Since crossing Stone Bridge was not going to be possible, only two passable routes remained to secure their flight over Sessalie's border: to scale the Great Divide by way of Scatton's Pass, which demanded a skilled climber's strength, perfect weather, and weeks spent at high altitude to enable the body to withstand the thin air. Or by trying the long and arduous loop through the southern ranges, which began with the harrowing perils of traversing a moving ice fall, risking the séracs and unstable fissures of the glacier at Howduin Gulch, and ended months later at Fingarra, a land whose location was still too far north to possess the requisite knowledge to repel an invasion by sorcery.

Anja sounded diminished as the harsh choices sank in. 'Do you think we could try to hide in the hills, then slip through when the fervour dies down?'

'Against shape-changers?' Mykkael splashed his face, then perched on a boulder and kneaded the knots in his calf. 'Time's a critical problem. Your sire can't die. He'll just be replaced by an heir who's suborned as a minion. That would leave you, your Grace, as the sole voice denouncing your brother's coronation. How long do you think a conquering sorcerer will suffer you to live in informed independence?'

The princess saw clearly; had already fled before the self-evident reason. If she tried to expose the truth to the court, she would face a creature who was not Crown Prince Kailen. Her false brother's ally would be the shape-changed *thing* who wore the semblance of Devall's heir apparent. Her royal suitor would stay tenderly insistent upon a state wedding. The will of the merchants would back him. For the greater weal of Sessalie, the marriage would prevail. The princess would find herself helplessly captive, or else hideously enslaved, with her own chancellors ruling against her.

'Howduin Gulch,' Anja stated, her resolute dismay all but lost in the gusting wind. 'By the glory of the trinity, I never imagined the hour I might actually freeze to death.'

'Your Grace, I won't let such a harsh fate befall you.' But the dread all but threatened to stop Mykkael's heart, that the oath of protection sworn to her sire might demand its own savage reckoning. Before the end, he might be forced to kill her cherished horses for their skins to keep her sheltered and living.

At that moment, Dedorth's glass lay trained on the ranges, focused on the progress of the scrub fire that crowned the flank of the hidden ravine. 'There,' murmured the High Prince of Devall amid the pitch dark of the cupola. Replete with satisfaction, he qualified using the voiceless communion exchanged between entities whose spirits shared obligation to the same demon. *'That's the place where Gorgenvain's long curse was thwarted from taking our prey.'* Aloud, he added, 'The search parties you plan to send out tomorrow should begin their sweep on that slope.'

Jewelled clothes stirred in the gloom as Devall's heir apparent straightened up to pass the glass to Sessalie's crown prince.

Kailen stepped over the sprawled corpse at his feet, scuffed a smear of spilled blood from his shoe, then bent in turn and peered through the instrument that Dedorth had been murdered for. 'Katmin Cut. That's rough country, up there. A desperate stretch of rock, scarred with slides.' Daily, the creature who wore the crown prince's flesh became more accustomed to human form. Soon he would not require the pretence of strong drink to mask his imperfect balance. He also grew more adept with the silent speech. *'Anja will have nowhere to go. The only route over the Great Divide kills even the hardiest travellers. She's unused to privation. An experienced search party ought to be able to overtake her and strike down her protector without undue trouble.'*

The high prince hissed, no human sound. *'Fool!'* He kicked the killed body in a fit of balked rage. *'This garrison captain you so lightly dismiss – Gorgenvain has fully tasted his scent. The report came back ugly. He's desert-bred stock from a powerful lineage, and he carries a terrible history.'*

'As a vagabond mercenary?' Kailen abandoned the glass. *'He's one man, alone, with a half-crippled leg. A guard with a steady crossbow can drop him.'*

'Is this so?' The high prince blinked eyes that flared sulphur yellow in the dark. *'I won't applaud till you drag in his carcass. This man, as you say, caused the Sushagos' demise. He helped destroy Quidjen. His command was the mercenary company hired by Prince Al-Syn and Perincar, who nearly defeated Rathtet. Gorgenvain said that this desert-bred all but delivered the victory into their grasp. The prince and his vizier*

would have prevailed had the royal family swallowed their vanity and heeded his plan for defence.'

Kailen shrugged. *'Why belabour close calls? Defeat sealed the conquest. The Efandi capitol fell to demonic forces.'*

'Yes. But the capture nearly expended Rathtet's supply of bound sorcerers. Most of his minions were destroyed as well. The original lineage that anchored the creche escaped final consumption, just barely. Do you think Rathtet himself would dare rest if he realized this "vagabond" captain of yours still survived?' The high prince rubbed his hands in agitation. *'Others would hunt in revenge, if they knew. Mykkael's close forebears made implacable enemies. The family your fighting cock captain descends from bred the shamans that Tocoquadi wasted three bonded sorcerers to eradicate. Until tonight, that bloodline was thought to be struck from the face of the world.'*

'Then we claim last glory.' Kailen's feral smile gleamed through the dark. He savoured the damp air, thick with fresh blood smell, and the sickly sweet odour of marzipan from the spilled plate of cakes the cook had sent up to tempt the scholar's finicky appetite. *'Gorgenvain will score the honour of closure, and Tocoquadi will owe him a debt. Mykkael's spirit will languish in perpetual torment. Or better, Gorgenvain could make use of the seed of his ancestry. Such get could found a creche of new sorcerers. Why not bind the bothersome creature as minion? An exquisite masterpiece of human anguish, to hold Anja captive and make her bear demonic children.'*

'The princess, I reserve for myself!' hissed the high prince in livid offence. *'I have anchored Gorgenvain's spell line through Devall. It's now up to you to extend his reach and his feeding ground, and secure his desire to claim Sessalie.'*

'We should go down at once. Or else take to the rooftop and devour your kill at our leisure.' The demonic spirit who played Crown Prince Kailen paced to the casement. He leaned into the mist, impatient to be gone, until his keen senses picked up movement and voices crossing the courtyard below. *'Someone comes.'*

* * *

The Fane Street physician knelt on the damp chill of the cobbles, an unlit torch braced between his knees. He answered Bennent's question without looking up from his effort with flint and striker. 'Well, the texts that exist are remarkably contradictory, not to mention scant unto rarity.' His second spark caught. He cupped his soft hands to the wavering flame, still expounding on his unpleasant subject. 'Kingdoms with sanctuaries have laws or decrees that consign proscribed texts to the fire. Tribal cultures with shamans have functional knowledge, but their initiates won't set that lore into writing.'

'Too dangerous,' Jussoud supplied from his place beside Taskin's litter. 'It was a man with an uninitiated mind who struck the first bargain with demons. A meddling fool, he bound over his mortal destiny to tap power from the unseen. The result has flung open the gateway to horrors. All sorcerers, and the lines that extend their foul works, descend from such dreadful mistakes.'

'How can I fight what I can't understand?' Captain Bennent cracked in frustration. Though bolstered by an escort of ten men-at-arms drawn from the roster at Highgate, he disliked the need for such secretive haste. The act of moving his king on a litter, wrapped in an anonymous blanket, made him feel foolishly vulnerable.

The guard captain sat on the remedy chest, and raked his nervous glance upwards. Late night fog had rolled up from the valley and swallowed all trace of the stars. The looming bulwark of Dedorth's tower was lost as well, the only tangible sign of its presence the moisture that dripped from the copper-clad roof. 'Every instinct I have says we're suicidal to risk sealing ourselves up in a place that has no escape route.'

'But you can't hope to battle a sorcerer, headlong,' Jussoud retorted. 'Sheer lunacy, even to try. Your unlucky casualties are not going to die. Each soldier fallen becomes a spirit enslaved, living coin to maintain the sorcerer's unholy pact with the demon who delivers his power from the unseen. The demon, in turn, keeps his bound minion alive, an unnatural immortality fashioned to fuel its insatiable appetite.'

'Trust Mykkael's experience. He gave you sound guidance.' The Fane Street physician straightened up with the cedar-laced torch brightly blazing. 'You must have a defensible refuge to hold out until help can be sent in deliverance.'

'What help?' The seneschal sniffed, displeased to be kept from his bed, and only reluctantly present to support the exhausted Duchess of Phail. 'Another sorcerer will just happen by and shoulder King Isendon's rescue?'

'Powers, no! Why do you think sorcerers' wars are so devastating?' The Fane Street physician handed the torch off to a guardsman, mopped his round face, then crouched to strike sparks to another. 'The demons that drive them are inveterate rivals. Two such bound minions upon the same ground will tear at each other, ripping the innocent earth to destruction.'

'Worse than using more fire to fight fire,' Jussoud allowed, sounding tired. Many sorcerer's lines had begun with a man who thought to dabble with danger for a cause; sound rulers cozened to buy bargains from demons for defence, only to discover themselves as evilly ensnared as the enemy they had striven to defeat. 'The less time we spend in the open, the better.'

Bennent reviewed the disparate party his skills had been charged to defend: a litter-borne king, a gravely wounded commander, two elderly, opinionated courtiers, and two mismatched healers, with only Vensic and the select pair of men-at-arms from the king's chamber able to bear weapons in active engagement. The ten guards just recruited carried no protective talismans. That made them no better than unshielded targets. Set under attack by the powers of hell, how could he mount a defence?

He must have spoken his frustration aloud, for the Fane Street physician served answer. 'The west has learned viziers, men who study lore for ways to balk sorcery. The tribes of the steppes and the southern desert train shamans, initiate talents who perceive the world of the unseen. They are the allies of the beset.' The last torch ignited. The remaining guardsman accepted its burden, while the flushed little scholar shoved up his slipped spectacles, and stood. 'You'll send a petition to ask for their favour. Or else join your cause with a kingdom or country willing to sign an agreement of shared defence. Mykkael's experience must see Sessalie's princess through, and then guide her to act as your realm's ambassador.'

The seneschal turned his chalky face, horrified. 'Rely upon *Myshkael*?' A disreputable desert-bred, lamed and on foot, armed with a sword and a handful of blow darts. 'Powers of mercy, we're lost.'

Vensic shook his head. 'Mykkael's a fit adversary. I wouldn't care to be wearing the shoes of the man who attempted to kill him.' He steadied the poles of Taskin's litter, prepared for Bennent's brisk order to march.

Inside the glow of five cedar torches, and five more alert guards who advanced with drawn swords, the company pledged to save Sessalie's freedom reached the postern of Dedorth's tower and started ascent of the worn spiral stair.

XXV. Encounter

CAPTAIN BENNENT LEFT TWO RELIABLE GUARDSMEN POSTED OUTSIDE THE TOWER DOOR. THEY STOOD UNDER orders to secure the entry, while the king's entourage filed inside, their progress delayed to a crawling pace as the litters were manoeuvred up the spiral stairwell. Outside, the mists slowly thickened. Droplets splashed down from the eaves overhead, slicking the courtyard cobbles. Sheltered from the cut of the wind, the smothering stillness seemed to diminish the distant shouts of the fire crews, labouring yet to douse the inferno that swept through the royal apartments.

Something scraped across metal, high overhead.

'You hear that?' The guardsman who spoke stepped out to investigate. 'Think it's a rat?'

'Up the tower?' his fellow said, dubious. 'On the *roof*, man? How could a blighted rat get up there?'

The faint scratching persisted, the sort of disturbance a rodent might make, gnawing the marrow from an old bone.

The other guard shoved back his helm. 'No varmint I've seen could climb a sheer wall.' He peered aloft, yet saw nothing through the choking mantle of mist. A fallen droplet splashed his upturned face, ice-cold, followed by a second that was sticky and warm. 'Mercy!' The soldier shuddered, then gasped, 'That's someone's fresh blood! Run! Shout up the stairwell and warn Captain Bennent. Tell him we've got dire trouble.'

The guardsman's cry arose from the base of the tower. Though the words were blurred to unintelligible echoes, the note of alarm carried clearly. Two litters borne in single file ascent effectively blocked the tight stairway. Completely cut off by the curve of the walls, Captain Bennent could do little but send the last man in line to investigate. He had to wait while his order was relayed downwards. Just past halfway up the narrow tower, he trailed his advance guard of four Highgate men, bearing swords and cedar-laced torches. Behind him, wheezing in sour complaint, came the seneschal of the realm, assisting Lady Phail's frail balance. The litters bearing Taskin and the king worked slowly upwards below them.

Bennent swore under his breath. As a tactical trap, this place was a living nightmare. His men were like dominoes poised in a chute, awaiting the first dropped marble.

'Stand fast,' he called to the bearers below. 'Pass word to halt down the line.'

The unwieldy column stalled in its tracks, the magnified scrape of hobnailed boots fit to set teeth and nerves on edge. More noise trailed upward, voices lost in the welter of echoes, as his worried scout addressed the rearguard. Bennent gripped his sword in frustration. He could not decipher the mishmash of words. Worse, the sentry must have left the lower door panel ajar. The updraught flared the guardsmen's held torches to rippling sheets of fanned flame.

The tangling confusion almost masked the patter of footsteps, descending the stair from above.

'Ware, forward!' called his leading guardsman.

'Report!' shouted Bennent. 'What's coming, above us?'

The front-line torchbearer responded with reassurance.

'Stand down. There's no threat. We're being joined by Prince Kailen.'

The crown prince addressed them a moment later. 'You guards! Douse those torches, at once! May the powers of the trinity preserve you from harm, didn't Lord Shaillon inform you? Cedar smoke acts as a beacon for evil. Would you draw in a sorcerer's spell lines?'

'There, so I told you!' the seneschal snapped. He abandoned Lady Phail to the support of her cane, then badgered his way past a sword-bearing guard to reach Captain Bennent's mailed elbow. 'We've dragged King Isendon through unspeakable hardship, all to no useful purpose!'

'Quiet!' cracked Bennent. To his vanguard, he added, 'Close ranks, douse nothing! I'll make my way up.'

The crown prince's startled reply floated down the narrow stairwell. 'Is that Bennent? Captain, are you seriously ordering the palace guard to stand against royal authority?'

'Highness, I act under direct command of your sire. Every cedar torch in this company stays burning.' The palace guard's ranking officer pressed upwards, spurs jingling, to back up his men at the forefront.

Poised above, Prince Kailen leaned on the rail of the landing that fronted the doorway to Dedorth's quarters. His left arm was raised, half shielding his eyes. Under the sudden, bright spill from the torches, any man's vision would become dazzled, if he had been using the glass in the darkened observatory upstairs.

'Who turned the king's mind?' Crisp, sounding irritated, the crown prince held his ground. 'The risk you are taking with Sire's life is unimaginably dangerous.' The flow of the draught wafted smoke up the stairwell. Kailen coughed, still protesting. 'Douse those torches, I say, on pain of treason.' As the fumes coiled higher, his Highness straightened and clambered several steps upwards. 'Why aren't you listening? His Majesty could take harm, even die for your bull-headed negligence!'

Bennent watched, chilled to caution. 'Stay close!' he

ordered his leading guardsmen. Then he passed word downstairs for the trailing members of the company to close up their position without straggling. He believed himself braced for whatever might come as he faced forward again, and addressed the disgruntled crown prince. 'Highness, pay heed to your sire's informed wisdom. Accept my protection and come down.'

'Madman! Fool!' Kailen's voice grated as though he had just inhaled pepper. 'You'll see us all slaughtered!' More smoke winnowed upwards. For a second, the prince's rich clothes seemed to billow, as though the form of the flesh underneath rippled into convulsion. He folded, gasping, fingers shoved through his hair.

'Mercy, what's wrong with him?' asked the torchbearer, confused. 'Has his Highness taken ill?'

'I don't know,' Bennent answered. Beyond doubt, the influx of torchlight and fumes seemed to be causing the unnatural affliction. 'Move up,' he instructed his uncertain guardsmen. 'Slowly. Carefully. Weapons ready! Hold those lit torches ahead of you.'

'Stay back!' The prince gagged through shut teeth, all but crushed to his knees as the smoke roiled over him. His face jerked and spasmed. His eyes seemed to shine, a yellow reflection that might have been tears, or something else that presaged an uncanny danger. 'On your life, Bennent, I beg you! Don't touch me!'

'What's happening!' the seneschal shrilled up the stair. 'Captain! Do something! His Highness appears to be choking.'

The guard captain stayed firm and ignored the plea.

'This is obstruction!' The seneschal clawed upwards, tried to shove past the guard, but found himself jerked short from behind. He glanced backwards, annoyed, and discovered Lady Phail standing on the furred hem of his council robe. The move was not oversight. Her insistent expression suggested his protest would fall on politely deaf ears.

'Trinity save us!' cried a guard, from above.

Faced forward again, the seneschal recoiled in revolted horror.

Through the billowing smoke, the smooth skin of Prince Kailen's face darkened as though touched by a blight. The growth spread, glittering like black glass, then sprouted into a stubble of pointed jet scales.

'Bright powers of daylight,' the seneschal shrieked. 'Your Highness, run! You're under attack by a sorcerer's catspaw! *Captain Bennent is casting a spell on you!*'

'Shut that raving idiot's mouth!' Jussoud called out from below.

'Lord Shaillon, be still!' snapped the Duchess of Phail. When the seneschal kept shouting, she raised her silver-tipped cane and jabbed the courtier's back. With his trailing robe still pinned by her jewelled shoe, the old man could not step forward to recoup his balance. He toppled on to his hands and knees, momentarily knocked speechless with outrage.

Before he could whimper, the nomad resumed his frantic instructions. 'Bennent! Right now! Your guardsmen must use the salt water and ashes!'

A bucket was passed hand to hand up the stair, followed fast by the pillowcase holding the charred remnants of the cedar that Vensic had burned in the warming pan.

'Hurry!' cried Bennent, unable to suppress a revolted shudder.

Before their shocked eyes, the crown prince was losing the semblance of his humanity. Each billow of torch smoke altered his shape. His handsome male features melted away, blond hair transformed to spiked scales, while lips and mouth distended and grew the muzzle and fangs of a predator. His bone structure become cruelly pointed and lean. Neat velvets and lawn shirt strained taut, and then shredded as the upper body enlarged with a grotesque bulge of muscle. The manicured hands curled beneath the remains of the dapper, voile cuffs were no longer a man's, but a hooked set of ripping, spiked talons.

The two guards bearing torches shrank, sweating and sick, while the swordsmen behind backstepped, dumbstruck.

'Hold your ground!' Bennent shouted, shaken to fear, as the *thing* in the stairwell crouched on its haunches, and clawed boots and breeches to shreds. No man, now, but wholly monster, it shrieked and launched to savage the guards at the forefront.

The demonic apparition charged down upon them, just as the passed bucket reached Bennent's hand. He doused the sloshing contents over the guards' heads, then snatched up the pillowcase, shoved in his arm, and lobbed a handful of ashes. The dry, gritted powder sifted out of the air, and clung to the salt-dampened skins of his two exposed point men.

The unmasked minion behind Sessalie's crown prince emitted a squalling screech. It wrenched its leap short, hissing and snarling with fury. The salt water and ash mix appeared to repel it. Wherever it encountered a dusting of ash, its gleaming jet scales became scalded.

Spared by the grace of Mykkael's instructions, the panicked lead guardsmen surged to attack with bared swords and live fire. The monstrosity scrabbled ahead of their rush, swiping its cinder-scored flesh. Smoke hazed it. Harried by the torches, it twisted in sinuous fury, lashed its tail, then streaked with a skitter of claws up the stairwell beyond the landing.

'After it, go!' Jussoud yelled from below. 'Wound it from behind, as you can. If you force it at bay, beware! It's likely to sprout wings. Bennent, if that happens, they'll need your bowman. Shoot to kill with the copper-tipped bolts.'

'He's too far downstairs,' the captain despaired. His line of march had prepared for assault from *behind*, with those men protected by talismans positioned as rearguard in the expectation that pursuit would arise from the palace. No one's ugly forethought had ever imagined Dedorth's tower might already be primed with an ambush. 'Call down!' he appealed to Jussoud. 'Have the archer's weapons passed upwards.'

Not all was lost. His lead guardsmen from Highgate had steadied their shocked nerves. They now advanced in well-disciplined step, armed with cedar-laced torches and swords. If ashes and salt served as natural banes, their banishing properties would not grant the men an impenetrably secure defence. Mere simples could not deflect a spell line with the shielding efficacy of a talisman. Yet the surprise incited by Mykkael's stopgap measures had wrested back room for hope. Given the courage to enact a prompt foray, four armed men might prevail and accomplish a dangerous kill.

'Stay close, keep together,' Bennent cautioned the duchess. He held the line, though his anguished frown bespoke his desire to bolster the rush of his guardsmen. 'Keep all torches lit. We'll regroup on the landing and take respite in Dedorth's chamber. Taskin and his Majesty can be settled in bed. We'll defend our position until we have word the top floor of the observatory is clear.'

'Lord Shaillon, pull yourself together!' Though shaken herself, Lady Phail helped the seneschal recover the wits to rise to his feet.

'Mercy!' The older man raised palsied fingers, brushed grit from his cloak, then distractedly rubbed his scraped palm, as though the raw sting might be dismissed as an errant fragment of nightmare.

'You're not going to wake up,' Lady Phail said, acerbic. 'Best face the unpleasant fact quickly.'

The seneschal stared upwards, searching the gloom of the upper stairwell. 'Powers of daylight! What was that monstrosity?'

'No power of daylight!' A quaver shot through the duchess's vexed tone. 'Nor was the foul spell cast by one of our own.' She planted her cane, squared thin shoulders and blinked, eyes damp in the haze of the torch smoke. 'I think we now know why our princess has fled. Small wonder she took no one into her confidence, with such evil at large within Sessalie.' Overcome, finally, the old woman blotted her lids with the back of her wrist.

As much in need of solace as she, the seneschal tucked her fingers over his dishevelled arm. 'I'm so sorry,' he murmured. 'You raised that boy. We all did, since the queen's death.'

'Such promise, all gone,' Lady Phail murmured. Assailed all at once by deep loss and regret, her inveterate bravery crumbled. 'Mercy deliver our poor Kailen!' Remiss at the last, her seamed cheeks streaming tears, the duchess faced down the stair. She tilted her head in crisp homage to Vensic, who bore up the poles of the commander's litter.

Their eyes locked through a moment of poignant honesty, and the shared torment of unspeakable tragedy.

Then, as though poised with her usual aplomb, the old woman awarded the son of a pig farmer a noble-born gentleman's courtesy. 'Young sir, your captain shall have my sincere apology for rank insult and thoughtless misjudgement.'

The garrison man flushed ruddy pink, then tipped her a heartfelt, grave bow. 'Then, my lady, for the sake of Mykkael's maligned honour, my task is made plain. I'll have to be sure you survive the debacle to address my captain in person.'

The cold blaze of stars did not change, or the wind, or the barren stone, locked in the tranquillity of earth element's silence. Yet something in Sessalie shifted, unseen. The change ruffled chills down Mykkael's spine and nipped gooseflesh over his skin.

The princess detected his hitched pause where she stood, watering her sweat-damp black horse at the cleft of the streamlet. 'What is it? Captain Mykkael?'

He stirred, ignored the sharp pang from his knee, then shoved to his feet all at once. 'Mount up, Princess.'

Unwilling to say more, he held out to see if she might protest or argue. Met by his braced quiet, she stared at him, nodded, then promptly made her selection. Some of his tension eased into approval, as she bridled and saddled the diminutive chestnut. Anja had gauged her six animals with a clear eye. The little mare seemed the most fit and rested.

Nor did she cavil at giving him royal orders, in turn. 'You ride the black, Stormfront. He's strong, never falters, and was probably foaled with the world's only set of iron nerves. He'll handle the nasty surprises in his stride. Once when the boys startled a snake in his path, he stomped the poor creature to paper.'

'Let us hope we won't need such staunch strength of character,' Mykkael said, his heightened uneasiness masked under soft-spoken courtesy. The loan of the gelding was a rare honor, he knew. Also a practicality plain as a steel nail tossed into a chest of gold jewellery. Not being Taskin, he could do little else except bow to her Grace's bidding. He caught up the prized animal's ornate headstall, prepared to treat with him as his noble breeding deserved.

Mykkael removed the belt from his surcoat and replaced it with a hacked-off rope length, then buckled the leather to the black gelding's chin ring to use for a rein. He had ridden with nomads often enough not to mind the lack of a bit or a saddle. Since sword and bow made a vaulting mount awkward, and the ache from his punctured thigh hampered his accustomed agility, he used the advantage of a high rock to settle himself astride.

Anja surveyed each move with critical eyes, then nodded to his tacit request that she handle the ropes leading the other two pairs of horses. As they clattered up the swept ridge under starlight, she pursued his reticent silence. 'Since you're thinking you might need your sword hand free, I ought to know what we're facing.'

Mykkael turned his head, a dark silhouette chisel-cut

against the clear sky. 'If I knew that, Princess, I would hope to use foresight, and plan better tactics than running.'

'I see.' Her gaze remained on him, fixed by a steel-clad purpose quite charmingly masked under impish determination. 'Since you have a tongue that could beat a carved statue for reticence, you don't leave me much opening for nicety. You are wounded, surely, in the leg?' His irritable glance downwards met her bright, pealing laugh. 'Yes. Don't look nettled. Your bandage has seeped. I know a fresh sword cut, don't bother to lie. The one on your hand is left in plain view, and you move like a man with a backache.'

Mykkael uttered an abrasive phrase in dialect, then added with stung dignity, 'I don't lie, Princess. I have in fact told you already. When I left the citadel, the enemy was using political pressure to divide your father's supporters. Some were incited to stop me. They failed. The scratches I suffer, meanwhile, are mine. The scar on my knee is an old one.'

Her probing regard did not shift, but sharpened to a keener perception. 'I saw your performance at last summer's tourney.' Not playful now, but deadly serious, she pressed, 'I don't know the man who could make you afraid.' When that leading statement also failed to draw him, she tried a frontal assault. 'What set you off, Captain? A moment ago, you looked fit to leap out of your skin.'

He still had no answer. The wardings he carried remained quiescent. Still hounded by the odd, nascent chill, Mykkael glanced over his shoulder. The view at his back made him rein up short. No good news, but now at least he had the means to defer this tenacious intent to expose him. 'Your Grace? Have a look.'

The valley below lay battened in mist, except for a distant, fuzzed ring that blazed like a brand of carnelian. Mykkael knew what he saw: the palace of Sessalie was set under demonic attack.

If Anja could not discern with his depth of knowledge,

she could scarcely miss the uncanny symmetry of the conflagration. She did not break down, or plead reassurance, but sat amid the warm jostle of her horses, her distress wrung to anguished silence. A moment passed; two; she forced shaken speech. 'That looks like the opened gateway to hell.'

'A wound on the earth, near enough,' Mykkael said, and this time, his acid bitterness rang through.

Anja pressed her mount up beside him. 'A sorcerer's balefire touched the palace aflame?'

The captain shook off the haunted recall of old ghosts, and the shadows of past apprehension, to give what reassurance he could. 'Thank the powers of your trinity, the blaze forms a ring. That means the long spell that raised the assault was shed by an active defence. Your sire is still safe.'

She peered at him closely. 'You suffer from witch thoughts?'

'Suffer?' He laughed. No northerner, ever, had phrased his affliction that way. His teeth flashed in a genuine smile. 'The tribal mother who disowned me at birth would more likely have counted the instinct a gift.' He tipped his head forward, still richly amused. 'After you, Princess. We need to keep moving.'

More shudders savaged him as Anja spurred past. In fact, he wanted her safe in a cave, with his warded sword guarding the entrance. Harrowing experience had well taught him not to disown the prompt of such spurious premonition. Nor would he erode his awareness by dwelling on logical doubts. He held his mind quiet as a pool of stilled water, and opened his senses to the bracing tang of the wind.

The next moment, a prickling grue raked his skin, and his anchored perception dissolved . . .

He was a crown guardsman, sword drawn, his other fist bearing a torch laced with cedar. He raced up a narrow turnpike stair in pursuit of a black scaled monstrosity. Hot breath rasped his throat. His mouth dried with fear. He rounded the last turn and reached the top floor of a tower observatory.

Amid crawling shadows thrown off by the flames, there were details, all wrong, and laced with a shrill sense of danger. The board floor held a spatter of fresh bloodstains. Yet the heedless swordsman pressed on with his rush, without taking time to investigate.

Beyond the bronze bands of the seeing glass, the fell creature he chased clawed on to the sill of the open casement. Through whirling smoke, and the flutter of flame light, its scaled form continued its horrific metamorphosis. A pair of leathery wings extended from its hunched back. Its vaned tail now wore a spiked knot of spines, which it slashed, raking to stab its oncoming adversary.

'Mercy!' gasped a second man, breathlessly arrived at the stairhead. He also was clad in a palace guard surcoat, and bearing both torch and bared sword. 'Take the thing down before it escapes!'

The pair spread out and advanced. Their raised blades gleamed by fire light. Intent on the demonic threat of the shape-changer, they all but tripped over the shed heap of clothing, abandoned to one side of the seeing glass. The left-hand man who had mired his foot was first to recognize the jewelled doublet that belonged to the High Prince of Devall. His Highness's shirt was there also, along with knit hose and dark breeches; even his boots with their stamped-gold toecaps. The ruby signet of Devall's heir apparent glinted, abandoned, on top.

The guardsman gasped, scared. 'Trinity spare us! Why would his Highness take off his clothes and leave his state seal in this place?' He poked the garments with an inquisitive foot, and laid bare a queer mark on the floorboards . . .

'No!' Mykkael hurled out of witch thought, his wrung senses spun through a hard spiral that left him sweat-drenched and clinging to the black gelding's neck. 'That's a sorcerer's short curse.' The cipher's infused lines formed a minion's chain. If its configured patterns were not ones he recognized, he still sensed their ominous undertone. A sorcerer's mark scribed in white river clay and blood was too ugly to be mistaken. 'Get out of there, now!' he gasped in distress. 'The binding connection is active!'

Yet no warning he spoke from the mountains could spare the two victims in Dedorth's observatory. Only Anja, mounted and riding close by, grasped at his forearm and shook him.

'What's wrong? Captain, what's happening?'

Fully restored to the windy heights, Mykkael bowed his head, tortured speechless. If the wardings about him maintained cool quiescence, his heart found no ease in their calm. He had stood in the path of too much disaster not to recognize the queer, sickly feeling that presaged the unfurling of demonic power. The lurch in the world's weave as the unnatural flux crossed dimensions ripped his mind into scalding recoil.

He heard Anja's cry, cranked shrill with distress, 'Merciful powers, *you knew that would happen*!'

He nodded, not needing to look as another sheet of balefire bloomed in the valley that cradled the citadel. This time the assault would not be shed by the grace of a standing ring of protection. Where the princess beheld that distant scourge as a flowering star of red light, he experienced the evil impact more fully through the gift of his wild talent . . .

The explosive eruption of spell-driven flame engulfed the top floor of the tower. Its rage consumed stone, the rare marvel of the seeing glass, and also the flesh of two living men whose tormented screams rang sharpened with the agony of the damned. The influx of the raw element surged forth from the sorcerer's mark. As though a hole had been torn through the world, it unleashed the fell fury of chaos. Anything in its path not instantly immolated reached flashpoint and ran molten, smelted metal and stone singeing the air into roiling heat. Amid a rain of liquid copper and slagged granite, the shape-changer perched on the flaming sill unfurled leathered wings and launched aloft, trailing a burning wake of shed cinders . . .

Breathing fast and hard, Mykkael shut stinging eyes, opened them, then took firm hold on his makeshift rein. He jammed down sick nausea, unclamped his scored hand, and soothed the black gelding's pawing unease. 'Shelter, now!' he snapped through scraped nerves. 'We have to find a cave, or a ledge. Somewhere under cover to stand in defence.'

'Say what you've seen,' the princess demanded. 'Let me know what sort of evil we face.'

'May you live, and never suffer the burden!' Mykkael faced forward, anguished, and urged the black gelding to a scrambling canter upslope.

The sorcerer's mark shook the tower observatory while Captain Bennent sought to cram the king's defenders into the shabby confines of Dedorth's private quarters. The tiny chamber was already bursting with the elderly scholar's belongings, its jumble of trestles heaped with unfurled star charts, and teetering stacks of books. The doors of the ambries gaped, stuffed with scrolls, beside candelabra on claw-footed stands, glued in place by old driblets of wax. The stuffed chair cleared off for Lady Phail disgorged a bent pair of spectacles, a squirrel's cache of mugs, three chewed quill pens, and several dried-up inkwells. On the armillary by the cobwebbed casement hung a mismatched pair of damp socks.

'Clean, at least,' pronounced the Fane Street physician, in enterprising search of a place to deposit the trunk of medicinal remedies. Jussoud laboured at speed to make space for Taskin and the king, since the tray left amid the unmade bed held the remains of the astronomer's supper.

With the floor space choked full, the men bearing the litters had been forced to hold back on the landing, the crates of food and sacks of assembled supplies dumped in disorder around them.

First warning of trouble, a vast, rushing wind screamed up the stairwell and hurled the king's blankets helter-skelter.

'Inside!' screamed Bennent, the flagged cloth of his surcoat clutched in one hand, and his unsheathed sword raised in the other. 'Move! Now!'

The unbearable screams of men burning, upstairs, entangled with his shouted orders. Within Dedorth's chamber, the candles snuffed out. Queer light blazed outside, raging orange, as the roaring fires of hell rampaged down, licking the darkness beyond the shut casement.

'Don't touch the walls!' yelled the Fane Street physician.

His saving cry came too late. Caught working the window latch to let in fresh air, one of the Highgate men-at-arms dropped dead on the floorboards.

'Get back!' the physician urged, frantic. 'Move away from all grounded stonework! A sorcerer's lines draw their current through air and earth. There must be a live craft mark, above us!'

'Pull together!' Jussoud called through erupting chaos, as maps and books flapped in the fierce updraught, and guardsmen blundered blindly into furnishings. 'Everyone! Move into a bunch!'

The panic-stricken rush to comply all but collided with Bennent's frantic efforts to harry the litters and bearers in from the stairwell. Vensic bundled the duchess out of her chair. Moved on trained instinct, he dragged the half-paralysed seneschal by the crushed pleats of his collar and pelted between tables, scattering books. He reached Jussoud and the physician by the doorway, which move brought the nine talismans fashioned by Perincar's lore into effective proximity.

The shield locked and sang. Blue light pealed out with

a lightning-sharp crack, widening into a sphere. The arcane defence touched the spelled conduit drawn through the tower's stonework and unleashed a burst of actinic static. Forces from the unseen collided with the vizier's geometry, and entangled with a booming, concussive report. The massive tower shook. Loose stonework rained down, hammering against the beamed ceiling. Molten stone and melted copper rained after, searing holes through the planking above.

The railing on the landing cracked and gave, with one man yanked back, saved from falling by Bennent's snatched grip on his mail shirt.

'Hold firm!' yelled Jussoud, while the world seemed to rock, and flaming cinders splashed against the glass casement. One of the roundels burst in a flying spray of smashed fragments.

Another deafening blast shook the tower. Then suddenly, all fell silent.

Eleven survivors stood in shaken, pale shock, with two more on braced litters, still breathing.

'Both the king and Commander Taskin are unharmed,' the Fane Street physician announced in a tremulous voice.

As Bennent stirred and surged towards the stair, Jussoud yanked him short. 'Stay here, Captain!' Distressed as no man had ever seen him, the nomad gathered the duchess's palsied hand and propped up the sagging seneschal. To snap Bennent out of brash shock, he said, bluntly, 'Your sentries downstairs are already dead, and the four men upstairs, consumed also. The whole top of the tower is probably gone. All that kept us alive was the closed proximity of Perincar's geometry. Lacking that grace, the structure that holds us would have gone up like a candle dropped into a forge flame.'

The Fane Street physician backed the nomad's disastrous assessment. 'Break the resonance of the copper talismans we carry, and believe it! Your king, and every last one of us, are going to die very horribly.'

'I hear you.' Bennent sheathed the sword he had drawn on blind reflex, then regarded the party left under his care to defend. 'Guardsmen!' he commanded, 'Clear Dedorth's quarters. We'll have to lie in for a siege, and hold out on the hope Captain Mykkael can win through with the princess.'

'Failed,' sent the minion, no longer wearing the semblance of the High Prince of Devall. Now a clawed monstrosity, the shape-changer crouched on the slagged rim of stone at the top of Dedorth's roofless tower, while its winged companion soared in balked fury over the site of the conflict. 'Our presence has been unmasked beyond salvage, with all hope of subtle conquest brought to impasse by a vizier's ninefold warding.' The news, and all it entailed, was heard by the bound sorcerer of Gorgenvain, lying wakeful in the king's bed in Devall. Curt orders returned on the breath of the moment, graven with the demon's imperative desire: 'Take down your antagonist, Mykkael, and after him, obliterate the last daughter of Isendon's lineage . . .'

XXVI. Pursuit

Mykkael sensed the backlash as the flux of the unseen recoiled through another ripple of change. A glance at the mist-covered valley below affirmed the sharp prompt of his instinct. The upsurge of a ring of protection had reduced the distant flare of red balefire to a raggedly flickering circle. The close defeat of the sorcerous assault left a dulled, sullen glow where unnatural forces had caused solid stone to run molten.

The immediate assurance given to Anja, that her royal sire survived, lent Mykkael no false peace of mind. On the contrary, he was forced yet again to revise his already desperate escape plan. King Isendon's victory would not buy him more time. The princess's plight was not going to gain respite. Any careful, staged passage across Howduin Gulch now became a sure route to disaster. Scatton's Pass, also, would take far too long, even had they carried the requisite ropes and equipment.

Trapped by a vicious quandary, Mykkael faced the impossible, last option: the fifty-league passage of sheer rock ravine, infested with kerrie nests, and savaged by the boiling froth of the flume that had pummelled the bones of every rash fool who ever attempted the crossing. Mykkael measured the hazards of riding Hell's

Chasm, and chose certain doom without flinching.

Better to die thrashed to ribbons on a rock spit, any horrible fate to stave off the risk of falling prey to a demon-bound sorcerer. Let his human failure buy Anja a natural death, and not the howling terrors he had glimpsed in the pit of Orannia's madness.

'You look grim as the judge forced to hang his own kin,' the princess observed at due length.

'I don't like the country,' Mykkael said, a sore truth. They were riding the knife-edged spine of the rim. The position left them ruthlessly exposed, with the horses forced to pick each precarious step with excruciating caution. Although the captain could have left matters there, Anja's resourceful character demanded better respect. 'Nor can I leave you in dangerous ignorance. Your false suitor has unmasked his true form, as well as the crown prince he suborned in liaison. They walk this world as hell's minions, but reclothed in the altered mortality of their stolen flesh.'

Anja covered her mouth with her wrist, her seat in the saddle stark straight as she absorbed the horrible, warped destiny that had befallen her brother, and also her dearest beloved: the young man she should have married in state ceremony, wreathed in the flowers of harvest. Her voice emerged muffled. 'You expect they'll attack?'

'One of them must, Princess. Inevitable tactics. The other will stay to hold your sire hostage until Sessalie falls under conquest.' Mykkael paused, measuring his words with much the same care as the horse underneath him took footing a brave course over the jumble of cracked rock.

Yet the princess's nimble mind leaped ahead of him. 'You seek a cave or a cleft, so you said. Then you're needing a guard on your flank?'

'Both sides, and behind,' Mykkael affirmed. 'With your Grace exposed at my back, I can't hope to fight off the assault of a winged predator.'

She received that dreadful disclosure with no more than a choked-off gasp. Darkness hampered his detailed review of her face. Mykkael could not tell if she was silently crying. Her slight hand on the rein never faltered. Hating the additional cruelty, he added, 'I'm sorry. We won't have much time to prepare.'

Anja tugged her cloak around her slim frame. 'There are caves not far distant, old lairs used by kerries.' To her credit, she faced apprehension without begging for useless reassurance. 'The caverns are found in the gulch that leads to Hell's Chasm, and to make matters harder, it's spring. We could run headlong into the fire and claws of a mated pair nesting a clutch.'

Mykkael tossed her an insouciant smile, as much to shake off the pervasive gloom of his doubts. 'Princess, if I can't defend you against a few kerries, my war-hardened skills aren't going to matter against the shape-changed get of a demon. Do you swim?'

'Oh, yes.' Her smile held the spontaneous fire of her indefatigable spirit. 'But only in private, and in the douce company of four attired maidservants.'

Mykkael laughed. 'My stark-naked sword blade will have to suffice to vouchsafe the lapse in propriety.'

'Better surety than the women, since the indolent creatures invariably used to fall asleep. Shai and I could have invited the stableboys. Once, to flout the rules, we nearly did.'

A steel shoe rang out in dissonance as the black gelding slipped. Mykkael gave on the rein, his reaction pure reflex. 'What held you to prudence, your Grace?'

Anja regarded him, her green eyes turned shrewd. An animate mischief suffused her flushed face by the starlit gleam off the ice fields. 'Taskin must have overheard the whispers in the tilt yard. I don't think it was coincidence he dropped his comment in my presence, that he hated to be forced to the task of whipping mere boys caught making lewd eyes at a princess.'

They had been brash adolescents, children who could have been scarred for life through the foolish play of two girls who lured them on by the heat of raw instincts. 'Shai and I had no intention of any serious misbehaviour,' the Princess of Sessalie admitted. 'Our prank was meant to give Lady Phail a livid fit, and I saw the horrid truth, that we would have used the stableboys as game pieces.' Even now, remorse showed in the wry set to her shoulders. 'That was the first time I was made to recognize that servants were people with feelings.'

'An *apology*, Princess, for the constraints of my station? Or is this some backhanded diplomat's warning to salve the inevitable bruises to my dignity?' Mykkael bridled at the insult, his carriage hackled stiff. 'What kind of an upbringing do you think I had, to require that high-handed slap on the wrist?'

She grinned broadly, the witch. 'How delightful to find the breathing man underneath the impervious swordsman. I would rather hear you talk without the provocation. What sort of snob do you think I am, *Captain*, to accept a protection that *might come to cost your life* as nothing else but my royal due?'

The strike caught him blindsided. Left speechless, and strangely touched in the heart, Mykkael shook his head. 'Mehigrannia have mercy,' he murmured the moment he managed recovery. 'What under the nine names of hell have I done to deserve your vicious wit? Perhaps I set too high a value on privacy?'

'If you do, it wasn't preference,' Princess Anja replied. 'Sessalie has treated you like a pariah, and such solitude has marked you with sorrow.'

That bold statement closed him like a netted clam. He clamped his heels and urged the black gelding ahead, his face set against the blast of the wind, until the cold burned his ears to red agony. They crossed over the ridge crest. He led, wrapped in silence. Only as the horses descended the back slope into a sheltered stand of pine, did the stinging surprise of the princess's onslaught relent. By then, the jab to his pride had cooled down enough. Mykkael could ponder her words without setting his teeth. Good-natured and something beyond rueful, he realized just how cleverly the royal minx had played him away from concern for her threatened welfare. He recalled he had been sounding her fears, and rejected her shameless deterrent.

As the horses wound through the storm-stunted firs, he offered truce, but not capitulation. 'Princess, if you want to dig up my history for diversion, that's demeaning.'

She grinned back with a candour fit to wrench a man to the soul. 'Only if you see me as Isendon's daughter. I'm a human being, first, a blood princess second, and a gently raised woman last of all. Please call me Anja. I would have my life unencumbered by formalities that don't have any meaning out of court.'

'Princess,' Mykkael said in gentle remonstrance, 'when have I given you less than your due as a human being first of all?'

He had done far more. The shaming force of his honesty threatened her with sympathy, and worse: his evident quality cried out to her need for close friendship. The isolation she saw in his outsider's face was in fact the reflection of her own secret loneliness. Too resilient for self-pity, Anja laughed at the trap she had spun for herself. 'A rotten influence, to be born royal. There are too many times when perception gets turned by the surfeit of admiring flattery.'

'That's hedging, Princess. If you're afraid, then *be afraid,*' Mykkael snapped with clipped force. 'If you're going to quit pretending, do it now and spare me the anguish.' Hardened by the awareness he could not grant her shelter by tempering his disclosures, he aimed his dart well, and struck. 'Don't make me second-guess the state of your mind. The distraction is a hindrance that could make or break the long odds of securing your survival.'

She stared at him, shuddered, then curled up on the

neck of her mare and started uncontrollably shaking. 'No one has ever lived through Hell's Chasm!'

This time, the ambush worked: her ragged terror burst through her tight barriers. As the onslaught of weeping stormed her reserves, he realized her bravery exceeded his first assessment: *somehow, at some point, she had guessed that Howduin Gulch was not going to pose a safe option*. Her intelligence was sharp enough to cut, which posed him a snagging difficulty. Given the arduous terrain lying ahead, too bright an imagination could break the active mind with overpowering dread.

The scope of his charge dwarfed all of his skills, left him humbled to rage for his helplessness. As a human being, first, the young woman on the chestnut mare was a treasure more than worth every sacrifice.

Mykkael let her savage anxiety wear down through the fiercely let salt of her tears. After a while, he laid a hand on her back, offering warmth and shared comfort. 'It's a very short step to arrive at a solution,' he said when Anja ran dry and stirred. She rallied quickly, her mind clear once again. The restored tilt to her chin bespoke a new determination to recover her plundered freedom.

When her wan smile resurged, the captain obliged and removed his tacit touch. 'We'll just have to become the first fools who live to blaze the trail.'

Pale gold wisps of hair snagged out of her braid streamed in the gusts off the heights. For one moment, in fast silence, Anja surveyed his immovable calm. 'You're not afraid, Mykkael?'

He owed her the truth. 'Not of the hazards that lie in Hell's Chasm.' For the sorcerer who pursued them with two shape-changed minions, she would see soon enough: the fear in him outstripped all words.

With that wrenchingly difficult turning behind, and the rock ridge that arose to the Howduin Gulch glacier dropping away at their back, the terrain for a while became easier. The horses made speed through a wracked stand of fir, and the gusts wore the fragrance of resin. The wheeling stars turned halfway between midnight and dawn.

Anja requested the chance to pause for the horses to rest and feed. Mykkael gently refused her. 'For your safety, Princess, we should not dismount.' Here, the harsh footing lay softened under thin soil and drifts of dead needles. They might have no better opportunity to make speed. The demonic creature the sorcerer had set on their trail would overtake their position. To be caught unprepared would bring them to certain disaster.

Therefore they wended their way downwards, into the bowl of the valley beneath the wild, raked rock of the heights. The massive glacier glimmered above them, a towering rickle of groaning ice that spilled into a jewel-toned lake. The sere ground grew a scatter of mosses and fern, stabbed through by spindled fir trees. Beyond the lake, the roaring flood of spring snowmelt carved the channel that plunged like a crack in the world, and framed the massive ravine of Hell's Chasm.

Although the easier path ran along the packed gravel shore, the riders made their way on the slope, under the thin cover of evergreens. Though the ermine that inhabited the forested vale were too small to draw hunting kerries, horses or strayed cattle posed a warm-blooded attraction. The great predators occasionally visited to roll in the ice. The glacier above showed their carved wallows, where they scoured off the parasites that burrowed into their ruff coats and nipped between their lapped armour of scales.

The horses made steady time in staged intervals at trot and walk, with Benj's hound limping alongside. As they traversed the rim of the lake, Mykkael was forced, once again, to admire their superb condition. Hard as he pressed them, they moved without flagging. Even in the thin air of the heights, they recovered their spent wind quickly. He noted their individual strengths and watched Anja counter their weaknesses. He marked them, each one, to glean deeper insight into her character, and also to know the hearts of the animals, whose tough sinew and courage must play their part to sustain a kingdom beset by dire peril.

Whoever had paired them had chosen well, the playful, inquisitive buckskin matched with delicate Covette, whose fiery nature restrained his rough teasing with tail lashes and flattened ears. Anja allowed her mount free rein to chastise her boisterous teammate. Whenever the posturing progressed to bared teeth, or a kick, a spoken reprimand curtailed the antics.

On the paired lead rope, trailing, Vashni's studdish bullying was balanced by Fouzette, a northern-bred mare with a sturdy frame and stoic patience that bordered on laziness. She wasted no move, planted each solid step with no-nonsense efficiency. What she lacked in grace, she made up for in broad-chested power and deep heartgirth, and a fitness like forged iron nails.

Stormfront had won Mykkael's admiration from the first snatched glimpse of a witch thought. When the gelding was not being pestered by his partnered mare's nipping head butts, he had the habit of peering behind, as though to size up his rider. Taken by his soft, round eye, and his odd, little satisfied snort as he faced front each time, Mykkael stroked his neck with appreciative fingers.

Anja noticed. 'You like that horse well, I see that much.'

The captain turned his head, his quick smile there and gone in the darkness. 'Who could resist?' Through the light talk, he kept his trained faculties tuned into ruthless focus. No rustle of wind through the boughs missed his notice, no snapped twig, and no scattered fragment of gravel. 'He's superb.'

The princess's reply held a hint of pure wickedness. 'Not to most men, he's not. In fact, he's got a widespread reputation for dumping puffed-up braggarts.'

Mykkael raised his eyebrows. 'Is that so?'

Anja nodded. 'You don't hang on his reins. Try that, you'll find out. Stormfront doesn't like brazen authority.'

'Do you ever for a minute stop testing a man?' Mykkael tipped up his face, his glance sweeping the open sky, and marking the turn of the stars. The tension behind his relentless vigilance could not help but set her on edge.

For of course, she had noticed the slope became steeper and rockier with each passing stride. Her response belied the gnaw of her doubts. 'Are you asking the woman or the Princess of Sessalie?'

'Both, of course.' A chill raked his skin. His move masked from view, Mykkael tested the strung tension on the bow slung over his shoulder.

'Then the answer is, seldom. Do men always measure themselves against power? Behind me stands the weal of a kingdom. Although I don't bear the burden of crown rule, I am seen as a figure attached to authority.' Anja stared forward, where the black fringe of the wood melded into the shadowed walls that narrowed into the impassable cleft. The lakeshore now wore slight ripples of current, with the throaty, distant boom of rushed water reflected off vertical cliffs. Her whispered appeal seemed a prayer to the brute elements. 'I have to survive this.'

'For the chance to gallop horses through the meadows to pick wildflowers, and wear bracelets that sing with small bells, and not least, for the passion you bring to your verses of poetry.' When she glanced at him, startled, the captain added, 'That's what I saw in your portrait, your Grace.'

In daylight, perhaps, her rush of embarrassment might have raised her fair skin to a flush. 'Has anyone said that you see far too much?'

'Not in my life as a mercenary.' The crawling chill that brushed over his senses ripped up a ruffle of gooseflesh. Mykkael urged the black gelding to a brisk trot, not liking the fact that the horses' steel shoes struck stray sparks off the flint-bearing rock. That moment, any small detail that might draw attention cranked his instincts to shrilling unease.

Anja spurred her pert chestnut. Well drilled to the lead rein, the other pairs followed without lagging. Perhaps drawing comfort from conversation, the princess picked up on the subtlety. 'Then you weren't a born recruit?'

'No.' Mykkael cast a tense glance over his shoulder; saw nothing but fir trees and pale stone. 'Your questions are better off held until later.' Pitched to the verge of *barqui'ino* reflex, he gave way to the cry of his primal hunch and unslung the bow from his shoulder. 'Watch for kerries.'

'Not the winged fetch of the demon?' The princess shortened the lead rein, drawing her horses in close.

Mykkael snapped off a negative headshake. 'Not yet, we can hope. My wardings aren't roused.' He measured her distance, and gained the insight that she undoubtedly understood archery. Her due care not to jostle the black gelding's balance meant she had ridden with huntsmen, or else had some skill at the butts.

He ventured the question. 'How well can you shoot?' Stormfront answered his heels, leaped over a gully, then shouldered through a stand of young aspen, ever closer to the gap where the coiling black current funnelled into the glacial lake's outflow.

'Provided the bow isn't over my strength?' Anja followed him, rattling over the loose pebbles piled up by the pressure of last winter's ice. 'I usually hit what I aim at, but then, bagging hare for some villager's table, one's hand doesn't usually shake.'

'Stick with the skinning knife, then. A small blade can be used to disable a talon. Cut the tendon at the back, just under the claw sheath. That's the best way to release any monster's clamped grip. Strike for the eye if you're bitten.'

The princess met his matter-of-fact instruction with an unnerved exclamation. *'You've fought kerries before this?'*

'No.' But he had twice killed a roc in the caldera of the

Vhael Wastes, and once driven off a king dragon bent on stalking the drovers who worked his supply train through Tirrage.

He had no chance to explain his experience. The next moment, a black shadow occluded the stars, to a whistle of sliced air off spread wings. If the kerrie had come to preen in the glacier, the rich, sweaty scent of Anja's six horses posed a morsel too tempting to pass up. The creature banked sharply, its tasselled tail streaming, and sleek feline hindquarters tucked under golden-shagged flanks. No question, the creature was hunting, its taloned foreclaws raked to extension.

'This way!' Mykkael shouted, driving Stormfront ahead through the thick stands of saplings lining the lakefront.

While riders and horses crashed through the greenwood, the kerrie swooped down in pursuit. Glimpsed through the treetops, the monster came on, its neck thickly maned and its lean belly armoured with scales. No ready target presented itself to the defending archer. The plate-sized orb of the beast's slitted eye was cased in a hardened, clear membrane, shielding its vision from the blasting, cold air, and the sparks trailing back from its horn-rimmed nostrils. The wind blew sour with the trace scent of sulphur from the fire sacs under its jowls. If it chose to spew, the volatile fluids it belched would vent flame from its razor-sharp beak.

Kerries by nature preferred to feed, raw. Yet if the creature that rushed down on wing-leather sails and bronze pinions could not stoop and strike through the branches, it would scorch its prey on the run, then land at leisure and gnaw on the charred meat of the carcasses.

Cursing for the bitter necessity, Mykkael grasped the black's mane, left-handed. The bow hung from his wrist, a slapping distraction that hampered the gelding's shoulder. He had to work fast, or risk breaking the weapon, as he leaned from Stormfront's back. Pressed to a flat gallop, he ripped the lead rein securing the last pair of horses from Anja's clenched fist.

'No! Powers have mercy!' She snatched at him, furious.

'Princess! We have to! Just ride!'

She reined her mare sideways, enraged fit to kill. 'Captain, please, no!'

Her cry of betrayal scored his heart like cold iron, but did not deter his intent. Too late for recovery, the sacrificed horses swerved away from their bunched fellows. Mykkael shouted. He drove the loosed animals leftwards and down, towards the open expanse of the lakeshore.

The volatile grey Vashni pounded away, dragging the less than willing Fouzette on the impetus of his hazed panic. Both horses galloped. They had worked in the bridle, matched together, for months. Fully extended, their powerful strides drove them over the rough ground, their cheek-by-jowl heads snorting trailed plumes of steamed breath.

Offered an unencumbered target, the marauding kerrie clapped down its wings and veered in bloodthirsty pursuit.

Mykkael dropped his makeshift rein. He snatched up the bow, yanked an arrow out of the jouncing quiver. To Anja, he shouted, 'Play them! Like wickets! Use their minds!'

Her face changed. She responded, and pealed out the voice cue for the halt. Then, wrung white with desperate hope, she repeated the command, louder. She hung every shred of her will on the call, that the horses' schooling might override their terror-stricken instinct to bolt.

Blessed Fouzette dropped on to her haunches, a sliding stop made at punishing speed. The sudden jerk caught Vashni short on his lead rein. He spun sideways, wrenched out of stride, while the kerrie whisked over his grey crest and missed its aimed strike. The killing, bared talons slammed into bare ground. Feathers slapped up loose stones, rattling through a bone-chilling bellow of rage.

'Jee!' shouted Anja. 'Jee! Now!' Tears streamed down

her face, pride and grief mingled as she watched her magnificent horses dare the murderous predator that spun in recoiling fury to rend them.

They answered, wheeled right, Vashni's mad scramble fought into breathtaking recovery. Ears back for the shame of missing his first prompt, he threw his heart into the game he had trained for, one that tested the limits of agility and obedience, with the prize of this match stark survival. As Fouzette reached her rhythm, the grey gelding blended his powerful stride into unison. He hurtled down the lakeshore, paired stride for stride with his sturdy, dependable teammate – as he had through countless afternoons in Gurley's back meadow, yoked to the mare by the arch of a wicket hoop, attached to their tandem harness. Fiery grey gelding and northern-bred bay, they poured out their hearts to lead the grand chase, as though they charged in safety over the greensward, opposed by a third horse and rider contending to snatch the target prize looped in the wicket sling.

Mykkael had his strung arrow sighted. Yet no opening for a clear shot presented as the kerrie sprang aloft and arrowed into thunderous, flapping pursuit. Air slapped off its vast, pumping wings and pounded gusts through the verge of the aspens. Such roiling wind would drive any arrow awry, even had the monster's scaled underparts granted a target for an archer taking aim through dense trees, from the back of a galloping horse.

'Wheel them again!' he told Anja, breathless. 'That kerrie can't turn with anything near your horses' agility.'

Anja's cry rang out clear and steady over the clatter of hooves. 'Haw! Haw, now!'

Bay mare and grey gelding dropped on to their hocks like paired dancers, the more agile Vashni digging into his counterstride on the outside, anchored by Fouzette's solid pivot. Again, the kerrie overshot. As its thrashing wings rose to brake, Mykkael snatched his moment and released.

His arrow arched out, clipped a twig, and glanced left.

Yet he had not waited to score his first effort. His next arrow was already nocked and drawn. The bow sang again before the first shaft dropped, clattering, amid the bare stone by the lakebed. The second shot did not go awry, but still missed the vulnerable moment of the kerrie's fullest extension. It caught the creature's right wing through the down-sweep, and lodged deep in the tissue between joints. If not a kill, the missile would hamper. The sting as the point tore through working flesh caused the enraged monster to spew molten fire.

'Go! Go! Go!' pealed Anja, exhorting her horses to gallop.

'Bring them back!' Mykkael ordered. 'Turn them under the trees if you can.'

This time, she gave him her trust without question. 'Jee! Vashni, Fouzette, here to me! *To me!*'

They responded, manes flying, and nostrils distended to show the red flare of the linings. The kerrie descended hard on their streaming tails, its lamed wing scarcely posing a hindrance.

'Too far out. They're going to be hit,' said Mykkael. 'Use your commands, try to dodge and win clear.'

'Whoa! Fouzette, Vashni, *Whoa!*' Anja halted the team, swerved them once, then twice, forcing the kerrie to fly wrenching manoeuvres to keep pace with their drilled co-ordination. The arrow-shot wing suffered under the strain. A spreading flood of scarlet now stained the bronze feathers on the underside of the tendons. As the horses spun again, Anja called. Their flat run veered upslope, as the captain required, then stayed on straight course for the treeline.

Now, the kerrie's driving strokes in pursuit showed a ragged, uneven rhythm.

'Oh, well done, Princess!' Mykkael reined up short. He nocked another arrow. While Stormfront stood in quivering obedience underneath him, he pulled the bow to full draw for the shot that would save, or the miss that was going to leave them burned meat in the beak of a merciless predator.

There, Mykkael held. Though his scourged back stung like vengeance, he tracked his aim through the dark lattice of branches. He held, as the teamed horses came pounding in; held as the kerrie swooped upwards to clear the wind-ravelled edge of the wood.

He released, point-blank. His arrow launched out, hissing, and thudded into the soft ventral muscle at the root of the monster's tail. Mykkael caught up his dropped rein, stabbed in his heels to roust the black gelding to flight. 'Turn!' He slapped the princess's mare, merciless in his need to get her away. 'Run!'

Anja slammed her mount into a tight pirouette, her cry for the horses milling in wild-eyed confusion beside her. 'Jee! Jee!' Exhorting, she urged the two still on lead ropes to move into pace with her mount. Running, now, her desert-bred chestnut pounding hard after Stormfront's lead, she threaded her reckless, galloping course through the thinning stand of aspen. Shouting, she summoned the loose bay mare and grey gelding pelting under the trees. 'Fouzette! Vashni! Haw! Haw now! To me!'

The frantic team swerved, caught their lead rein short on a sapling, just as the kerrie, squalling in mortal pain, crashed into the treetops over their heads.

'Go! Go! Go!' shrilled Anja. 'To me! Fouzette, Vashni, to me!'

As one horse, the pair reared. They ripped clear of obstruction, staggered on scrambling legs, then regained their shared balance and bolted.

'To me! To me! To me!' Anja's encouragement sawed through the crackle as the downed kerrie hurled fire, and exploded the saplings in conflagration.

Her horses responded, pounding in lathered terror through flaming boughs, and a white fall of cinders. Tails singed, hides scored and stinging, they galloped headlong after their guided companions.

Mykkael weighed the risk, turned them out of the wood. He swung right by the water, then whipped the small herd in a clattering dash down the packed gravel fronting the lakeshore. When Anja cried out, begging respite, he touched the rein, then angled Stormfront's long stride just behind her mare's streaming tail.

'Fly, Princess!' he exhorted her. 'Keep your horses together. Make for the head of the chasm. We can't stop, now. The kerrie is down, but a demon's minion flies the ridge just behind it. If we're not under shelter before it arrives, it will slaughter your brave teams on the run.'

XXVII. Trap

MYKKAEL MUST HAVE SEEN FOUZETTE'S LIMP BEFORE THEY FORDED THE FRESHET. UNTIL THEN, THE MARE'S high-spirited excitement had masked the onset of pain. The blood streaming from the gash on her left pastern had been hidden by her dark stocking. When she emerged on the far bank, hobbling three-legged, Anja noticed the ripped flap of skin, opened almost to the bone.

Her cry of dismay met Mykkael's deadpan calm. 'She and Vashni saved your life, Princess. I promise we'll do all we can for her.'

'What she needs is a lengthy soak in this stream. Cold water will keep down the swelling.' All but frantic to attend to the damage, Anja surged to dismount.

Her move was caught short by the captain's firm clasp on her forearm. 'No, Princess! Stay mounted. This place is unsafe. Your mare's wound won't swell as long as she's moving, and we can't make speed over this rough terrain, anyway.'

The princess resisted him, anguished. 'For mercy, Captain.' Her plea echoed off the rock cliffs, and rebounded through the tumble of rushing water. 'She's in terrible pain!'

Yet Mykkael remained adamant. 'The faster we reach

shelter, the sooner we can take steps to ease her.' He glanced over his shoulder, and scanned the black shore of the lake left behind, past the cut leading into the chasm. He saw no sign of Benj's best hound; had not, since the kerrie descended. The fires kindled by the monster's death throes stippled the basin in copper, beneath a star-scattered sky that stayed empty. The looming ice of the Howduin glaciers, and the snagged profiles of corniced peaks showed no trace of moving pursuit. If the shaman's mark on his sword hilt stayed mute, the sign gave him no reassurance. Mykkael's instincts remained nettled, as though the sorcerer's minion made a game of the hunt, lurking just outside range of his wards.

The streamlet where they had paused to regroup raced between the moss-capped boulders of a dell. Here, the vertical rise of the rim wall offered no cover, and no haven to stand off attack.

Mykkael stood by his initial decision. 'A pause in this place could cost us our lives. Princess, that injury has laid tendon sheaths bare. Fouzette's leg will stiffen, the longer we linger. I have seen enough suffering on campaigns to know she has no better choice but to bear up and go onwards.'

He spoke sound sense. She knew this. The streamlet's surrounds left no margin for flight. Another attempt by a hunting kerrie would end in bloodletting disaster. Mykkael clung to the rags of his patience. Orannia's straits had taught him too well that the heart could not always be reconciled with the brutal demands of necessity.

Soon enough, Princess Anja relented. The anger as she shook off his grasp reflected sore grief, and the wear of remorseless exhaustion. They pressed ahead to the stagger of Fouzette's lamed stride, and passed into the ever deepening gloom as the high rock of the gulch swallowed the sky on both sides. To the left, the black swirl of the current acquired white snags, torn by the jut of obstructing stones, and the crabbed limbs of wedged deadfalls.

The gusts that ripped down through the notch wore a fine spray of moisture, loud with the swelling thunder of unseen falls and leaping rapids. Guano streaked the overhead cliffs, where kerries had perched to dry out soaked wings, or seek nesting cracks in the ledges.

Again, Mykkael measured the turn of the stars. Perhaps two hours remained before dawn. Daylight would bring a small measure of reprieve, since kerries preferred feeding at night. The minions of demons also disliked strong light. Although they could fare abroad after sunrise, their senses were sharpest in twilight and darkness. The air and earth ties that channelled a sorcerer's long spell weakened as well, under the fire-sign influence of the sun. The assault he expected was most likely to strike before daybreak.

Mykkael scoured the gulch for a likely cave or deep crevice. If he could find a defensible site, he might widen his options, even waylay hell's minion, and trap it.

Anja broke the strung silence between them. At first, he thought she spoke out to redress the upset caused by Fouzette's laboured breathing. When the rush of the water forced her to speak louder, he realized *just what* direct question she asked of him.

'How bad is the injury to your back, Captain?'

Taskin's three stripes; blinding glory, how was he to explain that self-evident mark of chastisement? Or the scars underneath, brutal remnant of a more punishing ordeal, that his last campaign officer had taken amiss, not believing his account of the truth? Mykkael faced straight ahead, made aware of the sting that should have warned him Jussoud's dressings had torn through from the rigours of pulling the bow.

'Fouzette can still walk. My archery's dead accurate. What I call a scratch does not signify until my fighting strength is impaired.' She opened her mouth; he cut her off. 'Not your business, *your Grace*, unless I can't defend you. Which is obviously far from the case.'

His phrasing carried a shade too much vehemence. Too

late, Mykkael saw the clamped set to her jaw. His misjudgement had happened because he was tired, *and hurting, she saw that much, too clearly*. The lapse on his part only made him more slit-eyed and furious.

'How you hate it when somebody takes notice of you,' Anja observed at due length.

Revenge for the mare, Mykkael could but hope, or the acid-drawn prod of sheer boredom. He happened to be the sole target at hand to field her inquisitive interest.

Since her keen innuendo *could* force a response, he snatched at the shallow retreat. 'In my trade, the man who was noticed became the most likely enemy target. I don't like being shot at, with arrows or words.'

'I was not attacking,' said Anja, nonplussed. 'If my value is more in the world than a princess, then yours goes beyond being a soldier.'

'Does it?' Mykkael grinned. 'I've never been hired, except for my sword.'

She refused his insouciance. 'Yes, but who are you, beneath the trappings of your profession?'

He stonewalled her. 'A mercenary.'

'Who do you become, when you lay down your weapons?' She ducked a sprung branch, undaunted, still caring. 'Has no one but family ever loved you?'

He grinned the more broadly. This time well warned, and foreknowing his mistake, he dismissed her kindly meant overture. 'You'll have to see whether I talk in my sleep.'

The sorry truth lay too close to the bone: that his quarters in the keep contained only a cot, a trestle and stool, and one simple box of belongings. His Lowergate officers all knew that he slept with his hand on his sword grip. Not being Anja, they had never made comment on behaviour more suited to a hunted fugitive, or a man pursued by the pain of an active tragedy. He had no wish to dredge up the ghastly details. The Princess of Sessalie was not Jussoud, with a brother's blood kinship that tied family honour to the facts of Orannia's misfortune.

'Coward,' said Anja, the accusation served after a ruthlessly measuring pause.

Had she not been a princess under threat of cold sorcery, Mykkael would have laughed for the irony: of all the insults she might have tried, that one alone could not touch him. While silence was his preferred response, he could not afford the blind self-indulgence of risking her slightest contempt; not when the matter of her survival relied on her trust in his resources.

He inclined his head, deferential, and not smiling. 'Your Grace.'

'Blinding powers of daylight, Captain!' In darkness, her flush could be felt, and her fury.

Yet whatever else Anja intended to say, Mykkael pressed Stormfront ahead. Throughout the next hour, he presented her with the unflinching dignity of his back.

In that fashion, they rode down the throat of Hell's Chasm. The low ground of the ravine wended deeper into the narrowing channel carved out by scouring whitewater. The footing turned slippery, then treacherous. At each crook and turning, the bared shelves of the ledges grew shagged with moss. Although the crest of the spring melt had passed, the thrash of the cataract was deafening. The inexhaustible race of white foam misted the air with flung spray. That unending barrage of splashed moisture combined with the funnelled rush of the wind. Mounts and riders alike suffered the bone-hurting cold. Tails tucked, shoulders hunched, they plodded in silenced misery. The horses picked their way in single file, often sliding over the loose wrack hurled down in the spate of the thaws. The rock cleft reared up and towered on both sides, heaped at the base with smashed stone and split trees that had crumbled off the high rim wall.

Since the cavalcade moved more slowly than a human on foot, Mykkael slipped off Stormfront and signalled the princess to dismount. The piled boulders made punishing work for his knee. He had to lead each stride with his good leg, at the risk of turning an ankle. The encumbrance of the terrain gave him cold sweats, alongside the incongruous *fact* that the sorcerer's minion withheld from attack.

He chafed for the unease.

Such restraint made no sense, with the woman under his charge and six straggling horses forced to a tactical standstill. Mykkael fretted over the unfavourable odds, too well versed not to worry. No enemy ceded ground to no purpose. At each turn, he expected the trap that would set the final seal on their doom.

The crawling pace wracked his taut nerves, until, almost, Mykkael would have welcomed the whine of roused wards in the sword strapped over his back.

No such raised warning disturbed him. His limp degenerated to a lurching hobble, until he had to cling to Stormfront's mane to stay upright. Another league would bring his collapse, if he failed to find secure respite. The roar of the watercourse grew steadily louder, dire warning of worse ground ahead.

'We need to stop soon,' Anja called at last. Not for her own sake: the bay mare, Fouzette, was visibly flagging, dropped back from the rear of the column.

Mykkael nodded, distressed by the thought that they might have to snatch rest in the open. He was too spent to stand a reliable watch. That quandary posed a disastrous peril. To fall asleep without shelter, day or night, was to invite certain death. He wrestled the despair of outright defeat, when a crook in the chasm opened ahead. There, he found the site he had hoped for: the dark mouth of a cavern cut into the cliff wall, too low to be of interest to kerries, and with footing the horses could manage without stumbling.

He led them in, too exhausted to muster the grace of diplomacy as he enacted precautions to make sure of the ground. Keeping the princess and all of her horses inside the close range of his wardings, he explored by the light of a flaming, dry branch. The place was scarcely hospitable, strewn with brackish puddles and cobwebs. The only dry crannies were fragrantly sprayed, or else fouled by fish-eating muskrats.

Anja met Mykkael's anxious glance with a smile worn thin by fatigue. 'I can sweep out the animal droppings, and chase a few nesting spiders, but Fouzette's cut leg must come first.'

'I'll help tend your mare the moment I'm sure no sorcerer's minion has visited this place before us.' Mykkael passed over the lead holding Stormfront and Kasminna, shocked to discover the chill in her fumbling hand. The princess had endured uncomplaining for hours. Doubtless she had been frozen since the last stop at the spring. 'Stay behind me, your Grace.'

No help for the fact she must wait a bit longer before her discomfort could be redressed. Remiss for his failure, since the hazard of cold might fatally dull her reactions, Mykkael shed his surcoat and bundled the cloth over her shoulders forthwith. Then he moved ahead with drawn sword, the crude brand raised overhead. Back turned, all business, he began a meticulous inspection of the cavern's rock walls.

Every petty distraction was cast aside. Using all five senses, and sounding the well of deep instinct, the captain sustained his acute concentration until he was satisfied the place held no watchers, and no trace of a sorcerer's mark.

The princess's dumbstruck silence passed unnoticed until after Mykkael stood down. The cause raised dismay. For of course, the torchlight betrayed him. If a scatter of bloodstains had seeped through his surcoat, his shirt and jerkin must display graphic evidence concerning the state of his back. 'Let's have a small fire,' he suggested, flat crisp.

Anja stared at him, wide-eyed.

'Your mare's leg?' Mykkael reminded her, hoping the

intensity of her regard was evoked by the brand, which also provided her first clear-cut view of his desert-bred features.

'Fouzette. Yes.' Anja turned away, brisk. She helped him unfasten lead ropes, then watched in stout silence as he tied makeshift hobbles beneath the horses' front fetlocks.

'Sit,' he insisted. 'I'll care for Fouzette.'

For blessing, the princess was tired enough to obey him without foolish protest.

The cavern had driftwood, wedged in the cracks. Mykkael worked with the speed of a man who had foraged on the run, inside enemy territory. He gathered kindling and laid a discreet, smokeless blaze just inside the narrow entry. Although the mare's injury was no pleasant sight, he had tended worse. He used his sharp dagger, cut away the flap of torn skin, then mixed a dilute dose of his dart poison in warm water. The infusion numbed the exposed gash as he cleansed the dirt and stuck gravel. The contusion had most likely been caused by Vashni's trampling shoe. Bruising had made the mare lame, not direct damage to the ligaments and tendons exposed beneath the stripped flesh.

Anja helped bind the wound with a compress soaked in ice water drawn from the cataract. Relief coloured her voice as she secured the bandage, torn off the hem of the captain's surcoat. 'Brave Fouzette. She never once faltered. I expect she'll pull through with no worse than a scar, if we can hold down the infection.'

Mykkael said nothing. The suppressed quaver in the princess's tone showed that she knew well enough: a horse with a ripped leg would more likely be kerrie bait, in the course of their flight through Hell's Chasm. What else a mare with the blood-scent of a wound might become, he prayed Sessalie's princess might never find out. The wise course was to make an end of the problem, and let the carcass be washed far downstream.

Yet he could not embrace that grim proposition. More

than Anja's sentiment stayed his hand from the sword. Mykkael had never practised the thoughtless habit of using dumb beasts for convenience. Perhaps as a remnant of his tribal ancestry, he could not bring himself to destroy Fouzette's courage, which had saved both their lives in the breach.

'Rest,' he told Anja. 'I'll rub down the horses and fix something to eat.'

She rejected the suggestion, would have none of his solicitude, though in practical fact, the condition of the animals was of vital importance to his charge of defending her safety. She insisted he accompany her outside to stand guard, while she gathered the razor-edged marsh grass that grew at the verge of the gulch. Anja proceeded to wind and braid two stout wisps as competently as any stablehand. She handed him one, wordless, and together, they set to, burnishing the crusted sweat from fine coats. The day's exertion had come at high cost. Proud heads drooped with weariness. The staring bones of ribs and hips bespoke the sorrowful lack of high-quality grazing. Mykkael shared out the mixed grain with the animals, soaking his portion and Anja's into a gruel that he warmed in a cloth sack, slung from a string dangled over the fire.

The princess dozed where she sat, long before the grain had cooked enough to consume. He woke her when the first serving was ready, then watched like a hawk to see that she ate, and did not succumb to misplaced pity and sneak the hot mash to her horses.

For himself, he withheld a share from his ration, in case Benj's hound might come straggling in. Dalshie had not caught up since the chase with the kerrie, a sore point he dared not pursue. Best, if the dog had limped homewards. Far more likely, the chance she had fallen prey to the shape-changer, killed as a casual meal. Worse, if she should be claimed in possession, with her exceptional talent for tracking suborned as the tool of the enemy.

As long as he could, the captain sat wakeful, watching

until the stars paled above the black maw of the chasm. Sleep claimed him, inevitably, where he hunched beside the dying embers at the cave's entry. Knowing his limits, he had taken precautions. The strung bow and quiver of arrows lay beside him, and his unsheathed blade rested under his listening hand. Since exhaustion would only impair his sound judgement and rob the keen edge from his reflexes, he had no choice but rely on the shaman's ward in his blade to stand guard. Its vibration could be trusted to rouse him if the sorcerer's minion ranged close, or launched a surprise attack.

Mykkael woke to the mid-morning sun in his eyes. He pushed himself erect, rubbed the crust from his lids, then winced to the scream of stiff muscles. Movement roused the multiple complaint of his wounds. He hissed through shut teeth, raked a searching glance over the dank recess of the cavern. The disastrous discovery met his first sweep: only five horses remained in the rock cleft.

The rambunctious buckskin, Bryajne, had chewed the knots on his hobbles and strayed. Mykkael's warded sword would speak warning for inbound demons; not for a horse stepping over him on an inquisitive ramble outside.

Mykkael's soft-spoken swearing aroused Princess Anja from sleep.

'What's wrong?' She stirred from her curled refuge under his surcoat. Shoved erect, she flicked back wisps of tumbled hair and blinked to clear puffy eyesight.

Mykkael did not answer, but reached for the bow. He snatched an arrow from the quiver, set the nock to the string. With the notched shaft locked in place with his forefinger, he squinted past the bright fall of sunlight and into the shadowed ravine.

'Bryajne!' Anja's exclamation showed fond exasperation as she tossed off rumpled cloth and arose. 'The clown! I should have realized he would play the escape artist.'

She shouted the gelding's name, the cry split into echoes between the high cliffs of the chasm.

The good-natured gelding answered her call. Mykkael sighted the movement as the horse raised his head from a tough stand of sedge a stone's throw down the throat of the chasm. He whinnied, ears pricked. Content to abandon the unsavoury forage, he ambled upstream, no doubt expecting the carrot he often received as a handout.

Mykkael let the horse come. His watchful perception also encompassed the princess, who now approached his placed stance from behind, to welcome in her errant favourite. Endearing despite his bumptious head, the buckskin's sly antics could melt the hardest of hearts. Against hope, Mykkael leashed back his dread. He permitted Anja's eager advance, until necessity demanded precaution.

Before she could step past his guard at the entry, he clamped her wrist in restraint. 'Stay behind me, Princess. You must. That gelding has wandered outside the wardings, with no one awake to stand guard.'

'I don't see a thing wrong with him,' Anja insisted. 'The look in his eye is quite sane.'

'Your horse may be himself,' Mykkael agreed. 'That does not mean he is untouched, or harmless.'

She was not convinced; lacked experience to listen. Annoyed as her tug met his solid resistance, Anja whirled on him, furious. He never learned how her balked temper might revile him. The gelding had closed within fifteen yards, when the shaman's mark buzzed in his sword hilt.

Mykkael shouted. He dropped his protective grasp on her arm, raised the strung bow and hauled the nocked arrow to full draw. His release followed, seamless. He took the horse down with a shot through the neck, ripping through the great vein, then the artery just under the hollow where the jaw lapped over the throatlatch.

Death caused by bleeding was not pretty or quick. The buckskin horse staggered, screaming in shocked pain. His treble cry sounded eerily human. He reared, lashing out and shaking his neck. His mane snapped and flew to his panicked snorts, yet he could not dislodge the deeply set arrow. His thrashing forced the shaft's point to tear through the thick muscle, and finally, fatally, to entangle amid the interlocked bones of the spine. Pressure disrupted the nerves sheathed inside. Bryajne lurched sideways, his shining coat quivering. Within a few heartbeats, his splendid strength came undone, reduced to a jerking spasm that pitched him headlong to his knees.

Anja's tormented outcry shattered across the dying horse's wheezing shrieks. Heedless of danger, she bolted, determined to reach the stricken animal's side.

Mykkael extended his good leg and tripped her. She fell, weeping curses. Her palms ripped on cruel stone. He shoved her flat, his handling ruthless as she fought to rise. When she did not subside, he pinned her struggling shoulders on the explosion of *barqui'ino* reflex.

'Stay!' he gasped, breathless.

Her green eyes raked over him, stormed to reasonless fury. She was not going to listen, not going meekly to stay put as he asked, though his drawn sword came alive with the whine that signalled desperate danger. Mykkael let Anja go, then raced ahead to reach the downed gelding before her. He leaped over the shuddering horse, avoided the kicking thrash of shod hooves. Poised by the wither, he thrust the blade in a stabbing stroke through the crest just behind the buckskin's ears. The point pierced through the back of the skull, ending the animal's suffering. What seizures remained were the reflex of an expiring carcass.

'Anja, stay clear!' Mykkael knelt, his knee jammed into the soaked, streaming neck. He flipped back the black mane, and there, saw his dread fully realized.

Scribed on the hide, where the long hair had masked sight, the sorcerer's minion had patterned his craftmark. The short curse it carried was as virulent as anything the captain had witnessed in all his dread years of experience.

Worse, the headstrong princess had reached her slain horse. White with agony, she folded at Bryajne's head. His blood-splattered muzzle gusted his last breath in the grip of her desperately clenched arms.

'Bryajne! Bryajne!' Her grief unstrung thought. All riven loss, the pain for her lost brother and her beloved suitor became wrenched into razor-edged focus by the horse's violent passage.

Mykkael had *no choice, and no time to win distance.* The sword in his hand shrilled to a harmonic peak: the craft-mark laid to entrap them had wakened. Power welled up. An unstoppable force of demonic energy opened into the world as the spell-framed gateway surged active. The blinding, first spark hurled Mykkael beyond horror. He would have to shoulder the unspeakable risk, *could do nothing else, now,* except seek to ground the balefires as they erupted.

He raised his stained blade, drove it *down* through the clay spiral inscribed on the dead horse's neck. He rammed the steel through meat and bone until it slammed with a grate against the stone slab underneath. Keeping one hand clenched to the hilt, he reached, grabbed Anja's collar, yanked her up like a doll and jerked her against his braced flank. He pinned her there with all of his strength, unable to care if he bruised her.

Whatever she shouted, her words became lost. The maelstrom arose, bloomed and brightened into a fountainhead of loosed flame. The eruption reached resonance and became fully manifest, exploded like an untamed, hot star, a shrieking, clawing, *rage* of wrong forces that assaulted the unfurled net of his wardings. The conflagration spun wild, then snatched short, balked in midstream from its warped course of expansion. Mykkael fought to stay upright. Ripped by the very whirlwinds of hell, he kept his hand locked on the sword. His left arm crushed Anja, breathless, against him, while the song inlaid by the Sanouk shamans collided headlong with the sorcerer's curse of destruction.

The tattooed geometry seared into his scalp like etched acid, as the patterns laid down by two learned viziers aroused and strove to match, then recarve the forces of chaos unleashed. Mykkael held on. He clung to raw will, and to wailing, stressed metal, rocked half senseless as the uprushing powers were routed, then rechannelled back *through* him. He became the sealed vessel of fire itself. Every nerve, every born instinct of desert-bred heritage became torn into raging turmoil. He felt pummelled to rags, as the cascade of turned energies poured back down through the blade that transfixed the live craftmark. Solid ground shook. Stones crashed from the rim walls as the traumatized earth received the unnatural current and reclaimed its raw force in absorption.

Flame wrapped flesh and bone, a vicious scourge that surged to escape the wire-strung ties of the wardings. Active lines tangled with counter-spun patterns of guard, and plunged into vital contention. The wise safeguards invoked by two disparate viziers and a circle of initiate mystics sang out their peal of demand: to reseal the portal a sorcerer had wedged open to tap the fell forces of the unseen.

Mykkael clung to Anja, held her fast, though she struggled. Despite her shrill cries and her battering fists, he kept his hold on the vibrating sword grip. Both of their lives were cast into the breach. He must not give way, no matter how strongly his instincts shrilled ruin. No matter how desperately helpless he felt, *he must* bridge the gap between sanity and horror. He must let himself hang in trusting suspension above the abyss, while demonic powers threatened to drag him down into the limitless void. The cold-cast awareness abraded his will, that if the wards failed him, he would be lost, with Anja taken along with him.

Through the clash of the elements, Mykkael felt the sorcerer's purposeful groping. The ruthless, warped creature clawed, seeking purchase, pressing the limit of his extended reach to capture a hold upon Isendon's daughter.

That striving promised him limitless pain, then an unending fury for the claim to her spirit, denied. Mykkael tasted a hunger that savaged his mind, knew the voracious craving of an intelligence that desired to waste his warm flesh, then chain the steadfast flame of his being in torment for all of eternity. He howled in denial, refused the ending of hope, pinned all the while by the crushing awareness that he was no more than a moth set against the loosed blast of a gale.

Somewhere, everywhere, voices screamed along with him: all the sorry, damned souls claimed in thrall by the sorcerer's self-serving bargain. Bound to the insatiable demands of a demon, the warped creature must continuously wrest living spirits away from their natural mortality. Beyond lost, the sorcerer *knowingly* enacted such evil to sate an awareness that played him, then his minions, on puppet strings. Such power bought immortality in exchange for the coin of immeasurable human suffering.

Mykkael fought despair. He had known horrors, but none such as this: Devall had succumbed to *worse* than Rathtet. The sorcerer who bade for expansion through Sessalie was ruled by a demon who craved the demise of all rivals. It planned to defeat and consume its own brethren.

Mykkael sensed the vast forces that hounded him, shaken to unimaginable terror. Orannia's madness had reflected the hideous truth: that humanity's captive pain sourced a demon's inexhaustible strength. Its hoard of trapped spirits and its rooted foothold on land determined the scope of its dominance. This contender outmatched the rest for ambition; sought a spell line that would circle the earth, then expand until every soul born to woman became fodder to feed its ambition. Worse, the lines' origin *did not begin here*. Before this fair world, this demon's shape-changing pawns had taken another; and after this conquest, would reach between stars, seeking the next target to set under attack.

Against the dread sorcerer who enabled this demon's first foothold in Devall, one man's naked will seemed a cry of abject futility.

Mykkael wept, for grief. He trembled, while the storm raging through his marked sword blade bespoke the bared might of Gorgenvain, whose name was the essence of fear itself, and whose reach cast a terrible shadow across even the darkest realms of the unseen.

Then the short curse in the craft-mark exhausted its limit. The maelstrom of uncanny fires snuffed out, leaving a fair, sunlit morning marred across by the sickening taint of scorched meat. The clay pattern inscribed on the animal's skin had finally failed, having consumed its own substance. Bryajne's pierced neck had crisped to dry carbon where the weapon had rechannelled the destructive charge downwards into the earth.

Shaking, Mykkael withdrew his silenced steel. The blade slipped clear of papered ash without resistance. His palm was not burned. Throughout, the shaman-marked steel had stayed cool. Bared weapon in hand, he hauled Anja erect. She clung to him, limp, all the fight battered out of her by the impact of numbing terror. He caught her chin, turned her face, stared into her opened green eyes.

The pupils were black and distended. Tears were caught in her lashes. Yet the blank features he surveyed with desperate intensity showed him no worse than the stunned depth of her shock. He encountered none of the mindless torment that had caused Orannia's madness.

Where Perincar's geometry had fallen short under point-blank assault in Efandi, the resonant strength of the Sanouk song line had guarded the breach, even through the rampaging onslaught of grounding out a roused short curse.

A defender who found himself sorely beset could stake fragile hope on such footing.

Mykkael shut his eyes. All but unstrung by his shaken relief, he shouldered the princess's leaning weight. Though he felt her shrink in recoil from him, he blessed that first sign of recovery. If she hated him for ever for the arrow that had dispatched her luckless gelding, the penalty held no meaning beside the triumph of breathing survival. The Princess of Sessalie was alive; intact.

Her brave horse was dead.

For that sorrow, he had no words, and no balm of false reassurance. He could not apologize for the ugly event her sheltered young mind had just witnessed. A dangerous power had marked Isendon's heirs for destruction. The fell threat it carried dwarfed human perception. Mykkael swallowed, tasting the grit of bitter char. The trembling, raw aftermath struck all at once. Alone in Hell's Chasm, his frail resource seemed insufficient to stand foursquare in the breach.

'Princess,' he urged, his voice a scraped whisper. 'Come on. Let's get you away before passing kerries swoop down to feed on the carcass.'

The shock of the disturbance rippling over the unseen was sensed by the grand vizier's hired circle of shamans. They engaged a deep scrying, and uncovered the pattern of a scourge whose signature did not match the nine demons whose sorcerers walked abroad on the earth. Alarmed to encounter an unknown danger, they pursued the source, but lost the dread line as it grounded. To the emperor's capitol, they sent urgent word: a new peril stalked the cleft of Hell's Chasm, that might threaten their far northern border . . .

XXVIII. Cataract

AGAINST THE PRINCESS'S VEHEMENT WISH, MYKKAEL PROCEEDED TO SKIN THE DEAD HORSE. HE WORKED FAST, watching the sky for scavenging kerries. His methodical speed suggested he had done such grisly tasks of necessity many times in his past.

Or so Anja thought, where she sat, shuddering with nausea, deep inside the shaded cleft. She could not bear to witness the finish, as the flies swarmed and sucked at the raw, exposed meat of Bryajne's carcass.

Mykkael counted paces to ascertain the range of his wardings, then knelt at a rock spring to wash his befouled hands. Then, using field knowledge, he fashioned a bracing tea from the herbs he stocked in his scrip. He brewed the restorative in a cone of hard leather cut from his boot cuff, and heated the water by dropping in a hot pebble raked from his tiny fire.

At his urging, Anja sipped the concoction. If she was put off by the bitter taste, infused with the taint of boiled leather, the tincture soothed her stomach and eased the wrenching sobs she had stubbornly stifled to silence. She huddled, forlorn, in the shadow, while Mykkael scraped the fresh hide, and the inevitable hungry kerrie descended to devour the buckskin's remains.

Senses blunted by the warmth of full sunlight, the creature did not scent the living animals jammed inside the cave, but circled, cat-nervous and bugling. It landed at length, all shimmering bronze muscle slung on the feathered vanes of its wings. It snuffled, blew fire in riffling snorts, then sank its black talons into the dead horse's shoulder, and clamped the hindquarters in the murderous grip of rear claws. It took to the air, its prize clutched to its belly, to a gale wind of thunderous flapping.

It left behind the rank stink of sulphur, soon dispersed by the morning breeze. Where Bryajne had fallen, the stone showed a seared ring of slag, and dried blood snagged with circling flies.

By then, Anja's revolted tears had burned dry. She was not ready to move, yet. Mykkael did not press her, but stood silent guard at the cleft, knife blade working over the green hide. He cleaned the fat, then the hair, then rolled his handiwork into a bundle, lashed tight with a peeled strip of sinew. After that, he sat with his marked fingers rested upon the burnished steel of his weapon. He did not reproach his royal charge, or attempt to console her sore grief. His tacit trust, that her feelings were genuine, and not under his right to question, allowed her bruised dignity the footing she needed to begin the first step towards recovery.

He had saved her life, at unimaginable risk. That her horse should be mourned, and her privacy respected, bespoke an unprepossessing resilience of character; or not. The warrior who had slaughtered her hapless buckskin had launched his shaft with steel nerves, and no heart. Anja measured his posture. From the place where she sat, she could number the lines that exhaustion had scored into his rapacious features. Mykkael was not untouched, she decided. He looked like a man who ached to the bone, glass cast in the purview of solitude.

Curiosity as always outstripped her good manners. In the end, she could not resist prodding. 'Did you ever visit the Scoraign Wastes, or ride caravan through the desert?'

The captain turned his head, a dark shadow sliced into outline by the sunlit chasm outside. Against the harsh glare, she could not tell whether his expression showed offence, or contemptuous irritation. His soft-spoken reply stayed unruffled. 'No, Princess. Never. For me, that land was unsafe to travel.'

Her surprise moved him to qualify. 'The tribes adhere to an inflexible law. As an infant, exposed, I was outcast as a misfit. Given my self-evident breeding, but lacking the sanction of clan tattoos, I stand condemned in that country. A tribal warrior raised in tradition would be duty-bound to run his spear through my back.'

'Yet you speak the language.' Anja puffed a wisp of stuck hair from her lips. 'At least, I heard your fluent cursing.'

He grinned. 'Yes, but with a terrible accent. I learned the rough phrases a trader would use to drive bargains and share an oasis.'

The next question stabbed. 'Why do you answer? Did you hope to win my civil forgiveness?'

Mykkael sighed. The sword flashed, cold blue in sky-caught reflection, as he moved in attempt to lessen the discomfort of his damaged knee. 'I hope, first of all, to keep you alive to resent me or not, at your pleasure. And I answer your Grace because at heart, I have nothing to hide.' His careful regard searched her face through the gloom. 'Well enough to attack, well enough to ride on. Can you manage?' He stood up. Self-assured to the point of enacting his assumption, he sheathed his sword, then limped towards the horses with intent to unfasten their hobbles. 'I'd prefer not to linger where a sorcerer's mark has disrupted the natural currents that flow through the earth.'

'You talk like a shaman,' Anja said, rising.

He gave her his honest, velvet-grained laughter. 'Would you know, Princess? Have you ever met one?'

'Have I?' Her smile wobbled, which spoiled the humour, but not her steel-clad persistence. 'You could tell me.'

Bent to release the knots restricting Covette's dainty forelegs, Mykkael shook his head. 'Then be disappointed. I was fostered and brought up by a northern-born merchant. His wife lived with the inconvenience of my witch thoughts. She didn't like to encourage them. The wardings I carry were earned on campaign. Eishwin, who fashioned the first one, insisted he tapped into my desert heritage to bring the laid pattern to resonance. He talked like a vizier.' The flash of a smile was offered her way. 'I didn't fathom a single word of his inexhaustible theories.'

Anja knelt, checked Fouzette's bandage, which had grown disturbingly hot to the touch. She said a word, likely learned from a stablehand, that would have vexed the duchess who raised her. As the captain moved on to unfasten the hobbles on Vashni, she pressed her next question to divert her concern for her injured mare. 'Why didn't you stay with your family, trading?'

'A chance slip of fate.' His tone held no rancour, as if that bygone detail had long since grown distant and meaningless. 'Because I couldn't safely work the south passage, I was sent out with a close associate of the house to learn how to manage the exotic routes to the east. I was also expected to establish my own trading contacts. The customs of barter and exchange were complex enough to be interesting. On contacts, I fell shamefully short.'

Anja braced against Kasminna's head butts, guardedly ready to fend off the inevitable mischievous nip. 'You weren't suited for life as a merchant?'

His shrug as he straightened strove to dismiss the scab-crusted state of his back. 'At fourteen years of age, fast horses and huge, muscled nomads with swords posed the more riveting fascination.'

'But you would have matured,' the princess insisted. 'What made you abandon your upbringing?'

Mykkael must have sensed the quiet desperation

behind her chatterbox inquiries. His dark eyes met her open probe without flinching. 'In the course of my absence, the near family was stricken by an outbreak of virulent fever. Did I say they weren't young? The house fortune was inherited by a nephew, who had six grown children to carry the trade. By the time I returned, the presiding magistrate insisted there had been no written record. My claim was dismissed.'

'The nephew refused to employ you?'

Mykkael grinned outright. 'Actually, no. He made me a handsome offer. I declined.'

Her sandpaper edge progressed into bravery: her curiosity was not going to let up. 'In fact, you were likely to be assigned to the next caravan bound through the Scoraign?'

He laughed. 'Clever thought, but no. The truth is quite honestly boring.' He had been offered the position of desk clerk for his gift at translating languages. 'Which horse will carry your saddle, your Grace?'

'Covette.' Anja swallowed the pang, that the sensible choice *should have been her buckskin gelding*. 'The poor girl's not fresh, but with Bryajne gone, she'll be desolate and badly distracted.'

Mykkael nodded, approving. Had she named Vashni, he would have been forced to countermand her free preference. The grey was too tightly teamed to Fouzette. If pending danger should drive them to flight, the mare's lamed stride was too likely to cause her loyal companion to falter.

By logical default, he should ride Kasminna. Yet Mykkael made no move to claim the sorrel mare's headstall. Instead, he checked the knots, one by one, as the hobbles were retied into lead lines. The princess was left to saddle Covette by herself. Such unassuming humility, fast followed by that deliberate lapse from an accustomed royal prerogative, showed his steadfast respect for her human right to autonomy. The impact almost destroyed her reserve. When Anja handed off the mare's lead, throat tight with emotion, he accepted with a formal court bow that acknowledged the gift without speech.

'Leave Stormfront free,' she husked, turned away to preserve her strained dignity. 'He'll have to be trusted to follow his training.'

That risk made sound sense, since the black gelding was too powerfully strong to restrain in the heat of a crisis. If the horse lost his head to raw instinct and bolted, or if his footing gave way on a misstep, he would only drag his sorrel partner off balance, undermining the rider's defence. Taskin's sharp insight had taught Anja well, a point Captain Mykkael did not fail to appreciate as he fastened the unused lead into a crude surcingle, and lashed his rolled hide on to Fouzette's broad back.

Last of all, he reclaimed his tattered surcoat. Near enough to assist, *in case* Anja requested what he judged an unneeded assistance to mount, he donned the stained garment and readjusted his scabbard and sword harness.

'Please take the lead, Princess,' he said, his neat vault astride an achievement that masked the crippling halt in his knee. First-hand, she saw why Stormfront had agreed with him. His grasp on the rein was nonexistent as thistledown, and his cues to Kasminna, made in steppelands style with guiding leg and a balanced seat.

'You didn't learn your horsemanship from a merchant,' Anja said as the wily mare tested his measure, gave a startled snort, and stood fast.

'No.' Not smiling, Mykkael pressed Kasminna back on her haunches, then opened her stride from the shoulder to face daylight and finally move out. 'Sessalie trains mounted men to be lancers, which suits your defence, well enough. They can shock through a line in a siege, or mow down and break an interlocked shield wall that might challenge the span at Stone Bridge. But the wars where I hired demanded close infighting. A swordsman who relied on the reins became *ei'jien*.'

Since the *do'aa* term could not help but perplex her, Mykkael tipped his head. The gesture of deference was immediately betrayed, as sunlight exposed his faint smile of scorching amusement. 'That idiom roughly translates as "luckless, sitting target".'

Anja raised her eyebrows, resilience restored by his combative humour. 'We aren't *ei'jien* right now?'

That awoke his spontaneous laugh. 'No, Princess. I would have us be *seit shan'jien*, "the target with teeth that bites back".'

By late morning, they encountered the ripped carcass where something uncanny had dined on a slaughtered kerrie. Whether the fire-breathing predator had been naturally slain in the course of a territorial rivalry, or whether the sorcerer's shape-changer had dealt the huge creature its deathblow, the discovery sat ill with Mykkael. The grue chasing over his spray-dampened skin bespoke unclean implications. Not liking necessity, he asked the provocative question.

The princess informed him that the opportunistic kerrie would always feed upon carrion. The predators did not balk at consuming the flesh of their own kind. Available meat would not be left to rot unless something unusual or threatening aroused their overriding suspicion.

'You're troubled by this?' Anja had to shout over the deafening thrash of the flume, hurled up into fantails of whitewater against a crook in the narrowing channel.

'I've seen happier news,' Mykkael admitted, his reluctance to explain exacerbated by Kasminna's restive distress. Her wise equine instinct agreed with his hackled nerves, that all wholesome life should keep a safe distance from that mangle of gnawed bones and spilled viscera. The captain dismounted anyway, and handed the mare's reins off to Anja.

'Stay close,' he instructed, his dark face unreadable under the shadow of the ravine.

Still in full sunlight, and glad of the warmth streaming over her spray-damp shoulders, Anja caught his wrist in restraint.

The sinews she grasped leaped to instantaneous tension, then froze stone-still, unresisting. Mykkael tipped up his head. 'Your Grace?'

'You intend to investigate?' Her wide, worried eyes searched his features. 'Is that safe?'

His level regard seemed a cold reassurance. 'I am going to cut and salvage the wing leather. Horrid necessity. We're going to need something to braid into stout rope. A green hide will stretch. Wing leather won't. I can't imagine we'll find a material more strong and reliable.'

Anja did not release him. 'I asked, is it safe?'

'Life is not safe, Princess.' Mykkael gently unwound her choke hold on his wrist. 'This is Hell's Chasm, where use of a rope might mean your survival, or maybe that of your horses.'

Her green eyes held his, as fiercely relentless. 'And do you also plan to investigate?'

Mykkael sighed. He glanced away, while the pounding waters leaped and crashed, and gusts snapped the wet hem of his surcoat. 'What more could I find?'

His unexpected note of desolation chilled Anja down to the bone. She shifted a heel, sidled Covette, until once again, he must face her. 'What have you seen, Captain?'

To answer at all ran against his clear preference. Still, he gave the bared truth. 'My knowledge of lore is scant, at best, Princess. But this much I had from a dying vizier concerning the habits of shape-changers. The creatures do not slaughter wantonly. The captive essence they extract from devouring their kills is what allows the fell beings to shift form.' Watching her expression with a falcon's stripped focus, he added, most softly, 'I'm sorry.'

A moment of blanked shock, then the hammering impact: Anja reeled, grabbing mane for support. 'Oh, dear powers of daylight! Then Kailen, and also my high prince –'

His hand braced her rocked balance. Since he had no words for inconsolable horror, he gave a small tug to remind her of the lead lines that threatened to slip through her grasp. 'Bear up, your Grace. Let me do my work.' When the recovery he asked for escaped her response, he slapped the ends of Kasminna's reins to her thigh with a reproving, light sting. *'Anja! I won't take your blood on my hands as my destiny, or the failure, that I allowed you to die the same way.'*

She took charge of the mare.

'Watch for kerries,' he said.

Anja swallowed. 'All right.' Harsh reason resurged over deranging grief. 'Will that sword hilt give warning if a marauding creature is shape-changed?'

Again, Mykkael chose the thorn prick of honesty. 'I don't know.' The one time he had stood in the high prince's close presence, the established court protocol for royal audience had seen him stripped of his weapon. 'Princess,' he added, 'the sword doesn't matter. You can give warning by sight.'

A role she *must* play, if his back was to stay halfway guarded; she rose to match his high courage. Her spine straightened. Slight fingers closed, firm, on the rein ends.

'I apologize,' Anja said with strained dignity. 'Captain, you are no coward.'

He bowed. 'Your Grace.' Then he moved promptly off, the cat-fluid beauty of his warrior's stride undone by his marring limp.

Mykkael came alive to her, in that moment. Not as a hero, not as the paid captain of Sessalie's garrison, but as a man beset by a difficult quandary the less stout-hearted must name impossible. He stood guard for her fate, and his own, without arrogance. Even with scars and shortfalls in plain view, he was whole. The hands that wielded the skinning knife accomplished their revolting task, fast and sure. Anja saw his humility all too clearly. Dwarfed by the massive walls of the chasm, befouled by the corpse of a predator slain by an uncanny abomination, Mykkael should have seemed foolish and small. Instead, the will in him towered.

He lived as himself. Moment to moment, he surmounted his impaired strength through trained skill, and the unshakable self-trust of a man who had been put to the extreme test, and who had won triumph through the unflagging use of his wits.

Two kerries flew overhead. Uneasy within sight of the massacre, they circled, but did not alight. Anja minded the restive horses. She cajoled them steady until Mykkael returned, the unwieldy bundle of cut membrane draped over his shoulder, and tied with a length of scraped tendon.

'Princess, I ask you to let Fouzette bear the burden,' he said the moment he reached her. 'The load isn't nearly as heavy as it looks.'

When she did not argue, he looked at her straitly. 'Your Grace?'

Anja stirred out of suspended stillness. *Why, before this, had she never noticed the deep sorrow ingrained in his face?* Hoping her hesitation would be taken for grief, she gave her consent.

A fractional tension eased from his shoulders, that he need not contend with sentimental recalcitrance. His choice was not cruel, but strategic good sense. Fouzette had the stoic temperament to manage the unusual load without fuss. If flight became necessary, she was already slowed by her injured leg. By attempting to cosset one impaired horse, the risk of loss might shadow two. *Mykkael would spare Anja the agony of losing her teams, in every way that he could.* The hand that had pulled the bow for Bryajne had not been heartless, but driven to act out of inflexible expediency.

Anja used her voice to quiet Fouzette, while Mykkael strapped his horrific gleanings on to her back. He could not spare the time to be overly fastidious. Yet he did rinse his hands and clean off his knife before he remounted Kasminna.

His smile of encouragement remained sincere as he gestured downstream. 'Onwards. I promise your Grace, if we find the right pool, I'll try to spear trout for our dinner.'

They rode on, the horses picking their uncertain path between canted boulders, and through the drifts of back-fallen spray shot to gold by the shafts of noon sunbeams. The warm air seemed filled with the flitter of dragonflies, and the cheep of the black-and-white swallows nesting high in the cliffs. Then the sun passed the zenith. The chasm plunged into the chilly, premature twilight that extended through late afternoon. Only the crown of the rim rocks stayed sunlit, with the cloudless sky of high altitude an indigo ribbon between.

Anja rode, all her questions stunned silent, which raised more than one concerned inquiry from Mykkael. She noticed what had escaped her before: that the captain relied on her tone of voice more than words to measure her state of mind. He listened much the same way to the horses, and to the sword hilt strapped on his back. If the striking care behind such attentiveness might have begun as a trader's boy, brought up amid foreign cultures, the formidable skills he had displayed on the tourney field framed too stark an extreme. To see him move with a weapon in hand exposed what he was: a killer honed to an edge that eclipsed the humanity of his birthright.

The dichotomy sparked Anja's fascination, a puzzle that engaged her eclectic interest as never before.

Her observation underwent a rapt change in focus, while the daylight waned towards a sunset that must find them snugged down under cover. If the cavern walls had grown too narrow for the wingspan of diving kerries, the sorcerer's shape-changer would not be tied to any one form. Each crevice with its pocket of shadow might harbour an enemy ambush.

Mykkael's wary vigilance tightened to match the

increased chance of threat. Kasminna reflected his mood in her high-set neck and lifted tail. As the last sunlight licked the top of the cliff wall, dipping the rock faces scarlet, the desert-bred rode with his sword unsheathed, the flat of the blade lightly rested across his opposite wrist.

His senses detected no untoward warning, which did nothing to settle the uneasy clamour of his more subtle instincts.

The rush of the water grew louder, then swelled to a shattering roar that foreclosed all attempt at conversation. Mykkael kept his mount close behind Covette, often signalling for the princess to pause as he scouted past leaning boulders. Then the cavern crooked, and the race of the flume hurled itself off the edge of the world.

'Tie the horses.' Mykkael dismounted to reconnoitre on foot. Unasked, the princess went with him. The animals would be safe enough in the narrows, as they could not be, exposed on the rim. Beyond the cataract, the open sky teemed with wheeling kerries. Below the falls, the chasm widened into a vast stone basin, sliced at the skyline with snow-clad peaks. Tier upon tier, the stepped ledges were riddled with the caverns that sheltered the Hell's Chasm rookery.

'The Widow's Gauntlet,' Anja said, referring to the name given the site by an unknown, past prospector who had wisely turned back from the folly of a doomed enterprise. 'Unless the season has been lean, and the kerries are starving, we're not likely to see a mobbing attack where we're standing.'

Mykkael turned his head, his bared sword in hand. 'There's a reason?'

Anja nodded. 'Fortune seekers who've attempted to mine in the caverns sometimes try poisoning animals as bait in an effort to clear out the rookeries. Kerries are intelligent enough not to be tempted by domesticated stock if bad experience has shown them it's tainted. Provided they haven't forgotten the last incident, they'll watch, and hang back. With luck, they could leave us alone until they realize we don't match the exact pattern they hold in memory.'

'A strategic point,' Mykkael allowed. One they might have to press for advantage through the difficult, open terrain in the valley lying ahead. Intent, he resumed his close-up review of the landscape.

The head of the falls was relentlessly exposed, a lip carved into water-worn bedrock, raked clean by the surge of the thaws. The cliff wall near at hand posed an impasse, since the bend in the gorge skewed the jet of the falls into a pummelling vortex. The cataract slammed across the right wall of the channel. Age upon age of its scouring force had rinsed the rock satin-smooth. The only accessible route for the horses must be launched from the opposite bank, where the tumbled faults in the cliff face offered a precarious, zigzag descent.

'This is as far as we go before nightfall.' The crossing they must backtrack upstream to try could not be launched until morning. Beset by the thundering might of the cataract, Mykkael had to shout to be heard. 'There will likely be some form of hollow or cave under the ledge where the current spills over. Once I find the best way to get in, you must move your teams quickly. No looking back if they falter!'

Anja nodded. She swiped back the soaked hair plastered against her face by the barrage of wind-driven spray, then retreated to untie the horses. Until Mykkael signalled, she could but strive to meet his dauntless effort with courage.

The edge of the falls lay five paces distant, well inside the reach of his wardings. Anja was caught unprepared, all the same. A desolate feeling of emptiness half crushed her as the captain passed over the rocks out of sight. Alone as she had never been in her life, the princess was shocked to find herself shuddering through an onslaught of violent chills. Terror and cold could not fully explain this explosive storm of reaction. Such desperate, raw need lay outside her experience. The loss of her love for the High Prince of Devall had never touched her like this.

'Merciful powers of daylight!' she swore through her chattering teeth. 'This *cannot* be happening.' Her wretched denial brought no release. The worth she had come to attach to one man in the course of a single day outstripped every concept of decency.

The Princess of Sessalie railed at herself, stunned into dumbstruck fury. How could she have lapsed from the mores of state wisdom and due vigilance? Unconscionable, to realize she might fall prey to such an unguarded self-betrayal. Sessalie's future rode on her power to bargain. Every subject under her sire's crown relied on her honour to secure the protection of an alliance. Far wiser, to handle what must be done without wrenching the strings of her heart.

Anja tucked her crossed arms, aware she must find the strength from *somewhere* to blindside the captain's relentless perception. During her moment of preoccupied thought, Kasminna's boisterous head butt all but pitched her on to her knees.

Saved from a fall by Stormfront's black shoulder, she realized, distressed, that Mykkael was shouting. He had found a safe access into the cavern under the jet of the falls. Anja reddened, shamed to the quick for missing his urgent summons.

Fast as she recovered her paralysed wits, Mykkael's reaction outpaced her. He launched from the rocks. Not sparing his scarred leg, he reached her side with the seamless speed of unbound *barqui'ino* reaction. The lead ropes were snapped from her fingers. Then his hard, muscled shoulder slammed into her waist. Anja folded, draped over his back like a grain sack, with the back of her knees pinned under his iron forearm.

'Hai! Stormfront, Kasminna, to me!' He used his voice and the flat of his blade to prod the horses to moving flight. 'Hai! Hai! Covette, Vashni, Fouzette! Haw now! To me!'

Across the rocks, towards the thundering waters, he drove them in bunched, herd-bound urgency. No chance did he give them to balk or shy back. He hammered them, clattering, to a notch in the brink, then called upon Stormfront's inexhaustible nerve to lead the sliding plunge down the steep ledge. Swordsman and princess and five wild-eyed horses rammed through the roiling curtain of spray. They broke through, into fish-pungent air, whipped to windy turbulence by the rampaging spate of cold water. The noise deafened. Enclosed by the silvery shimmer of the falls, the shallow cavern was a mosaic of sheened puddles and gloom. Skin wet and shivering, Anja heaved in a taxed breath. Her indignant request to be set on her feet had no chance to be heard.

The shaman's mark upon Mykkael's bared sword came alive with a tingling buzz. Anja sensed the wasp hum of the warding as a stinging ache through her bones. In split-second response, the captain's hold shifted. She found herself hurled with jarring force over Stormfront's soaked back.

'Hold him!' Mykkael's shout pealed through the tumbling waters. 'Steady the others as best you can, or let them all go if they scramble! At all cost, bail off if the black gelding bolts.'

Anja scrambled, wormed, unhooked her hung ankle off Stormfront's scrabbling hindquarters. She seized his mane, achieved her erect balance astride, all the while calling out to steady the horses' jostling panic. 'Whoa! Whoa now!' Her cry sounded thin as a bird's through the roar of the cataract. Frantic, she persisted. 'Hold hard! Fouzette, Vashni, whoa now!'

The blessed bay mare answered her training. Eyes rolling white, her mane snagged with droplets, she flung up her blazed head and braced her planted legs, foursquare. Though Vashni battered into her shoulder, her broad-chested bulk blocked the narrow egress. The other horses jammed into milling turmoil, unable to shove past and take flight. Anja entrusted their fates to Fouzette's obedience. She slapped Stormfront's neck to get his attention, *made* him listen to her commands. She urged the trembling gelding with words, drubbed his flank with her heel, compelled him to wheel and face forward. She would see what lethal danger had roused the marked sword. Terrified as the horse underneath her, she refused the horror of being stalked from behind.

'Captain?' Hackled to gooseflesh, Anja sighted a flicker of movement past the soaked cloth of his surcoat. Patterned hide gleamed, pebbled with scales. The coiled viper that lurked in the gloom of a cranny launched a preemptive strike at Mykkael.

The eyes Anja glimpsed were no serpent's, but lit from within by the ephemeral spark of a power drawn from the unseen. *Like Devall's heir apparent, like her brother, what moved inside the skin of the creature was not any natural snake. Nor had its vile awareness been born under the clean light of day.*

'Beware, Captain!' she screamed, already knowing that words were too clumsy and slow.

The shape-changer must have laired in the cavern all day, waiting in cold-blooded ambush.

XXIX. Shape-changer

THE SHINING ARC CARVED BY MYKKAEL'S SWORD MOVED TOO FAST FOR THE EYE. HIS BLOW SHEARED OFF THE snake's head, but could not deflect its attacking momentum. The severed appendage maintained its trajectory, venomed fangs still extended. The strike should have taken Mykkael in the face. Except that his interposed body was gone, dropped into a crouching spin that blurred with the speed of trained reflex.

The launched threat sailed on, *unimpeded*, towards Anja's unguarded breast. The emptied span of air in between left no space to scream or react.

A sheet of flared silver, the captain's sword re-entered the scope of her vision. Too swiftly to follow, his cut scribed an arc, and thrust upwards with fearsome precision. The point jabbed the serpent head's lower jaw and speared through. The impaled skull jerked short of impact, a horrific trophy the size of a man's fist, snatched out of mid-flight.

Mykkael backstepped to absorb the unspent force of impetus. The cleaved air sang over moving steel as he reversed his extended stroke not a handspan from Anja's blanched face. He surged upright, flicked the noisome prize off the tip of his weapon. The serpent head landed, still snapping. His lightning-fast reflex stamped down a heel and crushed skull and jaws under his boot. The captain did not release the remains, even then. Ongoing threat faced him. The decapitated snake flailed in fatal spasm, and snapped a wrap around his bad knee.

Once, twice, his sword moved. Dulled steel scattered steaming blood. The severed coils parted. Mykkael turned the back of his wrist, slapped the upper coil as it let go. His strike batted its writhing, furious length under Stormfront's clattering hooves. The gelding snorted. Neck bowed, ears flattened, he trampled until the remains became chopped to red pulp.

Yet the dismembered fragments at Mykkael's feet did not shudder limp and fall lifeless. Instead, like the wakened shadow of nightmare, they flowed into uncanny change.

The scaled skin greyed, melted, sublimated into a wisping mist. The unclean emanation streamed along the ground, seeking, until it re-encountered its severed parts. Where the foggy clouds gathered, the substance of the felled serpent began to shift from scaled coils into something grotesquely man-shaped. The transformation gained speed as the tendrils of fog enveloped each part and reforged a cohesive connection.

Anja jammed back a whimper, then grabbed for the skinning knife, her effort already too late. The gore mashed underneath Stormfront's enraged hooves coalesced into quickened flesh. A monstrosity reformed as a human hand, grasping fingers attached to a forearm. The dreadful thing was alive and moving. It dragged itself in an insectile scuttle over the cavern floor. As though it sensed Stormfront's animal warmth, it snatched the black's fetlock, and hung on.

The princess screamed, 'Stormfront! Hold hard!' Her full-throated cry re-echoed off the rock walls, but the horse was too maddened to heed.

Anja clung, desperate, while the gelding beneath her stamped, spun and sidled across the cavern's treacherous confines. A fly caught in a wringer, she risked being crushed as the panic-struck horse fought to free his entrapped front pastern. When the shape-changer's clasp could not be dislodged, Stormfront went berserk.

His lunge to bolt should have shot him over the rim, straight through the white rush of the falls. Instead, a blurred form thrust in between. The horse crashed a glancing course off Mykkael, who hooked his left fist over the headstall and hauled the black's head hard around. The gelding skittered. Yanked short of his mindless plunge towards disaster, he spun. His streamered tail slashed through the jet of the falls and re-emerged, spattering droplets. The whiplash of unspent inertia slammed his heaving rump against the back wall of the cavern. Stormfront jounced into rebound. Anja fought his lurching strength as he bucked and scrabbled, hooves sliding on puddled stone.

The minion continued to mass into form. While the horse rampaged in lathered distress, it steadily drew and gathered its spilled essence, flowing into horrific change. The snake head dislodged from beneath Mykkael's boot plumped and rounded into a human skull. Naked bone grew a covering of skin, then a glossy shock of blond hair. Eye sockets and jaw fleshed over and mirrored the semblance of Kailen's fair features. The lids opened. Blue eyes rolled, intelligent, and located Anja, and the animate lips turned and *smiled*.

The princess screamed again, all but deranged by panic. She could not see Mykkael. Stormfront's mane slapped and blinded her. Whipped like a rag to the black's plunging neck, she just missed slamming into the cavern's low ceiling as the horse struck out its forelegs and reared. Even still, the evil hand clung. The gelding thrashed and staggered to throw off its clamping weight. Anja glanced downwards, her breath stopped with fright. For the detached fingers and forearm had *now been augmented, joined into a headless, bare torso.*

She fought to stay astride, and unhurt, while an evil beyond all imagining continued unfolding before her.

The shape-changer's essence streamed underfoot, drawing itself into an obscene replication of her brother's naked form. The head on the floor shoved off with its tongue, rolled itself sideways, until it found and was seized by the wandering hand. The gristly appendage crab-walked along, trailing a draggle of wristbones and sinew. It rattled across stone and through puddles, hauling the head by a gripped twist of hair. Self-aware, determined, it groped to close with the half-assembled monstrosity wrestling Stormfront's front leg.

Anja strove to master the black gelding, now transformed by his fear to a heaving juggernaut. She held her seat, flung and tossed; wrestled against the hampering disadvantage, that she rode with nothing beyond a headstall and single lead rein. She could not hold the horse, but only turn him in desperate, tight circles. The effort could not avert disaster. Stormfront's skating plunges inexorably drove him up to the verge of the brink, with its curtain of thundering water. Curbed by no more than a silver-bossed noseband, the gelding's crazed strength overmatched her.

Wet rope burned through her hands. 'Mykkael!' Anja shouted.

His sword was moving, already beset. Even through Stormfront's clatter, and the incessant din of the falls, she picked out the whine of the shaman's mark, its wasp-angry hum cut again and again as the whickering blade drove at speed through malformed flesh and air. Blood flew. A dollop splashed into Stormfront's soaked neck, scalding his hide like flung acid.

Through battering bedlam, half deafened by the gelding's shrill scream, Anja sighted the captain, *still on his feet*. The steel in his hand was a flying blur. Somehow, Mykkael had heard her. His warrior's perception encompassed her dire peril.

'Stay on Stormfront!' he shouted, still encumbered. An unseen sequence of strokes chopped and slashed. The shape-changer's bare legs and groin kicked and snagged, scissored in a wrestler's grip at his waist. When blows failed to break its incessant attack, Mykkael stabbed with precision, cut through a nerve, or a tendon. The appendages flopped loose, then fell away, streaming fog. His sword never faltered. A moving fan of smeared light, the blade cut their ephemeral connection again, and again, and again, snapping the stream as it sought to reform, and shredding the shape-changer's spellbound wraith into tatters of cobweb.

And still, the severed fragments came on, striving to assemble and reanimate. The hand with the head scrambled onwards. Though it might not have the full use of its eyes, it sensed warmth and spatial connection. Scuttling on nimble fingertips, quickened by a minion's intelligence, it darted this way and that, in vile effort to trip the princess's standing protector.

Mykkael leaped, one-legged, turned his weapon, and came down. His strike impaled Kailen's cheek on his blade. Where the steel touched, the shape-changer melted. Its jaw peeled away, sublimated back to mist. The dome of the cranium still remained, leering with unimpaired menace. Kailen's eyes rolled, imploring the severed hand. Fingers answered, then laboured to tug it towards shelter.

Mykkael reacted on the cascading fury of unleashed *barqui'ino* reflex. Steel sang, whistled downwards and crunched through the bone. The point pierced the skull and grounded with a shocked clang into bedrock.

Ward light blossomed in answer. The fog roiled back from the flare, whipping the stream of the shape-changer's essence into a blasting recoil.

Stormfront surged, staggering. Again Mykkael snagged the gelding's wet headstall. He jerked the crazed animal's neck in a bow, then ruthlessly rammed the foam-flecked muzzle into the black's sweated shoulder. Hooves skidded. The beleaguered horse lost his footing. His haunches went down and slammed on to rock, while his front limbs splayed out. Through the stinging tangle of mane, Anja saw the three-quarters complete body of the shape-changer lock its hold over the horse's bent foreleg. If the animal moved, if he followed the drive of his instinct and rose, the minion's obscene grip could twist and shatter the joint of his knee.

'No!' The princess pealed out a desolate command. 'Stormfront! Hold hard! Whoa now! Stormfront!'

One timely stroke of Mykkael's blade might free him.

Yet the desert-bred could not fight his way clear to respond. His saving effort was thwarted as the drumming, downed legs of the shape-changer lashed a crippling blow at his ankles. He evaded. Come whatever cost, he held the pinned cranium grounded to earth, all the while fumbling for *something* inside the scrip at his belt.

Anja clung to Stormfront's quivering back. 'Hold boy, hold hard.' She soothed the horse, desperate, while the eyes of her brother winked and postured in mocking parody. Still attached by a tendon, the tongue waggled in suggestive seduction.

She choked, revolted, her heart raced with terror as Kailen's hands, *Kailen's face* sought her ruin with diabolically enspelled ferocity.

As she watched, the resummoned hand gave up on its futile tugging. It let go of blond hair, scuttled backwards, and sprang. Crablike, nimble fingers hooked on to Mykkael's surcoat and climbed.

The captain shouted. He had no free hand to dislodge the fell thing that scrabbled over his clothing. The shape-changer's appendage snagged on to his harness, then shinnied upwards to throttle him. Mykkael held to his purpose, unswerving, until his searching fingers found the item he sought in his scrip. His raised fist emerged, clutching a small drawstring packet. He tore through the tied cloth with his teeth, then cast the freed contents into the nearest puddle.

White powder flew.

A scatter of granules raked Anja's damp face. Salt, she realized, the bitter taste sucked in with her burning, sharp breath.

As the mineral showered into the catchment of water, Mykkael turned his sword. He ignored the strangling grip at his throat, flung the cranium off his weapon point into the salt-treated puddle. The remnant landed with a sickening smack, nose downwards and snorting bubbles. Its substance sagged into jelly. The aware blue eyes burned with demonic hatred, then dissolved like run glass in a smelter's pot.

Mykkael drew his belt knife. He stabbed into the choking hand, drove the steel between the wristbones, and pried. The fingertips burrowed under his collar already plumed into smoke, half undone by chance contact with the vizier's tattoo at his nape. He caught the appendage as it shuddered loose, hurled it into a tumbling arc after the dismantled head. Not pausing to look to see how it landed, Mykkael spun with bared sword. He slashed at the calf of the disjointed leg, then leaped onwards to hack at the partial torso entangling Stormfront's right foreleg.

The thing sensed his approach. Perhaps warned by the warding note of the sword blade, it released the black gelding, and writhed into humping retreat. Too swift to prevent, it hurled itself, headless, over the verge, into the tumbling falls. The diced legs left behind sublimated into mist and streamed away in pursuit. Abandoned behind, the dissolute head and left hand boiled into a noisome sludge, entrapped in the salt-treated puddle.

'Whoa! Stormfront! Whoa, now!' Anja shouted.

The gelding surged, uncontrollable. In demented terror he regained his feet, hindquarters bunched to explode into blind flight. He met Mykkael's fist, a hammering blow at the jointure of chest and neck. His staggering recoil bounced him off the stone wall of the cavern. Mykkael dived in, dodged past milling forehooves and snapped the lead rein from Anja's locked fingers. He flicked the end in a whipcrack report in front of the crazed gelding's nose.

Stormfront shied and whirled left. Mykkael sprang back, nearly trampled. He braced his weight to the rein, hauled the horse's neck in a titanic pull. The impetus jerked Stormfront off balance. Clattering hooves skidded. His huge frame lost purchase. He half reared, neck bent, and keeled into a slow roll, with Anja caught like a burr against his back-falling neck and high withers.

A hand grabbed her, collar and hair; *yanked* her clear, as the horse came down like a mountain, rolling and thrashing in primal panic. Mykkael dropped Anja, hard, but safe, on chill stone. Sword drawn, he thrust past her. His face showed intense concentration. He closed, prepared to cut the horse down. No matter the cost, he *must* forestall the lethal danger posed by Stormfront's battering hooves.

The downed gelding rolled over, bellowing in helpless distress. His violent struggles were driven by the most basic of all equine instincts. Every survival urge he possessed insisted he must thrust to his feet and take flight.

Tear-blind, Anja could not wrench her gaze from the warrior who moved on her terrorized horse. She watched the sword, stunned outside thought, paralysed past reach of emotion. The stroke that *would kill* seemed inevitable. The gelding's ungovernable fit must be stopped before his inadvertent thrashing dealt them a crippling injury. Yet the blade did not fall. Its silvered length flicked upwards and back as Mykkael timed his opening, folded his lean frame, and hurled himself headlong against Stormfront's downed tantrum. His tucked body slammed into the horse, and pinned the black neck hard to the ground.

Anja shrilled a desperate command. 'Stormfront, hold hard!'

But the crisis was over. Danger was checked, with Stormfront saved. No horse could arise without lifting its neck. Mykkael bore down, fast-breathing and still. He held, while the horse's wrenching efforts to rise lost impetus, and finally ceased. The man raised his head. He said something breathless into the gelding's quivering ear. Then he stroked the steamed hide with his fingers. Over the roaring spate of the falls, the horse's taxed lungs forced moaning air through its larynx. The deep, laboured groans measured off passing seconds, while the black coat sweated and trembled.

Awareness of peripheral details resurged, as the hot rush of panic subsided. The four other horses cramped against the entry were milling and snorting in trapped fear. Shivering with nerves, miraculous Fouzette had held her braced stance at the bottleneck.

The discovery broke Anja to flooding tears.

At last Mykkael moved. Cautiously slow, he allowed the black gelding to raise his scraped head. The horse's eye ridge was skinned. He had bruised his lower lip. Bloodied foam trailed from his muzzle, and his eyes rolled white with hazed nerves. Yet on his release, he untangled his hooves, gathered his limbs and clattered back upright. Restored, shuddering, to his four legs, he shook like a dog and settled himself with a snort. Banged and shaken, he seemed otherwise unharmed.

The captain who had effected an impossible salvage hauled himself tenderly upright. His sword had gone quiet. The stained weapon stayed poised in his unrelaxed hand. He turned his head, first of all seeking Anja. She saw he was shaking worse than her horse. The wide-open eyes that raked over her still held a predator's focus.

'Captain,' she whispered.

He did not respond. The unnatural ferocity wound through his being did not subside. Wholly remade as the reflexive killer, he mapped his surroundings as though *all* that moved posed a potentially lethal target. That absorbed concentration made him a stranger, even as his shocked senses *must* show him that Sessalie's princess had come through unharmed.

Anja gathered her courage. 'Mykkael, I'm not hurt.'

His feral gaze tracked her without recognition. Yet after a drawn moment, he relented enough to rest his blade point down on the stone at his feet. The care he required to move without violence seemed all the more chilling, set against the blinding-sharp competence of the defence unleashed seconds before.

'Mykkael?' Anja ventured. 'Are you injured?'

'Don't come,' he husked. The skin at his collar was bleeding, scored over the darkening bruises left by the shape-changer's strangling assault. His tremors increased. Their brute force raged through him, shuddering in waves that set him swaying on unsteady feet. '*Barqui'ino* back-lash,' he gritted through locked teeth. 'A normal reaction to excessive adrenaline. It passes.'

A gimping step backwards allowed him to brace his seized posture against the stone wall. There, head bent, he waited, while the seizures came on and rocked him with ravaging force. Anja watched, helpless, as each ragged breath hissed through the strained cords of his throat.

To sit and do nothing seemed an intolerable cruelty. Anja placed her hand, shifted her weight to arise.

Mykkael's chin snapped up. His savage eyes pinned her. 'Don't come! I ask this.'

She swallowed. Hurting, she watched him battle himself. His bare-faced effort to recross the abyss that had distanced his ties to reason exposed an unbreakable patience. Mykkael had gone perilously far, to gain mastery over the knife-edged focus that gripped him. The unnatural shift left him a creature at war with the impact of magnified attributes. Anja wept to behold his wretched struggle, as he laboured to subdue the animal instincts that aligned his extreme state of clarity. The raced blood of that exquisitely tuned primal mindset did not release without penalty. Anja measured each shocking, strained second, as Mykkael reclaimed his intellect one disparate strand at a time.

'The horses,' she said, lamely. 'Someone should attend them.'

This time, her speech softened him, just a fraction. A fleeting frown crossed his blank expression, there and gone as stressed thought resurged to wring sense from her simple phrases. Comprehension became a minor victory, the first marker passed on a rough journey he surely had suffered few others to witness by choice. Mykkael ripped out a stiff nod. 'Go. Please move slowly.'

Anja effected a tender, first step. She paused at his flinch. He arrested the recoiling plunge back into *barqui'ino* trance, just barely. He shut his eyes, his grounding hand splayed against the cavern wall. The fist on his sword grip would not yet release. The pitched strain on his nerves stayed too volatile.

'Go,' he insisted. 'I am not out of hand.'

She went, though he tracked every step like a predator. Or perhaps in cold fact, she perceived him all wrong. *A loyal protector might look the same way, if his defensive instincts were still challenged.* Although the cavern appeared clear of hazard, Anja realized Mykkael's wardings might not be fully quiescent. Her task acquired the driven imperative, to recapture her unsettled horses.

She reached Stormfront first, caught up his dropped lead, crooning the familiar phrases to instil reassurance.

The black snorted and blew. He lowered his neck. Anja rubbed his lathered forehead, then edged past his shoulder and recovered Covette's looped reins. 'Kasminna, to me!'

The sorrel stamped, sniffing the cavern floor with uncertainty. On second command, she ventured one step. Then she froze, lacking Bryajne's solid presence as her accustomed anchor.

'Kasminna, to me.' Anja edged a cautious stride sideways, stooped, then retrieved the mare's trailing lead. With the jumpy creature brought firmly in hand, then coaxed in beside Stormfront and Covette, she dared to address her last team. 'Vashni, to me. Fouzette, hold hard.'

The flighty grey must be secured before the mare could be recalled from the entry. A stamped pewter shadow outlined by the falls, the gelding sidled. His eye still rolled white. Anja stared elsewhere, pretending boredom. She stuffed her hand in her breeches pocket, feigning a search for a carrot. Curiosity and habitual indulgence won out. The grey came around. He stretched his neck, snuffling at her wet clothes, and her easy reach to scratch under his jaw became a closed grip on his headstall.

Fouzette responded at first command. Once the princess had captured all five of her animals, she smoothed them down and checked them for injury. The creatures had suffered no worse than a few scrapes. Stormfront thankfully seemed little the worse for his sliding fall on the rocks. Already he shook out his wet mane, and started to lip at the puddles. Scant rations had worn him down to depletion. All the horses were spent from their nervous excitement. Their subsided calm reflected no less than the lassitude of starvation.

'You'll have hay and oats, all the grass you can eat,' Anja promised. 'We just have to get through Hell's Chasm.'

Kasminna dared a light nip at her sleeve. Anja slapped her off, gently, then risked a sidelong glance at Mykkael.

He stood, eyes shut, still propped against the cavern's rear wall. The tremors that plagued him now seemed more fine-grained. He had released his clamped grip from his weapon. The sword leaned upright beside him, uncleaned. At some point, unnoticed, he had torn a strip of rag from his surcoat.

'You're not hurt?' Anja inquired.

Mykkael looked up, more himself, but not smiling. His answer emerged, almost fluent. 'I was not bitten, if that's your concern.' He regarded the fouled puddle, which still steamed and smoked not far from his planted feet. 'A close call I prefer not to repeat.'

Anja forced a conversational tone. 'The shape-changer's dead?'

'No, sadly not.' The captain grimaced, as though the wisped fumes incited foul thoughts. 'We don't have the whole body. Even if we did, a fully fledged minion doesn't banish or die half so easily. We'll need a vizier or a trained tribal shaman to sever the creature's connections to the sorcerer who raised its formed will from the darkened realms of the unseen.'

Anja choked down a sick bolt of fear. 'That thing could come back?' She would not, *could not*, reconcile herself to an enemy wearing the semblance of her murdered brother.

Mykkael stirred, took up his fouled sword. As though soothed by rote habit, he plied his rag to the soiled blade. 'Princess, you are safe. The shape-changer's head is dissolved in salt water. So is a part of its arm. That binds its powers. It cannot shift form. The fragments that spilled over the falls might reassemble themselves, if they aren't too widely scattered. But headless, the construct that forms will be blinded and deaf. It can grope, but not mount an effective attack. My due course of vigilance should hold it at bay. Left as an animate, crippled corpse, it can't cause us serious harm.'

Still drenched from the dousing, tumultuous entry, Anja spoke through her chattering teeth. 'Well, even one-handed, it could pound us with rocks.'

'Sightless? It can try.' Mykkael straightened, sheathed his cleaned sword, then shrugged off the ache of some lingering discomfort. 'If these caverns have any ore veins bearing copper, I can doctor an arrow and stun it.' He pushed off the wall, took a shocking, gimped stride, then snatched a pause to resettle his balance. He assayed a next step, reached steadfast Fouzette, and set his hands to untie the noisome bundles strapped to her back. 'Forgive me, Princess. An unpleasant task remains to be done. I warn, you may not wish to watch.'

Anja swallowed. 'The shape-changer's head?'

Mykkael nodded. Under the filtered light through the falls, his expression stayed grim as iron. 'I'm sorry.' He chose the raw hide, used his dagger to slice off a yard length. 'Safety must come before nicety, in this case. The contents of that puddle will have to go with us and stay under constant guard.'

She coughed into her hand. 'What can I do?'

Startled, he regarded her, the crude square of horse-hide poised in his unsteady hands. 'By the nine names of hell, Princess! Are you sure?' The dawning hint of a smile resurged, sparked by his wry amazement. 'Very well. I've known seasoned fighters who were more faint-hearted. If you hold the hide taut, I will scrape.'

Anja lasted through the duration, just barely. While Mykkael lashed his unspeakable gleanings into a tight, secure packet, she crept off to seek respite amid the warm press of the horses. Dry heaves overwhelmed her within three steps. She doubled, reeled dizzy, as her empty stomach wrung itself inside out. A soft footfall approached. Mykkael's embrace gathered her in from behind, hooked under her arm, and resteadied her. His left hand, icy cold from a rinse in the falls, cradled her pounding, flushed forehead.

'We'll have a fire,' he said. 'Get you warm and dry. But first, some fresh air. The wardings are too short, I can't leave you alone. Can you manage a foray to fetch drift-wood?'

She ripped off a nod, between spasms.

'Your Grace,' said Mykkael, something more than impressed, 'let no one say you're a coward.'

His strong grasp raised her until she stood, propped against his right shoulder. Too breathless to question, that he should burden his sword arm assisting her wretched infirmity, she let him steer her wobbling steps to the cleft at the edge of the falls. He sat her down on a rock by the opening. Through the pause as he secured the horses with hobbles, the chill spray on her face braced her jangled nerves. Anja breathed in deep gulps of clean air, while her cramping nausea subsided.

Shortly, she was able to walk, even help gather the kindling caught in the boulders where the captain's limp gave him difficulty. They finished the task as the last daylight faded. Under the sky's lucent afterglow, streaked with the fire blooms of kerries, Mykkael made no protest as Anja shouldered her share of the load and worked her way back to shelter.

Much later, warmed under Mykkael's dried-out surcoat, Anja gnawed flaked trout from a stick, almost restored to contentment. The captain lounged across the raked coals, braiding tough strips of wing leather into a rope. He wove eight plies into a round plait, by his casual dexterity accustomed to finishing such an endeavour before.

'You implied you became a mercenary by choice,' Anja opened, her musing framed in a different tone from her barrage of questions that morning.

Mykkael looked up, the velvet-brown depths of his eyes rendered fathomless in the firelight. 'Oh, I chose, all right.' He leaned to one side, caught up a cut strip, spliced it seamlessly into his weaving. 'The decision was made with great storm and commotion. Everyone argued. My uncle forbade me. I left to study *barqui'ino*.'

Anja poked her cleaned stick into the embers, watching him by the flare as the wood caught. Chin cupped in her hands, she said, 'Why?'

He had marked the softening in her well enough. His quiet pause became weighted. Still, he answered. 'I realize, to prove I existed. Because my mother exposed me, I had no way to know where I came from. My northern upbringing was not who I was. I wrestled with the hollow question inside, until I became chafed to desperation. I wanted *barqui'ino* because the training was held to be the most demanding of all attainments.'

'Most trainees fail?'

His hands resumed, combed through the crossed-over strands, then deftly picked up their rhythm. 'All but a few.'

The spurt of the fire died back to a flicker, striking ruby glints off the falls. Mykkael's stubbled face seemed carved from dark sandstone, with the horses behind him a muddle of shadows, standing hipshot with lowered necks.

Anja pressed gently. 'And after your mastery?'

But this time, Mykkael shook his head. 'No, Princess. Enough.' He had blooded his young steel upon sorcerers' wars, no fit topic for conversation. 'You would do well to sleep while you can.'

Anja sighed. She could try. Despite the close-woven wool of the surcoat, the cold was likely to keep her awake. How foolish, if she confided her fear, that the looming dread of her nightmares paralysed her with unease.

Mykkael glanced up, startled. Witch thought had surely divined her distress. Anja, in turn, sensed the impact of that intrusively intimate recoil. As though he had reached out and touched her bared mind, she rebounded to flash-point perception. 'You want my eyes shut while you rebind your wounds!'

He blinked. 'Blinding powers of daylight!' Irritation hardened his rattled response. 'Your Grace. Should I not?'

Anja coloured. The blush made her eyes a most vivid green. 'You can't properly claim you can contend with an opened gash on your back. Captain, what are you guarding?'

'My dignity.' Mykkael's direct stare should have served as a firm deterrent. He had been a mercenary, hired by kings. No man lasted long in close royal service by playing the spineless sycophant.

'Do you cling to a principle we can afford?' Fire met live fire, across the fanned coals. Anja clamped dauntless fists over the falcon surcoat. 'If I try to sleep, Captain, how are you going to stay wakeful, or warm?'

He cursed in his ancestors' guttural tongue. 'Do as you please, Princess. For my part, discussion is ended.' Head stubbornly bent, he resumed his braiding. His face stayed stiffly set. He had to realize she would hold out until she had achieved her dissection.

For an interval, the silence stretched, brittle as glass. The coals hissed and flared, and the white water fell, slicing the night without let-up.

Then, without warning, the mark on the sword hilt roused and sang. Its sudden cry razed the air like tapped crystal. Mykkael surged to his feet amid an explosion of dropped braid and wing leather. Sword in hand, he glared outwards. His skin became pebbled with gooseflesh. Yet the note that chimed through the echoing dark was high, clear and sweet, with a ringing, melodic overtone.

The captain glanced wildly about, but saw nothing. No shadow moved, no sign arose to indicate lurking danger. The vibration struck off his shaman-sung steel did not build or sustain. With an eerie, light whisper, it simply diminished and faded away.

The night held nothing other than the rush of the cataract, jetting over smoothed stone. No smell lingered. Just the mineral tang of wet rock, and wood smoke, infused with the odour of seared trout.

Anja shivered. She tucked the tattered surcoat over her slender shoulders. 'What caused that?'

Mykkael shook his head, but failed to relax. 'I don't know, your Grace.' He ran questing fingers over the weapon's marked hilt, then shrugged off a grue that arose through his feet, and played itself through his locked frame. 'At no time have I heard the warding react to anything that way before.'

He limped from the fireside. His prowling footsteps stayed silent as he quartered the cavern twice over. His survey encountered no trace of a threat. The packet confining the shape-changer's leavings remained secure in his keeping. Except for pricked ears and turned heads, the horses evinced no distress.

Too riled to stand down, Mykkael stalked through a final round of inspection. He retired at last to the edge of the precipice. There, without ceremony, he laid down his sword and proceeded to unlace and strip off his trousers. Clad in shirt and smallclothes, he sat down on chill stone and began to unwind the stained poultice strapped to his thigh.

Night masked his dark form; but not the puckered shine of old scars, marked one after the other like a row of branded spear points. The imprints progressed with unsettling deliberation, up the sculpted muscle of his upper leg, and vanished under the shirttail that covered the more tender skin of his flank.

Anja sucked a breath of startled embarrassment.

'Princess?' He glanced over his shoulder, teeth bared in a combative smile. 'Puncture,' he stated in brazen challenge. 'Since you have neither manners or shame, let's end the excitement forthwith. The wound is quite clean. It was made by a sword. Cold water should do nicely to take down the swelling, a treatment I trust will make you nod off out of natural boredom.'

Anja discovered she lacked the effrontery to take up the thrown gauntlet, after all. Wrapped in the hard-used cloth of his surcoat, she huddled in silence, drifting from an uneasy catnap into the depths of oblivious sleep.

Both scryings failed. Though a second disturbance from the unseen had distressed the flow of the earth's flux, the circle of shamans gleaned little more than the emperor's vizier, although they sang a mighty power into their striving. A protector walked Hell's Chasm, they said, his person cloaked by a layered work of warding whose weaving had deafened their seers. Perplexity deepened. For when the tribal enclave retired, the elder among them dreamed a flawless line into the warrior's heart. He saw the man as a great, cloudy star, his light wracked and riddled by mishap and wounds, and the dross of his unshed tears . . .

XXX. Crossing

ANJA WAKENED TWICE IN THE NIGHT. THE FIRST TIME HER SLEEP RIPPED TO WHIMPERING SCREAMS, SHE ROUSED, drawn back from the darkness by a man's hand, cupping her tear-stained cheek. The same gentle touch stroked the damp hair from her temples. She realized she lay with her head pillowed against Mykkael's leg. He murmured a phrase that soothed her eyes closed. She submerged once again, lulled by the rhythm of his competent fingers, weaving a wing-leather rope.

Her rest broke the second time closer to dawn. She stirred, vaguely unsettled to find she no longer huddled on chill stone. The noise of the falls thrashed the air without let-up, and the captain was no longer braiding.

'Your Grace?' said Mykkael, crisply wakeful above her. 'You were shivering.'

He sat, his back propped to the cavern wall, her curled body cradled against his waist. The drawn sword in his hand rested across her lap, the war-battered steel of its crossguard glinting against the crumpled device on the garrison surcoat.

That moment, a near spurt of kerrie fire seared into the stream of the falls. Light flared through the cavern, sharp as the burst of a lightning flash.

Anja's reflexive surge to escape was arrested by Mykkael's tensed forearm.

'Lie still, Princess. You are quite safe. The creatures might taste our scent, but they can't fly or spit flame across falling water.'

Eyes shut, basked in his close warmth, Anja found she could not shed the image of the raised scars she had glimpsed, rowed across the bared skin of his thigh. 'Those marks were not sword cuts,' she accused, too drowsy to curb the brash confrontation she had murmured aloud.

'Sleep, Princess,' Mykkael said, unoffended. He smoothed the ripped cloth of the surcoat over her shoulders, easing her back into kindlier dreams with an effortless, blanketing calm.

She did not feel him slip from her presence. Aroused at daybreak to the smoke of a fire laid with the last billets of driftwood, Anja smelled fillets roasting over the coals. This time, Mykkael had speared a river pike. The hapless fish flushed over the rip of the falls had no chance against *barqui'ino* reflex.

The hunter himself seemed nowhere in evidence.

Anja pushed off the sheltering surcoat and sat up, to a spurt of stifled alarm.

'Princess?' The captain's voice issued from amid the horses, where he knelt to attend Fouzette's injury. 'Rise and eat. If we're to allow for a pause to seek fodder, we'll need to move out very soon.'

Hope raised Anja's spirits. 'Do you think we'll find grazing?' She peered through the gloom, caught her breath over the progress accomplished through his expert use of cold compresses, then measured the neat work he made of the leg wrap to draw the mare's swelling.

'The chasm is wider below the cascade.' Mykkael stood up and wiped his damp hands, his manner brisk with impatience. 'Any streamlet with good sunlight is bound to feed a pocket of tender spring grass.'

Anja shook out the tumbled folds of the surcoat, and

laid the garment across the cantle of her propped saddle. 'What about hunting kerries?'

The captain evaded a forthright answer. 'On that score, I have an idea. We'll test the result, but after we've forded the cataract.'

All but deafened by the thrash of the falls, Anja spotted the rope, finished off into gleaming coils of black braid. The use it might serve through the passage ahead wrecked the healthy pangs of her appetite. Beset by chills, the princess realized she had slept on the shrinking hope they could embrace the safe choice and turn back. The thundering force of the falls seemed an obstacle worthy of forestalling further progress. She had coddled the faint-hearted expectation that even Mykkael must shy back from running the Widow's Gauntlet.

'Eat.' The dauntless desert-bred knelt by his fire, spitted half of his cooked catch on a stick, and shoved the offering into her laggard hand. 'A sorcerer's shape-changer still dogs our heels. Your sire stands besieged, as we linger.'

Anja nibbled, scarcely tasting the morsel she made herself chew and swallow. 'You know he's alive?'

Mykkael looked sharply back at her. During the night, he had used his small dagger and shaved his dark face clean of stubble. 'At dawn, yes, he was. I had a witch thought, and saw Jussoud tending him. The Duchess of Phail was holding the king's hand.'

'Taskin stood guard for him?'

The captain turned smoothly away, intent on his portion of breakfast. 'An armed circle of defenders have taken refuge inside Dedorth's tower. The Commander of the Royal Guard was there at his Majesty's bedside.'

Though Anja received the distinct impression that Mykkael's seamless move had posed a minor avoidance, the anxiety at hand overshadowed her impulse to press him.

The perils of Hell's Chasm were lethal enough, without adding pursuit by a sorcerer. Ahead, every record agreed without variance, the ravine became brutally impassable. No misguided adventurers had ever won through. The ones who escaped outright slaughter by kerries had been battered to rags on the rocks, each one a name on a list of fatalities passed down for generations.

Yet the desert-bred captain who stayed wilfully set to make himself the exception finished his meal of roast fish. He gathered up his coils of rope, then calmly inquired which mount her Grace wanted bridled and saddled.

'Kasminna.' More shaken and sore than she cared to admit, Anja rose to match the necessity. She measured her animals' weaknesses and assets, and made the decision that might seal their lives, or their deaths. 'Stormfront will keep up if I ride his teammate, and your strength, on Vashni, should drive him on if Fouzette's bad leg slows her down.'

Too soon, the horses were readied. Anja accepted Kasminna's reins, aching for her animals' sad straits. The peppery sorrel was too starved and dispirited to do more than flatten her ears as her rider released the stirrups and mounted. The mare moved out after grey Vashni's lead, and clattered into the dousing plunge through the cleft. She emerged, soaked and snorting, into the twilight shade of the gorge, where a fresh morning sky painted the rocks with cerulean highlights.

Mykkael checked his bearings, then reined the grey back upstream. The race of the flume was still high with spring melt. He could not expect a tame crossing. The site he selected for least risk of hazard wrung the princess to stark trepidation.

The current narrowed to a raging, white span choked on the near side by a deep shelf of rock. The far bank rose out of a sluiced riffle of shallows, sucking over a potholed ledge. The cavern wall reared high above, cleaved by frost into cragged flaws and niches, and choked by a few tortured evergreens.

Mykkael completed his final assessment, then faced Anja's mute pallor without flinching. 'I can't pace out the distance to make sure of the wardings,' he said over the rampaging waters. 'Therefore, you'll carry my sword.'

Will ruled him as iron. He would part with the weapon without hesitation. While the horses snorted in bunched-up unease, he unslung the bow and hooked the tip on the quiver hanging against Vashni's shoulder. Then he stripped off his harness, passed the straps and sheathed blade into Anja's reluctant grasp. Still mounted, he assisted her shaking, cold fingers to tighten the buckles. The task was accomplished with startling speed. Belatedly, Anja discovered the reason. An additional row of holes had been punched, long ago, to accommodate somebody close to her size. 'You've done this before,' she accused, snatched breathless with apprehension.

He nodded. 'Just twice.' He yanked hard, made certain the straps were secure, then used the light cord unlaced from his cuff to lash the blade into the scabbard. 'Three times should be lucky.' The grim fact stayed unvoiced, that if the princess should be swept off and drowned, the shaman's mark founded his desolate hope that the shape-changer could not wreak a sorcerer's work upon her hapless dead body.

As the captain dismounted, handing off Vashni's reins, Anja regarded his upturned face with wide-eyed entreaty.

'Don't think,' said Mykkael. He unbuckled his belt, tossed his scrip and shed surcoat aside on the bank. 'I'll accomplish what must be done quickly.'

Clad in shirt and breeches, he approached the base of the cliff and pried out a loose stone with his dagger. On top, he stacked the grim packet holding the minion's captive remains. 'I can't risk a dunking,' he explained as he lashed the paired weight of stone and leather on to one end of his braided rope. He affixed several tight coils under the knot, and made them fast. 'The salt could wash through and release the bound contents.' If that particular misfortune happened, the terror that emerged would be too dire to contemplate.

Mykkael caught up Fouzette. He threaded the loose end of the rope over her back and between her wide-set forelegs to fashion a crude chest strap and surcingle.

Standing once more, his disquieting bundle laid to one side, he arranged the rope's coils in broad, open loops, where they would peel off without tangling. He spoke as he worked. 'Anja! Listen carefully. I will cross first. You'll count off seconds. If I go under for more than one minute, you'll back Fouzette and raise the rope taut. When I reach the far bank, I will throw back the rock. You will untie it and fasten the line to the ring under Kasminna's headstall. Leave two yards of extra line free at the end. That should be enough to knot around your chest at the armpits.' He stood, gripped her knee, and searched her face with determined brown eyes. 'Understand?'

She nodded, her throat too choked to reply.

He showed her the correct knot, made her repeat tying it twice. Once he was certain she would not fumble or slip, he gave her shoulder a light slap of encouragement. 'You'll do, Princess, more than very well. Now stand back. Lead the other horses well clear. Also make sure that Stormfront's secured. Let's sidestep the known pitfall, and forestall his impulse to tear loose and follow the mare.'

As Anja realized, dismayed, he had made no contingencies, Mykkael silenced her with a headshake. 'We do this just once. The lives of your horses rest in your hands, and I have not known you to fail them.'

He stepped back, a dwarfed figure in sadly soiled clothes who would stand or fall on lamed strength, naked will and ingenuity. Before Anja had mustered the resolve to go forward, Mykkael had taken his rock grapple in hand. He started it swinging. The whistling, tight circles compelled the princess to scramble clear and herd the horses against the cleft wall. When the hide tether sliced the air, then sang out with a whining hum, the captain raised his fist, and turned the spin horizontal. With the rock sling now whistling over his head, he payed out more line. His release was a masterwork of neat timing, no doubt perfected in siegecraft. The rock sailed over the chasm in a shot arc, trailing its runner of line.

It descended and caught in the first gnarled fir. Leashed momentum whipped the end in a caught spiral over the spindly tree. The snag sealed his commitment. No wishful tug could pull the line free. Mykkael would embark with no second chance. Either the rope was wound fast, or it would slip and break loose, or else tear up the evergreen, root and limb, the first time it came to be tested.

'Anja!' Mykkael shouted. 'Come steady your mare. If the line fails, you must not despair! If I should fall in, and if I stay under for more than a minute, you will work with the horse and draw up the slack. Don't stand at Fouzette's head. Hold her back from behind, or you'll risk being swept off your feet if she slides. Align her straight on. Try not to let her spin sideways.'

The captain backed the bay mare to harden the line. He tugged only once, to test its strung tension, then handed off Fouzette's lead to the princess.

'Don't think,' he insisted. 'Just breathe and stay focused.'

Mykkael left her no chance to build apprehension, but charged three running steps and launched off the ledge. He caught the line and swung himself hand over hand above the raging white race that tore down the throat of the chasm.

The captain had drawn himself halfway across, when the anchoring tree snapped its taproot. The line loosened and sagged. His feet struck the tossing rush of the flume, and the sudden, sharp jerk yanked Fouzette into a disastrous surge forward.

'Hold hard!' Anja screamed. 'Fouzette, hold hard!'

The mare answered, snorting. Her trembling hindquarters lowered to withstand the murderous drag at her forehand.

But Mykkael had already gone under. The beleaguered

fir tree trembled and bent, the lesser roots still clutched to the crag overtaxed by the drag of the current. The captain remained precariously tethered, though the foaming water had swallowed his form.

The princess looked on, wrung voiceless, as the braided black rope knifed downwards into the tumble. The pressure twisted and wrung at the stunted fir binding the end to the opposite shore. Bark and greenery peeled. A branch cracked and parted. Loose pebbles spilled down as the strained roots ripped up the thin soil.

Anja watched, her heart all but stopped, while the improvised rope still holding Mykkael sliced ever further from the near bank. A mote in a maelstrom, he was being dragged downstream by the raging spate.

She remembered to start counting. Unnerved and frightened, she ran through the sequence too fast. More pebbles cracked loose. A stricken glance at the tree showed its trunk wrung in half. Second by second, the stubbed base was tearing out of the crevice. The rope sliced the wild water, carving up spray. The current's brutal, swirling force swung Mykkael towards the far bank. If he could maintain his grip against its pummelling fury, if his strength held, and if the hide itself did not slide through his wet hands, he might have a chance to haul himself clear of danger. Provided the tree did not give way first.

The near bank posed no option. Even braced by Fouzette, the captain would be battered to rags against the undershot rim of the ledge.

Anja's count had cleared forty. Dread squeezed her chest. If she called on Fouzette, she saw right away, the precarious fir tree must fail. The roots, now peeled backwards, could not withstand even an ounce of additional strain. Sight fixed to the thrumming strand of the rope, Anja begged for reprieve from the elements. She held Mykkael's memory, rejecting tears, and compelled herself to keep his admonishment *to breathe.*

Tears blurred her vision, regardless. She caught

Fouzette's lead, prepared to drag in the line, when the whitewater at the far side kicked and splashed, thrown into savage recoil. A fan of spray shot from the moil of current. Then a dark hand emerged, sculpted with strain, still latched to the failing rope.

Mykkael reappeared, hurtled over and over in the tumble. He broke the surface, his head and face dashed under by the cataract of churned water. He ducked like a seal. Elbows tucked, he used legs and feet as a rudder, fought his clinging form in a slewing arc towards the shallows. Another haul on the line broke him clear of the murderous drag of the race. There he clung, trying to recover his stressed wind, spluttering and coughing up water.

'Mykkael!' Anja screamed out a warning. 'Look up! You must! The tree's giving way!'

He had already seen. If the line let go now, he would be lost. The slick, shelving rock that supported his hip hissed and boiled with sheeting, fast current. His attempt to fold on to one knee and gain purchase battered him once more downstream. The snagged fir tore again, raining pebbles. Another sharp tug would uproot it. The ledge where the captain languished was too slippery. If he tried to rise, he would be swept away. Each moment he relied on the line, the icy spate numbed the speed from his reflexes. Left no other choice, he dragged himself tenderly in, hand over inching hand. Each foot regained from the drag of brute elements, he seized from the poised jaws of fate.

Mykkael reached the far shore, scraped and bleeding, and all but stunned senseless. The knee of his breeches was shredded to rags. One of his boots had been torn away in the pummelling rush of the current. The wracked fir that had anchored him now hung straight down, with his improvised rock grapple dangling. The tied packet of peril that *must* be kept dry swung over the fast-rushing water.

Anja watched, breathless, as Mykkael discerned that

unfolding disaster. He kicked off his filled boot and surged to his feet in one seamlessly desperate motion. Steel flashed in his hand, though she had not seen the sheath that concealed the short dagger he kept for infighting. He jammed the blade into a crack in the stone, risked his weight to its steel, and drew himself up by the handle. His outflung fist snagged the swinging rope. He ducked the recoiling spin of the stone, let its momentum thud into the cliff wall. It shattered on impact. Face and shoulders, he was raked by the back-falling fragments. He clung through the battering. As the broken stone fell away, leaving the cord bindings uselessly slackened, Mykkael snatched like a cobra. When he lowered himself down, he had the salt packet with the shape-changer's remains once more in hand, tightly guarded.

He did not pause in triumph. The moment he had the burden stowed in the security of a dry crevice, he tugged down the splintered remains of the tree, and freed his length of snagged rope. He climbed again and whipped a tight half-hitch over a well-rooted tree bole. Once the trailing end of the line was reeled in, he tied on a new stone as a throwing weight. Then he coiled the slack, and hurled the line across the raced waters to Anja.

Mykkael did not call out in encouragement, or rush her to undue haste. The drawn tension on his face spoke more plainly than words: each second that kept him apart from his sword increased the potential for danger.

Anja caught up the icy, wet rope, and hauled the rock from its backsliding roll towards the water. She fought the pull of the slippery hide, skinned her knuckles working the stubborn knots free. Despite the terror clamped in her gut, she fastened the line to Kasminna's headstall. Then she knotted the trailing end to her waist exactly as Mykkael had taught her.

'All right!' Her tremulous shout arose thin as a gull's cry over the thrash of the flume.

The captain nodded his instant acknowledgement and

raised his cupped hands to shout. 'Lay the slack line on the upstream side! Then climb astride. Grab mane with both hands, gallop straight on and jump! Go! No thinking! Do as I say, now, Princess!'

Kasminna snorted, pawing, already aware her young handler was uneasy. Anja clambered astride, her blind state of fear underscored by stark common sense. The wise horse she rode would balk, if she faltered.

Anja swallowed. Trembling, she stroked the mare's neck, then balanced her weight for a running charge off the ledge. 'Kasminna! Ready!' She pitched the familiar command as though she prepared to launch a hot contest of steed wickets in the meadow.

The mare tensed beneath her, prancing with eagerness. Despite the strange setting, the start of a match was a well-known, beloved routine. The horse pricked her ears forward. Her muscles coiled with quivering anticipation.

'Kasminna, go!' shouted Anja.

The sorrel exploded forward. Her powerful stride unfolded and drove her headlong off the rim, then over the boiling torrent. The last thing Anja heard, through the whistle of air, and the foaming crash of the waters, was Stormfront's distressed whinny, that his herd mate departed without his accustomed support.

Then the mare struck. The shock of the icy, turbulent water slapped the breath out of Anja's chest. She gasped, stunned all but witless as she pitched into frigid immersion. The swift current hooked her clothes with battering force. Her body was torn off Kasminna's back. The locked clasp of her fists in wet mane buoyed her, barely. She sucked in a breath, before a hammering wall of white water drove headlong into her face. She swallowed a mouthful, nearly choked as the spate pummelled her lips and closed eyelids. She held on, overpowered and blinded, and robbed of all sense of direction.

The frightened horse fared no better. Kasminna pitched and thrashed through the froth. Head upflung, nose tipped skywards, she bucked the pull of the rope on her nose-band. Still, her stabbing hooves found no purchase. Swept downstream like a straw in a millrace, she rolled under, snorting in terror.

Through the cold and the dark, Anja thought she heard Mykkael's frantic shouting. She battled the greedy suck of the current. Her puny strength did not avail her. The remorseless force of the flume wrung her under. She could not twist her face to the surface. The drubbing eddies hurled her into chill darkness, pounding her down without let-up. She clung. Kasminna's struggles meant life. Anja felt her fingers inexorably sliding as her cramped lungs lost air, and the horse slammed, fighting, against her.

Then the shadowy deeps thinned around her. Sudden light burst and burned, and her head broke the surface, dashed with white fingers of foam. Her braid had wrapped around her wracked throat. She fought its wet choke hold, then felt her knees slam into a ledge of smoothed rock. One hand still gripped Kasminna's streamed mane. Anja clung like a limpet, while the mare dug in her iron-shod forefeet and scrambled. Her upflung head showered spray against the reeling sky overhead.

'Back up! Fouzette! Back, now!' Mykkael's shout sounded all but on top of her.

Anja coughed weakly. Cold water exploded from her filled nose and mouth. Somewhere near, a rope creaked taut. The stressed plies threw off moisture like plumed smoke.

Anja felt the jostling surge of the horse. She lost her last grip, slammed down and sideways into swirling water and rock. The fierce current clawed her, hauling at the deadweight of her filled shoes and soaked clothing. She hacked out a yell, felt the rope dig her chest. Then a ruthless pull from the tethering end snapped her ahead like a rag doll. A last, stinging wave slapped over her cheek. Then Mykkael's fist grabbed her collar, hauled her free of the rip, and flung her gasping upon the splashed ledge.

First thing, she pitched over and heaved up her guts. The horrid, cold gush of breakfast and river water gouted over her bleeding, grazed hands. Tears burned her eyes. Her lungs ached like bruised meat. Mykkael caught her up, tossed her over his raised knee, and pounded her back as she gagged. Her clogged airway emptied. Her limbs felt like a mangled stranger's. Shaking with shock, she shivered and retched, and fought in a raw gulp of air.

'The sword,' she gasped. 'Kasminna.'

'Both safe.' Mykkael cradled her against his wet shoulder, steel and all. His cold fingers were trembling as he cleared the heavy, drenched braid from her throat. 'You've done Sessalie proud as a princess.'

Anja freed a hand, pushed. 'The others.'

'We'll bring them.' Mykkael propped her upright, allowing the freedom her spirited pride would demand. 'Once you can stand, you'll help me.'

His tone was a level ribbon of steel, shocking her into recovery. Anja sat up, hampered by the unyielding burden of the weapon strapped on to her back. 'You aren't going back across!'

Mykkael released his supportive grip, warned off by her knifing anger. 'Someone must.' The chiselled set to his desert-bred features showed no softening change of expression. 'For one thing, the bow and arrows must stay dry. Nor can we leave the supplies in my scrip.'

Anja glared at him, horrified. 'Captain, no! If you try, you'll be battered to death where the water undercuts the far ledge!'

He grinned. 'I would if I planned to go swimming again.'

The tip of the sword scabbard clanked against stone as Anja shoved all the way upright. She arrived on her feet. White-faced and shivering, slightly rocked by the weight of the longsword strapped into the harness, she raised her chin, prepared to spit venom. Despite plastered hair and bedraggled appearance, she was every inch the crowned princess. Answers were expected, and prompt ones, to judge by the frown that snarled the cut silk of her eyebrows. 'Take back your weapon. Then show me.'

'I expect to.' Mykkael caught her wrists, restrained her rushed impulse to start unfastening buckles. 'Let's untie that safety rope first.' He reached with marked hands, began unlashing knots, his seal-wet head bent and still dripping. 'The sword stays with you, Princess, until I can make my way back.'

'Promise!' Anja repressed a violent shiver. She needed to rail at him, but words posed too daunting an effort. Sickness and strain had unstrung her. Wretchedly chilled, she could not stop shaking. 'You aren't going to swim.'

Mykkael bowed with crossed forearms over his chest, the formal royal salute he preferred. 'Your Grace, take my vow. The river is not going to have me.' He went on in swift terms to explain what he wanted, then proceeded to scramble up the near outcrop. There, he made adjustments to allow his fastened line to slide under friction, and affixed the retrieved end around the sturdiest of the remaining trees.

The captain's plan involved using the traction provided by two horses to create the crude principle of a block and tackle.

'You'll brace the line, so,' he said. 'Fouzette stands as anchor. I'll cross over the chasm, hand over hand, this time without a disaster.' He would not be immersed, except for his legs, and then, only for the final stretch where the slope of the line dropped too low to permit him full clearance. 'If I carry the middle of the rope across with me, and tie on the horses' headstalls, you'll have two trees taking the brunt of the strain, and the other end pulled by Kasminna.'

Anja swiped plastered hair from her cheek. 'How can you recover the centre of the line, once we've drawn the first animal across?'

'Not a difficulty.' Mykkael turned to Kasminna, and

began to fashion a makeshift harness and chest strap. 'I'll string lead lines together. Knotted on to the rope, they will serve as a feed string to drag the loop back.' With two horses pulling, the one crossing the current should be able to make the passage with a reasonable assurance of safety. The strategy seemed sound, as long as no animal panicked, and provided Kasminna and Fouzette, standing anchor, did not slip on wet rock or go down.

'The last horse,' Anja whispered. No fool, she had foreseen the pitfall. The final animal must swim unassisted. Fouzette, like Kasminna, must assay the crossing with no anchor on the far bank.

'You'll have four horses on this side,' Mykkael pointed out, his dark eyes unafraid as he watched her measure the catch. 'And myself. Fouzette's solid. If she can stand her firm ground at the end, I can cross back, hand over hand, just before her. Supposing the worst happens, and she fails at the last, you'll still have four horses to pull from this side. They should be sufficient to bring both of us through.'

Anja swallowed. 'If Fouzette gives way, Captain, you'll cut her rope.'

'She won't give way,' said Mykkael. Droplets scattered from his sodden shirt cuffs as he tested the last knot on Kasminna's improvised surcingle. 'Just imagine your bay lady standing with Vashni, stuffing her belly on marsh grass. How would you like to snack on roast trout while we dry ourselves off in the sun?'

XXXI. Siege

THE SENESCHAL OF SESSALIE PERCHED LIKE A NETTLED BIRD ON ONE OF DEDORTH'S TATTERED FOOTSTOOLS. Hands folded in prim disapproval, he spoke across the rapacious chess game Taskin played against the physician from Fane Street. 'I should go out. The council ought to be warned of the High Prince of Devall's doubtful motives.'

The outstanding contract for marriage seemed a dangerous thread to leave dangling. Yet Taskin languished next to the game board, uncommunicative, his eyes shut.

Undaunted by his freezing silence, or the click of the game piece as the physician advanced Dedorth's mouse-chewed white rook, Lord Shaillon cleared his throat and pressed on. 'His Highness's suit must be formally rejected. Your desert-bred captain was left wounded, you said. Should he fail to win through, Devall's heir apparent must not retain the implied standing to influence Sessalie's future.'

Taskin cracked open ice-blue eyes. He was currently propped up against pillows on the floor, while Jussoud, at the bedside, applied his knowledge as masseur to the king's intractable malady. Ignoring the seneschal, the commander glanced over the chessboard. Though even slight movement pained his strapped arm, he extended a finger and slid the black bishop two diagonal squares to the left. 'Check.'

As the seneschal drew breath, Taskin shifted his knife-point regard. 'I heard you the first time, Lord Shaillon.' His drained whisper lacked none of its caustic force. 'Go out, and you'll be a walking sacrifice. In the king's absence, and mine, you wield too much power. Can Sessalie afford to set you at risk of being claimed as a sorcerer's catspaw? I say not. My guardsmen will not let you pass.'

The seneschal jutted his chin, unintimidated. 'Without me, the council will argue the affairs of this realm to a standstill!'

'Let them.' Taskin tipped his head in ironic deference towards the bed.

'An intelligent tactic,' interjected King Isendon, roused and lucid under Jussoud's skilled ministrations. 'The rule of this kingdom is set under siege. Should I die in this tower, the state legalities are better left tangled. If we fall here, and Devall moves to upset my succession, my sealed record could still thwart him.' Crown heir Kailen destroyed meant Princess Anja must be left her clear right to inherit. 'I must believe my daughter can win free and sue for a southern alliance.'

The argument lapsed, leaving grief-stricken quiet, the fust of old books and Dedorth's frowsty housekeeping thickened by the aromatic smoke of burned cedar. The tight quarters had become a sore trial to the defenders besieged inside. Since Perincar's geometry and Mykkael's list of defensive banishings had stood off the initial assault, the sorcerer's watch spells ringed their refuge without surcease, probing for sign of a breach. Taskin's guardsmen shared vigil at the windows and door, which left the nine individuals carrying the vizier's talismans crammed into constant, close company. A chalked ring on the floor marked the limited range where the ninefold shield held to resonance. For any one of the bearers to stray past that distance would spell their defeat, sealing King Isendon's doom and inflicting a fate that would reach beyond death.

Allowed no expedient weakness to exploit, the focus of the sorcerer's attack appeared to have shifted elsewhere.

The perilous stand-off fallen since dawn chafed upon everyone's nerves. Lady Phail sensibly used the interval to catch up on sleep. The seneschal throttled his griped urge to pace, while the surviving sentries conscripted from Highgate stood fretful guard, and their wounded commander salved restless nerves by waging increasingly vicious campaigns on the chessboard.

'A soldier who took this long to counterstrike would become chopped meat on a battlefield,' Taskin barked at drawn length.

Never hurried for any man, the Fane Street physician paused to polish his spectacles. 'Healers by nature don't sacrifice without forethought. Knight takes rook.'

Eyes shut, Taskin smiled in evil triumph. 'Mate in two moves. You won't save your king. Reset the board. We'll play again.'

'A bit bloodthirsty, aren't we?' The physician fielded his latest defeat with good grace. Though he seemed content to accept a fresh challenge, even his dauntless optimism wore thin from the pressure of constant unease.

Under the thinning drift of the mist, nothing *seemed* untoward outside. The bell rang from Highgate to signal the change of the watch. The sweet clarity of the sunrise paean drifted down from the Sanctuary on the pinnacle. If the sorcerer's minion now stalked the chancellors in Sessalie's chambers of state, no word and no news reached the tower. After two overt assaults by cold sorcery, even the keenest mind could not guess how the council might have been soothed to placation.

The absence of the king, the crown prince and the duchess, as well as four ranking officers of the realm, must have been blamed on the fire that had struck the palace apartment. Yet no death knells had rung. The general populace had not been informed of a royal demise. Some semblance of legal decorum prevailed, since a change in succession demanded the proof of a body.

Shadowed by fearfully dire speculation, the select party immured with the king could do nothing but wait out their helplessness. They subsisted on mean rations and slept by turns in tight quarters, while the morning wore past like slow torture. The Duchess of Phail napped in her chair, her white head nested on a frayed bolster, while the off-watch men-at-arms slept, bearing weapons, and the handful of guard from the duty roster held the main door, and sparingly burned cedar in the grate.

'Powers of daylight look after my daughter,' the king prayed in a scraped whisper.

'Mykkael won't fail you, Majesty,' Vensic reassured him. Bent by the light of a tallow dip, he struck his knife upright and tipped the winkle of copper shavings just pared from a drawer pull into Dedorth's soot-streaked crucible. The melted metal would be used to treat arrow points, by Mykkael's instruction the best way to stun a sorcerer's fledged minion.

'One man, alone!' Bennent spoke from the shuttered window, where he kept uneventful lookout. 'What chance does that desert-bred have? I tell you, we ought to strike back while we can, and run Devall out of the kingdom.'

'Mykkael's experience has spared your life and the king's, three times over,' Taskin stated. 'If the warning he left with me held any substance, the high prince is already corrupt. Move on him now, and you could be challenging the primary tool sent to spearhead this sorcerer's invasion.'

'Well don't you think folk should be warned of the danger?' the seneschal pressed.

'They should not,' interjected the Fane Street physician, his plump hands staging pawns on the chessboard. 'Ignorance is the blessing that spares them, just now.' The horrible deaths of the apothecary and the seeress had established that fact beyond question. 'For myself, I shrink to contemplate the reason why this tower is no longer set under active attack.'

Lord Shaillon huffed in contempt through his nose. 'Personally, I prefer to enjoy the relief.'

'Shaillon, your lack of knowledge is dangerous.' King Isendon stirred on Dedorth's narrow bed, too tired for involved speech. 'Tell them, Jussoud.'

The nomad settled the moth-holed blanket back over the monarch's thin shoulders. 'As long as the royal family is held as the primary target, the sorcerer is still stalking. He wants Sessalie conquered without blood, in secret. If he's flushed out of cover in front of the populace, his presence would raise mass terror and fear. Then his work will have impact, and his invasion will draw notice. Tribal shamans often sense death and wars from a distance. The most gifted can read calamity in the movements of storms, even track down the source through skilled dreamers.'

Taskin took black, again without asking, and tapped impatient fingers until his more timid opponent played the first move. 'Tactics still suggest this enemy wants us trapped quietly. He'll have a design he wishes to hide. Some motive he prefers to keep secret. Be grateful we have our one man, alone.' Quite likely that captain's close guard on the princess was all that stood between Sessalie's people, and a disaster of unknown proportion.

A sandpaper whisper arose from the bed. 'Such a chance-met fly in the ointment, that we had a desert-bred captain on hire.' King Isendon sighed, eyes closed, his thinned hair wisped like silk on the pillow. 'I fear for Mykkael. As my daughter's protector, even the prowess of his reputation might not be enough.'

'He is shielded better than even he knows,' Jussoud offered in gentle remonstrance. 'I left him my gift of the Sanouk royal dragons.'

'Your silk sash?' interjected the Duchess of Phail, awakened and sharp with surprise. 'Why give up the token of your lineage and ancestry?'

The nomad inclined his head. 'I would say Mykkael needs the credential more than I do.' Whatever befell him, escorting a princess, while bearing the badge of old Sanouk royalty, he would not be misapprised as a ruffian.

'Well, you men can rely on your foreign killer and his sword.' Lady Phail settled back, arms crossed over the bed sheet she wore in place of a shawl. 'I'll stake my best diamond on our court ladies. They won't fall for Devall's smooth lies indefinitely. I doubt very much if they'll stay content to hand over Sessalie's independence.'

'Whatever the women might choose to try,' Taskin said, as he wiped the first white casualty off the game board, 'better hope no one in my guard's the next target chosen for coercion. This sorcerer's no soldier. Else he'd see fast as daylight that we're shielded from spellcraft, but vulnerable as babes to the first assault party backing a ram.'

The thunderous pounding rattled the door of Sergeant Cade's dwelling, a second-floor tenement overlooking an alley two streets down from the Falls Gate. The protest of the two posted guards clashed with a screech of female dissent. The fracas raged no more than a second. The browbeaten guardsmen were barrelled aside, and the panel burst open, slapping dust off the top of the dish cupboard.

A huge woman cloaked in ermine and flounced taffeta rammed out of the streaming mist. Her incensed invasion crossed over the threshold, while Cade's twin toddlers stared with huge eyes, and his infant daughter sat, sucking her fingers.

'Powers of daylight! Since when does a house arrest keep a man out of the kitchen?' Lady Bertarra advanced, jewels wrathfully swinging, while the floorboards creaked under her bulk. 'Sergeant!' she bellowed. 'Come out! As the late queen's niece, I will know what's happening within my family's kingdom!'

Cade's pert wife leaped up from her stool, all but dropping the lid of the butter churn. 'My lady?' That any court matron should call in this district framed an incomprehensible precedent.

'Your husband!' snapped Bertarra. 'Send for him. Now.'

Scared by the uproar, the child at the table started to wail.

Bertarra turned her head, startled. 'Oh, please! Hush, my button.' Still speaking endearments, the queen's niece pawed under her cloak. 'I haven't come to bring harm to your father.' Her ringed fingers emerged, clutching a half-dozen lemon drops twisted in waxed paper. She handed a sweet to the tearful girl, then offered the rest to her brothers. As one, the twins pounced, whooping with unbridled pleasure.

'You'll share those, you scoundrels!' admonished the wife. 'Tell the great lady thank you.' Plainly clothed and embarrassed, she gave up her rough seat. While her daughter's crying subsided to wonder, she extended a chapped hand to take Bertarra's furred wrap. 'Please be welcome, my lady, and forgive the rude manners. The children are beset with excitement. They've had low-country sugar just once, from their cousin's uncle whose second daughter married a sailhand from Dreish.'

Still puffing from her ascent to the garret, Bertarra shed her weighty mantle and sat, just as Cade poked his bald head through the back-chamber doorway.

Before his flustered wife could begin introductions, Bertarra plunged into ranting. 'The king, the crown prince, and the seneschal are all missing since the fire in the royal apartment! Commander Taskin's gone from his bed. Two days ago, he lay dying, and now, no one's home at his townhouse. We've got women with husbands in the palace guard whose men folk have failed to come home, and the High Prince of Devall has the council tied up behind closed doors in debate. As the oldest member of Isendon's family still at large, *I demand to know what is happening*!'

Cade entered, his laconic features flushed pink. Clad in shirtsleeves and breeches, he had been caught shaving, to judge by the stubble still prickling his neck. Eyebrows lifted, he measured the tonnage of jewels and silk crammed into his tiny kitchen, then managed to field the astounding invasion with a semblance of professional aplomb. 'My lady? Have you spoken to the new acting captain at the keep?'

Bertarra sniffed. 'That prig!' Earrings rattling, she drew herself up. 'Jedrey told me to be quiet and go home. As though there wasn't a crisis, and I had nothing better to do than nibble tea cakes and write invitations.'

Cade reached the trestle. He clasped his wife's shoulder in reassurance, then added with measuring thought, 'I'm under house arrest, were you aware?'

'For protesting that idiot's promotion, I know.' Bertarra fluttered a dismissive hand. 'Stennis, at the garrison, told me as much. He said your disgrace was political nonsense, that your jailers were My*sh*kael's, and that you could talk here more freely.'

Cade hooked a stool from the corner and sat down, his good-natured face tightly guarded. 'Stennis holds the day roster at the keep? He's still acting on Mykkael's left orders?'

Bertarra glared at him, miffed. 'Not openly. Though how anyone could overlook the reek of burned cedar is a mystery even a dunce isn't likely to miss. Sergeant! I came here for information, not to run on over lists and messages.'

'Then where's Jedrey?' demanded Cade, not wont to pause for mannered diplomacy with Sessalie's peace under compromise by a sorcerer. 'Is he still busy mustering men for an assault upon Dedorth's tower?'

'If that means flaunting his new rank above Highgate, and whispering over some plan set in motion by Devall's insolent marshal, then yes. Stennis was stalling, though he wished you to know, by mid-morning, he'll run out of excuses.' Bertarra narrowed her eyes at the half-clothed sergeant in seething exasperation. 'I *came here*,' she declared, 'to find out if there's a conspiracy afoot against Sessalie's royal family. Is it true there are sorcerer's minions mewed up in the observatory? Who burned off the roof? The ladies are worried. If the crown is in peril, they're anxious to help. But don't you *dare* act like the last braying ass, insisting the kingdom is peaceful!'

Cade met her tirade with his careful, slow smile. 'My lady, if I tell you that Mykkael was right all along, will your Highgate society listen?'

Bertarra snorted. 'Blinding glory, why not? The man may be uncouth, but everyone must now acknowledge he's competent. Taskin spoke for him, and so did the king. Desert-bred or not, since he took the garrison, the maidservants all say they can walk the Lowergate streets at night, safely.'

The wife made her decision, abandoned her butter, and graciously offered to brew tea. As though her hospitality sealed a decision, Cade drew his candy-smeared daughter on to his knee and started talking in earnest.

The last stage of the crossing over the flume did not occur without cost, though all five of the princess's horses arrived, safe and dripping, on the far bank of Hell's Chasm. They stood in a tight, dispirited bunch, coats steaming in the morning's chill shade, while early sunlight rimmed the crowns of the trees atop the towering rim wall. Still breathless from the effort required to draw Fouzette across the current, Mykkael reclaimed his sword and adjusted the fit of his harness. Since Anja could not fail to notice the blood streaking through his soaked shirt, he had no way to mask his discomfort. Taskin's three stripes stung his back like live fire, and the gash that crossed his left shoulder and chest had torn open from his exertion.

Aware of the princess's fixed, worried eyes, the captain tried to allay her concern. 'If you're nervous the bleeding might draw down a kerrie, I have an evasion in mind.'

Anja sucked in a shaken breath. 'You can hide from the

kerries all you like. But not me.' Surely he saw he would have to concede, give over his tightly defended privacy before risking a needless infection.

Finished fastening his harness, Mykkael retrieved his dry surcoat and scrip. 'Princess,' he stated, his tone beyond argument, 'I am not such a fool as to neglect a wound. But this is no place to dawdle with salves and fresh dressings.'

'What are you hiding?' asked Anja, point-blank.

Head bent, Mykkael rummaged among his supplies and pulled out a sealed wooden phial. A wicked smile turned his lips. 'A poacher's prized remedy for masking his scent when he sets the baits in his traps.'

While Anja tapped her foot, unwilling to sanction the slick change of subject, the captain uncapped the stopper. He sprinkled a sampling of the contents over the spread cloth of his surcoat, then bundled the garment over her head and enfolded her shivering shoulders. 'You'll forgive me, I trust, on the day of your wedding, when Sessalie's defence is firmly secured through a southern alliance.'

The indescribable stink struck the senses with the force of a physical blow. Anja recoiled, gagging. Slit-eyed and furious, she could not snatch the breath to upbraid his reviling prank.

Mykkael sidestepped her snake-fast attempt to land a slap on his cheek. 'Kerries,' he reminded. 'We can't smell like fresh meat. I assure you, the reek will wash off.'

Beset, every step, by her blistering glare, he proceeded to anoint himself and each of the horses. Then he retrieved his bow and stowed his coiled rope. Once Anja was mounted, he set a brisk pace back downstream towards the Widow's Gauntlet.

'Powers take the meddling high council!' Bennent cursed from his post beside the shuttered south window. 'Do you hear that?'

Outside, the echoes of an officer's orders rang off the

stone causeway that wound up to the observatory's cobbled courtyard, then turned in switched-back curves to mount the pinnacle behind the Sanctuary. 'Tell me that's not the Lowergate garrison's former night sergeant.'

Taskin raised his gaunt head from his pillow. 'Jedrey?'

'No less.' Bennent locked anguished eyes with his wounded commander. 'Listen. He's detailing a company to cordon the tower. Save us! These aren't Highgate lancers. We're facing attack by Mykkael's pack of common-born soldiers.'

'They can't. They wouldn't,' Vensic cried in shocked protest. Smudged with charcoal from his labour over the crucible, his good-natured face had gone white. 'Common or not, those men are well trained. Mykkael taught us as a company to think, and not just take orders like blind sheep.' He glanced, apologetic, towards the Duchess of Phail, then finished his thought in rough language. 'I can't believe the whole garrison would lie down like scared virgins for Jedrey's high-handed bluster!'

'Within this precinct,' said Taskin, 'they fall under my rank, no less subject to Sessalie's crown authority.'

On the bed, the king lay quietly sleeping, his gaunt hands stilled on the blankets. Before anyone could move to disturb that healing peace, Jussoud unfolded from his cross-legged seat on the floor.

'No. Don't wake him. If his Majesty shows his face at that window, he'll very likely be killed.' Point taken, the nomad's formidable glare shifted focus. 'Nor will you arise,' he added to Taskin, lest the commander should think to attempt the unwise intervention himself. 'No, don't argue, old friend. This goes beyond protecting your hurt shoulder. As an archer's mistake, or a minion's picked victim, you or King Isendon would be just as dead. Like it or not, the heart of the kingdom's rule is immured here. If Sessalie is going to stand firm for the princess, she can't withstand the loss of anyone in this company.'

The wisdom of prudence could not be argued. Even

through his white-knuckled rage, the commander grasped the stakes plainly. To Bennent and Vensic, and the determined handful of his conscripted sentries, he rasped, 'Stand down, soldiers. Until we actually see an attack, we can't do a thing but abide with our weapons held ready. If they ram us downstairs, the door will soon splinter. We're better off meeting their headlong assault right here at the upstairs landing.'

That way, words or blows must occur face to face, with cedar and shielding talismans at hand to unmask any man bound by spells, or coerced by the work of a sorcerer. A useless distress, to dwell on the uncertainty, that if Taskin's authority and the voice of crown sovereignty both failed, the attackers would simply retire below and fire the beams underneath Dedorth's quarters.

The choice to wait became no easier to bear, despite the clear-cut course of logic. The ongoing sequence of orders filtered through the latched shutters, closing Jedrey's men into position. Their numbers were inevitably bolstered by the High Prince of Devall's elite honour guard. Isendon's defenders endured the slow torment of anticipation, while the massive log ram was rolled in by wagon. They heard each called instruction, and the grunts of the labourers who hefted its weight into position before the lower entry. Though the activity could have been hampered with arrows, Taskin forbade direct action.

'These are our own men, entrapped by political pressure and Devall's insidious plotting.' Even faced with assault incited by foreigners, the few arrows at hand in the tower were insufficient to effect a changed outcome. Freed from the diversion of cut-throat chess, Taskin surveyed his guardsmen. He met each man's worried eyes, approving their unflinching fibre. 'Soldiers, don't for one second forget the true enemy,' he reminded them. 'We must conserve our copper-tipped shafts to strike down the sorcerer's minions.'

Beyond the gapped shutter, the relentless sun shone on

the team preparing to shoulder the ram in the courtyard. Their supporting troops formed ranks to back the first foray. Jedrey's self-satisfied praise rang through the clear air, while the gleam of the men-at-arms' helms and the blinding flare of gold accoutrements marked the high prince's strategically placed crossbowmen.

'Stay back from that window,' Bennent cautioned as a guardsman sought to peer outward. 'That lowcountry marshal wouldn't choose slackers to safeguard the heir to his kingdom.'

Yet even as Devall's crack archers spanned their weapons, and the front-rank officer exhorted his team to take up the ram, a disturbance flurried up from the causeway. Female voices arose, upbraiding a drover for what seemed an undue delay. An officer's shouted order to halt came unravelled to astonished outrage. 'You pestilent harpy, turn back I say! Now! This street is closed until further notice. Pack up your foolish offerings and go home!'

Helmets turned, flashing, on the front lines as the readied men jostled to stare.

'Upon whose authority may I not pass?' the woman yelled back, beside herself with impatience. 'These wagons will move straight through to the Sanctuary. There are poor children, babes and mothers in need, you rock-headed oaf. Your arrows and swords won't lose their sharp edge while we deliver bread for the hungry!'

Taskin lifted his head, his glance grown piercing. 'Bertarra?'

The Duchess of Phail coughed behind her ringed hand. 'None else, powers bless her.'

'Quite. Worth a spy's insights, and ten berserk soldiers.' The wounded commander's wry features showed sympathy for the officers under fire as the harangue outside erupted into a cat fight.

'I don't care how many towers you plan to put to the torch!' Bertarra howled. 'I have eyes, you tin nincompoop!

Looks to me like somebody did the task for you, or hasn't the roof already been gutted? Who do you have mewed up in there, anyway? No, Jedrey! The chancellors have mouthed that lame drivel all morning. I don't believe everything's under control! We've already had two unfortunate fires. Now you claim you're going to set *more* of them?'

Jedrey answered, too low to be heard. Whatever he said failed to placate the queen's niece.

Bertarra's voice reached the next piercing octave. 'Well, I say not! This is Sessalie, idiot. We're not plagued by sorcerers! Our poor king is dying, not dodging intrigues! And no foreign despot within his right mind mounts a war over barley and cattle!'

Jedrey's tone, rising, was cut short again, as Bertarra ran over him roughshod. 'Well, you're full of cow pies up to your ears! I don't give way on the orders of rabble, or bow to Devall's uppity marshal. He can stuff his gold braid! Yes, up his tight arse where it will hurt the most, for all that I care for his posturing! These wagons will pass. Afterwards, you can shoot all the crossbolts you like, and ram yourselves straight to oblivion!'

Poised like a discomposed cat in her chair, the Duchess of Phail raised her eyebrows. 'Does Bertarra have the other court ladies in tow?'

A thin spear of light pierced the gloom as Captain Bennent cracked the shutter. Shielded by the stone wall next to the sill, he stole a cautious glance downwards. 'Apparently so.' After a moment of tacit reconnaissance, he resumed, touched to awe. 'Blinding glory! No wonder she's got Jedrey flummoxed. Every matron from Highgate has come, bearing baskets. The wealthy society from the Middlegate is present as well, all decked out in their jewels and silk, and wearing white veils to accept the priest's blessing. They've also rolled in five loaded wagons, escorted by a tame pack of house guards.'

Just finished treating the last copper-tipped arrow,

Vensic burst into laughter. 'That's going to make chaos of Jedrey's fixed lines.'

'Already has,' said the palace sentry placed at the adjacent window. 'What a damnfool embarrassment! The ladies are barging straight through with their baskets.'

The next moment, a volley of curses arose, as fully armed men were scolded to shame, and jostled out of position. Without discharging their loaded weapons, Devall's crack archers could scarcely turn back the silk-clad invasion. Nor could a man from the Lowergate garrison gainsay the late queen's niece. Still bellowing imprecations, Bertarra accosted the outmatched front ranks, ploughed through to the causeway, then waved for her liveried contingent of house guards to follow through with the wagons.

'Vensic!' cracked Taskin. 'See those arrows distributed! Move, soldier! Hurry. If I'm not mistaken, those women are serious! They're launching a courageous, frontal assault, and those wagons weren't filled by the bakery.' Awarded a wise smile from the Duchess of Phail, the commander rousted his sleeping reserves, and positioned them at the windows with bows.

'Keep a hawk's eye and tight aim upon Devall's guard!' Taskin added, his whisper imperative. 'Also watch Jedrey. Some of those men will be more than catspaws. The ones suborned as minions won't stand interference. Before they let their sorcerer's plan become thwarted, they'll draw killing steel on the women.'

XXXII. Widow's Gauntlet

IF THE NOSE DID NOT NUMB TO THE SMELL OF THE POACHER'S CONCOCTION, THE KERRIES ALSO FOUND THE ODOUR repellent. The few that sailed down to size up the horses flapped and circled, and hissed plumes of smoke, but did not attack. Even with daylight blunting their senses, the breeze of their passage whipped overhead with dauntless frequency. Their hazing inspection reduced Anja to anxious silence. The creatures had hungry, reptilian eyes, and the sliced air fluted over their scales like a knife's edge parting a gale wind.

Tucked under the shade of a leaning boulder, while the horses grazed at the verge of a marsh, Anja cleared her raw throat, then wiped welling eyes with the back of a grimy wrist. The hair she had neatly rebound that morning flew in torn wisps at her temples, with her braid dried into a shrunken snarl from the morning's harrowing immersion. Dirty, scraped, and miserable with her own indescribable stench, the princess paused and looked back. The weight of the moment forced her to acknowledge the inspired scope of her victory.

The rickle of ledges at the head of the valley loomed upwards, sliced by the rebounding jet of the falls. Seen from below, the descent seemed to hold more beauty than hazard, spread like a tapestry embellished with gold thread under the fall of noon sunlight. Diminished with distance, the stark memory faded, of the harrowing, steep cliff, and the uncertain footing where the rock face had cracked from seasons of ice melt and frost. That all the horses had emerged unscathed seemed the work of a given miracle.

The accomplishment did not leave Mykkael complacent. He stood vigilant guard beside his strung bow, his hands busy doctoring arrows. Having scrounged for the copper-laced rock he required, he was shaving crumbles of verdigris ore into pine pitch, then moulding a layer of the particulate gum on to the shafts behind each flanged point. Although he seemed engrossed, a predatory tension infused his calm bearing, as thoughtlessly natural as breathing. A man who walked free through hostile territory, he recorded the play of the air through his skin, and attended the rasp of each insect and frog.

Mykkael did not look tired or hurt, only dangerous as the held spear that could be cast at an instant's notice. Anja strove to encompass that elusive awareness. Tested by her own uncertainty, she tried to measure the volatile nature of a spirit who could not be contained or predicted. She studied the living man, and encountered a presence, a potential whose imprint on the world could not be known through its state of pent stillness. The warrior himself could not be understood. His power could not be analysed. He could only be recognized by his impact, as movement and action begat consequence.

Anja ached to embrace that self-aware vitality. She desired the touch that would describe Mykkael's being with the same passion that drove her to try to capture the essence of a falcon within a written line of poetry.

The princess observed the transition as the bearing intensity of her regard hooked that superlatively tuned self-awareness. Mykkael raised his head. An inquiring gaze flickered over her. 'Your Grace?'

Words fell too far short of the question her burdened thoughts sought to express. As the shadow of another passing kerrie raked over the sunlit marsh, Anja blurted, 'Another man standing here with a bow would think of nothing but slaughtering monsters.'

Mykkael smiled. 'Because he could? Because they exist? Because they pose the possibility of inflicting a terrible death?' He slid his finished arrow back into the quiver, then reached for another shaft. 'An act made in fear is not the same thing as an action taken for necessity.' He regarded the kerrie, now past their position, as it banked with a crack of spread wings and whipped its streaming, kite tail to sweep over their vantage again. 'That creature is curious. It is also a predator, testing itself against the unknown. In that respect, the beast and I understand each other quite well.'

'I don't,' Anja said with wretched simplicity.

Mykkael thumbed up another dab of pitch, then set to with the knife and the ore. 'That is why you are a princess, and I am a man with a sword.' The arrow point flashed as he turned the shaft between his deft hands. Though he could have retreated into his busyness, he chose not to insult her intelligence.

'The thread of intent is a moving tapestry between me and that deadly creature. If the kerrie chooses to strike, then it dies, or I will. That is the certainty. Today, I am your defender, and it is the hunter. It must make the first move. That is the order I choose to enact, an important truth to remember. The attacker makes his choice *subject* to mine. If I know this, then I hold the clear-cut advantage, because I am always prepared. Response is more powerful in the *barqui'ino* mind, because it places the limitless potential of passive possibility foremost.'

He glanced at her sidelong. Her perplexity raised his quiet smile. 'Your sire rules. He has charged me to act, even kill, as your protector. My strength, my choice, my will, arise in answer to his Majesty's demand. Here is the paradox. I am the weapon a king has taken to hand, yet I am not his to possess. My power to act in his name *is not his*. I know this. He may not. Or he might forget, at his peril. Therefore, the gift of my oath to serve enacts the potential for dangerous consequence. If I misuse his Majesty's trust, the earned debt is entirely mine. If he misdirects me, there could be a dreadful cost. The balance becomes mine to guard, do you see? I choose when to strike or when to stand upon mercy.'

Anja shivered as the shadowing kerrie crossed between her and the sun. 'You stand upon mercy, more often than not.'

Mykkael's smile vanished. 'I am *barqui'ino*-trained. When I act, death follows. Mine, or your attacker's, that is the destructive certainty.' He slid the doctored arrow back into the quiver, then reached in fluid grace for another. 'Death has no repeal. It is a brute ending that leaves us the legacy of an inscrutable silence. Therefore, I understand the voice of mercy very well.'

The ruler in fact was not truly the master, and the ethic of choice stood or fell by the hand that commanded the sword. Anja regarded the desert-bred captain before her, whose strength and restraint had just redefined her with a mirror's unflinching honesty. She understood, watching him, that she would not bear a crown the same way, ever again.

She shivered, eyes shut. When she recovered, she encountered Mykkael's gaze, perhaps measuring. She was not brave in that moment, only daring. Like the kerries, curiosity ventured the question. 'What do you see?'

A genuine amusement softened his face. Yet whatever he might have said became lost as his skin ruffled up into gooseflesh.

'Witch thought!' she cried. 'You're having a vision?'

Mykkael managed to nod.

Eyes locked to his, Anja observed the shift as his awareness plunged into a depth beyond conscious reason. His mind went *elsewhere,* even as the trained pitch of his bodily reflex rose to the trembling forefront. Instinct warned against trying to touch him. Poised in a space only his mind could see, suspended above the abyss, he closed ready fingers over his sword hilt . . .

Sergeant Jedrey strode forward, shouting, unable to stop the silk-clad volunteers who had challenged his cordon. The women broke through and invaded the courtyard of Dedorth's observatory before Devall's exasperated marshal could gather his wits to intervene. Ahead of both men and their flummoxed officers, the enormous matron who had stymied the crossbowmen beckoned to her female colleagues.

'Ladies, act now!'

Each woman bearing a charity basket bent and whipped off the cover. Beside them, veiled collaborators whisked out flint and steel, striking live sparks to the contents. Flame blossomed. The fuel just ignited was not baked bread, but fronds of green cedar. *The smoke billowed into a spreading haze that engulfed the array of armed men. Some of them coughed. Irate expressions transformed into startlement, as though some of the garrison soldiers were slapped into a startled awakening. Others backed away from the fumes as though wary. Foremost among these were the Prince of Devall's smartly appointed honour guards.*

Yet their retreat became blocked from behind. The canvas covers masking five wagons unfurled to reveal a hidden contingent of soldiers rolled in from the Lowergate garrison. Others, salted into the ranks with the women, tore away their concealing white veils.

Smoke drifted, relentless, and immersed Devall's men. The contact touched off a hideous change, as crossbows fell from hands transformed into ravening claws, and faces dissolved into the fanged aspect of minions. Shouting erupted among Sessalie's guard. Before their startled, horrified eyes, winged monstrosities emerged out of human concealment, and shrugged off their false covering of armour and clothes. Man and monster closed into rending conflict, while the women flung baskets of blazing evergreen against the demonic attack. Claws raked. Teeth closed. Bloody mayhem ensued. The raw screams of the dying shattered the morning, as from Dedorth's tower, the first flight of Vensic's copper-tipped arrows hissed down in a vengeful swarm . . .

Mykkael's vision broke, unstrung by the disruptive awareness of Anja's rising alarm.

'What's happened?' The princess's frantic gaze searched his face. 'Captain, what did you see?'

The gyrating spin of turned senses required a moment to reorient. Mykkael shivered, unable to subdue his raw prickle of gooseflesh. Worse, the low thrum of his warded sword poured ranging chills down his spine. He sensed the close pressure as Perincar's geometry tightened down like a seal on the unseen air. Set under the protection's resharpened awareness, Anja's distress snapped like sparks through his unsettled nerves.

His onslaught of witch thought still bled chaotic images across his unshielded mind. His immediate surroundings seemed overlaid by a haze of run blood, punched through by the scream of copper-tipped arrows striking targets of corrupted flesh. Juxtaposed on these gleanings, he beheld Anja's struggle to handle a destiny outside her familiar experience.

'What did you see?' Still the princess, she showed her brave heart, and her selflessness. 'Has Sessalie fallen in my absence?'

'No conquest, not yet.' Mykkael qualified with delicate care. 'I glimpsed fighting, some bloodshed. A courageous attack by your sire's subjects has forced the sorcerer's minions to unmask.'

'Powers defend us!' Anja's ringing cry silenced the noontide drone of the insects. 'Are you telling me there are more shape-changers?'

'Minions, surely. Shape-changers? I think so, though

how many, I cannot guess.' Mykkael sensed mounting peril in the roused force of his wards. Yet he dared not voice the extent of the truth, that *all of the High Prince of Devall's armed guard had become hideously corrupted.*

'Your people have been resourcefully staunch,' he assured her. 'They have countered the threat of subjugation for a time. The sorcerer has not yet seized his sure foothold to lay down grounding power in Sessalie. He must still work his lines of attack over distance. But if his immediate effort is foiled, his invasion is far from disarmed. A setback against an assault by cold sorcery is not a long-term defeat.'

'This foothold,' Anja ventured. 'If the enemy achieves his triumph, what then?'

Mykkael shut his eyes. Honesty this time came sharpened by grief: the penalty exacted by a high prince's vain pride, and the glory and grace of the Efandi culture cast into desolate ruin. 'If Sessalie falls under the heel of this evil? A portal will be opened into the world,' he admitted, 'a hot connection to power that will serve to expand the demon's reach.' Cedar smoke, simples fashioned of copper and salt – the small charms and banishments would all cease to work. A whole kingdom would become stripped defenceless. The rock and soil that sustained earthly life would be claimed and for ever suborned by the powers of the unseen.

Anja clasped her scraped hands. 'My people are worthy of this adversary. I have to believe their strength can prevail, no matter the odds set against them.'

Mykkael inclined his head, bereft of encouragement as the pain of the moment shattered and reshaped this young, untried spirit with the cruel force of a hammer. Anja refused despair. She stood upon character, though her inexperienced hands were left empty. Shorn of all power, all comforts, all safety, she embraced understanding of what her role meant, as a royal. There and then, for no hope of personal gain, she shouldered the gift of a people's raw courage. 'Promise me, Mykkael! No matter what weakness should overtake me, never let me fall short.'

The captain could do nothing else except bow to her greatness. 'Your Grace, you shall bear my service.' He accepted her plea to stand guard in tribute, honouring the commitment that acknowledged the fact she was no more than human, and fallible.

'No choice, now, Princess. We have to press through.' Mykkael foresaw with pernicious clarity. First-hand, he had battled the miserable aftermath when the heart of a demon's creche became hazed. He had walked through the deadly entrapments, as desperation and wrecked plans turned the fell being's bound sorcerer to atrocities born out of rage. Inevitably, the brunt must fall upon Anja. Her freedom now posed the most urgent impediment to securing her kingdom in long-term conquest.

The wards Mykkael carried did not subside, but flared and pressed at his senses, set in flux by the rise of unnatural currents. The ground underfoot no longer felt safe, and the salt packet confining the shape-changer's trapped essence seemed to burn like a coal of liability. Spurred on by unease, Mykkael sheathed his knife. He bundled his unfinished arrows into a thong tie, and packed them back into his quiver. 'Whistle for your horses, your Grace. We can do little but run fast and far, before fresh pursuit overtakes us.'

Remounted at speed, the princess and Mykkael left the boulder-strewn hollow that cradled the marsh. The horses abandoned the grass with reluctance, yet Anja drove them on firmly. Kasminna accepted the hurried trot asked of her with a head-shaking fuss. Fouzette trailed her, resigned, while Mykkael rousted the small band from the rear. He handled Vashni with an expert touch, using herdsman's yips to turn Stormfront's efforts to wheel and break free, with Covette as his agile accomplice.

Down Hell's Chasm they pressed, while the overhead

sun branded scalding light over the towering cliffs. Amid that vast setting, stalked by circling kerries, the puny endeavour of two human riders seemed an act of abject futility. Progress was tortuous, with the scrambling clatter of the horses' strides swallowed by reaching silence. Their cast shadows flowed like spilled ink beneath them, leaving no mark to commemorate the princess who challenged the impossible on behalf of her threatened kingdom.

Mykkael forced the pace. Confronted by his charge's straight back, and a hardship that strained her sweet-natured intelligence, he could do no less, though exigency pained him. He could not evade the sorrowful cost, as harsh striving wore down and destroyed her young woman's innocence and beauty. Entrusted to temper her steel-clad resolve, *he could not back down*. At each stride, through each test of hostile terrain, he endured the price of his warrior's stewardship: of Anja's bright hair whipped into sad snarls, and the outrage to her unspoiled flesh, abraded to blistered exhaustion.

The princess had invoked the cruel burden of his service, with her survival pledged beyond compromise. Sessalie's populace rode on the balance, as well as the lives of who *knew* how many more innocents who inhabited the lands surrounding this kingdom's borders. *The charge Mykkael guarded was one unformed girl, when a sorcerer run rampant into new territory held the shattering potential to destroy lives by the countless thousands.*

No less than the excellence of all that he was demanded that *this one woman* should enact the full forfeit for the cause of the hapless many. Mykkael ached for necessity. As the forged sword must perform its harsh purpose, oh, he knew: he must force this proud princess to expend all her resource without thought of mercy or quarter.

Again, as he had done for Prince Al-Syn's daughter, he rose to the bitter, long odds. Although the ordeal yet to come should break Anja, heart or mind, he still must carry forward. His, the task to secure the unbroken integrity of her royal inheritance. The consequences were irrevocable, should he fail. If Anja *and* the captive remains of the minion fashioned from Prince Kailen's spirit were not brought under the arcane protection of a learned vizier, or a shaman, Sessalie's ground would lie open to conquest beyond mortal hope of redemption.

Mykkael denied the raw cry of his grief. Down the stone throat of Hell's Chasm, he pressured the horses to trot, where even a walk was imprudent. He walked, edging in zigzags over the unsafe, stepped ledges, where reason insisted no living horse should be risked. Anja cringed for their hazard. Sometimes, choked silent, she wept for the sacrifice asked of the animals, again and again, with no pause for praise or acknowledgement. Mykkael dared not slacken. He sat Vashni, cranked to a vigilance that pitched the grey into snorting, volatile tension. The demanding passage forbade conversation. Anja stayed game. Her unflagging spirit matched every demand as the way wended through arched rock, and seamed cliff, and ravine. Peril attended their precarious course over steep slopes and smashed boulders. Other times, they ploughed through sucking mud, where the melt-fed springs sluiced off the rock face and plumed in white sheets towards the flume.

Later, their path hugged the base of the cliffs, streaked with guano and heaped with the fly-buzzing bones dropped from the active kerrie roosts. While crossing one such unsavoury midden, hard under the site of a hatchery, Mykkael saw a kerrie fly in with a stunned buck gripped in its talons. The massive claws had drawn no blood, but cradled the unmarked prey in full flight with a chilling delicacy.

'Hunt training, for the young,' Anja explained, a quaver struck through her voice. 'As the hatchlings grow hardened beaks and sharp claws, the parents fetch them live game. Our foresters say the practice awakens the instinct to chase and kill.' While the horses picked their way over the noisome rubble of stripped carcasses, the princess shuddered. 'That deer will suffer, torn and shredded as the inexperienced nestlings indulge their first frenzy of bloodlust. This is the season we're apt to lose calves from the alpine pastures.'

The captain rode, war-wary, through the next narrows. Horrid as the habits of kerries might be, the creatures were straightforward predators. Their killing was clean beside the vile practice enacted by demon-bound sorcery. Mykkael turned an uneasy glance to the sky, noted the lowering sun, and once again pushed the pace.

Farther on, they had to coax the balked horses over a natural stone bridge spanning the cleft of a gorge. The structure sheared the winds into dissonance. Gusts wailed like damned souls through the vast chains of caverns, wrought by the might of forgotten cataclysm. The scree of smashed granite on the far side turned their course back down slope towards the flume. Here, granite boulders were jumbled like knucklebones, doused by flung spray as the current slammed through the serpentine channel alongside.

Always Mykkael's urgency pressed extreme limits. If the horses were fit and responsive through hardship, their agility became sorely tested. Walk or trot, they were constantly harried. Willing, they scrambled over the rough obstacles, disregarding their wiser instincts to fare over crumbling ledges, or creeping through fields of unstable boulders only safe for a sure-footed mule. The animals answered their training. Dauntless, they trusted their riders to guide them around the quicksands of the sink pools, while swooping kerries shadowed their progress, blowing fires that hazed them to trembling.

If Mykkael endured the snatched anguish of witch thoughts, showing wounded and dead back in Sessalie, Anja rode with her heart-stopping fear. She was horsewoman enough to perceive every hazard. One sliding misstep would end in disaster. She could give her brave animals nothing else beyond hoarse words of encouragement. She stroked Kasminna's sweat-soaked neck, raked over by chills as her thoughts grappled the horror of the less tangible menace that stalked her.

Time and again, Mykkael watched her falter. He measured each battle through desperate uncertainty, each bout to curb shaken nerves. She trusted he would not expend horseflesh needlessly. Despite her faith that his handling was imperative, the incessant demand could not turn her nature to callousness. The harsh use of her wicket teams distressed her far more than her own exhausted discomfort.

Whether the princess's profound quiet was caused by fatigued stupor, or whether she grasped his reluctance to outline the dangers that had forced their flight down Hell's Chasm, Mykkael could not guess. No reward existed in this terrible place for the virtue of Anja's resiliency. He brought up the rear, ever vigilant, while her fragile determination relied on his guidance, and surmounted the gruelling course, hour upon wearing hour.

Through the next pause to water at a spring, the princess caught him appraising her silenced anxiety. She sat her mare with hunched shoulders, unable to suppress her visceral flinch as a kerrie razed overhead. Buffeted by the breeze of its passage, the horses snorted and sidled, until she could no longer ignore her crowding suspicion. 'The trap scent's wearing off as the animals sweat.'

Mykkael nodded. He had noted the peril long since. 'We must extend the supply as long as we can.'

Anja assessed his hardened resolve. 'Blinding glory! What are you saying? We're not stopping at dusk?'

Understanding flooded Mykkael, sharpened by cruel awareness, that she had pitched herself to endure for *only that long*. She counted each breath and pushed forward, sustained by that promise of respite. A false hope he must inevitably tear down, as the sun sank past the horizon. There, courage failed him. He gave her the kinder silence of ambiguity, his distress diverted into a needless check on his bow and blade weapons. Yet even that resolute pretence of calm fuelled the princess's rising unease. In the end, her imploring green eyes forced his honesty. 'Your Grace,' he admitted, 'there can be no question. A pause at this point would kill us.'

'What do you know?' Anja whispered. 'What have you seen?'

Lady Shai, lying dead of a Devall man's sword thrust. The glass edge of that sorrow, he absorbed, beyond speech. 'Your Grace. We will face what occurs one obstacle at a time. To do otherwise would exhaust you with worry.'

Anja wavered, overdrawn by stark weariness as she grasped the fact that nightfall was not going to bring surcease. 'Not knowing is better?'

'But Princess, you do know.' Leashed by a patience he realized must infuriate her, Mykkael reached out and caught Fouzette's lead as the mare raised her dripping muzzle. He edged the stolid bay to one side to clear the bank for the black gelding. 'The next step is always before us, your Grace. Watch how you place your feet. Listen to what your horse tells you. Also, don't forget to give thanks for the sun. We could be making this passage under a drenching downpour. Without the blessing of today's clear sky, trap scent would be useless, and I could not rely on the bow.'

Fouzette stood, head drooping, her torn leg wrap oozing fresh blood. Neither was Anja unscathed. She had weeping sores on her knees. Mykkael saw the telltale stains on her breeches as she freed the stirrups to stretch her cramped calves. The strained set to her back would be due to pained hips from too many hours astride. His experienced eye read every sorrowful ache, as her mare shifted footing beneath her.

Although Anja made no complaint for herself, Mykkael

braced himself, ready. The terror and the relentless uncertainty *must* erupt into flashpoint rebellion. Confronted, each step, by Fouzette's tortured pain, Anja wrestled emotions her pressed resource could not sustain. Snapped at last by the cruelty, that the demonic assault that had unstrung her life must also savage her horses, she struck out in jagged despair.

'You think you'll win through this by the use of your *weapons*?'

'I don't know what I can, or cannot do,' Mykkael admitted, forthright. He regarded her closely. No anger showed in his face or his bearing. 'Nor will you, Princess, except through hindsight. If I counted the times I should have met death, I would have no joy left for living.'

Anja swallowed, ashamed. 'I'm sorry, Captain.'

He nodded. 'Leave it there, shall we? There's no foolishness in being afraid, or tired, or upset by distress or frustration. You can hurt with anger for your horses' suffering. Just don't lie to yourself. The emotion you choke when you think yourself helpless always turns in the hand. The original feeling that would prompt you to look for new resource becomes bottled, and sours to rage that *doesn't* assist your survival.'

Anja wiped her damp cheek on her sleeve cuff. '*Barqui'ino* philosophy?'

Mykkael returned a rueful shake of his head. 'Experience.' Most lately, a month spent flat on his back, raving with fever from a septic wound in his knee. His wry smile followed. 'The hard school that tends to repeat itself each time the lesson is forgotten. Your Grace, shall we ride from this place, and frustrate a few hungry kerries?'

Anja nodded. Beaten wordless, she gathered up her dropped reins.

The trial resumed, while the afternoon shadows lengthened. The cliff walls converged, once again narrowed down to a slit. Trot, walk, then trot on again, that rhythm interrupted by uncertain terrain, or by the snatched pauses to let the overblown horses recover their wind and heart rate. Worn himself, Mykkael held the pace without mercy. His sword hilt continued to whisper in warning. His viziers' tattoo plagued him also, raising prickles over his scalp. He rode, jarred by fragments of witch thought: *of flying things with sharp claws and red eyes; of women who shed grieving tears for their dead. He glimpsed Benj, snoring drunk with his feet propped on a basket, and saw Mirag's tight-lipped anxiety for the life of a son still in jeopardy. He felt the raw fire of Taskin's balked rage, to be strapped in bandaging and unable to stand in armed defence of his king.*

The whoosh of a passing kerrie ripped Mykkael back to focused awareness. He surveyed the surrounding country, a stepped vista of rock now turning shadowed and grim as the afternoon fled. Here, the cliff walls choked the channel down to a thundering millrace of foam. Buffeting gusts whistled through the pinched gap, and all but crippled his hearing.

The melodious note of the baying hound was almost missed in the tumult.

'Halt,' Mykkael said. 'Now!' His grip on Vashni's nose rope tightened. He had the unslung bow already in hand by the time Anja reined in beside him.

'What's wrong?' asked the princess. 'Is there trouble?'

Mykkael withheld direct answer. A crawling grue chased over his skin, provoked by his war-sharpened senses. 'Hold, Princess, very still. Stay at my back. For your life's sake, I beg you, don't move.'

He felt her unblinking stare, then her sharp intake of breath. She had noticed the hound. The baying cry was clearer, now, and bearing down by the moment.

Mykkael raised the bow, notching one of the ore-treated arrows from the quiver clipped at his flank. 'Not ours,' he whispered. No mortal dog could have crossed the flume's current, or escaped the predation of the chasm's swarming kerries. Smooth, silent, deadly, Mykkael slipped off

Vashni's back. He secured his footing on the slick rock, fingers pinched to his strung arrow. 'Stand fast, your Grace.'

He steeled his resolve, stilled his poised mind, then let go into *barqui'ino* awareness.

Sunlight still flooded the open country behind, butter-yellow against the twilit gash carved through the cliffs by the watercourse. Mykkael watched that opening. Soon enough, he sighted the hound, an abomination clad in Dalshie's black-and-tan body. The creature bounded down their backtrail with a heartbreaking show of exuberance. Where the man would have grieved for Benj's lost hound, inflexible training prevailed. The warrior raised and sighted his bow. Taut-nerved and silent, he waited.

The hound drove through the last of the open ground and entered the gloom of the narrows. Her blunt claws clicked on stone. Rock to rock, she sniffed and unravelled their scent. Her yawling cries as she gave tongue rebounded into the gorge. Through her oncoming noise, Mykkael noted Anja's rushed breathing. He felt the low vibrations in his sword shift upwards, humming into a whine as the wards shrilled an urgent warning. He drew. And still waited.

Whatever abomination wore the dog's flesh, it locked instantly on to his movement. Yapping with canine excitement, it raced in, tongue lolling, and white-tipped tail flagging welcome.

Mykkael held. The drawn bow etched a stilled line in the air. The arrow's tip seemed a nail fixed in time, pinning the moment in hesitation.

And the hound came. Barrelling through the gulch, leaping pooled spray and wet boulders, she bore down on the bunched horses. Closer, one saw the foam dashed from her muzzle. Closer still, one noted her eyes were vacant and utterly mad.

Vashni whuffed a hackled snort. Anja clamped back a whimper of terror, while the unnatural hound bounded nearer, a slavering parody of Benj's beloved Dalshie.

And still Mykkael held. He might have been stone, devoid of lifeblood and reaction.

Anja cried out, her fear overwhelming. As the ensorcelled creature raced towards her, she had no means to know whether her defender had been just as dangerously beguiled. Stilled as though ensnared by a spell, Mykkael held his drawn bow, but did not release.

'Blinding glory, *Captain*!'

He still did not loose.

The hound scrabbled nearer. Her hurtling rush was now almost on top of them. She coiled her hindquarters and sprang on to the ledge not five strides from Mykkael's set stance.

The warding invoked by the viziers' tattoo exploded. A blue ring of light sliced through the senses like the cut of a tempered blade. The eruption signalled Mykkael's chosen moment. His aimed arrow flew, then vanished across the raised line of active power.

The shaft struck its mark. Beyond that dazzling shower of light, something shrieked. The quavering cry raised the hair at the nape, and wrung the shocked mind into nightmare.

Then the bright curtain of wardings ripped out, doused like a gale-blown candle. The shot hound writhed on the rocks in her death throes, piteously whimpering, the shaft struck clean through her heart.

'Don't *move*,' Mykkael whispered. 'Your Grace, I implore you, stand strong.'

Shaking, her clammy hands clenched to the rein to restrain Kasminna's pawing unease, Anja ached with pity. Though she shut her eyes, no effort could silence the sound of the hound's dreadful torment.

'Captain! Show mercy, I beg you.' Her compassionate instinct cried out to dismount. She had taken game in the hunt too many times to condone the needless suffering of any wounded creature.

'That's no *dog*!' Mykkael lashed in reprimand.

His sword had not quieted. His adamance enforced the hideous *fact*, that the death which should follow his fatally placed shaft was taking abnormally long.

Warned of a danger beyond their far border, the shamans employed by the emperor's Grand Vizier immersed themselves into scrying. Their circle held trance with unbroken vigilance, from breaking dawn until dusk. Vision showed them a hound, no red-blooded creature, but a sorcerer's construct, unveiled as a monster as it was stunned on the point of a copper-tipped arrow. Warrior, they named the man with the bow. He whose presence they could not discern through the warding that masked him. The adversary stalking his flight through Hell's Chasm stood unveiled for one moment, as the spun continuity of cold-struck forces succumbed to the conductive matrix of copper. The vizier must receive the ill news at once: the pattern invoked was a shape-changer's line, outside the known reach of their wisdom . . .

XXXIII. Chasm

MYKKAEL DID NOT TAKE HIS EYES OFF THE WRITHING HOUND, STRUGGLING WITH DESPERATE, MORTAL PAIN that did not bring the surcease of death. To Anja, without turning, he said, 'Dismount, Princess, now. Change horses. Quickly!'

He tracked each sound to ensure she obeyed him: the chafe of her clothing as she slid from her saddle, then the tap as her soles touched on to firm ground. Her shuffling step bespoke her sore muscles, a setback that must disadvantage the speed of her reflexes.

'Can you do nothing to ease that hound's suffering?' she pleaded, as her tired hands fumbled with girth buckles.

Mykkael jerked his head, no. 'Much too dangerous.' He would have to cut out the hound's heart, if he could, to ensure the long curse that burned through its corrupt flesh would stay stunned and captive to copper. Yet the near threat of danger did not relent. The shaman's mark in his sword hilt stayed active. Its keening note razed through his bones, a clear warning the hound just dispatched was no more than the precursor blazing the trail. Something far worse would be following.

'Ready a fresh horse for me to ride,' Mykkael said, thankful his voice kept the semblance of calm. 'Choose carefully, Princess. Also, tie the bundles Fouzette's bearing on to Kasminna.'

The hound's piteous agony did not subside. Her whimpering cries drove Anja to shivering fury. 'Why can't you serve her the mercy stroke, Captain? I have to know!'

'Princess!' Mykkael snapped, his urgency knife-edged. 'Change mounts. *Do it now!*'

He dared *not* look aside to insist that she hear him. Bow in hand, arrows ready, he watched like a hawk down their back trail. The redoubled pressure of his viziers' tattoo tightened the skin at his nape. He put aside grief, every harrowing memory. *His run through Efandi left too many hard lessons*. Time did not permit speech. The forces that now used the hound for a beacon had no word in their language for mercy.

Quivering on the held edge of release, immersed in *barqui'ino* awareness, Mykkael stood guard. He chafed through each moment, as Anja transferred the surcingle and bundles, then saddled and mounted Covette. Her selection was wise. The little chestnut had the surest feet. Endurance was bred into the mare's desert lineage, making her the least likely to fail under stress and privation.

'I've tied your reins on to Stormfront's headstall,' the princess stated, subdued. 'He's ready to go when you are.'

'Now.' Mykkael spun with clipped haste. He accepted her cherished black gelding who was, yet again, the best choice. Stormfront had the strength to carry two riders, matched by the fire and heart of a fighter. The affray at the falls had well tested his mettle. He could be forced to stand his ground through the bloodshed and fury of battle.

Bow still in hand, Mykkael settled astride. He heard Anja's hissed intake of breath, and said, very softly, 'I know.'

He had seen them already: a swarm of black specks peppered the sky beyond the gap. Winged creatures of any kind must spell trouble. Large eagles avoided the

Widow's Gauntlet, and kerries by their contentious nature did not flock. 'We have to run, Princess. This site is too open and can't be defended.'

Anja wheeled Covette, all her arguments silenced. She dug in her heels, pitched the chestnut to a canter over slippery rock, while Mykkael dispatched hurried instructions. 'Fouzette can't withstand this. She'll fall behind. There can be mercy for her, but if so, you have to speak now.'

Anja turned her head. Her eyes showed stark horror. 'An arrow?'

Mykkael nodded. No kindness could lighten unbending necessity. 'One treated with copper into the heart.' He still carried dart poison. 'I can make the shot painless. She will drop fast, and no sorcery I know of will raise her.'

The tears spilled, whipped down Anja's cheeks by the breeze of the chestnut mare's passage. 'I can't hold her head?'

'No.' Mykkael saw no margin for compromise. 'Stop here, we die with her.' He must act, regardless. Yet the trust he preferred at all costs to preserve now relied on her willing consent. '*Don't* look, Anja!' as she twisted in her saddle for a desperate glance back.

Fouzette was already trailing, and the wards' ringing pressure informed well enough: the sorcerer's airborne sortie would be gaining.

Mykkael balanced Stormfront to effect intervention, but in the end, required no breach of integrity. Those slim, girlish shoulders quivered just once. The reply, when it came, was bravely regal, and delivered with clarity through the tumult as the horses thundered headlong down the narrows. 'Very well, Captain. If Fouzette must die, I would have you spare her from suffering.'

'Don't watch, Anja.' The captain's remonstrance this time came gentle, as he undertook the ugly task at grim speed, and treated the requisite arrow.

Mykkael dropped Stormfront back, chose his shot and his moment. The bow sang just once. The arrow arched out at point-blank range. The sturdy bay whose steadfast nature had thrice spared them, and whose bravery had stood down a kerrie's assault, missed her stride. She pitched out of balance as her forelegs buckled, but not on to cruel stone. Mykkael had not missed his timing. Fouzette crumpled into the foaming race of the flume, a more kindly embrace in fatality. Her sweated, dark coat melded into the spray. A rolled eye sought the bank in heartbreaking reproach. Then the current swallowed her under.

Vashni now ran bereft of his teammate. Mykkael slapped his grey rump. He used force as he must, and drove the flightier gelding ahead, while the animal's repeated, desolate neighs cast echoes between the rock cliffs.

His distress caused Anja to break discipline and glance back. Yet by then, there was no sign of trauma to see. The chasm was empty, her stout mare no more than a memory.

The narrows closed down to a chill, windy slit, overhung by the dirtied, aqua ice squeezed aside by the Howduin glaciers. Enormous blocks had sheared away, sometimes wedged between the walls of the cleft, where melt and weather carved hanging arches fringed with icicles, and dulled light scattered through glazings of pane ice. In these narrows, the flume rumbled and splashed, fouled with stones and mud as fragments upslope gave way and tumbled more substantial debris into avalanche.

Along with the hazards of slick stone and boulders, the horses now contended with frozen ground. They picked through splintered deadfalls, and the granular patches of snow that lingered in the deep recesses where sun did not penetrate. With night falling, the frigid air bit to the bone. Lathered coats were going to bring lethal chill, if impasse forced them to stop. Lacking fodder, the animals could not stay warm.

Already, Anja was starting to shiver. The wardings still hazed Mykkael to dire tension, incessantly warning the sorcerer's pursuit pressed ever nearer to closure. Whether the hound's copper-poisoned demise might delay them, or if such unnatural creatures must take pause to battle the territorial instincts of kerries, Mykkael had no way to guess. He distrusted blind luck. Their winded mounts could not hold the pace. Pushed to the crux, the captain knew he must make a stand, or forfeit his defence altogether.

'There!' He pointed towards a jumble of ice that had formed a crude buttress against the stone wall. 'Ride Covette on. Yes! Take her inside. Bunch the rest of the horses around you, and for the love of your sire, stay mounted!'

Harrying Vashni's reluctant trot, Mykkael drove the herd from behind. He pushed at their heels until they were crammed shoulder to shoulder inside the precarious shelter. The hollow was scarcely secure, formed as it was of unstable rime, undercut by the sluice of spring rains. Yet no better option existed, with his wardings pitched to the overriding, shrill urgency of a pursuit coming hard at their heels. *Barqui'ino* awareness heightened his senses to almost hurtful acuity. Tight though it was, the nook in the ice would forestall a strike on his flanks, and prevent an assault from behind.

Mykkael slid off Stormfront's back. He left the reins looped on the gelding's neck as he chivvied him in with his teammate. 'Stay astride,' he told Anja. 'Keep the horses as calm as you can. If they bolt, I can't hope to save them.'

He spared a fast glance, but could not read how she fared. Her face was a pale blur, lost in the gloaming.

When she spoke, her voice was too tired to show fear. 'Kerries can't fly here. The walls are too close for their wingspread.'

'I know.' Mykkael limped two short steps and snapped a dry bough from a nearby deadfall. He broke the wood into arm lengths, then jabbed each splinter upright in the ice. 'We're not hunting kerries, your Grace, a fine point upon which I have some experience.' Using torn strips from his surcoat, he wound the ends of each billet in rag, which he struck alight with the flint and tinder from his scrip. Under the flickering, wind-rippled flames, he readied his arrows in rows. The copper-marked ones he set to the left, with the untreated shafts opposed, on the right. Last, he tested the tension of the strung bow.

His final instructions were terse. 'Princess, hold fast. Not everything that you see will be real. Some things that move might seem like illusion. They're not. You may hear voices. Trust nothing they say. The wards in my presence are your only protection. Hide your eyes. Block your ears. Do whatever you must. Let me attend to your safety. Your sole task will be to stand without breaking.'

'Be *seit shan'jien*, Mykkael,' bade Anja. 'The target with teeth that bites back.' Cold, weary, terrified, Sessalie's princess gave him fierce words, where her Efandi counterpart in the same straits had muffled her sobs behind the torn silk of her headcloth.

Mykkael selected an arrow. Grim as struck bronze in the spill of the flames, he kicked away the loose gravel and set his feet. Then he notched the first shaft to the bowstring, aware he must be no less than *deit'jien tah*, 'the target that kills without quarter'.

Then the wave of the sorcerer's winged minions descended, and *barqui'ino* awareness left space for no thought at all.

They threaded the narrows in a whistle of sliced air, sinuous and agile and deadly. One saw the eyes, first, red as punched ruby, or orange as live coals, or yellow as fire in opal. They glinted out of the falling dark, lit to sparks as the torchlight caught them. The bodies were reptilian and scaled, and possessed by a murderous need to sate upon blood and slaughter. Where the size of a kerrie made its gliding strength ponderous, these creatures darted like swallows. They hurtled down the chasm in steeply banked flight at a speed that left a man breathless.

Mykkael aimed and shot. His arrow flew straight to the mark. The horror in front kited out of the air with a shriek. Wings flapping, it tumbled. The harrowing cry choked off as it splashed headlong into the flume. The bow sang again. Another shaft hissed skywards. A second abomination folded and slammed into the rock wall, to a rattling shower of gravel. More came behind. Mykkael shot them down, another, then another, nock, draw and release, a flow of continuous motion. His next kills ploughed the ledge a scant stone's throw away. Like the hound, each casualty writhed and thrashed, squalling in bone-chilling agony. Copper *could* stun them. That stroke of fortune raised Mykkael's hope, and also awakened sore grief. His accurate marksmanship would serve no mercy. As apparitions bound by the grip of spelled forces, these wrought minions could never receive the grace of a natural death.

Another bowshot, and another monstrosity plummeted out of flight. The distance had closed enough now to discern the unpleasant details. No two of the creatures seemed formed the same way. Some had fangs and claws, others insectile tails with needle-sharp stings. Some hissed or bellowed. Others swooped down in a silence Mykkael found all the more unnerving. The only consistency to their attack was their single-minded ferocity.

Arrow struck, another corruption cartwheeled downwards. This one's cry raised the hair, piteous as the wail of a hurt child. Mykkael stood unshaken. He had heard far worse. As he drew the next shaft in unbroken succession, aimed and let fly, he sensed the range, knowing: the incoming pack approached the far edge of the viziers' protections raised by his tattoo. Next second, the lead creature slammed into contact. Its horned head unravelled into a lick of queer flame, and a burst of maniacal laughter. The sound raised the skin into visceral revolt, and the breeze reeked of sulphur and burning. Mykkael watched, prepared, should the grace of his wardings fail to deflect. He listened to the strained note from his sword hilt. Yet the spurting flares of uncanny energies flowed into themselves and yanked back. In recoil, he watched, *horrified*, as the monster's fanged maw rematerialized into animate flesh.

No sorcerer's work he had encountered before could enact such a seamless recovery.

Mykkael noted the creature's snarling retreat, first warning he might face a stalemate. If the sorcerer's fell sending could not cross the barrier and maintain its form, neither did the viziers' geometry possess the commanding power to effect any lasting banishment. When his arrows ran short, he could be trapped in a stand-off. No way to tell, now, if the shaman's mark sung into his sword hilt held the lines to break through cold-struck bindings and compensate. He risked *far* worse danger, once he had to make closure, not any welcome development. For not all of the creatures that now wove and snapped in testing rage at the wardings would be the long-spelled design of an embodied apparition.

Several planted among them could be bone and blood shape-changers, beyond his known scope of experience.

Mykkael loosed his next shaft at near point-blank range. The sorcerous construct crashed through the warding and erupted into a fire burst. Cackling voices reviled his ancestry in three tongues he knew, and spat guttural curses clearly not human in origin. The next shaft he launched brought down something solid that struck earth at his feet, still raging with wounded fight. The bow was now useless. Mykkael ripped sword from scabbard, aware of the bright sting as the warded metal sang in his hand. He parried a clawed fist, sheared off the limb that swiped a rip at his ankle.

Contact raised smoke and spattering, hot blood that seared his cloth breeches like acid. Cut, parry, stab, parry, stab again. The brute horror grew back sheared limbs, and altered form twice before it finally gave way and collapsed. Its spasms fanned up a wind storm as its leathery wings walloped at the crevice, showering Mykkael's shoulders with dirt and ice. He ducked the debris, swung his sword upwards and severed the head, then kicked aside the snapping, downed jaws. Blade in hand, breathless but poised, he measured the next pair of eyes that advanced behind the hulked corpse just dispatched.

'*Baeyat'ji'in*, monster!' he shouted. 'I am ready.'

The inbound thing howled. Its ranging cry roused primal terror in the mind of any human-born creature. Mykkael fought the sickening clench of his gut. Streaming sweat, he heard Anja's gasped whimper. The sword in his hand seemed to shudder and wail, until he feared the stress of the warding might cause tempered metal to crack.

Spell-wrought fear such as this called for voice in redress. Mykkael laughed aloud, then hurled a taunt at the creature's bared teeth. 'I do not run from a wind made of lies! Begone, coward. Gnash your teeth for eternity. Do you think I care which?'

A furtive movement, just sensed, arose from the darkness *behind him*. Mykkael dared not shift his attention to glance back. 'Anja,' he whispered. 'For your life's sake, do as I asked and stay mounted!'

She had thrown away sense. Mykkael sighted her hand, in peripheral vision. She stood at his flank, reaching to grasp one of his readied arrows. Shaking, determined, moved by courage unparalleled, she must have retrieved the dropped bow.

He adjusted to compensate. No command he could give was going to deter her. When confronted with terror, some women cowered. Other ones charged like a lioness. 'The pull of the bow will be strong for your arm. You'll have to draw and loose quickly. Set your aim low, Princess. You know how the close-range arrow will arch.' He flexed his bad knee, still immersed in swift instructions. 'I'm going to charge, drop and roll. That creature will pounce. You must shoot for its chest as it leaps.'

Wood rattled on laminate; she had nocked the shaft.

'Brave lady,' said Mykkael. 'Don't mourn if you miss. The creature's glance will follow your arrow, even a shot gone badly astray. My strike will use the diversion.'

'Get ready,' Anja whispered through clenched teeth.

Mykkael raised his sword in a fractional salute. 'On your mark, Princess.'

He heard, very clearly, the creak of the bowstring as she flexed her shoulders, testing the tension required to draw. The bow *would* be difficult. Benj prided himself on his bullish strength. Yet brute muscle was as nothing beside the grit of this young woman's resolve. *Barqui'ino*-drilled reflex sensed her intaken breath as a texture, written in air across skin. Before words, Mykkael knew the moment she braced up her nerve and cried, 'Now, Captain!'

Already, he launched from the cleft. The winged monster sprang. The heavy recurve *whapped* in release, as he struck the ground, shoulder down and rolling under the arrow that hummed through the space overhead.

Anja did not miss.

The monster's bellow of rage scattered echoes the length of Hell's Chasm, simultaneous with the scream of the viziers' wardings, shocked to furious light at close quarters. Mykkael came to his feet underneath ten feet of coiling, venomous murder. He stabbed upwards. His thrust carried on by the force of momentum. His blade sheared through belly scales and bit deep enough to eviscerate. Mykkael rammed the cut home. Hot blood and offal splashed over his head. His sword shrieked complaint like bolt lightning. He could not see, could not hear, as shaman's ward and sorcerer's spell line entangled. The shape-changer's willed effort to reform its rent tissue came unstrung into billowing smoke. The fumes masked Mykkael's eyesight and stung his parched membranes as he coughed poisoned air from his throat. He might have been crushed, had the monster's hind leg not spasmed and smashed him aside. Landed, rolling, the bruise to his hip notwithstanding, he scrambled for balance and regained his feet.

War training and reflex carried on, before thought. While the shape-changer lay in copper-stunned range of his wards, he used his sword to cut tendons and hamstring. Once its dangerous thrashing had been subdued, he moved in, chopped the neck, and severed the head. He lopped the clawed feet, and also the spiked tail. Made aware of Anja's shocked regard as she pressed a limp hand to her mouth and averted her face, he scarcely took pause.

Such a thorough dismemberment was not done for spite. Awash in gore, Mykkael felt his skin crawl with the forces of the unseen. The sorcerer had active spell lines, still coiling through the carcass. The binding effect of the copper might not last. Alert to his danger, the captain understood he would have to take every part of the creature that might allow it to move, or else run the risk that it could resurrect in changed form and resume its appalling attack. As he dragged his horrific gleanings into a pile, he could not quell the suspicion, that *more than one entity had formed this monstrosity.* If so, he might not know until far too late, whether his barbaric remedy had succeeded in disarming the corpse.

He hacked through the chest wall, revolted to find the uncanny thing had three hearts. Had language answered his paralysed tongue, he would have begged Mehigrannia's mercy. Since *barqui'ino* focus overruled every civilized faculty, he resumed grisly work with the sword.

The hearts were gouged out. Mykkael moved on and recovered the cut head of the smaller monstrosity slain earlier. He did not allow himself respite until he had treated that second corpse to the same ruthless reckoning. Only then did he lower his arm and set his fouled blade back to rest. Hard-breathing, rushed all but berserk by the drive of excessive adrenaline, he touched the wet point to the ground and fought to recoup his scattered reason.

The shape-changer's remains posed a thorny problem. Lacking the salt he had used on the snake, he had little choice but to improvise a temporary banishment through live fire, laced with cedar ash from the packet kept in his scrip. He arranged the cremation forthwith. Wood from the deadfall must serve for the pyre, set alight with one of the torches, while Anja stood guard with her shaking grip glued to the bow.

'You were splendid,' Mykkael ventured, though his voice emerged gruff from the fumes as his select bits of carrion smouldered. Inside the ice cleft, the horses were milling. The princess must have taken steps to secure them. Although they snorted and stamped in distress, they stayed in the confines of shelter.

More sorcerous phantasms flitted through the unwarded surroundings, threading the notch high above. Their shrieks of frustration rang off the rocks. The rushed breeze of their passage fluttered the fire almost into extinction. Though they seemed unable to cause any harm, Mykkael was loath to rely on appearances. Too many times, he had seen sorcerous works transform to the shift in a pattern. Yet no horrors set down. Their wingtips dissolved into bursts of ephemeral smoke each time they grazed against the boundary of his wardings. Awash in their unnatural, flaring light, Anja looked like a street waif, the boy's shirt and jerkin too large for her shoulders, and the bow a man's weapon clutched in a doll's delicate hand.

'You're hurt,' she accused him.

Mykkael glanced down, saw his trousers were shredded. The flesh underneath seemed more bruised than bloodied. 'Not severely.' Yet he saw well enough, he would probably stiffen like vengeance the moment he stopped moving. His spattered sword still unsheathed in his hand, he thoughtfully braced his pulped flesh on the ice bank, that being the best available remedy to hold down the swelling. 'I've fought with worse.'

'That's how you measure the joy in your life?' Anja

forced speech through her chattering teeth. 'Whether or not you can fight?'

Some women charged danger like the wild lioness; small wonder they should not tame, afterwards. Mykkael would have preferred to give this one space, had he dared. Instead, he watched the small horde of long-spelled monstrosities weave and challenge the ward overhead. 'Shall I apologize for staying alive? No, Princess. Don't speak. Your anger is the natural response to a wrenching predicament. It's a savage force, better off freed.'

She blinked, sucked in an unsteady breath, *tried* to force her frayed nerves back in hand. 'Tell me there aren't going to be more of these *things*.'

'I can't make such a promise.' Mykkael fiercely wished the guard he maintained could have spared him the resource to measure her.

Anja's next effort sounded thin and forlorn. 'How can you do this, again and again?'

Mykkael managed to force a grin through the tangling grip of his tension. While the ribbon of sky over the clifftops lost the last glint of the afterglow, and the sword in his hand whined and murmured, he shrugged. 'Trust me, Princess, the alternative's a great deal less civilized.'

Her Grace all but flew at him. 'You are not a barbarian!'

'What I am,' Mykkael said, spattered head to foot in clotted filth, 'is not fit company for your sire's elegant salon.'

Anja drew herself up. Her green eyes stayed furious. 'You are better educated and better travelled than most of Sessalie's courtiers. You just don't wear masks well.'

Mykkael laughed, his good nature dispelling the last tremors of *barqui'ino* reaction. 'Then don't put a mask on me, your Grace.' He lifted the sword, deliberately wiped off the stained blood and faeces on his already befouled surcoat. Then he gave his slimed hands a vigorous scrub in the granular melt from a snow bank. 'Admire the pelt of the tiger, your Grace. Forget at your peril, he has teeth.'

'We're alive,' Anja stated. 'Safe.' The bow twitched in her hand. 'My applause, for the teeth.' Her erect balance suddenly wavered.

Mykkael took a limping step forward. He caught her up with a bracing grip the moment before her knees buckled. 'No,' he said sadly. 'We're not safe at all. But the heat from my fire will soon soften that ice bank. If I'm not going to bury us, we've no choice but to move on.'

Anja snorted. The sound was apparently a half-smothered guffaw. 'Now, see here!' She wobbled, gave up, and sagged back against him. 'Now I'm no longer fit company for Sire's salon, either. Oh, grant me the chance! I'd invite you for dancing. Together, we'd give the Duchess of Phail an apocalyptic case of the fright.'

Hysteria, battle nerves: Mykkael knew the signs. Carefully wary, he tempered his strength, slapped her cheek hard enough to shock her from desperate euphoria, back into her outraged senses. 'Princess! Bear up.'

She crumpled. Relieved to handle the expected reaction, Mykkael did not sting her pride further with comfort. As the storm broke and her tears welled over, he drew Anja back towards the ice cleft. There, he let her bury her misery in the curve of Covette's damp neck. He used the time, while she let loose and sobbed, and gathered up the remaining few arrows. Then he stripped the hobbles off Vashni and Stormfront, and unsnarled the incoherent mess of knots she had used to secure the mares' lead ropes.

When the moment came to ride on, and the princess turned from him, ashamed, Mykkael gave her embarrassment short shrift.

'I've seen many a hero walk off a battlefield, only to fall down and sob like a child. Look at me, Princess!' He waited, unmoving, until she must freeze, or give way and do as he bade her. 'Tell me to my face, what unnatural arrogance makes you believe royal birth should make you the exception?'

Anja snapped up her chin. 'This won't happen again.'

Mykkael stood back. He allowed her to mount on her own, all stiff back and sharp prickles. 'Don't make such a statement,' he admonished her as he resettled his sword and vaulted bareback astride Stormfront. 'I can't, myself. You'll damned *certain* slap me when I fall short and show you I'm no more than human.'

She arched her eyebrows. 'Slap you? I should! How long must I swallow the pretence that you're made of iron for the sake of your rock-headed pride? Or am I not to notice, you're bleeding again? Blazing glory, Mykkael!' The tears threatened, not born of hysteria this time. 'If you don't strip that shirt and clean out your hurts, I'm to watch like a fool while you take yourself down with wound fever?'

She was right. Mykkael found her intrusion a scalding irritation. When stymied by a self-righteous woman, he always preferred to submit and have the unpleasantness over forthwith. Though he knew his deferral would seem like an evasion, and probably cost dearly, later, the wardings he carried had not gone mute. Sorcery yet stirred through the air, and the ground, and danger was still present, and closing.

'We have to ride. Now, Princess!' Before she could protest, he cut her off. 'At the first reasonable moment, we'll seek proper shelter and stop.'

The concession he offered was not enough, Mykkael saw by one glance at her face. He would have to do more than capitulate. Hard set with distaste, he turned Stormfront's head and pressed onwards.

'Your Grace, my word, as sworn in your service, the moment I have your royal person secure, I'll let you attend the tiresome dressings yourself.'

XXXIV. Impasse

THE QUEER LIGHTS THAT FLARED OVER HELL'S CHASM THAT NIGHTFALL WOULD HAVE BEEN VIVIDLY CLEAR, IF Dedorth's glass had not been destroyed by a conflagration of sorcery. Beyond the Great Divide in the ranges, where the Grand Vizier's allied shamans did not require the use of a contrivance to view the natural world, or examine events at a distance, the ripple as power flowed from the unseen awakened the gifts of the seers. They sensed disruptions and ominous signs. The wise among them measured the portents and foresaw dire peril: an invasion to challenge Tuinvardia's northern border, over mountains considered impassable.

Afraid their warnings would meet disbelief, they dispatched an emissary to warn the Grand Vizier.

The audience was brought to the emperor's court by a woman clairvoyant, trained as a channel to receive distant messages with strict and reliable accuracy.

Under the airy glass-paned cupola of the Grand Vizier's painted chamber, she appeared child-sized, mantled in the gauze robes and circlet of her time-honoured profession. The flood of the alcove's candles exposed her distraught pallor. Yet she held her straight stance on the marble star beneath the Grand Vizier's dais, the hollow sphere of wrought copper used to amplify vision cupped in her delicate hands. 'My Lord Wisdom, I offer thee tidings from the circle of shamans sent to hallow the ground along the north border.'

The wizened vizier raised his bald head and regarded the emissary with gimlet eyes. 'Not good news, I see.' His sigh brought an apprentice scurrying with a pillow to ease his swollen feet. A snap of his fingers summoned two of the three master scribes he kept in constant attendance. Robes rustling, these left the labour of preparing updated amulets. They gathered beneath the dais to hear, ascetic faces lined with concern under sombre black caps with fringed lappets.

'Deliver the sending,' bade the Grand Vizier.

'Lord Wisdom, hear well,' the seer's channel opened. 'These words are Anzbek's, eldest from Jantii tribe's fox clan circle. His speech now follows: *"Wise one, we have sighted unfavourable portents that warn of a coming invasion. Winged minions wrought by a sorcerer whose demon's name is unknown fly down the gorge of Hell's Chasm."*'

The elder of the two master scribes raised his eyebrows. 'From the *north*! Has Anzbek gone mad?' Even the most powerful sorcerers avoided cold weather and altitude, that exposed all their delicate works to the stifling qualities of snowfall, and the unstringing chaos inherent in dwellings heated by wood fires.

'How can a new power arise to existence?' snapped the beak-nosed scribe at the trestle. The Nine demons might crossbreed a new innovation, but their Names and the sorcerers they held in sealed bondage had been exhaustively listed for centuries.

The seer's channel lifted her chin. 'Even so, Guardians.' She resumed, undaunted. 'Anzbek reads such a peril arising. His dreaming forecasts a danger beyond precedent. He further says this: his shamans have no phrase and no singing to banish the lines he encounters. Since he also expected the Lord Wisdom and masters might presume his sharp wits were failing, Anzbek chose to share counsel concerning the visions his circle has garnered. Be wary, he urges. The fragmented knowledge I bring thee in his name has been gathered at terrible cost to his scryers.'

'Anzbek's lore cannot sing a completion!' The Grand Vizier shoved straight in a disturbed glitter of beaded robes. Beside him, his master scribes exchanged startled glances. 'The night brings us ill news, indeed.' Ringed fingers flashed fire as the old conjurer beckoned the channel on to the dais. 'Thou carriest a sending? Pray show us.'

Gauze rustled. Shadows wavered as the candle flames swayed in the grip of an uneasy draught. The channel ascended the stair. At the Grand Vizier's bidding, she accepted the cushion just brought to cosset his feet. Then she knelt with the copper sphere offered between her cupped hands. The Grand Vizier laid his palms beside hers, fingers spread.

'As Anzbek sends,' the channel whispered, then bowed her head. She touched her circlet to the sphere and opened her mind to deliver the record of the tribal elder's true vision.

The Grand Vizier to the Emperor of Tuinvardia closed his eyes to receive. His brows hooked into a thunderous frown the first moment he accepted the contact. 'Shapechangers!' he said, shocked. His seamed face blanched. 'Ones able to meld and recombine, even dissolve at their sorcerer's will. They fly across the Great Divide through Hell's Chasm. The lines that reanimate them . . . are intensely complex.' He drew a vexed breath. 'Record this!'

The master scribe to his right rushed from the dais to the work table. Fingers flying, he assembled parchment, ink, and a quill pen with a fine, copper nib. He barely had the implement dipped before the Grand Vizier started dictation.

'East to west axis, parallel, doubled. North down to centre pin, then rise north-east, at twelve degrees. Arc to south, run a ground line, six point star at south, then a sunwards spiral, rising. End at heaven point. Lift the pen. Set down at west, now mirror the geometry at ninety degrees.'

'Murder and mercy!' murmured the master still seated. He had abandoned his labour over the talismans, stunned by the unprecedented pattern of ward now emerging, line by line, on the parchment. 'What *is* that thing?'

'Abomination,' whispered the Grand Vizier, never in memory so curt. His forehead broke into alarming sweat as he opened his eyes and fought his breath steady. 'One we may not have the wisdom to counter; would that Eishwin were still alive.'

'Eishwin?' The master scribe who remained on the dais cleared his throat in contempt. 'That lunatic hermit? But he only expounded on elementary design! A raw junior might consult his text. No one else would see fit to bother.'

The Grand Vizier's lips twitched. 'Basic text was the only knowledge the crafty old conjurer chose to write down.' Shaking his head, he said in strained quiet, 'Not all his workings were executed inside the lines of earthly dimension. The myth lingers, that Eishwin found ways to write as they say the most gifted of shamans can sing, in the language of light, that lies beyond eyesight.'

'Pure nonsense!' snapped the master still poised with the pen. All power of pattern was earth-based! How else to influence the subtle flow of the unseen through scribed lines, than to lock its expression in place through physicality's transfixing stability?

Again the Grand Vizier shook his bald head. 'I studied for years, and still the key to Eishwin's perception eludes me.'

Nor was he alone in his failure. The ignorant young might dismiss Eishwin's lore as absurdly simplistic. Only the most patient of the learned suspected the primal ciphers the conjurer left as his legacy might invoke powers outside of geometry. 'The Southern Council still holds debate on the subject.'

'An esoteric waste of time,' muttered the master scribe

taking dictation. He blotted the drying ink from his pen, his lips pressed tight with disdain. 'The known ways work best. Why trouble with pointless experiments?'

Earth patterns and copper invoked immobility, and froze consciousness into time. That made them reliably stable to work. Air and fire patterns were uselessly volatile. The action of water ran too subtle and slow. The way of the shamans inducted the mysteries through sound, and dissolved standing currents of flow. Yet the knowledge inherent in tribal tradition was kept closely guarded. The course of initiation such people followed demanded a lifetime of ascetic discipline. Just as well, that their nomad ways suited them for work far afield. The emperor's treasury held wealth enough to buy their help from the Scoraign chieftains. A circle of desert-bred shamans could sing empty-handed. Their lore could be worked in a scouring downpour, in wind storm, in snow, and in darkness. Oral tradition required no pattern books; used no pens, no parchment, no ingots of iron or copper. The tribe folk could patrol the most inhospitable canyons on foot, bearing little beyond a weapon to forage, and a headcloth and robe to stay warm.

The mere thought of leaving the comforts of court for a rough journey into the wastes raised the attendant scribes to consternation. They kept their irritable silence, while the Grand Vizier bent to resume communion with the channel's copper sphere.

'Pray the old ways work at all, in this case,' the old man whispered as, again, he closed his eyes to receive.

'Dictation,' he resumed at due length, though his voice shook. 'At east mark, scribe a half circle to west. Add a sine curve, rising, with the rhythm of the geometry to be one, two, three, five, seven, eleven, thirteen . . . the same again, but in mirror image . . .'

The pause that ensued seemed far too prolonged. At the bench, pen in hand, the master scribe prompted, 'My Lord Wisdom?'

His tacit query drew no response.

The next moment, the sphere shrieked in vibration. Heat followed. The channel yanked herself back with a cry. Forehead blistered, she released her clasped grip and cradled seared hands to her breast. The copper implement clanged down the stair, trailing a wisp of vile smoke.

The emperor's Grand Vizier made no sound at all. His limp palms draped over his mantled knees, and his robed body slumped, unsupported. All at once, he keeled over and pitched from his chair. The channel caught him, then lost her grip to burned hands. Crying, she fumbled, while the venerable conjurer toppled amid the heaped silk of his robes. His eyes stayed wide open, stilled in the spill of the candlelight. His unbreathing mouth gaped in sudden death, trickled with blood from a tongue bitten through in convulsion.

'First order of mercy!' shrieked the shocked scribe on the dais. 'What unspeakable evil could cause this attack?' Sunk to his knees, he cradled the purpled face of his mentor. Yet no succour availed. The Grand Vizier was gone, who had handled Tuinvardia's defence against sorcery through a half century of exemplary service.

His colleagues' distraught shouts brought the emperor's guards at a run.

The scribe at the trestle clutched his pen, as armed men crashed the doors and barged into the chamber. No chance was given to disparage the futility of their bared swords. The partially executed defence pattern on the parchment exploded into a whirlwind of conflagration. Screaming, both hands and sleeves set aflame, the vizier's most advanced master scribe collapsed before help could reach him.

In the deeps of Hell's Chasm, Mykkael and Princess Anja worked a cautious passage through a chain of ice tunnels. Here, where the gorge split the Great Divide, the continuous tumble of glacial debris often jammed the constricted watercourse. Each year, the raging force of spring melt waters drilled out the channel anew. With summer's approach, the spate had fallen. The verge offered a narrow, dangerous ledge carved out of compacted ice. Here, the passage became exceptionally hazardous for the horses. Even shod, the animals slipped and skidded. Glassy chips were gouged up by their hooves as they scrambled for purchase beside the boiling race of the current.

Here, even a skilled rider's weight might unbalance them. Mykkael insisted they proceed on foot. Still pursued by the weaving lights wrought by the sorcerer's long spell, he held the rearguard with drawn sword. The blade whined aloud. The viziers' tattoo at his nape stayed unquiet as well, a constant, spiking ache that chafed at his already volatile nerves. He lit the way with a torch, held left-handed, his reflexes cranked to *barqui'ino*-trained vigilance that reacted to every flicker and jerk of cast shadow. Nimble Covette had cast off a shoe. The bare hoof caused her two scrabbling falls, with only Anja's shouted commands warding off lethal panic.

To grasp the mare's reins and try to assist was to invite a disaster. Upon the slick ice, no footing was safe. At the first opportunity, Mykkael cut a stave from a deadfall. He lashed Anja's skinning knife on to the tip. Throughout his work, the lurid flares of sent spellcraft flashed and wove at the edge of the wardings. Their unsettling colours ghosted over his dark face, and the broken scabs of the sword cut marring his fingers.

'Use this,' he ordered. 'Right-hand side, between you and the water. Spike the blade into the ice like a walking stick. Princess, hear me! You don't take *even a single step* without securing your balance beforehand.'

Shivering, her face waxy blue from the cold, Anja nodded. She took the stave in numbed hands and pushed on. Utterly miserable, she withheld from complaint. She jabbed down the knife and moved ahead, while her heart drummed with terror and her frosted breaths plumed in the torchlight. Onwards she pressed, hurting down to the bone, yet too frightened to contemplate stopping. Behind her, Mykkael limped on watchful alert. His scarred knee, and the slap of the bootless foot he had strapped in green leather, demarked his halting progress. His war injury had stiffened, made worse by hard usage and uneven ground. Yet to pause was unthinkable, even to soak the inflamed joint in the ice melt. Not while the shaman's mark on the sword wailed its incessant warning.

'Princess! Princess, *stop now*!'

Mykkael spoke twice more, still unable to break through Anja's leaden exhaustion. She spiked in the stave, blindly absorbed by the rhythmic punishment of setting one step after the next.

'Your Grace, hold hard!' His insistent fingers bit into her shoulder. 'I should lead the way into the open.'

Anja edged to the side of the treacherous verge. Mykkael squeezed past with precarious care. The hide padding on his foot had torn through. Under the juddering light of the flame, Anja saw bloodied prints on the ice, caused by a gash on his toe. The hip he had bruised just as clearly gave him discomfort.

Yet the chance to seize respite stayed out of the question. The sword's mark buzzed its relentless alarm, and seen at close quarters, the captain's skin puckered with wave upon wave of raised gooseflesh.

'Witch thoughts?' Anja asked. 'What do you see?'

Mykkael's dark eyes flickered towards her, then away. He wrung out a gravel-rough answer. 'Nothing coherent.'

. . . an ancient vizier in a robe marked with symbols, lying dead in a ring of shocked faces; a vanguard of riders in exquisite, fine armour, riding hellbent over foreign terrain; an old man wearing tribal knots in his hair, rapidly speaking the desert variation of Scoraign dialect; then the dream-caught image of a warrior, himself? *wrapped in what looked like spun silver and shadow, and pursued by horrors fit to bring madness . . .*

'Mykkael?' Anja whispered. While the horses' breath

clouded around him, she closed a tacit hand over his forearm. 'Captain?'

. . . Jussoud, his deft fingers glistening with burn unguents as he treated a man whose flesh was seared beyond recognition . . .

Racked by a horrible, lingering chill, Mykkael unwound Anja's grip. He stared into her eyes, a glance that scoured for its depth of searching intensity. Then he touched her wrist to his forehead, a salute foreign to the northern manners practised in Sessalie. 'This is not Efandi,' he whispered. 'No sorcerer has *yet* seized a permanent hold on the land.' The scrape of his words seemed almost a litany, scarcely audible through the shear of the current over its milk-glass bed of ice.

To Anja, the captain's grasp felt alarmingly hot. She prayed the effect was no more than the contrast posed by her own numbed hand. 'Mykkael?'

He nodded, moved, stated, 'Ready the bow. Expect this, we're going to face ambush.'

Anxiously frightened, Anja called after him, 'How do you know?'

'Tattoo,' he gasped answer. 'It's a burning brand on me.'

The poised torch just as much of a weapon as the bared sword clenched in his grasp, he advanced towards the tunnel's gapped opening. Outside, the darkness hung like draped felt. Mykkael filled the aperture, shoulders cloaked in his spattered surcoat, and his hands chiselled bronze in the fluttering firelight.

Anja fumbled to unsling the bow. Shielded by Mykkael's readied stance at the forefront, she tugged the quiver at her hip into convenient reach. The scouring slap of whitewater filled the ice cave, with the horses' steamed presence crowding her back, loud with the scrape of shod hooves.

Mykkael's fingers tensed in the torchlight. The blade keened, a shrill note that shredded the mists combing off the arched ice overhead. He advanced a tight step, edged one foot on to the gritty rime of moraine laid bare by the thaws.

Something winged and weighty dropped, moving fast. Sword, torch and man exploded into blurred motion. The jerked flame fluttered down to a trailing coal, outlining the warrior against what appeared insubstantial as shadow and smoke. Yet his striking steel chimed. The minion antagonist he fought was unnervingly solid. Claws snatched the frayed hem of Mykkael's surcoat and opened a howling rip. Thrust, *clang*! slash, *clang*! the embattled rhythm of attack and riposte cast ringing echoes back down the cleft.

Anja laboured to close her chilled fist on the bow, then manipulate the nocked arrow. Her grip on the string seemed too numbed to draw, even had the captain's raging attack not foreclosed her clear view of a target. In darkness, the two-handed battle he sustained moved too swiftly for vision to follow.

The horses stamped and sidled, shaken from their exhausted torpor. Anja spoke, desperate to calm their distress before sliding hooves caused a mishap. She dared not look back, dared not loose the bow. Trembling amid the spun murk of the mist, she watched Mykkael's defence, a harrowing display of the *barqui'ino* mind that reforged the body into an engine of relentless ferocity.

The torch struck, raining a scatter of sparks. Teeth clashed and snapped, screeling into a ribbon of jabbing, sharp steel. Impact raised a sulphurous sizzle of flesh, and a horrific, keening howl. Mykkael's bootless foot came down on ice. He slipped, with the scarred leg unable to compensate. Down on one knee, his cleared sword scarcely wavered, its targeting point all but nailed into space, with his raised arm holding form overhead in a lightning-speed act of recovery.

Anja pulled the bow. She took aim at what appeared empty dark and released, both arrow and pent breath let go with a grunt. The shaft clashed into thc black shine of scales.

Its feathered nock vanished, hard followed by the streaked silver of Mykkael's stabbing blade. Fumes roiled. Smoke poured from the minion's rent flesh, deadly proof that he fought another marauding shape-changer. Leathered wings beat the air, scraped over rock and dislodged a stinging shower of gravel. Mykkael regained his stance and lunged into the pelting assault. Enfolded at once by billowing smoke, his sword dipped and flashed, backed up at each sally by the battering club of the torch shaft.

Through juddering light, and explosions of sparks as the blows thudded home, Anja tracked the captain's advance. She forced her shaking hand to string the next arrow. By the time she had the shaft firmly nocked, no clean shot was possible. Mist had obscured Mykkael's moving form. She heard steel clash and skitter, knitted into the minion's harrowing wails. Set amid failing light, the interlocked contest of man and monster was reduced to chaotic confusion.

That moment, an inrush of flying things pelted into the ring of the wards. They swooped down at suicidal speed, as though trying a concerted attack of sheer numbers to overwhelm its protection. Mykkael surely sensed the unpleasant effects. He shouted, perhaps seeking to turn the assault. Yet the wave of long-spelled abominations kept coming. They converged upon him, unfazed as their fellows struck the viziers' raised pattern and dissolved, bleeding flames in gyrating colours.

Since archery was futile, Anja stowed the bow and arrow to free her hands. The stick lashed with the knife could serve as a spear. That idea resolved, she began to advance, just as something coiling and heavy crashed with a bellow and carved up a scatter of gravel. Mykkael's sword clanged. More smoke roiled, clouding her sight, as claws scrabbled over wet rock. The struggle cut short with a thunderous splash. Mykkael reappeared, his steel glistening scarlet, and his left arm torn bloody under the dimmed glow of the torch.

Still immersed in *barqui'ino* awareness, he plunged out of the smoke, tossed the stubbed wood away, then seized the princess at scruff and waist. His fierce grasp hurled her astride, amid the bundles lashed on to Kasminna. Speech seemed beyond him. The flat of his sword spoke instead, slapping the sorrel's rump and startling her into a wild-eyed canter. In unbroken stride, Mykkael thrust past the grey gelding and remounted Stormfront. Through the lightning-burst flares as more accursed creatures crashed to destruction against the wardings, he belted his heels into the black gelding's sides and veered him hard after Anja's mare into the open darkness.

No sign remained of the horrific creature he had just driven into the spate. The black gorge of Hell's Chasm opened ahead, a sinister slit bisected by the roaring leap of whitewater. Anja had no choice but to entrust her safety to her mount's sharper eyesight. She clung for her life to the mare's wind-whipped mane, repeatedly calling to urge Vashni and Covette to press tired strides and keep pace.

'Shape-changer,' gasped Mykkael, his diction strangled by *barqui'ino*-induced adrenaline. 'Downstream.'

Anja finished his thought to clarify her understanding. 'You think the minion will reassemble?'

'Must. Very quickly.' Mykkael leaned out, yanked the lead rein with his free hand, and swerved Kasminna around an obstruction her distraught rider had missed. 'Run!'

He steered Stormfront's surging flight alongside the mare, riding bareback with a skill the princess suspected could only be matched in the heart of the eastern steppelands. He held the horses to their pounding charge, unwilling to let up as they leaped over potholes, and hammered headlong and stumbling across rimed ice and beached mounds of river stones.

Stormfront snorted a rattled warning and shied. The sword's warding shrieked. Kasminna leaped sideways, blowing with terror, as the stony ground seemed to heave into motion under her back-stepping hooves.

The violent swerve wrenched Anja off her seat. As the mare dropped on her haunches and spun away, urgent hands snatched at her clothing. She felt the vibrating cry as the warded sword's hilt gouged into the small of her back. Then blank air opened under her, and she slammed with a grunt across the withers of Mykkael's black gelding.

The precious, copper-tipped arrows slithered, falling out as the quiver upended. Anja shot out a forearm and pinned them. Through the lurch as Stormfront slid on his hocks and fought into scrambling recovery, Mykkael's left fist remained locked in her jerkin. Battered, face down, her braid whipping her cheek, Anja clung, jolted breathless. Single-minded, she rescued the arrows, her breast jammed to the captain's straining thigh. The bowstring grated and sawed at her collarbone at each surging, equine stride.

She could see little of the creature the captain confronted, beyond its horrendous talons. Through the violent gyrations of combat, she glimpsed scaled sinews, punch-cut against a spinning view of pressed gravel and gouged ice and raced water. Anja heard the captain's desperate, fast breaths, as the sword in his hand screamed and clove through *barqui'ino* attack forms over her head. Something heavy and hot seized her ankle, slapped away in a spray of liquid. The blade's warding shuddered complaint.

Anja shut her eyes. Dizzied to nausea by the stench of the captain's fouled surcoat, and the wildly tilting ground, she held like grim death to the sheaf of salvaged arrows. Her other fist clutched the cross-gartered ties binding the leathers to Mykkael's calf. She hung on to him, desperately mindful that his undisturbed balance was critical for accurate sword work. Both of their lives would be forfeit should she slide off centre, or fall off.

The bruising, rough ride drove the air from her chest each time Stormfront shifted direction. Mykkael kept his seat through superlative horsemanship, a sword wielded astride without use of stirrups a feat few men alive could achieve. Anja endured, from moment to precarious moment. Through the scatter of stones under Stormfront's hooves, she followed the clang and clatter of steel, aware that one man's pressured defence was all that forestalled an unspeakable fate. The spelled monster that hissed and snapped overhead lunged for its prey without quarter. She felt the whuff of its breath on her back, and winced to each clash of its teeth. If she chanced to be seized, her form would become a shape-changer's guise for a sorcerer to deploy at will. She could be worse than dead, with an imposter left to claim Sessalie's crown uncontested.

Mykkael twisted hard left. His sword struck moving murder. Anja felt the impact shock through his taut body. His hand on her jerkin convulsed with the force of his recovery, as he snapped his entangled blade free. Ducked under a sense of ponderous movement, her person snatched close and sheltered against a smoking pelt of hot fluid, she clung grimly as the captain stabbed in his heels and called out.

Stormfront responded, bunched and shot forward. A descending claw whistled close overhead. The sword clanged again, gave a sliding ring in deflection. Mykkael shouted. 'Jee!'

Anja braced, prepared, while the gelding wheeled sideways. Tail streaming, hooves pounding rough stone, he avoided the coiling slap of scaled tail, spiked at the end with barbed horns.

Vashni's shrill scream arose at their back. Anja turned her head, found her view obstructed by Mykkael's leg. Darkness masked even the partial glimpse of what mishap had just transpired. Claws scuffled on stone, milled through by the clatter of Stormfront's headlong flight. Then something massive splashed into the flume. The noises of struggle receded behind as the horses opened their stride, hazed into a panic-stricken gallop. Only two sets of hoof beats trailed after the valiant black gelding.

Poor Vashni's demise had opened the way to escape for the riders and the two mares.

Anja blinked through the burn of fresh tears, jounced against her protector. Above her, unending, the whining cry of the sword sustained its pitch through the scrape of Mykkael's raced breathing.

He did not pull up. Even when Stormfront's long strides devolved into a choppy canter, and his sweated coat streamed strings of lather, the desert-bred captain shouted to enforce the frantic pace.

'You'll kill him,' railed Anja, afraid for the gelding. Kasminna was flagging, and Covette, one foot shoeless, lagged dangerously far behind.

If Mykkael heard, he did not draw rein. Only when the next ice tunnel forced caution did he slacken from headlong flight. By then, the hard, running tremors brought on by *barqui'ino* recoil stormed through his overwrought flesh. Warned that his mind might not be coherent, the princess held on in agonized patience. Despite the fact that her midriff was bruised by the ridge of the horse's withers, she stayed passive in hope that her quiet would help restore the captain's hazed reason. In his prudent, right mind, surely Mykkael would choose to dismount, and light a torch to traverse the black maw of the passage.

Yet no respite came. Riding the razor's edge of raw reflex, the warrior stayed astride with drawn sword and drove Stormfront ahead without let-up.

'I'm not harmed,' Anja ventured.

Mykkael shuddered, head to foot, and managed a stilted reply. 'I know.'

Anja forced back the hot sting of tears, and doggedly pressed him again. 'If Stormfront slips, even once, we're both lost.'

All but deranged by the skittering slide as the black gelding's forehooves lost purchase, the princess endured with her breath stopped.

'We daren't pull up,' Mykkael stated at length. 'If that

vile thing overtakes us again, we're foredone.'

'You're hurt?' Anja asked, while the tremors whipped through him, aggravating his hitched shortness of breath. Her query went unanswered. Enveloped by the chasm's dank blackness, she could see nothing at all. Neither could she dispel her anxiety by touch. Not with her left hand clutching the arrows, and all her security dependent upon her grip on Mykkael's makeshift footwear. As Stormfront slewed again and again, scrambling for purchase on ice, she dared not risk loosing her grasp for even a fraction of a second.

No choice remained. Equine senses must be entrusted to secure Stormfront's imperilled riders.

Too long, they traversed the echoing dark, with the race of the current a blast of raw noise, and the horses' terrible, laboured breaths cruel proof of their overtaxed resource. By the time the far side of the tunnel emerged, a faint oval rinsed grey by starlight, Anja was shaking from overwrought nerves. Her hands were knotted with fiery cramps, and sweat slid in drops down her temples.

'Hyaa!' Mykkael's shout rousted Stormfront to a staggering trot.

Kasminna ripped out a startled snort, laid back her ears, and plunged after him, with Covette in limping pursuit.

'Are you crazy?' yelped Anja, pummelled again, her sick fear whipped on to wild outrage.

'Sword!' Mykkael gasped.

Too late, Anja realized: the angry, wasp hum of the steel had not slackened.

Horse and paired riders burst into the open. Mykkael shouted again, just as something huge missed its pounce from the back of the ice face. Stone rattled as it landed and launched into frenzied pursuit. The sword's warding screamed, and the spent horses bolted in a fresh burst of primal terror.

Left, right, left again, Stormfront changed his lead to thread through a maze of shattered boulders. He leaped the frothing seam of a freshet. The bough of a deadfall snagged his left side, gouging at Anja's legs. She hung on, lashed and battered. Mykkael, crouched above her, used his braced sword to fend off the stinging branches. The cavern around them had widened again, prime ground for a night-hunting kerrie.

Ahead, the change in terrain spelled disaster: the flume crashed down a laddered incline, then whirled with a thunderous roar into the black depths of a basin. Water exploded over the rim at the far side, streaming trailers of spray under starlight. The spillway of the falls overhung the sliced edge of the world, gateway to the impassable cliff that ended the run down Hell's Chasm.

The drop beyond was sheer, a vertical buttress that cleaved away into vacant air. There the rushing water plumed downwards, winnowed into veils like hurled dust, towards the distant floor of a canyon blanketed under white mist.

Anja beheld that vast drop off, then the gulf to the distant, far side. Upside down, the scope of the view set her mortal senses reeling. Recognition struck like a cry against silence, that she beheld her own certain death, and the bittermost ending of hope.

'We're defeated,' she gasped.

No human means could conquer an obstacle of such overpowering scale.

Her plaintive distress went unheard. Mykkael was not listening. Or else his awareness stayed riveted on the threat that still charged on the heels of the straggling horses.

He slapped the flat of his sword down on Stormfront's shoulder, turning him, hard, from the sloping drop towards the basin. The gelding slithered on stepped granite. Iron shoes scrabbling, he clawed himself into recovery, and snapped his hocks back under himself. Against chance-met failure, against futile ruin, the black horse rebounded. Dry grass, then brush, then needled branches slapped into Anja's dangling face. Eyes closed, skin stinging as thorns ripped her cheek, she plunged through the bruised evergreen fragrance of cedar. Then dank stone and darkness swallowed their striving. The horse's clattering gait dispersed into echoes cast back by a stone enclosure.

'Hyaa! Stormfront, forward!' Mykkael pressed the shivering horse into the black cavern carved out by the current in years when the basin swirled higher. The mares clambered after. Hooves splashed underfoot. The horses traversed a small streamlet or pool. Icy droplets splashed Anja's eyelids. Her dangling braid wicked up moisture. Then Stormfront's powerful body heaved underneath her as he surged upslope and arrived on a narrow, dry ledge.

Mykkael snatched the back of her jerkin. Without word or warning, he hurled her off the exhausted gelding's back.

Anja struck ground with a bitten-off cry, winded and scraped and on fire with outrage. The string of the slung bow sawed into her neck, while her salvaged arrows clattered around her.

The captain vaulted on to his feet just behind. 'Princess! See to your horses!' No time remained to speak of regrets. Sword raised, Mykkael scrambled on limping, fast strides to contend with the minion still bearing down from outside.

XXXV. Precipice

THE HORSES WERE NOW TOO EXHAUSTIVELY SPENT TO FALL PREY TO CHANCE MISADVENTURE. ANJA LEFT Stormfront's fallen reins trailing. Too winded to stray, the gelding could be trusted to recover at will in the company of his teammate. As Kasminna, and finally Covette, straggled in, sorely limping, the princess shoved aside pity for their battered plight. Consumed by necessity, she groped on hands and knees in the darkness, seeking her scattered arrows. She located three, ripped the bow from her shoulder, then pushed her bruised body back upright and rushed downslope after Mykkael.

Alone, he could scarcely defend the cleft's entrance with no more at hand than his sword.

She reached him, wrung breathless, and slid to a stop in a scatter of gravel. He held his blade raised. Eyes searching the darkness, he dug into his scrip, while, outside, the sorcerer's minion gave chase across the rock verge. It caught their scent with scarcely a pause, and veered into the brush at the mouth of the cavern. As before, the captain acknowledged Anja's presence without breaking his active focus. Never turning his head, he fished out the twist of leather holding his flint and dry tinder.

'Pluck a spray of cedar and light the green needles,' he

ordered, then offered the packet. His voice did not shake, or his hand, though the burgeoning wail of the sword signified urgent peril.

Awkward and fumbling, Anja juggled to free her burdened hands. 'The bow,' she gasped hoarsely.

'At my feet! Drop it!' Mykkael plucked the arrows from her clutched fist with the speed of a striking adder. 'The fire comes first!'

Anja shed the weapon with a clatter and shouldered the task he demanded. Limned against the swirling pool of the basin, the fell minion that hunted charged in. Its glimpsed form was black-scaled, and sinuously fleet under the thin gleam of starlight. Anja wrenched off an evergreen bough and doggedly wielded the flint. Cold and near panic had dulled her dexterity. She could scarcely command her dazed fingers.

Mykkael sensed her difficulty. While the sorcerer's sending hurtled upslope, the captain pinned the wasp hum of his blade flat to his side with his elbow. He snatched flint and striker out of her hands, and thrust a raked spark to the cedar. The frond caught. Flame blossomed, fanning a billow of smoke. Mykkael snapped another branch from a sapling, touched that alight also. Then he hurled the spill into the path of the oncoming monster.

Smoke spun on the wind. The creature bellowed and yanked back as though grazed by flung poison. Its sinuous form lost definition, then dissolved into whirling mist. Yet this time, the change brought no moment of respite. Warned by the relentless buzz of the shaman's mark, Mykkael secured his drawn sword and snatched up the bow. Fast as he moved, the shape-changer's tactic outmatched him. With diabolical speed, the minion recondensed and shifted into the known form of a man.

He stepped out of the night empty-handed and helpless, with no stitch of state finery upon him.

'Anja, beloved,' called the High Prince of Devall. Exquisitely handsome, clean-limbed as fine marble, he extended his opened arms in appeal, entreating the princess to spare him.

The bowstring twanged in release. Mykkael's aimed shaft slapped through defenceless flesh, simultaneous with Anja's choked outcry. Though reason insisted the fell creature was tainted, the wrenching sight of such beauty, cut down, stunned the heart with unparalleled savagery.

As the princess crumpled, hands pressed to her face, Mykkael left her side. He accomplished his butcher's work with the sword with what seemed an undaunted efficiency. While the princess wept for grief, mourning the suitor she once might have honoured in matrimony, the desert-bred captain who guarded her life disallowed any pause for condolence. Relentlessly silent, he destroyed the gristly remains there and then with a blaze set from dead wood and cedar.

The pyre burned bright, overseen by the ice-chip gleam of the stars. The roil of the chasm's black waters thundered on the stilled air, with no sanctuary rites to honour the dead, or sing the eulogy to grace passing royalty. Anja observed, shuddering in the windy cold, alone and distressed and uncomforted.

Mykkael prowled the brush at the mouth of the cavern. Though the whine of his blade had subsided to a whisper, he remained too cranked with tension to settle. He paused more than once to crouch in the shadows, forehead braced on crossed wrists at his sword hilt. The restless gesture seemed natural, until Anja realized the posture masked an ungovernable onset of dry heaves.

'Mykkael?' She arose, crossed the hard, stony soil, but no careful approach could disarm his flinching recoil.

On his feet, his weapon hilt cradled tight to his breast, he gasped, 'No. Princess, I beg you, go back and stand with your horses.'

'They don't need me.' Steadfast, Anja continued to offer her hand. 'Come away, Mykkael.'

He shook through a horrible, wracking tremor. 'You do

understand, that minion was no man.' Fear seized his voice, or an undisguised pain, from a source that could not be fathomed as he turned his face from her and finished, 'Nothing remained of the person you knew. Only an abomination.'

Anja realized she had seen more clearly than he. Through the gift that her sire described as a cold start, she had discerned the false apparition was not sourced in a human awareness. 'Captain, leave be,' she admonished. 'I already saw the distinction.'

But revolted nerves could not always be reconciled through logic. Mykkael coughed behind his raised wrist, the ripped shreds of his sleeve dark with blood. 'One doesn't grow hardened. If you can find comfort, the cedar is proof. Your suitor won't rise from these ashes tonight.'

Anja grasped his tensed fingers. 'Come away, Mykkael. The fire can accomplish its purpose without us.' Her tears came then, fast and hot in release as he permitted her touch, and allowed her to draw him aside.

The kerrie descended just as they turned to re-enter the mouth of the cleft. It swooped down in a rushing tumult of air from the cliff face above their heads. Mykkael hurled back into *barqui'ino* mind. His shove tumbled Anja ahead into shelter. The move marked the start of a seamless pivot as he spun to engage a defence. His effort appeared foredoomed at the outset, with the sword his sole weapon at hand.

Against fire and talon, one man with a blade would have to be sorely outmatched.

Choked silent by horror, Anja embarked on a hands-and-knees search to reclaim the dropped bow. Too late, she recalled she held no more arrows. Crushed to despair, she could only pause, numb, while the kerrie snap-folded spread wings in descent.

Its powerful, deadly strike seemed inevitable. Her valiant protector would be cut down before her anguished, stunned eyes. If Mykkael had regrets, his thoughts did not show. He did not cry out, or turn craven. Sword lightly raised, his stance set in readiness, he maintained his trained form. His battle-hard nerve engaged no wasted motion. Against the backdrop of plummeting predator and starred sky, his poised state of preparedness defied fate.

Mykkael held to life against all threat of ending, without rage, without recoil, without fear.

Had the kerrie been fixed upon human prey, that windy escarpment might have become the tragic site for a final stand. As events unfolded, the warrior's quiet acceptance itself framed his grace of salvation. Mykkael awaited his moment, *unmoving*; while the marauding creature ripped out of its plunge, aimed for its intended, first target. It struck the whirlpool in the basin with a splash that cast up an explosion of spray.

Massive pinions deployed, and fanned up a stinging barrage of forced air. Through back-bent brush and gust-flattened evergreens, Anja saw the predator arise from the depths with Vashni's corpse seized in mailed talons.

The dead gelding, not Mykkael, would be taken to sate its ravenous hatchlings. The kerrie soared upwards, bugling triumph. It carved a steep circle and dipped over the ledge, streaming flame and roiled sparks in its gliding wake as it soared down the night-dark canyon.

The severity of subsequent *barqui'ino* reaction left Mykkael unfit for close company. Every move, every breath made him flinch with hazed nerves. He countered the affliction the best way he could, and immersed himself in the frenetic activity of setting arcane defences. If Anja feared his efforts with fire and cedar ash might not be sufficient to repel the demonic forces that sought her destruction, she knew not to speak. The warrior drew steel at her least untoward movement. He could not be approached, far less withstand human contact or touch. His given promise to attend to his wounds must wait until the throes of raw backlash subsided.

Anja herself had small will to face her own toll of aches and bruises. To stave off the crushing despair of defeat, and escape morbid thoughts of the precipice that surely crushed every option but death, she bent her scraped knees and climbed back to her feet. Then she hobbled in aching, uneven steps to look after her exhausted horses.

They numbered three, of the six exceptional creatures she had sequestered in Farmer Gurley's back meadow. As hard-run survivors, how sorrowfully they had changed, standing with lowered heads, sides heaving, with their proud tails hanging limp and snarled and mud-stained. Anja ran her stinging, scraped fingers over the crusted salt matting their coats. She accounted the sad tally: of staring ribs, and sunken flanks, and the heartbreaking list of more hurtful damages. Never before had Kasminna been too dispirited to head butt and nip. Her hind fetlocks were puffy, and her near shoulder skinned bloody from a crash on the sticks of a deadfall. Covette had a bashed knee, hot and sore with tight swelling. Her bare hoof had split to the quick. She stood three-legged, unwilling to put weight on the crack. Stormfront, proud creature, had claw wounds in his neck. If Mykkael's superb horsemanship had spared his legs, the gelding was wretchedly muscle-sore.

Anja laid her cheek on the black's steaming side, too drawn and weary to weep. She had no liniments, no bran mash, no flannel leg wraps or restoratives. For her horses' suffering, she had no balm to bring them relief. Their sacrifice found her worse than empty-handed. Her fingers were too raw and clumsy with cold to manage girth buckles or knots.

'I can help.' Mykkael's clasp, still unsteady, closed over her shoulder and edged her gently aside. He assisted with the crusted ties binding his bundles of rope and rolled leather, removed Covette's saddle and bridle, then drew Anja away with the same uncompromised firmness he used to quell Kasminna's surliness. 'If you'll help tend the fire, your Grace, I can arrange the warm water you need to make you and your animals more comfortable.'

Anja stared at him, numb.

'Warm water.' The smile he offered was woundingly civilized. 'I can deliver my promise.'

He accomplished the feat by heating stones in the coals, then dropping them into a filled catch pocket in the stone ledge. Anja huddled to one side, stoking the blaze with the wood he had dragged from the deadfalls washed in and stranded at the high-water mark. Whatever harrowing end lay ahead, the princess would not lack for warmth. The supply of dry fuel proved blessedly plentiful. In the course of his rock shifting, Mykkael discovered the fact that kerrie wing leather resisted an unshielded flame. Delighted by that unsuspected advantage, he set to with a cut length of sinew, and a buckle tang ground sharp for use as an awl. Within a short time, he had fashioned a hide bucket. A sweet-smelling herb he kept in his scrip created a healing infusion. The balm would ease Covette's injured hoof, and rinse the crust from Stormfront's deep gashes.

'I can make more,' Mykkael reassured her, met by consternation as his bloodstained clothes reminded her that the horses were not alone in their need for a remedy. 'You ought to rest, Princess.'

Anja refused. Her own respite would be deferred until after her animals were tended. She would have each hurt doctored, each damp coat rubbed dry, and each mane and tail free of tangles. 'Once that's done, you made me a promise, Mykkael. I won't sleep until I see your injuries given the basic care you've neglected.'

He raised his eyebrows. 'In that case, we're going to require clean linen.' He blotted damp hands, looking mildly hopeful. 'Your Grace wouldn't balk at boiling laundry?'

She stared back, nonplussed. 'Your surcoat and shirt? Not at all.'

Mykkael bowed to her. He could do no less. Shown a

difficult challenge, King Isendon's daughter would take down her chosen target. 'Then by your wish, Princess, the horses come first.'

Mykkael limped and sat at the last, his game leg propped straight on a boulder. The poker-stiff set to his back disclosed the debilitating cramps that had probably gnawed him for hours. Despite the impassable setback posed by the gulf at the precipice, he had not stinted his care of the horses. The vantage he chose when he finally rested afforded a clear view of the cavern's entry, perhaps to allow him to stand wary watch. Or else he employed the evasive excuse to hold his fixed interest elsewhere. Head turned away, he tugged off his torn surcoat.

Anja accepted the soiled cloth from his hand. She rinsed off the ill-smelling muck in cold water before she shoved its bulk into the steaming bucket and stirred it about with a stick. 'You don't believe in futility, do you?'

'Your Grace?' He still did not face her. 'I don't intend to allow you to die here.'

Low spirits pressed Anja to sharpness. 'We have a choice?'

Mykkael surveyed her then. His dark eyes stayed shadowed. 'I promised you, Princess, and your sire before you. Why should you cast away hope?' Gaze on her, he unfastened his sword harness, then secured the sheathed blade, hilt laid ready to hand across his braced leg.

Anja swallowed. 'I don't see any way to escape.'

He raised his marked fingers, tugged loose the grimed lacings at cuff and collar. 'What meets the eye is the limited world. Our five senses don't fathom the greater part of existence.'

His persistent calm chafed against her despair. 'You don't have any plan.'

'Not yet.' Mykkael peeled off his shirt. 'When the time comes to act, there will be one. Until we are dead, we must trust in the future. There has been blood and striving to have come this far. Would you give Vashni, Fouzette and Bryajne the dismissal of your retreat?'

A great deal of the blood had been unequivocally his, Anja saw in silenced dismay. Through the stained ruin of Jussoud's pine-gum dressings, she mapped the bared sword cut across chest and shoulder, then the undressed gashes the shape-changer had clawed across an older slice on his left forearm.

'Princess?' Mykkael prompted.

She started, raised her glance from his hurts, and accepted his offered garment. 'Who tried to kill you?'

'In this case?' His desert-bred features turned taut and grim. 'A foreign enemy who wanted me dead. There have been a number of those in my history.' He worried the lifted edge of the dressing, then hissed through shut teeth for the unpleasant fact that the gum was not going to pull free without force.

'You'll need a hot cloth,' Anja said. 'Here, let me.'

He glanced up, his eyes snapped to live fire. 'Not yet, your Grace. Those rags have to boil, first. Leave me my due, for experience.'

His protest was scarcely enough to forestall her. In a strategic attempt to deflect conversation, he shifted his sword and arose. On his feet, his sore posture became all too evident as he yanked off his belt, still bearing the packet of the first shape-changer's salt-stunned remains. He tossed strap and bundle down at his feet. Then he stripped in one move to his smallclothes. The flurried, forced catch as he tossed Anja his shed breeches evinced his nettled distaste.

Yet like the fine sword brought out for inspection, he stilled in leashed tolerance for her review. Anja withstood the blazing intensity of his self-contained presence. Her survey brushed over the odd scrap of embroidered silk he wore wrapped at his waist, then moved on and tallied the score of his more intimate injuries: the opened weal on his thigh; the scraped bruise on his hip; and last of all the bandaged puncture she had watched him repoultice in the darkened hour before dawn.

Yet no present cut or bloodied abrasion could compare with the bared testament of his healed scars.

'Those weren't caused by sword cuts,' Anja gasped outright.

He did not need her glance to guess which past foray had raised her horrified comment. Amid the clean weals acquired in battle, the knotted, red burns left by a heated spear point were no pretty sight, though they had been branded in cruel, precise rows across the lean flesh of his flank.

Mykkael shrugged. 'A man wanted information I didn't have. He earned little else but my screams for his efforts.' Soft brown, his eyes remained on her as he finished in piercing rebuke. 'Truly, Princess, there are better distractions.'

Anja blinked, looked away, her left arm tightly clasped about her raised knees. She addressed his abstruse change of subject head on as she stirred the soiled breeches into the steaming water. 'Is this whole ordeal not the mask for a farce?'

Why clean a sword slash, or bind up a bruise in hot compresses? Why trouble to minister to any raw wound that would be given no grace to mend as the legacy left to a corpse?

Mykkael resettled himself across the fire, his marked hands clamped with gouging force on the muscles that seized his lamed knee. When he answered, his words bespoke razor-edged care. 'The last princess I guarded escaped death by sorcery, though her sire's wide realm was laid waste.'

Anja dropped the stick as though scalded. 'She survived?'

The captain bent his dark head. He nodded. 'She lives yet in safety. Why should you do less?'

The oddly hackled force of his statement raised Anja's

intuitive instincts. She stared at him, read the unquiet tension coiled through his naked shoulders. The insight unfolded too deep an awareness. 'She's alive. Pray tell, at what terrible cost?'

That thoughtless comment stung him too sharply. Caught without any ready defence, he recoiled and presented his back.

Anja's breath stopped.

The mistake snapped him short. Now compelled to confront a disgrace hurled beyond tactful phrasing to salvage, Mykkael answered her stunned shock, his tone pared curt. 'Taskin's earned justice, administered with fairness. Your Grace's safety required a breach of discipline on my part. Since the facts were exposed, the crown commander was duty-bound. He had no choice but to handle the matter according to form.'

'Three stripes?' Anja whispered. That surface dismissal seared away her last vestige of mannered restraint. 'Blinding glory, Mykkael!'

What were those few weals, but a pittance before the scars of a flogging that had savaged his flesh long before.

'Your Grace, I'm no felon!' Mykkael cracked back, irritable. For pride's sake, he held, not hiding the sight of the damage exposed in the firelight. With his face turned to shadow, he could not discern that her spilled tears held pity, and not the censure of speechless revilement.

The swift explanation ripped from him in fury, an unwanted reprise of a history he deeply preferred to expunge from the public record. 'I was fighting the Sushagos. Our position was desperate. We needed a man to pose as a deserter to gain trust in the enemy camp. Too long an entrenchment had soured our attackers with boredom. Their vindictiveness went beyond vicious. Since they were deeply suspicious of spies, the person we sent had to be more than convincing. My own second officer laid on those stripes. He protested the command, long and bitterly. At the end, he did as I asked because I was the only man standing who had the strength left to volunteer.'

Anja fell back on the steel of state discipline. Through distress, she forced her voice steady. 'You stood in defence at the siege of Evissa?'

Mykkael spun around, still too riled to face her. 'Your Grace, I broke the engagement by means of that foray. The garrison there stayed intact to win victory.' Self-absorbed in his rage, he sat once again. Sword recovered in hand, he glowered towards the egress that led to a precipice that *surely was* foredoomed to break him. 'Princess, you will not speak again of defeat. Cliff wall or castle, I will get you away. No sorcerer's demon will claim you.'

The rags, she decided, had boiled enough. Anja fished the torn shirt from the bucket. The instant the fabric cooled enough to be grasped, she shredded a strip off the hem. Aware Mykkael's senses would track every move, she gave him the courtesy of spoken warning before she approached.

'Captain, how could you cleanse any wound on your back? If you can truthfully tell me you would have freely asked for my help, then I will apologize with due humility.'

Tension fled all at once. He rested his forehead against his marked knuckles, shaken to sudden, wry laughter. 'Words,' he said finally, his diction half muffled. 'How often they can cut deeper than steel.' Erect once again, he matched her frank glance. 'Let me mend my ill manners. I ask your Grace for that kindness, here and now. Be still, Princess. You need not apologize. For you, as a ruler, there can be no worse nuisance than a man who won't redress his own errors of judgement.'

'Oh, there are worse plagues.' Anja grinned through the relief that threatened to unstring the feelings flooding her near bursting heart. 'Trust me, I've suffered far worse. You haven't seen Lady Bertarra trying to teach my ungrateful court maidens to dance.'

'Mehigrannia show mercy, your Grace.' Mykkael

smothered a smile. 'I have been spared. Count me profoundly grateful.'

He did not appear to resent her light touch as she set to with the rag. For all her neat care, he still sucked a sharp breath as she worked the neglected gum dressings away from his clinging scabs. Informed by her frozen pause, he turned his head and regarded her with reproach. 'You think I am stone? That I can't feel pain?'

Anja blotted the persistent tears that striped through the grime on her cheeks. She shook her head, wordless, tossed the used rag back into the pot to drive off its insipid chill. Mykkael did not press. His patience bridged the drawn interval while she fought to recover composure.

'You don't seem to feel fear,' Anja managed at length. 'At least, you didn't move, or shrink back when you faced down a kerrie that seemed bound to kill you.'

Mykkael reached out and clasped his hand over her shaking fingers. As soon as she steadied under the contact, he let go and faced forward again. 'I don't fear death. That is but one thing within the wide world, fraught with all sorts of uncertainties.'

Rag recovered, Anja wrung out the excess hot water. She dabbed the dirt from abused flesh and raw skin, her tender work veiled beneath drifts of steam. 'What do you fear, Mykkael?'

'Failure.' The admission came bald-faced. He would not elaborate. The rock-hard muscles under her hands evinced his adamant silence.

Somewhere, Anja realized, he *had* failed someone. Yet even the brazen nerve born to royalty balked at setting the unkind question. She chose not to force his unwilling disclosure. Mykkael might serve, but the crown did not own him. She would leave the seal on whatever sorrow had plundered the depth of his peace. Nor could she degrade his dignity further. She would handle only those injuries beyond his reach, and leave his competent store of experience to attend to the rest on his own.

His diligence on that score resulted in a rigorous round of cleaning, then an unpleasant soak under bracing, hot compresses for the bruised hip, the claw cuts, and the puncture. Mykkael left the older wounds open to let the new scabs harden and dry. 'We don't have the right unguents,' he explained as he wrung out and hung his cleaned clothes. At the last, he recovered the rag to scour the stains from his harness. 'Without a salve, a closed wrap would make the wounds fester.'

Long before morning, his concern of infection would surely become a moot point. Yet Anja was too weary to argue the issue with a male creature engrossed in blind stubbornness.

Exhausted at length, she drowsed by the fire. Mykkael woke her just once, to loan his cleaned shirt. 'So your own can be washed, if you wish it.' She accepted his offer, used the rag for a sponge bath behind the hung cloth of his surcoat. While the captain changed out the used water and boiled her clothes in his bucket, she found she could not make her eyelids stay open. She slipped into sleep, and in time, the dreamless blackness of total immersion spiralled her down into nightmare . . .

Through coiling mist, Bryajne came on, his black tail and mane streaming to the thrust of his powerful canter. Astride him, the rider who bore down was naked. Even armless and headless, she knew him as the brother fallen to usage by demons. Her tears launched the arrow from Mykkael's bent bow, and the shaft flew with vengeful accuracy. Heart-shot, Kailen tumbled beneath milling hooves, and blood ran like a cry through the darkness.

'Sweet Anja, my princess, Devall's future queen.' Her lost suitor's whisper arose with entreaty. 'What can your desert-bred warrior win for you? Why choose oblivion and an obscure death? You need not betray us. We can still return. You can marry in state and be adorned with my bride gift of rubies. Devall and Sessalie can still be joined in beneficial alliance . . .'

* * *

Anja's scream brought Mykkael to her side at a run. His strong hands braced her up as she wakened.

'What did you see?' His gaze was trained on her as her eyes fluttered open. The bow he had just cast aside clattered downwards and hooked over his upright, bent knee.

Anja swallowed, helplessly unable to stop shaking. She still wore his shirt. His dried surcoat, cast over her, kept off the cold. Though he had not slung his harness over the exposed scab on his chest, she did not fail to notice the ominous sign. The bared sword he had hastily thrust through his belt rang yet with diminished vibrations.

Her whisper came ragged. 'What did you just shoot?'

The word he uttered was no language she knew, yet his tone bespoke pity and sorrow. He folded his good leg, drew her shivering form close. The firm grip he tucked over her forehead pressed her ear against the raced beat of his heart. 'You heard voices?' he asked. His knife-edged wariness could never be masked, no matter how carefully he framed the pretence of gentleness.

Anja shook through an unwonted chill. Anguished, she repeated, 'Captain, tell me the truth. What unspeakable thing did your arrow take down?'

'Need you ask, Princess?' He brushed aside a loose wisp of her hair, and smoothed the slipped surcoat back over her shoulders. His considered silence suggested concern, an unbearable burden that wore him half desperate to contemplate. At due length, he addressed her stifled emotion. 'If you listen, beware. The whispers you heard only speak for the sorcerer. They will come again. If you let them drive you to conflict, they'll tempt you.'

'Kailen was my brother!' Anja shuddered as the captain's crossed arms surrounded her horror and drew her more tightly against him. She appealed to him, desolate. 'Is his fallen spirit truly not dead?'

'Princess, I'm sorry.' Mykkael tucked her head underneath his raised chin, the better to maintain his unrelaxed guard against the night's gathered darkness. 'Sessalie's crown prince is no longer human. He has spoken in dreams, yes? Then stay wary, I beg you. His words are false and his promises will never be what they seem.'

Lulled by the warmth of his intimate contact, Anja allowed her jangled nerves to be soothed. 'What harm could Kailen's poor ghost bring to me?'

'Your Grace, there lies a danger past reach of my weapons.' Mykkael shifted position to ease his scarred knee. Yet something more than a physical discomfort weighted his warning to grimness. 'If the wardings I bear give me certain protection, you have birth ties to kin that can't be revoked. The will of a demon now plays that connection to secure his claim to make conquest.'

He feared to explain the extent of her endangerment: that her survival made Sessalie's ground doubly vulnerable. For as long as her kingdom was threatened, and she remained untainted and free, her mind would be stalked and hunted. *Any* demon's bound sorcerer could make use of her blood lineage to strike through and suborn the minion that had been Kailen; then that seized foothold would be worked in turn to launch covert attack on a rival.

Too aware of the range of hideous consequence he had once spared the Efandi princess, Mykkael gave Anja his straightforward warning. 'If you succumb to this sorcerer's blandishments while asleep, I can do almost nothing to save you. Awake, aware, rely on this much. If I win through with the salt-trapped remains of the shape-changer's minion in hand, there will be a chance to enact a full banishment. That is your brother's sole hope of release, and your lasting promise of safety. Without trained assistance, Kailen's spirit can never be freed from demonic enslavement. If Tuinvardia has no skilled vizier to achieve this, there are others among the wise who would help in my name.' Mykkael's resolve rang through like sheared steel as he committed his heartfelt will. 'Princess Anja, if I ask, and I will, take my oath at this moment: all that can will be done to redeem your lost brother from darkness.'

Awareness touched through, of a grief locked inside him, a pain raw and deep as an unhealed canker kept wrapped and hidden from view. 'Whom did you lose?' Anja whispered.

He turned his face, sharply. She held, expecting the burn of his tears to spill through her pillowing hair. Yet no moisture came, no release. His voice remained dry as the desert that birthed him, a lonely phrase fashioned of wind. 'No one you know of.'

Yet the impact of that prior loss branded in him the imperative need *not to fail*. He would not yield a life he had sworn to defend, though the brute trial of Hell's Chasm made his task a hopeless mockery.

Anja turned in his arms. She tilted her head, kissed the hollow of his throat with all of her passion unleashed. 'Let there be an hour of joy before death. Mykkael, I beg, let me give this for both of us.'

His hands caught her shoulders, cupped her form as though precious. Then, speechlessly shaken, he slipped his fingers upwards and cradled her face. He stared down at her, stripped by a turbulent distress that cut through to his well-guarded heart. 'On my sword, Princess, *you are not going to die*. Nor am I free to accept such a terrible gift.'

Anja gripped him. 'For all I know, Sessalie has already fallen to sorcery!'

Mykkael shut his eyes, shook his head. Not untouched, nor inhuman, he was trembling also. 'No, Princess. Anja, please, no. End this folly. You know by the voices you heard in your dream that Isendon's rule is not broken. Witch thought shows me Taskin, on guard at the king's side. Your sire's charge of protection still binds me to your defence.'

The brave words were sincere. Yet the wrenched conflict in the captain's expression firmed Anja's resolve by the honest force of its agony. 'You are more than the warrior, Mykkael! Just as I am human, and not immune to love behind the state mask of the princess.'

His hands tightened. 'If that's true, Anja, then you will wait! Survive Hell's Chasm. If we win through, if I bring you into Tuinvardia unscathed and living, only then can I set down my sword. Give your heart as you wish, and to whom you wish, then. But until you have reached a vizier's safe haven, *I remain bound to your service.*'

The gist of his earlier words by the marsh resurged with uncompromised clarity: that the honour of kings stood or fell by the hand of the warrior entrusted to bear arms on the field.

Mykkael's strength was unimpeachable and his gentleness beyond protest, as he eased himself clear of her offered embrace. There, he paused. Her trembling hands remained clasped in his own. He sustained her filled eyes without flinching. 'Your Grace, you are beautiful. I have seen no woman whose generosity can match your magnificence. But my pledge has been sworn. I can accept nothing of personal ease until my crown oath to your sire sees closure.'

She smiled through the spilled blur of her tears. 'No princess has ever been served with so bright and cruel an integrity. Nor, if you die here, has any crown in the nations ever commanded as steadfast a champion. You are not surpassed. That becomes your last epitaph. Should you starve for a line that is destined to pass out of living memory with me?'

'A sorrowful blessing,' Mykkael acknowledged, no less gruff as he released her at last to resume the dropped charge of his weapons. 'Forgive my ingratitude. Tonight must stay desolate. I do know your worth. If I fail to deliver the free gift of tomorrow, or if I win through, there can be no reprieve from this quandary. Better by far, Anja, to have witnessed your political marriage as Sessalie's princess. My name has no meaning, apart from my sword. I should have beheld nothing more than the dream painted into your portrait. Best, if your Grace had never known the nature of my close company.'

The channel conveyed desperate word back to Anzbek, that the emperor's Grand Vizier had perished while striving to fashion a pattern to guard Tuinvardia's threatened north border. The tribe's dreamer garnered more in his wandering sleep: of cedar fires burning an unconscionably foul spell line, and a fair-haired princess's tears. The warrior still lived, enveloped in the silver-edged shadows no scryer's talent could pierce. When the shaman's circle had shared these grim tidings, Anzbek spoke. 'The signs all converge. Hope lies in the warrior's wardings. He carries the songs to secure our salvation. This princess, by blood, holds the key to alliance that can bind Sessalie's ground under Tuinvardia's protection. Our future now hangs on the thread of two lives. Sing for mercy and strength, that they might survive . . .'

XXXVI. Ordeal

THE NIGHT SLOWLY WANED. ANJA STAYED WAKEFUL, TOO HARROWED TO RISK THE DANGERS THAT MIGHT STALK her in dreams. Mykkael's adamant service constrained him from comfort. He kept his strict distance, engrossed with a contrivance fashioned from tied rope and wing leather. Twice more, his sword's wardings clamoured in warning. Each time, he hazed off the renewed assault. The sorcerer's minions were held in lurking retreat by clouding the cleft's entry with cedar smoke. The evasion was stopgap. The enemy need do no more than keep them pinned down. A blind fool could see the fuel of evergreen would scarcely last beyond daybreak.

Light-headed from hunger and too little rest, Anja donned her cleaned clothes and huddled in silenced misery. Though she made no complaint, her gloomy despair did not escape the captain's keen vigilance.

'We'll be leaving at dawn,' he ventured at due length, returned on what seemed a routine trip to build up the failing fire.

Anja gave a dispirited poke at the coals with the stick lately used to hang laundry. 'You've designed us a plan.'

Mykkael's pause suggested the unusual weight of his reticence. 'I've mapped out a tactic.' His innate honesty would not let him mask the bald truth. 'If the odds aren't encouraging, they're not suicidal. I have measured the risks the best way I know, with the outcome by no means a sure failure.'

'I trust you,' murmured Anja. 'How could I not?' Yet his reluctance continued to burden the stillness, and his glance bent aside in avoidance. She drew a tight breath. Her own nerve faltered before broaching the obvious necessity. 'If we're climbing, I realize, my horses can't go.'

'We're not climbing.' Busy reclaiming his last treated arrows, Mykkael smoothed a marred fletching between competent fingers. 'To try such a feat in this warren of kerries would be irredeemable folly.' He confronted her squarely. 'Your Grace.' Reclad in the tattered cloth of his surcoat, with his harness in place, he should have worn the guise of the captain, invincible in his field-battered trappings. Instead, he appeared uncharacteristically irresolute. Despite this, his phrasing stayed swift and direct. 'The horses can't go. Princess, you must choose the fate that your absence bequeaths them.'

Here, Sessalie's royal demeanour outmatched him. King Isendon's daughter had been raised and tempered for the hour she must decree life or death for the weal of a sovereign nation. Crown blood to sworn captain, she responded. 'I would not have the animals suffer. Please grant them the mercy you gave to Fouzette. Only this time, I would stand at your side and hold their heads through their moment of crossing.'

'Princess.' Mykkael bowed to her. He fetched his strung bow, selected three arrows, and doctored the points with the dart venom kept in his scrip. Ready too quickly, he faced her with an expression like hammered iron. 'The act should be done near the mouth of the cavern, where kerries can clean up the carrion.'

Through her glass-edged onslaught of grief, Anja was nonetheless able to follow his cold line of reasoning. The ugly practicality Mykkael suggested would spare the remains from falling to usage by demons.

Her words emerged as a tortured whisper. 'Let's have this over with.' She managed the courage to lead the first step, and unfasten the horses' hitched lead ropes.

Even starving and worn, the three animals raised their heads, and whickered their acknowledgement of her presence. They followed her, trusting. Covette's lurching limp and Kasminna's mild lameness clopped a ragged refrain to Stormfront's almost unimpaired stride. The slight stiffness that lingered from last night's rough flight scarcely marred his panther-smooth grace.

Anja arrived at the site the captain selected. Her ravaged heart let the horses nibble the dry grass, while her numbed mind scarcely noted the laced bundles of wing leather left snugged in a niche to one side. Dead to curiosity, she had no attention to spare for Mykkael's nightlong hours of endeavour. She had no eyes to see past the proscribed lives of her beloved horses. Ripped to the verge of unquenchable tears, she bundled her chestnut mare's blazed head against the front of her jerkin. 'Covette first,' she said, all but strangled. 'The cracked hoof pains her worst. She is suffering.'

Mykkael stepped in close. His back turned to her shoulder, he ran a fierce hand down the chestnut mare's crest. His resolute body shielding, that she would not see his arrow as it struck, he bent the bow, held his breath and released.

No kindness could mask the snick as the point punched through living flesh. Covette jerked in startlement. The spider venom worked mercifully fast, masking the bright edge of her agony. The mare jerked again as the shaft lodged and settled. She swayed on her feet. Then with a mortal, shuddering spasm, her hindquarters crumpled. Mykkael steadied her shoulder as she went down. His hand, unerring, felt for the raced pulse in her neck. Head bent, he waited through the hung moment of passage. As the valiant chestnut's heart slowed to ragged rhythm and finally stopped, he straightened, still wordless, and signalled the bittermost end.

On her knees by the side of her stricken animal, Anja wept, unable to move.

Mykkael caught her up, eased her back to her feet. 'We must hurry,' he said, softly urgent. 'Although there's no blood, the kerries won't be far behind us.'

He positioned himself at Kasminna's shoulder, viced to patience as Anja responded. She let the inquisitive mare lip at her sleeve, not minding if she was bitten. Yet her indulgence passed unrequited. The next arrow bit deep. The proud sorrel grunted. Ever the rebel, she would not yield her life lightly. Her braced forelegs resisted the drag of the poison. Nose to the ground, her dark eye wide and puzzled, she trembled. A dribble of foam slid from her slackened muzzle. She folded at last. Anja crooned nonsense into her ear, while her noble frame quivered and sighed out her final, warm breath.

Wretchedly sobbing, Anja shoved off Mykkael's touch. She thrust to her feet unassisted, and stood before Stormfront on the visceral blast of her anger. What was her worth, as princess or as human, that these dumb, trusting beasts should give up their lives for a horror outside their natural understanding? They had served her, unstinting. Where came the right, to demand of their grace the ultimate, ruinous sacrifice?

'Shoot quickly,' gasped Anja, wrenched to ragged self-hate. 'For I can no longer endure this.'

Craven, she buried her face in black mane, her arms locked to her gelding's scabbed neck.

Time stretched, hung, spun out with the wind a soughing whisper through standing evergreen. 'Shoot,' Anja said, tortured. 'End this, I beg you.'

She heard, at her back, the slight rustle of cloth. She braced, heart torn beyond bearing. And still, nothing happened. Mykkael had lowered the drawn bow. 'I can't.'

His voice sounded seized, as though he fought tears. 'Mehigrannia show mercy, I can't.' As his hand failed him, he let go of the arrow that promised Stormfront a clean, painless death.

Anja spun on him, wild. 'Did you think I loved Covette or Kasminna any less?'

He shook his head, speechless. Her attack scarcely fazed him. Had a kerrie descended, it might have taken him uncontested in the shock of his deadlocked reaction.

'I can't finish this.' The admission ruffled his skin into gooseflesh, while the sound of his own utterance seemed that of a displaced stranger. He gestured, struck helpless. Before Anja's betrayed pallor, he forced out the raw speech to explain.

'This animal is not crippled or impaired by hurt. His spirit is that of a fighter, like mine.' Arms crossed at his chest, as though to bind up his faltering will, Mykkael stated, 'My instinct implores me to let this brave creature stay on his feet. His will is all fire. Can you not see? This horse should die fighting, as I would.'

Anja glared, shaking, her regard without quarter. 'You would risk my best gelding to demons?'

Mykkael stared at his hands, which were trembling. 'Even so. I can't kill him. Not without wounding a part of myself.'

Gripping the lead rope in white-knuckled fists, Anja straightened. With her disordered hair and her ragged, boy's jerkin, she was no less in that moment than Sessalie's ruling princess. 'What would you do if I granted you Stormfront's fate? Look at me, Captain!' Firm in her right to wield royal prerogative, she waited until he obeyed her. 'Answer my question!'

Mykkael matched her demand. If he shed no tears, his eyes showed an anguish that ripped through all pride and pretence. With his human soul stripped woundingly naked, he still answered without hesitation, 'I would rub his coat with cedar ash and entrust him to meet his own fate.'

For one second more, Anja weighed his resolve. Then she passed magisterial judgement. 'So be it.' She handed over the black gelding's lead rein. 'I make you the free gift of him. Stormfront is yours. Treat with him as your conscience dictates.'

Mykkael crossed his forearms and bowed to her. Then he caught up her icy, numbed fingers and closed them back over the gelding's headstall. 'Take this prince of horses and lead him inside. Dust him down with the ashes in my stead, your Grace. Cover him well. I require that help if I am to finish what must be done to deliver you from Hell's Chasm.'

As Anja froze, unable to act, or face the pitiful forms of the mares now sprawled in limp death on the rocks, Mykkael caught her rigid shoulders. He dealt her a bracing, light shake. 'Your Grace. Go. Now. I have ugly work to complete, and I implore you to leave. Trust my word when I say that you don't want to be here to watch what has to happen.' He gave her a firm push towards the cavern.

Forced to step forward, or fall on her face, Anja unlocked planted feet. Stormfront followed. His blazed head turned once, a puzzled inquiry to see why his companion mares were not following. His desolate whinny broke Anja's heart. She took charge, caught his silver-bossed cheek strap, and led him away. Through blinding tears, she did not look back. She did not see Mykkael draw his skinning knife and kneel down on the ledge beside the slain hulk of her sorrel.

The captain was forced to work swiftly, because of the blood. His hands knew their task well. The brutal experience of hard campaigns had well taught him how to gut a dead horse, and clean out its entrails and viscera. Befouled to the elbows, Mykkael dragged out his prepared cache of wing leather, then lined the emptied cavity of the mare's abdomen. He punched the holes between ribs that would bind up the carcass with improvised lacings of rope.

He well understood he had no time to spare. Kerries were bound to descend, any moment, to drag off the carrion. A fast rinse sluiced the gore from his fingers and wrists. Resolute, he moved on to fetch Anja.

Mykkael found her crying, her face buried in Stormfront's ash-streaked mane. 'Come away, Princess. Our moment can't wait.' He used his knife to slice through the lead rope. Once the horse was set free, he bundled the princess's grieving form to his side, then steered her ahead without compromise.

Her stumbling steps reached the mouth of the cavern. Anja smelled the blood first, then the stink of spilled viscera. Jerked back from his hold, she beheld her brutalized mare. The intelligence that framed her most difficult asset grasped the gist of his chosen intent.

Her face drained to white ice. Yet the impact of her shocked disbelief stunned her for only a moment.

'No! No!' She spun and slammed into him. 'No, Mykkael, I can't do this!' She pounded a fist against his unyielding chest, heedless of the flesh wound her fury might savage. 'Put me down without pain as you did for my horses! Don't risk me, oh, merciful *grace*, Mykkael! I beg you, don't even think to expose me as kerrie bait!'

The captain locked his arms. Beyond pity, he pinned her frantic struggles against him. Head bent, trained hands too quick for her thrashing fight, he caught her face in a vice grip and kissed her.

Startlement hurled Anja into wild confusion. In the unguarded moment while sense and reason stood diverted, he betrayed her young trust. The duplicitous finger he stroked at her neck pressed down and pinched critical bloodflow. Lips still pressed to hers, he allowed her no quarter; gave her no chance to fight the enormity of what was happening. While her eyelids fluttered and her pupils dilated, he held on, trained to sense the forerunning tremor as her limbs slackened. Then he released the pinched arteries. He tapped his clenched knuckles in a precise blow at her nape with just enough force to fell her.

Unconscious, Princess Anja of Sessalie sagged into the clasp of his arms.

Time fleeted. Above, Mykkael sensed shadows slicing the grey pall of daybreak. Interested kerries were already circling. Spurred by straight fear into *barqui'ino* reflex, he bent and tucked Anja into Kasminna's gutted abdomen. Nestled into his improvised lining of wing leather, he prayed to his goddess that Sessalie's princess would stay reasonably safe. Outside the dire mischance of a fall, no encounter with kerrie fire should harm her. When she wakened and struggled, no matter how dreadful her panic, *she must not tumble out*. Mykkael whispered a plea for her royal forgiveness, while his flying fingers threaded the readied ropes tight. In moments, he had the princess secured inside the laced ribs of the carcass.

Air whistled, above him. Mykkael sensed the kerrie's stooping descent. He snatched up the bow, then retrieved the arrow once readied for Stormfront's unfinished deliverance. His hurried touch rechecked the rope on the makeshift sling he had fashioned to bear his live weight. Scant seconds ahead of the predator that dived in to seize his laid bait, he leaped into the rock cleft and wormed into the sack he had sewn out of wing leather. In the last, frantic second, Mykkael strapped his waist with the line he had fixed as a safety.

Then the crux was upon him.

The kerrie touched down like the shadow of doom. Buffeted by its turbulence, Mykkael huddled with stopped breath. His skin streamed icy sweat within the suffocating cover of wing leather. If he had misjudged, if the creature he had lured was not starved for meat, it might balk and notice the odd set of his ropes, under the heaped entrails left as a decoy. It might tear up the carcass in a frenzy of rage, or refuse the doctored meal altogether.

Thought suspended, Mykkael awaited the drive of primal instinct that *should* prompt the kerrie to pluck up the carrion laced with the scent of fresh blood. Pinned by the agony of irreversible decision, he watched the predator fold knife-edged, bronze wings. Armoured talons clashed as the beast stalked and spun, snuffling the breeze with its tasselled tail lashing. Crested head raised, suspicious eye darting, it inspected the ledge at the verge of the basin, then scouted the skyline for rivals.

Finding none, it trumpeted and spat flame, and shook its leonine neck ruff. Then it bent its terrible, scissor-sharp beak, and with a horrific delicacy, snapped up the spilled viscera. The taste whetted its appetite. One stride, and it loomed overtop of the carcass. With a dreadful, finicky strength, its huge talons lifted, settled, bore down. Claws like curved hooks pierced through sorrel hide, and grasped the slabbed muscle at shoulder and croup.

The kerrie bellowed and unfolded broad wings. Its first, driving downbeat hammered the air and launched it to upward flight. It rose amid a gale of ripped wind, bearing the horse in its talons. The attached braid of rope slithered and whumped taut. The strung leather sack containing Mykkael was jerked headlong out of the crevice.

He was dragged, bounced, rolled in a bruising tumult across obstacles of brush and stone. The fear froze his heart, that his improvised rope might snag and snap under the strain. Yet the plaited line held him. The ground spun away in a dizzying rush. His stomach turned over in the wrenching lurch as the airborne predator lofted his slung body upwards. The kerrie clapped down spread wings, then soared over the precipice, angled to glide on the lifting breeze wafting off the high cliffs of the canyon.

Mykkael caught his raced breath. Far below, the diminished landscape reeled under him as the kerrie veered south towards its rookery. *Everything* now relied on his strength, his agility, and his trained skill to bear weapons in adversity. If his hand, or his wits, or his courage failed now, or if mischance led his tactic amiss, the princess could die screaming, torn apart by the ravenous maws of vile hatchlings, or far worse. Spirit from flesh, she could be flayed into madness, then hurled into bondage for all of eternity. She could still fall as a defenceless pawn to the sorcerer who spearheaded a demon's invasion.

Her hope of escape irretrievably committed, Mykkael braced his strung nerves. Suspended in the rocking, unstable sling, he freed his hands and readied his weapons.

The blackout faint soon released Anja's smothered consciousness. She awakened, strapped into tight confines, whirled dizzy and flooded with nausea. The pervasive smell of bloodied meat overwhelmed her turned senses. She choked down her panic, scarcely able to stir amid the wing leather binding her folded limbs to her chest. Aware with sick fury that she had been strapped into the carcass of her dead mare, she gagged for breath.

Mykkael had left her the barest slit opening to let in fresh air. Through the turbulent whistle of wind from outside, she felt the buffeting force of the kerrie's wing beats. Her effort to peer through the crack showed a reeling view of the canyon below, the shine of flat water coiled across a distanced tapestry of scrub landscape. Anja coughed. Her skin flushed to chill sweat. The surging lift as the predator turned towards the cliff face upended her unsettled gut.

Before she threw up, Anja shoved her face to the gap. She swallowed back the taste of churned bile. The slight change only served to unveil the horrid extent of her straits. She sighted the slender, whipped line of black rope, then the man, suspended above the abyss in a makeshift sling cut from wing leather.

Horror lanced through her. 'Earthly powers, *Mykkael*!'

The fear that followed all but unstrung her mind, for what she saw, the monster who bore Kasminna's carcass must inevitably notice as well. Kerries had rivals. They were wont to snatch game from the claws of their adversaries. Mykkael had taken an *unconscionable* risk to surmount the dead end at the precipice. Worse, how was he to survive the inevitable crash landing, when the predator that bore them swooped down and alighted upon its inhabited nest in the rookery?

Anja wrestled with drowning horror as her imagination ran rampant. Her desert-bred captain would be crushed, torn apart, or smashed wholesale. The sling gave him no shred of protection. Already, the kerrie swung into approach. The pinnacle with the rookery's snagged eyries unfolded into clear sight. The excited squawks of the hatchlings arose, shrill and thin on the morning air.

The kerrie banked into a circling descent. Spurred by mortal terror, Anja forced her constricted forearms upwards. She wedged her working fingers into the slit and pried at the roped flesh to widen her range of view.

'Mykkael,' she entreated.

Though her voice emerged muffled, he had to hear. The line suspending him was barely a spear shaft in length. If he did not respond through the thundering wind as the kerrie plunged earthwards, he was not oblivious to the predicament that rushed to confront him. Huddled into the sling, he had positioned his bow. His arrow was nocked to the string. As Anja watched, he flexed his shoulders and drew. He took careful aim, striving to compensate for the gyrating swing of his vantage. Anja's breath caught. The shot he undertook carried desperate, long odds. Chance must play an equal hand to all of his years of trained skill. No matter how seasoned, the warrior must realize that he danced the knife-edge between flagrant risk and sure death.

Mykkael trusted his own measure. He took steady

aim, but not without sign of stressed tension. Anja saw the sheen of sweat on his brow. She had never known a man's face could reflect such savagely intense concentration.

Undone by dread, her shaken will faltered. She could not bear to watch. Eyes shut, she huddled in blood-reeking darkness, and waited for the loosed arrow that would determine the course of her fate.

Mykkael sighted his target. The drag of the wind at his wrist, and the yawing drift of the sling fouled his sighted line. Again and again, he corrected his aim. He resisted impatience; rejected defeat. Against rising frustration, he steadied the drawn shaft, and damped the breeze humming through the taut string. Too much relied on caprice and blind chance: that Benj's rambling on the habits of kerries held truth, and their talons would reflexively bind to a kill in the same fashion as large birds of prey. That a low dose of dart venom would induce the predicted response in a half-avian monster: slow its reaction and mar the fine balance required for spatial co-ordination. If, in harsh fact, a nerve poison drawn from spiders would affect the dread creature at all.

The list of unknown variables could do nothing but spoil the nerve of the archer who measured his mark.

Mykkael turned his face, blotted streaming sweat on his shoulder. He induced the tight focus of the *barqui'ino* mind, gauged the drift of his arrow, then judged his moment and released.

The shaft launched, a close shot into the blood-rich muscle of the predator's pumping wing. The shaft smacked home, sunk down to the fletching. Mykkael braced just in time. The monster recoiled from the needle-sharp sting, and rolled into a lurching wingover.

Mykkael gripped the hurled sling with desperate hands to avoid being tossed out like flotsam. As the upended world whipped in violent recoil, he clung, while the enraged kerrie righted. It screamed with rage. Then its crested head swivelled downwards. The massive, honed beak snapped at the trailing rope in an effort to shed its bothersome human cargo. As the tug of the wind, and the considered placement of the sling's tether balked its reach, it convulsed the bulging sacs behind its jaw and hurled a crackling plume of live flame.

The warrior evaded incineration, just barely. Balled up behind shielding wing leather, he ducked his head. The sheltering membrane grew scaldingly hot. His gripped knuckles seared to raised blisters, and he retched from the smell of singed hair. Hurled this way and that as the kerrie wrenched to unload him, he coughed on the oily fumes thrown off by the monster's incendiary breath. Below him, the roosting ledges tilted and rushed ever closer. If the poison set by his arrow failed now, he would smash into a nest of blood-frenzied, ravenous hatchlings.

Eyes tearing on smoke, Mykkael battled despair. He would not escape injury on the hard rocks, or the spiked dead wood that shored up the eyrie. Long before he could cut himself free, he would find himself torn limb from limb by the predator's immature young.

Worse, Anja had roused. He had seen her fingers plying the crack he had left to allow her to breathe. Her inevitable state of trapped panic posed a cruelty beyond contemplation. Tossed and spun by the kerrie's buffeting flight, Mykkael understood he must take futile action. Before the creature hurled downwards to seize its firm stance on a roost, he must risk its fire, climb up the rope, and try to force an alternative landing.

Yet as he groped for the knife to cut himself free, the kerrie's flight suddenly wobbled. The huge wings above broke their rhythm, then faltered in mid-air. The creature shook its ruffed head, beak parted in panting distress.

The poison was working. Warned as a shudder played through the rope, Mykkael risked a glance outwards. He saw with jolting dread that the cliff wall encompassed his entire field of view. The roosts with their white streaks of guano were all but on top of him. With juggernaut speed, the kerrie plummeted in. It came on too recklessly fast to secure any chance of safe landing.

Survival, now, relied on its instinct for self-preservation. Either it would succumb to confusion and collide headlong with the rocks, or it would seize the more sensible choice and pour its failing strength into a glide. Rather than suffer a suicidal crash into the roost's narrow precipice, it *must* attempt the less critical descent, and alight on the open terrain of the vale.

Mykkael forced his breaths even. The sling that suspended him was spinning too wildly to allow a last-ditch intervention. The fate of Anja and Sessalie now rode on the winds of chance-met design.

Whirled breathless with strained nerves and fright, Anja saw the uprushing ground through the laced slit in the carcass. She had heard the release of Mykkael's bent bow; felt the thump of the arrow's impact. The wavering dip of the kerrie's impaired flight turned her stomach. Fighting down nausea, fist pressed to her mouth, she had squeezed her eyes closed to shut out the harsh moment of impact against the reared cliffs of the roost.

Then the kerrie effected a clumsy, banked turn. Wind whistled through its taut pinions as it struggled to brake. Too panicked to look where it tried to set down, Anja heard and felt the drag of the sling as it thrashed through a low stand of trees. Then the trailing rope snagged in green limbs and hooked fast. The monster jerked short in full flight and upended. It slammed downwards, struck earth on its back, and released its clutched grasp on the carcass. Anja felt herself spun upside down. Hurled end over end, until her tumbled senses lost all sense of direction, she whimpered and bit her tongue. Then the dead horse that enclosed her ploughed into the ground with a thump that knocked her breathless.

Shock momentarily darkened her eyesight. Her over-flexed wrist burned from a sprain. The slit in the mare's abdomen showed a close-up view of shag moss and round pebbles. A trickle of water, not seen, ran over more rocks close by. Lashed to terror by helplessness, Anja screamed Mykkael's name.

She could hear the kerrie thrashing nearby. Its spat fires flung drifts of black smoke on the breeze. A kicked rattle of rocks, and the clash of its beak evinced its ongoing struggles. But whether it battled a wounded man, or shuddered in the agonized throes of distress from an arrow, Anja could not determine. Coughing oily soot, half choked by nausea, she strained and shoved in crazed need to burst free of the imprisoning carcass.

'Mykkael!'

He did not come. She would not see rescue. The captain was surely smashed bloody and dead. Anja forced back hysterical sobs and flogged her mind for the means to escape. No solution presented itself. She had no blade or cutting tool on her, not even the skinning knife lost in the gorge. The lapse meant she had no option left but her teeth. She would have to try to gnaw through the wing-leather rope.

'Blinding merciful *powers*!' Her ugly predicament could get no worse. The vile, black sinew revolted her nose. It must inevitably upend her gut as she sampled its sickening taste.

Braced for the worst, whipped on by desperation, Anja shoved her tear-streaked face towards the slit.

Fingers reached through, brown and strong, and restrained her. 'Your Grace, hold fast! Let my knife cut you free.'

'Mykkael!' Undone by her savage flood of relief, Anja hammered at the mare's ribs with trapped fists. *'Damn you, Mykkael!* I told you I wouldn't endure this!'

His blade snipped the first rope, then parted the next with deft haste. 'Yes, I heard you.' The clipped words sounded strained. 'You can pummel me later.' A tug jerked the carcass. The laced ties slithered loose. Another few slashes cleared the bindings away. Mykkael grabbed her shoulder and yanked. Still bundled in the gory wrapping of wing leather, Anja should have landed, secure, clasped into the captain's locked arms.

His effort went wrong. He fumbled her weight, pinned her to his bent body and let her slither to earth with a grunt. Her fleeting, disconcerted view of his face showed his bronze flesh drained to grey pallor.

'What's wrong?' she demanded.

'Ribs,' Mykkael gasped. 'Cracked some, on landing.' He forced a breath through the jerk of seized chest muscles, and added, 'We have to run.'

Smoke streamed on the wind. A stand of nearby trees had caught fire. The stink of smouldering hair and charred feathers surely signalled the kerrie's demise.

Yet Mykkael drove her on to her feet, wildly urgent. 'The monster's not dead. My arrow won't work deep enough to dispatch it. Come on!'

Belatedly, Anja reasserted her balance. Only as her step met firm ground did her scattered awareness reorient. She realized with giddy exhilaration that she stood on the floor of the canyon. The silhouette of the cliff walls reared overhead, blurred by the haze of the burgeoning dawn.

Wonder unstrung her. 'We're over the precipice. Clear of Hell's Chasm and over the Great Divide.' The way to Tuinvardia lay open before her, with no insurmountable obstacle left to obstruct their passage into the western plains.

'Kerries!' Mykkael snapped. He clamped a blistered hand on her wrist and dealt her a frantic shove forward. 'This dropped carcass is no less potent a lure. We're still under threat of predation.'

Nor would the sorcerer's minions rest, now. Without knowing the Name of the demon that bound them, the captain had no means to estimate how far they must flee to outdistance its line of reach. Anja roused at last, her complacency shattered before Mykkael's driving concern. The last arrow was spent, and the bow had been smashed amid the tumult of landing. Now, Mykkael possessed little else but his sword and his wardings to secure their journey towards safety.

XXXVII. Trial

THE PRINCESS FOUGHT TO RECOVER HER BURNING, SHORT BREATH. WORMED INTO A NOOK UNDERNEATH A CLUSTER of tumbled boulders to escape hot pursuit by a kerrie, she still clutched the wing leather under her arm. Since Mykkael insisted on keeping the trophy, she had been required to carry the load to keep his hands free to bear weapons. The sprint to reach shelter left her beaten limp. Anja could do little else but draw gulps of air, and wait for her spinning senses to settle.

'Just a bit further,' Mykkael encouraged her from the darkness behind. As though he expected her flare of rebellion, he tapped on the heel of her shoe. 'Witch thought,' he gasped, his explanation clipped short by the hitch of his battered ribs. 'Don't balk now, Princess. There's a much better place to take respite.'

Anja spat out a clinging cobweb. Nursing her painfully swollen wrist, she shoved the wing leather ahead and edged forward. Something slimy slithered under her hand, most likely a startled salamander. Anja whispered a shaken curse. The encounter scarcely bolstered her confidence in a rock pile just as likely to harbour a nest of venomous snakes. If her hackled instincts clamoured for her to back up and escape, she had the captain's straits to consider. His laboured progress evinced his discomfort. Any prone crawl through close quarters would grant his injuries little surcease. Nor would the tight confines permit him the space to slip past her and take the lead.

The princess elbowed ahead, inch by inch. True to Mykkael's promise, within a few feet, the tortuous passage opened up into a void. The jumbled boulders let in dusty streamers of light, with just enough space to sit upright.

Anja cleared the narrows and made way for Mykkael. He emerged with strained difficulty and crouched on the earth floor, one hand braced to prop his torso erect, while his forearm stayed clutched to cracked ribs. Nonetheless, he kept vigilance, tracking the frustrated bellows of the predator their dash to the bolt hole had thwarted. The downed struggles of its poisoned fellow had swiftly attracted a horde to sate themselves on its weakness. An immature male too inexperienced to fight for a share of the carcass had circled the site, then chased the two humans to earth.

'I'm sorry, Princess,' Mykkael ground out at length. 'If we're not to stay penned, we'll have to use trap scent.' Outside, the new day had lifted the mist. Broken sun pierced a thin cloud cover. Lacking the need to mask any horses, enough potion remained to maze the predators' light-impaired senses and cover the start of their southward journey through the canyon.

Yet the void left behind by the wicket teams' absence did little to balance that life-saving asset.

'Stormfront,' broached Anja between panted gasps. 'You used him! Kept him living as a diversion.' Like that treacherous, surprise kiss: a cold-blooded act that made her ache to strike out at the self-contained warrior before her.

Mykkael measured her blaze of resentment. He chose to address her straightforward pique concerning the gelding foremost. 'Not entirely, no.' Though a simple confession would have served to vent the worst of her festering anger, he had too much respect to belittle her feelings by sheltering behind a falsehood. 'Sometimes I must honour my deeper instincts. For Stormfront, I could not loose the bow.'

'Why?' Anja pressured. 'Was his future foreseen by a witch thought? Did you have any sure reason to spare him?'

Mykkael glanced down, though not in regret. Gloom masked his subtle expression. Outside, the incessant rattle of rocks bespoke the kerrie's balked efforts to root out its fugitive prey. Since the gaps in the sheltering stone overhead allowed the beast wind of their scent, the captain grimaced and shifted his weight. He dug into his scrip and fetched out the dregs of Benj's repellent trap potion. After he loosened the cap with his teeth, he answered the question left dangling. 'I had no good reason then, and no empty promise to leave with you now. Your Grace, I won't justify my broken nerve. I could not kill the horse. He became your diversion. Understand this much, and clearly. I have sworn a crown oath. Beware of your gifts, Princess. For I will wring use out of every advantage to ensure your continued survival.'

Anja stiffened to shout at him.

He cut her off, merciless. 'Admittedly, you are now still alive to revile my choice of tactics.'

'Alive!' Unable to contain her explosive fury, Anja ground her fists against her tucked knees. 'Oh yes, we survived an unconscionable risk! How close did I come to being shredded by hatchlings? No, don't answer, Mykkael! That horror did not happen by the grace of sheer luck! How *dared* you defy my free will on this matter? Tell me, Captain!' Green eyes narrowed, the princess looked wild enough to spit in contempt at his feet. 'What would you have done if your overweening folly had ended in failure?'

He maintained his fixated gaze on the ground. Yet the fingers supporting his crouch had turned rigid, and his carriage was not relaxed.

'Answer me, Captain!' Anja's anger swelled in her, wounded hurt and emotional recoil built to an ungovernable rage. 'Did you have a contingency plan for defeat? Or would you in your idiot glory of male pride have stood by as I perished, screaming?'

'In my scrip,' Mykkael said, 'I still carry one blow dart.'

Shock reeled her off balance. Anja sucked in a ragged, stunned breath. 'Merciful powers!' Yet even that stark admission held no power to deflect her fury. 'You let down Stormfront,' she snapped, her ardour still savaged by his past night's adherence to duty. 'Do you love me enough to have lost your nerve, if my straits had demanded a mercy stroke?'

He did look up, then, his regard sparked to searing self-honesty. 'Princess, I don't know. I can't answer that question.'

'You betrayed me!' accused Anja.

Though Mykkael knew very well she condemned his brazen handling of her affections, his nature when stubborn was adamant steel. She had backed him as far to the wall as he was prepared to allow her. *He would not apologize.* Neither would he grant her the one glimpse she craved, of clear insight into his heart. Instead, he adhered with unwavering form to the unanswered fate of the horse. 'You told me that gelding doesn't like snakes. Princess, I entreat you to look there for hope.'

To make certain the contentious subject stayed closed, he upended the opened phial at speed and sprinkled her hair and her clothes.

Once the kerrie grew bored of rooting up stones, princess and captain abandoned the bolt hole and turned downstream towards the emperor's realm of Tuinvardia. They followed the riverbed, where the gravel-strewn verge offered the easiest footing. Mykkael moved badly, despite the tight strapping improvised to bind up his cracked ribs. The rough ground overtaxed his scarred knee, and the constant need to keep vigilant guard pitched his wary senses to snapping. In the canyon's flat lowlands, with roost sites on both sides, the predation of kerries posed a constant threat.

Mykkael's limp could do nothing but steadily worsen. Lines of pain and fatigue etched his features. He pressed onwards, undaunted. As morning wore on, he expended his waning resource without reservation or complaint. Anja watched him wrestle the looming certainty that the seizing cramps in his leg must eventually come to impair him. Unable to walk, unfit to wield weapons, his oath to defend King Isendon's daughter would soon be an empty promise.

After a trying passage across a dry wash, Anja could no longer bear to watch his determined, halting step. 'We should rest,' she entreated.

Mykkael shook his head, no. He answered, his speech gritted with the sawing discomfort of who knew how many other contusions left by his jounced fall through the treetops. 'Rain's coming. We dare not pause.'

The low clouds overhead were steadily gathering, piled up by moist wind from the south. The drizzle that threatened to blow in by nightfall was bound to rinse off the trap scent. Their last ploy to deter the questing feints of the canyon's infestation of kerries was not going to withstand a soaking. Yet more than weather hackled Mykkael's deep instincts. As his dark skin ruffled up into gooseflesh, he moved with one hand gripped to his sword hilt.

Whether he suffered from witch thoughts or the arcane prompt of his wardings, the grim depth of his silence spoke volumes. Anja was too unutterably worn to make even half-hearted inquiry. Her best effort required her to keep moving, and avoid pointless conversation.

Even so focused, even so brave, her leaden despair overwhelmed her.

The bleak landscape offered no sign of habitation or safe harbour. Its barren expanse of open floodplain and brush extended to the horizon, clumped with hillocks whose crowns of scrub trees showed the patched scars of fire, where kerries had engaged in their savage rites of spring courtship. No game moved in the coverts. Even Mykkael was moved to make comment, that the mud at the river's edge bore no tracks left by deer, mice or hare. Hungry and silent, he plodded ahead, well accustomed by war to the stresses of privation.

Anja had no such hard experience to buoy her. Never so sore and tired in her young life, she strove to bear up. Her step dragged, regardless. As noon brought a sky dimmed under clouds, with more ominous banks piling up to the south, she fell back upon brute determination. The sloppy fit of her shoes chafed her feet, until both of her heels rubbed to blisters.

For all that, her limp was less pronounced than Mykkael's. At last, beyond hope, Anja reached the point where further effort seemed meaningless. She realized the captain's bad leg had locked. He now moved hunched over, often using his hands to raise his scarred knee over even the most trivial obstacles. Descending a mild slope, he almost fell down as his quivering muscles betrayed him. Undone by pity, the princess stopped her raw outcry behind a closed fist.

Such punishment could not be allowed to continue. Anja reviewed her dearth of wise options. The kerries that stalked them were circling nearer. The bold ones raked past, claws ripping the wind to a whistle of air, while the breeze off their wingtips flattened the gorse with the violence of their passage. Inevitably, one of the large males dipped close and hurled an eruption of flame in their path.

Mykkael recoiled to hair-trigger wariness. When the next beast stooped over them and spat its volatile fuel above their heads, he shouted, 'Anja, get down!'

His war-sharpened response already acted to compensate. He reached out, shoved the princess flat on bare stone. His crouched pose shielded her body, with the salvaged wing leather bundled over his sheltering shoulders.

The kerrie passed over them, raining fire. The barren outcrop they traversed offered no prospect of safety. As the incendiary vapour burned away to an oily pall of black smoke, Mykkael dragged Anja back to her feet.

'Run,' he gritted.

They managed no more than a half dozen paces. When the second pass came, Mykkael took a longer time, rising. The effort taxed him to grunting distress. Still, he straightened, erect. Sweeping the sky for the next sign of threat, he blotted the beaded sweat from his brow, lips clamped with determined ferocity. Then he extended his hand and assisted Anja up off her knees.

'We need a bolt hole,' she scolded, point blank.

When he tugged the straps of his harness to rights, and flatly refused her suggestion, Anja tried using her evident weariness to make him back down and seek respite.

He would not hear reason. His dark, shadowed eyes remained fixed upon her, all the spontaneous grace of his humour erased by unyielding demand. 'No, Princess.'

Anja whirled aside, hands pressed to her face to mask the moisture flooding her lids. Unlike him, she would *not* grasp at unfair advantage. Royal pride and straight character would not let her turn her woman's tears against him as a weapon.

The quiver that rocked her braced shoulders betrayed even that sorry intent. Mykkael's arms closed around her, his offered comfort kept tenderly light to avoid jostling his damaged ribs. 'Princess. Bear up. No matter how bad things appear at this pass, I promise you, I have endured worse.'

Anja choked back a sob of despair. 'Merciful powers, Mykkael! By now, you have to be lying.'

Her head pressed against the warm hollow of his throat, she felt him swallow. His answer brushed through her fouled, tangled hair. 'Your Grace, how I wish that I was.'

He could never discount the intent of her enemies. No choice was possible, except to sustain. They had been marked as the prey of a sorcerer, a creature slaved to the vile will of a demon, whose insatiable craving for pain and conquest was never going to abate.

Anja sniffed. She rubbed her damp cheeks, and assailed him with logic. 'Apparitions are no longer dogging our trail. Don't you think we've outlasted this sorcerer's reach?'

'I can't promise that we have.' Mykkael released his tenuous clasp. Uneasy habit restored his hand to his sword hilt. Eyes turned aloft, still tracking the shuttling weave of the kerries as they dived at close rivals and scrapped in querulous spats of flame overhead, he shared his stark premise. 'Our ploy at the canyon has most likely broken the enemy's hold on our trail. At twilight, when the barrier between this world and the unseen becomes thinnest, the sorcerer will spin lines of seeking. I won't know until then if we have gained enough distance to escape a short curse laid by the creature's bound minions.'

How could he divulge the unbearable truth? The horror of Kailen's fate had already rendered the sister a game piece. Kin ties to her brother laid the invading enemy open to an unsettling vulnerability. Without learned protection, Anja would now be stalked by every other warring demon who contended for supremacy in the nether realms.

No stubborn pride, no act of courage, and nothing akin to sane reason drove Mykkael. Anja regarded the stripped planes of his face, and there glimpsed the abject terror that would pressure him past human limits.

'Some fates,' he said faintly, 'are too ugly to contemplate. I beg you, your Grace. Find the strength you don't have. For both of our sakes, carry onwards.'

Anja reforged her shattered equilibrium and straightened. She took another step, then another. At each subsequent stride, she resisted the impulse to block her ears. She tried not to hear Mykkael's scraping limp as he marshalled his spent resource and held his place, guarding her back.

The kerries circled above them, relentless. Kept staunch by no less than her simmering anger, Anja felt she should welcome the creatures' murderous appetite. At least as a bone in the teeth of a predator, she would win a petty victory. The sorcerer's deathless desire to trap her would suffer a backhanded setback.

Wings rushed overhead. Another hackled male banked and dived in aggressive pursuit. As it ripped overhead, its beak opened to lash them with fire, Mykkael snatched for the wing leather draped from his shoulder.

Just then, an earth-shaking bellow sounded above the gouged seam of the river course. The huge male sheared off. Its violent manoeuvre flattened the reedbeds and rattled the dry brush on the bank, then winnowed the thickets on the far shore in the blast of its turbulent wake. The captain stopped, listening, as with one mind, the opportunistic kerries that trailed them peeled away like a flock of scared pigeons.

'What is it?' Anja asked, hating the thin, lost sound of her voice.

Mykkael shook his head. 'I don't know.' He drew his sword. Plunged by hazed nerves to *barqui'ino* awareness, he caught her wrist and pressed his gimping stride forward.

Anja easily kept pace with his dragging leg. Scrambling, together, they surmounted the next hillock. Huddled amid the rocks at the crest, the tatter of wing leather pulled over them, they were suddenly combed by a cracking wind as a low-flying kerrie streaked over them. The creature was a massive, adult female, identified by her chevron-marked tail vanes, and by the lack of furred crest at her neck. Her trumpeting cries sounded over the vale. With enraged, darting rushes, she looped to and fro, chasing the pack of scavenging kerries and making them scatter.

'She's guarding young,' Anja breathed to Mykkael, too frightened to move or speak loudly. 'Most likely a fledgling.

The mothers defend them as they learn to fly, and guard their first efforts to hunt.'

But Mykkael was not watching the ground, or the brush. His incredulous gaze stayed fixed skywards.

'Do you see?' He pointed towards the rampaging female.

Anja followed his gesture, then picked up the faint equine whinny of distress. The predator held Stormfront clenched in her talons, an unmarked prize borne in for her offspring to hunt on the open ground by the riverbed.

'Stormfront!' Hands pressed to her lips, Anja shuddered. Before her wide eyes, the monstrous creature descended into a thunderous hover, then opened the terrible trap of her claws and released the black horse to run free.

'Merciful grace! Mykkael, do something.' Beneath their exposed vantage, a sinuous form flapped pin-feathered wings and hurled itself with raucous cries from the thickets. Stormfront sighted the movement, bucked once, and bolted. Fast as he sprinted, tail curled in terror over his hindquarters, the young kerrie's bumbling charge outmatched him.

'Mykkael!' implored Anja. 'Act, I beg you. The poor gelding's going to be shredded alive.'

'I can't take him down for you,' the captain said, desolate. 'Not with safety. We don't have the bow.'

'Then get ready with your poison and dart!' Whipped on by her unsated, venomous anger, Anja hurled back the loose cover of wing leather.

Mykkael moved to deter her. Slowed by the disastrous cramp of his ribs, this time, he could not react soon enough. His lightning snatch failed to pull her back down, or forestall her piercing shout.

'Stormfront! To me! Hai, Stormfront!'

The black gelding heard her. Obedient to his training, he swerved. Straight as a shot arrow, he raced down the vale, ears flat and tangled tail streaming. The fledgling came also. Naked head raised, beak parted for murder, it changed course with harrowing speed, intent on its fleeing prey. No obstacle thwarted its bloodthirsty rush. Large as a bull and bent upon slaughter, it must seize its brought meal, or go hungry. If its short, gliding efforts with immature wings could not yet sustain airborne flight, its co-ordination on level ground was formidably lethal. It had fire sacs as well, and blazing green eyes, fixed on the horse in the glittering frenzy of bloodlust.

Mykkael snapped out a curse in guttural consonants. 'Stay here! Lie low in the rocks, and don't move.' He pressed his drawn steel into the princess's startled grasp. Then he muttered a prayer in straight language begging for Mehigrannia's mercy, and snatched up the torn scrap of wing leather.

Too late, Anja measured the scope of her folly. *The captain had warned that the guarding protections he carried would not reach past fifteen paces.* If the shaman's mark sung into his blade was not sufficient to guard her, he could do nothing to spare her, should the sorcerer strike in his absence. Nor could Mykkael avoid intervention. Not with the panicked horse pounding in, luring the fledged kerrie and the certain wrath of its protective mother down on them.

The warrior had no time to pick his way off the outcrop. His scarred knee must disastrously slow him. With the wing leather bundled around his frail form, he jumped, tucked and rolled down the slope of loose scree. He fetched up at the bottom, sprawled in the path of the galloping horse, and the bounding rush of the predator.

The impact slammed the wind from his chest. Muscle cramps triggered by his jarred ribs curled his form in a quivering knot. Hands pressed flat to earth, he fought to arise. Even from Anja's vantage, above, his rigid strain was apparent as he battled through pain to command his recalcitrant body. On his feet, staggering, left arm pressed to his side, he mantled his shoulders in wing leather. He knotted the tattered hide under his throat, then flung up his head in a dogged, lamed effort to set his balance in readiness.

His toll of injuries would not let him straighten. Nonetheless, he called Stormfront to him.

Steel flashed in both fists. He had drawn his knives: the curved dagger Anja had seen him use to skin game, and another one, smaller and thinner, yanked from a concealed sheath that must have been masked inside the laced seam of his belt. The cutting edge of its blade did not shine. The glint of the metal seemed oddly dulled, as though coated over with varnish.

Anja's heart all but stopped as Stormfront bore in. She pulled in her shallow, raced breaths through an onslaught of choking fear. Pressed to chill rocks, she watched Mykkael's stand, wrenched by the punishing cost of her idiocy, and on fire with hope that his left-hand weapon might have been treated with poison.

Barqui'ino-*trained, surely he stood a chance.*

Yet the odds appeared insurmountable, as his monstrous adversary surged in pursuit of the haplessly tiring horse. While Stormfront approached the base of the rise, Mykkael dug in his toes. Anja had observed the same gesture before, as he made sure of his footing. Aware the slight motion foreran his first move, she tracked his poised figure, unblinking.

Mykkael waited until the inbound gelding was almost upon him, then shouted the familiar command string. 'Stormfront, whoa! Hold hard! Stormfront.'

Ruled by drilled habit, the black dropped his hind-quarters into a braking slide. Gravel scattered under his scrabbling hooves. Through the stopped second as his pounding run slackened, the fledgling kerrie launched into a soaring spring.

The instant its talons left the ground, Mykkael threw out his arms, and hazed the oncoming horse off.

Stormfront shied. Already settled on to his hocks, he

reacted on reflex and spun hard to the right. The young kerrie yawed its wings, head turned and scrawny neck extended in an awkward effort to compensate. Mykkael followed through with a flicked throw of his knife. The blade flew at short range, its hurled impact augmented by the speed of the predator's charge. Keen steel impaled the fledgling's exposed fire sac, then drove on through into its throat.

Volatile fluid spewed on to the ground, gouting flame; and also, seeped into the knife cut sliced between the cartilage bands of the monster's windpipe. The influx dribbled a caustic stream over sensitive internal tissues. The kerrie gurgled a bellow of surprised pain. Its tumbled crashlanding ploughed over Mykkael, who had dropped into a protective crouch to avoid the uncontrolled slash of its talons.

As the warrior was milled under, the fledgling squalled murder. It flapped and thrashed in wild agony. Its distressed cries raised deafening screams from above, as its mother folded her wings and hurled down in vengeance-bent fury.

The Princess of Sessalie blinked streaming eyes. Whipped by gusting wind, she sighted the man, his surcoat entangled in the blind clench of a talon. Locked in a struggle to spare his frail life, he fought to drive himself into precarious shelter underneath the stricken fledgling.

'You once slew a roc,' she whispered entreaty. 'You told me yourself that you hazed off a dragon to salvage a critical supply train.' Surely the desperate tactics used then could assist with this lethal predicament.

Anja swallowed, her mouth dry as dust. Against hope, she pleaded, 'Don't let my stupid, childish pique become the mistake that will kill you.' The profligate waste of a gifted man's valour tore her wide open and shamed her. She had truly learned *nothing* from Taskin's sage counsel concerning the unjust punishment that might befall through her arrogance as a royal. 'Mykkael,' Anja gasped, 'whatever happens, survive this!'

Then the dread shadow fell. The female kerrie alighted to defend her wounded young. Her evil head snaked, and the gaped beak slashed down in a harrowing strike. She darted and stabbed, missed and missed yet again. Her vision was repeatedly obscured by the battering wings of her offspring. Mykkael still fought, unscathed. Caught like a burr beneath the fledgling's scaled belly, he offered too small a target.

The balked mother shrieked her rage and frustration. A sidewise swipe of her head bowled her squalling youngster over. As the flailing fledgling toppled, topsy-turvy, the warrior was left exposed. He clung, one fist clenched to the taloned leg's pin feathers, and the other one glued to the haft of his smaller blade.

The female kerrie raised hooked claws. Her lightning-fast snatch plucked him away. As her talon closed over him, Mykkael jabbed in the knife. Her mailed clasp recoiled. Instinct ruled her reflexive reaction. Her attempt to stamp down, or apply crushing pressure, would just serve to drive his steel deeper.

Anja damped back her screams, knuckles jammed to shut teeth. She dared make no sound. Whatever befell now, she must not add to her tragic mistake: any shrill outcry might draw in another inquisitive predator. Stormfront had fetched to a halt to one side. His thin flanks heaved and his distended nostrils showed linings of red. Foam spattered from his dripping muzzle. He was utterly spent; momentarily safe, as long as he did not move.

Saved, as her human protector was not, trapped in closed battle with an enraged, adult kerrie. Where another man in his straits would have seized on the monster's flinching hesitation and snatched the opening to batter his way free, Mykkael wrapped his arm around the beast's armoured leg. Undaunted, he bore in, and hacked with the knife. His effort sawed past tendons like cables, then thrust razor steel into the tissue between. Anja shared his grim concentration. Bound by willed purpose, he sought the pulse of the deep artery.

The female kerrie howled her pain. Thrashing her wings in a battering storm, she raised her maimed talon and clashed her beak to pluck out, or burn, the verminous creature whose stinging persistence lit her nerves to searing, bright agony.

Mykkael must have sensed her oncoming strike. He let go and rolled clear, just as her flame-spewing jaws snapped and bit in vain effort to free his jammed knife blade.

A wing slammed the ground, whipped up flying stones that near crushed him. The captain wrenched himself sideways. In the maelstrom of torn brush and loosed fire and smoke, he was a scrap of tossed flotsam, wrapped in a bloodied surcoat. The kerrie's wing battered his tucked frame again. The whoosh of the pinion tips slapped down and tumbled him head over heels towards the rise of the hillock.

Through her stifled terror, Anja realized the monster was dying. Whatever fell poison Mykkael used on his blade, its effects unstrung the predator's co-ordination. Yet the shuddering tempest of the female's death throes only redoubled their peril. Rival kerries would soon be descending to prey on her weakness and feed.

Her fledgling had also shuddered into collapse, internally burned by its volatile secretion until it succumbed to suffocation. Its ejected faeces flecked the ground in rank spatters as it twitched and rolled in extremity. Anja shoved upright on quivering knees, alive to the imperative danger. She snatched up Mykkael's sword and scrambled downslope, knowing she had scarcely minutes to roust up her wounded protector and find a secure cranny for shelter. The reek of fresh carnage dispersed on the breeze, added to the enticing scent of a lathered horse run to exhaustion. The ravenous kerries prowling the cliffs by the rookeries would quickly catch wind and take notice. They would wheel and converge, fighting each other with fire and beak and savage claw, crazed beyond caution with bloodlust.

Anja sprinted downslope. Sliding through gravel, uncaring whether her rush threw her down in a headlong tumble, she dropped to her knees beside the tattered bundle of cloth and scraped limbs fetched sprawling amid the low brush. 'Mykkael!'

He was up on one elbow, and struggling to arise. Blood seeped through the front of his surcoat. The small, spreading stain was low on his belly, result of a puncture or claw cut. The wound's position was desperately grim, Anja knew at first glance.

Tears flushed her lids. She blinked them back, furious. 'Mykkael, bright powers forbid!'

Jaw clenched with agony, he raised his eyes to her face, the set to his drawn features obdurate. 'Catch Stormfront,' he grated. 'I have trap scent still left. The flask's in my scrip. Get it out. Use what's left. Anja, hurry.'

As she drew back, unwilling to risk her fumbling hands too near the hurt on his abdomen, he barked with impatience. 'Princess, do it!' His eyes pleaded. 'I've been mauled, but there's still the chance the result won't be fatal.'

When her choked gasp denied this, Mykkael muttered an incoherent phrase concerning Sanouk dragons, and Jussoud's gift of a sash.

'Captain, don't speak.' Anja bent at his side, sought with shaking hands to carry out his bidding. As her seeking fingers unfastened his scrip and sorted the disparate contents, she glimpsed a scarlet-stained edge of bright silk beneath the rent in his surcoat. The tissue-thin cloth had been driven deep into the puncture.

'Seasoned soldiers wear silk to draw embedded arrow points,' Mykkael informed her with desperate clarity.

This time, Anja grasped his obtuse meaning. If the kerrie's talon had not pierced the fabric, the gash would be clean. He might not succumb to the wasting death from wound fever induced by the tainted claws of a predator.

'We can't know if we don't survive.' Mykkael hazed her on, adamant. 'Go. Call back Stormfront. Work quickly.'

Anja searched out the phial. She squeezed his clenched hand and left him the sword, aware he would need the blade as a prop to assist his pained effort to stand.

Stormfront came at first call. He was wretchedly limping. Anja checked his bad leg, and wept to discover that he had injured a tendon. If he walked far now, the tear could grow worse, until at last, the exertion crippled him. She doused him with trap scent, then tore off her belt, binding his hot fetlock and foreleg in leather to support the damaged tissue.

Mykkael's halting step arrived at her shoulder as she buckled the makeshift wrap tight. Anja shot straight, appalled to discover he could move at all with the gravity of his injuries. He had retrieved his curved knife. The dropped scrap of wing leather trailed from his shoulder, and his streaming face looked like death.

'Get on,' snapped Anja. 'I'll brace your knee as you mount.'

'Stormfront's lame,' Mykkael whispered. 'To ride would be cruelty.' The stark alternative haunted, that the merciful choice would be to use a dart, and put an end to the brave gelding's suffering.

'No!' Anja rubbed her wet chin with the back of her sleeve, while her eyes brimmed and spilled all over again. 'No, Mykkael! Please. Stormfront will bear you. Lacking your instincts, he would already be dead. He's your horse. Let him help your survival!'

When he drew back, either dizzy with shock, or suspended in agonized hesitation, she seized the front of his surcoat. 'Mykkael, I beg you, *get on*! If you don't stay alive, I won't find the will to keep breathing!'

XXXVIII. Circle

IF NOT FOR THE DIVERSION OF TWO DYING KERRIES, ANJA COULD NOT HAVE BORNE MYKKAEL AWAY ON THE BACK OF the exhausted, lamed gelding. The best Stormfront could manage was a ragged walk. The slow pace felt like torture, with the dregs of the trap scent scarcely sufficient to mask the redolent sweat that steamed from his coat.

Anja wended her wary way through the scrub, stumbling over roots and small stones. One step to the next, she sensed each of Mykkael's rasped breaths like a knife blade scraping her nerves. He rode with his elbows clamped to his sides, wrists braced against the horse's high crest, and his hands knotted into black mane.

'I've killed you,' said Anja.

His laboured whisper came back reproachful. 'You haven't. Princess, I'm not close to dead.'

Yet the inexorable, spreading stain on his surcoat belied the assurance that he could stay upright much longer.

Ruled by his oath, Mykkael addressed the stark points of survival forthwith. 'We have to find some sort of shelter, your Grace. The scent of my blood could draw kerries. Turn Stormfront out of the riverbed.'

Anja stared at his sweating face, horrified. 'Go *towards* the cliffs? Mykkael, that's madness!' How could they seek refuge beneath the high ledges infested with active rookeries?

Yet the captain insisted. 'We have to try. This time, a rock pile is not going to serve.' The river bank was too flat and barren for the cave they required to spare Stormfront. There, Mykkael at last bowed to sound sense. He could no longer walk. Although sadly lamed, the black horse provided his sole chance to stay upright and moving.

Anja dared not indulge in disheartened fear or trepidation. She measured the captain's insecure seat, afraid as he swayed, and the impaired reaction of his swordsman's balance barely snatched him short of a fall. Such misfortune could end only in disaster. If he lost consciousness and tumbled off Stormfront, the princess realized she lacked the strength to drag his limp bulk back astride.

Worse yet, his seasoned gaze touched upon her and read every looming fear. His expression reflected wretched distress as he gathered himself for another strained effort to speak.

Anja cut him short. 'Don't say you've seen worse, Mykkael!'

The forced ghost of his former smile twisted one corner of his mouth. 'This is almost as bad as it gets.' He shifted cramped fingers, shut his eyes, then compelled himself to complete a sweep of their immediate surroundings. Ahead, the river meandered between vertical stacks of stone, the weathered flanks of the lower slopes mottled dun with tattered stands of scrub woodland and spiny vegetation. 'Turn east, just a bit. Yes, I ask, trust my instinct. Anja, please. Do not stop this horse! *For your life's sake you have to listen.*'

Scoured by the cut of the wind, the princess did as he bade her. The necessity drove her to flinching remorse. Each of Stormfront's jolting, hitched strides dealt the warrior an unmerciful jostling. He was streaming cold sweat. Internal bleeding and the relentless loss of fluid would be causing his reeling dizziness.

'You need to drink water,' the princess informed him.

Well aware the suggestion framed an imperative, Mykkael said, 'Soon. Listen first.'

The decision chilled Anja. She doused her fierce protest. Too experienced not to recognize the limited reach of his resources, the captain must know and *would* gauge to the fine, bitter edge, just how long he could trust himself to stay aware. Since obedience was the only relief in her power to grant him, Anja faced firmly ahead and placed one aching foot after the next. As Mykkael mustered the strength to instruct her, she held stalwart, unable to bear the desperate sight of his suffering.

'Anja. Record what I say into memory. The warding sung into my sword is Sanouk, from the eastern steppelands. The connection will have meaning to the viziers in Tuinvardia.' At her sharply turned head, he nodded encouragement. 'You'll get there. Just listen. Your brother's remains must stay guarded at all costs. Perincar's pattern tattooed at my nape will still function, whether I'm living or dead. The older lines done by Eishwin will not. They are tied into my ancestral heritage, and they must fade if my spirit should leave the flesh.'

Anja's grief was too savage. 'Mykkael! No. I won't drag your dead carcass!'

His dark eyebrows arched. In a tortured effort at humour he said, 'I rather thought you should flay off the skin. I salvaged my knife for the purpose.' When her choked silence threatened to devolve into dispirited misery, he fell back upon searing honesty. 'You can count on my will to stay living, your Grace. Yet I must consider my duty foremost. No matter how dedicated, the best warrior born can still fail.'

'Then stop talking!' snapped Anja. 'I don't have your knowledge of sorcerers and war. Alive, you can help me. Dead, you're no use. Mykkael.' She paused to contain her relentless anxiety. 'Sessalie's people, and I, still depend on you. Just stay alive. If you insist I must find a cave under the rocks of a kerrie roost, you'll hear my request, and not nag me with cruel distractions.'

'Your Grace.' His whisper emerged too complacent.

Her anxious glance found him slumped against Stormfront's neck, his eyes wide open and fixed, as though his sight faded with faintness. 'I forgive you,' he added. 'Stormfront's life was well worth the risk taken with mine.'

Which words woke her fury. 'You will not leave me, Mykkael. Nor will you shame the gift of this fine horse, whose courage will bear you for as long as it takes. Together, we will see you through to Tuinvardia and into the care of a healer.'

'Your Grace,' the captain said faintly. 'On reaching safety under the charge of my sword, you already carry my oath.'

Anja walked. Stormfront limped alongside her. Mykkael's sawing breaths came and went. The promise of help seemed a distant, vain dream, with the horizon rolling away into featureless haze. No sign of habitation broke the desolate terrain. Overhead, the scud of grey cloud was still massing. The river rippled with ominous whitecaps, snapped up by a rising breeze. Anja folded her arms, huddled into her filthy jerkin. She matched her step to Stormfront's plodding stride, while the air silvered under the first veils of drizzle, and the rocks glistened pewter with moisture. Against the pall of the oncoming storm, the cliffs rose like dull iron, with the wheeling kerries over the rookeries reduced to knifing, swift shadows.

The princess paused only once, to drape Mykkael's slack form with the salvaged tatter of wing leather. His skin was damp and too warm to her touch. Hoping the gravid sensation of heat was provoked by her own chilled hands, Anja laid her palm on his forehead. There she encountered the scalding flush that presaged the onset of wound fever. Whether the captain had succumbed from the initial sword puncture, or yesterday's neglected gashes, or the disastrous bout with the kerries, did not matter. Mykkael was sinking, with no skilled hand within reach to offer him comfort or succour.

Anja could do *nothing else* but keep moving. The stricken crown officer left in her care seemed the last life in the world, while her past experience as Princess of Sessalie seemed a dream whose importance had vanished. What shaped the meaning of a man, or a people, or a horse, if the devouring hunger of a sorcerer's lines could destroy joy and laughter, and rob the last hour of hope?

No answer arose. Only sere desolation. Anja stroked Stormfront's sodden forelock. She made no more empty promises concerning mashed grain and comforts. As the weeping, cold rain soaked into her clothes, and dripped from the bedraggled ends of her hair, the trap scent must slowly rinse off. Scavenging kerries would track their damp warmth. Hunting and hungry, they would soon descend, and the end would be swift and terrible. Anja slogged ahead anyway. She gimped on sore feet, while the afternoon started to fail, and her borrowed shoes stretched from the puddles. Slipping, trudging, pummelled numb by fatigue, she moved with her arm braced on Stormfront's shoulder. She kept time to the draw of Mykkael's tortured breath, and the horse's irregular hoofbeats.

'No!' The captain's sharp word held ringing distress. 'No, Orannia, don't do this.'

Anja lifted her drooping head, grabbed the brown fist clenched like iron in Stormfront's soaked mane. 'Mykkael, what's wrong?'

'If she dies,' he gasped, breathless, 'the sorcerer's demon will claim her!'

Thrust past the first, ugly start of her fear, Anja realized he was raving. 'Mykkael,' she entreated, 'Mykkael, I'm not harmed. The wards in your sword hilt are silent.'

But the voice he heard in delirium was not hers. He did not respond to assurance. Words poured from him in an anguished torrent, fuelled by heartsick memory. 'As her family, I beg you, assist me! Do not allow her to take her own life and become for ever consumed. Please, no! I don't care how she cries, or what torment she suffers in madness. You must stand strong, as I have. Guard her, each minute. Don't give her life over to Rathtet without fighting.'

Anja stroked his wracked face, and laid her cheek on his forearm. 'Hush, Mykkael.' Her woman's touch seemed to calm him. 'Whatever princess you speak for, she's safe.'

He subsided. The last word he whispered held shattering sorrow, and a clarity cruel as glass. 'Orannia.'

Anja could do no more than press onwards, coaxing Stormfront's choppy stride towards the encroaching cliffs. Daylight was fast fading, sped on by the gloom of the storm. As sunset approached, no clinging remnant of trap scent would deter the kerries' night-hunting acuity.

Under the rock face, the streaming water splashed into shallow catch basins. The sloped verges were surrounded with lush groves of trees, and tangles of late-blooming wildflowers. Their sodden colour did little to restore Anja's courage. She had gone beyond tired. Wending a dispirited course under the dripping evergreens, she was chilled and wet, and starting to shiver. The rock wall to her right showed no trace of an opening. The marshy tussocks around her were broken by flooded gullies and split stone, a trial to Stormfront's lameness. Mykkael's raving had lapsed into ominous quiet, the rasp of his breathing grown shallow and thin. Anja touched his hand, and found the clenched fingers icy. Fear rode her, that he was slipping away.

He needed rest, and a fire for warmth. Yet her ongoing search encountered no safe place for respite. She kept on, without other option, except to sit down and give up in the rain.

That moment, cold as tapped crystal, the shaman-sung pattern etched into the sword hilt sang out a note of clear warning.

Anja stopped Stormfront. Planted against his steamed

shoulder, she fastened wet fingers around Mykkael's wrist, as the sword in his harness continued to ring, and terror hazed her to trembling.

'Captain,' she whispered. 'Beware, there is sorcery.' Torn apart by harrowing dread, she did not expect him to answer.

Yet the queer, thrumming cry of the blade had cut across his mazed senses. Mykkael stirred and sucked in a hitched breath. He raised his bent head and made a brave effort to survey the dripping slope under the cliff face. After a moment, a frown marred his brow. 'Do you smell the breeze, Princess?' he whispered. 'That's no kerrie's fire, but wood smoke.'

Anja had not picked up the detail. Light-headed from hunger and adrift in bleak misery, she was never so keenly attuned to the nuance of the open wilds. She gripped Stormfront's cheek strap, blinking through misted lashes, but could detect no glint of a nearby blaze.

That moment, in front and behind, the soaked leaves of the thickets rustled and shed their strung burden of droplets. Furtive movement closed on their position *from all sides*, driving Mykkael to wild anxiety. His clawing effort to clear his sheathed sword was clipped short by a spasm of agony.

Stormfront was too worn and crippled to run. Anja stood exposed, while the surrounding wood came alive with the emergent forms of twelve people. They were clad in tanned pelts and deer hide. Oddments of carved bone swung from their belts, and their shoulder-strapped bundles of belongings. Each held a straight spear with a leaf-shaped steel point, and a grip made of cross-wrapped leather.

Except for one, in the lead, an unarmed old man who carried a slender wood staff.

'Don't move,' Mykkael grated. 'We're pinned down.' He jammed his hands against Stormfront's crest and forced his cramped posture back upright.

While he battled to secure his reeling balance, his sword hilt fell ominously silent.

Anja huddled against the drooping black horse and surveyed the ring of queer foreigners who had crept up and set wary ambush. They made no overt move towards violence. The spears stayed upright. The bone-handled knives at their hips remained sheathed, while their dark-skinned, foreign faces inspected captain and princess with scouring interest.

Held straight by royal bearing, Anja regarded them back.

Six were wizened elders. These wore ornate bracelets on their forearms and wrists, fashioned of silver and copper. Two pairs were young warriors, of exquisite, lithe build. The other cloaked forms appeared to be female. Man, woman or elder, their faces had the same sharp-edged leanness, the same angled jaw and high cast of cheekbone. They could have been stamped from the selfsame mould as the desert-bred captain beside her.

Anja stared at their elderly leader. The white hair at his temples had been laced into braids beneath a peaked snakeskin headdress. He carried no weapon. His simple, cut staff bore no decoration. Despite his exotic, uncivilized clothes, his weathered features bespoke a commanding presence. Caught like a stunned rabbit under his gaze, Anja realized that Mykkael might have looked so, had he the chance to live out his years to the dignity of advanced age.

Stormfront tossed his soaked mane and snorted. The movement jostled the captain, and broke the uncanny quiet settled over the glen like a spell.

'They're tribal,' breathed Mykkael. 'Scoraign shamans, beyond doubt.' His wet skin ruffled up into gooseflesh as though his mind went on fire with witch thought.

'Mercy,' gasped Anja. 'Mykkael, you told me they'd kill you for being an outcast.'

He unfastened a clenched hand and touched her to

silence. 'Let me handle this, Princess. Despite their stern customs, they won't be discourteous.' Unsteady with pain, braced upright on Stormfront, he raised his closed fist to his forehead in trembling salute.

The elder in front returned the same gesture. His spill of white hair blew in the damp wind. His attendant circle made no forward move. The warriors stood with stilled hands on their spears, apparently not concerned for the hour, or the predations of night-hunting kerries. The old man's dark eyes raked the princess's protector, avid as piercing black glass. He did not speak. His tradition insisted the male stranger on horseback should be the first to declare himself.

Mykkael strove to match that implicit demand. Erect as his injuries would allow, alert though his ears rang with fever, he addressed the elder in the poorly accented southern dialect used by the caravan traders. *'She is Princess Anja of Sessalie, descended of King Isendon and Queen Anjoulie. Of her line, she is both the last born, and the last, after her sire who is failing. You behold the heir who must bear the light of her ancestry unto the next generation. Her nation is under assault by cold sorcery. Her people have no vizier to defend them, and no shaman to hallow the ground. If you will accept her and grant her protection, my first charge to her sire will be fulfilled.'*

The ancient man measured him. Bone-thin and graceful, with hands that revealed the hard wear of a lifetime clasped to his stave, he said nothing for a drawn moment. Then, as though each word had been carefully weighed, he said, *'Warrior, behold, you are heard. I am listening.'*

'There is more.' Mykkael inclined his head. *'This woman's brother, Prince Kailen, has been bound beyond death by a shapechanger. The creature's dissolved head and right arm remain in my hands, prisoned in leather and salt. My oath of service to Sessalie's crown demands my vigilance, until his Highness's spirit can be redeemed. I ask, might Tuinvardia's knowledge achieve his safe passage through banishment? My life is pledged*

to stand guard, that Isendon's son should not fall to further ill use as a sorcerer's abomination.'

No move from the elder; the warriors maintained their motionless poise. Their stark expressions revealed their harsh understanding. To a man, they realized the gravity of the peril this outsider had brought to their country. The shamans behind exchanged unsettled glances, while darkness loomed, and the gathered mist drifted. Rain trickled and fell. In due time, the ancient inclined his head towards Anja, granting leave for her consultation. Then he settled to wait in strict form, while Mykkael shared a whispered translation to summarize the exchange.

After the princess's nod to her spokesman, the aged shaman deigned to give answer. *'Warrior, tell the woman you guard, we accept her. She will be given the same care as our Jantii tribe's daughters, until presented to Tuinvardia's emperor. If our circle should fail, and her enemy triumphs, all shall weep, for our own will have fallen before her.'*

Mykkael saluted, fist to forehead again. *'You do her high honour, as the line of her ancestry deserves.'*

Anja, listening, did not grasp the strange words. She could but watch as the old shaman addressed the captain again.

'Warrior! For the burden you carry, named as Isendon's son, fox clan circle will undertake a deliverance, but at a price. To attempt this banishment, you must grant us the song line that Jantii tribe does not possess. Give my people the patterns sung into your wardings if we are to try to achieve what you ask.'

Mykkael caught a hitched breath. He shut his eyes through a moment of reeling dizziness, then murmured in clipped words to Anja, 'Princess, you shall have learned help. Let me make the arrangements, and pray that Prince Kailen may be redeemed along with you.'

'What are the demands, Mykkael?'

He jerked his chin, no; refused the pause to enact explanation. The entreaty on his stripped face suggested his lucid awareness was slipping away. If he should succumb, she would have no one else to treat for her. Anja rested her hand on his knee, and gave him her tacit consent.

Mykkael bowed his head to the elder forthwith. Besieged by pain, he bound over the price that was asked without hesitation. *'Take all that I have, beginning with this blade I carry.'*

Too stricken to unbuckle his harness, he bent. His face turned in wrenching appeal towards Anja. Aware that his gesture presaged a surrender, but not knowing what terms must be served, the princess was forced to draw the weapon on his behalf. At his firm bidding, she laid the battered blade on the ground at the old man's feet.

Mykkael fought a wringing shiver and straightened. The next phrase he spoke came through ragged, while Anja stood trembling behind Stormfront's drooped head. She listened to each foreign syllable in tense, agonized silence.

'A Sanouk circle sang the white ward on that hilt. Begin there.' Even pressed to the bittermost edge of endurance, the grace of Mykkael's ear for language shone through. His gutturals had instinctively altered to match the living example before him. *'My nape bears the tattooed patterns of guard wrought first by Eishwin, then augmented by Perincar to fight Rathtet. Into your hands, I commit my live flesh, bearing these protections as you require.'*

The elder raised his stave, then thumped the end to the earth's breast to seal a pact of honour with the mounted stranger before him. *'Warrior! I am Anzbek, born to fox clan's mothers. Let my name and ancestry bear witness to Jantii tribe's pledged half of the circle.'*

Anja saw Mykkael's locked fingers whiten. She felt the terrible spasm that raked him shudder through Stormfront's neck. She dared not move, even to offer her hands. Though the next moment brought his collapse, his bearing decried any effort to help. Whether he fell off the back of the horse, the princess could not in that moment have risked the affront to his dignity.

Mykkael had to fight, now, for the breath to frame speech. He had lost all aplomb. In appeal before Anzbek, threadbare with emotion, he set seal to his share of the bargain. '*Elder, I am Mykkael. I have name, but no claim to ancestry. Let the sword at your feet and the gift of Sanouk regard stand for my half of the circle.*'

Anzbek touched his fist to his brow. Then he raised his staff in salute and announced to the tribesfolk assembled around him, '*Jantii people, bear witness! This pledge is accepted.*' He bent and collected the sword, and clasped the marked hilt to his breast.

'*Hail, Mykkael! You do us great honour!*' His sharp eyes glittered. '*Hear my praise, warrior! Know that your run through Hell's Chasm has restored our hope, and that of the brothers we serve in Tuinvardia. The line of song that your valour has bequeathed shall be sung with reverence by fox clan circle's children. For as long as life lasts, their grandchildren will preserve the notes after them, and their offspring, throughout generations to come.*'

The old shaman spun his staff. He thumped the base to the ground, setting seal to an oath his tribe must uphold for as long as their descendants walked on the earth.

The young warriors slapped their opened palms to their spear shafts. They broke their poised stance and pressed forward. Yet as their crowding attentions closed in, Mykkael reeled. Stormfront sidled to his sharp shift in weight. Before the captain's lurching slide should pitch him off the black gelding's back, Anja lunged and braced up his limp weight.

'*He must not ride further,*' Anzbek pronounced, still speaking in Scoraign dialect. He gestured a hurried command to his tribesmen. '*My brothers, ready your spears.*'

Yet as the elder shaman reached out to grasp Stormfront's headstall, Anja jostled the gelding away.

The old man snapped short. Startled by her vehement hostility, he folded his hands on his staff, then jerked his chin for his spearmen to hold in restraint. '*Does this warrior's bargain not please you?'* he inquired in stiffened surprise.

Anja did not know a word of the language. She had heard Mykkael speak, but had grasped little beyond their demand that he yield up his sword. 'No spears!' Embarrassed that her protest must be phrased in Sessalie's clipped tongue, she flushed and said lamely. 'Forgive me.' Although convinced she could not make herself understood, she was bound by state courtesy to apologize. 'I don't speak Scoraign dialect. Even so, I won't let you kill him.'

The elder responded in stilted northern. 'Kill him?' He raised grizzled eyebrows. His dark features clouded, while the air surrounding his peaked snakeskin hat seemed oddly limned in a soft, grainy light. 'The warrior has promised the songs in his wardings! Do you forbid him this choice?'

Anja swallowed. Her stance stayed arm-folded and adamant. 'Mykkael told me himself, if he dies, Eishwin's pattern will cease to guard against sorcery. If you desire the protections he carries, have your warriors put up their spears. For this man's life's sake, I will not back down. Not being armed, I can do no more than beg the grace of your reprieve.'

The elder grunted. The stave in his fist stayed grounded to earth as he shrugged with frowning puzzlement. For a drizzle-soaked interval he studied the princess's face. In dirt and weariness, he would read exhaustion, and hunger, and trials of harrowing uncertainty. Whether or not he grasped the gist of her speech, his shining black eyes seemed to measure the conflict she held in her heart.

At length, he addressed her. His tone stayed polite. 'Princess Anja, you have been named and set under our protection.' His accent was inflected with a musical lilt that rendered the phrase gravely pleasing. 'We certainly realize your Mykkael is hurt. The spears of our warriors will only be used to fashion a litter to bear him. Jantii people have knowledge of wounds and their treatment. Stand aside. If you value this man's pledge as we do, you must stand down and allow our healer to treat him.'

When she hesitated, still uncertain, his humour resurged and transformed his stern features with laugh lines. 'Daughter, do you fret for the beast? He is our sacred relation as well. His hurts will be tended with mindful care.' Gently, firmly, he captured her chilled hand. 'Give the rein, Princess. Let Anzbek of the fox clan circle extend Jantii tribe's hospitality.'

Presumptuous at the last, he pried her frozen fingers off the black gelding's headstall. 'Go with the women,' urged Anzbek. 'Our elders will attend to the warrior, while the young men look after the lame horse.'

A tender, shy touch brushed at Anja's stiff shoulder. One of the women stood at her side, her approach unnervingly soundless. 'Come away, Princess. We have a fire. You must take food and shelter in a cave in the rocks not far off.'

'Kerries,' Anja protested, still resisting. 'There are roosts in these cliffs. The creatures will prey on the horse.'

The desert-bred woman smiled and tapped a contrivance made of cord and carved wood, looped on a thong at her belt. 'Not to worry. Our people know what to do when such flying marauders come hunting.'

Anja regarded the warriors, closed in and awaiting her permission. Their fierce expressions were not unfriendly. The six elders, also, watched her next move. Ripped by indecision, she turned her soaked head, and finally surveyed Mykkael. His limp frame bore upon her sprained wrist, the unconscious bulk of his weight more than her failed strength could sustain. The shallow draw of his breath brushed her neck, the rhythm now broken and ragged. The relentless drizzle beaded his skin, wisped to raised steam by his fever. Whatever binding promise he had yielded along with his sword, he had appeared to meet his fate willingly. Untreated, he would certainly die of his wounds. When these Scoraign people stripped off his clothes, they would discover the fact he was outcast by his lack of tribal tattoos.

The spear thrust demanded by their strict tradition would at least grant a clean end to his suffering.

Night was fast approaching. Too starved and tired to argue, or strike out through the wilds on her own, Anja accepted the inevitable last choice. She must follow the example set by Mykkael before her, and accept the shamans' protection.

Pride set her back straight. If she would cast herself upon Jantii tribe's mercy, she would show no less than the steel of her royal dignity. She gave the elder her magisterial nod. As the warriors stepped in to lift Mykkael from her, she delivered her formal, last word. 'Treat this man kindly. He has served his oath to my sire with great courage. For the sake of his honour, which has placed my safety foremost, I must accept his agreement.'

Anzbek thumped his staff.

The warriors bore in. As the captain's slack frame was eased from Anja's shoulders, she swayed, wrung to sudden light-headedness. The tribal woman instantly offered an arm and steadied her failing balance. As saving hands guided her step through the gloom, the princess glanced backwards just once.

Two of the warriors stood guard beside Stormfront, weapons held at the ready. Their vigilant stance was fluid as Mykkael's must have been, before the misfortune of war had crippled his knee. Anzbek oversaw the grey-headed elders, who folded the wounded captain into the warmth of their own shed mantles. Their handling was firm, and showed respect for his injuries as they lowered him on to their makeshift litter. Steel spear tips glinted. Voices murmured and exclaimed in thick dialect. The rolling gutturals had a rhythmic beauty, if one had an ear for the music. Movement flurried as a tall spearman broke away and scolded someone unseen in the underbrush.

A wiry young boy Anja had not seen earlier slithered sheepishly out of a tree. Called to heel by Anzbek's brisk gesture, he unreeled an object strung on a plaited string.

Moments later, the gusting breeze of a scavenging kerrie winnowed over the trees. The boy spun the contrivance over his head and whirled it in gyrating circles.

A keening note sawed through the night air. Put off by the ear-splitting sound, the predator sheared away, huffing smoke.

'Come, sister,' entreated the woman in her accented northern. 'You are weary and tired. My people will fetch you hot water to bathe. While you soak your hurts, let us clean the unpleasant smell off your clothes and arrange for your rest and comfort.'

Amid drifting consciousness, King Isendon of Sessalie dreamed. A wizened shaman sat with his daughter, Anja, his gnarled hand placed at her heart. Ancient eyes closed, a battered sword on his knees, he raised his voice and started to sing. The failing monarch felt each note as the kin tie to his heir rang out in summoned vibration; and all over the kingdom under his rule, the gathering darkness of the sorcerer's lines broke apart and scattered like vapour. The sweet notes pealed on until nary a shadow remained. When at due length the feat was accomplished, the king woke to find Jussoud bent above him. 'Did you hear?'

The nomad nodded, wonder shining in his grey eyes.

'Fetch Taskin,' said the king, very clearly.

The commander's voice answered, close by. 'Your Majesty, I am with you.'

King Isendon smiled. 'Captain Myshkael brought my daughter to Tuinvardia alive. The allies she treats with have spared us.' This said, the old monarch drew his last breath and, content, his exhausted heart rested.

XXXIX. Deliverance

THE OLD SHAMAN LIFTED HIS HAND FROM THE SWORD HILT THAT HAD ENABLED THE WARDINGS SUNG BY Sanouk shamans for protection to be woven into Jantii circle's singing. He opened black eyes. Before him sat the young princess whose bloodline had provided the bridge to cleanse the demonic incursion that had threatened Sessalie's unspoiled ground. She was cleaned and fed, though scarcely rested, with borrowed clothes of Scoraign design, and her pale hair shining by firelight. As the surrounding shamans stirred out of trance, the eldest nodded his proud acknowledgement of their night's difficult work.

Now the identity of the unknown invader could be addressed with safety.

Anzbek spoke. 'The demon that tried to force conquest in Sessalie, and extend his reach to despoil Tuinvardia is known as Gorgenvain. Of Nine, he is Tenth. Let his Name and the song to dispel the powers of his bound sorcerers be recorded for all of eternity.'

The deed was finished, with the dread spell lines broken, that had sought to destroy Anja's people. If the Kingdom of Devall yet stayed enslaved, the future was not without hope. The warrior had brought them Perincar's patterns tattooed on to his scalp. He also carried the earlier mark invoking his desert-bred ancestry, drawn with Eishwin's unequalled finesse. Scoraign elders possessed the initiate awareness to access the mysteries behind their own heritage. The combined sum of Mykkael's wardings could forge them the new songs to enact an aggressive attack. The vizier's master scribes owned the knowledge to decipher the wisdom inherent in Perincar's legacy. The lore books in the emperor's libraries would help them define the geometry, and configure the powerful banishments needed to counter Gorgenvain's bid for expansion. Short curse, or long spell, with Tuinvardia's assistance, Devall's conquered ground might be freed.

Yet the young princess who had helped bring three nations' salvation remained unconsoled, though her gratitude for the circle's deliverance was phrased with heartfelt sincerity. Her green eyes still reflected deep sorrow, the source for which was the warrior.

'Let me see him,' she entreated. 'Promise me Mykkael will live!'

Anzbek sighed. With the sword still cradled across reverent knees, he called upon vision, and weighed Anja's anguish. Her birth gift of beauty was no longer untouched. The face she showed to the world had been pared to strong womanhood by the forces of grief and adversity. 'Daughter, no wisdom in my possession can promise the course of the future.'

His eyes upon her shaded with pity, he gathered the steel, and his staff, and arose. Ancient though he was, and despite the late hour, he moved easily.

'Come, daughter. You shall visit your warrior.' Old hands raised the sword, and gave it into the princess's keeping. 'I award you the honour,' said Anzbek. 'You shall restore this treasured weapon to Mykkael's side. Our people now share its song of bright warding. The gift of Sanouk protection should now be returned to the man who received it.'

* * *

They had laid the warrior on a bed of soft furs, behind a rough screen to lend privacy. The curtain had been fashioned from his torn surcoat. Although the device had faded with washing, Sessalie's crown and falcon blazon shone like old blood in the firelight.

Mykkael lay motionless, stripped of his clothes, and covered in the dusky colours of the Scoraign elders' borrowed mantles. His marked hands were still. His features seemed a grave mask in bronze, with the cleaned swath of silk embroidered with dragons pillowed under his head.

Anja stepped past the two warriors who stood vigil. She sank to her knees by the man who had served as her sworn protector and laid his longsword flat by his side. The battered steel seemed as hard used as his body, that now appeared scarcely breathing.

Grief blinded her. She blinked, but could not stop flooding tears. Hands raised to stem her unbearable sorrow, she gasped through her muffling fingers, 'Don't tell me he's dying. Surely your healers hold hope for him?'

The old shaman regarded her, solemn in his peaked snakeskin hat, and his air of matchless dignity. 'He is not for you, Princess. Will you leave him to us?'

Anja swallowed with difficulty. 'Leave him? How can I? He said your kind would kill him because he did not merit tribal tattoos.'

Anzbek stared at her, thunderstruck. 'Not *merit*?' He gripped his birch staff, his brows snagged into a frown. 'Princess Anja of Sessalie, are you naming this warrior an outcast?'

Anja met the shaman's glaring black eyes, aroused to spitfire anger. 'I name him my captain, and cherish his value. Unlike your tribes from the Scoraign, the life in his body is dear to me.'

Utterly taken aback, Anzbek jerked a fast gesture to the paired warriors, who now bristled. 'Hold!' he commanded, staying the fists aggressively gripped to their spears.

Due care must be taken. This princess was young, and

bravely impulsive. She was also raggedly tired. She may not have intended to slight Jantii tribe's hospitality, or use words that inferred a killing offence. Anzbek knelt and looked into her eyes, and there, read a fear too fierce to be tamed.

'Daughter,' he said gently. 'How do you presume our Scoraign people have wronged him?'

'He is of your own blood,' Anja stated with heat. 'Explain why his mother would expose him at birth.'

Anzbek folded his legs and sat down, his plain stave laid crosswise over his lap. 'Did she in fact? Why don't you tell me the facts as you believe they occurred?'

Anja coloured. Where was her right, as Sessalie's princess, to speak of Mykkael's private origins? And yet, she must. Her brash outcry had broached the matter headlong, and foreclosed the chance for tactful diplomacy. Princess enough to stand as ambassador, she addressed her duty unflinching. 'Mykkael told me he was abandoned beside a caravan route as an infant. Northern traders found him, half starved and alone. Their family took him under their roof and raised him as one of their own.'

Anzbek absorbed this with stilled deliberation. Then he signalled his tensioned warriors to stand down. When he gave his considered response, his heart was not angry, but sorrowful. 'The names of Mykkael's parents are forgotten, this is true. The line of his ancestry is not known to us. This is our loss.'

Anzbek stared towards the fire. He murmured a prayer for the flames to consume his regret, then admitted the rest of his failure. 'I cannot recover the story of the misfortune that turned this man's path far astray from the clan that might have embraced him.' He stroked Mykkael's forehead, the contact all reverence. 'I can say this much. Seer's talent such as this warrior harbours is never exposed to the desert! If his birth mother was raised in tradition, if she followed the way of her tribe, she would have faced death before being parted from a child with such shining potential. More likely her infant was left to a caravan because her own life was threatened. She would have been pressed by starvation, or enemies, to have sacrificed a son as gifted as this one.'

When Anja bowed her head in raw anguish over the warrior's chest, Anzbek reached out and took her clenched hands into his aged clasp. 'Daughter, Mykkael is not outcast. If you claim the right to stand for his lost family, and appeal to Jantii people for his adoption, you must first release him from Sessalie's service. Then fox clan circle would gladly sing him a name in tradition, and grant him his tribal tattoos.'

Anja paused, drawn up short. Pinned under the ancient shaman's regard, she must see beyond spoken words. Agree, or refuse, the authority had been taken into her hands. The answer she gave could never be simple. If Mykkael died, he would receive last rites among strangers, but be granted the honour of kin. If he lived to resume his crown captaincy in Sessalie, and rejoined the court at her side, he would need no such barbaric markings. His desert-bred features already bespoke his foreign blood with a burdensome clarity. Just for being what he was, he seeded distrust and uneasiness amid Sessalie's ingrown society.

King Isendon's commission and the Lowergate garrison had always been too small a domain to contain him.

Anja gave way at last, unable to sustain the piercing awareness revealed in the shaman's wise eyes. 'Mykkael is dying,' she whispered. 'How should my choice matter if he does not rise from this sickbed?'

Anzbek nodded. 'You are right to be anxious.' His sage nature admired her forthright character, that dared to face the difficult truth. Since the young woman showed him her unflinching courage, the shaman related the facts as fox clan circle's healer had told them.

'Mykkael is strong and resilient. He has recovered from many past injuries that would have defeated a lesser spirit.

Of his hurts, all are minor, except for the claw puncture low in his belly. That is the source of the fever he suffers, and that, he must battle if he is to walk in the sunlight. The poisons that sicken him rise from within. Princess, his life now hangs by a thread. Take hope from the fact he has been two days, fasting. His gut was empty at the time he was savaged. Our herbal infusions have flushed the rent clean. We have stitched the ripped bowel with boiled sinew, and kept the wound open for drainage. Your Mykkael could yet live if he can surmount the infection.'

Anja closed her eyes. Dread and uncertainty robbed the serenity from her pale, northern beauty. Sunlight against shadow, she bent her gaze to the warrior, her longing a blaze like new flame. 'Mykkael is the strongest man I have known. What kind of life could your people give him?'

Anzbek squeezed her fingers. Then he blessed her braced strength, that dared to examine the future with selflessness. 'I discern two paths, and a choice to be made, but my wisdom cannot lend you guidance. For that, you must wait until morning and place an appeal to Jantii tribe's seer.' The shaman unfolded his clasp and freed her chilled hands. Arisen, staff in hand, he waited amid the limitless peace of his silence.

For long moments, nothing moved but the dance of the fire the healer had left burning for light. Princess Anja of Sessalie surveyed the face of the man who had delivered her from the terrors of sorcerers, and the harrowing trials of Hell's Chasm. Mykkael lay far removed, adrift in unconsciousness. Since words were useless, and tears served him mean tribute, she bent, kissed his lips, and reluctantly rose to her feet.

Anzbek steadied her stumbling step as she pushed past the curtain, abandoned to grief. His self-contained presence led her back to the women, who would see that she rested until daybreak, when the seer could be summoned for consultation.

* * *

The clouds cleared by morning. Under the cold light of dawn, the elder seer greeted Anja, clad in weathered hide and a belt of carved shells, passed down for untold generations. He clasped her young hands under the dripping boughs, beside the stilled verge of a catch basin under the cliffs. Ripples fled over the water's bright surface, ephemerally fleeting as mortal lives, that were just as swiftly erased from the changing face of eternity. Surrounded by greenery and singing birds, the soothsayer gazed into the princess's eyes.

His first words broke the pristine silence like a knife cut of pure despair. 'Keep the warrior as yours, he will die of his injuries.'

Anja yanked back. 'But that makes no sense!' By her understanding of human nature, a spirit would strengthen when embraced by love, and wane away in its absence.

A flicker of sunlight brightened the high rim of the rock face overhead. A kerrie launched from its roost, spouting flame. As deeply inscrutable as time itself, the desert-bred seer withheld comment, wrapped in his mantle of deer hide.

'Why?' Anja entreated, scraped raw by her sorrow. 'Why would Mykkael leave this world, when I care for nothing but giving him royal position and joy at my side?'

The seer watched her, still silent. His dark eyes were forthright as the blade on a Scoraign spear, that could warn without drawing blood.

Exposed by that terrible, impartial patience, the princess curbed anger that was hers alone. Like Anzbek, the old seer would leave her to sort out her feelings. He would let her declare herself without taking undue offence. No girl, but a woman raised for crown rule, Anja determined to carry the riddle beyond the self-blinded pain of her heartache. 'What will the future bring if I should give Mykkael up?'

The seer tipped his grey head to watch a small sparrow alight on a twig. As though the tracks of the world's fate rode upon the seeds it flew home to its nestlings, he said, 'Your loved one may live, and perhaps find his happiness. As warrior, he will choose his own hour of death. Let him go, and I can tell you the wounding he suffers will not compel his release.'

The tiny bird flitted. Burdened by Anja's cruel distress, the seer gathered his robes and perched on a mossy boulder.

'Daughter,' he said gently, 'life is not simple. The ties on a strong man's spirit are seldom straightforward, or free. Your warrior believes himself bound to the weal of your kingdom. Do you see? That commitment is forcing his sacrifice.'

She was young, and a maiden. Her disbelief importuned him. 'He will die,' said the seer. 'In your heart, you know this.'

That desolate truth hurt beyond all bearing. Yet Anja rejected the complacency of defeat. She did not require an old man's gift of vision to sense the ebb of an indefatigable vitality. Mykkael, in his wisdom, saw more clearly than she. If he lived, he understood the full import of what she would ask. Tied by the oath he had sworn to her sire, he could do no less than stand guard throughout her triumphant return. On arrival in Sessalie, his heroic deeds would demand the accolade of crown gratitude. Anja's young love would chain him to her side. And there, he would languish as an embarrassment, penned amid the stilted ways of a hidebound northern society. Mykkael's *barqui'ino* mind and razor-sharp ethics made him too honest a cipher. The crown council would never abide the clarity that walked in his presence. Highgate's titled families would never accept him.

When the stillness itself commanded response, Anja dared the same question she had broached to Anzbek the evening before. 'What life will Mykkael have if I leave him?'

The seer shook his head. 'If you give this man up, his

future will no longer be yours, but his own. Though you ask, I cannot interpret his path. Not after his step becomes parted from yours.'

Anja clasped her arms, anguished. 'If I set him free, what is there for me?'

'Give me your hands,' said the seer, not unkindly. 'That is a choice I can show you.' He gathered her chilled fingers into his own, which were seamed and warm as brown earth. Then he looked deeply into her eyes. 'Anja of Sessalie, you will leave this place to forge an affiliation through marriage, and wed an emperor's son, the youngest Prince of Tuinvardia. The pair of you will make your home in the mountains, and rule as King Isendon's successors.'

'Marriage,' whispered Anja. After Devall, and Mykkael, the prospect seemed bleak.

Shown her jagged-edged trepidation, the elder inquired, 'Do you fear the young prince is not comely, or that he might be of unsound character?'

Anja sighed. With her fingers still clasped in the elder's calm touch, she regarded the pool, and the fugitive rings carved by the falling droplets. 'I don't need to know.'

Yet the inner voice clamoured through her resignation. This emperor's son might be beautiful and kind, or he could be ugly and mean. The difference seemed moot. He would not be Mykkael. The seer's steady presence impelled her to acknowledge that stifled fragment of honesty. Love refused to stay mute. Though the pain cut like glass, the Princess of Sessalie firmed her will and crushed down her passion with silence.

The blazing flame in her heart must not blind her. Days ago, before the terrors of a sorcerer had impelled her flight through Hell's Chasm, she had once confided to her best friend Shai, that she would have gladly married a monster, if Sessalie's people should benefit. The young woman who now watched the sunrise on the far side of the Great Divide had touched horrors that destroyed goodness and life. She wept in mourning for a dead brother. If the untried spark of her idealism had seared away under hardship, the core of her upright integrity remained. The heritage of her royal lineage was not revocable. Still, she held the weal of a nation in the palm of her unsteady hand. A crown relied on her power to bind an alliance. Her duty was clear, whether the emperor's son was appealing, or plain, or a wastrel.

The seer smiled, then released her as though in salute. 'Brave Princess, you shall not choose without sight.' He raised his finger and tapped her forehead.

The morning world rippled. Water and dewfall blurred into dream. *Anja beheld a wide plain. A party of horsemen rode under the crisp snap of Tuinvardia's banners. They were led by a young man with reddish hair and blue eyes, splendidly tall in chased armour. He sat his fine horse with impeccable skill, his clean-cut, handsome features lively with laughter as he caught a ribbing from the troop captain at his right hand.*

Then the brief vision fled, leaving the fathomless gaze of the seer, regarding her with expectancy.

'He is younger than I am,' Anja blurted, overcome by the boy's similarity to her lost brother, Kailen. The crown prince's vivacity would be sorely mourned. How easily the incumbent council in Sessalie might come to love this brash son of Tuinvardia's emperor.

'In fact the young man has a year more than you.' The seer's seed-black eyes sparkled with a surprisingly caustic amusement. 'As the emperor's fifth son, Prince Trigal's importunate humour has yet to be tempered. He will mature quickly. If you take him as husband, his well-spoken character will swiftly be put to the test. He would rise to match you. Any man must. The passage you survived by the sword of your warrior has sharpened you to discernment. You know what it means to be vibrant and living, and to treat with hard choices fearlessly.'

'Mykkael's example would have me choose peace for my people. Let his crown oath to serve be released.' Anja straightened her shoulders with resolve. 'I will honour the strength of his sacrifice, and marry for Sessalie, and rule as Tuinvardia's ally.'

The seer bowed to her. Then he turned, and Anja discovered that Anzbek waited at the far edge of the glen. The eldest dreamer seemed already aware that she had reached her anguished decision. His snakeskin cap was perched atop his white head, and his regard showed tranquillity as she left the seer's presence, and strode from the pond's verge to meet him.

'Daughter,' he addressed her in his accented northern. 'We have a patrol of four warriors prepared to move south down the canyon. Fox clan circle must bear urgent word back to court. Vital patterns they carry must be received by Tuinvardia's next grand vizier. You can go now, and meet Prince Trigal's armed company. Or you can wait here, until the emperor's mounted escort can be summoned to receive you in state.'

Anja drew a painful, shuddering breath. 'Mykkael, has he wakened?'

The ancient shaman shook his head, no.

'Then let it be now,' whispered Anja through the aching shimmer of her pent-up tears. 'Delay will make parting no easier.'

After the brave young princess departed, Jantii tribe's fox clan circle prepared to sing for the great warrior's deliverance. The shamans waited until the new day warmed the ground. When the lingering damp of last night's rainfall dried from the rustling leaves, they bore him from the cave on a litter of spears. Four warriors stood guard at the cardinal points as they laid him naked on the green verge at the edge of the pool, in the flood of the morning sunlight. Birth to death, a man only borrowed his skin. Earth mother's embrace would acknowledge him.

His Sanouk-marked sword they placed at his right hand. At his feet, symbol of the harsh path he had trodden, they arranged his falcon surcoat, and the shred of scraped hide that had lately contained the shape-changer's perilous leavings. By these tokens, they signified his release from a charge accomplished with unswerving strength. His other hand, they left empty, freed for the future that was his choice alone to receive. At his head, Anzbek held his planted stave, to keep the place of his ancestors, whose clan name they did not know, and therefore could not invoke to watch over his spirit.

Under his nape, against the warding tattoos that defended the land from Gorgenvain's shadow, they placed the tattered silk with the Sanouk royal dragons, for remembrance that they were not first among the world's people to acknowledge his signal worth.

'Let the circle be joined. Grant this warrior our song, for the healing or release his spirit requires for completion.' Anzbek led the pitch that wove the first note through the sacred hush of the clearing. Amid birdsong and the whisper of wind, the other singers joined in.

Then the wizened elder who acted as spokesman and healer knelt at the warrior's side. He extended his hands, palms turned downwards, and evoked the listening silence to sound out the flow of the life force. He would map the cords of love that bound Mykkael to survival, and reaffirm those that were worthy. The ones that persistently tied him to pain, the circle's raised song could dissolve, as his spirit granted permission.

Eyes closed, the healer probed gently. His sensitive touch traced the bars of strong energy arising from Mykkael's heart. With tender care, he tested each one. Of those that mattered, he found seven. Two held clear potential to strengthen his will. Two more framed regrets. One, shining bright as a chain, still enslaved him. And two more, again, held the power to kill him, as they leached the stream of his vitality.

The healer addressed the least difficult, first. Deft in wisdom, he opened the song and began.

His chosen register awakened the powerful lines that spoke of kin ties and fellowship. Around him the circle of initiate elders framed the imperative chord to quicken the tone into potency.

Far off in Sessalie, Jussoud raised his head. His silver eyes glinted with pleased recognition, as he acknowledged the distant, bright contact sourced by the Scoraign shamans. He gave his reply without hesitation. 'I will speak for Mykkael. He is the adopted son of the Sanouk dragon. His name is welcomed, and his star shines with honour alongside those of my ancestry. His place in my heart is a brother's. As my own blood, I will cherish him.'

The circle received the sincerity of the steppeland nomad's affirmation, and used its colour to augment their song. The rich chord they braided burgeoned and burned, woven into an exultation.

Bathed in a haze of glimmering light, the healer's brown hands moved onwards and traced the tension in the next binding. His sustained note changed key, and called on the aspect that bespoke shared wisdom and teaching.

One of eight chosen men appointed to keep the Sanctuary vigil over King Isendon's bier, Sergeant Vensic, just promoted to crown commission, lapsed into a moment of daydream. 'Mykkael is my mentor, the uplifting example who raised me from the drudge of the farmyard. He showed me how to discover my gifts, and instilled the discipline of self-achievement. For his inspired standard of leadership, I honour him.'

The shaman's phrased melody affirmed the tie, then enriched its resplendent tonalities. To the solemn acknowledgement of professional competence, they unveiled the gift of Vensic's admiration and loyalty.

The healer's touch tested with tacit care, next pressing against the inflexible strings that anchored the warrior's regret. He sang for the first, and the circle followed his line, rousing the dissonance of a tragic conflict, engendered when an oath-sworn priority had entangled with an upright crown officer's imposed duty.

Commander Taskin cursed his forced inactivity, then the strapping that bound his right arm, though the chubby physician who poked at his bandage insisted his shoulder was healing. Imperious, impatient, he dismissed the prompt of the shaman-sent dream with his usual brisk dispatch. 'Captain Mykkael? Damn his ungodly prowess with a sword! His loyalty was ever beyond my reproach. For her Grace's survival, I forgive him.'

The circle responded, and mellowed the discord that carried the sorrow of bloodshed. Under their singing, the scar of regret was reforged to the martial beat of a competent commander's awed respect.

Again, the healer's touch shifted. While the sunlight streaming into the glen smote through the enveloping glow spun by the singers' weaving, he listened again with stilled subtlety.

His next note summoned the first of the ghosts.

Prince Al-Syn appeared, aggrieved as he had not been in life. His graceful, ringed hands clasped the sceptre inscribed with the penultimate patterns of guard laid down by his court vizier, Perincar. The wardings shone blue, that had once failed to spare a kingdom engrossed in its arrogant complacency. His answer to the song that called his shade to redress the cry of his doom re-echoed with woeful remorse. 'For Mykkael, the bravest and best of the captains who stood to Efandi's defence? Tell him that I lament the ruin caused by the folly of my royal pride. I beg the grace of his forbearance for the cost he paid in blood and suffering to spare the life of my only child.'

For the knot of sorrows Prince Al-Syn's error bequeathed, the shamans sang of requital. One after the other, they struck the clean notes that transmuted the horror that had overcome Mykkael's valiant company, and the twenty-five of his finest men lost to a desperate retreat. When the echoing resonance of terror had been quelled, and the grisly event lay detached into distanced memory, the healer extended his touch yet again.

His following note struck the chain of bound duty and drew forth a monarch just departed.

King Isendon of Sessalie already understood that his daughter was saved, with the threat to his realm cleared and broken. To the peace of that knowledge, the Scoraign seer raised his gift and sang into the future: of a kingdom's succession secured in alliance with the Emperor of Tuinvardia. Anja would wed Prince Trigal before harvest. War would follow, as the two allied nations sent armed troops and learned viziers marching into the lowcountry. The engagement would be savage, but brief, and the gratitude bought by Devall's restoration would win Sessalie her right to seaport access in perpetuity. 'Captain Mykkael?' The late king addressed those who petitioned his shade with magisterial surprise. 'The man never failed any sovereign who employed him. He has served my royal oath with the utmost integrity. With gratitude, I release him.'

The shaman's melody sang dissolution, and freed the sworn tie to crown service. In the glen, the circle of elders rested. Their pause gave thanks for the world's sunlight, and rejoiced for the warrior, who now breathed more easily within their shield of spun light. When at length they resumed, Anzbek bade them join hands, for ahead lay the shadows that tugged hardest, weighing the heart and draining the passion Mykkael required to live.

The healer poised his trembling hands, then sounded the note for the final, most dangerous summonings. His tone called in love, with a purity that scalded, and a haunting overtone that keened like tapped glass with despair and desolation.

On foot, trudging under noon sun in the company of tribal warriors, a blonde-haired princess turned her head, and looked backwards with opened, green eyes.

'Did you love me?' said Anja.

This time the burden of the reply fell to the stricken warrior. He appeared as a faded shadow of himself, yet his answer was instant, and true. 'Of course, your Grace. I ached to possess you the moment I dreamed of the spirit I saw in your portrait. But your strength of character would have been wasted alongside a man of the sword. Your people revere you. Their need for your peace is more pressing than mine, that has been too well tempered for war. Anja, brave heart, you were never for me. Therefore I held your love briefly and lightly, like the butterfly poised in the opened hand once inscribed in a verse of your poetry. Return in triumph to Sessalie. My witch thoughts will watch you ride spirited horses and pick wildflowers in the high meadows. Princess, I beg you to marry in state. Bear your crown with courage, and forget me.'

'No, Mykkael.' Anja's smile was bittersweet, and her beautiful eyes, changed for ever by poignant regret. 'Marry I must, but not to forget you. The artist who once fashioned my likeness shall paint yours as well. The portrait will hang over the throne within Sessalie's great hall of state. There, your bared sword will hold the true steel of your ethics over the heads of my chancellors. Your name is inscribed in my nation's history. Warrior, your story shall be told, and retold to my royal children and grandchildren. Your part in their legacy shall be remembered for as long as Isendon's blood reigns.'

Of Anja, the shaman circle sang of parting, tenderly softened by the passing of years. They shifted the enduring burden of sadness, and enhanced the rich depths of shared intimacy, selfless honesty and grace, until the glen rang with the haunting purity and altruism of wise choice.

Lastly, the healer stalled in hesitation. His poised touch now tested the current bearing the most grievous binding of all. He glanced, uncertain, towards Anzbek, who nodded.

'Mehigrannia sends the light of her mercy as a balm to all human suffering.' The elder dreamer bowed his white head, his grasp firm on his planted staff. 'What has been started shall finish here, whether this singing begets life or death.'

The healer gathered himself one last time, and began. The note he struck emerged as a whisper, then swelled and gained force, until his throat spilled a cry of passionate sorrow over the morning quiet. Pierced by its poignancy, the circle of Jantii shamans gathered and sustained the difficult intonation. Tears spilled from their knowing, experienced eyes, as they sang of terror and pain and enslavement, and wove the fabric of dark refrain that comprised Orannia's madness.

The notes built and rolled, their forceful beat like war drums and distant thunder. Anzbek, who guarded, sharply lifted his head. His fierce gaze narrowed as he measured the conjured sound, and the steel thread of discord laced through its depths raised his skin into violent gooseflesh. As eldest, and dreamer, he sensed the ominous, unnatural forces that bespoke active spell lines spun by a sorcerer. Worse, he could name the bound creature's demon, an ancient, unforgotten evil preserved with strict vigilance in the legacy of Jantii tribe's memory.

His shout ripped the close-woven chant of the singers. 'Cease!'

One word smashed the burgeoning ring of cruel power, and left desolate, ringing silence. For a heartbeat, no voice spoke but the sough of the wind. Then the ancient shaman sank to his knees. He lowered his white head. The thin braids at his temples trailed on the ground, as he touched his forehead against Mykkael's brow.

'Ah, warrior,' he said in his gentlest whisper. 'Fox clan circle recall the lines for Rathtet.'

There and then, out of gratitude, he started the old song of warding, leading the banishing phrase that resurged as the circle rejoined him. The chant swelled and resounded. As Anzbek dreamed to enact the grand healing, their powerful harmony burned to moving light, then bridged over distance, sustained by the patterns stitched into the heirloom embroidery tucked beneath Mykkael's head.

Far off, in the eastern steppelands, sheltered under a painted tent, a raven-haired Sanouk princess stirred awake and opened her silver-grey eyes. The old matron who tirelessly guarded her life sat erect, and beheld the dawning miracle of her restored sanity. 'Orannia? Granddaughter?'

Tears spilled down the woman's creased cheeks. 'Granddaughter,' she repeated, astounded. Then the startled elation that lifted her heart was seared through by the gift of a witch thought. 'I see your man, Mykkael, astride a black horse, guarded by our Sanouk royal dragons. He comes, his arms open to meet you.'

In the glen, while the circle of Scoraign shamans repeated that grateful refrain, Princess Orannia responded. Her voice shot new light through the weave of the dream, and the notes were all of rejoicing.

'My heart beats with gladness, for the name of Mykkael. I will love him. Pray send him speedily home.'

Epilogue

THE NOTES SWELLED INTO A MIGHTY CHORD, THEN BLENDED TO UNISON AND DWINDLED TO SILENCE. THE song for the warrior's healing was done. The seer broke the circle and summoned his gift. His face bright with gratitude, he spoke for Mykkael's future, and foretold a long life, both vital and vibrant.

Yet when the shamans arose, and the guarding spearmen offered their mantles to bear up the hero's sleeping form, Anzbek planted his staff and forbade them.

'We are not finished. This man may marry into Sanouk, and bring up his children in steppeland heritage. Yet he is a son of the Scoraign desert. Although his ancestry has been forgotten, let him not make his way in the world without the acknowledgement his beginnings have sadly denied.'

Still murmuring in wonder, the shamans re-formed their circle. Next, Anzbek delved into his mantle and produced a phial of obsidian dye, then a brush fashioned from the fine hair clipped from the black gelding's forelock. 'Let today's inscriptions be done in paint. When Mykkael recovers awareness and strength, the honours rightly bestowed on this hour can be awarded with formal ceremony. As he wishes, he shall bear proper Scoraign tattoos.'

The healer accepted the dye and hair-brush. His warm acquiescence came touched by dismay, for he had no line of beginning. 'What story shall be told of Mykkael's blood origins? What design should be set at his navel?'

Anzbek spoke without hesitation, having given the matter his circumspect thought. 'The sign for his mother's clan need not be left blank. None can deny he is Scoraign-bred. He shall be given the mark of all tribes, set into the sacred circle. This relationship has been justly earned. For the patterns that ward against the Tenth Name, all our people owe him for protection.'

The surrounding elders thumped the earth with their hands, and sang the note for appreciation.

'The marks of origin shall be done as described,' the healer agreed. Though surprised by the daring departure from form, he nodded his earnest approval. 'Tell me, what name shall I paint him?'

'His own,' Anzbek replied. 'For he has marked his worth on the world's weave alone. The nations who carry his debt for their sovereignty do him honour as Mykkael already.'

Then the eldest Jantii dreamer lifted his staff and called the circle to listening silence. With reverence, he recited the accolades, by which Scoraign people would know the inner spirit of the one reborn to a name on this day.

'Mykkael is a warrior! Let his heart bear the sign of the sword, turned upright, the alignment given to mercy. His left wrist, which must show those gifts granted at birth, will bear the eye of the seer. On his right wrist, for the path he has chosen through life, place the arrows of high honour and sacrifice, configured between the stars for endurance and courage, and the sun's triumph of lasting victory. He has been sorely tested, this man. His history of service is written in scars that require no further embellishment. May his union with Orannia grant him fine children and much laughter, as they grow to maturity and bring him the wealth of happiness and strong grandchildren.'

Anzbek raised his birch staff to the sky, and song arose at his bidding. The gathered shamans offered the warrior their pealing tribute, as the healer set his brush to the dye, and began to record Mykkael's heritage. The elder took pride in his work on that day, while Jantii tribe's fox clan circle bore joyful witness.

Birth to death, Scoraign people only borrowed their skins. Henceforward, Mykkael would be graced with the symbols to honour that ancient tradition. To trace such marks on the living man was to acknowledge his presence. Each chosen tattoo would reflect for all eyes the intangible flame of his being, that endured, as his deeds would endure, beyond the frail bounds of mortality.

Glossary

Al-Syn-Efandi – Prince of Efandi, whose realm was overrun by a sorcerer.
Anja of Sessalie – Princess of Sessalie, youngest child of King Isendon and Queen Anjoulie, sister of Crown Prince Kailen.
Anjoulie – deceased Queen of Sessalie, wife of King Isendon, mother of Anja and Kailen.
Anzbek – Scoraign tribal elder, dreamer of Jantii's fox clan circle.

baeyat'ji'in – *do'aa* term meaning 'beware of me'.
barqui'ino – a rare form of martial arts, which shifts the awareness to a primal state of focused clarity.
Benj – poacher and woodsman of Sessalie, husband of Mirag, father of Timal.
Bennent – First captain of the Royal Guard, second in command to Taskin.
Bercie – palace wine steward's wife in Sessalie.
Bertarra – the late Queen Anjoulie's niece.
Beyjall – a foreign apothecary who lives in the citadel.
borri'vach – an idiom used as a curse in Scoraign dialect, meaning 'to douse the problem with sand'.
Bryajne – a buckskin gelding.
Bull Trough Tavern – tavern and brothel in the Falls Gate district of the citadel.

Cade – Lowergate Garrison's day sergeant.
Cafferty – assistant to the Fane Street physician.
Canna – maidservant to the Princess of Sessalie.
Cockatrice Tavern – a tavern in the Falls Gate district of the citadel.
Collain Herald – court officer of Sessalie.
Covette – a chestnut mare of desert breeding.
Crossroads Market – an unlicensed assembly of squatter vendors outside the citadel walls.
Crown Advocate – ambassador for the King of Devall who stood as spokesman for the High Prince's suit for marriage.
Cultwaen Highlands – a country to the west, with advanced knowledge of sorcery.

Dalshie – Benj the poacher's lead hound.
Dedorth – scholar of Sessalie.
deit'jien tah – *do'aa* term meaning 'the target that kills without quarter'.
Devall – a wealthy coastal kingdom situated in the northeastern lowcountry, whose High Prince sues for the hand of the Princess of Sessalie.
do'aa – the *barqui'ino* term for an enclave of learning, under a master teacher, whose students are sworn to life loyalty.
Dreish – a coastal town.

Ebron – a lancer of the Royal Guard.
Efandi – a kingdom in the southeast, overrun by hot sorcery.
ei'jien – *do'aa* term meaning 'luckless sitting target'.
Eishwin – a vizier who fought in the wars that defeated the Sushagos.
Evissa – town in the southeast that was besieged by the Sushagos sorcerers.

Falls Gate – a postern in the outer wall of Sessalie's citadel, that leads into the disreputable quarter of town.
Fane Street – a lane in the Falls Gate quarter of the citadel.
Farrety – a lord of Sessalie.

Fingarra – a kingdom in the mountains that lies south and east of Sessalie.
Fouzette – a northern-bred bay mare.

Gance – a kingdom to the northeast.
Gorgenvain – name for the tenth demon.
Great Divide – the high range of mountains that run north to south, and are impassable except in a few places near the southern coast.
Grigori – a lancer of the Royal Guard.
Gurley – a farmer in Sessalie.

haw – voice command to turn a horse to the left.
Highgate – the portal leading into the third and highest tier of Sessalie's citadel, holding the king's palace, the Sanctuary, and the homes of the old blood nobility.
Howduin Gulch – a rift and a glacier in the ranges lying southeast of the citadel.

Indussian – refers to Indus, a kingdom known for its healing arts.
Isendon – reigning King of Sessalie.

Jantii – a tribe from the Scoraign Wastes.
Jedrey – noble-born sergeant who serves on the night roster of the Lowergate garrison.
jee – a voice command to turn a horse to the right.
Jussoud – Sanouk nomad who serves the Royal Guard as masseur and healer.

Kaien – master of a *barqui'ino do'aa*.
Kailen – Crown Prince of Sessalie, brother to Princess Anja, son of King Isendon and Queen Anjoulie.
Kasminna – a sorrel mare.
Katmin Cut – a pass leading into the upper ranges, west of the citadel in Sessalie.
kerrie – a winged, fire-breathing predator inhabiting the ranges, that preys upon large game and cattle.
Kevir – a lancer of the Royal Guard.

Lindya – widowed daughter of Commander Taskin.
long spell – the line of power strung by a demon-bound sorcerer. See Appendix for further detail.
Lowergate – the keep that houses the citadel's garrison, and also, one of the fortified entrances through the lower tier wall.

Mantlan – a kingdom famed for its wool, dyeing and carpets.
Marshal of Devall – commander of the high prince's honour guard.
Maylie – a prostitute employed in the Bull Trough Tavern.
Mehigrannia – goddess of the Scoraign tribes.
Middlegate – the portal through the middle wall of the citadel, which separates the merchants' district from the lower town.
Mirag – wife of Benj the poacher, mother of Timal.
Mistan – a lancer of the Royal Guard.
Muenice – a noble of Sessalie.
Mykkael – a desert-bred foreign mercenary, who serves as Captain of the Lowergate Garrison.
My*sh*kael – a lisped pronunciation of Mykkael's name, an affectation common to Highgate society.

Orannia – daughter of the Sanouk royal line, who once served in Mykkael's company.

Paunley – a soldier of the Lowergate garrison.
Perincar – court vizier to Prince Al-Syn-Efandi.
Phail – a duchess in the Kingdom of Sessalie, King Isendon's mistress since the queen's death.
Pinca – a dialect spoken in the east.

Quidjen – Name of one of the Nine demons.

Rathtet – Name of one of the Nine demons.

Sanouk – a nomad tribe from the eastern steppes.

Scatton's Pass – the difficult, high-altitude route over the Great Divide, that the mountaineer Scatton was first to cross.
Scoraign Tribes – inhabitants of the wastes to the south.
Scoraign Wastes – desert in the southern lands.
seit shan'jien – a *do'aa* term meaning 'the target with teeth that bites back'.
sennia – a beverage brewed in the eastern steppes from beans of the Sogion plant.
Serphaidian – the three related languages spoken on the eastern steppes.
Sessalie – a tiny, isolated kingdom located in the mountains on the eastern side of the Great Divide.
Shai – a lady who is Princess Anja's maid of honour.
Shaillon – the lord who is Seneschal of Sessalie.
short curse – a mark fashioned by a sorcerer's minion, to raise a circle of destruction.
Sogion – a wild bean plant common to the eastern steppes, used for medicinal purposes.
sorcerer's mark – the form inscribed of white river clay mixed with blood, urine, or spittle, that enables a sorcerer's short curse.
Stennis – sergeant of the Lowergate garrison.
Stone Bridge – the guarded span over the river where the trade road leads into the Kingdom of Sessalie.
Stormfront – a black gelding.
Sushagos – Name for one of the Nine demons.

Taskin – Commander of the Royal Guard in Sessalie.
Tavertin – a lord of Sessalie.
Timal – son of Mirag and Benj the poacher.
Tirrage – a kingdom in the southeast.
Tocoquadi – Name for one of the Nine demons.
Trade Gate – the third entrance through the lower wall of the citadel, where the trade road spans the lower moat.
Trakish – a dialect spoken in Kingdom of Trake.
Trigal – fifth son of the Emperor of Tuinvardia.
Tuinvardia – empire in the southwest, over the Great Divide.

Vangyar – a horse thief in Sessalie.
Vashni – a grey gelding.
Vensic – breveted sergeant of the Lowergate garrison.
Vhael – a wasteland with volcanic calderas.

Appendix Notes

On Demons and Sorcery

The hierarchy of the demonic sorcery that preys upon the human kingdoms in this book runs as follows:

Power arises from demons, who are named, and who rule and contend as rivals within the nether realms of the unseen. To affect the material world, they must first snare and bind a sorcerer. This would be a human who desired to wield power, or receive longevity, who did not balk at paying the consequences. Such a person would have enacted a ritual to open a portal, or make contact with the nether realm, and treat with a demon to acquire power. Such pacts by their nature bound the human to demonic service. The payoff would be might and immortality. In exchange, the human would enact the will of the demon, at risk of the penalty of falling to eternal torment.

A sorcerer would be closely tied to his portal, or source of contact with the nether realms. To expand his power base, he would create minions, or living subjects, bound into subservience. These would enact the work to enlarge his territory, since conquest of new ground provided the human victims that fed the demon, augmenting its powers in the nether realms.

A long-established sorcerer might have more than one human realm under minion control, to provide for the demon he served. Such sorcerers could be bred, to create more bound souls, and establish a crèche. If a crèche was large enough, and the demon powerful enough, the sorcerer's portal could be expanded, and the actual ground of the earth be suborned into demonic service. This would create a hot contact, or permanent portal between the nether realms and the physical world, and enable the demon to deal directly in its quest to feed upon life. A hot contact would also allow a source for demonic beings to incarnate in physical form, and work the bidding of the nether realms without requiring a human sorcerer to stand in liaison. Crèches of sorcerers whose demon had claimed a hot contact could then leave their point of origin, vastly more powerful than before.

A sorcerer's bound minion could operate within a limited range of the sorcerer. Over distance, the spell lines that fuelled them would break down by attrition. The power derived from the demon, as source, and would be channelled into the physical world through the sorcerer's works, then be passed on to the minion by a spell line, woven through existing energy channels in the air, and the earth. A minion could augment and direct the forces running along these spun spell lines to enact the demon's will, within a set range. He could 'tie' on a catspaw, or work a spell of compulsion upon an unsuspecting victim, to bind their will or otherwise move them to act in the demon's interest. He could also create other minions; however, this required much power, and the spell line from the initial sorcerer could only channel so much available force at once. The power and talents of a minion might vary widely, and cover a range of effects, as would the characteristics of the creations, apparitions, and sendings it would spin from the sorcerer's spell line.

A short curse, or sorcerer's mark, differs from a spell line. This would be a pattern of geometry, laid down by demonic intent, but powered by the minion who drew it. It would be painted with white river clay, to draw the demon's power through the earth, then mixed with a bodily fluid to wed its properties to the minion or sorcerer creating it. The fluid would link it to their being, and thus activate, or raise the mark into resonance. It would then 'burn', or fuel itself, off the minion's life force, taking only enough to remain in a state of active readiness. Lacking that connection, the mark could not function, since it works independently from a spell line. A short curse requires contact with a live victim, or animal, to 'trigger' its effects. Proximity or contact would link the minion and the victim through the geometry, with the spirit of the latter subsequently claimed by the demon, who then can flow destructive power directly into the site where the mark was drawn. The phenomenon would last only as long as the victim's aura holds connection to its dying flesh. Once the living spirit is consumed, the demon would lose connection to the site, which is why a short curse quickly consumes itself. If a sorcerer's mark is grounded after triggering, the victim who becomes consumed to destruction (in forfeit), would be the minion whose connection raised the mark to resonance.

A watcher's mark would be a demonic geometry laid into air as a passive device for listening. It would be held active by a hair, or a nail clipping, or a bit of dead skin, left behind by the minion who set it.

A last note: the English word 'sorcerer' may originally have derived from the French, *sourciers*, a meaning for which was used in connation with dowsers, who were 'finders of sources', and has no such evil connotation as my usage of the word for the purpose of this work of fiction.

On Martial Arts

The particulars of *barqui'ino* training, and the *do'aa*, are entirely fictional, and not derived from any actual existing discipline or school of teaching.